ALSO BY SIMON R. GREEN

BLUE MOON RISING

SIMON R. GREEN

A ROC BOOK

ROC
Published by New American Library, a division of
Penguin Group (USA) Inc., 375 Hudson Street,
New York, New York 10014, USA
Penguin Group (Canada), 90 Eglinton Avenue East, Suite 700, Toronto,
Ontario M4P 2Y3, Canada (a division of Pearson Penguin Canada Inc.)
Penguin Books Ltd., 80 Strand, London WC2R 0RL, England
Penguin Ireland, 25 St. Stephen's Green, Dublin 2,
Ireland (a division of Penguin Books Ltd.)
Penguin Group (Australia), 250 Camberwell Road, Camberwell, Victoria 3124,
Australia (a division of Pearson Australia Group Pty. Ltd.)
Penguin Books India Pvt. Ltd., 11 Community Centre, Panchsheel Park,
New Delhi - 110 017, India
Penguin Group (NZ), cnr Airborne and Rosedale Roads, Albany,
Auckland 1310, New Zealand (a division of Pearson New Zealand Ltd.)
Penguin Books (South Africa) (Pty.) Ltd., 24 Sturdee Avenue,
Rosebank, Johannesburg 2196, South Africa

Penguin Books Ltd., Registered Offices:
80 Strand, London WC2R 0RL, England

Published by Roc, an imprint of New American Library,
a division of Penguin Group (USA) Inc. Previously published in a Roc mass
market edition.

First Roc Trade Paperback Printing, September 2005
10 9 8 7 6 5 4 3 2 1

Copyright © Simon R. Green, 1991
All rights reserved

ROC REGISTERED TRADEMARK-MARCA REGISTRADA

Printed in the United States of America

To my mother and my father who were always there when I needed them.

In those days there were heroes and villains, and darkness walked the earth. There were dragons to be slain, captured Princesses to be saved, and mighty deeds were accomplished by knights in shining armor.

Many tales are told of that time, tales of steadfast bravery and derring-do.

This isn't one of them.

CHAPTER ONE

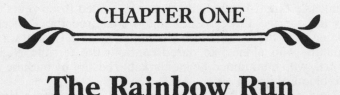

The Rainbow Run

Prince Rupert rode his unicorn into the Tanglewood, peering balefully through the drizzling rain as he searched half-heartedly for the flea hiding somewhere under his breast plate. Despite the chill rain, he was sweating heavily under the weight of his armor, and his spirits had sunk so low as to be almost out of sight. "Go forth and slay a dragon, my son," King John had said, and all the courtiers cheered. They could afford to. They didn't have to go out and face the dragon. Or ride through the Tanglewood in full armor in the rainy season. Rupert gave up on the flea and scrabbled awkwardly at his steel helmet, but to no avail; water continued to trickle down his neck.

Towering, closely packed trees bordered the narrow trail, blending into a verdant gloom that mirrored his mood. Thick, fleshy vines clung to every tree trunk, and fell in matted streamers from the branches. A heavy, sullen silence hung over the Tanglewood. No animals moved in the thick undergrowth, and no birds sang. The only sound was the constant rustle of the rain as it dripped from the lowering branches of the waterlogged trees, and the muffled thudding of the unicorn's hooves. Thick mud and fallen leaves made the twisting, centuries-old trail more than usually treacherous, and the unicorn moved ever more slowly, slipping and sliding as he carried Prince Rupert deeper into the Tanglewood.

Rupert glowered about him, and sighed deeply. All his life he'd thrilled to the glorious exploits of his ancestors, told in solemn voices during the long, dark winter evenings. He remembered as a child sitting wide-eyed and open-

9

mouthed by the fire in the Great Hall, listening with delicious horror to tales of ogres and harpies, magic swords and
rings of power. Steeped in the legends of his family, Rupert
had vowed from an early age that one day he too would be a
hero, like Great-Uncle Sebastian, who traded three years of
his life for the three wishes that would free the Princess
Elaine from the Tower With No Doors. Or like Grandfather
Eduard, who alone had dared confront the terrible Night
Witch, who maintained her remarkable beauty by bathing in
the blood of young girls.

Now, finally, he had the chance to be a hero, and a right
dog's breakfast he was making of it. Basically, Rupert blamed
the minstrels. They were so busy singing about heroes van-
quishing a dozen foes with one sweep of the sword because
their hearts were pure, that they never got round to the
important issues; like how to keep rain out of your armor,
or avoid strange fruits that gave you the runs, or the best
way to dig latrines. There was a lot to being a hero that the
minstrels never mentioned. Rupert was busily working himself into a really foul temper when the unicorn lurched
under him.

"Steady!" yelled the Prince.

The unicorn sniffed haughtily. "It's all right for you up
there, taking it easy; I'm the one who has to do all the
work. That armor you're wearing weighs a ton. My back's
killing me."

"I've been in the saddle for three weeks," Rupert pointed
out unsympathetically. "It's not my back that's bothering
me."

The unicorn sniggered, and then came to a sudden halt,
almost spilling the Prince from his saddle. Rupert grabbed
at the long, curlicued horn to keep his balance.

"Why have we stopped? Trail getting too muddy, perhaps? Afraid your hooves will get dirty?"

"If you're going to be a laugh a minute you can get off
and walk," snarled the unicorn. "In case you hadn't noticed, there's a massive spider's web blocking the trail."

Rupert sighed, heavily. "I suppose you want me to check
it out?"

"If you would, please." The unicorn shuffled his feet, and
the Prince felt briefly seasick. "You know how I feel about
spiders . . ."

Rupert cursed resignedly, and swung awkwardly down from the saddle, his armor protesting loudly with every movement. He sank a good three inches into the trail's mud, and swayed unsteadily for a long moment before finding his balance. He forced open his helmet's visor and studied the huge web uneasily. Thick milky strands choked the narrow path, each sticky thread studded with the sparkling jewels of trapped raindrops. Rupert frowned; what kind of spider spins a web almost ten feet high? He trudged cautiously forward, drew his sword, and prodded one of the strands. The blade stuck tight, and he had to use both hands to pull the sword free.

"Good start," said the unicorn.

Rupert ignored the animal and stared thoughtfully at the web. The more he looked at it, the less it seemed like a spider's web. The pattern was wrong. The strands hung together in knotted clumps, falling in drifting streamers from the higher branches, and dropping from the lower in thick clusters that burrowed into the trail's mud. And then Rupert felt the hair on the back of his neck slowly rise as he realized that, although the web trembled constantly, there was no wind blowing.

"Rupert," said the unicorn softly.

"We're being watched, right?"

"Right."

Rupert scowled and hefted his sword. Something had been following them ever since they'd entered the Tanglewood at daybreak, something that hid in shadows and dared not enter the light. Rupert shifted his weight carefully, getting the feel of the trail beneath him. If it came to a fight, the thick mud was going to be a problem. He took off his helmet, and put it down at the side of the trail; the narrow eyeholes limited his field of vision too much. He glanced casually around as he straightened up, and then froze as he saw a slender, misshapen silhouette moving among the trees. Tall as a man, it didn't move like a man, and light glistened on fang and claw before the creature disappeared back into the concealing shadows. Rain beat on Rupert's head and ran unheeded down his face as a cold horror built slowly within him.

Beyond the Tanglewood lay darkness. For as long as anyone could remember, there had always been a part of the Forest where it was forever night. No sun shone, and whatever lived there never knew the light of day. Mapmakers called it the Darkwood, and warned: *Here Be Demons*. For countless centuries, Forest land and Darkwood had been separated by the Tanglewood, a deadly confusion of swamp and briar and sudden death from which few escaped alive. Silent predators stalked the weed- and vine-choked trails, and laid in wait for the unwary. And yet, over the past few months, strange creatures had stalked the Forest Land, uneasy shapes that dared not face the light of day. Sometimes, when the sun was safely down, a lone cottager might hear scratchings at his securely bolted doors and shutters, and in the morning would find deep gouges in the wood, and mutilated animals in his barn.

The Tanglewood was no longer a barrier.

Here Be Demons.

Rupert fought down his fear, and took a firmer grip on his sword. The solid weight of the steel comforted him, and he swept the shining blade back and forth before him. He glared up at the dark clouds hiding the sun; one decent burst of sunshine would have sent the creature scuttling for its lair, but as usual Rupert was out of luck.

It's only a demon, he thought furiously. *I'm in full armor, and I know how to use a sword. The demon hasn't a chance.*

"Unicorn," he said quietly, peering into the shadows where he'd last seen the demon, "you'd better find a tree to hide behind. And stay clear of the fight; I don't want you getting hurt."

"I'm way ahead of you," said a muffled voice. Rupert glanced round to find the unicorn hiding behind a thick-boled tree some distance away.

"Thanks a lot," said Rupert. "What if I need your help?"

"Then you've got a problem," the unicorn said firmly, "because I'm not moving. I know a demon when I smell one. They eat unicorns, you know."

"Demons eat anything," said Rupert.

"Precisely," said the unicorn, and ducked back out of sight behind his tree.

Not for the first time, the Prince vowed to find the man who'd sold him the unicorn, and personally do something unpleasant to every one of the swindler's extremities.

There was a faint scuffling to his left, and Rupert had just started to turn when the demon slammed into him from behind. His heavy armor overbalanced him, and he fell forward into the clinging mud. The impact knocked the breath from him, and his sword flew from his outstretched hand. He caught a brief glimpse of something dark and misshapen towering over him, and then a heavy weight landed on his back. A clawed hand on the back of his neck forced his face down, and the mud came up to fill his eyes. Rupert flailed his arms desperately and tried to get his feet under him, but his steel-studded boots just slid helplessly in the thick mire. His lungs ached as he fought for air, and the watery mud spilled into his gaping mouth.

Panic welled up in him as he bucked and heaved to no avail. His head swam madly, and there was a great roaring in his ears as the last of his breath ran out. One of his arms became wedged beneath his chest plate, and with the suddenness of inspiration he used his arm as a lever to force himself over onto his back, trapping the squirming demon beneath the weight of his armor.

He lay there for long, precious moments, drawing in great shuddering breaths and gouging the mud from his eyes. He yelled for the unicorn to help him, but there was no reply. The demon hammered furiously at his armor with clumsy fists, and then a clawed hand snaked up to tear into Rupert's face. He groaned in agony as the claws grated on his cheekbone, and tried desperately to reach his sword. The demon took advantage of his move to squirm out from under him. Rupert rolled quickly to one side, grabbed his sword, and surged to his feet despite the clinging mud. The weight of his armor made every move an effort, and blood ran thickly down his face and neck as he stood swaying before the crouching demon.

In many ways it might have been a man, twisted and malformed, but to stare into its hungry pupilless eyes was to know the presence of evil. Demons killed to live, and lived to kill; a darkness loose upon the Land. Rupert gripped his sword firmly and forced himself to concentrate on the demon simply as an opponent. It was strong and fast and deadly, but so was he if he kept his wits about him. He had to get out of the mud and up onto firm ground; the treacherous mire gave the demon too much of an advantage. He took a cautious step forward, and the demon flexed its claws eagerly, smiling widely to reveal rows of pointed, serrated teeth. Rupert swept his sword back and forth before him, and the demon gave ground a little, wary of the cold steel. Rupert glanced past the night-dark creature in search of firmer ground, and then grinned shakily at what he saw. For the first time, he felt he might have a fighting chance.

He gripped his sword in both hands, took a deep breath, and then charged full tilt at the crouching demon, knowing that if he fell too soon he was a dead man. The demon darted back out of range, staying just ahead of the Prince's reaching sword. Rupert struggled on, fighting to keep his feet under him. The demon grinned and jumped back again, straight into the massive web that blocked the path. Rupert stumbled to a halt, drew back his sword for the killing thrust, and then froze in horror as the web's thick milky strands slowly wrapped themselves around the demon. The demon tore furiously at the strands and then howled silently in agony as the web oozed a clear viscous acid that steamed where it fell upon the ground. Rupert watched in sick fascination as the feebly struggling demon disappeared inside a huge pulsating cocoon that covered it from head to toe. The last twitching movements died quickly away as the web digested its meal.

Rupert wearily lowered his sword and leaned on it, resting his aching back. Blood ran down into his mouth, and he spat it out. Who'd be a hero? He grinned sourly and took stock of himself. His magnificent burnished armor was caked with drying mud, and etched with deep scratch marks from the demon's claws. He hurt all over, and his head beat with pain. He brought a shaking hand up to his face, and then winced as he saw fresh blood on his mailed gauntlet. He'd never liked the sight of blood, especially his own. He sheathed his sword and sat down heavily on the edge of the trail, ignoring the squelching mud.

All in all, he didn't think he'd done too badly. There weren't many men who'd faced a demon and lived to tell of it. Rupert glanced at the now-motionless cocoon, and grimaced. Not the most heroic way to win, and certainly not the most sporting, but the demon was dead and he was alive, and that was the way he'd wanted it to be.

He peeled off his gauntlets and tenderly inspected his damaged face with his fingers. The cuts were wide and deep, and ran from the corner of his eye down to his mouth. *Better wash them clean,* he thought dazedly. *Don't want them to get infected.* He shook his head and looked about him. The rain had died away during the fight, but the sun was already sliding down the sky toward evening, and the shadows were darkening. Nights were falling earlier these days, even though it was barely summer. Rain dripped steadily from the overhanging branches, and a dank, musky smell hung heavily on the still air. Rupert glanced at the web cocoon, and shivered suddenly as he remembered how close he'd come to trying to cut his way through. Predators came in many forms, especially in the Tanglewood.

He sighed resignedly. Tired or no, it was time he was on his way.

"Unicorn! Where are you?"

"Here," said a polite voice from the deepest of the shadows.

"Are you coming out, or do I come in there after you?" growled the Prince. There was a slight pause, and then the unicorn stepped diffidently out onto the trail. Rupert glared at the animal, who wouldn't meet his gaze.

"And where were you, while I was risking my neck fighting that demon?"

"Hiding," said the unicorn. "It seemed the logical thing to do."

"Why didn't you help?"

"Well," said the unicorn reasonably, "If you couldn't handle the demon with a sword and a full set of armor, I didn't see what help I could offer."

Rupert sighed. One of these days he'd learn not to argue with the unicorn.

"How do I look?"

"Terrible."

"Thanks a lot."

"You'll probably have scars," said the unicorn helpfully.

"Great. That's all I need."

"I thought scars on the face were supposed to be heroic?"

"Whoever thought that one up should have his head examined. Bloody minstrels . . . Help me up, unicorn."

The unicorn moved quickly in beside him. Rupert reached out, took a firm hold of the stirrup, and slowly pulled himself up out of the mud. The unicorn stood patiently as Rupert leaned wearily against his side, waiting for his bone-deep aches to subside long enough for him to make a try at getting up into the saddle.

The unicorn studied him worriedly. Prince Rupert was a tall, handsome man in his mid-twenties, but blood and pain and fatigue had added twenty years to his face. His skin was gray and beaded with sweat, and his eyes were feverish. He was obviously in no condition to ride, but the unicorn knew that Rupert's pride would force him to try.

"Rupert . . ." said the unicorn.

"Yeah?"

"Why don't you just . . . walk me for a while? You know how unsteady I am in this mud."

"Yeah," said Rupert. "That's a good idea. I'll do that."

He reached out and took hold of the bridle, his head hanging wearily down. Slowly, carefully, the unicorn led him past the motionless cocoon and on down the trail, heading deeper into the Tanglewood.

Two days later, Rupert was back in the saddle and fast approaching the boundary between Tanglewood and Darkwood. His aches had mostly died away, thanks to a pouch of herbs the Court Astrologer had forced on him before he left, and though more than once he found himself wishing for a mirror, the wounds on his face seemed to be scabbing nicely. All in all, Rupert was feeling a little more cheerful, or at least only mildly depressed.

He was supposed to kill a dragon, but truth to tell nobody had seen one in ages, and they'd pretty much passed into legend. Rupert had become somewhat disenchanted with legends; they seemed to dwell on the honor and the glory and leave out the important parts, like how you killed whatever it was without getting killed yourself. "Because your heart is pure" isn't a lot of help when you're up against a dragon. *I bet mine breathes fire,* thought Rupert dismally. He was working hard on a great new rationalization that would let him turn back almost honorably, when his bladder loudly called itself to his attention. Rupert sighed and steered the unicorn over to the side of the trail. That was another thing minstrels never mentioned.

He quickly dismounted, and set about undoing the complicated series of flaps that protected his groin. He only just made it in time, and whistled nonchalantly as he emptied his bladder against a tree trunk. If his diet didn't improve soon, he'd be the only hero going into battle with his fly undone . . .

That thought decided him, and as soon as he'd finished what he was doing, Rupert set about discarding his armor. He'd only worn the damn stuff because he'd been assured it was traditional for anyone setting out on a quest. *Stuff tradition,* thought Rupert happily, his spirits soaring as piece by piece the battered armor dropped into the trail's mud. After a little thought, he decided to hang onto the steel-studded boots; he might want to kick someone. Clad finally in leather jerkin and trousers and his best cloak, Rupert felt comfortable for the first time in weeks. Admittedly, he also felt decidedly vulnerable, but the way his luck had been going recently, he'd only have rusted up solid, anyway.

"I hate grass," said the unicorn moodily.

"Then why are you eating it?" asked Rupert, buckling on his sword belt.

"I'm hungry," said the unicorn, chewing disgustedly. "And since we ran out of civilized fodder weeks ago . . ."

"What's wrong with grass?" Rupert inquired mildly. "Horses eat it all the time."

"I am not a horse!"

"Never said you were . . ."

"I'm a unicorn, a thoroughbred, and I'm entitled to proper care and attention. Like oats and barley and . . ."

"In the Tanglewood?"

"Hate grass," muttered the unicorn. "Makes me feel all bloated."

"Try a few thistles," suggested Rupert.

The unicorn gave him a hard look. "Do I even faintly resemble a donkey?" he inquired menacingly.

Rupert looked away to hide a grin, and discovered a dozen goblins had moved silently out of the shadows to block the trail. Ranging from three to four feet in height, scarecrow thin and pointed-eared, they were armed with short, rusty swords and jagged-edged meat cleavers. Their ill-fitting bronze and silver armor had obviously been looted from human travellers, and their unpleasant grins suggested only too clearly what had happened to the armor's previous occupants. Furious at being caught so easily off-guard, Rupert drew his sword and glared at them all impartially. The goblins hefted their weapons, and then looked at each other uneasily. For a long moment, nobody moved.

"Well don't just stand there," growled a deep voice from the shadows. "Get him!"

The goblins shifted unhappily from foot to foot.

"Have you seen the size of that sword?" said the smallest goblin.

"And look at those scars on his face, and all that dried blood on his armor," whispered another goblin respectfully. "He must have slaughtered a dozen people to get in that much of a mess."

"Probably chopped them into chutney," elaborated the smallest goblin mournfully.

Rupert swung his sword casually back and forth before him, light flashing the length of the blade. The goblins brandished their weapons in a half-hearted way and huddled together for comfort.

"At least get his horse," suggested the voice from the shadows.

"Horse?" The unicorn threw up his head, rage blazing from his blood-red eyes. "*Horse?* What do you think this is on my brow? An ornament? I'm a unicorn, you moron!"

"Horse, unicorn; what's the difference?"

The unicorn pawed the ground, and lowered his head so that light glistened on his wickedly pointed horn.

"Right. That does it. One at a time or all at once; *you're all getting it!*"

"Nice one, leader," muttered the smallest goblin.

Rupert shot an amused glance at the unicorn. "I thought you were a sensible, logical coward?"

"I'm too busy being angry," growled the unicorn. "I'll be afraid later, when there's time. Line these creeps up for me, and I'll skewer the lot. I'll show them a shish kebab they won't forget in a hurry."

The goblins began surreptitiously backing away down the trail.

"Will you stop messing about and kill that bloody traveller!" roared the voice from the shadows.

"You want him dead so badly, you kill him!" snapped the smallest goblin, looking busily around for the nearest escape route. "This is all your fault anyway. We should have ambushed him while he was distracted, like we usually do."

"You needed the combat experience."

"Stuff combat experience! We should stick to what we're good at; sneak attacks with overwhelming odds."

There was a deep sigh, and then the goblin leader stepped majestically out of the shadows. Broad-shouldered, impressively muscled, and very nearly five feet tall, he was the biggest goblin Rupert had ever seen. The goblin leader stubbed out a vile-looking cigar on his verdigrised bronze chestplate, and glared at the tightly packed goblins huddled together in the middle of the trail. He sighed again, and shook his head disgustedly.

"Look at you. How am I supposed to make fighters out of you if you won't fight? I mean, what's the problem? He's only one man!"

"And a unicorn," pointed out the smallest goblin.

"All right, one man *and* a unicorn. So what? We're footpads now, remember? It's our job to waylay defenseless travellers and take their valuables."

"He doesn't look defenseless to me," muttered the smallest goblin. "Look at that dirty big sword he's carrying."

The goblins stared at it in morbid fascination as Rupert tried a few practice cuts and lunges. The unicorn trotted back and forth behind him, sighting his horn at various goblins, which did absolutely nothing to improve their confidence.

"Come on, lads," said the goblin leader desperately. "How can you be frightened of someone who rides a unicorn?"

"What's that got to do with anything?" asked the smallest goblin. The leader murmured something of which only the word "virgin" was clearly audible. All the goblins peered at Rupert, and a few sniggered meaningfully.

"It's not easy being a Prince," said Rupert, blushing fiercely despite himself. "You want to make something of it?"

He took a firm grip on his sword and sheared clean through an overhanging branch. The severed end hit the ground with an ominous-sounding thud.

"Great," muttered the smallest goblin. "Now we've really got him angry."

"Will you shut up!" snarled the goblin leader. "Look; there's thirteen of us and only one of him. If we all rush him at once, we're bound to get him."

"Want to bet?" said an anonymous voice from the back.

"Shut up! When I give the word, charge. Charge!"

He started forward, brandishing his sword, and the other goblins reluctantly followed him. Rupert stepped forward, took careful aim, and punched the goblin leader out. The other goblins skidded to a halt, took one look at their fallen leader, and promptly threw down their weapons. Rupert herded the goblins together, backed them off a way, well out of range of their discarded weapons, and then leaned against a convenient tree while he tried to figure out what to do next. They were such incompetent villains he really didn't have the heart to kill them. The goblin leader sat up, shook his aching head to clear it, and then clearly wished he hadn't. He glared up at Rupert, and tried to look defiant. He wasn't particularly successful.

"I told you thirteen was unlucky," said the smallest goblin.

"All right," said Rupert. "Everyone pay attention, and I'll tell you what I'll do. You agree to get the hell out of here and stop bothering me, and I'll agree not to turn you over to the unicorn in small, meaty chunks. How does that sound?"

"Fair," said the smallest goblin quickly. "Very fair."

There was a lot of nodding from the other goblins.

"Do we get our weapons back first?" asked the goblin leader.

Rupert smiled. "Do I look crazy?"

The goblin leader shrugged. "Worth a try. All right, sir hero; you got yourself a deal."

"And you won't try to follow me?"

The goblin leader gave him a hard stare. "Do I look crazy? It's going to take me weeks to turn this lot back into a fighting force, after what you've done to them. Personally, sir hero, I for one will be extremely content if I never see you again."

He got to his feet and led the goblins back into the trees, and within seconds they had vanished completely. Rupert grinned and sheathed his sword. He was finally getting the hang of this quest business.

An hour later, the light faded quickly away as Rupert left the Tanglewood and crossed into the Darkwood. Far above him, rotting trees leaned together, their leafless interlocking branches blocking out the sun, and in the space of a few moments Rupert passed from mid-afternoon to darkest night. He reined the unicorn to a halt and looked back over his shoulder, but daylight couldn't follow him into the Darkwood. Rupert turned back, patted the unicorn's neck comfortingly, and waited for his eyes to adjust to the gloom.

A faint silver glow of phosphorescent fungi limned the decaying tree trunks, and far off in the distance he thought he saw a brief flash of light, as though someone had opened a door and then quickly closed it, for fear light would attract unwelcome attention. Rupert glanced about him nervously, ears straining for the slightest sound, but the darkness seemed silent as the tomb. The air was thick with the sickly sweet stench of death and corruption.

His eyes finally adjusted enough to show him the narrow trail that led into the heart of the Darkwood, and he signalled the unicorn to move on. The slow, steady hoofbeats sounded dangerously loud on the quiet. There was only one trail through the endless night; a single straight path that crossed the darkness from one boundary to the other, cut so long ago that no one now remembered who had done it, or why. The Darkwood was very old, and kept its secrets to itself. Rupert peered constantly about him, one hand resting on the pommel of his sword. He remembered the demon he'd fought in the Tanglewood, and shuddered suddenly. Entering the Darkwood was a calculated risk, but if anyone knew where to find a dragon, it was the Night Witch.

Assuming she was still alive, after all these years. Before Rupert set out on his journey, the Court Astrologer had helped him delve into the Castle Archives in search of any map that might lead to a dragon's lair. They didn't find one, which pleased Rupert no end, but they did stumble across the official record of Grandfather Eduard's encounter with the Night Witch. The surprisingly brief tale (surprising in that the most recent song on the subject lasted for an interminable hundred and thirty-seven verses), included a passing reference to a dragon, and a suggestion that the exiled Witch might still be found at her cottage in the Darkwood, not far from the Tanglewood boundary.

"Even assuming that I am daft enough to go looking for a woman whose main interest in life is forcibly separating people from their blood," said Rupert, dubiously, "give me one good reason why she should agree to help me."

"Apparently," said the Astrologer, cryptically, "She was rather fond of your grandfather."

Rupert studied the Astrologer suspiciously and pressed him for more details, but he refused to be drawn. Rupert trusted the Astrologer about as far as he could spit into the wind, but since he hadn't a clue of how else to find a dragon . . .

Gnarled, misshapen trees loomed menacingly out of the gloom as Rupert rode deeper into the endless night. The only sound was the steady rhythm of the unicorn's hooves, and even that seemed somehow muffled by the unrelenting dark. More than once Rupert reined the unicorn to a sudden halt and stared about him, eyes straining against the darkness, convinced that something awful lurked just beyond the range of his vision. But always there was only the dark, and the silence. He had no lantern, and when he broke a bough from one of the dead trees to make a torch, the rotten wood crumbled in his hand. With no light to guide him, he lost all track of time, but eventually the closely packed trees fell suddenly away on either side, and Rupert signalled to the unicorn to stop. Ahead of them lay a small clearing, its boundaries marked by the glowing fungi. In the middle of the clearing stood a single dark shape that had to be the Witch's cottage. Rupert glanced up at the night sky, but there was no moon or stars to give him light, only an empty darkness that seemed to go on forever.

"Are you sure this is a good idea?" whispered the unicorn.

"No," said Rupert. "But it's our best chance to find a dragon."

"Frankly, that doesn't strike me as such a hot idea either," muttered the unicorn.

Rupert grinned, and swung down out of the saddle. "You stay here, while I check out the cottage."

"You're not leaving me here on my own," said the unicorn determinedly.

"Would you rather meet the Night Witch?" asked Rupert.

The unicorn moved quickly off the trail and hid behind the nearest tree.

"I'll be back as soon as I can," Rupert promised. "Don't go wandering off."

"That has to be the most redundant piece of advice I've ever been offered," said the unicorn.

Rupert drew his sword, took a deep breath, and moved cautiously out into the clearing. His soft footsteps seemed horribly loud on the quiet and he broke into a run, his back crawling in anticipation of the attack he'd probably never feel, anyway. The Witch's cottage crouched before him like a sleeping predator, a dull crimson glow outlining the door and shuttered windows. Rupert skidded to a halt at the cottage and set his back against the rough wooden wall, his eyes darting wildly round as he checked to see if he had been followed. Nothing moved in the ebon gloom, and the only sound in the endless night was his own harsh breathing. He swallowed dryly, stood quietly a moment to get his breath back, and then moved over to knock, very politely, at the cottage's door. A bright crimson glare filled his eyes as the door swung suddenly open, and a huge bony hand with long curving fingernails shot out and grasped him by the throat. Rupert kicked and struggled helplessly as he was hauled into the Witch's cottage.

The bent old woman kicked the door shut behind her, and dropped Rupert unceremoniously onto the filthy carpet. He sat up and massaged his sore throat as the Night Witch cackled fiendishly, rubbing her gnarled hands together.

"Sorry about that," she said and grinned. "All part of the image, you know. I have to do something fairly nasty every now and again, or they'll think I've gone soft. What are you doing here, anyway?"

"Thought you might be able to help me," husked the Prince.

"Help?" said the Night Witch, raising a crooked eyebrow. "Are you sure you've come to the right cottage?" The black cat crouched on her shoulder hissed angrily, and rubbed its shoulder against the Witch's long gray hair. She reached up and patted the animal absentmindedly.

"Give me one good reason why I shouldn't turn you into a frog," demanded the Witch.

Rupert showed her his sword. The Witch grinned nastily. "Sheath it, or I'll tie it in a knot."

Rupert thought about it a moment, and then slipped the sword back into its scabbard. "I believe you knew my grandfather," he said carefully.

"Possibly," said the Night Witch airily. "I've known many men in my time. What was his name?"

"Eduard, of the Forest Kingdom."

The Night Witch stared at him blankly, and then all the fire seemed to go out of her eyes. She turned slowly away, and moved over to sink into a battered old rocking chair by the fireplace.

"Yes," she said finally, almost to herself. "I remember Eduard."

She sat quietly in the rocking chair, staring at nothing, and Rupert took the opportunity to get to his feet and take a quick look around him. The cottage was filled with a dull, unfocussed light that seemed to come from everywhere at once, though there was no lamp to be seen. The walls leaned away from the floor at different angles, and bats squealed up in the high rafters. A cat's shadow swayed across a wall without a cat to cast it, and something dark and shapeless with glowing eyes peered out from the empty, smoke-blackened fireplace.

Rupert studied the Night Witch curiously. Somehow she didn't seem quite so impressive when she wasn't actually threatening him. Rocking quietly in her chair, with her cat in her lap, she looked like anybody's grandmother, a shrunken gray-haired old lady with a back bent by the years. She was painfully thin, and suffering had etched deep lines into her face. This wasn't the Night Witch of legend, the raven-haired tempter of men, the terrible creature of the dark. She was just a tired old woman, lost in memories of better times. She looked up, and caught Rupert's eyes on her.

"Aye, look at me," she said quietly. "I was beautiful, once. So beautiful men travelled hundreds of miles just to pay me compliments. Kings, emperors, heroes; I could have had my pick of any of them. But I didn't want them. It was enough that I was . . . beautiful."

"How many young girls died to keep you beautiful?" said Rupert harshly.

"I lost count," said the Witch. "It didn't seem important, then. I was young and glorious and men loved me; nothing else mattered. What's your name, boy?"

"Rupert."

"You should have seen me then, Rupert. I was so lovely. So very lovely."

She smiled gently and rocked her chair, eyes fixed on yesterday.

"I was young and powerful and I bent the darkness to my will. I raised a palace of ice and diamond in a single night, and Lords and Ladies from a dozen Courts came to pay homage to me. They never noticed if a few peasant girls went missing from the villages. They wouldn't have cared if they had.

"And then Eduard came to kill me. Somehow he'd found out the truth, and he came to rid the Forest Land of my evil." She chuckled quietly. "Many the nights he spent in my cold halls, of his own free will. He was tall and brave and handsome and he never once bowed to me. I showed him wonders and terrors and I couldn't break him. We used to dance in my ballroom, just the two of us, in a great echoing hall of glistening ice, each chandelier fashioned from a single stalactite. Slowly, I came to love him, and he loved me. I was young and foolish, and I thought our love would last forever.

"It lasted a month.

"I needed fresh blood, and Eduard couldn't allow that. He loved me, but he was King, and he had a responsibility to his people. He couldn't kill me, but I couldn't change what I was. So I waited till he slept, and then I left my palace, and the Forest Land, and came here to live in the darkness, where there's no one to see that I'm not beautiful anymore.

"I could have killed him and kept my secret safe. I could have stayed young and lovely and powerful. But I loved him. My Eduard. The only man I ever loved. I suppose he's dead now."

"More than thirty years ago," said Rupert.

"So many years," whispered the Witch. Her shoulders slumped, and her crooked, twisted hands writhed together. She took a deep breath and let it go shakily, then looked up at Rupert and smiled tiredly. "So you're Eduard's kin. You have some of his looks, boy. What do you want from me?"

"I'm looking for a dragon," said Rupert, in a tone he hoped suggested that, if at all possible, he'd really rather not find one.

"A dragon?" The Witch stared at him blankly a moment, and then a broad grin spread slowly across her wrinkled face. "A *dragon!* Damn me, but I like your style, boy. No one's had the guts to hunt a dragon in years. No wonder you weren't scared to come calling on me!" She studied him admiringly while Rupert did his best to look modest. "Well, dearie, this is your lucky day. You're looking for a dragon, and it just so happens I have a map that will lead you right to one. A real bargain, I can let you have it for the knock-down price of only three pints of blood."

Rupert gave her a hard look. The Witch shrugged.

"Worth a try. Since you are Eduard's kin, let me revise that offer. The map's yours, free of charge. If I can remember where I put the damned thing."

She rose up slowly out of her chair, spilling the cat from her lap, and hobbled away to investigate the depths of a battered oak filing cabinet in a far corner. Rupert frowned uncertainly. He'd fully intended to kill the Night Witch if he got the opportunity, but although she spoke casually of murdering so many young girls that she'd finally lost count, somehow he just couldn't bring himself to do it. In a strange kind of way he actually felt sorry for her; her long years alone in the Darkwood had punished her enough. More than enough. The Witch was suddenly before him and he jumped back, startled, as she thrust a tattered parchment scroll into his hands.

"There you are, boy, that'll take you right to him. If you get that far. To start with, you've got to pass clean through the Darkwood and out the other side, and there's damn few have done that and lived to tell of it."

"I got this far," said Rupert confidently.

"This close to the Tanglewood boundary there's still a little light," said the Witch. "Beyond this clearing, there's nothing but darkness. Watch your back, Rupert. There's a cold wind blowing through the long night, and it smells of blood and death. Deep in the Darkwood something is stirring, something . . . awful. If I wasn't so old, I'd be scared."

"I can take care of myself," said Rupert tightly, one hand dropping to the pommel of his sword.

The Witch smiled tiredly. "You're Eduard's kin. He thought cold steel was the answer to everything, too. When I look at you, it's almost like seeing him again. My Eduard." Her voice suddenly shook, and she turned her back on Rupert and limped painfully over to sink slowly into her rocking chair. "Go on, boy, get out of here. Go and find your dragon."

Rupert hesitated. "Is there . . . anything I can do for you?"

"Just go," said the Night Witch harshly. "Leave me alone. Please."

Rupert turned and left, closing the door quietly behind him.

Sitting alone before her empty fireplace, the Night Witch rocked gently in her chair. After a while her eyes slowly closed, and she fell asleep. And she was young and beautiful again, and Eduard came to her, and they danced together all through the night in her ballroom of shimmering ice.

Several days' travel later, Rupert had finished the last of his provisions. There was no game to be found in the Darkwood, and what little water there was, was fouled. Thirst burned in his throat, and hunger was a dull ache in his belly.

Since leaving the Night Witch's clearing he had left all light behind him. The darkness became absolute, and the silence was oppressive. He couldn't see the trail ahead, the unicorn beneath him, or even a hand held up before his eyes. Only the growing stubble on his face remained to show him the passing of time. He grew steadily weaker as the unicorn carried him deeper into the Darkwood, for although they stopped to rest whenever they grew tired, Rupert couldn't sleep. The darkness kept him awake.

Something might creep up on him while he slept.

He passed a shaking hand over his dry, cracked lips, and then frowned as he slowly realized the unicorn had come to a halt. He tried to ask what was wrong, but his tongue had swollen till it almost filled his mouth. He swung painfully down out of the saddle, and leaned against the unicorn's side until his legs felt strong enough to support him for a while. He stumbled forward a few steps, hands outstretched before him, and grunted with pain as thorns pierced his flesh. More cautious testing revealed that a thick patch of needle-thorned briar had grown across the narrow trail. Rupert drew his sword, and was shocked to find that he'd grown so weak he now needed both his hands to wield it. He gathered the last of his strength, and with awkward, muscle-wrenching cuts, he set about clearing a path through the briar. The unicorn slowly followed him, the proudly horned head hanging tiredly down.

Time after time Rupert struggled to raise his sword for another blow, fighting the growing agony in his chest and arms. His hands and face were lacerated by the stubborn thorns, but he was so tired he barely felt the wounds. His sword grew heavier in his uncertain grasp, and his legs trembled with fatigue, but he wouldn't give in. He was Rupert, Prince of the Forest Kingdom. He'd fought a demon and braved the Darkwood, and he was damned if he'd be beaten by a patch of bloody briar. He swung his sword savagely before him, forcing his way deeper into the briar, and then cried out as a sudden burst of sunlight threw back the night.

Rupert brought up a hand to shield his eyes from the blinding glare, and stumbled forward. For a long time, all he could do was squint painfully through his fingers while shocked tears ran down his cheeks, but finally he was able to lower his hand and blink in amazement at the scene spread out before him. He'd emerged from the Darkwood high up on a steep hillside, and down below him sprawled a vast patchwork of tended fields; wheat and maize and barley, ripening under a mid-day sun. Long lines of towering oaks served as windbreaks, and sunlight reflected brightly from shimmering rivers. Slender stone walls marked the field boundaries, and a single dirt road meandered through them on its way to the huge, dark mountain that dominated the horizon, its summit lost in clouds.

The mountain called Dragonslair.

Rupert finally tore his gaze away from the ominous crag and peered dazedly about him. His breath caught in his throat. Not a dozen yards from the Darkwood's boundary, a fast-moving stream bubbled up from a hidden spring, leaping and sparkling as it tumbled down the hillside. Rupert dropped his sword, staggered forward, and fell to his knees beside the rushing water. He dipped his hand into the stream, brought his fingers to his mouth, and licked cautiously at them. The water was clear and pure. Rupert felt fresh tears start to his eyes as he leant forward and thrust his face into the stream.

He gulped thirstily at the chill water, coughing and spluttering in his eagerness, and then somehow found the strength to draw back from the stream. Too much water at first would only make him sick. He lay back on the springy grass, feeling comfortably bloated. His stomach growled, reminding him that he hadn't eaten in days either, but that could wait a while. For the moment, he felt too good to move. He watched as the unicorn drank sparingly from the stream and then turned away to crop contentedly at the grass. Rupert smiled for the first time in days. He raised himself on one elbow and looked back the way he'd come. The Darkwood stood brooding and silent behind him, and the bright sunlight didn't pass an inch beyond its boundary. A chill breeze blew steadily from the rotting, spindly trees. Rupert grinned savagely at the darkness, and tasted blood as his cracked lips split painfully. He didn't give a damn.

"I beat you," he said softly. "I beat you!"

"I helped," said the unicorn. Rupert turned back to find the animal looking worriedly down at him. He reached up and patted the unicorn's muzzle.

"I couldn't have done it without you," said Rupert. "You were there when I needed you. Thanks."

"You're very welcome," said the unicorn. "Now then, I'm going to graze on this wonderful grass for some time, and I don't want to be disturbed until I've finished. Is that clear?"

Rupert laughed. "Sure. You go ahead; the sun's high in the sky, and I've an awful lot of sleep to catch up on. Afterwards . . . I think I'll show you how to tickle trout."

"Why should I wish to amuse a fish?" asked the unicorn, but Rupert was already fast asleep.

It took Rupert and the unicorn almost a month to reach Dragonslair mountain. Regular meals and fresh water did much to restore their health and spirits, but the Darkwood had left its mark on Rupert. Every evening, as the sun dipped redly below the horizon, Rupert would build a large fire, even though the nights were warm and there were no dangerous beasts in the area. And every night, before he finally allowed himself to sleep, he carefully banked the fire so that there was sure to be light if he woke before the dawn. His sleep was restless, and plagued by nightmares he chose not to recall. For the first time since he was a child,

Rupert was afraid of the dark. Each morning he woke
ashamed, and cursed his weakness, and swore silently to
himself that he'd not give in to his fear again. And every
evening, as the sun went down, he built another fire.

Dragonslair drew steadily closer and more imposing as
the days passed, and Rupert became increasingly uncertain
as to what he was going to do when he reached the mountain's base. According to the Night Witch's map, somewhere near the summit he'd find a dragon's cave, but the
closer he drew the more impossible it seemed that any man
could climb the towering basalt wall that loomed darkly
before him, filling the horizon. Yet, despite all his doubts,
despite the unreasoning fear that tormented his nights, Rupert never considered turning back. He'd come too far and
been through too much to give up now that his goal was
finally in sight.

*Go forth and slay a dragon, my son. Prove yourself wor-
thy to the throne.*

The early morning air was still cold from the night's chill
when Rupert rode into the foothills. Thinning grass and
stunted shrubbery soon gave way to bare rock, pitted and
eroded by long exposure to wind and rain. A pathway cut
into the mountainside itself led steeply upwards, and the
unicorn cursed steadily under his breath as he picked his
way carefully along the uneven path. Rupert kept his eyes
fixed firmly on the path ahead, and tried not to think about
the growing drop behind him. The trail grew steadily narrower and more treacherous as they ascended, and was
finally interrupted by a wide patch of shifting scree. The
unicorn took one look at the gently sliding stones that
blocked the path, and dug his hooves in.

"Forget it. I'm a unicorn, not a mountain goat."

"But it's the only way up; it'll be easy going after this."

"It's not the going up that worries me, it's the coming
down. Probably at great speed, with the wind rushing past
me."

Rupert sighed, and swung down out of the saddle. "All
right. You go on back, and wait for me by the foothills.
Give me two days. If I'm not back by then . . ."

"Rupert," said the unicorn slowly, "You don't have to do
this. We could always go back, and tell the Court we couldn't
find a dragon. No one would know."

"I'd know," said Rupert.

Their eyes met, and the unicorn bowed his head to the Prince.

"Good luck, Sire."

"Thank you," said Rupert, and turned quickly away.

"You be careful," muttered the unicorn. "I'd hate to have to break in another rider." He turned carefully around on the narrow path, and cautiously headed back down the mountainside.

Rupert stood a moment, listening to the slowly departing hoofbeats. The unicorn would be safe enough in the foothills. If scree hadn't blocked the trail, he would have found some other excuse to send the unicorn back; what remained of the quest was Rupert's responsibility, and his alone. There was no need for both of them to risk their lives. Rupert shook himself briskly, and studied the vast patch of scree before him. It looked treacherous. Forty feet across, but barely ten feet wide; one wrong move and the shifting stones would carry him clean over the edge. Rupert glanced briefly at the drop, and swallowed dryly. It was a long way down. If he were to slip, he'd probably reach the foothills before the unicorn did. He grinned sourly, and stepped lightly out onto the scree.

The packed stones shifted uneasily under his weight, and Rupert held his breath as he waited for them to settle. Slowly, step by step, foot by foot, he moved across the scree, taking his time and testing each part of the scree cautiously before committing his weight to it. Despite all his efforts, the sliding stones carried him closer and closer to the edge, and Rupert knew he wasn't going to make it. The gusting wind plucked fussily at his cloak, and he felt the scree stir under his boots. He shifted his weight slightly to compensate and the scree ran like water beneath him, carrying him remorselessly toward the escarpment's edge. Rupert threw himself flat, digging his hands deeply into the scree, and he slowly slid to a halt with one foot hanging over the edge. He could hear stones falling, tumbling down the side of the mountain.

Barely five feet of scree stood between him and solid rock, but it might as well have been five miles. Rupert lay still, breathing shallowly. He couldn't go on and he couldn't go back; the slightest movement could mean his death.

Rupert frowned as an answer occurred to him. A slight movement couldn't save him, but a lunge with all his strength behind it just might. It might also kill him. Rupert grinned suddenly. What the hell; if the scree didn't get him, the dragon probably would. He pulled his legs carefully up under him in one slow, controlled movement, and dug his feet into the scree. The shifting stones carried him a little closer to the edge. Rupert took a deep breath and lunged for the solid rock beyond the scree. He landed awkwardly, the impact slamming the breath from his lungs, but one outflung hand grasped an outcropping of rock, and he held on tightly as the sliding scree carried his body out over the long drop. For a moment he hung by one hand, feet searching helplessly for support, loose stones showering down around him, and then his free hand found a hold, and slowly he pulled himself up onto hard, solid rock. Rupert staggered a few feet away from the edge and then collapsed, shaking with reaction, his heart hammering madly. The unyielding stone path beneath him felt marvelously comforting.

He rested a while, and then clambered painfully to his feet. His whole body ached from fighting the scree, and he'd torn his hands on the jagged rock. Without the water canteens he'd left with the unicorn, Rupert couldn't even clean his wounds, so he did the next best thing and ignored them. He hoped like hell they wouldn't get infected; he was a long way from the nearest healer. He shrugged the thought aside, turned his back on the scree, and trudged tiredly along the uneven path that would lead him eventually to his dragon.

Some time later the trail suddenly disappeared, replaced by a seemingly endless series of narrow steps cut into the sheer rock face. Rupert turned away from the sight, and looked out over the long drop, taking in the view. Beyond the many miles of tended fields, the Forest seemed very small, and very far away. Rupert sighed once, regretfully, and then turned back to the steps and began the long climb.

The steps were crooked and uneven, and pain blazed through Rupert's legs and back as, for hour after hour, he fought to maintain his pace. The stone stairway stretched out behind and before him for as far as he could see, and after a while Rupert learned to keep his head down, and concentrate only on those steps directly ahead of him. The air grew steadily colder as he made his slow way up the mountain, and the driving wind carried sleet and snow from the summit. Rupert huddled inside his thin cloak and struggled on. Vicious gusts tugged at him as he climbed, and the bitter wind blew tears from his eyes. The cold numbed his hands and feet, his breath steamed on the chill air, and still he climbed, step after step after step, fighting the cold and the surging wind and his own pain.

He was Prince Rupert of the Forest Kingdom, and he was going to face his dragon.

The stairway ended in a narrow ledge before a vast cave mouth. Rupert stood swaying on the ledge, ignoring the freezing wind that wrapped his cloak about him, and the harsh breathing that seared his throat and burned in his chest. The cave gaped before him like some deep wound in the sheer rock face, filled with darkness. Rupert moved slowly forward, fatigue trembling in his legs. The Night Witch's map hadn't lied; he'd finally found his dragon. Ever since leaving the Court, he'd wondered how he'd feel when he finally had to face the dragon. If he'd be . . . scared. But now the time had come, and he didn't feel much of anything, if truth be told. He'd given his word, and he was here. He didn't believe he could beat the dragon, but then he never had. Deep down, he'd always known he was going to his death. Rupert shrugged. The Court expected him to die; maybe he'd live, anyway, just to spite them. He drew his sword, and took up the best position he could on the narrow ledge. He tried not to think about the long drop behind him, and concentrated instead on the correct form of the challenge.

All in all, he'd never felt less heroic in his life.

"Hideous monster, I, Prince Rupert of the Forest Kingdom do hereby challenge ye! Come forth and fight!"

There was a long pause, and then finally a deep voice from far inside the cave said, "Pardon?"

Feeling slightly ridiculous, the Prince took a better grip on his sword and repeated his challenge. There was an even longer pause, and then Rupert dropped into his fighting stance as the dragon emerged slowly out of the darkness, filling the cave mouth with his massive bulk. Long sweeping wings wrapped the creature like a ribbed emerald cloak, clasped at the chest by wickedly clawed hands. A good thirty feet from snout to tail, with light slithering caressingly along his shimmering green scales, the dragon towered over the Prince, and studied him with glowing golden eyes. Rupert hefted his sword, and the dragon smiled widely, revealing dozens of very sharp teeth.

"Hi," said the dragon. "Nice day, isn't it?"

Rupert blinked resentfully. "You're not supposed to say anything," he told the dragon firmly. "You're supposed to roar horribly, claw the ground, and then charge upon me breathing fire."

The dragon thought about this. Two thin plumes of smoke drifted up from his nostrils. "Why?" he asked finally.

Rupert lowered his sword, which was becoming heavier by the minute, and leaned on it. "Well," he said slowly, "It's traditional, I suppose. That's the way it's always been."

"Not with me," said the dragon. "Why do you want to kill me?"

"It's a long story," said the Prince.

The dragon grunted. "Thought it might be. You'd better come on in."

He retreated into his cave, and after a moment's hesitation Rupert followed him into what quickly proved to be a tunnel. In a strange way, he felt almost angry that he hadn't had to fight; he'd spent so long preparing for the moment, and now it had been taken from him. He wondered if the creature might just be playing with him, but it seemed unlikely. If the dragon had wanted him dead, he'd be dead by now. He stumbled clumsily on down the tunnel, a cold sweat beading his brow as the light fell away behind him. The unrelieved gloom reminded him of the Darkwood, and he was glad when the darkness soon gave way to the cheerful crimson glow of a banked fire. He hurried toward the light, and burst out of the tunnel mouth to find the dragon waiting patiently for him in a huge rock chamber easily five hundred feet across, the walls of which were covered with the largest collection of preserved butterflies Rupert had ever seen.

"I thought dragons collected hoards of gold and silver," said Rupert, gesturing at the hundreds of highly polished display cases.

The dragon shrugged. "Some collect gold and silver. Some collect jewels. I collect butterflies. They're just as pretty, aren't they?"

"Sure, sure," said the Prince soothingly, as sparks glowed hotly in the dragon's nostrils. He sheathed his sword, sank down onto his haunches opposite the reclining dragon, and studied him curiously.

"What's the matter?" asked the dragon.

"You're not quite what I expected," Rupert admitted.

The dragon chuckled. "Legends rarely are."

"But you can talk!"

"So can you."

"Well yes, but I'm human . . ."

"I had noticed," said the dragon dryly. "Look, most of the legends, that we're big and strong and nasty and eat people for any or no reason, all those stories were made up by dragons, to frighten people away."

"But . . ."

"Look," said the dragon, leaning forward suddenly. "One on one I'm more than a match for any human, but no dragon can fight an army." The huge creature hissed softly, golden eyes staring through Rupert at something only they could see. "Once, dragons filled the skies, masters of all that was. The sun warmed our wings as we soared above the clouds and watched the world turn beneath us. We tore gold and silver from the rock with our bare claws, and the earth trembled when we roared. Everything that lived feared us. And then came man, with his sword and his lance, his armor and his armies. We should have banded together while we still could, but no; we fought each other, and feuded and squabbled, and guarded our precious hoards. And one by one we fell, alone. Our time had passed."

The dragon lay brooding a moment, and then shook himself. "Why did you come to challenge me?"

"It's supposed to prove me worthy to be King."

"Do you want to kill me?"

Rupert shrugged, confused. "It'd be easier if you were the monster you're supposed to be. Haven't you slaughtered women and children, burned property to the ground, and stolen cattle?"

"Certainly not," said the dragon, shocked. "What kind of creature do you think I am?"

Rupert raised an eyebrow, and the dragon had the grace to look a little sheepish. "All right, maybe I did raze the odd village, devour an occasional maiden, but that was a long time ago. I was a dragon; they expected it of me. I'm retired now."

There was a long pause. Rupert frowned into the gently crackling fire. This wasn't at all what he'd expected.

"Do you want to kill me?" he asked the dragon.

"Not particularly. I'm getting a little old for all this nonsense."

"Well, don't you want to eat me?"

"No," said the dragon firmly. "People give me heartburn."

There was another long silence.

"Look," said the dragon finally, "Killing me is supposed to prove your worth, right?"

"Right," said the Prince. That much he was sure of.

"So, why not bring back a live dragon? Isn't that an even braver thing to do?"

Rupert thought about it. "That might just do it," he said cautiously. "Nobody's ever captured a real live dragon before . . ."

"Well then, that's our answer!"

"Don't you mind being captured?" asked Rupert diffidently.

The dragon chuckled. "I could do with a bit of a holiday. Travel to strange lands, meet new people; just what I need." The dragon peered about him and then beckoned for Rupert to lean closer. "Er . . . Prince . . ."

"Yes?"

"Do you by any chance rescue Princesses? Only I've got one here, and she's driving me crazy."

"You're holding a Princess captive?" yelled Rupert, jumping to his feet and clapping a hand to his swordhilt.

"Keep your voice down!" hissed the dragon. "She'll hear you! I'm not holding her captive; I'll be glad to see the back of her. Some Court's elders sent her up here as a sacrifice, and I hadn't the heart to kill her. She can't go back, and I can't just throw her out. I thought maybe you could take her off my hands . . ."

Rupert sat slowly down again and rubbed gently at his aching brow. Just when he thought he was getting the hang of things, somebody changed the rules.

"She's a real Princess?"

"Far as I know."

"What's wrong with her?" asked Rupert warily.

"Dragon!" yelled a strident voice from a side tunnel. The dragon winced.

"That's what's wrong with her."

The Princess burst into the cavern from one of the side tunnels, and then stopped short on seeing the Prince. Rupert scrambled to his feet. The Princess was dressed in a long flowing gown that might once have been white, but was now stained a dozen colors from dried mud and grime. She was young, barely into her twenties, and handsome rather than beautiful. Deep blue eyes and a generous mouth contrasted strongly with the mannish jut of her jaw. Long blonde hair fell almost to her waist in two meticulously twisted plaits. She was poised and slender and easily six feet tall. As Rupert considered the right courteous words with which to greet a Princess, she whooped with joy and rushed forward to throw her arms around him. Rupert staggered back a pace.

"My hero," she cooed, bending down to nuzzle his ear. "You've come to rescue me!"

"Well, yes," muttered Rupert, trying to break free without seeming too discourteous. "Glad to be of service. I'm Prince Rupert . . ."

The Princess hugged him fiercely, driving the air from his lungs. *I was safer with the dragon,* thought Rupert, as bright spots drifted before his eyes. The Princess finally let him go, and stood back to take a good look at him.

He couldn't have been much older than her, she thought, but the recent scars that marred one side of his face gave him a hard, dangerous look. His long slender hands were battered and torn, and covered with freshly dried blood. His leather jerkin and trousers had obviously seen a great deal of use, his cloak was a mess, and all in all the fellow looked more like a bandit than a Prince. The Princess frowned dubiously, and then her mouth twitched; all in all, she probably didn't look much like a Princess, either.

"Where's your armor?" she asked.

"I left it in the Tanglewood," said Rupert.

"And your steed?"

"At the base of the mountain."

"You did at least bring your sword?"

"Of course," said Rupert, drawing the blade to show her.

She snatched it out of his hand, tested the balance, and swept it through a few expert passes.

"It'll do," she decided, and gave the sword back to him. "Get on with it."

"Get on with what?" asked Rupert politely.

"With killing the dragon, of course," said the Princess. "That's what you're here for, isn't it?"

"Ah," said Rupert, "The dragon and I have talked it over, and I'm going to take him back to my Castle alive. And you too, of course."

"That's not honorable," said the Princess flatly.

"Oh yes it is," said the dragon.

"You keep out of this," snapped the Princess.

"Gladly," said the dragon.

"Who's side are you on?" demanded Rupert, feeling he needed all the help he could get.

"Anybody's who'll rescue me from this Princess," said the dragon feelingly.

The Princess kicked him.

Rupert closed his eyes a moment. When he got back to Court, he intended to give the minstrels some explicit instructions on how to sing their songs. This sort of thing needed to be pointed up more. He coughed politely, and the Princess swung angrily back to face him.

"What's your name?" he asked.

"Julia. Princess Julia of Hillsdown."

"Well, Princess Julia, you have two choices. Come back to my Castle with me and the dragon, or stay here on your own."

"You can't leave me here," said the Princess. "That wouldn't be honorable."

"Watch me," said Rupert.

Julia blinked, and then peered at the dragon, who was staring at the cavern ceiling and blowing different colored smoke rings from his nostrils.

"You wouldn't leave me here alone. Would you?"

The dragon grinned widely, his many teeth gleaming crimson in the firelight.

Julia glared at him. "You wait," she muttered ominously.

"Can we make a start now, please?" asked Rupert. "My unicorn's only going to wait two days for me to return."

"You ride a unicorn?" asked the dragon. Rupert glanced at the Princess, and felt his face grow hot.

"It's not easy being a Prince. It's to do with Bloodlines; the last thing any dynasty needs is bastard pretenders to the throne popping up all over the place. So unmarried royalty have to be kept . . . pure."

"Right," said the Princess. "That's why the elders sent me up here."

The dragon coughed tactfully. "Is it far to your Castle, Rupert?"

Rupert started to answer, and then had to grab Julia's arm for support as his head suddenly started to swim. His legs trembled violently, and he sat down quickly to avoid falling.

"What's the matter?" asked Julia, as she helped Rupert lower himself to the cavern floor.

"Just need a bit of a rest," he muttered groggily, passing a shaking hand across his aching temples. "Hot in here. I'll be all right in a minute."

The dragon regarded the Prince narrowly. "Rupert; how did you get up the mountain?"

"Followed the trail until the scree blocked it. Then I sent my unicorn back, crossed the scree, and used the stairway."

"You came all that way on foot? In this weather?" Julia looked at Rupert with new respect. "I came in mid-summer. I had an escort of seven guards and a pack mule, and it still took us the best part of four days to manage it." She took his battered hands in hers, and winced. "You're so cold you can't even feel your wounds, can you? You must be frozen to the bone; it's a wonder you were still on your feet."

Rupert shrugged uncomfortably. "I'm all right. Just a bit tired, that's all."

Julia and the dragon exchanged a glance.

"Sure," said the dragon. "Look, why don't you warm yourself at the fire a while, and then I'll fly you both down. It's a lovely day for flying."

"Sure," said Rupert drowsily. "Lovely day . . . for flying." His chin sank slowly forward onto his chest, and sleep rolled over him like a tide. The Princess lowered him gently to the floor, wrapped furs around him, and then washed and bandaged his hands. Rupert knew nothing of this, but for the first time since leaving the Darkwood, his rest was free of nightmares.

*   *   *

A few hours' sleep did much to restore him, and all too soon Rupert found himself perched awkwardly on the dragon's shoulders, hugging the creature's neck like he'd never let go. The Princess Julia was sitting right behind Rupert, and holding him just as tightly, if not more so.

"I hate heights," she confided in a small voice.

"You're not alone," Rupert assured her. He looked around at the dark clouds filling the sky, and shivered as a bitter wind swept over the narrow ledge outside the cave mouth. "If this is a good day for flying, I'd hate to see a bad one."

"Ready?" asked the dragon, flexing his wings eagerly.

"Uh . . ." said Rupert.

"Then hold tight," called the dragon, and running quickly forward, he threw himself off the ledge and fell like a stone. The wind whistled past them as they hurtled down, and Rupert squeezed his eyes shut. And then the breath was knocked from him as the dragon suddenly spread his wings, and with a series of bone-shuddering jolts, the fall quickly became a controlled glide. After a while, Rupert cautiously opened his eyes and peered past the dragon's neck to take in the view. He then rather wished he hadn't. The cultivated fields far below lay stretched out like a pastel-shaded patchwork quilt. The Forest lay to the North, with the Darkwood clearly visible, like a canker feeding on the body of which it was a part. Rupert swallowed with a suddenly dry mouth as the base of the mountain rushed up to meet him at harrowing speed. On the whole, he just might have preferred to walk down after all. The dragon's massive wings beat strongly to either side of him, and then stretched to their full extent as the creature soared in to a slightly bumpy landing that jarred every bone in Rupert's body. The dragon folded his wings and looked about him.

"There you are. Wasn't that exciting?"

"Exciting," said Rupert.

"Does you good to feel the wind rushing past you," said the dragon. "Uh . . . you can let go of me and get down now, you know."

"We're getting used to the idea slowly," said Julia. "My stomach still thinks it's up in the clouds somewhere."

She carefully unwrapped her arms from Rupert, and then the two of them helped each other down from the dragon's back. The solid earth beneath their feet had never seemed

so welcome or so comforting. The dragon had brought them
to the start of the mountain trail, and Rupert looked around
him. As he'd expected, there was no sign of the unicorn.

"Unicorn! If you're not back here by the time I count ten
I'll turn you over to the Royal Zoo to give rides to children!"

"You wouldn't dare!" said a shocked voice from behind a
nearby outcropping of rock.

"Don't put money on it," Rupert growled.

There was a pause, and then the unicorn stuck his head
out from behind the rock and smiled ingratiatingly. "Welcome back, Sire. Who are your friends?"

"This is the Princess Julia. I rescued her."

"Ha!" said the Princess, loudly.

"And this is a dragon. He's coming back with us to the
Castle."

The unicorn disappeared behind the rock again.

"Unicorn, either you come out or I'll send the dragon
after you. Even worse, I might send the Princess after you."

Julia kicked him in the ankle. Rupert smiled determinedly,
and vowed to do something unpleasant to the first minstrel
he met singing of the joys of adventuring. The unicorn
trotted reluctantly into view, halting a safe distance away
from the dragon.

"Oh, you've decided to join us, have you?" asked Rupert.

"Only under protest."

"He does everything under protest," Rupert explained to
the Princess.

"I heard that!" The unicorn stared unhappily at the dragon.
"I don't suppose there's any chance that thing is a vegetarian?"

The dragon smiled. His pointed teeth gleamed brightly in
the sunlight.

"I thought not," said the unicorn.

The Darkwood brooded before them, darkness envelop-
ing rotting trees in a starless night that had never known a
moon. The path Rupert had cut through the briar lay open
before him, and he studied the narrow gap with horrid
fascination, cold sweat beading his brow. Through all the
many weeks it had taken him to reach Dragonslair mountain
and return, he'd been unable to shake off the gut-deep fear
the darkness had imposed on him. He shivered suddenly as
the chill breeze drifting from the decaying trees brought to

him the familiar stench of corruption. His hand dropped to his swordhilt as though searching for some kind of comfort, or courage. His breathing grew harsh and unsteady as the horror mounted within him.

Not again. Please, not again.

"The Darkwood," said Princess Julia, her voice tinged with awe. "I thought it was just a legend, a tale to frighten children on dark nights. It smells like something died in there. Are you sure we have to pass through it to reach the Forest Kingdom?"

Rupert nodded briefly, afraid that if he tried to speak his voice would betray how much the mere sight of the darkness unnerved him. They had to pass through the Darkwood. There was no other way. But still he hesitated, standing stiffly beside the unicorn, unable to make the slightest move toward entering the long night that had tested his soul and found it wanting.

"I suppose I could fly you and Julia over," said the dragon slowly, "But that would mean abandoning the unicorn."

"No," said Rupert immediately. "I won't do that."

"Thanks," said the unicorn.

Rupert nodded curtly, his eyes fixed on the never-ending darkness.

"Come on," said the Princess finally. "The sooner we start, the sooner we'll be out the other side." She looked at Rupert expectantly.

"I can't," he said helplessly.

"What's the matter?" snapped the Princess. "Afraid of the dark?"

"Yes," said Rupert softly. "Oh yes."

Julia stared at him in amazement, taking in his pale face and trembling hands.

"You're kidding, right? You can't be serious. Afraid of the *dark?*"

"Shut up," said the unicorn. "You don't understand."

"I think perhaps I do," said the dragon. His great golden eyes studied the darkness warily. "The Darkwood was old when I was young, Julia. Legend claims it has always been here, and always will; darkness made manifest upon the earth. For any who dare to enter, there are dangers for both body and soul." The dragon stared into the darkness a while, and then looked away uneasily. "What happened to you in the Darkwood, Rupert?"

Rupert struggled for words that could express the true horror of the darkness, but there were no words. He simply knew, beyond any shadow of doubt, that if he entered the Darkwood again he would die or go mad. With an effort that shook him, Rupert tore his gaze away from the darkness. He'd faced the Darkwood once; he could do it again. Rupert clung to the thought desperately. The long night had marked him, but it hadn't broken him. Perhaps this time the journey would be easier to bear. He had food and water and companions. There was firewood for torches.

If I turn back now, I'll always be afraid of the dark.

Rupert took a deep, shuddering breath and let it go.

"Rupert," said the dragon, "What happened to you in the Darkwood?"

"Nothing," said Rupert hoarsely. "Nothing at all. Let's go."

He urged the unicorn forward, but the animal hesitated, and looked back at him.

"Rupert; you don't have to do this . . ."

"Move, damn you," Rupert whispered, and the unicorn followed him silently into the Darkwood. Julia followed the unicorn, and the dragon brought up the rear, the needle-thorned briar rattling vainly against his armored hide.

Night slammed down as they crossed the Darkwood's boundary, and Rupert bit his lip to keep from crying out as the darkness swept over him. The familiar country sounds of bird and beast and wind were gone, replaced by a still, sullen silence. Out in the dark, demons were watching. He couldn't see them, but he knew they were there. All his instincts shrieked for him to light a torch, but he dared not. Light would attract the demons, and the surrounding briar made his party a sitting target. He hurried forward, wincing as thorns stung his outstretched hands. The trail seemed narrower than he remembered, but the briar finally fell away, and Rupert whispered for the party to stop a moment. He fumbled the tinderbox from his backpack, and after several false starts, he lit a single torch. The dancing flame seemed strangely subdued, as though the Darkwood begrudged even that much light within its domain. Decaying trees lined the narrow path, gnarled and misshapen. Their branches held no leaves, and gaping cracks revealed rotten hearts, but Rupert knew with horrid certainty that somehow they were still alive.

"Rupert . . ." said Julia.

"Later," he said roughly. "Let's go."

The company moved slowly along the twisting trail in their little pool of light, heading into the heart of the darkness.

They hadn't been moving long before the first demon found them. Crooked and malformed, it crouched at the edge of the torch's light, watching from the shadows with blood-red eyes. Rupert drew his sword, and the demon disappeared silently back into the darkness.

"What the hell was that?" whispered Julia.

"Demon," said Rupert shortly. The scars on his face throbbed with remembered pain. He handed Julia the torch and moved forward to stare about him. Faint shuffling sounds hovered on the edge of his hearing, and then, slowly, the torchlight showed him glimpses of twisted, misshapen creatures that crouched and scurried and slithered both before and behind the company. Glowing eyes stared unblinkingly from the shadows of the rotting trees. Rupert hefted his sword, but the cold steel had lost all power to comfort him.

"It's not possible," he said numbly. "Demons never hunt in packs. Everyone knows that."

"Obviously these demons don't," said the dragon. "Now get back here, please. You're a little too far from the rest of us for my liking."

Rupert fell back to join the company. The demons pressed closer still.

"Why don't they attack?" said Julia quietly.

"Don't give them ideas," muttered the unicorn. "Maybe they just can't believe anyone would be stupid enough to walk into such an obvious trap. I can't believe it and I'm doing it."

"They're afraid of the dragon," said Rupert.

"How very sensible of them," said the dragon.

Rupert tried to smile, but it felt more like a grimace. It took all his self-control not to strike out blindly at the gathering demons. Fear writhed in his gut and trembled in his arms, but he wouldn't give in to it. Not yet. Unlike the darkness, the demons could be fought. He took a firm grip on his sword, and stepped forward. The demons faded back into the darkness and were gone. Julia sighed slowly in relief, and the torchlight was suddenly unsteady as she finally allowed her hands to shake. Rupert glared about him into the unresponsive darkness, angry that the demons had backed away from a confrontation, denying him the comfort and release of action. He slammed his sword back into its scabbard, and led the company on into the endless night.

Some time later they reached a small clearing, and stopped for a while, to get what rest they could before continuing. Julia built a fire in the middle of the clearing while Rupert set torches to mark the perimeter. The need for caution was past; it was clear the demons could find the party whenever they chose. Rupert lit the last torch and retreated quickly back to the blazing fire. The leaping flames threw back the dark, and the fire's warmth eased the chill in his bones. Rupert frowned as he sank wearily down beside Julia; he didn't remember the Darkwood being this cold on his first journey through. He didn't remember this clearing, either. He shrugged, added another branch to the crackling fire, and pulled his cloak tightly about him. On the other side of the fire, the unicorn lay dozing in the shadows. The dragon was off in the dark somewhere, probably frightening demons. Rupert glanced covertly at Julia. The Princess sat huddled under the only spare blanket, shivering and holding out her hands to the dancing flames.

"Here," said Rupert brusquely, taking off his cloak. "You're cold."

"So are you," said Julia. "I'm all right."

"You sure?"

"Really."

Rupert didn't press the point.

"How much longer before we get out of the Darkwood?" asked Julia, as Rupert refastened his cloak.

"I don't know," he admitted. "Time passes differently here. On my first trip it could have been days or weeks; you lose all track of time in the dark. At least this time we've food and water and firewood. That should make a difference."

"You crossed the Darkwood without light or provisions?" Julia looked at Rupert with something like respect, and then looked quickly away. When she spoke again, her voice was carefully neutral. "What's your Castle like, Rupert?"

"Old," said Rupert, and smiled. "You'll like it."

"Will I?"

"Of course. Everyone'll make you very welcome."

"Why should they?" said Julia softly, staring into the fire. "I'm just another Princess without a dowry. Seven sisters stand between me and the throne, even assuming the elders would have me back. And they won't."

"Why not?"

"Because . . ." Julia looked at him sternly. "You won't laugh?"

"I promise."

"I ran away. They wanted me to marry some Prince I'd never met, for political reasons. You know."

"I know," said Rupert. "Bloodlines."

"So I ran away. I didn't even reach the frontier. They already had seven Princesses, and they didn't need an eighth, so they sent me to the dragon's cave." Julia glared into the fire. "My father signed the warrant. My own father."

Rupert put a comforting hand on her arm, but she jerked away.

"Don't worry," he said lamely. "Everything'll work out. I'll find a way to get you home again."

"I don't want to go home; as far as they're concerned I'm dead! And sometimes I wish I was!"

She jumped up and ran off into the darkness. Rupert got up to go after her.

"Don't."

Rupert looked round to find the dragon watching from the shadows. "Why not?"

"She doesn't want you to see her crying," said the dragon.

"Oh." Rupert shuffled uncertainly, and then sat down again.

"She'll be back in a while," said the dragon, moving forward to squat beside him.

"Yes. I'd help her if I could."

"Of course you would. Julia's not a bad sort. For a human."

Rupert almost smiled. "We all have our problems."

"You, too?"

"Of course; why do you think I came on this damn quest?"

"Honor, glory, love of adventure?"

Rupert just looked at him.

"Sorry," said the dragon.

"I'm a second son," said Rupert. "I can't inherit as long as my brother's alive."

"And you didn't want to kill your own brother." The dragon nodded understandingly.

Rupert snorted. "Can't stand the fellow. But if I declare against him, the Forest Land would be split by civil war. That's why my father sent me on this quest. You were supposed to kill me and rid him of a vexing problem."

"Your own father sent you out to die?"

"Yes," said Rupert softly. "My own father. Officially, it was a quest to prove me worthy to the throne, but everyone knew. Including me."

"But then, why did you go through with it? You didn't have to face me."

"I'm a Prince of the Forest Kingdom," said Rupert. "I'd given my word. Besides . . ."

"Yes?"

Rupert shrugged. "My family's other major problem is money. We're broke."

"Broke? But you rule the country! How can you be broke?"

"The Land's just had its second famine in a row, the Barons are refusing to pay taxes, and if our currency was any more debased you could use it as bottle caps."

"Oh," said the dragon.

"Right. Oh."

"So bringing me back alive isn't going to help you much."

"Not really," admitted the Prince. "Apart from the hoard you were supposed to have, dragon's hide is worth a lot of money, you know. So are dragon's teeth. And as for dragon's . . ."

"I know what they're worth, thank you," said the dragon huffily. "I value them myself, rather."

Rupert blushed and looked away. "Well, you see my problem."

"I'll think about it," said the dragon.

"Will you two shut up and let me sleep," muttered the unicorn blearily.

The Princess came back out of the darkness with slightly puffy eyes that nobody commented on, and settled herself by the fire.

"What were you two talking about?" she asked.

"It seems the Prince's family is financially embarassed," said the dragon.

"Broke," said the unicorn.

"Maybe when this is over I should go on another quest," Rupert said gloomily. "Look for a pot of gold at the Rainbow's End."

"If you do, you can walk," said the unicorn.

"Rainbow's End," said the dragon slowly. "It's not just a legend."

"You mean it's real?" asked Julia.

The dragon hesitated. "Sometimes."

"How do I find it?" asked Rupert.

"You don't; it finds you." The dragon frowned, struggling for the right words. "Rainbow's End is a state of mind as much as a place. If you reach it, you can find your heart's desire, but that may not be what you think it is. There's a spell . . ."

Everyone froze as a branch snapped somewhere out in the dark, and then they surged to their feet. Rupert drew his sword and Julia pulled a wicked-looking dagger from her boot. The unicorn pressed close beside the dragon, nervously pawing the ground. And then, one by one, the torches at the clearing's perimeter guttered and went out, and darkness welled forward like a tide.

"They've found us again," said Rupert.

A figure stepped into the clearing. Tall, spindly and corpsepale, it squatted at the edge of the firelight, clawed hands twitching restlessly at its sides. Faintly glowing eyes stared unblinkingly from a broad toadlike head. As the company watched in horrified fascination, more demons crept forward out of the dark. Some walked on two legs, some on four, and some crawled on their bellies in the dirt. Firelight gleamed redly on claw and fang. No one creature was shaped like any other, but all had the mark of foulness on them, a darkness in the soul. Rupert raised his sword and moved forward, and the toad demon came to meet him, loping horribly fast across the uneven ground. Rupert dropped into his fighting stance, and then swayed aside at the last moment to let the demon rush by him. His sword swung out in a long arc and bit deeply into the creature's back. Dark blood spurted, and the demon fell, writhing silently on the

ground until the unicorn slammed down a well-placed hoof.
The watching shapes melted back into the darkness.

"What are our chances?" muttered Julia.

"Not good," Rupert admitted, swinging his sword back
and forth before him. "There's too many of them."

"But we've got a dragon with us," Julia protested. "Everyone knows dragons can't be killed, except by heroes
whose hearts are pure."

"Legends," said the dragon wearily. "I'm old, Julia. Older
than you can imagine. My eyesight's poor, my bones ache in
the winter, and I haven't breathed fire in years. Don't even
know if I still can. No, Julia; dragons die just as easily as
any other creature."

"Are you saying we've no chance at all?" asked Julia
softly.

"There's always a chance," said Rupert, hefting his sword.

"Not that way," said the dragon. "You'll have to make
the Rainbow Run."

"What are you talking about?" snapped Rupert, eyes still
fixed on the lurking shadows among the rotting trees.

"Rainbow's End. I know a spell that will take you right to
it. If you're strong enough. Any man who can run down the
Rainbow will find his heart's desire; whatever that might
be."

"Try the spell," said Julia. "I won't let those things take
me alive. I've heard stories."

Rupert nodded grimly. He'd heard stories, too.

"Look out!" yelled Julia. Rupert howled his battle cry
and swung his sword two-handed as demons burst from the
Darkwood's concealing shadows. His blade flashed in short,
vicious arcs, slicing through his opponents like overripe
wheat. Blood flew on the air, but the demons never made a
sound, even when they died. The Darkwood silence was
broken only by the stamp of feet on earth, and the chunk of
Rupert's blade as it bit into flesh. The dragon reared up to
his full height and slammed into the demons, rending and
tearing. The dead and the dying lay piled around him on the
bloodied earth, and still they came. Julia drove her dagger
into a demon's bulging eye and kicked the twisting corpse
aside. The unicorn moved quickly in to protect her, his
hooves and horn already dripping gore. Rupert spun and
danced, his sword tearing through flesh with murderous

skill, but for every demon that fell another rose out of the dark to take its place. A growing ache burned in his arms and back, and every time he swung his sword it seemed a little heavier. Rupert didn't give a damn. The bottled-up frustration of months on end found an outlet in his fury, and he grinned like a wolf as his sword rose and fell in steady butchery.

And then it was over. The demons melted back into the safety of the darkness, leaving their dead behind them. Rupert stared about him as he slowly lowered his sword, his harsh breathing aching in his chest. Blood and death lay scattered across the clearing, and as his anger ebbed away, Rupert felt tired and cold and just a little sick. He'd been taught the use of a sword, as befitted his station, but his newfound joy in killing disturbed him. To take pleasure in slaughter was the demon's way. The blood dripping from his blade suddenly disgusted him, and he sheathed his sword without bothering to clean it. He swallowed dryly, and looked round to check how his companions had fared in the battle. The dragon seemed pretty much unscathed, though his claws and teeth gleamed with a fresh crimson sheen. The unicorn's white coat was dappled with blood, little of it his own. Julia was cleaning her dagger in a businesslike way, but her hands were shaking. Rupert shook his head slowly. Without rage to keep him moving, fatigue left him weak and trembling, but already he could hear faint rustlings and stirrings in the dark beyond the clearing. He turned to the dragon.

"Use the damned spell," he said gratingly. "Another rush like that, and they'll roll right over us."

The dragon nodded. "It's all down to you, Rupert. First you'll see a light in the distance, like a beacon, and then the Wild Magic will show you a path. Follow it. That's the Rainbow Run. What you'll find depends on you."

Rupert stared out into the dark, and a voice deep inside him said, *I can't.* It had been hard enough to go back into the Darkwood armed with light and friends, but to give them up and go off into the darkness on his own . . . *Haven't I done enough? I can't go back into the dark! I'm afraid!*

"Rupert?"

I'm afraid!

"Set the spell," said Rupert.

"Get ready," said the dragon. "I need a moment to prepare."

Rupert nodded stiffly and moved away to join the unicorn.

"Look after the Princess for me, will you?"

"With my life," promised the unicorn. "When there's no other choice, I can be heroic, too, you know."

"I never doubted it." The Prince smiled.

The unicorn shuffled his feet uncertainly. "All in all, I've been on worse quests, Sire."

"I hate to think what they must have been like."

"Will you shut up," said the unicorn affectionately. "And mind your back on the Rainbow Run. I've grown accustomed to having you around to gripe at."

Rupert hugged the unicorn's neck, and turned away to find Julia waiting for him. She offered him a handkerchief.

"A lady's favor," she said. "The hero always carries a lady's favor."

"I always wanted one," said Rupert softly. He tucked the silk square inside his tattered leather jerkin. "I'll bring it back safely."

"Bring back some help, that's the main thing." She leaned forward suddenly and kissed him. "And come back safe yourself, or I'll never forgive you."

She hurried off into the shadows. The Prince raised a hand to his lips. There was one thing the minstrels hadn't lied about. The dragon came forward.

"Are you ready?"

Rupert looked out into the darkness. *I'm afraid. But I gave my word.*

"Ready as I'll ever be. You?"

The dragon nodded. "The spell is set."

Rupert drew his sword, hefted it, and then handed it to the dragon. "Give this to Julia. It'll only slow me down when I'm running."

"Of course," said the dragon.

"A light!" yelled the unicorn. Rupert whirled to look. A crimson glare showed deep in the Darkwood.

"That's it!" cried the dragon, but Rupert was already off and running. He burst through the demons at the clearing's edge and was gone before they could stop him. A trail formed before him in the darkness, seeming to glow and sparkle beneath his pounding feet. A demon leapt out of the dark to block his path, only to scream and fall back as light flared up from the trail to engulf it. Rupert shot a quick glance at the motionless body and ran on. Behind him he heard the first sounds of battle as the demon host fell on his companions. He forced himself to run faster. The Darkwood trees rushed past him. The path glowed bright against the dark. Breath burned in his lungs, ached in his chest, and a cold sweat ran down his sides as his arms pumped, but he was beyond pain, beyond fear, driven only by a desperate need to somehow save his friends. He didn't know how long he'd been running, but the trail still shimmered ahead of him, and the beacon seemed to draw no nearer. *It's not how fast you run,* a voice whispered inside him, *It's how badly you need it.* Fatigue shivered through his aching legs, and he saw with horror that the path was slowly fading away. He drove himself even harder, crying aloud at the pain that stabbed through him, and then he tripped and fell headlong as the path guttered and went out.

I'm sorry, Julia, he thought despairingly as the dark washed over him. *I so wanted to be a hero for you.*

Light roared against the darkness. Rupert staggered to his feet as vivid hues cascaded down around him. His ears were full of the thunder of a mighty falls. Time seemed to slow and stop. Brilliant colors burned into Rupert's eyes as he threw back his head and raised his hands to the glory of the Rainbow.

And then the Rainbow was gone, and the night was darker than before.

For a moment Rupert just stood there, entranced by the splendor of Rainbow's End, and then slowly he lowered his head, and looked about him. Where the Rainbow had touched them, the gnarled and twisted trees were straight and true, and leaf-strewn branches framed a hole in the overhead canopy through which moonlight streamed, forming a pool of light around the Prince. And there before him on the ground lay a sword. Rupert stooped down and picked it up. It was an ordinary, everyday sword with sharp edges and a good balance. Rupert smiled bitterly as the darkness gathered around him. The treasure of Rainbow's End . . . just another legend. From far off the sounds of fighting came to him, and Rupert turned to find the shimmering trail waiting to lead him back to his beleaguered friends. He hefted the sword once and then ran back through the Darkwood.

He burst back into the clearing, and for a moment all he could see was a mass of leaping, clawing demonkind. The dragon surged back and forth, firelight glowing ruddy on his flailing wings and tail. Blood streamed from his terrible teeth. Julia crouched behind the dragon, sword in hand, moving always to keep the fire between her and the demons. Her robe was soaked in blood. There was no sign of the unicorn. As Rupert hesitated at the clearing's edge, a demon ducked under the dragon's guard, knocked the Princess to the ground and stooped over her. Rupert screamed and ran forward. A demon leapt toward him. He cut it in two and ran on without pausing. More demons came to block his way. His sword seemed weightless in his hand, and demon blood fell to the ground like a ghastly dew.

He reached the demon's side to find the Princess busily gutting the demon that had attacked her. She looked up as he joined her, and wiped at her face with a bloodied hand.

"Took your time, didn't you?"

Rupert grinned, and they stood back-to-back, swords at the ready, as the demons came at them again. Julia wielded her sword with surprising skill, her face grim and determined. Rupert spun and danced, his sword licking out to kill and kill again, but he knew it was hopeless. The darting, leaping creatures swarmed out of the dark in seemingly endless numbers, and he was already exhausted. Eventually, they were bound to pull him down. The company's only chance for survival had been the Rainbow Run, and he'd failed. Rupert gasped as demon claws raked across his rib cage. He cut the demon down, but he could feel blood running down his side in a thick stream. His head swam dizzily, but the pain kept him from fainting. More demons pressed forward, and Rupert knew he was no longer fast enough to stop them all. He silently cursed the missing unicorn to hell for his cowardice in deserting the party to their fate, and took a firm grip on his sword. He hoped it would be a quick death.

And then the dragon raised himself in all his ancient glory, and fire blazed on the night. Demons curled up and fell away like scorched leaves as the dragon's flaming breath washed over them. Others fell to roll on the ground in silent agony before lying still. The dragon's awesome head swayed back and forth, his fire scouring the clearing of demonkind, and then the flame flickered and went out.

In the last of the light, Rupert watched the survivors fall back to join others of their kind, waiting in the darkness beyond the clearing. More demons. There were always more demons. Rupert slowly lowered his sword and leaned on it. He dared not sit down for fear he'd never get to his feet again. *His strength is as the strength of ten, because his heart is pure.* Minstrels. Rupert sighed softly. Julia sat suddenly down beside him as her legs gave way. Her eyes were glazed with fatigue, but somehow she still found enough strength to hang onto her sword. Anger stirred in Rupert afresh as he realized not all the blood on Julia's dress came from demons. He stared horrified as he took in the terrible extent of her injuries, and swore silently. If he hadn't taken her from the dragon's cave; if he hadn't brought her into the Darkwood; if he hadn't left her to go chasing after a legend . . . If. *You're a brave lass, Julia,* Rupert thought wearily. *You deserved better than me.* He stared out into the darkness; looking at Julia hurt too much. He could hear the demons gathering. There seemed no end to their numbers. Rupert turned to the dragon, crouching exhausted by the fire. One wing hung limply, half torn away, and golden blood ran steadily down his heaving side. The dragon slowly raised his great head and studied the blood-spattered Prince.

"Did you reach the Rainbow's End?"

"Yes," said Rupert. "It was very beautiful."

"What did you find there?"

"A sword. Just an ordinary sword." Rupert couldn't keep the bitterness from his voice as threw the sword onto the ground before him. The dragon studied the sword, and then looked away.

"The Wild Magic is often . . . capricious." He stared out into the darkness. "The demons are almost ready. One last attack, and it will all be over."

"We can't just give up," Rupert protested. "We've beaten them off twice . . ."

"I'm hurt, Rupert," the dragon said simply. "I'm too old for all this nonsense."

Rupert shook his head, searching for some kind of anger

to hold back his growing despair. "What happened to the unicorn?"

"He's over there," said the dragon.

Rupert followed the dragon's gaze. Not a dozen feet from the fire, the unicorn lay stretched out and unmoving, half-hidden under a pile of demon bodies.

"Unicorn!" Rupert staggered over to his fallen steed and knelt beside him. The unicorn tried to raise his bloodied head, and couldn't.

"Will you keep your voice down? My head hurts."

Bloody rents crawled along the unicorn's flanks, and his rib cage had been smashed in. His horn had been broken off at the base, leaving only a jagged stub.

"I'm sorry," said Rupert. "I'm sorry."

"Not your fault," said the unicorn. His voice broke, and he coughed a bloody foam.

Rupert started to cry.

"Stop that," said the unicorn gruffly. "You should see the other guy. Did you find the Rainbow's End?"

Rupert nodded, unable to speak.

"Well, how about that. Some quest, eh, lad? They'll sing songs about us forever."

"And get it all wrong," said Rupert.

"Wouldn't surprise me," said the unicorn. "I think I'll take a little rest now, lad. I'm tired."

"Unicorn?"

"I'm so tired."

"Unicorn!"

After a while, Julia came and crouched beside him.

"He lost his horn for me," said Rupert bitterly. "What did I ever do for him, except lead him into danger?"

"He was your friend," said Julia, gently.

She couldn't have hurt him more if she'd tried.

"Rupert!" cried the dragon. "Demons!"

"I brought your sword," said Julia as they rose painfully to their feet, and she offered Rupert the sword he'd found at Rainbow's End. Rupert glared at the sword, and felt a slow, steady rage burn within him. All around him he could see demons spilling into the clearing, bringing the darkness with them. Firelight gleamed on fang and claw. The dragon stood ready to meet them, crippled but undefeated. Julia stood before him, bloodied but unbowed, waiting for him to

take his sword and fight at her side. And the unicorn lay
dying at his feet.

He was your friend.

Rupert reached out and took the sword. Anger and sorrow surged through him as he realized there was nothing left
for him to do except die bravely, and take as many of his
enemies with him as he could. He raised the sword above
his head, and then all his rage, all his anguish, all his
determination seemed to flow up into the blade and out, out
into the long night and beyond, like a great shout of defiance against the dark. Light burst from the blade, filling the
clearing. The demons cowered and fell back, and then turned
to flee as, with the thunder of a mighty falls, the Rainbow
slammed down into the Darkwood.

Time seemed to slow and stop. Brilliant colors scorched
back the night, scything through the demonkind, who fell to
the blood-soaked ground and did not rise again. And still
the shimmering light poured over them, until their misshapen forms melted and flowed into the broken earth and
were gone. And then the Rainbow · was gone, and once
again night held sway over the Darkwood.

In the sudden silence, the crackling of the campfire seemed
very loud. Moonlight filled the clearing, falling through a
wide hole in the overhead canopy, and the surrounding
trees stood straight and whole where the Rainbow's light
had touched them. Rupert slowly lowered the sword and
studied it, but it was just a sword again. *Well*, he thought
finally, *it seems some legends are true . . .*

"Can anyone explain to me why I'm not dead?" asked the
unicorn.

"Unicorn!" Rupert turned quickly to find the animal climbing shakily to his feet. His wounds had healed, leaving only
faint scars, and blood no longer ran from his mouth and
nostrils. Rupert gaped at the unicorn, and then quickly
checked his own wounds. He had an interesting collection of
scars, but he didn't hurt any more. He felt great.

"I'm fine, too," said an amused voice behind him, and
before Rupert could turn round, Julia gave him one of her
best bear hugs to prove it. She put an arm across his shoulders while he got his breath back, and then ran over to
hug the dragon, who was flexing his healed wing experimentally.

"Will somebody please tell me what's going on?" demanded the unicorn.

"I called down a Rainbow and saved your life," said Rupert, grinning from ear to ear.

"Ah," said the unicorn. "I always knew you'd come in handy for something."

Rupert laughed, and carefully sheathed the rainbow sword. Joy bubbled up in him like water from a long-forgotten well. And then his laughter died slowly away as he studied the unicorn more carefully.

"What's the matter?" asked the animal, frowning.

"There's something different about you," said the Prince thoughtfully.

"I feel fine," said the unicorn, twisting his head round to study himself as best he could.

"Oh dear," said Rupert, as he finally realized.

"What is it?"

"Uh," said Rupert, searching frantically for a tactful way to approach the subject.

"Hey," said Julia, as she and the dragon came over to join them, "what's happened to the unicorn's horn?"

"My *what?*" The unicorn went practically cross-eyed trying to find it, but all that remained was a nub of bone in the center of his forehead.

"The demons broke it off when you were injured," Rupert explained. "Apparently the Rainbow only heals wounds; it doesn't regrow things you've lost."

"My *horn!*" shrieked the unicorn. "Everyone'll think I'm a *horse!*"

"Never in a million years," Rupert assured him.

"In the meantime," said the dragon, "May I suggest we get the hell out of here? We're a long way from the Darkwood's boundary, and no doubt there are still demons to be found in the dark."

"Right," said Julia. "The nightmare's over, but the night goes on forever."

"Not forever," said Rupert softly, and his hand dropped to the pommel of the rainbow sword. "Every night comes to an end eventually."

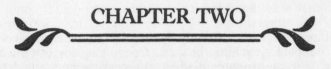

CHAPTER TWO

Homecoming

Some two months later, Rupert, Julia, the dragon, and the unicorn were travelling wearily down the long, winding road that led to Rupert's Castle. Rupert rode his unicorn, while Julia rode on the dragon's shoulders. The Prince and the Princess both wore leather jerkin and trousers, topped by a thick fur cloak. The weather had turned suddenly cold in the last few months, and a chill wind blew constantly through the Forest.

"Home is the hero," said Julia. "Shouldn't there be a band playing, or something?"

"The first minstrel I see had better start running," said Rupert. "I've had it with minstrels."

The dragon coughed tactfully. "I hate to bring this up, Rupert, but you were sent out on your quest in the hope you'd bring back a dragon's hoard of gold and gems. Or at the very least, parts of a dead dragon, which are apparently worth almost as much. Instead, you've brought back a live dragon, worth not a lot, a Princess without a dowry, and not a single gold coin to show for all your admittedly remarkable adventures."

Rupert grinned. "There's always the rainbow sword."

Julia looked at him aghast. "You're not going to sell it, surely?"

The Prince shrugged. "The Forest Land needs the money more than I need a magic sword. Royalty has its responsibilities, remember?"

"I remember," said Julia. "It'll be hard, going back to all that nonsense. Back to formal gowns, and etiquette, and

Ladies-in-Waiting to stop you doing anything that might be fun."

"I'll be there, too," Rupert promised.

Julia smiled. "That'll help," she said, and reached down to squeeze his hand briefly.

Tall, majestic oaks lined the road they travelled, heavy branches ablaze with the bronzed tatters of autumn leaves. It was barely evening, but already the sun was low on the sky. Rupert frowned as the chill breeze stirred the trees; winter looked to be coming early this year. As if the Forest didn't have enough problems . . . He shook his head slowly and breathed deeply, savoring the familiar rich scents of wood and leaf and earth that filled the air, telling him he was nearly home. Home. The word roused many memories, few of them happy. Rupert reined the unicorn to a halt, and turned to the dragon.

"Uh, dragon . . . I think it might be better if you were to . . . well . . ."

"Make myself scarce for a time?" The dragon smiled, revealing row upon row of pointed teeth. "I understand, Rupert. We don't want to panic everyone rigid just yet, do we?"

Rupert grinned back at the dragon. "Quite. They're going to find it hard enough pretending they're happy to see me again, without having to cope with you as well."

"Fair enough," said the dragon. He crouched down, and waited patiently while Julia carefully dismounted. The dragon then moved unhurriedly off the road, stepped into the surrounding trees, and vanished.

Rupert's jaw dropped. "I didn't know dragons could make themselves invisible."

"We can't," said a disembodied voice from far back in the trees, "But we're very good at camouflage. How else do you think we find food? When it comes to sneaking up on things from behind, thirty feet of dragon isn't exactly inconspicuous, you know."

"Fine," said Rupert. "Fine. I'll see you later, then, after I've had a chance to sort things out with the Court. Oh, and dragon . . . if you come across any small, fat, stupid-looking birds, don't eat them. They're a protected species, by order of the King."

"Too late," said the dragon, indistinctly.

Rupert shook his head resignedly. "Ah well, it's about time we thinned out the dodos again." He turned to Julia, who was waiting impatiently in the middle of the road.

"If you've quite finished," she said, ominously, "It is getting late . . ."

"Oh sure," said Rupert. "The Castle's just down the road; we're almost there." He hesitated, and then swung down out of the saddle.

"What are you doing now?" asked Julia.

"Well," said Rupert awkwardly, "It'd look rather bad it I came back riding the unicorn while you had to walk. You'd better ride him the rest of the way."

"No thanks," said Julia.

"I really think it would be better . . ."

"No," said Julia, firmly.

"Why not?"

"Because I *can't* ride a unicorn, that's why not!"

Rupert looked at the ground, and scuffed some dirt with his boot.

"Oh," he said finally.

"And what's that supposed to mean?"

"It means he's thinking," said the unicorn. "Always a bad sign."

"So I'm not qualified to ride a unicorn," said Julia. "Big deal."

"Unfortunately, around here it is," said Rupert. "Unicorn; you've gone lame."

"No, I haven't," said the unicorn.

"Yes, you have," said Rupert. "That's why both Julia and I are walking."

"I suppose you want me to limp," said the unicorn.

"Got it in one," said Rupert. "And do it convincingly, or I'll see you're fed nothing but grass for a month."

"Bully," muttered the unicorn, and walked slowly away, trying out various limps for effect. Rupert and Julia exchanged a smile, and followed him down the road.

The crowding trees soon gave way to a clearing, a moat, and the Castle. Rupert stopped at the edge of the moat, and frowned at the raised drawbridge; normally, the Castle was only sealed during states of emergency. His frown deepened as he took in the empty battlements, and he mentally reviewed the Forest land they'd passed through since leaving the Darkwood. There couldn't have been a war or a rebellion, or they'd have seen burnt-out farms, and bodies lying in the fields for the gore crows. Plague? Rupert shivered suddenly as he realized he hadn't seen a single living soul since his return, but common sense quickly pointed out that at the very least there'd have been sulphur fires burning, and crosses painted on doors.

"What's wrong?" asked Julia.

"I'm not sure." Rupert peered up at the gatehouse over the Keep. "Ho the gate! Let down the drawbridge!"

While he waited impatiently for an answer, Julia turned her attention back to the Castle.

"It's not very big, is it?" she said finally.

Rupert smiled wryly. He had to admit that to the casual eye, Forest Castle wasn't all that impressive. The stonework was cracked and pitted from long exposure to wind and rain, and the tall, crennelated towers had a battered, lopsided look. And yet, somehow the familiar crumbling battlements and ivy-wrapped walls still had the power to stir him deeply. The Castle had stood firm against wars and pestilence, against darkness and decay, guarding his ancestors as they guarded the Land. Fourteen generations of the Forest line had been raised within those walls, fourteen generations of service. Rupert sighed quietly. Sometimes the past seemed heavy on his shoulders. But even though he'd spent most of his young life praying for a chance to escape from the Castle, when all was said and done it was still his home, and he was glad to be back.

"The Castle's much more impressive once you get inside," he assured the Princess.

"It would have to be," said Julia.

"We've four separate wings of a thousand rooms each, twelve banquet halls, three ballrooms, the servants' quarters, guards' quarters, stables, courtyard . . ."

Julia stared at the modestly sized Castle before her, no more than three hundred feet wide, and barely a hundred high. "You've got all that? In *there?*"

"Ah," said Rupert casually. "The Castle's bigger on the inside than it is on the outside."

"How did that happen?"

"Cock-up at the architects," said Rupert, grinning.

"A thousand rooms to a Wing," muttered the Princess. "How do you heat the place?"

"Mostly we don't," Rupert admitted. "I hope you brought some thermal underwear."

"How many rooms are there altogether?"

"We're not actually sure," said Rupert, beginning to wish he'd never brought the subject up. "Some rooms are only there on certain days. And nobody's been able to find the South Wing since we lost it thirty-two years ago. It averages five thousand, two hundred and fourteen rooms in the autumn. I think. Still, not to worry; you're perfectly safe, as long as you stick to the main corridors."

He was saved from Julia's response by a coarse voice from the gatehouse.

"Oi! You by the moat! On your way, or me and the lads'll use you for target practice."

Rupert glared up at the shadowed embrasures over the portcullis. Once inside, he'd have a few sharp words with the Officer of the Watch. No doubt there'd be a right old panic in the Keep once they recognized his voice.

"Let down the drawbridge, fellow!" he called grandly, striking a regal pose.

"Get lost," came the answer. The unicorn sniggered audibly. Rupert's hand dropped to his swordhilt.

"Don't you know who I am?" he asked tightly.

"No," said the voice. "Don't care much, neither."

"I am the Prince Rupert!"

"No, you're not," said the voice.

"Are you sure you've got the right Castle?" Julia asked sweetly.

"Unfortunately, yes," said the unicorn. "Now you know why we're always so glad to be away from it."

"I tell you I am the Prince!" howled Rupert, very much aware of how all this must look to the Princess.

"Leave it out," said the voice boredly. "Everyone knows young Rupe got sent off on a quest to kill a dragon. He is missing, presumed dead. Now beat it, you pair of tramps, or we'll string our bows and the dogs'll get their dinner early."

"Tramps!" screamed Rupert. "I'll kill him! I'll kill them all!"

"Easy, easy," soothed Julia, hanging determinedly onto Rupert's arm to stop him drawing his sword. "He does have a point, you know; we're not exactly dressed as royalty."

Rupert glanced at their battered and travel-stained clothing and scowled even more fiercely.

"Guard! This is your last chance!"

"Push off, peasant."

Rupert was all set to explode on the spot when a determined voice carried clearly from the trees behind him. "Stand fast, Prince Rupert; I'll fix him."

There was a slight pause, and then thirty feet of annoyed dragon erupted out of the trees, showering Rupert, Julia, and the unicorn with leaves and broken branches. The dragon's powerful wings brought him quickly to the raised drawbridge, and held him in position as his wickedly clawed feet reached out and dug in, rending the thick wood like so much paper. The guard in the gatehouse had a brief but clearly audible fit of the vapors, and then ran away, screaming for help. The dragon's wings beat strongly as he threw his weight against the windlass holding the drawbridge up. Light shimmered on his emerald scales as great muscles bunched and corded. There was a sudden squealing of chains, and Rupert, Julia, and the unicorn stood well back as the drawbridge slammed down across the moat. The dragon glided down to join them, while Rupert and Julia applauded loudly.

"Nice one," said the unicorn. "Now they'll probably send the whole bleeding army out to fight us."

Rupert led his party across the drawbridge, which shuddered under the dragon's weight. Something stirred in the moat, and Julia peered dubiously at the shifting scum covering the murky waters.

"Do you keep crocodiles in your moat, Rupert?"

"Not any more," said Rupert absently, keeping a watchful eye on the huge double doors at the other end of the Keep. "We used to, but then something set up housekeeping in the moat and ate them all."

"What was it?"

"We're not sure," said Rupert. "It doesn't really matter; if it can eat crocodiles, it can certainly guard a moat . . ."

The massive oaken doors swung slowly open before them, and Rupert led his party out of the Keep and into the Castle's courtyard. He stopped just inside the inner gates and stared about him, frowning. Even this late in the day there should have been traders at their stalls, haggling with a bustling crowd of villagers and townsfolk. There should have been conjurers and gypsies, knife-sharpeners and tinkers, beggars and priests. There should have been guards at the gates, and men-at-arms watching from the battlements. Instead, the vast empty courtyard lay still and silent before him. No braziers or torches disturbed the courtyard's gloom, and the shadows seemed very dark. Rupert moved slowly forward, his soft footsteps unnaturally loud in the quiet.

"Where the hell is everybody?"

His words echoed hollowly back from the towering stone walls around him, and there was no reply.

"I've seen livelier graveyards," muttered Julia.

"If I see anything that looks even remotely like a cross painted on a door, I'm leaving," said the unicorn, rolling his eyes nervously. "Something's wrong here; I can feel it in my water."

"Oh shut up," snapped Rupert. "If there was a plague they wouldn't have opened the gates to us, dragon or no dragon."

"I take it things aren't normally this . . . peaceful," said the dragon.

"Not usually, no," said Rupert tightly. He came to a halt at the bottom of the long flight of steps leading up to the main entrance hall, and glowered warily at the closed entrance doors. "There must have been some kind of emergency in the Land. Something so menacing that the Castle itself had to be stripped of its defenders, and then sealed against the outside world." He stared up at the unmanned battlements and catwalks, and shivered suddenly. "But what kind of threat . . ."

"The Darkwood," said a quiet voice.

Rupert spun round sword in hand as torchlight spilled suddenly into the courtyard. At the top of the flight of steps, a tall, imposing figure swathed in shining chain mail stood half-silhouetted before the slowly opening entrance-hall doors. Broad shoulders topped an impressively muscled frame, and the torchlight glowed ruddy on the huge double-headed axe in his hands. Julia drew her sword and moved protectively in beside Rupert as a dozen armed guardsmen burst out of the hall to reinforce the silently watching figure.

"Friends of yours?" said Julia casually.

"Not necessarily," said Rupert.

For a long moment nobody moved, and then the tall figure lowered his axe and smiled.

"Welcome home, Prince Rupert."

"Thank you, sir Champion. Good to be back." Rupert bowed slightly, but didn't sheath his sword. "Surprised to see me?"

"Just a little." The Champion stared thoughtfully past Rupert's shoulder. "I see you found a dragon."

"That's right," said Rupert calmly. "Now do you want to get rid of those guards, or shall I tell him supper's on?"

The Champion laughed, and dismissed the guards with a wave of his hand. They disappeared back into the entrance hall as the Champion strode majestically down the steps to greet Rupert and his party. Prince and Champion stared at each other thoughtfully, and Julia frowned as she realized neither man had put aside his weapon yet. The Champion worried her. He had to be at least forty, but he carried the massive war axe as if it was a toy. Old scars patterned a hard, unyielding face, and his constant slight smile wasn't reflected in the cold, dark eyes. *Killer's eyes,* thought Julia, and shivered suddenly. Just standing there, he made her feel . . . uneasy.

"Well," said Rupert softly, "What's the situation these days?"

"No change, Sire," said the Champion. "I still may have to kill you."

"For the good of the Realm?"

"Yes, Sire. For the good of the Realm."

They locked eyes, and Rupert looked away first. The Champion glanced at Julia.

"And who might this be?"

"The Princess Julia," said Rupert.

The Champion bowed slightly. "If you'll excuse me a moment, Sire, I'll see that a room is made ready for your guest."

He turned and made his way unhurriedly back up the steps to the entrance hall. Rupert swore under his breath and sheathed his sword with unnecessary violence. Julia glanced uncertainly after the departing Champion, and then sheathed her sword too.

"What was all that about him killing you?" she asked quietly.

"I'm a second son, remember?" said Rupert grimly. "My brother's first in line for the throne, but there are any number of factions within the Court ready to use me as a figurehead in their grab for power. The Champion's duty is to preserve the Realm; he'd cut me down in a moment if he thought it would prevent a civil war. I've known that all my life. I was supposed to die on the quest, and save everyone a lot of bother. Instead, I've come back at a difficult time, and he's afraid I might try to take advantage of the situation, whatever it is."

"Would you?" asked Julia. "Take advantage, I mean."

"I don't know," said Rupert. "I suppose . . ."

"Quiet," said the unicorn. "He's coming back."

A handful of courtiers and Ladies-in-Waiting jostled for position at the entrance hall doors as the Champion made his way back down the steps, accompanied by four armed guards, wearing scarlet and gold colors. Julia's hand dropped to her sword again.

"It's all right," said Rupert quickly. "They're just an escort."

Julia glared suspiciously at the guards, and then seemed to relax a little, but Rupert noticed uneasily that her hand still rested on the pommel of her sword. A polite cough drew his attention back to the Champion waiting patiently before him.

"Yes, sir Champion?"

The Champion studied Rupert at length. "Interesting scars you have on your face, Sire."

"Cut myself shaving."

"And what happened to your armor?"

"I left it in the Tanglewood. It got in the way."

The Champion shook his head slowly. "I've sent word of your arrival to the Court, Sire. I think you'd better pay your respects to your father."

Rupert winced. "Can't it wait?"

"I'm afraid not." The Champion's voice was polite, but his cold, inflexible gaze allowed no room for disagreement. "As you may have gathered, Sire, we have a problem on our hands."

Rupert nodded warily. "You mentioned the Dark-wood . . ."

"Yes, Sire. It's spreading."

Rupert stared at the Champion in disbelief. The Darkwood's boundaries hadn't shifted by so much as an inch in centuries. "How fast is it moving?"

"Half a mile a day. The Tanglewood has already fallen to the long night, and demons are loose in the Forest. The Darkwood will be here in a matter of months. Unless we find a way to stop it."

"Stop it? You couldn't even slow it down!" Rupert didn't know whether to laugh or cry. He fought down an impulse to grab the Champion and shake some sense into him, and struggled to keep his voice calm. "We came back through the Darkwood, sir Champion. The place is crawling with demons. We were lucky to get out alive, and we had a dragon with us."

"We have trained soldiers," said the Champion mildly.

"Oh yes?" said Rupert, "Where?" He glared pointedly round the deserted battlements, but the Champion's gaze didn't waver.

"Demons have been attacking the outlying farms and villages, Sire; we've had to send out every guardsman and man-at-arms we can spare to protect them. The outermost settlements are being evacuated, but since no one dares travel by night, it's a slow process. Too slow. Every night we lose more men. The demons have grown . . . cunning."

"Yes," said Rupert quietly, remembering. "They hunt in packs now."

"That's not possible," said the Champion flatly.

"Bull," said Julia. "I saw it with my own eyes."

"Demons don't co-operate," the Champion insisted, ignoring Julia.

"They do now," said Rupert. "Why have you sealed the Castle?"

"Demons have been here," said the Champion. "When night falls, they appear at the clearing's edge, watching from the shadows, their eyes glowing in the night like coals. So far they've made no move against the Castle, but every night there are more. It's as though they're . . . waiting for something."

Rupert bit his lower lip thoughtfully. If the Darkwood was still months away, what were demons doing so far ahead of the darkness? And where were they hiding during the day? He shook his head slowly in disgust.

"Since I've had the most recent experience of the Darkwood, I suppose that makes me an expert . . . I'd better see my father."

"Yes, Sire. The Court is waiting. With respect, Sire, don't expect too much. Every faction in the Court seems to have its own plan for dealing with the Darkwood, none of them worth a damn. Your father listens to all of them, which is why nothing's been done. Try to make him understand, Sire; there are decisions that must be made. He can't go on putting them off."

Rupert stared at the Champion thoughtfully. He was being set up for something; he could tell. The last time everyone started calling him Sire, he'd ended up travelling through the Darkwood in search of a dragon.

"Where's Harald?" he asked suspiciously. "He's always been the practical one of the family."

The Champion shrugged. "I don't think your brother really believes in the Darkwood."

Rupert snorted. "I'll change his bloody mind for him. All right, take me to the Court. No, wait a minute; I've a bone to pick with you. That guard at the gatehouse . . ."

"Has been replaced," said the Champion. "Now, Sire, I think we've wasted enough time here. The Court is waiting."

"Let them," said the dragon. "I want a word with you."

His massive head swung down till the great golden eyes were on a level with the Champion's. The armed escort fell back in disarray, but the Champion stood his ground.

"Rupert is my friend," said the dragon. "You threatened to kill him." Bright sparks glowed suddenly in the dragon's nostrils, and two thin plumes of smoke drifted up on the still evening air. The Champion didn't move a muscle.

"I have my duty," he said steadily.

"To hell with your duty," said the dragon.

The Champion glanced at Rupert, who was watching the scene with undisguised glee. All his life he'd walked in the Champion's shadow, knowing he lived or died at that man's whim. Now the shoe was on the other foot, and he intended to enjoy it while it lasted. The Champion took in Rupert's grin, and turned reluctantly back to the dragon.

"If anything happens to Rupert," said the dragon, "I'll level this Castle to the ground. Got it?"

"Got it," said the Champion. "Anyone ever tell you your breath stinks of sulphur?"

"Dragon!" said Rupert quickly, as the creature's claws

flexed ominously. "I appreciate the thought, but much as I hate to admit it, we need him."

"Thank you," said the Champion, dryly.

The dragon glared at the Champion a moment longer, and then pulled back his head. Smoke continued to seep from his nostrils as he ostentatiously sharpened his claws on a convenient piece of brickwork. The Champion glanced at Rupert.

"I think you'd better teach your pet some manners, Sire."

Rupert shrugged. "When you're thirty feet long and breathe fire, who needs manners? And sir Champion; don't ever call my friend a *pet*. You might upset him."

The dragon smiled widely. The Champion studied the many rows of gleaming serrated teeth, and pointedly turned his back on the dragon.

"If you're quite ready, Sire, your father . . ."

"I know," said Rupert. "He hates to be kept waiting. Let's go, Julia. Julia?"

"Over there," said the unicorn.

Rupert looked round just in time to see Julia knee a guardsman in the groin and punch out a Lady-in-Waiting.

Julia had been having an interesting time. Fed up with being ignored by everybody, she'd wandered off on her own to see what there was to see. She hadn't got far before being intercepted by a delicately pretty Lady-in-Waiting in her late thirties, and a bored-looking young guardsman.

"A Princess?" said the Lady Cecelia, glancing disparagingly at Julia's battered leather jerkin and trousers. "From . . . where, precisely?"

"Hillsdown," said Julia, taking in the Lady Cecelia's ornate gown with a sinking heart. Intricately stitched, and studded with hundreds of semiprecious stones, the shaped and padded gown covered the Lady from shoulder to ankle, and was so heavy she could only move in little mincing steps. The massive flared cuffs were wide enough to swallow a small dog, and the bulging cleavage was at least partly supported by the ribbed corset responsible for the Lady's tiny waist. The Lady Cecelia looked rich, aristocratic, and gorgeous. And she knew it.

I don't give a damn, thought Julia. *I'm not wearing a corset.*

"Hillsdown," said the Lady Cecelia thoughtfully. "Possibly I'm mistaken, dear, but I always thought Hillsdown was a Duchy. And strictly speaking, a Duchy isn't entitled to have Princesses. Still, country titles aren't like the real thing, are they? I mean, they don't count for anything in Polite Society." She bestowed a gracious smile on Julia, to underline the point that whilst Julia might not be a part of Polite Society, the Lady Cecelia most definitely was.

I'd better not hit her, thought Julia. *Rupert's got enough problems as it is.*

She leaned forward and studied the Lady Cecelia's dress closely. In addition to the corset, there were definite traces of bone stays built into the dress itself, to help maintain the hourglass figure.

"How do you breathe in that thing?" asked Julia.

"Daintily," said the Lady Cecelia, coldly.

"Does everybody dress like this?"

"Anybody who is Anybody. Surely even country gentry know High Fashion when they see it?"

I'm not going to hit her, thought Julia determinedly.

"You arrived with young Rupert, I believe," said the Lady Cecelia.

"That's right," said Julia. "Do you know him?"

"Oh, everyone knows Rupert," said the Lady Cecelia, with an unpleasant smile. The guard at her side sniggered.

Julia frowned. "Did I say something funny?" she asked, ominously.

The Lady Cecelia giggled girlishly. "Rupert, my dear, is a Prince in name only; he'll never inherit the throne. That falls to his elder brother, Prince Harald. Ah, dear Harald; now *there* is a Prince. Tall, handsome, charming, and a devil on the dance floor. And when it comes to the Ladies . . . oh my dear, the tales I could tell you about Harald . . ."

"Never mind Harald," said Julia. "Tell me about Rupert."

"Prince Rupert," said the Lady Cecelia crossly, "is no earthly use to anybody. He can't dance, or sing, or write poetry, and he has absolutely no idea how to treat a Lady."

"Right." The guard grinned. "He still rides a unicorn."

"He's not a real man," purred the Lady Cecelia, "Not like my Gregory."

The guard smirked, and flexed his muscles under the Lady's admiring gaze.

"Rupert," said the Lady Cecelia, "Is a dull, boring . . ."

"Spineless little creep," said the guard. And they both laughed, very unpleasantly.

So Julia quite naturally kneed the guard in the groin and punched the Lady Cecelia in the mouth.

On the other side of the courtyard, Rupert watched in amazement as the guard sank to his knees, and the Lady-in-Waiting stretched her length on the courtyard floor. One of the Champion's escort drew his sword and started forward. Rupert kicked the man's feet out from under him, and set his sword point at the guard's throat.

"Nice moves," said the Champion. "You've improved, Sire."

"Thank you," said Rupert tightly. "Keep an eye on this clown while I take care of Julia." He sheathed his sword, and hurried over just in time to stop Julia slamming a boot into the Lady Cecelia.

"Julia, not here! Please, come with me to the Court and meet my father. There are lots of people there you can hit, I'll be happy to point them out to you, but don't waste your spleen on amateurs like these. The real creeps wouldn't be seen dead outside the Court."

Julia sniffed angrily, but allowed Rupert to lead her away.

"I suppose they insulted you," said Rupert.

"Something like that," said Julia.

"Forget about it," said Rupert soothingly. "I'm sure they won't do it again."

"Never," promised a faint male voice from the ground behind them.

Rupert grinned, and shook his head. It was obvious that Julia wasn't going to take easily to being a lady again.

The Champion bowed to Julia as she and Rupert rejoined him. "If you will follow me, Princess Julia, the Court is this way."

Julia inclined her head regally, accepted the Champion's proffered arm, and allowed him to assist her up the steps to the entrance hall. The four guardsmen followed at a discreet distance. Rupert turned to the dragon and the unicorn.

"I thought the escort was for you," said the dragon.

"Hardly," said Rupert. "Well, don't just stand there; come with me to see the King."

"You want both of us?" said the unicorn timidly.

"Damn right," said the Prince, smiling. "I'm going to

need all the support I can get. Now let's go and look after Julia. Before she kills someone."

Rupert paced impatiently up and down the Court's narrow antechamber, shooting seething glances at the securely locked double doors that led into the Great Hall itself. The Champion had gone in first to inform the King that his son had finally arrived, and then, as so many times before, the ancient doors had been slammed in Rupert's face. Once again, the Court was busy deciding his future. *Whatever they want, the answer's no,* thought Rupert determinedly. *I didn't survive the Darkwood just to get killed off by my own scheming relatives.*

He stopped pacing and listened at the doors. A constant hubbub seeped through the solid wood, indicating that most of the Court were still present, despite the late hour. Rupert grinned. Courtiers hated having to work late; it interfered with the important things of life, like hunting, drinking, and wenching. Rupert stretched slowly, and thought longingly of the deep-mattressed bed waiting for him in his room. But, tired as he was, he knew he wouldn't be able to sleep until he'd discovered what new deviltry the King and his Court had come up with. He threw himself into one of the exquisitely uncomfortable chairs provided, and looked to see what his friends were doing.

Julia had her dagger out, and was using the family portraits for target practice. Her aim was pretty good. The dragon was lying partly in the antechamber, and partly in the outer hall. He was practicing blowing smoke rings from his nostrils, and chewing absently at a centuries-old tapestry Rupert had never liked much anyway. The unicorn was . . . Rupert winced.

"Unicorn; couldn't you have done that before you came in?"

"Sorry," said the unicorn. "I get nervous inside strange buildings, you know that. I keep thinking the roof's going to fall on me."

Rupert shook his head, and looked back at the closed double doors. How many times had he stood before those doors, waiting for permission to speak to his own father? His mind drifted back through yesterday, and found nothing pleasant there. Born seven years after his brother, Rupert had been a surprise to everyone, and bad news to most. A

King needed a second son as insurance in case something happened to the first, but two healthy adult sons meant nothing but trouble. Rupert had known that from an early age; everyone had taken great pains to make it clear to him. He scowled, as memories crept out of the shadows. The tutors, who beat him for being brighter than his favored elder brother. His instructors-at-arms, who beat him for not being as strong as his brother. The courtiers, who flattered or insulted him according to the fashion. The Barons, who intrigued in his name. And the Champion, whose cold dark eyes were full of death.

Foxfire moss glowed steadily in several lamps hanging from the low ceiling, but the antechamber was still full of shadows, as though darkness had followed him into the Castle. Rupert leaned back in his chair and sighed, wearily. Out in the Forest it had all seemed so simple and straight-forward. He had to go back to the Castle because the Forest Land needed him. He smiled bitterly. The Forest didn't need him. It never had. The only people who'd ever needed him were Julia, the dragon, and the unicorn. His friends. Rupert's smile softened at the thought, and he rolled it back and forth in his mind, savoring it. He'd never had friends before. His position had kept him apart from other children, and his family . . . His mother died when he was five years old. His brother insulted and tormented him. And his father sent him out on a quest, to die.

Rupert shook his head to clear it. He'd passed through the Darkwood twice, fought off demons, and called down a Rain-bow. Stuff his father, stuff the Court, and stuff the bloody Champion. They'd tried to get rid of him, and it hadn't worked. He was back, and they could like it or lump it.

"How much longer?" asked Julia, retrieving her dagger from an ancestor's eye.

Rupert shrugged. "They like to keep me waiting; it helps put me in my place."

"And you put up with that?"

Rupert looked at Julia, and then at the unicorn and the dragon.

"I always used to," he said thoughtfully, "But things have changed since then. Dragon . . ."

The dragon looked up from sharpening his claws on a handy suit of armor. "Yes, Rupert?"

"See those double doors?"

"Yes, Rupert."

"See how many matchsticks you can make out of them."

The dragon studied the doors a moment, and then grinned broadly. He surged to his feet, and reached out to tap the doors with one clawed hand. They shuddered under the dragon's touch, and nodding solemnly, he backed carefully out of the narrow antechamber and turned himself around in the hall outside. Rupert, Julia, and the unicorn squeezed themselves into a far corner as the dragon cautiously introduced his rear end into the antechamber. He peered over his shoulder to check his friends were safely out of the line of fire, and then lashed out with a vicious swing of his tail. The doors exploded inwards, splinters flying on the air like grapeshot. Rupert nodded with satisfaction as screams and curses erupted from the packed Court. *Slam the doors in my face, will they?* He grinned, and ducking past the dragon's tail, moved forward to check the damage. One door hung crookedly from its only remaining hinge, whilst the other had given up the ghost entirely and was lying facedown on the floor. Rupert took a deep breath and stepped forward into the gap where the doors had been. The Court's uproar died away to an astonished silence.

Rupert looked about him. Several hundred assorted courtiers and Ladies-in-Waiting stared back with a fair mixture of fear, outrage, and curiosity. Half a hundred foxfire lamps shed their silver glow across the Court, while at the far end of the vast, spacious Hall, the last of the evening light fell through gorgeous stained-glass windows onto a massive throne, set high on a raised dais and carved in its entirety from a single block of oak. Sitting on that throne, unruffled and unmoved, was his father, King John IV. The King's great leonine head seemed almost too heavy for his frail body, and his richly patterned robes and proud golden crown couldn't disguise the ragged mop of gray hair and uncombed beard. Even on his better days, Rupert's father still looked like he'd been dragged through a hedge backwards. And yet, despite the strong impression of age and tiredness that hung about him like an old, familiar cloak, King John carried himself with dignity, and his deep-set eyes were calm and steady.

At his side stood Thomas Grey, the Court Astrologer.

Tall, broad-shouldered, and darkly handsome, the black-clad magician had every aspect of regality save the barest essential; noble birth. Born the son of a blacksmith, he'd been the King's companion since childhood, and on John's ascension to the throne, Thomas Grey had cut short a promising career at the Sorcerers' Academy to return and stand at his friend's side.

Rupert disliked the man intensely; he smiled too much.

The courtiers watched with hostile eyes as the Prince moved forward into the Court, his footsteps echoing loudly on the hush. He stopped almost immediately and turned to the Court usher, who was still staring slack-jawed at the ruined doorway.

"Well, don't just stand there, usher; announce us."

"I think they know we're here, Rupert," said an amused voice behind him. Rupert grinned, but shook his head firmly.

"That's not the point, Julia. We have to be announced."

"I have absolutely no intention of announcing you," said the usher haughtily. "You can't come barging in here and . . ." His voice died away as the dragon's head peered interestedly over Rupert's shoulder. Color drained from the usher's face as the dragon squeezed his bulk slowly through the doorframe, widening it somewhat in the process. The usher swallowed heavily.

"Announcing you right away, Sire."

He stepped hastily forward and, striking his best formal pose, declaimed; "Prince Rupert of the Forest Kingdom, second in line to the Forest throne, defender of the weak, warrior of the Realm, and collector of lesser taxes!" He then glanced nervously back over his shoulder and added in a smaller voice ". . . and friends . . ."

Julia curtsied daintily, and then realized she was still holding her dagger. She grinned, and lifting her trouser to show a generous amount of leg, she stuffed the weapon unconcernedly into the top of her boot. The dragon smiled widely, light gleaming prettily on his pointed teeth. Several of the nearer courtiers had a sudden attack of modesty, and faded quickly back into the crowd. The unicorn bobbed his head nervously, and christened the door-jamb.

"Do that again," muttered Rupert, "and so help me I'll tie it in a knot."

"Rupert, dear fellow, so good to see you back safe and

well," boomed a deep voice from the rear of the Court. Rupert turned to see an aisle open up in the courtiers as his brother, Harald, came striding confidently forward to greet him. Tall, classically handsome, and loaded with muscle, Harald looked every inch a hero out of legend, and he knew it. He clapped Rupert on the shoulder and shook his hand firmly. They both tried for the knuckle-crusher and Rupert lost, as always.

"Interesting dragon you've brought us, dear boy," said Harald brightly. "But you are supposed to kill them first, you know."

"You're welcome to try," smiled Rupert, surreptitiously trying to shake the blood back into his fingers. Harald glanced at the dragon, who was licking his lips with a long forked tongue and eyeing the elder Prince hungrily.

"Perhaps later," said Harald, and turned quickly away to smile charmingly at Julia. "Well, Rupert; at least your taste in women has improved. Aren't you going to introduce us?"

"I have a feeling one of us is going to regret this," said Rupert. "Princess Julia of Hillsdown, may I present my brother, Prince Harald of the Forest Kingdom."

Used as he was to violent reactions to his friends, Rupert was still rather taken aback when the entire Court gasped with what sounded suspiciously like shock. Julia took one look at Harald's outstretched hand, and let fly with a scream of pure rage. Harald looked at Julia's right hand, and his jaw dropped. He fell back a pace, making helpless little shooing motions with his hands. Julia was all set to lunge at Harald and punch him out, but Rupert recognized the build-up and grabbed her from behind.

"Now what's the matter?" he demanded wearily. "Can't you get on with *anyone?*"

"It's him!" shrieked the Princess, fighting to break free.

"I know it's him!" snapped Rupert. "I introduced you, remember?"

Julia suddenly stopped struggling, and Rupert warily released her.

"You don't understand," she said dully. "He's the Prince I was supposed to marry; the one I ran away from."

Rupert closed his eyes briefly in disgust. Every time he seemed to be getting the hang of things . . .

"Why didn't you say something earlier, Julia?"

"I never knew his name, Rupert. They never told me. I was promised in marriage when I was still a child; the ceremony was supposed to take place once I came of age. Your father and mine exchanged rings of engraved white gold as a token of the arrangement. I've worn mine since I was four years old, and Harald is still wearing his. I saw it on his hand. It bears exactly the same design as mine."

Rupert glared at his brother, who was busily gathering the remaining shreds of his composure.

"Is that right? You're supposed to marry her?"

"Well yes, dear boy, at least I was, but . . ."

"But what?"

"Well, she did run away, after all," said Harald huffily. "That being the case, father quite naturally arranged another marriage for me, with one of the Barons' daughters. Nice little filly. Damn fine dowry, and good political connections. Now, thanks to you . . ."

"Thanks to you, Rupert," said the King, his dry even voice cutting effortlessly across Harald's, "since the contract with the Duchy of Hillsdown still stands, technically, the original marriage will have to take place after all. Any other disastrous news you'd like to share with us?"

"Give me a moment," said Rupert. "I'm sure I can think of something."

Harald stalked off to have several quiet words with the King, while Rupert did his best to mollify the fuming Julia.

"I'm not marrying him," she snapped furiously. "I'll enter a nunnery first."

Rupert's mind boggled at the thought of Julia in a nunnery, but he strove to remain calm.

"You won't have to marry him," he promised soothingly. "I'll sort something out."

Julia sniffed, unconvinced, and studied Harald dubiously. "He's your brother; what's he like?"

"Rich, good-looking, and successful with women. Three good reasons to hate anyone. Harald, however, is also a pompous, meticulous, occasionally hard-working twit who thinks fun should be outlawed for everyone not actually of noble birth. When I was a boy, he made my life hell. I still have some of the scars. Basically, he's a hard-headed, ruthless creep who'll make a great King."

"Your average Prince," said Julia solemnly, and Rupert had to grin.

The Court, meantime, had finally gathered its collective wits together. Rupert's return alone would have provided the courtiers with enough gossip to last out the year, but his dramatic entrance via an exploding doorway was an unexpected bonus. The arrival of Julia and the dragon had sent them into a positive frenzy of speculation, though as yet nobody had quite worked up the nerve to formally introduce themselves to either the dragon or the Princess. In fact, there was much lively discussion as to which of the pair it would be safest to approach first. A few braver souls had started to edge casually forward when everyone suddenly discovered what happens when thirty feet of dragon breaks wind. The nearest courtiers fell back in disarray, desperately clapping perfumed handkerchiefs to their noses, and there was a general rush to open windows. Rupert and Julia looked at each other resignedly. It was obviously going to be one of those days.

The King was on his feet, rage darkening his face. "Get that dragon out of my Court! Get him out before he does it again!"

The dragon did it again. Rupert glared at him.

"Must you?"

"Yes," said the dragon firmly.

"Are you going to do it again?"

"Possibly."

"Then go outside and do it; there's a whole Castle to choose from."

The dragon shrugged indifferently. "Can't be bothered. I think I'll take a little nap instead." He stretched his massive wings, sending several courtiers diving to the floor for safety, and then he curled up in the middle of the Court, his chin resting comfortably on his tail. The great golden eyes closed, and he was soon snoring steadily, like a thundercloud with indigestion.

"Has your friend finished now?" asked the King icily, settling back onto his throne.

"I hope so," said Rupert. "But let's keep our voices down, and let sleeping dragons lie."

The King sighed, and shook his head slowly. "Approach the throne."

Rupert did so, followed by Julia. The Astrologer stood to

the King's left, Harald to his right. They both bowed politely to Julia, who ignored them. The King stared silently at Rupert for some time.

"Rupert; can't you do anything right?"

"Not a lot," said Rupert. "Sorry I couldn't oblige you by getting killed during the quest, but being dead is so boring."

"I was referring to the dragon," said the King.

"Sure you were," said Rupert coldly. The King didn't look away.

"I did what was best," he said softly.

"You mean what the Astrologer told you was best."

Thomas Grey bowed formally, but his pale blue eyes glittered dangerously. "I advise the King to the best of my poor ability," he said silkily. "We both felt a successful quest might do much to help your standing in this Court. A Prince who had slain a dragon would, at the very least, be somewhat easier to arrange a marriage for."

Rupert grinned mockingly. "What's the matter; still a glut of second sons on the market?"

The Astrologer started to say something, but was cut off by the King, who was studying the unicorn narrowly, and frowning.

"Rupert; what happened to the unicorn's horn?"

"He lost it in a fight."

"Careless of him," said Harald. They all looked to see if he was joking. He wasn't.

"Harald," said the King, "Why don't you start thinking about what you're going to wear to your wedding. You know debate isn't your strong point."

"Neither's thinking," muttered Rupert.

"At least he would have had more sense than to bring back a live dragon," snapped King John. "Or a Princess we were well rid of. Now we'll have to go through with the damn marriage, or Hillsdown will break off diplomatic relations."

"I'm not marrying Harald," said Julia defiantly.

"You will do as you're told," said King John, "Or you can spend the time until your wedding day in the dirtiest, most dismal dungeon I can find."

Julia locked eyes with the King, and she was the first to look away. She turned uncertainly to Rupert.

"Are you going to let him talk to me like that?"

"He's my father," said Rupert.

There was an awkward pause.

"It's not the end of the world, your highness," said the Astrologer smoothly to Julia. "There's no need to rush things; after all, the marriage needn't take place immediately. I'm sure that once you've got to know Harald you'll find him a decent, upstanding young man who'll make you a fine husband. And remember, he will be King one day."

"If there's a Kingdom left," said the Champion.

Everybody jumped. The Champion had moved silently forward to stand on Rupert's right. He'd left his war axe behind, but he now carried a sword on his hip.

"I see you're still good at sneaking up on people," said Rupert.

The Champion smiled. "One of my most useful talents." He turned and inclined his head slightly to King John. "Your majesty, we do have a serious problem to discuss. The Darkwood . . ."

"Can wait a minute," said the King peevishly. "I haven't finished with Rupert yet. Rupert; you were supposed to bring back the valuable parts of a dead dragon and at least some of his hoard. Haven't you brought back *any* gold?"

"No," said Rupert. "There wasn't any."

"What about the dragon's hoard?"

"He collected butterflies."

They all stared at the sleeping dragon. "Only you, Rupert," said the Champion quietly. "Only you . . ."

"Haven't you brought back anything of value?" asked the King.

"Just this," said Rupert, drawing his sword. Everyone studied the gleaming blade warily.

"It has a strong magical aura," said the Astrologer dubiously. "What does it do?"

"It summons rainbows," said Rupert, just a little lamely.

There was a long pause.

"Let's talk about the Darkwood," said King John. "Suddenly, it seems a preferable topic of conversation."

"Suits me," said Rupert, sheathing his sword.

"Time is running out, your majesty," said the Champion earnestly. "We've already lost three of the outlying villages to the demons, and every day more of the Forest falls under the shadow of the long night. The trees are dying, and rivers are fouled with blood. Babes are stillborn, and crops rot before they can be harvested. Demons run ahead of the Darkwood, slaughtering all in their path. My men are dying out there, just to buy us a little more time. I respectfully beg your permission to levy the Barons and raise an army. We must make a stand against the darkness, while we still can."

"So you keep telling me," said King John testily, "But you know as well as I that the Barons won't supply me with men for an army, for fear I'd use it against them. The way they've been acting lately, I just might. No, sir Champion; an army is out of the question."

The Champion shook his head stubbornly. "I must have more men, your majesty."

"The Royal Guard . . ."

"Aren't enough for what needs to be done!"

"They'll have to be," said the King flatly. "All my other guards and men-at-arms are scattered across the Kingdom, protecting my people and keeping the roads open. Shall I recall them to build you an army, and leave the villages and towns to be overrun by the darkness?"

"If need be," said the Champion evenly. "You don't cure a disease by treating its symptoms. The demons are born of darkness; the only way to stop the long night spreading is to lead an army into the Darkwood and destroy its heart."

Rupert's stomach turned suddenly as he realized what the Champion was saying. If the guardsmen were recalled, that would leave the villages unprotected, and the demons would roll right over them. A cold sweat beaded his brow as he remembered the leaping, clawing demonkind surging into the Darkwood clearing where he and Julia stood back-to-back, sword in hand. He remembered waiting to die, and hoping it would be quick. The demons were of the dark, and knew nothing of honor or mercy. Villagers armed with scythes and pitchforks wouldn't stand a chance against the darkling tide that swarmed ahead of the Darkwood. Blood would fly on the night air, and the screams would last till morning . . .

"There has to be another way," he blurted, glaring at the Champion's impassive features.

"There is," said Thomas Grey. "When might of arms is not enough, there is still magic."

The Champion smiled contemptuously. "Same old song, Astrologer. All your prophesies and illusions won't rid us of the Darkwood; sooner or later, it always comes down to cold steel."

"You talk as if the dark were some wild animal, to be dispatched with sword and lance," snapped the Astrologer. "Darkness can only be dispelled by light; white magic against black, reason against ignorance. Send an army into the Darkwood, and you'll never see it again."

They stood glaring at each other across the throne, the Champion proud and tall in his gleaming chain mail, and yet somehow his broad, muscular frame seemed almost dwarfed by the dark, imposing presence of the black-clad Astrologer. His icy blue eyes were full of a secret knowledge, and an aura of power and foreboding hung around him like a shroud. Rupert studied him, puzzled. In the few short months he'd been gone from the Court, Thomas Grey seemed to have grown in stature and influence. Not to mention bravery; there were few indeed who dared to contradict the Champion to his face. Rupert frowned. The Astrologer was too confident for his liking; magic might be the only answer to the darkness, but only a full sorcerer could hope to turn back the Darkwood. And Thomas Grey wasn't a sorcerer.

"Your majesty!" called a resonant, commanding voice from among the nearest courtiers. Rupert turned to look as a short fat man in gorgeous gravy-stained robes pushed his way forward. Sharp, piggy eyes peered from under plucked eyebrows, and his rouged mouth was pursed in a constant scowl. He stopped opposite the Champion, and bowed perfunctorily to the throne. "Your majesty, as Minister for War, I really must protest . . ."

"All right," said the Champion equably, "You've protested. Now beat it, we've got work to do."

The Minister's face flushed with rage, but his voice was cold and hard. "Whether you approve or not, sir Champion, I am the King's Minister for War. Address me in such an insolent fashion again, and I'll have you flogged."

The Champion's hand dropped to his swordhilt. The Minister paled suddenly and fell back.

"Sir Champion," said the King, "Draw on one of my Ministers and I'll have your head."

For a moment it seemed the Champion would ignore him, but the moment passed, and he took his hand away from his sword. The Minister started breathing again.

"He insulted me," said the Champion.

"You insulted my Minister," said the King icily. "An insult to him is an insult to me. Is that clear?"

"Of course, your majesty," said the Champion, inclining his head slightly. "I live only to serve you."

The King turned his attention to the Minister. "If you have something to contribute to the discussion, Lord Darius, by all means do so."

"Your majesty is most gracious," said Lord Darius, glaring at the Champion. "It seems to me that both sir Champion and the Astrologer have overlooked the most obvious answer to our present difficulties. Since neither force of arms nor magic can hope to stand against the Darkwood, we must clearly fall back upon the one remaining course of action: diplomacy."

There was a short pause. Rupert didn't know whether to laugh or cry.

"The man's insane," said the Champion. "Talk with demons? You might as well argue with the thunderstorm. Demons kill to live, and live to kill."

"For once, I agree with sir Champion," said the Astrologer, staring coldly at Lord Darius. "The Darkwood is the incarnation of darkness upon the earth. All that thrives within it is evil. Demons are not living creatures such as we; they exist only to serve the Darkwood."

"They don't just serve the Darkwood," said Darius softly. A sudden silence fell over the Court. Rupert stared at the Minister with growing horror as he realized what Darius was implying.

"You can't be serious," said the Astrologer.

"Why not?" said Darius. "How else do you explain the Darkwood's sudden growth? There's only one possible answer. The Demon Prince has returned."

"A legend," said the Champion, too quickly. "A tale told to frighten children."

"Some legends are true," said Rupert quietly, but only Julia heard him. She took his hand, and squeezed it briefly.

"Men have struck deals with the Demon Prince before," said Darius, persuasively. "Why else would demons haunt the Castle grounds night after night, so far from the Darkwood? They're waiting for us to go to them and make a compact!"

"I'll strike no bargains with the dark," said King John.

"But what if we give the Demon Prince what he desires . . ." The Minister's voice died away beneath the King's cold, angry gaze.

"What do you suggest, Minister? That I surrender the villages to him, in the hopes he'll spare this Castle?"

"Why not?" said Darius flatly. "As sir Champion has already pointed out, what are the lives of a few peasants against the security of the Forest Kingdom?"

"This is madness!" roared the Champion. "I meant we should fight the darkness, not surrender to it! Set a blood sacrifice for the Demon Prince and we'll never be free of him!"

"Such a plan would destroy us all!" grated the Astrologer. "We either stand against the dark or fall beneath it!"

"Your majesty, as Minister for War I must protest . . ."

"SHUT UP!" yelled Rupert. A sudden silence fell across the Court as everyone looked at Rupert in surprise, having forgotten in the heat of the argument that he was still there.

"Thank you, Rupert," said King John. "It was getting a little noisy. According to the Champion, you actually passed through the Darkwood on your quest."

"Twice," said Rupert curtly.

A ripple of barely suppressed laughter ran through the Court. The Minister for War sniggered openly, his dark little eyes sparkling with malicious glee.

"Oh come now, Rupert," said Lord Darius, dropping a podgy hand on Rupert's arm. "Surely you don't expect us to believe you passed through the Darkwood *twice?* Even with a dragon in your party, the demons would have ripped you to pieces."

"They tried," said Rupert evenly. "We got lucky. Now get your hand off my arm, or I'll feed you your fingers."

The Minister removed his hand with exaggerated care, and bowed sarcastically.

"And how many demons did you meet in the Darkwood, sir hero? Ten? Twenty?"

"Too many to count," said Rupert angrily. "Demons hunt in packs now."

"Nonsense," snapped the Astrologer. "Everyone knows demons haven't the intelligence to work together. They prey on each other when food grows scarce."

"I was there," said Rupert grimly, struggling to remain

calm. "There were hundreds of the bloody creatures, fighting side by side."

"Hundreds?" sneered Darius, his gaze openly contemptuous. "Don't waste our time with such obvious lies. You were never in the Darkwood. I've no doubt the Princess Julia was most impressed by your pretty stories, but don't think to deceive us as well. You're a coward and a failure, and everyone here knows it. Now run along, and tell your tales to the scullery maids. You've no business here."

Rupert drove his fist into the Minister's sneering mouth. The Court gasped as Darius fell backwards into the crowd and lay still. A guardsman moved forward to restrain Rupert, and Julia kicked him between wind and water. The guard bent in two, and Julia rabbit-punched him. More guards came forward, and the Champion drew his sword. Rupert and Julia drew their swords and stood back-to-back. For a long moment, nobody moved.

"Think you're up to it, lad?" said the Champion, softly.

"Maybe," said Rupert. "You said yourself I'd improved, and Julia's pretty good with a sword, too. Who knows; we might just get lucky."

"You'll never be that lucky." The Champion grinned, moving forward. His eyes were cold and hard and full of death.

"Enough!" roared the King, surging to his feet. "Sir Champion, sheath your sword. That's an order! Guards, return to your places; I'm in no danger."

The Champion looked at the King a moment, and then sheathed his sword, his face calm and expressionless. The guards moved reluctantly back to their positions, and the King sank back onto his throne.

"Rupert, Julia; please put down your swords," said King John evenly, his eyes darting from one to the other. "You are under my protection in this Court, and you have my word you will come to no harm here."

Julia glanced at Rupert, who nodded slowly. They sheathed their swords, and everybody relaxed a little. A small knot of courtiers gathered around the feebly groaning Lord Darius.

"Somebody help the Minister for War back to his chambers," said the King, and two of the courtiers half-led, half-carried Darius away. The King hid a smile behind a raised hand, and leaned back in his throne. "Now, Rupert . . ."

"No, no, and no," said Rupert firmly. "No, I will not lead an army into the Darkwood to fight the demons; no, I will not lead a diplomatic party to talk to the demons; and no, I don't have any sense of duty or honor. I think that covers everything."

Julia nodded solemnly.

"Rupert, I assure you . . ." King John began, but Rupert cut in quickly, knowing that if he started being reasonable now, he was lost.

"Forget it. I don't care what you've got lined up for me, the answer's no. I've done my bit; let somebody else put their head on the block for a change."

"Rupert, if there was anybody else . . ."

"There is; Harald."

His brother looked up from idly buffing his nails, and shook his head amiably. "Afraid not, dear boy; I'm needed here. Sorry."

"Blow it out your ear, Harald."

There was a slight pause, as everyone pretended not to have heard that.

"Rupert," said King John firmly, "I quite agree that you've earned a rest. Unfortunately, the task I have for you is both urgent and vital, and it cannot wait. Tomorrow morning . . ."

"Tomorrow morning!" shrieked Rupert. "I've only just got back! I don't believe this. I just do not believe it; I've been back in the Castle less than an hour, and already you're trying to get rid of me again. What's the bloody rush?"

"We're running out of time," said Thomas Grey. "There's a Blue Moon rising."

Dark murmurs rustled through the Court as the young Prince stared blankly at the Astrologer.

"There hasn't been a Blue Moon for centuries," said Rupert slowly, and then a dim memory came flooding back to him, and his eyes widened. "Wait a minute; according to some legends, the first time a Blue moon rose, the Darkwood was born . . ."

The Astrologer nodded grimly. "Once in a Blue Moon, magic is loosed in the world. Wild Magic, to create or destroy, strong enough to reshape reality itself on the night the Blue Moon is full. We have seven months until that night; seven months in which to find an answer to the darkness. If we fail, the Darkwood will spread over all that is. Civilization will fall, the long night will have no ending, and the world will belong to the demons."

For a long while the Court stood silent, shaken by the Astrologer's dark vision.

"There must be something we can do," said Rupert haltingly.

"There is," said the Astrologer. "Prince Rupert; you must journey to the Dark Tower, and there summon the High Warlock."

Rupert stared at the Astrologer.

"I should have volunteered to lead an army against the Demon Prince," he said finally. "It would have been safer."

"But you'll do it," said King John.

"Of course," said Rupert bitterly. "You knew that before I came in here."

"Wait a minute," said Julia, moving quickly forward to stand between Rupert and the King. "What's going on here? Rupert; who is this High Warlock?"

"A sorcerer," said Rupert shortly. "Very powerful, and very deadly. Exiled years ago. He doesn't take kindly to visitors."

"You don't have to go," said Julia, laying a gentle hand on his arm. "You've done enough."

"No," said Rupert tiredly. "Father's right; there is no one else . . . they can spare."

"Then I'm going with you."

"Oh, I say," said Harald. "I'm afraid I can't allow that."

"Shut your face, creep," said Julia. Harald gaped at her, and the courtiers had a coughing fit. Julia ignored them, her eyes pleading with Rupert as he slowly shook his head.

"I can't take you with me, Julia. Not to the Dark Tower. There's no one I'd rather have to guard my back, you know that, but I can't let you risk your life for me again. I've no right. You'll be safe here . . . as long as you keep Harald at arm's length."

"But . . ."

"No, Julia." Rupert met her gaze unyieldingly, and she looked away.

"It's not fair," she said quietly.

"No," said Rupert. "It isn't." He turned to the King, who studied him narrowly.

"Well, Rupert; it seems you and the Princess Julia have grown somewhat fond of each other."

"Yes," said Rupert.

"She's promised to Harald," said King John. "The contract was signed long ago."

"I know my duty," said Rupert. "I've always known my duty. That's the only reason I'm going on this mission. And what's more, if I've got to go calling on the High Warlock, I want a full troop of guards to back me up."

"They'll be ready for you first thing tomorrow morning," said the King.

"And I want the Champion to lead them . . ." said Rupert.

"An honor to ride at your side, Sire," said the Champion.

". . . under my orders," said Rupert.

The King hesitated, and then nodded. "It's your expedition, Rupert. But I strongly suggest you listen to the Champion's advice at all times."

"As long as it is advice," said Rupert.

"Of course, Sire," said the Champion, bowing.

He's calling me Sire again, thought Rupert dourly. *Things must really be desperate.*

"All right," he sighed finally. "Sir Champion; we start at first light tomorrow. Though how we're going to persuade the High Warlock to come back with us I don't know."

"He's our only hope," said the Astrologer.

"Then you'd better start making white flags," growled Rupert.

"I don't see any need for further discussion," said the King hastily. "Court is dismissed!"

The courtiers filed slowly out, chattering animatedly as they headed for the gap where the double doors used to be. Rupert turned to Julia, who turned her back on him.

"Julia . . ."

"We should never have come back to the Castle, Rupert."

"I did what I thought was best."

"I know," said Julia tiredly. "It's not your fault."

Rupert took her gently by the arm and turned her round to face him. "Julia; I didn't save you from the demons just to lose you to my brother. Now let's get out of here. I'm tired, and I've got to be up early tomorrow."

Julia studied him a moment, and then smiled reluctantly. "It has been a long day, hasn't it? Let's go."

"Excuse me," said Harald, moving elegantly forward to block their way. "But if anyone is to escort the Princess Julia to her chambers, it should be me. I mean to say, dammit, she is my fiancé."

"Harald," said Rupert calmly, "I am not in the mood for this kind of nonsense. I rarely am in the mood, and take it from me, right now I am less in the mood than ever before, if that's possible. So get out of my way or I'll feed you a knuckle sandwich. Even worse, I might let Julia do it."

Harald looked at Julia thoughtfully. She smiled sweetly at him, and let her hand rest casually on the pommel of her sword. Harald bowed to her, and then smiled politely at Rupert.

"How brave you've grown, Rupert, now you've a dragon to back you up. Assuming you survive your journey to the Dark Tower, do hurry back; I want you to be best man at my wedding." He grinned as Rupert flushed angrily. "I thought you'd like that, Rupert. I'll see you tomorrow, Julia; we have so much to . . . discuss."

He stepped back, bowed to them both, and swept majestically out of the Court. Rupert and Julia watched him go.

"Nice brother you've got there," said Julia. "Really knows how to twist the knife."

"Yes," said Rupert. "Still, we mustn't be too hard on him. He hasn't got long to live."

"Why not?"

"Because one of these days I'm going to kill him."

Julia chuckled earthily. "Can I help?"

They laughed together, and then went to awaken the sleeping dragon. Rupert called to him, yelled in his ear, and even rapped on the creature's bony forehead with his fist, but the two thin plumes of smoke rising from the dragon's nostrils didn't even waver. Rupert sighed, walked round to the rear of the dragon, took careful aim, and delivered a mighty kick. The dragon slowly opened his eyes, and Rupert jumped up and down for a while holding his foot in both hands. The dragon rose grumpily to his feet and peered blearily around him.

"Julia; where is everybody?"

"They've all left."

"Pity; I was just starting to feel a little peckish. Why is Rupert hopping up and down and muttering to himself?"

"I think it's some kind of folk dance," said Julia solemnly.

"Oh," said the dragon doubtfully. He studied Rupert carefully, and then looked away. "Where's the unicorn?"

"Hiding," said a melancholy voice from behind a hanging arras. "Every time Rupert has to speak to his family he ends up in a foul temper, and he takes it out on me."

"Get out of there, unicorn," snapped Rupert, hobbling over to lean on Julia.

"See what I mean?" said the unicorn, emerging cautiously from behind the tapestry. "If you've run out of people to upset, Sire, could we perhaps go now? In case it slipped your attention, we haven't eaten since first thing this morning, and my stomach thinks my throat's been cut."

"Of course," said Rupert. "I'll get you all the grass you can eat."

"Oh, whoopee," said the unicorn.

They headed for the shattered doorway, Rupert still leaning companiably on Julia.

"Just my luck," muttered the unicorn.

"What?" asked Rupert.

"All that effort I put into practicing my limp, and nobody even mentioned it."

Rupert and Julia looked at each other, spluttered with laughter, and led the dragon and the no-longer-limping unicorn out of the Court.

King John watched the last of the dragon's tail slither out the doorway, and then he sighed wearily and sank back in his throne. Thomas Grey lowered himself cautiously onto the steps leading up to the throne. His knees cracked loudly as he sat down. Both King and Astrologer looked suddenly older.

"Doesn't the Court seem larger without Rupert's friends in it," said the King.

Grey laughed. "Not to mention quieter."

"I like Julia," said the King. "She's got spirit. And Rupert seems to have developed a powerful right hand."

"At least he got that idiot Darius off our backs for a while."

"Quite," growled the King. "That's what you get for making Ministerships hereditary."

"Not one of my better ideas," Grey admitted. He yawned suddenly.

"Don't," said the King. "You'll start me off, and there's work to be done yet. At least, I assume there is."

"I'm afraid so," said Grey. "To start with, we've got to change all the arrangements for Harald's wedding."

King John closed his eyes and groaned loudly. "As if they weren't costing enough all ready."

"And we've got to work out some way of politely informing Baron Oakeshoff that Harald isn't going to marry his daughter after all."

"Pity about that," said the King. "Now the Barons will be more trouble than ever. Have we had *any* taxes from them yet?"

"Not a penny," said the Astrologer. "They're not going to pay up as long as they think they can get away with it, and we can't use the Royal Guard to persuade them until the demons stop attacking us."

"And the Champion expects them to give me an army," sighed the King.

"Politics never was his strong point."

"He's loyal to the throne," said King John. "That's why I made him Champion. Do you know, Thomas; after all these years he still makes me nervous. There's something almost inhuman about a loyalty that's never questioned. He's killed over a hundred men at my command, and never once asked why."

"When a Champion starts asking questions, it's time to get a new Champion," said Grey dryly.

The King laughed, but there was little humor in the sound. "Life wasn't always this complicated. Do you remember when I first came to the throne, Thomas?"

"Aye, John; must be all of thirty-five years since the High Warlock placed that crown on your head. In those days there was still gold in the coffers, the Barons knew their place, and the Darkwood was just a patch of ink on the maps, little more than a legend."

"A long time ago, Thomas." The King tugged pensively at his straggling gray beard. "Where did it all start to go wrong? I've done my best down the years, but for every problem I solved two more sprang up to take its place. When I came to power, the Forest Kingdom was a rich land, a healthy land; a power to be reckoned with. We had such plans, you and I . . . Now look at us; two old men fighting our own Barons just to hold the Land together.

"We're all that's left of the old order, Thomas. On the

day I was crowned, a hundred and fifty knights bent their knees and made the oath of fealty to me. Where are they now? Dead and gone, all of them, lost in one stupid little war or another. All my brave knights . . . Now chivalry is no longer fashionable, and honor is a thing of the past. Times change, and I've lost the ability to change with them.

"It's been so long since I could rest, Thomas. So long since I could sleep at night without my troubles invading my dreams. So long since my poor Eleanor died . . ."

Grey leaned back against the King's leg, and they sat quietly together a while; two old friends, remembering happier days.

Shadows filled the Court as night slowly fell. King John stared out across the vast, empty hall with its wood-panelled walls and soaring rafters, and ghosts came to stand before him in their shining armor, swords held aloft as they silently roared their loyalty to the throne. All the heroes of his Realm, the questors and champions, the stalkers and avengers of evil, dead and gone down the many years. King John sat staring at an empty Court, and one by one the ghosts left him, until all that remained was his throne, and his Kingdom.

"You know," said King John finally, "it's not so much making bad decisions that bothers me; it's just that I spend days on end weighing up the pros and cons, and I still make the wrong decision!"

The Astrologer chuckled quietly. "That's why you keep me around, John. I may not be the High Warlock, but my small magics do come in handy now and again."

"Indeed they do, Thomas." The King ruffled the Astrologer's hair affectionately. "What would I do without you?"

They sat together in companiable silence, the King's brooding eyes fixed on yesterday.

"Fifty-five isn't old," he said suddenly. "I'm not as young as I was, but I don't *feel* old."

"Time catches up with all of us eventually," said the Astrologer.

"You seem to be putting up a good fight," said the King tartly. "Look at you; your back's as straight and your hair as dark as it was forty years ago."

"I dye my hair."

"And you wear a corset."

"Only sometimes."

"Only when you're chasing a new wench." The King chuckled evilly. "Man your age should have more dignity."

"Every man should have a hobby," said the Astrologer complacently.

The King laughed, but his habitual frown soon returned. "What is the matter with the Barons anyway? They've never been this bad before."

"It's the Darkwood, John. Our wealth comes from mines run by the Barons; it's their gold and silver and copper that keeps our economy afloat. But since the Darkwood has spread its boundaries, more and more of the mines lie beneath ground fallen to the long night. Demons are crawling up out of the pits and spilling into the main workings. Miners are afraid to go down into the dark. Some mines have had to be sealed, for fear of what might emerge from the deepest shafts."

The King scowled thoughtfully. "I hadn't realized things had got so out of hand."

"You can't be expected to keep track of everything, John."

"Perhaps if I sent the Barons more guards . . ."

"No, John; we can't afford to lose any more men. We're thinly enough spread as it is. We can't really spare that troop of guards you're sending with the Champion and young Rupert."

"I know," said the King, "But if we didn't let Rupert have them, I really think he wouldn't go."

"Yes," the Astrologer said smiling. "He's finally learning . . ."

They shared a smile, and then the King frowned again, and looked away.

"They'd better bring back the High Warlock," he said softly. "After the mess we've made of things, he's our only hope."

CHAPTER THREE

Duels

Thin trailers of mist curled lazily on the chill morning air as Rupert saddled his unicorn in the courtyard. The dawn sun had barely crept above the horizon, and the sky was still splashed with blood. Not the best of omens for the journey ahead. Rupert grinned tiredly, and then leaned briefly against the patiently waiting unicorn as a yawn stretched his jaw to its limit. According to his water clock, he'd had almost six hours' sleep, but it seemed he'd barely laid his head on the pillow before a servant was shaking him awake.

A lukewarm bath and a cold breakfast hadn't improved his temper, and being studiously ignored by his own troop of guards was the last straw. Rupert cursed under his breath as the bitter cold numbed his fingers, making them clumsy on the harness. A buckle slipped from his grasp, and he grabbed awkwardly for it. Although his back was to the guards, he could hear some of them laughing. He flushed hotly as he tightened the cinch, sure he was the butt of their humor. *One joke,* he thought angrily, *just one and I'll feed the man his chain mail, link by link!* Rupert smiled sourly, and shook his head. Not yet out of the Castle gates, and already he was thinking of attacking one of his own guards. He closed his eyes a moment and breathed deeply, searching for some kind of calm. There was a long journey ahead of him, with plenty of time for him and his guards to test each other's measure.

Assuming they survived long enough.

Rupert brushed the thought aside, quickly fastened the last few straps, and then turned and stared casually about

him. Half a hundred guardsmen and their mounts milled
back and forth in the courtyard, interspersed with hurrying
servants and grooms. Flagons of mead and cheap sweetmeats were being warmed over flaring braziers by gaudily
clothed hawkers, and here and there small knots of men
spoke quietly with hooded priests. A dozen guards were
fighting mock duels under the Champion's watchful eye,
and the towering stone walls echoed to the ring of steel on
steel. Other guards stood and watched, polished their swords
with oiled rags, and practiced looking evil. Rupert found
their obvious competence both intimidating and comforting.
He pulled his cloak about him, and stamped his feet to keep
warm. His breath steamed on the still morning air. Rupert
frowned; it shouldn't be this cold so early in the autumn.
The Darkwood must be closer than anyone thought . . . he
let his hand drop to the pommel of his sword. The sooner he
got this journey started, the better.

And yet he hesitated, watching the duelling guardsmen
thrust and parry, their swords flashing brightly in the gloomy
courtyard. Sweat glistened in the guards' faces, and their
breathing grew harsh as they drove themselves ever harder,
searching for the elusive first blood the would decide the
duel. Rupert remembered all too clearly the many times
he'd fought in this courtyard, in the early morning chill.
Bitter memories surfaced, of standing awkwardly under his
tutor's disdainful gaze, wrapped in ill-fitting chain mail and
carrying a sword that seemed far too heavy for his skinny
arms. His duelling partner had been a lean muscular guardsman, almost twenty years his senior and many times his
better. Between them, the tutor and the guard slowly turned
the young Prince into a swordsman. He paid for the knowledge with blood and humiliation. Rupert scowled thoughtfully; he might never be the expert his brother was, but he'd
learned tricks in his hard school that were often overlooked
in Harald's more standard lessons.

Rupert had never given in to the temptation to show off
his skill with a sword. Now and again the two brothers
would engage in a formal duel, under the Champion's criti-
cal eye, and Rupert always lost. It was safer that way. As a
merely competent fighter, he was no threat to Harald's
position, so he suffered the scars and the jeers silently. But
he never forgot them. Rupert's mind drifted back from

yesterday, and he studied again the straining, grunting guardsmen as they practiced with sword and buckler. He was surprised to find them not nearly as impressive as he'd first thought. They were strong and cunning, but their tactics were limited and their stamina negligable. They were good, but a sudden excitement surged through Rupert as he realized that, just possibly, he was better.

Rupert frowned suddenly as he recognized one of the guards, a tall wiry man with dark, saturnine features. Rob Hawke was a Bladesmaster, a swordsman trained to such a point of expertise that he was unbeatable with a sword in his hand. He was also stubborn, crafty, and so insubordinate that only his extremely rare skill with a blade kept him from being expelled from the Royal Guard. Rupert scowled thoughtfully, and wondered how many other bad apples the King had landed him with.

A sharp voice suddenly cut across his thoughts, and he looked round to see Harald standing beside the Champion. Rupert studied his brother warily as he realized Harald was wearing full chain mail, and carrying a steel-bossed buckler. He was also smiling.

"Rupert, dear fellow; thought you might fancy a little sword practice before you go, just to warm your blood a trifle. Well, brother, what do you say?"

It's a set-up, thought Rupert disgustedly. *He's well-armored and rested. I don't even have a shield.*

He glanced round as silence fell quickly over the crowded courtyard. The other duels had been stopped, and the guardsmen were watching interestedly to see what his answer would be. It was obvious that everyone expected him to make some excuse and back out of it. That was the sensible thing to do. Harald intended Rupert to pay in blood for insulting him in front of the entire Court, whilst simultaneously undermining what little respect the guards had for their new leader. It was a good scheme; any other time it might even have worked. But not this time. For once in his life, Rupert intended to win. He chuckled suddenly at his own eagerness, and for the first time Harald seemed uncertain. Beside him, the Champion remained impassive.

"Thank you, brother," said Rupert loudly, his voice echoing clearly from the massive stone walls. "I could use the exercise."

He turned his back on his brother, removed his cloak, and dropped it over the unicorn's saddle.

"Are you sure this is a good idea?" muttered the unicorn.

"No," said Rupert cheerfully. "And I don't give a damn."

"Some times I don't understand you at all."

"That makes two of us."

The unicorn sniffed audibly. "Watch your back, Rupert."

Rupert nodded, and then strode confidently over to where Harald stood waiting, sword in hand. Rupert's sword whispered from its scabbard as the guardsmen moved to form a circle round the two Princes.

"I seem to have caught you without a shield," said Harald.

"That's all right," said Rupert. "I don't need one."

Harald took in Rupert's relaxed stance and steady gaze, and glanced quickly at the Champion, who shook his head slightly.

"You must have a shield," Harald insisted. "It must be a fair combat."

"It will be," said Rupert. "Now do you want to talk, or fight?"

An amused murmur ran through the watching guards, and Harald flushed hotly. He sank into his fighting stance with the naturalness of long practice and moved cautiously forward, studying Rupert narrowly over the rim of his buckler. Rupert came to meet him, his trained eyes searching out weaknesses in Harald's stance, potential awkwardnesses that could be exploited. Harald was clearly more used to the stylized techniques of the mock duel than the cut and thrust of a blood fight; he'd grown soft, whilst Rupert's experiences in the Darkwood had honed his skill to a razor's edge. Rupert grinned broadly as all the old bitterness of having to lose to Harald surged through him. This time, Harald was in for a fight he'd remember for the rest of his life. Rupert's grin widened as he moved lightly forward, his sword licking out to test for holes in Harald's defense.

For a while the only sounds in the courtyard were the stamp and scuff of booted feet on the bare stone, and the occasional rasp of blade on blade. Breath steamed on the chill air as the two brothers circled each other warily, and then Harald lunged forward, his sword flashing in a bright arc for Rupert's unshielded ribs. Rupert parried the cut easily, stepped inside the blow and kicked Harald in the knee. Harald lurched to one side as his leg betrayed him, and Rupert slammed a knee into his gut. Harald bent forward over his pain, almost as though bowing to Rupert. Air whistled in his throat as he fought for breath. Rupert darted back out of range and allowed his brother time to recover; he'd waited a long time for this victory, and he saw no reason to rush it. The guards had responded to the brief exchange with interested murmurs, and out of the corners of his eyes Rupert could see money changing hands. He grinned tightly, and then his brother came to meet him again. Harald's sword and shield were steady, but he favored his left leg. Rupert felt a grim laughter stir within him. Harald was already beaten, even if he didn't know it yet. Cold-bloodedly, Rupert set out to prove it.

His sword sang through the air as he swung the blade double-handed, and blow by blow, cut by cut, he drove Harald backwards round the circle. Splinters flew from Harald's buckler as Rupert pressed home his attack, his sword flashing past the shield's rim to draw blood from a dozen minor cuts. Harald bobbed and weaved and cut viciously at Rupert's unprotected head and body, but always he was thrown back with fresh blood seeping into his chain mail, as Rupert showed him every skill and dirty trick he knew. Rupert was the better fighter, and now he and everybody else knew it. The guardsmen applauded and cheered every move, and Rupert laughed aloud as he drove his brother back. A sudden impatience took him, and slamming aside Harald's buckler, Rupert smashed the sword from his brother's hand, kicked his feet from under him, and then set the point of his blade at Harald's throat as he lay helpless on the blood-splashed cobbles.

"Yield," said Rupert hoarsely.

"I yield," said Harald quietly, bitterly.

Rupert stared down at him for a long moment, and then stepped back. He'd beaten his brother, just as he'd dreamed for so many years, but somehow it didn't quite feel real yet. The applauding guards fell silent as Harald rose painfully to his feet, his shield arm hanging limply at his side. His immaculate chain mail was scarred and bloodied, and he left his battered sword where it lay. Blood trickled unnoticed down his face as he smiled coldly.

"I should have had you killed years ago, Rupert. If by

some miracle you survive the journey to the Dark Tower, don't come back. I won't make the mistake of fighting fair again."

He turned his back on Rupert and limped away, slapping aside the helping hands guards offered him. Rupert watched him go. After all the years, all the insults, all the pain, he'd finally beaten his brother. It didn't feel as good as he'd thought it would. He shrugged, and grinned round at his guards. They seemed strangely subdued, almost as though they were waiting for something . . . A sudden suspicion flared in Rupert's mind, and he'd just started to turn when a mailed fist slammed into the small of his back, sending him sprawling to the ground. He made it to one knee, and then a steel-clad boot buried itself in his gut. He writhed on the cold ground, sobbing with pain.

"Never drop your guard, Rupert," said the Champion calmly. "You know better than that."

His boot lashed out again, catching Rupert on the hip and sending him rolling into the feet of the silently watching guards. He lurched to one knee and reached for his sword. The Champion's boot slammed down again, but this time Rupert was ready for him. Instead of snatching back his fingers he continued the movement, caught the Champion's ankle in both hands, and twisted him off-balance. The Champion fell heavily, and by the time he regained his feet Rupert was waiting for him, sword in hand.

"Now that's more like it," said the Champion approvingly. His sword licked out to open a shallow cut on Rupert's left cheek, and then the Champion had to jump back out of range as Rupert's blade sheared through the chain mail over his ribs. The Champion glanced down, and saw blood seeping through his armor.

"Getting old, Champion," said Rupert thickly. "There was a time you wouldn't have given me a chance to recover."

The Champion smiled. "I'm still good enough for you, boy. Come on; let's see what you can do."

Rupert moved cautiously forward, his sword sweeping back and forth before him. The two fighters circled each other warily, and then came together in a flurry of steel too fast for the eye to follow. They sprang apart and circled each other again, their steel-clad boots striking sparks from the bare stone. Blood rilled down from a wide cut on

Rupert's forehead, filling his eyes with crimson. The Champion had another bloody rent in his chain mail. Rupert wiped blood from his eyes with the back of his hand, and couldn't parry the Champion's attack in time. Fresh blood trickled down Rupert's sword arm, making his grasp slippery. And so the fight went on. Rupert used every trick he knew, all his strength and skill coming together in an exhibition of swordsmanship that had the guardsmen crying aloud in appreciation. Again and again he threw himself at the Champion, his sword a bright blur on the still morning air as it rose and fell, rose and fell. Rupert gave everything he had, and it wasn't enough.

He never stood a chance.

The Champion parried his every blow, allowed Rupert to tire himself out, and then moved in with a flurry of hammering blows that left Rupert lying battered and helpless facedown on the blood-smeared cobblestones. He was dimly aware of the Champion crouching before him, and then tears started from his eyes as a strong hand grabbed a handful of hair and lifted his head up.

"Sorry, Sire," said the Champion quietly. "But you should have know better than to beat Harald in public. Next time, you will know better." The hand released Rupert's hair, and the cobblestones jumped up to meet his face. The Champion's voice seemed to come from far away. "We ride in half an hour, Sire; I expect you to be in your saddle and ready to leave. If you're not, I'll have you strapped to the unicorn."

He walked unhurriedly away, and one by one the guards followed him, leaving Rupert curled around his pain. The courtyard chatter slowly resumed. For a long while Rupert just lay there, and then there was the sound of running feet, and two gentle hands were holding his shoulders. He cried out wordlessly, and shrank away from the hands, afraid of more pain.

"Rupert, love; what have they done to you?" said Julia.

Rupert's mind slowly cleared, and he became aware of Julia kneeling beside him.

"What happened, Rupert?"

"I wanted to win," he said thickly, and spat blood onto the cobblestones. "Just once, I wanted to win. Help me up, will you?"

Slowly, leaning heavily on Julia's supporting arm, he got

to his feet, and she guided him over to the nearest wall so that he could lean against it. His head swam madly, and he stood quietly while Julia cleaned the worst of the blood from his face with a silk handkerchief.

"Waste of good silk, that," he said, trying to smile.

"Who did this to you?" demanded Julia, her voice shaking with fury.

"The Champion," said Rupert. "I shouldn't have turned my back on him."

"I'll kill him!" said Julia, and Rupert quickly grabbed her wrist.

"No! Don't even think it, Julia. He wouldn't kill you, but he'd have no compunction about scarring you a little to teach you a lesson. You're good with a sword, lass, but I'm better, and he walked all over me and didn't even raise a sweat." He realized he was still holding her wrist painfully tight, and let her go. "I'm not badly hurt, Julia, except in my pride. He was careful not to do any real damage. I should have known he wouldn't let me get away with beating Harald."

"You beat Harald?"

"Yeah." Rupert grinned, wincing a little as fresh blood seeped into his mouth. "I beat him. I did everything but sign my initials on him."

Julia laughed, and clapped her hands together. "Oh, I'd love to have seen that!"

"Bloodthirsty wench," Rupert growled, and then laughed as she nodded demurely.

"Why did the Champion attack you?"

"Partly to keep me in my place. Partly to undermine my authority with the guards. And partly because he has to prove he's still the best, even after all these years as Champion. As he's got older, he's needed to prove it more and more."

Julia frowned thoughtfully. "I think I'll have a word with the dragon about this."

"Thanks for the thought, but no. I want to beat him myself."

Rupert pushed himself away from the wall and breathed deeply until his head steadied. Pain still simmered in his muscles, flaring up if he moved too quickly, but it was bearable. He'd hurt worse in the Darkwood. He looked round for his sword, and Julia handed it to him without having to be asked. He smiled his thanks, slipped the blade into its scabbard, and then took his first good look at Julia.

Somebody had clearly decided to take the young Princess in hand. Julia now wore a long flowing gown of midnight blue, with gold and silver piping. Diamonds flashed from rings and bracelets and necklaces, and they'd taken away her sword. Her long blonde hair had been piled up on top of her head and carefully arranged in the latest High Society style. Expertly applied cosmetics softened the harsh planes of her face without disguising them. All in all, Rupert thought she'd never looked lovelier. Even though it was a totally unsuitable outfit for visiting a filthy courtyard at the break of dawn.

"I like the dress," he said solemnly.

"I look like an idiot," grumbled Julia. "All I need to finish the job is a cap and bells. The dress is too tight, my shoes are crippling me, and this damn hairdo is giving me a headache. What's more, the thick wooly underwear they forced on me itches like crazy." She went to scratch herself and only then realized she was still holding the bloodstained handkerchief she'd used to clean Rupert's face. She sniffed, tucked it unconcernedly into her flared sleeve, and glared at the Prince accusingly. "You were going to sneak off without saying goodbye, weren't you?"

Rupert shrugged awkwardly. "I don't like goodbyes. They always seem so final."

"Rupert," said Julia slowly, "Just how dangerous is this High Warlock?"

"Very. The last messenger we sent him came back transformed."

"Transformed? Into what?"

"We're not actually sure. Remember the crocodiles that used to live in the moat?"

"You mean whatever ate them is . . ."

"We think so."

Julia scowled thoughtfully. "And the High Warlock's our only hope against the Darkwood?"

"Looks like it."

"Than we're in deep trouble."

Rupert nodded solemnly, and Julia had to laugh. Rupert grinned, glad he'd finally broken her grim mood.

"Well, Julia; how are you getting on with Castle Society?"

"Settling in. Slowly."

"Hit anybody recently?"

"No one important."

Rupert laughed. "That's all right, then."

They stood together a while, neither of them sure what to say for the best, and then Julia leaned forward and kissed him. Rupert took her in his arms, and held her close. He could feel her heart beating against his. After a while, he pushed her gently away.

"It's almost time to go, Julia."

"Yes."

"I'd take you with me if I could."

"I understand."

"Wait for me?"

"Of course. Do you still have my favor?"

Rupert reached inside his jerkin and pulled out a very battered and blood-stained handkerchief. "My lady's favor. I wouldn't be parted from it for all the Forest Kingdom." He looked up and found there were tears in Julia's eyes, too. He turned quickly away, and stared out across the packed courtyard as he put the handkerchief away again. He heard Julia move in close behind him, felt her breath warm the back of his neck as she spoke.

"No goodbyes, Rupert. Just . . . come back safely. Or I'll never forgive you."

There was a pause, and then he heard her turn and walk away. He wished there was something else to say, but there wasn't. He put his hand over his heart, and felt the soft pressure of the handkerchief under his jerkin. It seemed the minstrels weren't always wrong, after all. He grinned, and made his way across the courtyard to rejoin the unicorn.

"Are you all right now, Rupert? You look a bit flushed."

"I'm fine. Fine."

"Julia's gone?"

"Yes."

"I like her," said the unicorn.

"So do I," said Rupert.

"I had noticed," said the unicorn, dryly.

Rupert laughed, and put his cloak back on. "Ready to move out?"

"Ready as I'll ever be. Why isn't the dragon coming with us? I'd just started to get used to him."

"He's resting. I think the demons hurt him more than he'll admit. The Rainbow should have healed him, but I suppose he's just . . . not as young as he was. Last night, it was all he could do to walk to the stables. I'll miss him, but he's not up to a long journey, let alone fighting off demons."

"Demons?" said the unicorn sharply. "What demons?"

"Well, when we go back into the Darkwood . . ."

"The Darkwood? Nobody said anything to me about going back into the Darkwood! Right. That's it. Get that saddle off me, I'm not moving."

"We're only going into it a little way . . ."

"So I'll suppose we'll only be killed a little bit. Forget it!"

"Look, unicorn, either we go and fetch the High Warlock, or the Darkwood will come looking for us. It's that simple."

"There has to be another alternative."

"Like what?"

"Run away?"

Rupert laughed, and patted the unicorn's neck. "Are all unicorns as chicken as you?"

"The ones with any sense are. The only reason unicorns are so rare is that most of us haven't the sense to come in out of the rain. Or to stay clear of humans."

Rupert studied the unicorn thoughtfully. "You're my friend, aren't you?"

The unicorn shifted his feet. "Yeah, I suppose so. I've got used to having you around."

"I have to go back into the Darkwood again. It's my duty."

"I know," sighed the unicorn resignedly. "And I have to go with you."

Rupert patted the unicorn's neck again. "Thanks. I'd hate to have to do it without you." He frowned suddenly. "Unicorn . . ."

"Yes?"

"I just realized . . . all this time we've been together, and I don't even know your name."

The unicorn turned his head slowly, and fixed Rupert with a blood-red eye.

"My name? I'm a slave, Prince. Slaves don't have names."

The courtyard seemed suddenly colder, and Rupert looked away, unable to meet the unicorn's steady gaze.

"You're not a slave . . ."

"No? You think I wear this saddle and bridle by choice? I was taken from my herd by men with ropes and whips. They beat me till they broke my spirit, and then they sold me to you. That's not slavery?" The unicorn laughed bitterly. "You've been good to me, Rupert. I'm fond of you, in my way. But I'm still a slave, and you're still my master. And slaves don't have names. I used to have a name. When I was free, I had a name." The unicorn's voice dropped to a whisper. "One day, I'll have a name again."

"I'm . . . sorry," said Rupert lamely. "I just . . . never thought about it before." He looked up to meet the unicorn's gaze. "I led you into the Darkwood, and nearly got you killed. You could have run off and left me anytime, but you didn't, because I needed you. You're my friend, unicorn. If you don't want to come with me, you don't have to. But I wish you would."

Man and unicorn stared at each other.

"Climb aboard," said the unicorn finally. "We've a long ride ahead of us."

Rupert nodded, set his foot in the stirrup, and swung up into the saddle. Not back twenty-four hours, and already on his way again. *Julia was right*, he thought suddenly. *We shouldn't have come back to the Castle. We were happy together, out there in the Forest. We didn't know about Harald's marriage contract, or the spreading Darkwood. I could have loved you, Julia. I could have loved you, then.*

He sighed and shook his head, and then looked up as the slow clatter of approaching hooves caught his attention. The Champion drew up beside him, astride an armored charger. The horse stood a good ten hands taller than the unicorn, and carried the heavy armor with nonchalant ease. *Impressive*, thought Rupert. *Great for jousting. But not a lot of use against a pack of demons.*

"Expecting trouble, sir Champion?" he asked, solemnly.

"Always, Sire. I take it you're ready to leave?"

"Of course. You did an excellent job, sir Champion. I'm hurt, but not actually damaged."

"I try to be professional."

"One of these days . . ."

"You'll what, Sire? Slip poison in my cup, or a dagger in my back? I doubt it; that's not your way. You want to beat me sword-to-sword, like you did Harald. And you'll never be good enough to take me that way."

"Don't put money on it," said Rupert calmly. "There was a time Harald thought the same."

The Champion gave him a hard look, but said nothing. For a long moment the two men stared at each other, feeling the change in their relationship, and for the first time Rupert realized that he wasn't afraid of the Champion any more. For as long as Rupert could remember, the Champion had seemed to him the personification of death; a cold-eyed killer with a bloody sword who would one day come for him as he had come for so many others. But not any more. Rupert had gone sword-to-sword with him under the worst possible conditions, and he'd drawn blood twice. He might have lost the fight, but nobody had let the Champion's blood in over twenty years. The man was good, very good, but he wasn't unbeatable. *And one day,* thought Rupert, *I'm going to prove it.* He grinned mockingly at the Champion, who studied him thoughtfully, and then turned his horse away.

"One moment, sir Champion."

"I'm busy, Sire."

"I don't give a sweet damn how busy you are, sir Champion; you turn your back on me again and I'll have your head."

The Champion turned his horse back, and then dropped his reins to leave his sword hand free. A slight smile jerked at his mouth. "I think you forget your place, Rupert."

"Do I? Last evening, my father ordered you to accept my authority during the journey to the Dark Tower. Are you going to break your word to your King?"

The Champion sat very still, and Rupert sensed wheels turning behind the impassive face. Then the Champion looked down, and took up his reins again, and Rupert knew that he'd won.

"My word is my bond, Sire," said the Champion slowly. "On this journey, you command."

"Good," said Rupert, trying to keep the relief out of his voice. "Because if you try to undermine my authority over the guards again, I'll cut your throat while you're sleeping."

"Threats aren't necessary, Sire. I gave my word."

Rupert nodded ungraciously. "Have you told the men we'll have to pass through the Darkwood to reach the Warlock's Tower?"

"Aye," said the Champion. "I've never actually travelled through the long night, Sire. What's it like?"

Rupert let his mind drift back. He remembered fear and pain that weighed on him still, like chains wrapped around his soul. "It's dark," he said finally. "Dark enough to break anyone."

The Champion waited a while, and then realized Rupert wasn't going to say any more.

"I'll assemble the men, Sire. You'll want to address them before we set out."

"Do I have to?"

The Champion raised an eyebrow. "It is customary to brief the men on what dangers they'll be facing, Sire."

"Oh, yeah. All right; line them up, sir Champion."

"Right away, Sire."

The Champion rode off. Rupert watched him bark orders to the aimlessly milling guards, and strove to collect his thoughts. How the hell was he supposed to explain the dangers of the Darkwood to men who'd never even seen it? Most Forestmen never set foot in the long night; the Tanglewood saw to that. Rupert scowled thoughtfully; according to the Champion, the Tanglewood had fallen to the darkness, and demons roamed the Forest Land at will. Rupert shrugged, and let his hand drop to the pommel of the rainbow sword. If all else failed, he'd just have to summon another Rainbow.

The guardsmen slowly assembled before him in ones and twos, their horses stamping and whinnying in their eagerness to be off. Breath steamed on the chill morning air, and the odd shaft of sunlight gleamed golden on shining chain mail. The guards looked hard and competent, and Rupert's heart sank a little as he realized they'd never understand the true horror of the Darkwood until they met if face-to-face. It was too personal a horror to bear explanation. But he had to try.

"The Darkwood," he said finally, "Is dangerous. Always. Even when you can't see the demons, be sure they're watching you. There's no light, except what we take in. There's no usable food or water, except what we collect beforehand. I've passed through the Darkwood twice, and each time it came close to killing me. I had a dragon with me on the second journey, and it didn't make a blind bit of difference."

He paused and looked about him, the echoes of his voice dying quickly away in the courtyard's silence. The guards stared impassively back, their eyes wary, but perhaps just a little respectful. In all Forest history, no man had passed through the Darkwood twice and survived. *And I'm going to try it again,* thought Rupert sourly. *I must be mad.* He smiled grimly at the guards before him.

"It's a hard, bloody journey to the Dark Tower, my friends, and you'll be facing the worst odds of your career. Most of you won't be coming back. But we have to go; the Forest is depending on us to bring back the High Warlock. If we fail, darkness will spread over all the Land, and there'll be nothing left to come back to. If we make it, they'll sing songs about us forever.

"Anyone who wants, can back out now. The Darkwood's no place for unwilling heroes. But for once in your life, you have a chance to make a difference; the Forest Land needs you. And I need you."

He looked around, his breath caught in his throat as he waited for their answer. And one by one, the guards drew their swords and held them aloft in the ancient warrior's oath of fealty. Rupert slowly nodded his acceptance, unable to hide how much the gesture meant to him, and half-a-hundred swords crashed back into their scabbards.

"Sir Champion!"

"Aye, Sire?"

"Let's go."

Rupert headed the unicorn toward the inner gates. The Champion fell in beside him, and the guards followed close behind in tight formation. The huge oaken doors swung slowly open, and massed hoofbeats shook the thick stone walls as Rupert led his men through the Keep. And then the portcullis lifted, the drawbridge slammed down across the moat, and Rupert and his party rode out into the early morning mists.

Rupert shivered, and wrapped his cloak tightly about him. He'd been travelling all morning, but though the mists had finally cleared, the day grew no warmer. A dull, blood-red sun glowered down from the dark, overcast sky, ominous with the threat of thunder and sudden storm. A heavy frost had bleached the grass verges of the trail he followed, and the uneven ground was hard and unyielding beneath the unicorn's hooves. Stark leafless trees stood brooding to every side, and silvered cobwebs shrouded what little greenery remained. No animals moved among the trees, and no birds sang. The Forest lay still and silent in that bleak afternoon, and the dull muffled hoofbeats from Rupert's troop of guards seemed an unwelcome intrusion on the unnatural quiet.

Rupert beat his fists together to get the blood moving, but the cold still gnawed at his fingers, despite his thick leather gloves. He'd long ago lost all feeling in his feet. *It's barely autumn,* he thought dazedly. *It's never been this cold so early in the year . . .* The bitter wind lashed his face, chafing his cheeks raw. Rupert felt a familiar chill growing in his bones, and knew that the wind had its beginnings in the endless night. The Darkwood's influence moved ahead of it, falling like a blight on land soon to be claimed by the darkness. Rupert started to shiver, and for a long time he couldn't stop.

The Champion suddenly put up a hand, and the column of guards came to a ragged halt. Rupert reined in his unicorn and stared quickly about him, his hand resting on the pommel of his sword.

"Why have we stopped, sir Champion?"

"We're being watched, Sire."

Rupert frowned. "I don't see anybody."

"They're here," said the Champion softly. "They're waiting for us."

For a long moment, nobody moved. The guards sat stiffly in their saddles, eyes testing the Forest shadows, ears straining for the slightest noise. The gaunt, spectral trees crowded about them, guarding ancient secrets in an impenetrable gloom. The only sound was the whinnying and snorting of the restless horses, and the low murmur of the wind in the bare branches. And then Rupert felt his hackles slowly rise as he made out dim, furtive movements in the shadows ahead.

There was a susurrus of steel on leather as the guards drew their swords. *Demons,* came the murmur, passing swiftly through the ranks, *Demons in the shadows.* Rupert drew his sword, and swore under his breath as he realized his buckler was still securely fastened to his backpack. He fumbled at the straps, his eyes straining against the gloom ahead. Half a dozen lancers moved forward to flank him and the Champion, light gleaming on the deadly steel shafts. Rupert slipped on his buckler, glanced at the Champion, and then urged the unicorn forward. The troops moved with him, slowly gathering speed.

Demons in the Forest. Demons by daylight. The Darkwood must be closer than we thought.

Rupert shook his head quickly to clear it, and hefted his buckler to a more comfortable position. He realized he could barely feel the swordhilt with his numbed fingers, and tightened his grip. And then a single tiny figure darted out into the trail ahead, and raised both its hands in surrender.

"We give up!" it called plaintively. "Honest!"

Rupert brought his unicorn to a sudden halt, the guards piling up behind him. A sudden suspicion entered his mind, and a broad grin spread slowly across his face as out onto the Forest trail stepped a great crowd of goblins. Their leader took one look at Rupert and winced visibly.

"Oh no. Not you again."

The other goblins peered shortsightedly at Rupert, and then crowded together in the middle of the trail, shaking in every limb. There was a general dropping of weapons, and several of the smaller goblins burst into tears.

"Friends of yours?" asked the Champion.

"Not exactly," said Rupert. He gestured for the goblin leader to approach him, and the goblin did so reluctantly.

"It's not fair," he said bitterly, glaring up at Rupert. "I've spent weeks turning that bunch of knock-kneed idiots into a crack fighting unit. I've taken farmers and herders and leechmen and turned them into warriors. Two days ago we fought off a demon pack. Morale's never been higher. And then what happens? *You* come along and demoralize the whole damn bunch without even using your sword! It's not fair!"

"Calm down," said Rupert.

"Calm down? It's not enough that you've become a legend among us, as the only human ever to have defeated a whole pack of goblins. It's not enough that some of that pack are still having nightmares about you. It's not enough that goblin mothers now frighten their children with tales of the nasty human who'll come for them if they're naughty. Oh no, not content with all that, you decide to hunt us down with a whole troop of guards! What are you going to do for an encore; set fire to the Forest?"

Rupert grinned. It was obvious that the goblins he'd scared off had built him up into a mighty hero, to justify their running away. Maybe legends had their uses after all.

"What are you doing so far from your home?" he asked, and the goblin leader scowled.

"The Tanglewood's gone," he said gruffly. "The dark came, and demons overran the narrow paths. They wrecked our homes and butchered our families. We ran before them, carrying what we could. Goblins aren't brave; we've never needed to be. It's not in our nature. But after what we've seen, some of us have learned to hate.

"We're an old race, sir hero, remnants of an earlier age. It was a simpler time, then. No humans to make us afraid, no Darkwood to blight our Forest. An age when magic was strong in the world, and cold iron lay safely in the ground, no danger to the small folk. Then man came, using steel against our bronze, forcing us from our ancient homes. We created the Tanglewood with the last of our magic, and made it our new home. Few of us survived the move; we live long and breed slow, and we don't like change.

"We're not fighters, sir hero; it's not our way. We don't even make good footpads, as you no doubt remember. We farm, and tend our herds, and leave the world be. All we've ever asked is to be left alone. But now the night is spreading, and our day is finally over. Once, our numbers were beyond counting. Then there were thousands of us, living in the Tanglewood. Now there are hundreds, and we have no home. So we're going to the Forest Castle. We may not be strong and brave or carry cold steel, sir hero, but we can fight, and if the Castle will shelter our families, we'll defend it with our lives."

The goblin leader glared defiantly up at Rupert, as if expecting an insult or a blow for his presumption in claiming his people to be warriors. Rupert looked past him, and saw that the listening goblins had drawn strength from their leader, and were standing calmly in the middle of the trail, awaiting Rupert's answer. They were not proud or brave, but there was something about them that might have been dignity.

"Go to the Castle," said Rupert, his voice breaking a little. "Ask admission in my name; Prince Rupert of the Forest Kingdom. Your families will be safe there, and the King can always use warriors like you."

The goblin leader stared at him, and then nodded briefly. "And where might you be off to, sir hero?"

"We're going to the Dark Tower," said Rupert. "To summon the High Warlock."

The goblin leader's mouth twitched. "I don't know who I feel more sorry for; you, or him."

He turned on his heel and marched back to his waiting people. More goblins emerged from the Forest shadows; women and children, carrying what few possessions they had left. The goblin leader coaxed and bullied his people into a single ragged line, and then led them past the silently watching, somewhat bemused troop of guards. Slowly, wearily, the goblins headed down the dirt trail that led to Forest Castle.

"I take it you've encountered these . . . persons . . . before," said the Champion.

"Several of them tried to kill me in the Tanglewood," said Rupert. "I showed them the error of their ways." He realized he was still holding his sword, and sheathed it.

"I see," said the Champion. His tone of voice made it clear that he didn't.

Rupert grinned, and then looked down as somebody tugged impatiently at his stirrup. The smallest goblin smiled cheerily up at him.

"Good day, sir hero; remember me? Thought I'd just say thanks. Our glorious leader's pretty damn good at fighting, but he's not much of a one for the social graces. Not that I'll hear a word said against him, mind; it's thanks to him we've learned to kill demons. We saw off a whole pack of them, not so long ago."

"Wait a minute," said Rupert slowly. "You people fought a pack of demons? Where?"

"Place called Coppertown," said the smallest goblin. "Chopped them demons into chutney, we did. Not very tasty, mind; all bone and gristle. Now then, don't you worry about the Castle, sir hero, we'll look after it for you. We know all kinds of nasty things to do with boiling oil."

"Wouldn't surprise me in the least," said Rupert. "About Coppertown . . ."

"Nice little place, that. Many's the night me and the lads would steal calves and chickens from the townspeople. Not any more, though."

"Why not?"

"Demons," said the smallest goblin. "Ripped the village's guts out, they did. No more humans. All gone. Can't stop, sir hero; got to catch up with the lads. Have a nice trip."

"Thank you, sir goblin. But remember; if I hear you've molested one lawful traveller between here and the Castle, I'll personally have you strung up by the heels for the moat monster to gnaw on. Got it?"

"Oh sure," said the smallest goblin. "Us Forest folk got to stick together. Oh yes. Definitely. Not even one?"

"Not even one."

"Spoilsport," said the smallest goblin. He grinned, bowed quickly, and hurried after his friends. The guards watched the goblins depart, and glanced respectfully at Rupert. Anyone who could intimidate an entire pack of armed goblins without even raising his voice was clearly a leader to be reckoned with.

"Coppertown," said the Champion slowly. "We could be there by evening."

"You know the place?" asked Rupert.

"Small mining town, Sire. Eight hundred people live there, including half a company of guards. It's not possible Coppertown could have fallen to the darkness . . ."

"The Darkwood must be closer than anyone thought," said Rupert. "Eight hundred people . . . we'd better check it out."

The Champion nodded grimly, and led the way deeper into the Forest.

The sun was sinking fast when Rupert and the Champion rode into Coppertown. No lights glowed in the miners' houses, and the narrow streets were full of shadows. The guards eyed the silent houses warily, and eased their swords in their scabbards. Muffled hoofbeats echoed hollowly back from the thick stone walls, the dull sound eerily loud in the quiet. The horses tossed their heads and whinnied nervously. Rupert stared about him as he led his men deeper into Coppertown, and the unshuttered windows stared back like so many dark, unseeing eyes. There was no sign of violence or destruction, but every house lay still and silent and abandoned. Somewhere out in the growing dusk, a door banged lazily as the wind moved it, and there was no one to shut it. Rupert signalled for his men to stop, and reined in his unicorn.

"Sir Champion . . ."

"Aye, Sire?"

"Hold my unicorn. I'm going to check out one of these houses."

"I'd be more use guarding your back, Sire."

Rupert studied the Champion a moment, and then nodded shortly and swung down from the unicorn. There was a general rustling of chain mail as the guards drew their swords and moved quickly to block off both ends of the street. Rupert unstrapped the lantern from his saddle and struggled to light its candle with flint and steel.

"Rupert . . ." said the unicorn.

"Ah," said Rupert, "You've finally decided to stop sulking and talk to me."

"I have not been sulking! I've been thinking."

"About what?"

"You mostly. You've changed, Rupert."

"Oh yeah? How?"

"Well, you used to have more sense, for one thing. There could be any number of demons hiding in these houses."

"I know," said Rupert, grinning broadly as the candle-wick finally caught. "That's why I'm going to check one out." He closed the lantern and held it high as he moved cautiously forward to study the nearest house. The unicorn made as though to follow him, and then stopped and turned away as the Champion joined Rupert before the gaping doorway.

"Ready, Sire?"

"Ready, sir Champion."

Rupert padded forward, slipped silently past the open door, and then slammed it back against the wall in case there was something hiding behind it. There wasn't. The heavy crash echoed loudly on the still air, and the timbered

ceiling creaked in sympathy. Rupert moved away from the
door and stared about him, the Champion close behind.
Dirty straw matting covered the earth floor, and the bare
stone walls were discolored by lichen and running damp.
The smoke-blackened hearth held nothing but a little coal
and some ashes. Four mismatched chairs, one obviously a
small child's, surrounded a roughly hewn table. Wooden
platters had been set, as though for a meal. The whole room
couldn't have been more than ten feet square, and the
ceiling was so low Rupert kept wanting to duck his head.
The smell was appalling.

Rupert wrinkled his nose in disgust. "How can people *live*
like this?"

"They're a miner's family," said the Champion, "which is
just another way of saying poor. If a miner doesn't dig
enough ore to meet the overseer's quota, he doesn't get
paid. If he meets the quota too easily, they raise it till he
can't. Wages are low, and prices are high; the overseers run
the only stores. A miner digs enough copper in a day to feed
his family for a year, but the penalty for stealing ore is
death."

"I didn't know," whispered Rupert. "I just never . . .
thought about it . . ."

"Why should you?" said the Champion. "You have your
responsibilities, the poor have theirs; that's the way of things."

"Nobody should have to live like this," said Rupert flatly.

"We can't all live in Castles, Sire. Somebody has to mine
the copper."

Rupert glared at the Champion, and then they both froze
as a door slammed shut somewhere above them. The Champion hurried over to the only other door at the back of the
room and pulled it open, revealing a narrow, rickety stairway. He peered up into the dark, and then slowly mounted
the stairs, each step creaking loudly under his weight. Rupert glanced round the empty room, and then followed the
Champion, sword at the ready.

The stairway led to the second floor; the same tiny room,
this time containing two simple beds, separated by a hanging curtain, only half drawn. The Champion pushed the
curtain back to reveal a window, the flimsy wooden shutter
banging in the wind. He shook his head, put away his
sword, and closed the shutter. Rupert frowned at the two

beds; they appeared to have been made up, but not slept in. He thought about looking underneath them, but they were too low to hide anything but a chamberpot. He held his lantern high and stared about him. Something lying on the far bed caught his eye, and he moved over to get a better look. It was a child's toy; a ragged cloth doll, with crudely drawn features. Rupert sheathed his sword, and picked the doll up.

"Sir Champion; look at this."

The Champion studied the doll, and frowned. "It's well past a child's bedtime."

"Right. So where is she?"

The Champion shrugged. "With her family. Whatever happened here, I'd say they left together, of their own free will. There's been no fight or struggle in this house."

Rupert scowled. "The goblin said Coppertown had been visited by demons."

"Goblins," said the Champion, "have been known to lie, on occasion."

Rupert looked at the doll in his hand, and then thrust it under his jerkin and headed for the stairway. "I want every building in Coppertown searched, sir Champion. Get the guards moving, while there's still some light left."

"They won't find anything."

"Do it anyway!"

"Yes, Sire."

The Champion followed Rupert down the stairs, his silence clearly indicating his disapproval. Rupert didn't give a damn. All right, maybe the goblin had lied to him; certainly demons would have left more traces of their passing. But there had to be some good reason why eight hundred people would just walk out of their homes and disappear into the falling night. Somewhere in Coppertown there was an answer to all this, and Rupert was going to find it.

He stalked through the house and out into the street. The evening was fast becoming night, the darkening sky streaked with crimson from the setting sun. The Champion barked orders to the waiting guards, and soon the town was alive with running figures. The distant sound of banging doors carried clearly on the still air, and lanterns danced through the empty houses like so many will-o-the-wisps. And one by one the guards returned, having found nothing and no one. Coppertown lay silent and deserted beneath the ebon sky.

"This is a mining town," said Rupert finally. "Where's the mine?"

"Just down that road, Sire," said the Champion.

Rupert shook his head resignedly. "We might as well check it out; it's the only place we haven't looked."

"Aye, Sire. It's not far; half a mile at most."

Rupert looked at him thoughtfully. "How is it you know this place so well?"

"I was born here," said the Champion.

A pale sliver of moon shone in the starless night as the Champion led Rupert and the column of guards down a steep hillside. Lanterns hung from every saddle, glowing golden against the dark, the pale light barely sufficient to show the path the Champion followed. Tall crooked shadows loomed menacingly out of the darkness as the company wended its way through the sparse trees. The wind had finally dropped, but the night air was bitter cold. The slope flattened out suddenly, and the Champion reined in his horse.

"This is it, Sire. The mine."

Rupert held up his lantern, but the dim light hid more in shadow than it revealed. The mine workings looked old; centuries old. A few ancient half-timbered buildings surrounded a main entrance barely wide enough to admit three men walking abreast. The Champion swung down out of the saddle and stood quietly, his cold dark eyes fixed on the entrance. After a while, Rupert dismounted and moved forward to stand beside him.

"I was ten years old when my father first took me down below," said the Champion quietly. "The motherlode was running out, and the Barons had cut our wages, to reduce the overheads. My family needed the money, and there was always work for children down the mine. The tunnel that led to the main face was so small my father had to crawl through it on his hands and knees. All I had to do was duck my head. The only light came from the candles in our caps, and the air was thick with dust. That first day the shift was only six hours, but it seemed forever.

"I ran away, that night. I thought I was brave, but I

couldn't face another day down the mine. I haven't been
back here in over thirty years, but that mine still has a hold
on me. Funny, isn't it, after all these years."

Rupert shot a quick look at the Champion, but he seemed
to have finished. The Champion's face was mostly lost in
shadow, but it seemed as calm and impassive as ever. Rupert looked away. He didn't know why the Champion was
telling him these things; it wasn't as though they were close,
or even friends. Rupert studied the mine entrance before
him. It was hard to think of the Champion as a boy; a child
who laughed and cried and ran away from a darkness he
couldn't bear.

"Sir Champion . . ."

"We'll check the buildings first," said the Champion evenly,
and moved away to give the orders.

Light soon flared from a dozen torches set around the
main entrance. Guards moved silently through the darkness,
searching for traces of the missing townspeople. The buildings proved to be empty, but strange scuff marks were
discovered in the tunnel leading down from the main entrance. Rupert entered the tunnel and knelt beside the
marks, studying them as best he could in the dim light from
his lantern. They weren't tracks as such; it looked more as
though something indescribably heavy had lain briefly on
the tunnel floor, crushing and packing the earth tightly
together. Rupert frowned; whatever was responsible for
those traces, it definitely wasn't demons. The Champion
came back out of the tunnel darkness, and Rupert rose
quickly to his feet.

"Have you found anything?"

"Not yet, Sire. They're in the mine somewhere."

"We can't be sure of that, sir Champion."

"I'm sure," said the Champion flatly. "Something called
to them. Something called to the townspeople, and they left
their houses to come here, to the mine. Men, women and
children; so many they must have had to wait their turn to
file through the main entrance. They're down there somewhere, in the dark, waiting for us to join them."

Rupert glanced at him sideways. If he didn't know better,
he'd swear the Champion was cracking up. The man had
always been a little unstable, but. . . . Farther down the
tunnel, a guard cried out in horror. Rupert ran forward, the

Champion at his side, and the guard came out of the darkness to meet them, his face drained of all color. He'd lost his sword and his lantern, but he was carrying something in his hand.

"What's happened?" snapped the Champion. The guard stumbled to a halt. His mouth worked, but he couldn't speak.

"What have you found?" asked Rupert. The guard shook his head wordlessly, and handed Rupert a red shoe. Rupert frowned. It was small, too small to be anything but a child's. It seemed strangely heavy in his hand. He looked into the shoe, and then fought back the urge to vomit. The child's foot was still in the shoe, neatly severed at the ankle. The shoe was red from dried blood. Rupert passed the shoe to the Champion, who studied it calmly.

"Did you find anything else?" Rupert asked the guard.

He shook his head. "I couldn't . . . I couldn't see much; it was too dark. But the smell . . . the smell's pretty bad." He swallowed dryly and stumbled away, heading for the surface.

"He's young," said the Champion absently. "First tour of duty. Never struck a blow in anger, like as not. He'll get over it."

"Yeah, sure," said Rupert. His stomach lurched as the Champion casually threw the bloodstained shoe to one side, and he quickly looked away. "Quite a few of my guards seem equally young, sir Champion. I take it they're all equally inexperienced?"

"Pretty much, Sire."

"No wonder the King let me have them."

"You're learning," said the Champion.

Rupert smiled tiredly, and for a moment they stood together, staring down the tunnel into the darkness.

"Well," Rupert said finally, "There's nothing more we can do here. Let's get back to the town."

The Champion frowned. "Back to Coppertown?"

"It's better than being trapped out in the open," said Rupert. "If there are demons here, we'll be safer behind stone walls."

"They didn't help the townspeople much," said the Champion. "Aren't you curious about what's down there in the dark?"

"Not a lot," said Rupert.

"There could be somebody still alive, deep in the mine."

"It's not very likely."

"No, Sire. But it is possible."

"Yes," Rupert sighed regretfully, "It is possible, sir Champion. What do you think we should do?"

"We must go down into the dark," said the Champion calmly, "And either save the townspeople, or avenge them."

Rupert felt a sudden surge of empathy for the Champion. In his own way, the Champion was as scared of the mine as Rupert had been of the Darkwood. And like Rupert, the Champion wasn't going to be stopped from doing what he felt was right, just because was afraid.

"All right," said Rupert. "Tell the guards what's happening, and get me four volunteers to come with us. Have the rest set up a perimeter and mark it with torches. If there are any demons prowling, they'll steer clear of the light."

"Four volunteers, Sire?"

"This is going to be a scouting party, sir Champion, not an attack force. Time for that when we know what we're up against. And I want *real* volunteers, mind."

"Of course, Sire." The Champion smiled slightly and headed for the exit, to talk to the guards.

Rupert grinned, and then stared down the tunnel into the darkness. The darkness stared back, giving nothing away. Rupert drew his sword, and hefted it. The Rainbow Run seemed a long time ago. *I don't have to do this*, he thought slowly. *It's stupid to risk my life for a few hundred missing townspeople. My mission to the High Warlock is far more important.* He sighed regretfully, knowing he didn't really have a choice. *No, I don't have to do this. But I'm going to. As long as there's a chance we can save somebody, I can't walk away and leave them to the dark.* He studied his sword thoughtfully. If there were demons in the mine shafts, he could always call down another Rainbow.

The Champion came back with four guardsmen, each carrying a sword in one hand and a lantern in the other. The extra light served mainly to emphasize the narrowness of the tunnel. Rupert noticed that the Champion had left his lantern behind, in order to have both hands free to carry his massive war axe.

"Ready, Sire?"

"Ready, sir Champion. You know this mine, so you'd better lead the way."

"Of course, Sire." The Champion strode calmly down the tunnel, into the dark. Rupert followed close behind him, lantern held high, and the four guardsmen brought up the rear. Rupert stared worriedly at the Champion's back; the man was too determined not to let his old fear of the mine rule him. That kind of singlemindedness could lead to him doing something foolhardy and get them all killed.

The tunnel sloped steadily downwards, and Rupert hunched forward a little to avoid bumping his head on the lowering ceiling. The walls were pitted and scarred, supported here and there by thick timbers disfigured by moss and rot. Fat clumps of white fungi gathered where the walls met the floor, and a faint sickly sweet smell tainted the air. Rupert scowled. The smell bothered him; it seemed strangely familiar. The Champion's confident pace soon slowed, and he peered about him almost hesitantly, as though troubled by unwelcome memories. Rupert could hear the guards muttering behind him, and every now and again there was a muffled curse as they lost their footing or forgot to duck their head. Rupert glared into the darkness before him, but the lantern's pool of light didn't extend more than a few feet beyond the Champion.

The tunnel suddenly widened out into a cavern, a good hundred feet in diameter. Set roughly in the center, a wide shaft fell deep into the earth. Positioned over the pit was a heavy duty windlass, from which hung a thick sturdy rope that disappeared down into the shaft. The Champion gestured for the guards to work the windlass, and Rupert realized he was looking at a simple elevator. He moved over to the shaft's edge, and peered gingerly down into the pit. The sickly smell was immediately stronger.

"Smells like something died down there," muttered one of the guards disgustedly, as he sheathed his sword and helped take the strain on the wheel. The rope snapped taut, and then slowly began to wrap itself around the overhead windlass as the elevator rose reluctantly from the bottom of the shaft. Rupert moved back from the edge, frowning unhappily as he finally realized why the smell had seemed so familiar; it was the same stench of decay he'd found in the Darkwood. He watched the rope gather on the solid steel spindle for several minutes, and tried to visualize how far down the shaft must go. He gave up after a while. The answer disturbed him. He moved over to join the Champion.

"Is this the only way down?" he asked quietly.

"Aye, Sire," said the Champion. "One of the guards will go down first, to spy out the situation. Once he's given the all clear, I'll send back for more guards to work the windlass, and then we can follow him down."

Rupert scowled. "I don't like leaving one man down there on his own."

"You're a Prince," said the Champion. "You have no right to risk your life unnecessarily."

Rupert raised an eyebrow at him, and then looked away as the elevator platform finally lurched into view. One of the guards cursed softly, and another blessed himself. The solid oak platform was scarred and burned as though with acid, and the last few yards of the rope were scorched and discolored. The guards hurriedly made fast the windlass, and then everybody froze as a sound drifted up out of the shaft; a long, sliding sucking sound, culminating in a deep bass grunt that seemed to shiver through the very stone of the cavern.

Rupert moved forward, and stared grimly at the battered wooden platform. "Stand ready, sir Champion. I'm going down."

"No, Sire," said the Champion firmly. "It's too great a risk."

"That's why I have to go. Whoever sank this shaft let it fall too far; they've woken something deep in the earth that should never have been disturbed. Cold steel isn't enough against creatures of the dark, sir Champion; you need a magic sword. Like mine."

The two men stared steadily at each other.

"You swore to follow my orders," said Rupert softly, and the Champion bowed slightly.

"Step aboard, Sire. We'll lower you a few yards at a time. Sing out if you hit any trouble, and we'll bring you straight back up. If you're too far down to be heard, slap the rope twice with the flat of your sword."

Rupert nodded, and stepped gingerly onto the platform. The rope creaked, but the scarred wood felt solid enough under his feet. "Lower away, sir Champion."

"Aye, Sire." The Champion joined the guards at the wheel, and the elevator sank jerkily into the shaft.

Rupert carefully placed his lantern on the edge of the platform, so as to have one hand free. The walls of the shaft moved slowly past him, gleaming dully in the pale golden light. Rupert sniffed the close air, and grimaced. The stench of corruption was growing stronger. He remembered the red shoe, and tightened his grip on the rainbow sword. The platform descended steadily into the pit, and the lamplit cavern above was soon nothing more than a shrinking circle of light. Rupert shifted nervously from foot to foot, and tried not to think about how much farther he still had to go before he reached the bottom of the shaft. He glanced into a shadowed cavity in the left hand wall as it rose past him, and then yelled for the guards to stop the elevator. The platform sank another few feet and then slammed to a halt. Rupert grabbed the shuddering rope to keep from falling, and then looked for the cavity, but it now lay just beyond his reach.

"Are you all right, Sire?" The Champion's voice seemed faint, and very far away.

"I'm fine!" Rupert yelled back. "Raise the platform a little; I've found something!"

There was a pause, and then the elevator rose gradually back up the shaft. Rupert snatched up his lantern and waited impatiently as the wall cavity fell slowly within reach.

"Hold it!" The elevator jerked to a stop, and Rupert moved forward to peer into the cavity. A human skull, broken and distorted, gleamed yellow in the lamplight. It could have been a recent death, or it could have lain there for centuries; Rupert had no way of knowing. Either way, it was a bad omen. Rupert hefted his sword uncertainly, and then yelled for the Champion to continue the descent.

The elevator fell for what seemed like hours. Rupert clutched his sword so tightly his hand started to ache, and he had to force himself to loosen his grip. The air grew thick and moist, and the cloying sweet stench turned his stomach. Again and again, Rupert told himself there was no chance any of the townspeople could still be alive. But he had to be sure. He glanced back up the shaft, but no trace of the cavern remained, save for a dim speck of light far above him, like a single star on a moonless night. And then the platform slammed into solid rock, and Rupert was thrown to his knees by the impact. The elevator had finally reached the bottom of the shaft.

Rupert called up to the Champion that he'd arrived safely, but there was no reply. Rupert shrugged, and looked about him. A series of tunnels led off from the base of the shaft, each opening barely four feet high. Rupert chose the largest tunnel mouth and crawled gingerly forward on hands and knees, holding the lantern out before him. Moisture beaded the dark stone walls, gleaming brightly in the pale golden light. Rupert scrambled awkwardly on into the darkness, and tried not to think about the vast weight of rock hanging over his head. His back ached from the unaccustomed strain of moving on all fours, and the sword in his hand seemed to grow heavier and more of a nuisance with every bruise it earned him. The tunnel floor was suddenly wet under his hands, and Rupert stopped as a horrid thought struck him. His stomach lurched as he looked down, suddenly certain he'd find the stone slick with freshly spilled blood, but there was no trace of crimson in the thick, viscous slime that lathered the floor. Rupert frowned, put down the lantern, and rubbed a little of the stuff between his fingers; the slime was clear as water and very slippery. He brought his fingers to his nose, sniffed cautiously, and then snatched his hand away. The slime stank of death and decay.

The tunnel seemed suddenly full of the stench, and Rupert scrubbed his fingers on his jerkin until he was sure they were clean again. His breathing was harsh and unsteady, and his knuckles whitened as he clutched his lantern and his sword. The familiar stench and the dark crowding around him had thrust him back into the Darkwood, and once again fear threatened to overthrow his reason and leave him lost and alone in the darkness. He flailed out with his arms as panic took him, and they slammed into the tunnel walls. The solid unyielding rock was strangely comforting, and he drew strength from its inflexible reality. His breathing gradually slowed to normal, and he even manage a small smile at how close the dark had come to sending him back to the edge of madness. He might still be scared of the dark, but it couldn't break him. Not just yet, anyway.

He stared down the narrow tunnel before him, and held up his lantern. The floor was covered with glistening slime for as far as he could see. Rupert gnawed his lower lip uncertainly. He wanted to go on, if only to prove to himself that he could, but when all was said and done this was supposed to be a scouting party, and he ought really to go back and tell the Champion what he'd found. The slime worried him. Demons left no such trace to mark their passing. Rupert started to edge slowly back down the tunnel, and then froze. Far ahead in the tunnel darkness, someone was singing.

The voice was male and female, both and neither, and it called to Rupert. It promised light and love, friendship and protection, all he ever wanted and more besides. The voice was sweet and smooth and slick, and Rupert trusted it. The voice called, and Rupert crawled slowly forward, into the slime. His hands slipped and he fell forward, the hard impact driving the breath from his lungs. He gasped for air, and the sweet stench of decay filled his nostrils, shocking him awake.

Rupert froze in horror as he realized what he'd been doing. The voice still sang, beckoning and cajoling, but Rupert fought it, refusing to believe its lies, even when it offered him his most secret dreams. And in the end he won, possibly because he had been lied to so many times before, and no longer believed in anything much; not even his own dreams. Rupert lay stretched out on the tunnel floor, covered in evil-smelling slime, and finally understood why the people of Coppertown had left their homes and descended into the depths of the pit.

The voice rose and fell, roaring and wailing as it realized its failure. Rupert clutched his sword, and lay perfectly still. He knew he ought to blow out his lantern and hide in the dark, but he couldn't bring himself to do it. The voice squealed and gurgled and then died away to a horrid sucking sound, ending in the short bass grunt Rupert had heard earlier. The sudden silence seemed to ring in Rupert's ears as he strained to hear more clearly. Far off in the distance, a little girl started to cry.

Rupert swore softly, letting his breath out with a rush. It had to be a trick, and a pretty damn obvious one at that. But there were children missing, and if by chance one had survived, and was wandering lost in the tunnels, looking for help . . . Rupert shook his head helplessly, trapped in an agony of indecision. He remembered the red shoe, and shivered, and then he remembered the child's doll he'd found, still tucked inside his jerkin. He could feel it, pressed against his chest by the tunnel floor. He sighed resignedly, knowing he didn't really have a choice. If there was even the slightest chance the child was still alive, he had to find her, or he'd never forgive himself. He edged slowly forward into the darkness, grimacing as the cold slime oozed between his fingers.

The slime glistened dully under the golden lamplight, and Rupert noticed uneasily that the walls and ceiling of the tunnel were also coated with the stuff. He struggled on, slipping and sliding, and holding his sword blade carefully clear of the slime. The little girl was still crying; a lost, lonely sound. Rupert stopped for a while to get his breath back. Crawling on his hands and knees was awkward as well as tiring, and his back was killing him. He'd been crawling for what seemed like ages, but the crying hadn't drawn any closer. He glanced back the way he'd come, but the tunnel entrance was lost in the darkness. He looked ahead, and frowned; he had to be close to the main workings by now. He suddenly realized the child had stopped crying. He waited, listening, and the silence dragged on. *She could be anywhere,* thought Rupert. *I've got to find her before the voice does.*

"Hello?" he called softly. "Where are you? Don't cry, love; I've come to help . . ."

The voice screamed in triumph, and Rupert's blood ran cold as he felt the tunnel floor shudder beneath him. Something was coming, something large and indescribably heavy. A strange pressure built on the air, pressing lightly against Rupert's face as he stared into the dark. He realized there was no child, and never had been. But then he'd always known that, deep down; he just hadn't wanted to believe it. He scrambled backwards down the tunnel, his arms hammering against the tunnel walls in his haste. Whatever owned the calling voice hadn't been able to see his lantern, so it had tricked him into calling out. And now it knew where he was.

He fought his way back to the tunnel entrance, thrown back and forth by the shaking rock beneath him. A deep, throbbing grunt sounded out of the darkness, horribly close, and then Rupert fell backwards out of the tunnel and into the elevator's cavern. The lantern flew from his hand and rolled across the floor, the pale golden light flickering ominously as it came to rest by the elevator platform. Rupert scrambled onto the platform, grabbed the lantern, and screamed for the Champion to pull him up. Wet sucking sounds echoed from the tunnel entrance. Rupert struck the elevator rope twice with the flat of his sword, put down the lantern, and stood ready to face whatever it was that pursued him. The deep bass grunt sounded again, close and horribly eager. The platform suddenly lurched beneath him, and then rose slowly up the shaft.

Rupert yelled for the guards to pull faster, and clutched desperately at his sword. Whatever had called to him in the tunnel was of the dark, and the only answer to darkness was light. He had to have a Rainbow. He took his sword carefully in both hands, and raised it above his head. All his fear and hate and desperation came together in him as he screamed defiance to the dark, but the Rainbow didn't come. The sword was cold and lifeless, and Rupert somehow knew, beyond any shadow of doubt, that this time he was on his own. There wasn't going to be any Rainbow. Rupert slowly lowered the sword, and stared at it numbly. No one had ever told him the blade could be used more than once; he'd just assumed it. And he'd assumed wrong. Rupert's hands suddenly began to shake, and he panted for breath as panic welled up within him. Until now, he hadn't realized how much he'd come to depend on the rainbow sword; knowing he had that extra ace up his sleeve had given him a confidence and security he'd never known before. Rupert shook his head violently, forcing back the growing panic. All right, so the sword was useless; he'd just have to face the dark the hard way, that was all. He'd done it before, he could do it again. And then a thick slobbering grunt came from directly beneath him, and something slammed into the underside of the platform, throwing him off-balance.

"Pull faster!" Rupert screamed to the guards, "Pull me up! Pull me up!" The platform lurched beneath him, tipped to one side, and then fell back as the elevator finally began to pick up speed, leaving the creature behind. Rupert stared anxiously up the shaft as the widening circle of light drew steadily nearer. It was going to be close. He snatched up the lantern and readied himself to jump clear the moment the elevator reached the winch cavern. Deep in the shaft, the creature grunted; hungrily, eagerly.

It's still following me up the shaft, thought Rupert dazedly. *What is it? What the hell is it?*

The platform burst out of the shaft and into the cavern. Rupert threw himself to one side and hit the ground rolling, somehow still hanging onto his sword and lantern. He lurched to his feet and yelled a warning to the startled guards at the wheel, and then something crashed into the stationary platform from below. The solid wood shattered into splinters as the creature of the dark roared up out of the mine shaft. Silver gray and shining with its own eerie light, it erupted into the cavern and fell upon the guards. They didn't even have time to scream. At first Rupert thought it was some monstrous worm, but then he saw how the shimmering flesh spread out as it surged beyond the confines of the elevator shaft, and he realized the creature had no shape as such, simply becoming what it needed to be to fulfill its purpose. The Champion was suddenly at his side, grabbing him by the shoulder and almost throwing him into the tunnel that led to the surface. Rupert snapped out of his daze and sprinted along the tunnel, the Champion close behind. Rupert glanced back once; the glowing, pearly flesh had filled the cavern and was spilling into the tunnel after them. Rupert swore harshly, and ran faster. The Champion lifted his lantern to judge the distance ahead.

"We're not going to make it, Sire. We have to stand and fight."

"It'll kill us!"

"If you've a better idea, I'm open to suggestions."

Wet sucking sounds echoed behind them, and the creature grunted like some vast hog at its trough. Rupert glared about him as he ran.

"The tunnel supports!" he said suddenly. "The wood's half-rotten anyway; cut through enough of them and the roof will collapse. That should slow the creature down!"

He skidded to a halt and hacked at the nearest support with his sword. The blade sank deep into the rotting wood and stuck fast. Rupert cursed, and worked it free. The Champion sliced clean through the opposite support with one blow of his war axe. Rupert cut again and again at the stubborn timber, and finally sheared it through. The roof creaked once, and a little dust fell into the tunnel. The Champion cut through another support. Rupert glanced back down the tunnel and froze. The creature was fast approaching, surging forward like a flash flood. Frothing and writhing, it filled the tunnel with its eerie gray light. Deep within the semitransparent flesh floated the limp bodies of the guards, turning slowly end-over-end, and Rupert finally knew what had happened to the people of Coppertown.

Behind him, the Champion sheared through a thick timber support, and the roof creaked ominously. The sudden sound snapped Rupert out of his reverie, and he ran on down the tunnel to attack another support with his sword. The decaying wood fell apart on the first blow, and the roof sagged. Dust fell in thick streams as the rock overhead groaned and shifted. Rupert and the Champion ran on, and the tunnel roof came crashing down behind them. A thick cloud of dust billowed around them as they headed for the surface, and the sound of falling rock continued for some time.

Rupert staggered out into the fresh night air and sank exhausted to the ground. The Champion stood beside him a moment, breathing evenly, and then moved away to tell the waiting guards what had happened. Rupert sat with his back propped against the half-timbered base of the main entrance, and listened to the gentle rumble of settling stone. He would have been hard pressed to name a part of him that didn't ache, but he was alive and intact, and that was enough to set him grinning like he'd never stop. He breathed deeply, savoring the clear air after the constant stench of the pit. He realized he was still holding tightly onto his sword and his lantern. He put the lantern down beside him, and studied the sword thoughtfully. It seemed the magic was gone from the rainbow sword, and in a strange way Rupert was almost glad. The last time he'd stood against the dark, a Rainbow had come down to save him; this time, he'd had to do it himself. And knowing that he'd been able to meant a great deal to him. He considered for a moment giving up the rainbow sword in favor of a blade more suited to combat, but decided against it. The sword had a good edge and a good balance, and he was used to it. Rupert sheathed his sword, and stretched slowly. It felt so good to be alive.

The constant rumbling deep within the tunnel showed no sign of abating, and Rupert frowned despite himself. Countless tons of fallen rock stood between him and the creature of the dark; there was no way in which it could get past such a barrier . . . Rupert grabbed his lantern, clambered painfully to his feet, and stared into the tunnel darkness, a horrid certainty growing within him that the fight wasn't over yet. He thought back on what he'd seen of the creature, and his scowl deepened. It had no shape save that dictated by its surroundings, and when it moved, it frothed and undulated as though its unnatural flesh was some strange mixture of solid and liquid, or perhaps even something else entirely, with the properties of both. In his mind's eye Rupert saw again the solid oak platform burst asunder as the creature smashed right through it without even slowing.

Rupert swore softly, under his breath. He knew the creature was dead, crushed into pulp under tons of fallen rubble. He knew it, but he had to see it himself, to be sure. He drew his sword, held his lantern high, and moved back into the tunnel, squinting through the slowly settling dust that choked the air. The Champion was suddenly at his side.

"Where are you going, Sire?"

"Just down the tunnel a way."

"It isn't safe, Sire."

"If that tunnel isn't sealed, none of us are safe. I'm going to take a look."

The Champion studied him, and then bowed slightly. "Very well, Sire. Wait just a moment, and I'll detail a few guards to accompany us."

"No!" Rupert checked himself, surprised at his sudden anger, and when he spoke again his voice was calm and even. "We took four guards with us on our first investigation of this mine, sir Champion. Now they're dead. I never even knew their names. What's left of that tunnel roof could come down at any minute, and I'll not put any more of my men at risk unless I have to. I'm only going back in because I need to be sure."

"Then I'll come with you," said the Champion. "I need to be sure, too."

Rupert nodded, and headed down the tunnel into the darkness, the Champion at his side. The tunnel air was still thick with dust, and the roof and walls creaked ominously.

Rupert and the Champion soon reached the cave-in; a ragged wall of fallen stone and earth and broken timber. The Champion stared dubiously about him as Rupert moved cautiously forward to inspect the massive barricade. He prodded the wall here and there with his sword, but nothing gave by so much as an inch. Silence filled the narrow tunnel, broken only by the soft whisper of earth trickling down from cracks in the lowering roof.

"Come away, Sire," said the Champion quietly. "It's all over."

"No," said Rupert. "I don't think so. I can hear something . . . something moving . . ."

He backed quickly away, still staring at the wall of fallen debris, and then a single boulder at the top of the barrier slowly teetered and fell forward into the tunnel. And through the gap it left slithered a long rope of glowing silver flesh. From beyond the barrier came a deafening roar of triumph and bloody hunger, culminating in a vast sonorous grunt. The Champion hefted his war axe uncertainly and glanced at Rupert.

"If the cave-in didn't hurt it, I don't see what more we can do, Sire. Let's get out of here; if we can get to the horses, we might be able to outdistance it."

"No!" snapped Rupert. "We have to stop it here! At least the tunnel keeps it to a manageable size; if it reaches the surface . . ."

The Champion nodded, and grinned suddenly. "I never did believe in running away from a good fight. What are your orders, Sire?"

The barrier began to fall apart as glowing silver-gray flesh enveloped the smaller rocks and digested them. More and more of the creature flowed into the tunnel as Rupert glared furiously about for an answer. The creature was of the dark, and the dark must always fall to the light; the rainbow sword had failed him, but perhaps his lantern . . . He darted forward and carefully place the lantern in the path of a probing silver tentacle. The tentacle ignored the lantern and lashed out at Rupert. He swung his sword double-handed, and it slashed easily through the pallid flesh, meeting only the faintest resistance. Rupert smiled grimly as the severed end splashed to the floor, and then he spun round as the Champion shouted a warning. Broad cracks had spread across the barrier, and the creature was breaking through in a dozen places. Rupert and the Champion fell back, and the creature flowed after them. A silver tentacle rolled over the lantern, engulfing it in a second, and Rupert's heart fell. And then the creature screamed and flung the tentacle from it, as the silver flesh burst suddenly into flame. The discarded tentacle writhed feebly as the fire consumed it, burning fiercely until nothing remained but an evil stench on the air. Rupert grinned savagely as the answer came to him. Fire; man's oldest ally against the dark.

"Oil lamps!" he yelled to the Champion. "Get me some oil lamps!"

The Champion nodded quickly, and sprinted back to the surface. Rupert hefted his sword and studied the creature warily by its own eerie light. The barrier blocking the tunnel was riven in a dozen places, and silver-gray flesh oozed through the narrow fissures in a steady flow. Stone and earth and timber creaked ominously as the creature pressed its awful weight against the barrier, and Rupert knew it was only a matter of moments before the mounting pressure would burst the wall asunder, and the creature would come roaring down the tunnel like a flash flood. If the Champion wasn't back by then, Rupert knew that running wouldn't be enough to save him. He started to retreat cautiously down the tunnel, and the Champion came to meet him with a dozen guards, all carrying oil lamps.

"Right," said Rupert crisply, "Empty the oil out onto the floor, then go back for more lamps. Move it; there's not much time!"

The guards exchanged glances but did as they were told, and soon the tunnel floor was awash with oil. Deep in the dark, the creature grunted hungrily as the stone and earth barrier heaved and cracked apart. Rupert sent the guards back to the surface, and studied the pool of oil that lay between him and the creature.

"Think there's enough, sir Champion?"

"If not, we'll soon find out, Sire."

Rupert laughed, and turned to face the Champion. "Give me your lantern, and then get out of here."

"Lighting the oil is my job," said the Champion evenly.

"Not this time."

The two men looked at each other, and then the Champion bowed slightly.

"I'll wait at the entrance, Sire. Don't be long."

Rupert nodded his thanks, and the Champion turned and padded silently back down the tunnel. Rupert sheathed his sword, knelt beside the pool of oil, and watched the barrier slowly fall apart. He wasn't really sure why he'd sent the Champion back; he only knew this was something he had to do. If only to prove to himself that he didn't need a magic sword to be brave. The stone and earth of the barrier began to shake, and Rupert opened the lantern and took out the candlestub. He glanced at the pool of oil, and hesitated. If he stooped down to light the oil with the candle, the sudden flames would engulf him too, but if he threw the candle, it would probably go out before it hit the oil. And then the creature roared with triumph as it finally burst through the barrier, and surged down the tunnel toward him.

Rupert wavered uncertainly as the glowing silver tide came sweeping forward, dark shadows that had once been men floating half-digested within the creature's bulk. Some of the shadows were no larger than children. That thought gave him the answer, and Rupert grinned fiercely as he pulled from inside his jerkin the cloth doll he'd found abandoned back in the miner's house. He dipped the doll's head in the oil, stood up, and then touched the candle to the doll's head. It burned steadily, glowing gold and crimson against the dark. Rupert looked up. The creature was almost upon him, filling the tunnel from floor to ceiling and wall to wall. Its deep sonorous grunts had taken on a hellish, unnerving rhythm that seemed to shudder through his bones. Rupert threw the burning doll into the oil, and then turned and ran for the surface.

Intense heat scorched his back as the oil caught, and the tunnel was suddenly full of light. And then the creature screamed shrilly, so loudly that Rupert stumbled to a halt, his hands clapped to his ears. He stared back down the tunnel and saw the creature burning, brighter than the brightest lamp. It writhed and heaved as the fire coursed through it, consuming the creature from within. It tried to retreat back down the tunnel, but the fire followed, and the flames grew brighter still, until Rupert could hardly see for the blinding glare. He turned and ran for the surface again, driven away by the searing heat, and then a vast explosion picked him up and threw him down the tunnel, and all the light was gone.

For a time, he lay still on the packed earth of the tunnel floor, just glad to be alive. His head ached, and his ears rang from the explosion, but otherwise he seemed largely unhurt. He rose painfully to his feet, half choking on the thick evil-smelling smoke that filled the narrow tunnel, and slowly he made his way back through the darkness, and out into the night. The waiting guards cheered as he stumbled out of the main entrance, and Rupert raised a hand tiredly in response and then sat down quickly before he fell down. The guards laughed, cheered him again, and then moved away to start preparations for the journey back to Coppertown. Rupert leaned back against the entrance wall, and let the tiredness take him. He felt he'd earned a rest, at least for a while. The Champion came and stood over him.

"I take it the creature burned, Sire."

"Yes," said Rupert. "It burned."

'Do you think it's dead?"

"They say fire purifies . . . No, sir Champion, it's not dead. We've just hurt it, and driven it back, back into the depths, into the dark and secret places of the earth from which it came."

Rupert rose slowly to his feet, stared briefly into the mine entrance and then turned his back on it. The cold wind blowing was clear and fresh, dispelling the stench of corruption and decay like a passing memory.

"You didn't have to stay and light the oil," said the Champion slowly. "That was well and bravely done, Sire."

Rupert shrugged uncomfortably. "You did pretty well yourself, sir Champion."

"I did my duty, nothing more."

Rupert thought of the Champion's fear of the mine, but said nothing.

"A pity we couldn't save any of the townspeople," said the Champion.

"It was already too late when we got here," said Rupert. "There was nothing we could have done. Not much of a homecoming for you, was it?"

The Champion watched the guards mill back and forth, his face as impassive as ever. "Forest Castle is my home,

Sire, and always has been. What are your orders for the mine?"

"Have the guards bring down the tunnel roof again, sir Champion; I want that entrance completely blocked. I doubt it'll stop the creature getting out, but it should stop it enticing any more victims down into the mine."

The Champion nodded, and moved away to give the orders to the guards. Rupert watched him go, and let his hand rest on the pommel of the rainbow sword. Now the blade had proved itself worthless as a weapon against the dark, his mission to summon the High Warlock became more important than ever.

The wind seemed suddenly colder. Rupert stared up at the new moon; already it seemed tinged with blue, like the first hint of leprosy.

CHAPTER FOUR

Allies

Princess Julia paced impatiently back and forth in the Court's narrow antechamber, bored out of her mind. King John had sent for her half an hour ago, but despite all her shouting and kicking, the double doors leading to the Great Hall remained securely locked. Julia threw herself into a chair and scowled at the world, fed up to her back teeth. There was no one to talk to, nothing to do, and since they'd taken down all the portraits she couldn't even while away the time with a little target practice. Julia sighed disgustedly, folded her arms, and cursed Rupert to hell and back for riding off and leaving her.

He'd been gone almost three months, and Julia missed him more than she cared to admit. She'd done her best to settle into the Court and its Society, but like so many times before, her best hadn't been nearly good enough. Her willingness to knock brickdust out of anybody dumb enough to insult her twice had earned her a certain grudging respect, but few friends. Those Ladies of Julia's age and station had tried their utmost to make her feel welcome, but they didn't really have much in common with the young Princess. Their main interests were gossip, fashion, and the best ways of catching a rich husband, while Julia didn't give a damn about romantic or Court intrigue, threw away her fashionable shoes because they pinched her feet, and threatened to become violent if anyone even mentioned her forthcoming marriage to Prince Harald. She much preferred riding, hunting, and sword-drill, pastimes which scandalized her peers. It's not *feminine*, they protested faintly. In reply, Julia said something extremely coarse, and all the young Ladies found sudden compelling reasons why they had to be somewhere else.

After that, Julia found herself left pretty much alone.

At first, she spent a lot of time exploring the Castle. She quickly discovered that the same door needn't lead to the same room twice; that some doors were entrances, some were exits, but not all were both; and that some corridors actually folded back upon themselves when you weren't looking. Julia found all this intensely interesting, but unfortunately she tended to get lost rather a lot, and after the fourth search party King John made her promise not to stray from the main corridors without a guide. And that, for all practical purposes, was that.

Like their master the Seneschal, who governed the day-to-day running of the Castle, the guides shared a strange mystical sense that told them where they were in relation to everything else. This meant that not only could they not get lost, but they knew where any given room was at any given time. In a Castle where directions depended on which day of the week it was when you asked, such gifted people were invaluable, and therefore rather scarce on the ground when you needed them. Julia reluctantly gave up her explorations, and went back to challenging the guards at sword-drill.

The King then provided her with a chaperone. Julia quickly discovered the easiest way to deal with that sweet gray-haired old Lady was to run her off her feet. After three days of running round the Castle at full tilt just to keep Julia in sight, this worthy Lady told the King flatly that the young Princess had no need of a chaperone, as there wasn't a man in the Castle fleet enough of foot to catch up with her.

Which was not to say that nobody tried. The main contender was of course Harald, who seemed to think that their arranged marriage already gave him certain rights to her person, if not her affections. A few jolting left hooks taught him to keep his distance, and sharpened up his reflexes wonderfully, but he seemed to regard it all as part of the game and wouldn't be put off. Julia supposed she was meant to find this flattering, but she didn't. Harald was charming enough when he wanted to be, but when he wasn't flexing his muscles for her to admire, he was dropping heavy hints about his vast personal wealth, and how all the Forest

Kingdom would be his one day. In return, Julia tried to drop little hints concerning how she felt about him; like hitting him, or trying to push him off the battlements. Unfortunately he still didn't seem to get the message. Julia avoided him as much as possible, and for the most part they'd settled on an armed truce, with an unspoken agreement never to use the word *marriage*.

But she was still bored, and even a little lonely. The Ladies-in-Waiting weren't talking to her, the courtiers had disowned her, and the guards wouldn't duel with her any more because it made them look bad when they lost. So, when King John summoned her to Court, she went. It was something to do.

Julia glowered at the closed Court doors, and her hand dropped to her side, where her swordhilt used to be. Her scowl deepened as her hand clutched aimlessly at nothing. Even after all this time she still felt naked without a sword on her hip, but the King had been adamant about her not wearing a sword in the Castle, and she'd grown tired of arguing. And so the sword Rupert had given her in the Darkwood now lay locked away in her bedchamber, unused except for sword-drill. Julia sighed moodily. It wasn't as if she needed the sword, anyway. And she still had her dagger, tucked securely into the top of her boot.

Julia slouched in her chair, and stared gloomily round the antechamber. She was tempted to just get up and leave, but her curiosity wouldn't let her. King John had to have some good reason for suddenly requiring her presence at Court, and Julia had an uneasy feeling that when she found out what it was, she wasn't going to like it. So she gritted her teeth, and stayed put. She smiled slightly as her roving gaze fell upon the locked double doors again. The carpenters had done their best, but though the sturdy oaken doors had been carefully rehung, nothing short of total replacement would ever hide the deep scars and gouges left by the dragon's claws.

Julia frowned as the steady murmur of raised voices continued to seep past the closed doors. The courtiers had been shouting at each other when she first arrived, and it seemed they were still going strong. The sound was just loud enough to be intriguing without being understandable, and Julia decided she'd had enough. She leapt to her feet, glared round the sparsely furnished antechamber, and then grinned evilly as an idea struck her. Keep her waiting, would they? She studied the hanging tapestries for a moment, pulled down the ugliest, and stuffed it into the narrow gap between the doors and the floor. She then removed one of the flaring torches from its holder, knelt down, and carefully set light to the tapestry.

It burned well, giving off thick streamers of smoke, and Julia replaced the torch in its holder, and waited impatiently for the Court to notice. For a time the flames leapt and crackled to no effect, and Julia had just started to wonder if a little lamp oil might not help things along, when the Court fell suddenly silent. There was the briefest of pauses, and then the silence was broken by piercing shrieks and yells of "Fire!" Julia smiled complacently as through the doors wafted the unmistakable sounds of panic; swearing, shouting, and running in circles. The doors flew open to reveal Harald, who nodded to Julia and then emptied a pitcher of table wine over the burning cloth, dousing the flames instantly.

"Hello, Julia," he said casually. "We've been expecting you."

She pushed past him. He grinned and goosed her, and then ducked quickly to avoid the dagger that nearly took his ear off.

"That one wasn't even close," he chided her, staying carefully just out of reach as he led her through the flustered courtiers. "Does that mean you're mellowing toward me?"

"No," said Julia. "It means I need to practice more."

Harald laughed, and brought her before the throne. King John glared at her tiredly.

"Princess Julia; why can't you knock, like everyone else?"

"I've been kept waiting for almost an hour!" snapped Julia.

"I do have other business to attend to, apart from you."

"Fine; I'll come back when you've finished."

She turned to leave, and found the way blocked by half a dozen heavily armed guards.

"Princess Julia," said the King evenly, "Your attitude leaves much to be desired."

"Tough," said Julia. She glared at the guards, and then

turned reluctantly back to the throne. "All right; what do you want?"

"For the moment, just wait quietly while I finish my other business. Harald can keep you company."

Julia sniffed disdainfully, hitched up her ankle-long dress, and sat down at the bottom of the steps leading up to the throne. The marble step was cold, even through the thick carpeting, but Julia was damned if she was going to stand around until the King was ready to talk to her. It was a matter of principle. Harald came and sat down beside her, still keeping just out of arm's reach. Julia smiled slightly, drew her dagger from the boot, and cut tic-tac-toe lines into the carpet between them. Harald grinned, drew a dagger from his boot, and carved a cross in the center square. King John decided not to notice.

He closed his eyes briefly, and then turned his attention to the three men waiting before his throne with varying degrees of patience. He'd had dealings with Sir Blays before, but the two other Landsgraves were new to him. All three had arrived together, which implied the Barons had finally agreed on a common course of action, but judging from the way the three Landsgraves watched each other all the time, it was an uneasy alliance at best. King John smiled slowly, and settled back in his throne. Divide and conquer, that was the way. Get them arguing among themselves, and their own vested interests would tear them apart.

He studied the three Landsgraves carefully, taking his time. It wouldn't do to have them thinking they could rattle him. Sir Blays took the center position; a short, stocky man with close-cropped gray hair and deep, piercing eyes. Calm, sober, and soft-spoken, he cultivated an air of polite consideration, which fooled only those who didn't know him. King John had known him for almost twenty years.

The impressively muscled figure waiting impatiently to the right of Sir Blays had to be Sir Bedivere. Rumor had it he'd killed a dozen men in duels. There were whispers he'd provoked the duels deliberately, for the sport of it, but no one had ever said that to the man's face. He was young and darkly handsome, in a self-indulgent way, and the King didn't miss the weakness that showed in Sir Bedivere's puffy eyes and pouting lower lip. Some day he'd be a possible replacement for the Champion; if he lived that long.

The quiet, timid figure to the left of Sir Blays was Sir Guillam, a man so ordinary in appearance as to be practically invisible. Tall rather than short, and perhaps a little on the skinny side, his round open face had no more character in it than a baby's. His thinning hair was a mousey brown, neatly parted in the center. His pale gray eyes blinked nervously as he shifted uncomfortably under the King's gaze, and King John hid a smile behind his hand. Sir Guillam was a familiar type; he'd obey whatever instructions he'd been given to the letter, mainly because he wasn't bright enough to do anything else. Such emissaries were easy to confuse, and even easier to manipulate. And then Sir Bedivere stepped suddenly forward, and bowed deeply to the throne.

"Your majesty; if I might beg a moment of your time . . ."

"Of course, Sir Bedivere," said the King graciously. "You are the new Landsgrave of Deepwater Brook demesne?"

"Aye, Sire; I speak for the Copper Barons."

"And what do they wish of me this time?"

"Only what they've always wished, Sire; justice."

A ripple of laughter ran through the courtiers, dying quickly away as the Landsgrave stared coldly about him. Easily six foot six in height, his broad shoulders and massive frame might even have given the Champion himself pause. Sir Bedivere swept the packed Court with a challenging gaze, and then dismissed them all with a contemptuous toss of his head, as not worthy of his attention.

"Justice . . ." said the King mildly. "Could you be more specific?"

"The Copper Barons must have more men, Sire. Demons are overrunning the mining towns, destroying everything in their path. Refugees line the roads, more every day. We can't even feed them all, let alone give them shelter when the night falls. Already, there have been riots in the towns. Most of our guards are dead, killed trying to hold back the demons. What few men we have left can't hope to maintain law and order. The Copper Barons respectfully demand that you send a substantial part of your Royal Guard to help drive back the darkness that threatens us."

The King stared at the Landsgrave. "So far, I have sent your masters almost five hundred guardsmen. Are you telling me they're all dead?"

"Yes," said Sir Bedivere. A shocked murmur rustled through the courtiers.

"They died fighting demons?"

"Aye, Sire."

"How many of the Barons' own men rode out against the dark?"

Sir Bedivere frowned. "I don't quite see . . ."

"How many!"

"I really couldn't say," said the Landsgrave shortly. "A great many guards had to stay behind to protect the town and maintain order . . ."

"I see," said the King. "My men died, while the Barons' guards stayed safe behind stout town walls."

"This is all quite irrelevant," said Sir Bedivere calmly. "My masters require more men from you; how many troops will you send?"

"I have no men to spare," said the King flatly.

"Is that your final answer?"

"It is. My men are needed here. The Barons must defend themselves, as must I."

"They don't have a Castle to hide in," said Sir Bedivere loudly.

Silence fell across the Court, the courtiers struck dumb by the open insult. Such a remark from a Landsgrave was almost a declaration of treason. Everyone looked to King John for his reaction, and it took all his years of experience and diplomacy to keep his visage calm and unmoved. A quick glance at Blays and Guillam had shown the King that he would find no support there. Their faces and their silence said more plainly than words that Bedivere spoke for all of them. The King had always known that sooner or later the Barons were bound to take advantage of the situation and turn against him, but he hadn't thought it would be this soon. Whatever happened here today, whatever decision he made, the Copper Barons couldn't lose. If he sent them men he couldn't spare, that would be a clear sign of weakness, and they'd just return with even more outrageous demands. If he refused to help, the Barons would use that as an excuse to topple him from his throne, and replace him with someone more to their liking. Someone they could control. Sir Bedivere had been sent for just one purpose; to insult and humiliate King John before his Court, and make it plain to one and all that the real power in the Forest Land now resided with the Barons.

"It's easy to be brave behind high stone walls," said Sir Bedivere, an unpleasant smile twisting his mouth. "My masters have only town walls and barricades to protect them from the demons. We demand you supply us with more men!"

"Go to hell," said the King.

Sir Bedivere stiffened, and for a moment a red glare showed in his eyes, as though a furnace door had suddenly opened and closed. In that swift crimson gleam the King saw rage and hunger and a madness barely held in check, and he shivered, as though a cold wind had blown over him.

"Brave words, from an old fool," said Sir Bedivere, his voice harsh and strained. "My masters will not accept such an answer. Try again."

"You have my answer," said the King. "Now leave my Court."

"Your Court?" said the Landsgrave. He glanced round at the hushed courtiers and grim-faced guards and men-at-arms, and then laughed suddenly; a dark, contemptuous sound. "Enjoy it while you can, old man. Sooner or later, my masters will send me back to take it away from you."

"Treason," said the King mildly. "I could have your head for that, Landsgrave."

"Your Champion might," smiled Sir Bedivere. "Unfortunately, he's not here."

"But I am," said Prince Harald, rising suddenly to his feet, sword in hand. The courtiers murmured in approval as Harald moved forward to stand between his father and the Landsgrave. Julia smiled, and surreptitiously transferred her dagger to her throwing hand, just in case one of the other Landsgraves tried to interfere. Sir Bedivere studied Harald a moment, and then laughed quietly. The red glare came and went in his eyes, and he reached for his sword.

"No!" said the King sharply. "Harald, please put away your sword. I appreciate the gesture, but he would quite certainly kill you. Please; sit down, and let me handle this."

Harald nodded stiffly, slammed his sword back into its scabbard, and sat down beside Julia again. She gave him a quick nod of approval, and he smiled sourly. The King leant forward in his throne, and studied Sir Bedivere narrowly.

"Landsgrave; you have much to learn. Did you really think you could threaten me in my own Court and get away with it? You're a fool, Sir Bedivere, and I do not suffer fools gladly. You now have a simple choice; bow your head to me, or lose it."

The Landsgrave laughed, and Thomas Grey stepped forward to face him. The Astrologer raised one slender hand, and Sir Bedivere's laugh became a scream as a sudden agony burned in his muscles. He tried to reach for his sword, but the searing pain paralyzed him where he stood.

"Kneel," said the Astrologer, and Sir Bedivere fell forward on all fours, tears of agony and helpless rage streaming down his face. The two other Landsgraves watched horrified as the giant warrior cried like a child.

"And now, bow to your King," said the Astrologer, and Sir Bedivere bowed. King John looked down at the sobbing, trembling Landsgrave, and found no pleasure in the sight. Instead, he felt tired and soiled and just a little sick.

"Enough," he muttered, and the Astrologer lowered his hand and stepped back beside the throne. Sir Bedivere collapsed, and lay shuddering on the rich carpeting as the pain slowly left him.

King John looked slowly round his Court, but the courtiers for the most part avoided his gaze. Those few who didn't look away showed a profound horror and disgust at what the Astrologer had done in his name. King John sighed, and glanced at the black-clad figure standing patiently beside his throne. The dark, saturnine features were calm and relaxed, with only the faintest of smiles playing around his mouth. *Thomas, old friend,* thought the King suddenly, *What's happening to us? We once swore we'd die rather than use such magics as these.* The thought disturbed him, and he shook his head querulously, as though annoyed by a buzzing insect. His gaze fell upon Sir Bedivere, struggling to raise himself on one knee. The King gestured to two nearby men-at-arms.

"Help the Landsgrave to his feet."

"No!" gasped Sir Bedivere. "I don't need your help!"

Slowly, painfully, he got his feet under him. He rested there a moment, breathing harshly, and then rose clumsily to stand swaying before the throne. His legs trembled uncontrollably, but somehow he still held himself proudly erect.

Dried tears showed clearly against the pallor of his face, but his steadfast refusal to be beaten by his own weakness leant him a kind of dignity. And then the red glare filled his eyes, and he threw himself at the King. He just made it to the steps, and then the Astrologer raised his hand, and a bolt of lightning slammed into the Landsgrave, hurling him back from the throne. The blinding flash dazzled everyone for a moment, and when they looked again, Sir Bedivere was lying in a crumpled heap some twenty feet from the dais. Where the lightning had struck him in the chest, the intense heat had melted away his chain mail and seared through the jerkin beneath. Thin wisps of smoke rose from the scorched leather. Sir Blays knelt beside the fallen warrior and checked his pulse and breathing.

"He's alive," he said finally. "His armor protected him."

The King gestured to the two men-at-arms. "Get the Landsgrave out of here. Have my surgeon attend him."

The men-at-arms hurried forward, picked up Sir Bedivere between them, and carried him out of the Court. King John shook his head wearily, leant back in his throne, and eyed the two remaining Landsgraves dourly.

Sir Guillam blinked unhappily at the King and smiled tentatively, obviously out of his depth. A faint sheen of perspiration glistened on his brow, and he constantly shifted his weight from one foot to the other, like a small child too shy to ask his way to the privy. King John frowned, and studied Sir Guillam more carefully. The man couldn't be entirely useless, or the Barons wouldn't have sent him. The King's frown deepened as he considered the various possibilities. Sir Bedivere had already tried to kill him, so Sir Guillam could be a back-up assassin, versed in spells or poisons or curses. He could be a spy, sent to contact any disloyal elements within the Court. He might even be a highly skilled diplomat, behind the timid facade. King John smiled tightly; there was only one way to find out . . .

"Sir Guillam."

"Aye, Sire?" The Landsgrave started violently, and peered shortsightedly at the King.

"You are new to my Court."

"Aye, Sire; I'm the new Landsgrave for the Birchwood demesne. I speak for the Silver Barons."

"And what do they wish of me?"

Sir Guillam glanced furtively at the sternly brooding Astrologer, and swallowed dryly. He smiled nervously at the King, and ran a finger round the inside of his collar, as though it had suddenly grown too tight.

"The Silver Barons also ... require ... assistance, Sire. They need, uh . . ."

What little confidence he had left seemed to desert him entirely, and he fumbled quickly for a parchment scroll tucked into his belt. He unrolled it, found he'd got it upside down, grinned foolishly in embarrassment, turned the scroll the right way up, and read from it aloud.

"My masters instruct me to inform you that they are in dire need of the following; seven troops of guardsmen from your own Royal Guard; four troops of conscript militia; weapons, mounts and supplies for these troops . . ."

"That's enough," said the King.

"There's a great deal more yet," protested Sir Guillam.

"Really?" said the King. "You do surprise me. Answer me a question, my noble Landsgrave."

"Of course, Sire."

"Why are you here?"

Sir Guillam blinked confusedly, gestured helplessly, and nearly dropped his scroll. "I represent the Silver Barons, Sire; I carry their words to you."

"No, Sir Guillam; I meant why did they select *you* as the new Landsgrave? You don't appear to have had much experience in this line of work."

"Oh no, Sire. Before my appointment, I was Chancellor of the Exchequer to Baron Ashcroft."

The King winced. An accountant; that was all he needed. On the whole, he'd rather have faced another assassin.

"Pass your list on to my Seneschal, Sir Guillam; he'll supply you with whatever weapons and provisions we can spare."

"There is also the slight matter of eleven troops . . ." Sir Guillam's voice trailed away as the Astrologer chuckled darkly. The Landsgrave smiled weakly. "We could compromise and call it seven . . ."

"No compromises," said the King. "And no troops. Do you wish to argue the point?"

"Oh no, Sire," said Sir Guillam hastily. "Not in the least. Not at all. Absolutely not."

He rolled up his scroll, bobbed a quick bow to the King, and then stepped back to hide behind Sir Blays. The King nodded politely to the third Landsgrave, and Sir Blays bowed formally in return. Control and discipline showed in his slow, deliberate movements, and his voice was calm and even as he glared coldly at the Astrologer.

"Your powers have increased since I was last here, sir Astrologer, but don't think to intimidate me. I don't frighten that easily. I am Sir Blays of Oakshoff demesne. I speak for Gold."

The King inclined his head slightly. "You are welcome in my Court, Sir Blays. Do you also demand troops from me?"

"I carry my master's words," said Sir Blays carefully. "We must have more troops if we are to stand against the dark. Our borders have fallen to the long night, and already demons swarm across the land like so many rabid wolves. We can't hold out much longer; even the stone and timber of our Keeps are no defence against the darkness when it falls. You know my words are true, Sire."

"Aye," said the King tiredly, "I know. But my answer must remain the same, Sir Blays; I have no more men to send you."

"I will carry your answer to my master," said the Landsgrave slowly, "But I tell you now; he won't accept it."

"He'll accept it," said the Astrologer calmly. "He has no choice."

"There's always a choice," said Sir Blays. His quiet words seemed to ring ominously on the silence, and for a long moment nobody said anything.

"Very well," said the King finally. "You came to this Court to petition my help, noble Landsgraves, and whilst it is not in my power to grant you what your masters desire, I can perhaps offer them a message of hope and comfort. Even as we speak my Champion and my youngest son, Prince Rupert, are on their way to summon the High Warlock, that he may return to the Forest Land and set his sorceries against the darkness."

"You'd bring him back?" asked Sir Blays softly. "After what he did "

"It's necessary," said the Astrologer.

"Desperate situations call for desperate remedies," said

the King. "I have therefore also decided to reopen the Old Armory, and draw the Curtana from its scabbard."

For a long moment everyone just stared at him, frozen in shock as though carved from marble, and then the Court erupted into bedlam. Suddenly it seemed everyone was shouting and cursing, fighting desperately to be heard over the deafening clamor. Those courtiers nearest the throne surged forward angrily, and had to be driven back at swordpoint by the men-at-arms. And still the uproar mounted merging into a solid wave of sound that echoed and re-echoed from the high-timbered ceiling.

Julia stared in bewilderment at the heaving, frightened mass that had once been a Court. Shock and outrage were stamped on every face, underpinned here and there by naked fear. She turned to Harald, who seemed almost as confused as her.

"Harald; what the hell's going on?" The din was such that she had to practically bellow in his ear to be understood, and even then he just shook his head curtly. She searched his face for an answer, but as the first shock passed his features quickly became an impassive mask. Only the whitening knuckles on his dagger hilt betrayed the depth of his feelings.

"Enough!" thundered the Astrologer suddenly, and fire roared up around him, smoking thickly on the stuffy air as the flames sought in vain to consume him. His night-dark cloak belled out like spreading wings, and an awful knowledge seemed to stir within his icy, impenetrable eyes. An all-pervading silence fell across the Court, broken only by the crackling of the dancing flames surrounding the Astrologer. He glanced round the quiescent Court, and smiled grimly. The leaping flames flickered and went out, and once again Thomas Grey seemed nothing more than a lean old man dressed in black.

"Thank you, sir Astrologer," said King John evenly. "Now listen well, my noble Lords and Ladies; I will not tolerate these disturbances in my Court. Any more such outbursts, and my headsman will earn his pay. I will have order in this Court! Is that clear?"

One by one the courtiers knelt and bowed their heads to their King, and then the men-at-arms, and even the Astrologer, himself, until in all the Court only two men remained standing; the Landsgraves of Silver and Gold. Sir Guillam trembled when King John's gaze fell upon him, but although he couldn't meet the King's eyes, he wouldn't kneel. King John knew better than to try and stare down Sir Blays; they'd known each other too many years.

The King leaned back in his throne and studied the two men thoughtfully. There was a time Sir Blays would have taken his own life to prove his loyalty to the Forest Land, and cut down any man who questioned it. Set against his past fealty, his refusal to bow was practically a declaration of war. The King turned his attention to Sir Guillam, and frowned. Scared half out of his wits, and still the man defied him. Why? King John closed his eyes, and sighed tiredly. He knew why. Frightened as he was, Sir Guillam was far more frightened of the Curtana.

I have to do this, King John thought stubbornly. *It's necessary.*

He opened his eyes and stared cynically out over the sea of bowed heads before him. The sight did not impress him in the least; they bowed because they were afraid of the Astrologer's magic, not because they were loyal. The King smiled grimly. If he couldn't have loyalty, he'd settle for fear. He had a war to wage, and with the darkness pressing closer all the time he could no longer afford to be choosy over which weapons he used.

"Rise," he growled finally, and the Court scrambled to their feet amid a rustle of silks and the clatter of chain mail. A rebellious murmur started among a few of the courtiers, only to die quickly away when the King frowned. He smiled sourly, and then turned to glare at Sir Blays, who stared calmly back.

"So, noble Landsgrave; you object to my drawing the Curtana."

"The Sword of Compulsion has been forbidden to your majesty's line for over four centuries," said Sir Blays coldly.

"The situation has changed since then," said the King reasonably. "The darkness must be stopped, and since we can't hope to do it by force of arms . . ."

"The Curtana is forbidden!" said Sir Blays stubbornly. "A King rules by the consent of his people, not because he has a magic sword that compels their obedience. We've already seen how your Astrologer uses such power. For all his faults, Sir Bedivere was a warrior; he fought and bled for you in a dozen campaigns. And your pet sorcerer treated him like a rabid dog! So you think the Barons will stand idly by while you employ such power?"

"When the King wields Curtana, the Barons will do as they're told," said the Astrologer silkily, and for a long time nobody said anything.

"Your majesty!" said a deep, resonant voice from among the courtiers, and the King groaned silently.

"Yes, Lord Darius?"

"With your permission, Sire; I think I may have a compromise that will satisfy both you and the noble Landsgraves."

"Very well, Lord Darius, approach the throne. But if this compromise is anything like your last brilliant idea, you'd be much better off staying where you are."

The Minister for War chuckled appreciatively as he made his way forward, his plump figure moving with surprising grace as he threaded his way through the wary courtiers. He stopped before the throne, took up a position carefully midway between the Landsgraves and the King, and bowed to them both. King John frowned impatiently.

"Well, Lord Darius?"

"It seems to me, your majesty, that Sir Blays and Sir Guillam are mainly concerned as to how the Curtana is to be used. If you could perhaps explain a little of your strategy . . ."

"A King doesn't have to explain anything," said the Astrologer. "A loyal subject obeys without question."

"Of course, of course," said Lord Darius quickly. "I merely seek to clarify matters, nothing more."

"It's a reasonable request," said the King mildly. "And if it will help to set Sir Blays's mind at rest . . ." He glanced at the Landsgrave, who nodded stiffly. "Very well. As Sir Blays has already pointed out, the nature of the Curtana is to compel obedience. I propose to turn this power on the demons, and force them to return to the darkness from which they came. It's a simple enough solution to the problem."

"Almost elegant in its simplicity." Lord Darius smiled. "Would you not agree, Sir Blays?"

"It might work," said Sir Blays grudgingly. "If the Curtana can affect nonhuman minds. Far as I know, no one's ever tried that before. But even if it does work, what happens to the sword after the demons have been routed?"

"Afterwards, it will be returned to the Armory," said the King. "And there it may stay till the end of time, as far as I am concerned."

"Indeed, indeed," said Lord Darius, smiling and bobbing his head and clasping his podgy hands across his vast stomach. "I fear, however, that the noble Landsgraves will require more concrete evidence of your majesty's intentions."

"You dare?" roared the Astrologer, stepping forward.

Lord Darius paled, but stood his ground. "Your majesty . . ."

"Let him speak," said the King, and the Astrologer resumed his position beside the throne.

Lord Darius bowed gratefully. "When all is said and done, your majesty, a sword is just a sword. Since you agree it should never be used again, might I suggest hat once the demons' threat has been disposed of, the Curtana should be publicly melted down and destroyed, once and for all."

The King frowned thoughtfully. "My instinct is to say no. The sword has been in our family for generations, and might be needed in the future . . . but I see your point. The Curtana is too dangerous a weapon to be trusted with anyone. Would such an answer satisfy the Barons, Sir Blays?"

"It might," said Sir Blays carefully, "but I speak only for Gold."

King John smiled coldly. "Where Gold leads, Silver and Copper follow. Isn't that right, Sir Guillam?"

The Silver Landsgrave bobbed his head nervously. "I'm sure my masters will find it an excellent scheme, Sire."

"Then I'll consider it," said King John. "You'll have my answer before you leave tomorrow."

Sir Blays nodded, his face carefully impassive. "Thank you, Sire. Our business now being at an end, with your permission Sir Guillam and I will withdraw to our chambers. It's been a long day."

"That it has," said the King. "Very well, my noble Landsgraves; you are dismissed."

Sir Guillam and Sir Blays bowed to the throne, turned, and left the Court. The courtiers watched them go, and muttered quietly to each other.

"Be silent," said the Astrologer, and they were.

"Before I dismiss this Court for the day," said King John, "I have a pleasant duty to perform. Princess Julia . . ."

"Ah, you've remembered me at last," sniffed Julia. "I was beginning to think I was invisible."

"Julia, my dear, you are never far from my thoughts," said the King earnestly. "Harald; I trust you've been keeping the Princess entertained?"

"Oh sure," said Harald. "She's getting quite good at tic-tac-toe. A little more practice, and she'll be able to beat me without cheating."

Julia stabbed at his foot with her dagger, and grinned as he moved it quickly out of range.

"If you've quite finished," said the King, "I have an announcement to make."

"Then get on with it," said Julia.

The King sighed quietly to himself, and then stared out over the Court. "My Lords and Ladies, I announce this day the betrothal of my eldest son, Prince Harald, to the Princess Julia of Hillsdown. I wish them every happiness and all good luck."

"He's going to need it," muttered a voice at the back.

Julia was on her feet in a second. "I'm not marrying Harald!"

"Yes, you are," said the King. "I've just announced it."

"Then you can damn well unannounce it!"

"Princess Julia," said the King, entirely unperturbed, "You can marry him willingly or unwillingly, but whatever you say and whatever you do, your marriage will take place four weeks from today. Harald is a fine young man and a credit to his line. I'm sure that, under his tutelage and discipline, you will become a credit to him and to this Court."

"I'll kill myself first!"

"No you won't," said the Astrologer. "You're not the type."

Julia glared angrily about her, and then turned her back on them all as she found herself blinking away angry tears. "We'll see," she muttered shakily. "We'll see about this . . ."

King John ignored her, and looked out over his Court. "My Lords and Ladies, I thank you for your kind attention. Court is now dismissed."

The courtiers bowed and curtsied to the throne, and then

filed slowly out through the double doors, unusually quiet and subdued. At a nod from the King, the guards and men-at-arms followed them out. Julia moved away from the throne, and then looked up to find Harald standing before her. She couldn't seem to work up the energy to hit him.

"What do you want?" she asked tiredly.

"Julia . . ." Harald hesitated. "Do you really love Rupert?"

Julia shook her head slowly. "I don't know. Perhaps. Why?"

Harald shrugged. "I don't know. Look, Julia; this marriage is going ahead whether we want it or not. I don't expect you to love me, girl, but am I really such a bad match? I'm not an ogre, you know. Well, not all the time, anyway." He waited to see if she'd smile even a little, but she didn't. Harald sighed, and shook his head. "One way or another, Julia, you will be my wife. Get used to the idea. I'll talk with you again, later."

Julia watched him leave the Court. Her head spun with plans to escape from the castle, but once outside the walls, there was nowhere to go. By all accounts the Forest Land was overrun with demons. If the dragon had been strong enough to go with her . . . But he wasn't. His wounds still hurt him, and he slept most of the time. Julia swore quietly to herself, but she knew she couldn't just go off and abandon him. Or Rupert, for that matter. Julia scowled. It was all Rupert's fault, anyway. If he hadn't brought her back to this Castle and then abandoned her, to go running off to be a hero again, and get himself killed . . .

Julia squeezed her eyes shut, and dug her nails into the palms of her hands. She wouldn't cry in front of the King, she wouldn't . . . After a while, she opened her dry eyes and stared unseeingly at the empty Court.

Wherever you are, Rupert, be safe. And get back here, fast.

King John watched the Princess leave, secretly admiring her calm and poise. He waited until the double doors had closed behind her, and then slumped exhausted in his throne.

"That has to be one of the longest sessions we've ever had," said the Astrologer, lowering himself carefully onto the top step of the dais.

"Right," said the King wearily. "I swear this damn throne gets more uncomfortable every day."

"At least you get to sit down," said the Astrologer wryly. "I've been on my feet for the past ten hours. My back's killing me."

The King chuckled sympathetically. "We're getting too old for this, Thomas."

"Speak for yourself," said the Astrologer, and the King laughed.

They sat for a while in companiable silence, watching shadows gather in the silent Court. Light spilled through the gorgeous stained-glass windows, and dust motes swirled lazily in the golden haze. The King tugged thoughtfully at his shaggy gray beard, and glanced at the Astrologer.

"Nice act you put on for the Landsgraves, Thomas."

"Thank you, John. I thought it went rather well."

"Did you have to make Bedivere crawl like that?"

Thomas Grey frowned. "Come on, John; the man's a killer. The barons knew that when they sent him. He would have killed you."

"I know," said the King shortly. "But no man should have to crawl as he did. It made me feel . . . dirty."

"Look, John, we spent most of last night working on this. The only way to keep the Barons in line is to make them more frightened of us than they are of the dark. Now how am I supposed to scare them if I don't use my powers? It's not as if I hurt the man, John; I just forced him to do what he should have done, anyway."

"And the lightning bolt?"

"Mostly illusion. There was enough power there to knock him cold, but that's all."

"You're missing the point, Thomas. The whole reason for drawing the Curtana was to prove to the Barons and the Court that we're not helpless against the dark; that we do have more powerful weapons we can use against the demons. After what you did to Sir Bedivere, no one's going to give a damn about the demons; they'll be to busy worrying about whether the sword's going to be used on them."

"Damn," said Grey. "I'm sorry, John, I didn't think . . ."

"As it is, it's touch and go whether we dare draw the Curtana now, never mind the Infernal Devices. If the Barons even suspect we intend drawing those swords as well . . ."

"We'll have open rebellion on our hands. I do take your point, John, but we've got to have those swords. The darkness will be here soon, and we can't afford to rely on the High Warlock. We can't even be sure he'll come."

"He'll come," said the King. "You know he'll come."

There was an awkward silence. Grey cleared his throat uncertainly. "I know how you feel about him, John. But we need him."

"I know."

"Maybe he's changed. He's been away a long time."

"I don't want to talk about it."

"John . . ."

"I don't want to talk about it!"

Thomas Grey looked into his old friend's eyes and then turned his head away, unable to face the ancient rage and bitterness and sorrow he had found there.

"Tell me about the Infernal Devices," said King John. "It's been years since I had to read up on the bloody things."

"Apparently there were once six of these swords," said the Astrologer quietly. "But only three remain to us; Flarebright, Wolfsbane and Rockbreaker. No one's dared draw them for centuries."

"Are they as powerful as the legends say?"

Grey shrugged. "Probably more so. Every source I can find was scared spitless by them."

"That's as may be," growled the King. "But both they and the Curtana are still sheathed in their scabbards in the Old Armory. And the Old Armory is in the South Wing. And we haven't been able to find that since we lost it thirty-two years ago!"

"The Seneschal says he can find it," said Grey calmly, "And that's good enough for me. He's the best tracker this Castle's ever had."

"Yeah, maybe," said the King. He scratched half-heartedly at his ragged mop of hair, and sighed wearily. "There are times, Thomas, when I wish your title wasn't just honorary. Right now it would be very useful to have someone who actually could foresee the future."

Grey laughed. "Sorry, John, but my title's nothing more than a legacy from our superstitious ancestors. When all's said and done, I'm just an astronomer. Show me a sheep's entrails and all I could tell you is what kind of soup they'd make."

The King smiled, and nodded slowly. "Just a thought, Thomas, just a thought." He rose stiffly to his feet, and glanced round the empty Court. "I think I'll turn in now. I get so damn tired, these days."

"You've been working too hard. We both have. You ought to give Harald more responsibility; let him handle some of the routine matters. He's of an age where he could easily take some of the burden off our backs."

"No," said the King shortly. "He's not ready yet."

"You can't go on putting it off, John. We won't always be here to guide him; age is creeping up on us."

"In my case, it seems to be positively sprinting." The King gave a short bark of laughter and started down the dais steps, waving aside the astrologer's offered arm. "I'm tired, Thomas. We'll talk about this tomorrow."

"John . . ."

"Tomorrow, Thomas."

The Astrologer watched the King walk slowly across his empty Court. "Tomorrow may be too late, John," he said quietly, but if the king heard him, he gave no sign to show it.

"You could be King, Harald," said Lord Darius.

"I will be King," said Harald. "I'm the eldest son. One day, all the Forest Land will be mine."

"You'll be King of nothing if you wait to inherit the throne."

"That's treason."

"Yes," said Lord Darius pleasantly. "It is."

The two men smiled, and toasted each other with their goblets. Harald nodded his acceptance of the vintage, and the Lady Cecelia leant gracefully forward and filled his glass to the brim. The Prince smiled his thanks, settled himself more comfortably in his chair, and glanced round Darius's chambers. From the tales he'd heard of Darius's lifestyle, Harald had expected lush and sumptuous quarters, buried under thick carpets and rich tapestries. Instead, he found a quiet, somber, almost austere room whose floor and walls were bare polished wood, warmed only by a single fire. One wall lay hidden behind a massive bookcase, whose shelves were tightly packed with works on politics, history and magic. Harald raised a mental eyebrow. It seemed there was more to the Minister for War than met the casual eye. The Prince sipped at his wine and studied Lord Darius over the goblet's rim. There was a basic squat ugliness to the man's face that all the careful makeup, plucked eyebrows, and oiled hair couldn't disguise, and when he dropped his public mask his face set into uncompromising lines of cold determination.

This man is dangerous, thought Harald calmly. *He's ambitious and ruthless; a useful combination in any field, but especially so in politics. Probably sees himself as a Kingmaker.*

He turned his attention to Lord Darius's wife, the Lady Cecelia. She smiled slowly, and met his gaze with a stare of open appraisal. Hair dark as the night tumbled down over her bared alabaster shoulders, outlining and emphasizing her delicately pretty face. Sensuality smoldered in her dark eyes and pouting lips. She had changed from her intricately ornate Court gown into a simple silk wrap that revealed tantalizingly brief glimpses of upper thigh every time she moved. *Tasty,* thought Harald. *And not exactly backward in coming forward, even with her husband present.* Not for the first time, Harald wondered what Darius and Cecelia saw in each other. There was no doubt they made a formidable political team, but her affairs with the younger guardsmen were common gossip. Darius must have known, but he never said anything. *Takes all sorts to make a world,* thought Harald sardonically.

"Well, my Lord Minister for War," he said politely, "This is all very pleasant, I'm sure, but what exactly do you want from me?"

Darius smiled at the Prince's bluntness, and sipped unhurriedly at his wine. "As yet, very little, Sire. But rest assured that my friends have your best interests at heart."

"Really?" said Harald amusedly. "How very interesting. I was under the impression your *friends* had the interests of the Forest Land at heart. That is, after all, why I'm here."

"By helping you, we help the Land," said Darius earnestly. "Your father is no longer fit to be King. He has abandoned the Barons to the darkness, insulted and attacked the Landsgraves in open Court, and now he threatens to draw the Curtana! He must know the Barons won't stand for that. He's all but inviting a rebellion."

"The Barons need a King," said Harald calmly. "They

haven't enough men to make their separate stands against the Darkwood, and they know it. Their only hope is an army; a single armed force strong enough to throw the darkness back. They tried bullying the King into giving them more men, only to find he doesn't need their support any more. Assuming, of course, that the Curtana will work on nonhuman minds. If it doesn't, it'll be too late to try and raise an army. Small wonder the Barons are desperate. If the sword doesn't work, we all go down into the darkness. If it does work, King John could become the greatest tyrant this Land has ever known. With the sword of Compulsion in his hand, his merest whim would become law. However, with King John overthrown, who would control the army? The Barons don't trust each other, as any one of them could use the army to make himself King.

"So; the Barons need a King, but they don't want King John. And that, my Lord Darius, is why you requested my presence here tonight. Isn't it."

Darius studied the Prince narrowly. "You show a keen grasp of the situation, Sire. I didn't realize you had such an interest in politics; in the past you've always seemed more concerned with other . . . pursuits."

Harald laughed. "But then none of us are always what we seem, are we, dear fellow?" The habitual blandness fell suddenly from his face, revealing hard, determined features dominated by piercing dark eyes. "I may act the fool, Darius, but don't ever take me for one."

"Why pretend at all?" asked the Lady Cecelia, frowning prettily.

"It disarms people," said Harald. "They don't see me as a threat until it's too late. Besides; it amuses me."

His face relaxed into its usual lines of vague amiability, but his eyes remained cold and sardonic. Darius smiled uncertainly, his mind racing as he struggled for the right approach to use with this new, unexpected, Prince Harald.

"Your father undoubtedly means well, Sire, but he is an old man and his mind is not what it was. He listens too much to his pet Astrologer, and not enough to those courtiers whose privilege and responsibility it has always been to advise him. With the darkness already gathering outside our walls, we can't afford a King who'd gamble all our lives on a single magic sword that might not even work. If the King won't listen to reason, he must be made to listen."

"You're talking about my father," said Harald softly. "If I thought you were threatening him . . ."

"We're not," said Darius quickly. "There's no question of the King coming to any harm."

"You're forgetting Sir Bedivere."

"A mistake, I promise you. I don't think any of us had realized just how unstable the man had become."

Harald looked at him coldly.

"Please believe me, Sire," said Darius slowly, "The King will not be harmed. My associates and I have a great deal of respect for what he achieved in the past. We merely feel that the pressures of his position have grown too great for him, in his old age. The Forest Land needs a younger, more capable ruler. Such as yourself, Prince Harald."

The Prince just smiled at him. A silence grew between them.

"Do we have your support?" asked Darius. He could feel a cold sweat forming on his face, though the room was comfortably warm. The Prince sitting opposite him wasn't the man he'd thought he knew, and Darius began to wonder if perhaps he and his friends had made a horrible mistake. One word from this cold-eyed stranger to the Royal Guard, and a great many heads would roll from the bloodstained block before morning. Darius shifted his weight in his chair, casually dropping one pudgy hand onto the hilt of the poisoned dagger he carried sheathed beneath his sleeve.

Harald lifted his empty glass. The Lady Cecelia leant forward and poured him more wine. Her silk wrap parted slightly, allowing Harald a brief glimpse of her impressive cleavage. Harald sipped at his wine, and smiled sardonically.

"You have my support," he said finally, "but for my reasons, not yours."

"Your reasons," said Darius uncertainly.

"I want to be King," said Harald. "And I'm tired of waiting."

Darius smiled, and moved his hand away from the dagger. "I don't think you need wait much longer, Sire."

"Good," said Harald. He sipped at his wine thoughtfully. "Why did you come to me, Darius? Surely Rupert would have been a better choice; he has so much more to gain then I do."

"Rupert has become an unknown factor," said Darius. "His time in the Darkwood changed him. He's become stronger, more forceful, more . . . independent. He's always been loyal to the Land, but he's made no secret of the fact that he puts ethics before politics. A rather naive attitude in a Prince, and altogether untenable in a King. Besides; I don't think he and I could ever work amicably together."

"He doesn't like me, either," said the Lady Cecelia, pouting elegantly.

Harald put down his glass and rose to his feet. "I support you in principle, Darius, but for the moment that's as far as I go. Arrange a meeting for me with your . . . friends, and I'll talk with them. If I'm to commit treason, I want to know who my fellow conspirators are. All of them."

"Very well," said Darius. "I'll have word brought to you when we're ready."

"Soon," said Harald. "Make it soon."

"Of course, Sire," said Darius, and Harald left. Darius poured himself more wine, and was surprised to find that his hands were shaking.

"Insolent puppy," he growled. "He should be grateful for the chance we're giving him."

"Kings aren't noted for their gratitude," pointed out the Lady Cecelia tartly. "He'll come around. He's young and greedy, and not nearly as bright as he'd like us to think."

"Don't underestimate him," said Sir Blays, stepping out from behind the bookcase as it swung slowly open on its concealed hinges. Sir Guillam and Sir Bedivere followed him into the room, and the bookcase swung shut behind them.

"We don't have to worry about Harald," said Darius. "He wants to be King, and we're his best chance."

"This morning I might have agreed with you," said Blays thoughtfully, sinking into the chair opposite Darius. "Now, I'm not so sure. I always said there was more going on in that Prince's head than anyone ever gave him credit for, and unfortunately it seems I was right. The old Harald was no problem; we could have handled him. This new Harald; I don't know. He must have realized that, once we've put him on the throne, he'll never be anything more than a figure-head for the Barons."

"Undoubtedly he has," said Darius complacently, folding his fat hands across his stomach. "But what can he do? If he betrays us to the Royal Guard, he loses his chance to be King. He might never get another. And once we've place him on the throne, he'll soon find he needs us more than ever. The odds are that Prince Rupert will be back by then, along with the Champion and the High Warlock. No, gen-tlemen; Harald needs us, and he knows it. If we work it right, he'll always need us."

"The High Warlock worries me," said Blays. "What if he and the Champion decide to overthrow Harald in favor of Rupert?"

"From what I remember of the High Warlock, he won't give a damn who sits on the throne, as long as they do what he tells them. He never was much interested in politics."

"And Rupert and the Champion?"

"The Champion has always been loyal to the eldest son," said Darius slowly. "And he's never had much time for Rupert. I don't think the Champion will be a problem. In fact, with a little persuasion he might even take care of Rupert for us."

He looked up, and realized Sir Guillam and Sir Bedivere were still standing. "Do sit down, gentlemen; you make the place look untidy."

Guillam bobbed his head quickly, and sat down on the edge of the chair nearest him. He smiled briefly at Darius and Cecelia, as though apologizing for his presence, his pale blue eyes blinking nervously all the while. Bedivere stood at parade rest, his back straight and his hand near his swordhilt. He made no move to seat himself. Darius studied him narrowly. Bedivere had replaced his damaged chain mail and jerkin, and apart from a slight paleness to the face, no sign remained of the ordeal he'd suffered at the Astrologer's hands. And yet, despite his calm features and relaxed stance, he was no more at ease than a cat waiting at a mousehole. There was a deadly stillness to the man, as though he was merely waiting for his next order to kill somebody. *Who knows,* thought Darius, *maybe he is.*

Blays brushed disdainfully at a length of cobweb clinging to his sleeve. "You really should do something about your bolthole, Darius; the acoustics are appalling and the walls are filthy."

"It was also very draughty," said Guillam petulantly. "The length of time you kept us waiting there, I wouldn't be at all surprised if I caught a chill. What is that place, anyway; the tunnel we were in seemed to go on for miles."

"It does," said Darius. "It's a part of the air vents." He sighed quietly as he took in the Landsgrave's puzzled face, and decided he'd better explain, if only for the sake of good relations. "Sir Guillam, you must have already noticed that my chambers, like the majority of rooms in this Castle, have no windows. It is therefore vitally important to keep air circulating throughout the Castle, if it is not to turn bad and poison us all. The many vents and tunnels within the Castle walls are designed to draw in fresh air from the outside, and carry out the foul air. Over the years I've spent a great deal of time exploring and mapping the endless miles of air vents within the Castle; more than once they've proved an invaluable asset when it came to . . . gathering information."

"I suppose it beats listening at keyholes," said Blays sourly.

Darius smiled politely. "If nothing else, Sir Blays, you must admit that the air vents do provide an excellent escape route for us, should the need arise."

"Maybe," said Blays. "but you'd better do something about that bookcase door; it's far too slow to open and close. In an emergency, it's be no bloody use at all."

Darius shrugged. "The counterweights are very old, and I lack the expertise to repair or replace them. As long as they still serve their purpose . . ."

"What about the migration?" said Blays suddenly. "Will that affect you?"

"I haven't moved from these chambers in fifteen years," said Darius calmly. "No one knows the secret of the bookcase but you and I."

"Migration?" said Guillam, frowning. "What migration?"

"I'll tell you later," said Blays. "Now, Darius . . ."

"I want to know now!" snapped Guillam.

Darius looked to Blays, expecting him to put the other Landsgrave in his place, but to Darius's surprise, Blays swallowed his irritation and nodded curtly to Guillam. *Interest-*

ing, thought Darius. *It would appear Sir Blays isn't as much in control of things as he'd like everyone to think.*

"You have to remember," said Blays to Guillam, patiently, "that because the interior of the Castle is so much greater than the exterior, it causes certain unique problems for the occupants. One is the lack of windows and fresh air. Another is that with so many layers of stone between the inner and the outer rooms, there can be extreme differences in temperature within the Castle. The thick stone walls retain heat, so that the innermost rooms are always the warmest. Thus, in summer the King and the higher members of High Society live on the outskirts of the Castle, where it's coolest. When winter comes, they move to the center of the Castle, where it's warmest. Those in the lower strata of Society live in a reverse manner. And those who hover somewhere between the two extremes, like Darius, don't migrate at all. Is everything clear to you now, Sir Guillam?"

"It sounds very complicated," said Guillam.

"It is," said Darius. "That's why the timing of our rebellion is so important. With the migration well under way, the general confusion will work to our advantage."

"Thank you," said Guillam politely. "I understand now."

"Then perhaps we could please get down to business," said Darius heavily. "We do have a great deal to discuss."

"Like what?" said Blays. "Our orders were to insult and isolate the King and sound out Prince Harald, and we've done that. Far as I'm concerned, the sooner we're out of here, the better. I don't like the company I'm keeping these days."

"We were also ordered to be discreet," snapped Guillam, flushing slightly. "Now, thanks to Bedivere's stupidity, the King is bound to go ahead with the drawing of the Curtana!"

"He would have, anyway," said Blays.

"Not necessarily! We might have talked him out of it!" Guillam shook his head in disgust. "At least you kept your wits about you, Darius. If the King agrees to the Curtana's destruction, we might come out of this ahead yet."

"You really think the King will give up the Curtana?" asked Blays incredulously.

"I don't know! Maybe. If we can keep this muscle-bound oaf on a leash, perhaps . . ."

"Oh, stop whining," said Bedivere. Guillam spluttered

wordlessly, outraged, and then Bedivere turned and looked at him. "Be quiet," said Bedivere, and Guillam was. The crimson glare burned openly in Bedivere's eyes, and Guillam could feel all color draining from his face. His hands were trembling, and his mouth was suddenly very dry. Bedivere smiled coldly, and the madness faded slowly from his eyes, or at least as much as it ever did.

"You'll never come closer," he said softly, and then he turned away from the shattered Landsgrave, and once again stared off into the distance at something only he could see.

Darius studied the silently brooding warrior a moment, and then took his hand away from his poisoned dagger. He sighed quietly. Berserkers were all very well in battle, but there was no place for them in councils of war. When Darius had first been told of Sir Bedivere, having a Landsgrave who could double as an assassin had seemed like a good idea, but now he wasn't so sure. The man was clearly out of anyone's control, and once the rebellion was over, he'd have to go. Assuming Bedivere held together that long . . .

"This meeting that Harald wants," said Blays suddenly, breaking the awkward silence. "Is it possible?"

"I suppose so," said Darius, "But it's a hell of a risk. I don't like the idea of all of us gathered together in one place; if anyone should betray us . . ."

"You can always post men-at-arms to see that we're not disturbed."

Darius sighed resignedly. "Very well. But I still don't like it."

"You don't have to like it," said Blays shortly. "Just do it."

There was a slight pause.

"Would anyone like a glass of wine?" asked Cecelia. Blays and Guillam shook their heads. Bedivere ignored her.

"I suppose King John does have to die?" said Blays slowly, and everyone looked at him.

"You know he does," said Guillam. "As long as he's alive, he's a knife at our throats. There'd always be someone plotting to put him back on the throne. He has to die."

"But if Harald ever suspects . . ."

"He won't," said Darius. "King John will be killed during the initial fighting, while Harald is occupied elsewhere.

Bedivere will do it, in such a way as to throw suspicion on the Astrologer."

Bedivere stirred. "Do I get to kill him as well?"

"We'll see," said Darius, and Bedivere smiled briefly.

"I've known John a good many years," said Blays. "He's not been a bad King, as Kings go."

"As far as our masters are concerned," said Guillam, "A good King is one who obeys the Barons."

"Times change," said Blays sourly, "And we change with them." He shook his head, and slumped back in his chair.

"John has to die," said Guillam. "It's for the best, in the long run."

"I know that," said Blays. "My loyalty is to Gold, as it has always been. By theatening to draw the Curtana, John threatens my master. I can't allow that."

"No more can any of us," said Guillam.

"It's a pity, though," said Blays. "I always liked John."

"He has to die," said Darius, and there was enough bitterness in his voice that all three Landsgraves looked at him curiously.

"What have you got against John?" asked Blays. "Your fellow traitors I can understand; they're in it for the power, or the money, or a chance to settle old scores. But you . . ."

"We're patriots," said Darius coldly.

Blays smiled. "They might be, but you're not. You're in this for your own reasons."

"If I am," said Darius, "that's my business, not yours."

There was a ragged whisper of steel on leather as Bedivere swiftly drew his sword and set its point at Darius's throat.

"You've been holding out on us," said Blays, smiling unpleasantly. "We can't have that, can we?"

"We need your fellow *patriots* to ensure that Harald's Court will toe the line," murmured Guillam, "But we don't necessarily need you. When all is said and done, Darius, you are a go-between. Nothing more. And go-betweens shouldn't keep things to themselves, should they? I really think you ought to tell us about these other *reasons* of yours."

Darius met their gaze unyieldingly. A thin rivulet of blood ran down his neck as Bedivere pressed lightly with his sword. For a moment the tableau held, with no one giving way. Blays and Guillam exchanged a glance, and Guillam

nodded at the terrified Lady Cecelia. Blays grabbed a handful of her hair and bent her head sharply back. Both her
screams and her struggles ceased abruptly as Guillam pressed
a dagger against her throat. She started to whimper, and
then stopped as the blade cut into her skin.

"Well?" said Blays.

"I wanted revenge," said Darius, so quietly that it took
the Landsgraves a moment to understand what he'd said.
Blays gestured for Guillam to put away his dagger, and
released Cecelia. Bedivere took his sword away from Darius's throat, but made no move to sheath it.

"I never wanted to be Minister for War," said Darius. "I
inherited the post from my father. No one gave a damn
what I wanted to do with my life; nobody cared that I had
no training or inclination for the work. I could have been a
sorcerer; I had the talent. I had the power. The Sorcerers'
Academy offered me a place even before I reached a man's
years. But the King and my father wouldn't allow me to go.
I would be the next Minister for War, and that was all there
was to it.

"I did my best, to begin with, but somehow my best was
never good enough, so after a while I just stopped trying.
And the King and the Astrologer and the Champion have
taken it in turns to insult and ridicule me because I'm no
good at a job I never wanted, anyway. After the rebellion,
Harald will probably grant me whatever post I want, but
that isn't why I've done all this. I want revenge. I want
revenge for all the years of abuse I've suffered, for all the
insults I've had to swallow. I want to see everyone who ever
laughed at me broken and humbled."

"You will," said Blays. "You will."

"I want to see the King die!"

Bedivere chuckled darkly, and sheathed his sword. Darius
nodded his thanks shakily, and then reached out and took
Cecelia's hand as she ran over to kneel beside his chair. A
spot of blood stained the high collar of her dress, from
where Guillam's dagger had nicked her throat. Blays rose to
his feet.

"I don't see the need for any further discussion. Lord
Darius, arrange for a meeting between Prince Harald and
your fellow patriots. The sooner he commits himself to our
cause, the better. And make sure everyone attends. It's

time we sorted out our friends from our enemies." Blays smiled coldly. "I'm sure I don't need to tell you what to do if anyone tried to betray us to the King."

"I'll take care of any problems," said Darius.

"I'm sure you will. Good night, my Lord and Lady. Sleep well."

He bowed slightly, and then turned and left. Guillam and Bedivere followed him out. The door swung slowly shut after them. Cecelia waited a moment to be sure they'd really gone, and then made a rude gesture at the door.

"They think they're so smart," she said, dismissing the Landsgraves with a contemptuous sniff. "By the time you've finished working on Harald, you'll be the power behind the throne, not the Barons."

Darius patted her hand soothingly. "Let them think they're in charge for the time being, my dear. It does no harm, and it keeps the Barons happy."

"And after the rebellion?"

"Afterwards, it shouldn't be too difficult to prove to Harald who really killed his father . . ."

Cecelia laughed, and clapped her hands together impishly. "And with the Landsgraves discredited, who else can he turn to for support, but us? Darius, dear heart, you're a genius."

Darius smiled, and sipped at his wine. "Have you been able to entice Harald into your bed yet?"

"Not yet."

Darius raised a plucked eyebrow. "Are you losing your touch, my dear?"

Cecelia chuckled earthily. "I'm beginning to wonder. Court gossip has it that he's infatuated with the Princess Julia. I suspect the novelty of a woman who knows how to say no intrigues him. Still, he'll get over that. And I'll have him in my bed if I have to drag him." She frowned thoughtfully. "King Harald. It sounds well enough, and with us behind him he'll be great in spite of himself."

"I wonder," said Darius softly. "We're taking a lot on ourselves. If anything should go wrong . . ."

"Dear cautious Darius," said Cecelia. "Nothing's going to go wrong. You've planned it all so carefully. What could go wrong now?"

"I don't know," said Darius. "But no scheme's perfect."

Cecelia sighed, rose to her feet, and brushed her lips across Darius's forehead. "It's been a trying evening, dear. I think I'll go to bed."

"Ah yes; how is Gregory?"

"Still having problems from when Julia hurt him, but I'm helping to cure that."

Darius chuckled, and Cecelia smiled at him affectionately. "Dear Darius. Sometimes I wish . . ."

"I'm sorry," said Darius. "But you know I've never been interested in that sort of thing."

"It was just a thought," said Cecelia. "We make a good team though, don't we?"

"Of course," said Darius. "Brains and beauty; an unbeatable combination. Good night, my dear."

"Good night," said Cecelia, and hurried off to her tryst.

Darius sat quietly in his chair, thinking of the meeting he had to plan for the Prince Harald. There was much to do.

What the hell am I doing here? Thought Julia as she followed the Seneschal down yet another dimly lit corridor, but she already knew the answer. With so many worries and problems crowding her head, she'd had to find something to do, or go crazy. The Seneschal's expedition to rediscover the lost South Wing had seemed a heaven-sent opportunity, but she was beginning to have her doubts. She'd been walking for what seemed like hours, mostly in circles, through what had to be the most boring corridors Julia had ever seen. She was beginning to think the Seneschal was doing it on purpose.

He hadn't seemed all that pleased to see her when she'd first approached him about the expedition, but then, the Seneschal rarely seemed pleased about anything. Tall, painfully thin and prematurely bald, his aquiline features were permanently occupied by doubt, worry, and a frantic desire to get as much done as possible before everything fell apart around him. He was in his mid-thirties, looked twenty years older, and didn't give a damn. His faded topcoat had seen better days, and his boots looked as though they hadn't been polished in years. He was fussy, pedantic, and bad-tempered, and those were his good points, but he was also the best damn tracker the Castle had ever known, so everybody made allowances. Lots of them. When Julia first found him, he was scowling at a large and complex map, while a dozen heavily armed guards waited impatiently and practiced looking evil. One of the guardsmen spotted Julia approaching, and tapped the Seneschal on the arm. He looked up and saw Julia, and his face fell.

"Yes? What do you want?"

"I've come to join your expedition," said Julia brightly, and then watched interestedly as the Seneschal rolled up his eyes and shook his fists at the ceiling.

"It's not enough the maps are hopelessly out of date. It's not enough that my deadline's been brought forward a month. It's not enough that I've been given twelve neanderthals in chain mail as my guard! No! On top of all that, I get landed with the Princess Julia as well! Forget it! I'm not standing for it! I am the Seneschal of this Castle and I will not stand for it!"

"I knew you'd be pleased," said Julia.

The Seneschal seemed torn between apoplexy and a coronary, but finally settled for looking terribly old and put upon. "Why me, Princess? It's a big Castle; there are hundreds of other people you could annoy. Why not go and persecute them instead?"

"Now don't be silly," said Julia briskly. "I promise I'll try really hard to be helpful and not get in the way."

The Seneschal winced. "Must you? You always do so much more damage when you're trying to be helpful." He noticed the storm clouds gathering on Julia's brow, and sighed resignedly. "Oh, all right then. If you must. But stay close to me, don't go off on your own, and *please,* Princess, don't hit anyone until you've checked with me first."

"Of course not," said Julia innocently. The Seneschal just looked at her.

Which was why, some time later, Julia was boredly following the Seneschal down a dimly lit corridor somewhere at the rear of the Castle, and rapidly coming to the conclusion that this had not been one of her better ideas. And then the Seneschal took a sharp right turn, and everything changed. With all its many corridors and halls, it was inevitable that parts of the Forest Castle would fall into disuse, and Julia felt her interest reviving as it became obvious that nobody had walked this corridor in years. The wood-panelled walls were dull and unpolished, and thick spiderwebs shrouded the empty lamps and wall brackets. The Seneschal called a halt while two of the guards lit the lanterns they'd brought with them, and then he led the party on down the corridor. Julia drew the dagger from her boot and carried it in her hand. The dim light and the quiet reminded her uncomfortably of the Darkwood.

The corridor eventually branched in two, and the Seneschal stopped the party again while he consulted several maps. Julia moved cautiously forward and studied the two branches. The left-hand fork seemed to curve round and head back the way they'd come, whilst the right-hand fork led into an unrelieved darkness that raised the hackles on the back of her neck. Julia shook her head to clear it, and made herself breathe deeply. The Darkwood was miles away. A little darkness couldn't hurt her. Julia clutched tightly at the hilt of her dagger, as though for comfort, and smiled grimly. Even after all this time, she still needed a lit candle in her room at night, before she could sleep. Like Rupert before her, the long night had left its mark on Julia. Her heart jumped suddenly as she realized there was someone standing beside her, and then it steadied again when she recognized the Seneschal.

"Which way?" she asked, and was relieved to find that her voice was still steady.

"I'm not sure yet," said the Seneschal testily. "According to all the maps, we should take the left-hand branch, but that feels wrong. That feels very wrong. No, to hell with the maps; we have to go right. Into the darkness."

"I might have known," muttered Julia.

"What? What was that? I do wish you wouldn't mumble, Princess; it's a very annoying habit."

Julia shrugged, unoffended. The Seneschal's perpetual air of desperation made it impossible for anyone to take his remarks personally; he was so obviously mad at the world, rather than whoever he happened to be addressing at the time.

"Why are we looking for the South Wing, sir Seneschal?"

"Because, Princess, it has been lost for thirty-two years. That's lost, as in missing, unable to be found, vanished from human ken; absent without leave. It may not have been a particularly impressive Wing, as Wings go, but we were all rather fond of it, and we want it back. That's why we're out looking for it. What else should we do; throw a party to mark the thirty-second anniversary of its loss?"

"No, sir Seneschal," said Julia patiently, "I meant, why are we looking for it *now?* You've managed without it all these years; why is it suddenly so important?"

"Ah," said the Seneschal, and peered dubiously at the Princess. "I suppose if I don't tell you, you'll just make my life even more of a misery."

"Got it in one," said Julia cheerfully.

The Seneschal sighed, glanced furtively at the waiting guards, and then gestured for Julia to lean closer. "It's not exactly a secret, but I'd rather the guards didn't know what we're after until they have to. I'm sure they're all perfectly loyal to the King . . . but why take chances?"

"Get on with it," said Julia impatiently, intrigued by the Seneschal's uncharacteristic nervousness.

"We're looking for the South Wing," said the Seneschal quietly, "because that's where the Old Armory is."

Julia looked at him blankly. "Is that supposed to mean something to me?"

"The King intends to draw the Curtana," said the Seneschal, "And the Curtana is in the Old Armory."

"Got it," said Julia. "I'm with you now."

"I'm so glad," said the Seneschal. "Anything else you'd like to know?"

"Yes," said Julia dryly. "If this Curtana is as powerful as everyone makes out, how is it that no one's tried to find the Old Armory before, and take the sword for themselves?"

"Over the years, a great many people have tried."

"So what happened to them?"

"We don't know. None of them ever came back."

"Terrific," said Julia. "I notice you didn't tell me any of this before we set out."

"I thought you knew," said the Seneschal.

"Assuming we get to the Old Armory," said Julia, "a prospect that seems increasingly unlikely the more I think about it, I take it you will be able to recognize the Curtana when you see it?"

The Seneschal stared into the darkness of the right-hand corridor, and smiled grimly. "The Curtana is a short sword, not more than three feet in length, and it has no point. Going back several hundred years, it used to be called the

Sword of Mercy. It was presented to each Forest King at his coronation, as a symbol for justice tempered by compassion. And then James VII came to the throne. He took the Curtana and set a touchstone within its hilt—a sorcerous black gem that enslaved the minds of all who beheld it. Legend has it that the Demon Prince himself gave King James the stone, but records of that time are scarce. It was a time of murder and madness, in which the Curtana became the Sword of Compulsion, a symbol of tyranny. No one has drawn that blade since James was overthrown, but it's said that even sheathed, the sword has an aura of blood and death and terror. I've never seen the Curtana, Julia, but I don't think I'll have any problem recognizing it."

The Seneschal turned away and glared at the waiting guards, who were peering into the darkness ahead and hefting their swords warily. "And now, if you've run out of questions for the time being, Princess, I think we should press on, before those neanderthals start carving their initials into the woodwork."

He paused just long enough for each guardsman to light his lantern, and then strode confidently forward into the gloom of the right-hand corridor. *Damn the man*, thought Julia as she and the guards hurried to catch up with the Seneschal, *There's a lot to be said for bravery and heroism, but this is getting out of hand. First he tells me horror stories about previous search parties that never came back, and then he goes marching off into the dark without even bothering to send in a few scouts first.* Julia scowled, and shook her head. *I should never have let them take away my sword . . .*

The party's footsteps echoed hollowly back from the dust-covered walls, but even that small sound seemed to carry eerily along the quiet corridor. The guards huddled together and held their lanterns high, but still the darkness pressed hungrily against the sparse pool of light the lanterns cast. In the constant gloom, it was hard to judge distances, and Julia began to wonder if the corridor had an end, or if the damn thing just went on forever. She looked back the way she'd come, but the original junction was already lost to the darkness. There was a faint scurrying sound on the edge of her hearing, but no matter how hard she concentrated, she couldn't seem to place where it was coming from. *Probably rats*, she thought, hefting her dagger. *After thirty-two years, they probably think they own the place.*

"How can anyone lose a whole Wing?" She asked the Seneschal, more for the comfort of the sound of her voice, than because she cared about the answer.

"It seems one of the Astrologer's spells went wrong," said the Seneschal absentmindedly, while dubiously studying a map in the light of a guardsman's lantern. "No one's quite sure exactly what he was up to, and since he's still too embarrassed to talk about it, the odds are we'll never find out, but apparently there was a massive explosion, and then in the space of a few moments all the doors and corridors that used to lead to the South Wing suddenly . . . didn't. Those people who were in the Wing were able to get out, but nobody could get in. Legend has it that there were a few people unaccounted for, who never got out."

"What a horrible thought," said Julia, shivering despite herself.

"If you don't want to know the answers, don't ask the questions," said the Seneschal testily. "Now quiet, please; I'm trying to concentrate."

Julia swallowed an angry retort, and the Seneschal went back to frowning over his map. The air grew steadily more stifling and oppressive as the party pressed on into the darkness, and Julia glared about her as the faint scuffling noises seemed to hover at the edge of the lamplight. The guards heard it too, and one by one they drew their swords. *It's only a few rats,* Julia told herself sternly, but her imagination conjured up images of people watching from the darkness. Men and women, grown strange and crazy in their isolation. Children, who'd never known any other world than the South Wing. Julia took a firm grip on her dagger. *Even rats can be dangerous,* she thought defensively.

And then Julia stumbled and almost fell as the floor lurched violently and dropped away beneath her. The corridor walls seemed to recede into the distance and then return, sweeping in and out in the space of a moment. Her sense of left and right and up and down reversed itself and then spun her dizzily round and round before snapping back to normal. A sudden darkness swallowed the lanternlight, and she could hear voices crying out in fear and anger, but only faintly, as if from a great distance. She felt she had to keep moving, but every step seemed harder than the one before, and her muscles ached with the effort it took to press on. A hideous pressure built within and around her, trying to force her back, but Julia wouldn't give in. That wasn't her way. The pressure reached a peak, but Julia could feel there were people in the darkness with her, helping her to fight back. She drew on their strength, and they drew on hers, and together they threw themselves forward. And then the light came back, and the world was steady again.

Julia sank onto her haunches and breathed harshly as her head slowly cleared. She was exhausted and wringing with sweat, as though she'd been running for hours on end, but when she glanced around she found she was still in the same dark corridor. The only light came from a single lantern, held by a guard crouching beside her who looked almost as bad as she felt. Julia frowned suddenly, and looked back the way she'd come. The Seneschal was leaning weakly against a wall, glowering at one of his maps, but there was no trace of the other eleven guards.

"What the hell happened?" demanded Julia, climbing shakily to her feet after waving away the guard's proffered hand. "And where are the other guards?"

"The South Wing is trapped inside some kind of barrier," said the Seneschal thoughtfully, as he carefully refolded his map and tucked it into his coat pocket. "Presumably set up when the Astrologer's spell backfired." He glanced down the corridor, but the impenetrable dark gave nothing away. The Seneschal sniffed, and turned his back on it. "The other guards must still be on the other side of the barrier. Typical. Damn guards are never around when they're needed."

Julia fought down an impulse to grab the Seneschal by the shoulders and shake some sense into him, and smiled at him reasonably. "Sir Seneschal, we can't just leave them there . . ."

"Oh, they'll be safe enough; we can pick them up on our way back. It's their own fault, anyway. We broke through that barrier because we refused to be beaten, and because at the end we worked together. The other guards weren't up to that. A pity, but never mind. We've made it into the South Wing, and that's all that matters. The first people in thirty-two years . . . Well, come on; there's no point in standing about here, there's work to be done."

And with that, the Seneschal grabbed the lantern from the guard's hand and stalked off down the corridor without even a backward glance, leaving Julia and the guard to hurry after him. Julia studied the guard covertly as they followed the Seneschal deeper into the South Wing. He was short and stocky, with a compact muscular frame and heavily muscled arms. All in all, he looked rather like a giant who'd been cut off at the knees. He couldn't have been much more than forty, but there was a certain grimness to his face that made him seem a lot older. His broad, heavily-boned features were capped by a close-cropped hair of so light a blond as to be nearly white, and there was a wary watchfulness to his eyes that Julia found reassuring. Whatever happened, this guard wasn't the kind to be caught unawares.

"My name's Bodeen," he said suddenly. "In case you were wondering."

"I hadn't realized I was staring," said Julia.

"You weren't," he assured her. "But there's not much I don't notice."

"Keep that attitude," said Julia, "and we may all get out of this alive."

They both chuckled quietly, but there was more tension than humor in the sound. The Seneschal stopped suddenly, gazed thoughtfully at a side turning, and then plunged into it. Julia and Bodeen followed. The Seneschal led them through a baffling series of twists and turns, down corridors and up stairways, in and out of spiderwebbed doors and passages, until the Princess had lost all sense of time and direction. She began to feel strangely disorientated, as though she was standing still and everything else was moving around her.

Bodeen padded silently at her side like a cat on the prowl, his eyes constantly searching for possible dangers. Anywhere else, Julia would have found such behavior intensely irritating, but ever since she'd entered the South Wing she'd had the feeling someone was watching and waiting in the dark beyond the lantern's light. No matter where she looked, or how quickly she turned her head, she never saw anyone, but still the feeling persisted, gnawing unmercifully at her nerves until she could have screamed from sheer frustration.

She clutched her dagger hilt until her knuckles ached, and cursed herself for a fool for ever having volunteered to join the Seneschal's party. She glared at his unresponsive back, and then had to pull up short to avoid crashing into it as he came to yet another sudden halt. He stood still a moment, his head tilted back like a hound searching the air for an elusive scent, and then he slowly lowered his head and turned to face her.

"Something's wrong," he said quietly.

"How do you mean?" asked Julia, unwilling to voice her own fears aloud, in case they sounded ridiculous.

"I'm not sure." The Seneschal looked about him, and then shivered suddenly. "Whatever spell the Astrologer attempted all those years ago, it must have been a damn sight more powerful than he was willing to admit. It's still here, echoing in the wood and stone, trembling on the air."

"You mean we're in danger here?" asked Bodeen, raising his sword warily.

"Yes. No. I don't know!" The Seneschal frowned unhappily at Bodeen and Julia, as though expecting them to come up with an answer, and then turned his back on them. "We're wasting time. The Treasury isn't far. Let's get on." He communed briefly with his inner sense, and then strode confidently down a side corridor, leaving the guard and the Princess to hasten after him or be left behind in the dark.

The silence bothered Julia more than anything, and not just because it reminded her of her time in the Darkwood. The endless quiet seemed to smother every sound, as though the silent Wing resented any disturbance. Bodeen methodically swept the darkness with his gaze, checking every door and passageway they passed, but there was never any sign to show the party was being watched or followed. And yet, in some strange way, it was the very absence of any sign or sound that convinced Julia they were not alone. All her instincts screamed to her of danger, near and deadly, and she knew with a deep inner certainty that something evil watched and waited in the darkness beyond the light. A blind panic welled up within her, and she crushed it ruthlessly. She'd be scared later, when she had the time.

The corridor grew suddenly narrower, the walls crowding in out of the dark. The Seneschal's lantern shed a dull yellow glow over faded tapestries and portraits of men and women long dead. He stopped suddenly before a closed, ornately carved door, and frowned thoughtfully. All at once, Julia felt a presence close at hand; something dark and dangerous and horribly familiar. She shot a glance at Bodeen, who was staring back the way they'd come. He hefted his sword with casual competence, but didn't seem particularly worried. Julia glared at the closed door, and shuddered in spite of herself. There was something awful on the other side of that door; she could feel it in her bones. She licked her dry lips, and hefted her dagger.

"Are you all right?" asked Bodeen quietly.

"I'm fine," said Julia, shortly. "I've got a bad feeling about this place, that's all."

Bodeen nodded unsmilingly. "It's just the dark. Don't let it throw you."

"It's not just that! Don't you ever listen to your instincts?"

"All the time. But mostly I trust my eyes and ears, and so far I haven't seen or heard one damn thing to suggest there's anyone in this Wing except us, and a few spiders."

Julia shook her head stubbornly. "There's something in here with us. And we're getting closer to it all the time."

"If you two have quite finished," said the Seneschal acidly, "you might possibly be interested to learn that we're almost at the end of our journey. Beyond this door lies the South Tower, and beyond that lies the main entrance to the Treasury."

Julia frowned. "Are you sure?"

"Of course I'm sure!"

"Then why have you kept us waiting all this time?"

"Because the door doesn't *feel* right!" snapped the Seneschal disgustedly. "I *know* this door leads to the South Tower, but . . . I keep getting the feeling that it doesn't!"

"Are you saying we're lost?" asked Julia, her heart sinking.

"Of course we're not lost! I'm just not entirely sure where we are."

"Terrific," said Bodeen.

The Seneschal glared at the door, and then reached cautiously for the handle. Julia tensed, and held her dagger out before her. The Seneschal glanced quickly at Julia and Bodeen, and then eased the door open a crack. Bright light flared round the edges of the door, throwing back the darkness. Julia and the Seneschal fell back, startled by the sudden glare, and Bodeen moved quickly forward to stand between them and the door. He waited a moment while his eyes adjusted to the new light, and then gave the door a quick push with his foot. It swung slowly open, and Bodeen whistled softly as bright daylight flooded into the corridor.

"Come and take a look," he said slowly. "You're not going to believe this . . ."

Julia glared about her warily, before moving over to join the Seneschal at Bodeen's side. Her sense of imminent danger had faded to a vague unease, but she still couldn't shake the feeling they were being watched. *Nerves*, she told herself angrily, and looked through the door. She blinked dazedly into the light for a moment, and then realized she was looking out into an endless sky. Clouds floated before her, soft and wet and puffy, so close she could almost reach out and touch them. She looked up, and then gasped as her stomach lurched. Far above her, a hundred feet and more, lay the ground. The view was upside down. Julia closed her eyes, and waited for her stomach to settle before looking again. Heights didn't usually bother her, but the upended view's casual defiance of the natural order of things disturbed her deeply.

"Interesting," she said finally, forcing herself to look up at the ground.

"Yes, isn't it," said the Seneschal happily, and Julia was disgusted to note that not only he was looking up and down with no sign of distress, he was actually smiling while he did it. "It's a view from the South Tower, Princess, or at least from where the South Tower used to be. If you look down, or rather up, you can see the moat quite clearly. Fascinating. Absolutely fascinating. It's not just an illusion, you know; somehow, within this doorway space itself has been inverted. I can feel it most distinctly. I suppose if someone were to step through this door, they'd fall up, rather than down."

"After you," said Julia, and the Seneschal chuckled. Bodeen stared up at the ground, frowning.

"If the Tower's been missing all this time," said Julia slowly, "Why hasn't anyone noticed it before? It should have been obvious from the outside."

"Actually, no," said the Seneschal, still studying the view. "The Castle's exterior is mainly illusion."

"At least now we know what happened to the other parties," said Bodeen suddenly, and Julia and the Seneschal stepped carefully back from the door before turning to look at him.

"Obvious when you think about it," said the guard calmly, still staring out into the sunshine. "Like you, sir Seneschal, they must have decided to enter the Treasury through the South Tower. It was the main entrance, after all. Unfortunately, their trackers weren't in your league. They had no way of knowing the door had become a death trap. So, blinded by the light, they just walked right in and fell to their deaths."

"But . . . someone would have found the bodies," protested Julia.

Bodeen shrugged, and turned away from the door. "Like as not they ended up in the moat, or near it. And the moat monster's always hungry."

"We can't be sure all the parties came this way," said the Seneschal. "And even if they did, I can't believe none of them would have survived the trap."

Bodeen smiled grimly. "Maybe there are other traps we haven't found yet."

For a long moment the three of them just stared at each other, and then the Seneschal shrugged, and turned away to stare through the doorway.

"All right," said Julia, "Where do we go now? We can't get to the Treasury this way."

"Actually, I rather think we can," said the Seneschal. "I've just had an idea."

Julia looked at Bodeen. "Can't you just feel your heart sinking?" Bodeen nodded solemnly.

"The South Tower may be missing," said the Seneschal, "but the door that leads to the treasury is still there. I can see it, just a little farther along what is now the outer wall. Even more to the point, there's a stairway that connects these two doors, built onto the wall."

"A stairway," said Julia. "Is it intact?"

"Mostly. The supports that held it in place seem to have vanished with the Tower, but it looks secure enough. As long as we're careful."

"Let me get this straight," said Julia. "You expect us to go out that door, crawl along an unsupported crumbling stairway, carefully ignoring the hundred-foot drop, just to reach another door that's probably locked, anyway?"

"Got it in one," said the Seneschal.

Julia looked at Bodeen. "You hit him first. You're nearest."

"You won't be in any real danger," said the Seneschal hastily.

"Damn right I won't," said Julia. "I'm not going."

"Princess Julia," said the Seneschal firmly, "I am going. So is Bodeen. If you wish to stay behind and wait for our return, or if you want to try and find your way back through the dark without me, that is up to you."

Julia glared at him, and then rounded on Bodeen, who shrugged helplessly.

"Sorry, Princess; the Seneschal's in charge."

Julia turned away in disgust. "All right; let's get this over with."

The Seneschal chuckled irritatingly, and moved over to look out the doorway. He craned his neck to get a better view of what lay above the lintel, and then nodded happily. "The stairs begin directly above the door. The only problem's going to be the gravity switch, but as long as we get a good grip on the lintel first . . . Well, don't just stand there, Bodeen; make a stirrup for me."

The guard moved quickly forward and cupped his hands together. The Seneschal set his foot in the stirrup, positioned his weight carefully, and then took firm hold of the lintel with both hands. He glanced quickly out the door, and then nodded to Bodeen. The guard lifted as the Seneschal jumped, and Julia gasped as the Seneschal's body flipped gracefully end over end through the doorway. He shot upwards out of sight, his hands still clinging fiercely to the lintel. There was a long silence, and then the hands suddenly disappeared.

"Are you all right, sir?" called Bodeen hesitantly.

"Of course I'm all right!" yelled the Seneschal crossly. "Give me a chance to get a little farther along the stairs, and then send out the Princess. And tell her to watch her step; it's slippery out here."

Julia looked at Bodeen, and swallowed dryly.

"Take your time," he said understandingly. "There's no rush."

"What gets me is we volunteered for this," said Julia, and Bodeen smiled.

"It beats collecting horse manure for the gardens. But only just. Ready?"

Julia nodded, slipped her dagger back into her boot so as to have both hands free, and then set her foot in the stirrup Bodeen made for her. She tried for a firm grip on the lintel, but her fingers slipped on the smooth wood, and she had to stop and rub her hands dry on her dress before she could get a grip she trusted. She took a deep breath, let it slowly out, and nodded to Bodeen. He smiled reassuringly, and Julia jumped.

Gravity changed while she was still in midair. Up was suddenly down, and her head swam madly as she found herself hanging by one hand from the bottom of the door. Beneath her kicking feet there was nothing but air, and she didn't dare look down. She reached out with her free hand, and stubbed her fingers on the rough stone of the stairway. She grinned fiercely, grabbed hold, and pulled herself up onto the first step. It was broad and wide and seemed comfortingly solid. She pressed herself against the Castle wall, and looked around. The stairway stretched out before her, jagged and broken and punctuated here and there by yard-wide gaps in the stonework. Some fifty feet away, farther down the wall, the Seneschal was crouched before another door, his brow creased in thought.

"Sir Seneschal," called Julia sweetly, "I'm going to get you for this."

The Seneschal looked around unhurriedly. "Ah, there you are, Princess. I would have come back to help you, but I'm afraid I got distracted by this door. I was miles away."

"I wish I was," muttered Julia. The gusting wind tousled her hair as she stared uncomfortably at the view spread out below her. The Forest sprawled greenly across the horizon in which ever direction she looked, and it was hard for Julia to imagine such an ancient and magnificent sight falling to darkness and decay under the long night. She strained her eyes until they ached, but as yet there was no sign of the Darkwood itself. She wondered if Rupert had passed through the darkness yet, on his way to the High Warlock. She tried to remember exactly how long he'd been gone, and felt vaguely ashamed when she found she wasn't sure. Julia scowled, and turning away from the Forest, she concentrated on the stairway before her. One problem at a time. Her frown deepened as she realized much of the stonework was cracked and pitted from its long exposure to the wind and rain, and several of the steps hung at crazy angles from the Castle wall, apparently only held in place by a little mortar and accumulated pigeon droppings.

"Is it safe for me to come out yet, Princess?" called Bodeen plaintively, and Julia started guiltily as she realized how long she'd kept the guard waiting.

"All clear!" she yelled quickly, and scrambled down onto the next step so as to give him more room. She'd barely made it before Bodeen came flying upside-down through the door, somersaulting in midair as the gravity changed. His grip on the lintel never even looked like slipping, and in the space of a few moments he was crouching gracefully on the top step, and looking interestedly down at the view.

"Do stop hanging around," called the Seneschal. "The Treasury door isn't locked."

Julia glanced across just in time to see him tug energetically at the door. It opened outwards, nearly knocking the Seneschal from his perch in the process. He quickly regained his balance, stared dubiously into the dark opening, and then jumped into it, flipping head over heels upwards as he went.

That man has nerves of steel, thought Julia. *Either that, or absolutely no sense of self-preservation.*

She glared at the weathered, rough-hewn steps that lay between her and the Treasury door. There were only a few gaps wide enough to require jumping, but the steps on each side of the breaks looked decidedly precarious. Julia looked down, and then wished she hadn't. The drop seemed to get longer every time she looked. She studied the battered stairway, and cursed under her breath, so as not to upset Bodeen. If the Seneschal hadn't already made the journey, she'd have called it impossible. As it was . . . Julia sighed, gathered up her long dress, and tucked the front and back ends securely into her belt. The wind was cold on her bare legs, but she had to be able to see where her feet were. She glared dubiously at the next step down, and then lowered herself cautiously onto it. The stone creaked warningly under her weight. Julia waited a moment for it to settle, and then moved on to the next step. Slowly, she made her way down the stairway, one step at a time, testing each slab of stone carefully before committing her full weight to it. Time and again she stood motionless while the ancient stonework groaned and shifted beneath her, and crumbling mortar fell away in sudden little streams. Julia was aware of Bodeen hovering close behind her in case she fell, but after a while she had to order him to stay farther back. The stone steps couldn't hold both their weight.

The first jump was the hardest. An entire block of six steps had broken away, leaving a jagged-edged gap of some fifteen feet. The steps on either side looked none too secure, and Julia reluctantly decided that her best bet was a running start. She climbed back two steps, took a few deep breaths to settle her nerves, and then launched herself at the gap, trusting to speed and luck to get her safely across. For a brief moment there was nothing but open space beneath her, and then her feet slammed heavily onto the far step. She fell forward and clutched anxiously at the uneven stonework, but the great stone slab barely shifted an inch. Julia let out her breath in a great sigh of relief and, rising cautiously to her feet, she moved down onto the next step to give Bodeen enough room for his jump. He made it easily, landing in a catlike crouch that barely stirred the stonework. The two of them shared a grin, and then continued on down the stairs, one step at a time.

The wind was rising steadily, a bitterly cold wind that seemed to strike clean through to the bone. Julia couldn't stop shivering, and in her eagerness to get out of the cold she hurried down the last few steps without bothering to check them first. The icy wind tugged and buffeted her as she stood staring at the final gap in the stairway. It was only a yard or so wide and, once over, it was only two more steps to the Treasury door. Julia checked that her dress was still tucked securely in place, studied the distance to the far step, and then jumped the gap easily. The stone gave lightly beneath her as she landed, and then tore itself free from the Castle wall with a roar of rending stone and mortar. Julia threw herself forward, and just caught the edge of the next step as the first slab dropped out from under her. She watched it tumble lazily end-over-end on its long way down to the dirty green waters of the moat, and tried not to think of how many other people might have ended up there. She clutched fiercely at the rough stone step, and waited for her heart to settle.

"Hang on, Julia," said Bodeen quietly. "I'll jump across, and then pull you up."

"No! Stay where you are, Bodeen!" Already Julia could feel the step shifting. There was no chance of it supporting the guard's weight as well. Slowly she pulled herself up over the edge of the step, stopping every few seconds to let the shifting stone settle. Her arm muscles ached unbearably, but she didn't dare hurry herself. Eventually she was able to hook one knee over the edge and then, with one heart-stopping lunge, she hauled herself up onto the step. For long moments she just lay there in an ungainly heap, feeling the stone creak and groan and grow still beneath her. Her heart hammered furiously against her breastbone, and sweat trickled down her face and sides despite the chill wind. *When I get inside*, she decided shakily, *I am going to brain the Seneschal with the nearest blunt instrument.* She eased herself down onto the next step, and only then got to her feet and turned to look back at Bodeen, watching anxiously from the far side of the gap.

"All right, Bodeen, come across. But aim for this step; I don't think the other will take your weight."

Bodeen nodded calmly, and made the jump look simple. The stone slab absorbed his landing with only the faintest of tremors, and Julia turned her attention to the open Treasury door before her. *After all I've been through to get here*, she thought slowly, *the Treasury had better be worth it.* She took one last look at the Forest spread out below, and then stepped through the doorway.

Once again, gravity changed while she was still in midair, and she only just got her feet under her in time. She looked around for the Seneschal, and then had to jump to one side as Bodeen came somersaulting in. He landed awkwardly, and Julia put out a hand to steady him. He moved quickly away, and Julia was surprised to note the man was actually blushing. She grinned as the answer hit her, and carefully rearranged her dress so that her legs were once again modestly covered. Bodeen concentrated all his attention on shutting the Treasury door, until he was sure it was safe to turn around again.

"It didn't bother you on the stairway," said Julia, amusedly.

"That was different," said the guard firmly. "Here, it wouldn't be at all proper. I mean, what would the Seneschal say?"

"Something vexing, no doubt," said Julia, staring curiously about her. As her eyes grew used to the gloom, she realized they were in a vast hall, illuminated only by the sparse light that trickled past the edges of the many shuttered windows. The timbered ceiling towered above them, choked with cobwebs. Thick streams of the dirty gossamer hung from every surface, though there was surprisingly little dust. Tightly packed bookcases lined the walls, and dozens of chairs stood before dozens of desks, all joined one to the other by their cobweb shrouds.

"I wonder what this place was," said Julia.

Bodeen shrugged. "If this was the Treasury, I suppose this could be the old counting house."

"Right first time," said the Seneschal, appearing suddenly from a doorway to their left. "Who knows how many tons of· gold and silver and copper passed through this room? The whole wealth of the Forest Kingdom must have passed through here at one time or another."

Julia's eyes gleamed suddenly. "Do you suppose," she said demurely, "that any of the gold and silver and copper might still be around?"

The Seneschal chuckled. "Who knows?"

"I'm beginning to be glad I came," said Julia, and Bodeen nodded solemnly.

"Let's find the Old Armory first," said the Seneschal dryly. "Then perhaps we can consider a little treasure hunting. This way, Princess."

Julia grinned, and she and Bodeen followed the Seneschal through the side door into the next room. Julia stopped just inside the door, and wrinkled her nose as the smell hit her. The darkened antechamber would have seemed small and dingy even when it was still in everyday use, but after thirty-two years of neglect the place stank of damp and decay. There were no windows, the only light the familiar golden glow of the Seneschal's lantern. Mildew and wood rot speckled the wall panelling, and what had once been a rich, deep pile carpet crunched dryly under Julia's feet as she moved slowly into the room. A single chair lay overturned in a corner, cocooned in spiderwebs. The Seneschal turned as though to say something to Julia, and then froze. From somewhere close at hand, quite distinct amid the silence, came a furtive scurrying sound. It was too loud and too heavy a noise to be rats.

Julia drew her dagger, and Bodeen drew his sword. The Seneschal silently drew their attention to the door on the far side of the antechamber that stood slightly ajar, and the three of them crept quietly over to stand before it. The scurrying had stopped as quickly as it had begun, but Julia couldn't help feeling there was something horribly familiar about the sound. It wasn't just that she'd heard it before, on her journey through the South Wing; it was as though there was something about the sound she ought to recognize, but was afraid to. Julia scowled, took a firm grip on her dagger, and peered cautiously through the door's narrow gap. All was silence and darkness. Julia glanced at Bodeen, who looked at the Seneschal for his orders. There then followed a short conference between the three of them, consisting mainly of looks, shrugs, and scowls, until Julia lost her patience and kicked the door wide open.

The door flew open on squealing hinges, and slammed heavily against the wall. The echoes seemed to go on forever, but nothing came to investigate the sound, and after a while Julia padded silently into the room, followed closely by the Seneschal and Bodeen. The still air was dank and oppressive, with a faint scent of rot and decay that grated on Julia's nerves. The Seneschal held up his lantern, and then all three gasped as the lanternlight shimmered on gold and silver and precious jewels, scattered here and there across the floor, like a small child might leave his toys after he'd grown tired of playing with them. Stout oaken treasure chests lay on their sides, broken open and spilling their contents onto the floor. The lids of the chests had been torn clean away, the wood scored and split as though by claws. *Must have used a crowbar*, thought Julia dazedly. *Well, at least now we know we're not the only ones here.* She glanced quickly round, but there was nowhere for anyone to hide in the cramped little room that met her gaze. The Seneschal moved away to check the first of the room's two other doors, and Bodeen quickly sheathed his sword, knelt down beside the nearest chest, and started stuffing handfulls of assorted jewels into his pockets. Julia grinned, and crouched beside him.

"Don't load yourself down too heavily," she said dryly. "We may still have to fight our way out of here."

"Take what you can, when you can; that's always been my motto," said Bodeen calmly. "And any one of these jewels is worth more than they pay me in a year. Besides, there's no one here to fight, Princess."

"Somebody must have broken open these chests," said Julia. "And fairly recently, at that."

"How can you tell?" asked Bodeen, frowning.

"No cobwebs."

Julia left him thinking that over, and moved away to study a pair of sheathed swords mounted on a wall plaque. If there was to be any fighting, Julia wanted a sword in her hand. She tucked her dagger back into her boot and, brushing away the cobwebs, she pulled one of the swords from its scabbard. The blade shone brightly, even in the dim light, and the balance was exceptionally good. She tried the edge on her thumb, and raised an eyebrow when it drew blood.

Behind her, the Seneschal paused at the room's only window, and then tugged at the closed shutters until they swung slowly open on protesting hinges. Light flooded into the room, and the carpeted floor was suddenly awash with dozens of scuttling spiders darting back and forth, driven mad by the sudden light after so many years of darkness. Bodeen yelped shrilly and jumped up onto a chair, but the spiders quickly disappeared into a hundred nooks and crannies. Bodeen looked carefully around to make sure they were all gone, and then climbed down from the chair with as much dignity as he could muster. Julia shook her head wonderingly. So much fuss over a few spiders. Now *rats*, that would have been different . . .

And then she and Bodeen both spun round sword in hand as the Seneschal cried out in pain and horror. He dropped his lantern as he staggered back from the open second door, blood rilling down his chest, and then the demons erupted out of the darkness beyond the door and fell on him hungrily, swarming all over him like flies on a piece of meat. Julia and Bodeen charged forward, yelling their war cries and, incredibly, the demons retreated back into the darkness from which they'd come, leaving their prey behind.

Julia and Bodeen hauled the Seneschal to his feet. He was covered in blood and his eyes didn't track, but at least he was still breathing. Julia quickly looked around for the lantern, and snatched it up, but the fall had put it out. She cursed briefly, and then helped Bodeen drag the Seneschal back toward the antechamber door. The demons watched from their darkness, but made no move to follow them.

"We've got to get out of here!" said Bodeen shrilly.

"Right," said Julia evenly. "Just back steadily toward the door. No sudden moves, nothing that might upset them. Take it easy, and we'll get out of this in one piece yet."

"But they're demons! You saw what they did to the Seneschal!"

"So what!" snarled Julia. "Ram a yard of cold steel through them and they'll die just as easily as any man! I ought to know, I've done it before; remember?"

"How many of the damn things are there?" asked Bodeen more quietly, and Julia relaxed a little.

"A dozen, no more."

"Why aren't they coming after us?"

"Beats me. Maybe the sudden light from the window blinded them, and they don't know how many of us there are."

"Once they realize, we're in trouble."

"Right. How much farther to the door?"

Bodeen glanced back over his shoulder. "Nearly there, Princess. How's the Seneschal?"

"I don't know. He's in pretty bad shape."

"How bad?"

"Bad enough. And he's the only one who knows the way out of here."

"Terrific," said Bodeen.

They'd almost made it to the open door when the demons burst out of their darkness. Their eyes glowed bloodred, and their twisted pallid shapes came flying through the dim light like so many misshapen ghosts. Julia and Bodeen threw the Seneschal into the antechamber, and then sprang through after him. Bodeen slammed the door shut in the demons' faces, and then sheathed his sword and hung onto the door-knob with both hands to keep them from pulling the door open.

"Lock it!" he yelled to Julia.

"There's no key!"

"How about bolts?"

There were two, top and bottom. They were both rusted into place, and Julia wrestled the top one loose as the door heaved and shuddered under the demons' assault. There was the sound of claws tearing into wood. Julia slammed the top bolt home, and then turned quickly to the bottom bolt. It snapped off in her hand, rusted clean through. Julia and Bodeen looked at each other.

"That door isn't going to hold them long," said Bodeen quietly.

"It doesn't have to," said the Seneschal. "We've got to lead them into the counting room."

Julia and Bodeen spun around to find the Seneschal getting unsteadily to his feet. His face was pale, and streaked with drying blood, but his eyes were back in focus. Bodeen moved quickly over to support him, and the Seneschal nodded his thanks.

"The demons will break in here any minute. Bodeen, help me through that door into the counting room. Princess, you follow us, but stay in the doorway so that the demons can see you. When they have, you can fall back to join us. Don't let them lose sight of you, but don't let them catch you, either. Got it?"

"Not really," said Julia. "Are you sure you know what you're doing?"

"Of course," snapped the Seneschal testily. "I always know what I'm doing. Now give me the lantern."

Julia and Bodeen exchanged a glance. The antechamber door trembled as the demons hammered on it.

"What the hell," said Julia, handing the lantern to the Seneschal. "A short life, but an interesting one. Get him out of here, Bodeen. I'll hold the doorway."

Bodeen nodded curtly, and half-led, half-carried the Seneschal out of the antechamber and into the counting room. Julia turned back to face the shaking door. The only light in the narrow little room came from the open door before her, and Julia hefted her sword uncertainly. Silhouetted against the light, she made an obvious target. She frowned, and then backed away from the groaning door to stand hidden in the shadows of the open counting room door. She'd let the demons see her when she was good and ready, and not before. And then the straining bolt finally tore itself free from its socket, and the antechamber door flew open. The corpse-pale demons poured into the antechamber like maggots oozing from a game bird that had been left hanging too long. Their eerie pupilless eyes glowed crimson in the gloom as they peered hungrily about them for their prey. Julia stood very still, and waited patiently for something to come within range of her sword.

The demons sniffed at the still air, and then lowered their misshapen heads to the floor, like so many hounds searching out a scent. The sight might have been funny if it hadn't been so horrible. And then either they found a trail, or Julia made a sound without realizing it, for one by one the demons raised their heads to stare unblinkingly in her direction, and Julia knew the shadows weren't deep enough to hide her. She stepped quickly forward to block the doorway, sweeping her sword back and forth before her. Light gleamed dully the length of the blade. One of the demons leapt forward, and Julia cut it down with one stroke of her sword. The creature fell to writhe silently on the thick carpet, and then the other demons were upon her.

The Seneschal had told her to lead the demons back into the counting room, but Julia knew that once she fell back through the doorway, they'd roll right over her. The narrowness of the door meant the demons could only come at her in twos and threes, but it was only a matter of time before the sheer weight of numbers would wear her down, and she'd have to retreat back into the counting room. And then they'd take her.

Julia swung her sword with all her weight behind it, and demon blood flew on the air as a growing ache built in her muscles. She ripped open a demon's belly with a sideways sweep of her blade, and then had to fall back a step to avoid the clawed hand that narrowly missed her throat. She realized she was no longer protected by the doorway, and fell back again as the demons surged forward. And then Bodeen was beside her, adding his sword to hers.

The demons fell back before the two flashing blades, and Julia leapt aside as Bodeen slammed the door shut in their faces. Julia looked quickly for the bolts, and swore harshly when she realized there weren't any. Bodeen set his back against the door as the first claws began ripping into the wood.

"When I give the word," he said calmly, "head for the outer door."

Julia nodded, and then looked round just in time to see the Seneschal pull the outer door to, plunging the room into darkness. Julia bit her lip and hefted her sword.

"I hope somebody knows what they're doing," she said loudly, and wasn't all that reassured when the Seneschal just chuckled dryly.

"Get ready," said Bodeen. "I can't hold them . . ." The door surged open a few inches, pushing him back. A clawed hand snaked past the door, glowing palely in the dark. "Now, Julia! Go now!"

Bodeen jumped back, and Julia ran for the outer door. The demons flew after her, ignoring Bodeen as he hid behind the opened door. Julia got to the outer door and pushed it open. Bright sunlight flooded into the room. The Seneschal grabbed her arm and pulled her to one side, but the demons just stumbled on, blinded by the sudden light. Julia grinned savagely as she finally understood. She attacked the demons from the side while Bodeen harried them from the rear, and it was the easiest thing in the world to drive the nine surviving demons through the door and out into the long drop.

Julia lowered her sword and sank wearily to the floor. Her head ached fiercely, and her arms were as heavy as lead. Fatigue shivered in her legs and, just sitting there with her back pressed against the wall, Julia felt like she could sleep for a week. She shuddered at the thought. It had been bad enough lying in bed at night, knowing that while she slept the Darkwood drew steadily closer, but somehow she'd always thought the Castle's thick walls would keep her safe from demons. It came hard to her, to realize that nowhere was safe any more. Julia clutched her sword fiercely, and wondered if she'd ever dare sleep again.

Bodeen bent over her, and whistled softly as for the first time he saw the blood on her face and arms. "Princess, you're hurt."

"Cuts and bruises, Bodeen, nothing more. Help me up."

He helped her stand, and then waited patiently as she leaned heavily on his supporting arm until her head cleared.

After a while she pushed him away, and turned to the Seneschal, who was busily relighting his lantern with flint and steel.

"How are you feeling, Sir Seneschal?"

"I've felt better, Princess." He finally coaxed his candle alight, and closed the lantern. "It probably looks worse than it is."

"You looked pretty bad when we dragged you out from under those demons," said Bodeen, and the Seneschal grimaced.

"Don't remind me. I thought my time had come."

"You should rest for a while," said Bodeen.

"I'm all right," snapped the Seneschal. "Don't fuss. There'll be plenty of time to rest when we get back; right now, I'm more worried about the Armory. I hate to think how much damage the demons could have caused there. How the hell did those creatures get into the castle?"

"Somebody let them in," said Julia simply. "We have a traitor among us."

For a moment, they just stood and stared at each other. Bodeen scowled, and the Seneschal shook his head dazedly. Julia smiled grimly.

"Remember the demons who wait and watch outside our walls at night? Well, now we know where they hide during the day."

"I just can't believe it, Princess," said the Seneschal slowly. "Who'd be mad enough to bring demons into the Castle itself?"

"More to the point," said Bodeen suddenly, "why bring them into the South Wing?"

The Seneschal's head snapped up, his eyes wide with horror. "Of course; the Armory! The bloody Armory!"

He turned and ran out the side door and into the antechamber. Julia and Bodeen exchanged a startled glance, and then plunged into the darkness after him. They followed the Seneschal through dozens of dimly lit rooms and corridors, his lantern bobbing ahead of them like a beckoning will-o-the-wisp on a moonless night. Julia soon lost all sense of direction, and concentrated on running. She had a strong feeling that, if she stumbled or fell, the Seneschal would just leave her behind.

The Seneschal finally came to a halt before a pair of

massive oaken doors, easily eight feet tall, and almost as wide. The carved and curlicued wood gleamed dully in the golden lanternlight as he reached out and pushed gently at the left-hand door. It swung smoothly open at his touch, the counterweights creaking loudly on the silence. For a moment the Seneschal just stood there, staring into the darkness beyond the doors, and then his shoulders slumped and all the strength went out of him. He staggered, and would have fallen if Julia and Bodeen hadn't been there to support him.

"What is it, sir Seneschal?" asked Julia, scowling worriedly. "What's so important about the damn doors?"

"Don't you understand?" whispered the Seneschal, staring sickly at the open door. "The Armory's been breached! The Curtana's unguarded . . ."

He shrugged free of Julia and Bodeen, and led them into the Old Armory. Beyond the massive doors lay a towering hall so vast the Seneschal's lantern couldn't begin to light it. Julia started as a suit of armor loomed up out of the darkness, and then relaxed slightly when she realized it was only an exhibit. Dozens of huge display cases lay scattered across the hall, showing swords and axes, longbows and lances, main gauches and morningstars, in all their variations. Julia peered raptly about her as she moved slowly through the vast, dark hall in her narrow pool of light, awestruck by the sheer size of the collection. Rupert's ancestors had built up the Armory over twelve generations, weapon upon weapon, until now it would have taken more than one man's lifetime just to catalogue it all. Julia felt her hackles rise as for the first time she realized just how ancient Forest Castle was.

The Seneschal stopped suddenly before a dusty wall plaque, set in a deep recess that hid it from casual view. The single silver scabbard it bore was tarnished and begrimed from long neglect, but there was no sign of the sword it once held. The Seneschal sighed tiredly.

"It's gone," he said heavily. "Curtana's gone."

"But the Sword of Compulsion's our only hope against the demons," said Bodeen. "Who'd be mad enough to steal it?"

"Somebody who stood to gain if the castle fell," said the Seneschal. "And these days, that description covers an awful lot of ground."

"All this way," said Julia, too tired even to be bitter. "All this way for nothing. Come on, sir Seneschal, let's get out of here."

"Of course, Princess; the King must be told." The Seneschal turned his back on the empty scabbard, and stared out into the darkness. "Somewhere in this Castle there's a traitor. We've got to find him, Princess. We've got to find him and the Curtana, before it's too late."

'Perhaps it already is," said Bodeen quietly. "Perhaps it already is."

Julia stared out of the stables at the falling rain, and sighed dejectedly. The afternoon was barely over, but it was already growing dark. The rain had been falling for over an hour; a steady persistent drizzle that wore at the nerves, and worked its way down even the tallest chimneys to make the fires splutter and steam. Water gushed from the drainpipes and the overhanging guttering, turning the courtyard into a sea of mud. It dripped through the many cracks in the thatched stable roof, and pattered noisily on the straw-covered floor. The stable creaked and groaned as the rain hit it, and Julia stared out the open stable door and sighed again, perhaps in sympathy. Behind her, the dragon stirred.

"You should be in your room, resting," he said sternly.

Julia smiled, but didn't look round. "I'm all right. A few more interesting scars to add to my collection, that's all. The Seneschal took the worst of it; I don't know how he stayed on his feet long enough to get us out of the South Wing. The surgeon took one look at him and ordered him to his bed, but he wouldn't go until he'd spoken to the King. Bodeen and I were all that was holding him up, but he wouldn't give in. He's a tough old bird, that Seneschal. Didn't pass out until he'd told the King everything he knew and suspected about the Armory break-in. Bodeen and I carried him back to his rooms. He's sleeping now. Tough old bird."

"You should get some rest yourself," said the dragon. "I can smell the pain and tiredness in you."

"I couldn't sleep," said Julia. "Not yet. I need to talk to someone."

"What is it this time?" said the dragon gently. "Someone threatening to make you take etiquette lessons again?"

"Hardly. I've been excused from lessons since all my tutors refused to enter the same room as me unless they were granted an armed escort first."

"What is it, then? What's troubling you?"

"I don't know." Julia turned away from the stable door, and moved over to sit down beside the dragon. The thick layer of straw softened the earth floor as she leaned back against his huge, comforting side. The falling rain became a pleasant background murmur, and the constant drip of water from the thatch was strangely soothing. The scent of freshly scattered hay hung heavily on the air, rich and earthy, and the dragon could feel Julia's muscles slowly relaxing.

"Dragon," she said finally, "What happened to the horses that used to live here?"

"Delicious," said the dragon solemnly.

Julia elbowed him sharply in the side, and he grunted obligingly, through she doubted he actually felt it. "You didn't really eat all those lovely horses, did you?"

"No, Julia; I moved in and they moved out. At the gallop, as I recall."

Julia laughed, and snuggled back against his smooth scales. Sometimes it seemed the dragon was the only friend she had left in the world; an island of calm in an ocean of storms. After Rupert had left, the dragon had wandered aimlessly round the Castle, sleeping where he felt like it, and eating anything that didn't either run away or actively fight back. Eventually he'd settled down in one of the old stables, and showed every sign of staying there as long as someone brought him his meals regularly. The Castle staff quickly volunteered to take care of that, and heaved a collective sigh of relief. Between the dragon's appetite and Julia's sudden rages, they'd never done so much running and dodging in their lives.

"How are you feeling?" Julia asked the dragon, and he shrugged slightly.

"Better, I suppose. Casting the spell to summon the Rainbow Run took a lot out of me. Then the demons swarming over me, tearing at me with their fangs and claws. And finally I had to breathe fire, and that hurt me, Julia; hurt me deep down inside. By the time Rupert called down the Rainbow I was dying, and it seems there's a limit to how much even the Wild Magic can do. It saved my life, but only

time can heal me. I'm going to have to hibernate soon, and
sleep until I'm healed. If I can still heal. Magic is going out
of the world, and magical creatures like myself are having a
harder time of it." The dragon smiled sadly. "Or perhaps
I'm just getting old, even for a dragon. I haven't seen or
heard of another of my kind in over three hundred years.
perhaps I'm the last. The last dragon in the world of men."

"Three hundred years," said Julia slowly. "Didn't you
ever get lonely?"

"As a rule, dragons aren't particularly gregarious. We
each have our territories and our hoards, and we guard
them both jealously. But yes; there have been times this last
century when I would have welcomed the sight of another of
my kind. It's been so long since I soared on the night winds
with my brethren . . . so very long."

"When all this is over, we'll go and look for some more
dragons," said Julia.

"Yes," said the dragon kindly. "When all this is over."

Julia stared up at the thatch overhead, and listened to the
falling rain. "Dragon, do you think there's something . . .
wrong with me?"

"No. Why?"

"It's those damn Ladies-in-Waiting. They make me feel
like a freak, because I don't want to get married and settle
down to raising a family. I'm not ready for that. Not yet."

"Then don't," said the dragon.

Julia scowled. "It's just that sometimes . . . sometimes I
wonder if they're right. If there is something wrong with
me. All my friends and most of my sisters are married, and
they seem happy enough. Mostly. Maybe they're right. Maybe
I am missing out on something. I just don't see why I have
to give up being *me* to get married. I'm supposed to marry
Harald, but all he wants is a combination lover and serving-
maid. Well, he can forget that for starters. And if he gooses
me one more time, I'll raise his voice with a well-placed
knee."

She broke off suddenly, and frowned thoughtfully. "You
know, that's part of what I mean. If I'd said that to a
Lady-in-Waiting, she'd have had a fit of the vapors and
called for her smelling salts. Being blunt and direct isn't just
unfashionable, it's unfeminine. Do you think I'm unfeminine?"

The dragon chuckled. "Julia, I'm hardly an expert on

human behavior, but it seems to me that if you'd been just another helpless domesticated female, you'd never have survived the Darkwood. Or your journey through the South Wing this afternoon."

"Damn right," said Julia. "So why can't they just leave me alone "

"You're a Princess," said the dragon. "You have responsibilities. Even I know that."

Julia sniffed disdainfully, picked up a straw from the floor, and chewed on the end. "A Princess. And because of that I'm not supposed to think or feel or hope? Because of that I have to take orders from everyone on how to dress, how to talk, how to act? Because of that I have to marry a man I don't love? I'll see them rot in hell first!"

The dragon slowly turned his head to get a better look at her. "We've finally come to what's really bothering you, haven't we?"

"Yes," said Julia quietly. She looked at the straw in her hand, and threw it away. "Rupert should have been back ages ago."

"It's a long trip, there and back. And from what I've heard, the High Warlock will take a lot of persuading."

"I should never have let him go back into the Darkwood. You know what that place is like."

"Yes," said the dragon softly. "I remember." He flexed his wings slightly, and Julia reached up to scratch the recent scar tissue.

"Do you still have nightmares?" she asked suddenly. The dragon shook his head. "I do, sometimes. Only now I dream about Rupert, dying, alone in the darkness."

"Rupert can take care of himself," said the dragon.

Julia sniffed. "You could have fooled me."

"Do you love him, Julia?"

Julia stared out the open stable door. "Looks like the rain's finally going off."

"You haven't answered my question."

"I know."

"Humans," said the dragon, and chuckled wryly. "If you care for him, why not tell him?"

"Because he's not here! He went off and left me behind!"

"He could hardly take you with him into danger, could he?"

"He could have if he'd wanted to! I'm as good with a sword as he is! Anything would have been better than leaving me here. He's not coming back, dragon; I know it. The demons finally got him, and I wasn't there to help him . . ." Julia pressed her face against the dragon's side, and let the tears come.

The dragon lifted a wing and wrapped it gently around her, holding her close until the tears finally slowed and stopped.

"You're tired," he said softly. "Why don't you go back to your rooms and rest?"

"I don't want to go back to my room," Julia said to the dragon's side. "I'm afraid of the dark. Of the demons."

"Then stay here with me. Sleep. You'll be safe here, I promise you."

"Thank you," said Julia, so quietly only a dragon could have heard her. She settled herself against his side, riding his slow breathing, and soon she was asleep.

"Humans," said the dragon, affectionately. He lowered his great head onto his tail, and waited patiently, watchfully, for the night to pass.

CHAPTER FIVE

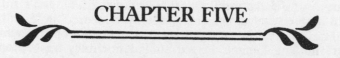

The Dark Tower

Deep in the Darkwood, in the hidden heart of the unending night, there lay a clearing. Far above, the inward-leaning trees bowed down to darkness, mingling and intertwining their gnarled misshapen branches until the bower was safely protected from the light of day. Phosphorescent lichens spotted the tree trunks, spreading a dull, eerie blue light. Fungi and oily mosses carpeted the clearing floor, in the middle of which stood a single, rotting tree stump, roughly fashioned into the shape of a throne. And in that darkness, on that corrupt throne, the Demon Prince.

In his way, the Demon Prince seemed human. He resembled a man, but his features were blurred, his delicate fingers ended in claws, and his burning crimson eyes showed no trace of human thoughts or feelings. He looked like a man because it amused him to do so. Once he had looked like something else, and might again, but for now he lived in the world of men. If *lived* could be applied to a creature that was never born.

Even seated, he was obviously unnaturally tall, and slender to the point of emaciation. His pale flesh had a lambent pearly gleam, and he dressed in rags and tatters of purest black. He wore a battered, wide-brimmed hat, pulled down low over the eyes, and as he sat upon his throne like some terrible carrion crow, he gnawed lazily at something that still feebly kicked and squealed. The Demon Prince had no need to eat but he liked to kill, and was compelled by his nature to terrify.

Surrounding the rotting throne, filling the clearing like so many crooked shadows, lay the demons of the Darkwood, abasing themselves before their Lord. They sat or crouched or lay upon their bellies in the dirt, watching if they had eyes, listening if they had ears, or just . . . waiting. They were of the dark, and the dark was patient.

A glowing silver sphere suddenly appeared before the throne, shimmering and pulsating as it floated on the stinking air. The Demon Prince smiled horribly, fresh blood trickling down his chin, and threw aside his meal. Two demons squabbled briefly over the remains. The Dark Lord beckoned languidly to the glowing sphere, and it drifted closer.

"Master," said a quiet voice from the sphere, and the Demon Prince grinned bloodily.

"Yes, my dear traitor; I await your report." His voice was soft, sibilant and subtly grating on the ear.

"Prince Rupert and his party approach the boundary of your Kingdom, Master. They intend to pass through the long night on their way to the Dark Tower. You must stop them before they reach the High Warlock . . ."

"He is of no consequence," said the Demon Prince amusedly. "No man can stand against the dark. Or perhaps you think otherwise?"

He slowly closed one hand into a fist, and agonized screams echoed from the sphere. The waiting demons shifted uneasily, disturbed at any threat of violence from their Lord. The Demon Prince opened his hand, and the screams died away, to be replaced by labored, tortured breathing.

"I'm sorry, Master, I . . ."

"You forget your place, my dear traitor. Once, you sought power over me, but now your body and soul are mine, to do with as I please. Fail me, and I will transform you into the least of my demons. Obey me in all things, and all the kingdoms of the world shall be yours . . ."

"Yes, Master. I am your most faithful servant."

"You are my slave." The Demon Prince rested his chin on his bony hand and stared thoughtfully at the floating sphere. The wide-brimmed hat plunged his face into shadow, an impenetrable darkness in which only his burning eyes still showed. "Well, traitor, do you have the Curtana?"

"Yes, Master. It's safely hidden, here in the Castle."

The Dark Lord chuckled quietly, and the demons stirred.

"You have done well, dear traitor. Without that sword, they have no hope against me. I have the touchstone. I have the unicorn's horn. I have my pretty demons. And now, after all the many centuries, the Blue Moon rises, and my time comes around again."

"But what of the High Warlock, Master?"

The Demon Prince closed his hand, and again screams rang from the sphere. "For all his learning, and for all his power, the Warlock is just a man. I have faced such men before, and broken them at my pleasure."

He slowly opened his hand, and the screams stopped. For a time, the only sound in the clearing was the heavy, ragged breathing from the sphere. The Demon Prince smiled.

"Return to my work, slave. Be my eyes and ears at Court. Be my darkness in the heart of their light."

The sphere shimmered and was gone, and once again darkness lay across the clearing, broken only by the dim blue glow of the phosphorescent lichens. The Dark Lord stared out over his waiting demons, and laughed softly.

"Soon," he promised them. "Soon . . ."

Prince Rupert reined the unicorn to a halt, and stared grimly at the Darkwood boundary before him. Darkness hung on the air like a curtain, marking the new beginning of the long night. Rupert shivered, and pulled his cloak tightly about him. Lowering clouds hid the midday sun, and the bitter wind was thick with sleet. The air was tainted with the smell of corruption, and the surrounding trees were gaunt and twisted, withered and malformed by the approaching night. Their dessicated bark was flecked and mottled with a dozen kinds of lichen and mold, and dead leaves choked the ancient trail.

Behind him, Rupert could hear his guards shifting nervously as they got their first good look at the Darkwood. He frowned, and gestured for the Champion to join him. The sooner he led his guards into the long night, the better— before the darkness destroyed what little confidence they still had. Rupert glared through the driving sleet, unable to tear his gaze away from the rotting trees that bordered the Darkwood. He could feel his hands shaking, and the smell of his own sweat was strong in his nostrils. He'd hoped this journey would be easier. He'd already survived the darkness twice. He had a troop of guards to back him up. But still his breath caught in his throat, and his heart hammered against his breastbone. His hands closed tightly on the unicorn's reins until his knuckles showed white, and he shook his head quickly to clear it. He was going back into the Darkwood come what may, and this time he'd leave the demons a sign to mark his passing they'd never forget.

The Champion guided his armored war horse in beside the unicorn, and nodded briefly to Rupert. "So this is the Darkwood," he said slowly, a strange excitement stirring in his cold dark eyes. "It's everything you said, Sire, and more. It's like a nightmare thrust into the day, a pathway to Hell itself."

Rupert raised an eyebrow as he turned to face the Champion. "Are you telling me you've never seen the Darkwood before?"

"I'm afraid so, Sire. As Champion, my duties have always kept me close to the Castle, and the Darkwood hasn't been a real threat to the Forest for centuries; the Tanglewood saw to that. I've read all the reports, of course, but . . ."

"Yes," said Rupert. "I know."

The Champion studied him closely, as though seeing him for the first time. "And you braved that darkness twice. No wonder you came back changed." He turned away before Rupert could comment, and brought out a leather map from one of his saddle panniers. Rupert waited impatiently while the Champion unrolled the map, and then he leaned over to point out their position.

"You can see for yourself, sir Champion; we have to go through the Darkwood. There's no other way. Head East, and we come up against the Starshade Mountains; West, and we'll have to cross the Brightwater rapids. Either route will cost us weeks of travel we can't afford. But, if our intelligence reports are right, the Darkwood's spread pretty thinly here. We should be able to punch our way through and out the other side in two or three hours, if we're lucky."

"And if we're not lucky, Sire?"

"Then we won't make it at all," said Rupert evenly.

The Champion grinned suddenly, and turned to study the darkness waiting before them. "Has it occurred to you, Sire, that the Darkwood may have been left deliberately thin, as a temptation to travellers?"

"Oh sure," said Rupert. "It's almost certainly a trap. That's why speed is so important; we have to get in and out before the demons even know we're there."

The Champion shrugged resignedly, and rolled up the map. "A pity. I was hoping I'd get the chance to try my steel against a demon or two."

Rupert rubbed briefly at the thick scars that marked the right side of his face. "It's an overrated pastime. If the demons find us, sir Champion, we're as good as dead. All of us."

"I'm sure they seemed fierce enough when you had to face them alone, Sire, but . . ."

"You didn't understand the Darkwood until you saw it," said Rupert harshly. "You won't understand the demons until you've seen them gather in the darkness. Now get the men ready to move off; we've wasted enough time talking. I'm not sure how the horses will react to the long night, so to begin with everybody walks, leading their horses on a short rein. Light every lantern and oil lamp we've got, and strap them to the guards' saddles. From the moment we enter the Darkwood, every man carries his sword and buckler at the ready, but our only real defense against the darkness will be the light we bring in with us."

"Don't you think you're being a little overcautious, Sire?"

"No."

"Very well, Sire. Which path do we follow through the Darkwood?"

"According to all the legends there's only ever been one path, and that's miles away. No, sir Champion; we hack our way into the Darkwood, and cut out a path for ourselves as we go. It shouldn't be too difficult; those trees are rotten to the core."

The Champion studied him narrowly. "If there are any demons nearby, they'll be bound to hear us, Sire."

Rupert shrugged. "I've tried stealth, sir Champion. It doesn't work. Our only hope is speed."

The Champion nodded impassively, thrust the map back into his pannier, and moved away to give the guards their orders. Rupert turned his attention back to the Darkwood boundary, and then had to look away. The darkness brought back too many memories. He looked instead at his guards, already dismounted from their horses and searching for flint and steel to light their lanterns. The men seemed calm enough, but the horses were nervous. They stamped their hooves and tossed their heads, their snorting breath steaming on the chill air. They seemed fascinated by the darkness, but rolled their eyes wildly if any guard tried to lead them closer to the boundary. Rupert frowned, and called to the guards to wrap cloaks or blankets round the horses' heads, to keep the animals from panicking when they were led into the Darkwood.

The guards nodded respectfully, and moved quickly to obey. Seeing the Darkwood close up had impressed the hell out of them, and knowing that Rupert had already been through it twice and survived suddenly meant a great deal more to them than it had. Rupert smiled grimly. The guards might see him as some kind of expert, but he knew better. He swung down out of the saddle and strolled casually among them, talking quietly and calmly, and answering what questions he could about the Darkwood. His answers weren't exactly reassuring, but the guards listened carefully to everything he said, laughed politely at his jokes, and without actually saying anything themselves, made it very clear that they appreciated his not lying to them about the dangers ahead. Several of the men clapped him on the back, and told him they'd had worse leaders. Rupert went back to his unicorn with tears stinging his eyes. He'd never been more proud of his men, or felt less worthy to lead them.

Finally everything was ready, and Rupert leaned against the unicorn's shoulder as he looked his guards over one last time. Lamps and lanterns hung from every saddle, glowing palely in the daylight. Smoke drifted on the air from half a dozen torches. Swords gleamed dully in every guardsman's hand. The horses stirred restlessly, disturbed by the Darkwood's stench, but the thick cloth around their heads kept them manageable. Rupert bit his lip thoughtfully, checking for anything he might have forgotten. Provisions wouldn't be a problem this trip, but he'd had the guards fill their canteens from the nearby brook, just in case. Rupert sighed. Everything that needed to be done had been done. Anything else would just be an excuse, to help him put off the moment when he'd have to go back into the Darkness again. The darkness that had laid its mark upon him.

He shook his head angrily, and looked to the Champion, who stood waiting patiently at the Darkwood boundary, his huge double-headed war axe in his hands. The two massive blades flashed brightly as the Champion hefted the axe. He looked at Rupert inquiringly, and grinned when Rupert nodded curtly. The Champion took a firm grip on the axe's oaken shaft and turned to face the darkness. For a moment he hesitated and then, with one swift movement, he raised the axe above his head and brought it savagely down on the first Darkwood tree. The steel blade sank deep into the rotting wood, and the stench of corruption was suddenly worse. The Champion jerked the axe free and struck again, shearing clean through the tree. The trunk was hollow, eaten away from within. The Champion worked on, swinging the giant war axe effortlessly, and then he stepped forward into the Darkwood, and the darkness swallowed him. The sound of his axe cutting into rotten wood could still be heard, but only faintly, as though from far away. Rupert gestured to the first half-dozen guards, and they set about widening the new path into the darkness.

Rupert watched uneasily as their swords rose and fell in a steady rhythm, cutting quickly through the decaying wood. The scars of his face ached fiercely, throbbing to the rhythm of the swordblows. He didn't have to go back into the darkness. He could still change his mind, and go the long way around. Rupert clenched his hands until the nails dug painfully into his palms. He'd beaten the Darkwood before; he could beat it again. He had to. If only because his men trusted him to get them through safely. He realized he was holding the unicorn's reins too tightly, and slowly relaxed his hands.

"Rupert," said the unicorn quietly, "Are you sure this is a good idea?"

"No," said Rupert. "If you've got a better one, let's hear it."

The unicorn sniffed, and tossed his head. "I'm just the transport; who listens to me?"

"Don't start that again," said Rupert wearily. "You're my friend, and right now I need all the help I can get. If there was any other way to reach the Dark Tower in time, I'd take it. Do you think I want to go back into the darkness?"

"No," said the unicorn softly. "I know you don't. I don't want to, either."

"We don't have any choice," said Rupert, his voice not as

firm as he would have liked. "If the Blue Moon rises before we get back, there'll be nowhere to get back to. The High Warlock may be our last chance to stop the long night."

"The rainbow sword . . ."

"Saved us once. It can't help us again. I tried to call a Rainbow back in the Coppertown mine, when I was being chased by that creature. Nothing happened."

"Hardly surprising," said the unicorn. "How's a Rainbow supposed to get to you when you're hidden away down in the depths of a mine?"

"I thought of that," said Rupert tiredly. "I've tried to summon the Rainbow a dozen times since, but nothing's ever happened. What magic there was in the sword is gone."

"Great," said the unicorn. "Just great. I notice you didn't mention this before we got to the Darkwood."

"Must have slipped my mind," said Rupert innocently.

The unicorn snorted, and kicked at the muddy trail with his hoof. "No dragon, no rainbow sword, and we're going back into the darkness. We must be mad. Ah well; if nothing else, maybe we'll find the demon that thieved my horn. I feel naked without it."

"You're always naked," said Rupert.

"You can go off people, you know," said the unicorn.

Rupert chuckled briefly, and then looked up as one of the guards called to him. They'd finished widening the path. Rupert took a deep breath, let it go slowly, and led his unicorn and his men into the Darkwood.

Night slammed down as Rupert crossed the boundary. The wind and the sleet couldn't follow him, but the darkness was even colder; an icy chill that sank into his bones and gnawed at them, until it seemed he'd never feel warm again. As more and more guards crossed the boundary into the Darkwood, their lamps and lanterns helped push the darkness back, and Rupert began to breathe more easily. Not far ahead, the Champion and his guards pressed steadily forward in their own little pool of light, slowly and methodically opening up a new trail into the Darkwood. Rupert hefted his sword and stared about him, but the dim lamplight couldn't penetrate far into the endless gloom. Gnarled misshapen trees glowed golden under the light, and every now and again a twisted branch would stir slightly, though no wind blew in the long night.

"How are you feeling?" asked the unicorn quietly.

"Lousy," said Rupert. "I keep feeling we're being watched."

"We probably are."

"You're a great comfort. Can you see anything out there?"

"No."

Rupert scowled unhappily. "They know we're here. I can feel it. It's just a matter of time . . . With luck, we'll be out of here in an hour."

The unicorn snorted. "Since when have we ever been lucky?"

Cutting the path was slow, hard work, and as the company pressed deeper into the Darkwood, their pace soon slowed to a crawl. The guardsmen crowded together, glancing uneasily about them as the dark brooding oppression of the long night sank slowly into their souls. Their usual joking and horseplay soon vanished, replaced by a wary, watchful silence.

Rupert changed the trail cutters as soon as they showed signs of tiring, but there was a limit to how fast the guards could fell and drag aside the closely packed trees. The sound of steel cutting into rotten wood was eerily loud on the quiet, but still there was no sign of the demons. The waiting wore at Rupert's nerves, and it was all he could do to stop himself jumping at every sudden sound or movement. The slow march continued, and he began to worry that the candles in the lanterns wouldn't last the journey. He tried to figure out how much oil there was left for the lamps, and then bit his lip when he remembered he'd used most of it to burn the creature from the Coppertown pit. He swore softly, and checked the candle in his own lantern. Less than an inch of stub remained; half an hour, at most. Rupert frowned. Perhaps that was the demons' plan; wait until the company lost its light, and then attack under cover of the darkness. Rupert called for the men to stop and rest, and moved over to join the Champion.

"I really don't think it's wise to stop, Sire," said the Champion quietly.

"We're using too much light," said Rupert shortly. "Either we cut back now, or we'll finish our journey in darkness."

The Champion nodded thoughtfully. "I'll order the lamps doused. The lanterns can give us what light we need. When they're exhausted we'll switch back to the lamps." He looked at Rupert warningly. "The men won't like it, Sire."

"They'll like the dark less," said Rupert. "Anything's better than the dark."

The Champion looked into Rupert's haunted eyes, and looked away. "I'll give the order, Sire."

He turned away and moved quietly among the guards, and one by one the lamps went out, and the darkness pressed close around the shrinking pool of light. Several of the men stirred restlessly, and a few glanced angrily at Rupert, but nobody said anything. Rupert was too tired and too worried to give a damn. After a while, the Champion came back to stand beside him.

"We have a problem, Sire. We've lost seven men since we entered the Darkwood."

For a moment Rupert just looked at him, not understanding, and then his blood went cold, rushing through him like a chill wind. "Seven? Are you sure?"

The Champion nodded grimly. "There's no trace of the men, their horses, or their equipment; no sign to show they were ever with us. They were taken quietly, one at a time, and nobody heard or saw a thing."

Rupert swore harshly, and kicked at the dusty ground. If the demons had found them already . . . "From now on the men work in pairs; one cuts trail while the other guards his back. There can't be more than a handful of demons out there, or they'd have attacked us openly by now. It'll take them time to summon more. If we can move fast enough, we might get out of here alive yet."

"With no sky or stars to guide us, we can't be sure we're cutting a straight path," said the Champion slowly. "Press ahead too quickly, and we could end up travelling in circles."

Rupert looked back the way they'd come. The sparse light showed only a few feet of the trail they'd cut. He shrugged angrily. "Sir Champion; the way we're spread out we'd soon notice a bad curve in the trail, and we're not going to be in the Darkwood long enough for a subtle curve to make much difference."

And so the company moved on into the long night. The dark pressed close around them, muffling all sound and dimming the light they moved in. One by one the candle-stubs in the lanterns guttered and went out, and were replaced by oil lamps, and still the company cut their way through the decaying trees, with never a sign to show they were any nearer to the Darkwood's far boundary. They lost no more men to the dark, but still Rupert could feel the pressure of watching eyes on his back. The scars on his face throbbed with remembered pain, and only his pride kept him from peering constantly into the darkness. His lantern guttered, and he scrabbled in his backpack for an oil lamp. And then everything hit them at once.

The earth boiled and writhed beneath the company's feet as dozens of corpse-white arms thrust up out of the ground and snatched at the guardsmen's legs, pulling them down to what lay waiting in the burrows under the earth. Long sticky strands of blood-red gossamer uncoiled from high in the rotting trees and lashed down to wrap themselves around the bewildered guards, dragging them with a horrid ease back up into the far branches of the trees, where the lamplight couldn't reach. Blood ran down the treetrunks, and the guards' screams carried clearly on the still air until they were suddenly cut off. Small scurrying creatures poured out of the darkness in their hundreds and swarmed all over the screaming horses, eating them alive.

Rupert and the Champion stood back-to-back, killing anything that came within reach of their weapons. Out of the corner of his eye, Rupert could see the unicorn rearing up again and again, shaking off the swarming creatures and pulping them under his flailing hooves. In the space of a few moments, a dozen guardsmen had been snatched from the trail, but even as Rupert howled his anger the trail before him erupted as a blood-spattered guard fought his way back out of the burrows. More guards followed him, and one dropped down from the branches overhead, looking eagerly around for something else to kill.

Dark twisted shapes came running and leaping out of the darkness, falling on the guards with fang and claw and glaring hungry eyes. The guards formed a defensive ring around the few surviving horses and the unicorn, and slowly fought the creatures back. Swords and axes gleamed brightly in the lamplight as they rose and fell. Blood flew through the air and ran thickly on the ground. Rupert swung his sword double-handed, grunting and growling with the effort of his blows. For every creature that fell before him, another rose to take its place, and Rupert grinned savagely as he cut them down. The darkness had finally given him an enemy he could fight, an enemy that could be faced and defeated. Rupert and the Champion and the guards strove against an enemy that outnumbered them ten to one, and still they wouldn't give in to the dark. They stood their ground and fought side-by-side, and suddenly the creatures of the dark gave way before them, and faded back into the concealing shadows from which they'd come.

Rupert slowly lowered his sword and looked warily about him. No arms reached up from under the earth, no strands hung down from the trees, and the surrounding dark was still and silent. Scores of the little scurrying creatures lay crushed and broken on the ground, but all the horses were dead, including the Champion's war horse. Its armor hadn't been much protection after all. The Champion knelt beside his fallen steed and patted its shoulder gently, as though apologizing. Rupert looked quickly around for the unicorn, who moved slowly over to join him. Angry scratches bloodied the animal's flanks, but otherwise he seemed largely unhurt. Rupert sighed wearily, and leaned against the unicorn's side a moment before turning around to inspect his guards. Of the forty-six men who'd followed him into the Darkwood, only thirty remained. He'd lost seven men while cutting trail, and nine more during the battle. Rupert swore quietly and glared disgustedly at the blood-spattered sword in his hand. Another Rainbow might have saved his men, but the rainbow sword was just a sword, while the Darkwood was still dark.

The Champion came and stood beside him, leaning casually on his war axe. "It seems I was wrong, Rupert; demons do hunt in packs after all."

Rupert smiled tiredly. "Nine men, sir Champion. We've lost nine more men."

"We were lucky not to have lost a damned sight more. What are our chances of making a break for it?"

"Pretty low. We can't be far from the boundary, but the demons would be on us before we could cut another foot of trail."

"We could retreat back down the trail . . ."

The Champion's voice fell away as demons moved forward out of the dark to crouch at the edge of the lamplight.

Hundreds of the twisted creatures surrounded the company, and hundreds more moved unseen in the darkness beyond the narrow pool of light. The faint scurrying and slithering sounds carried clearly on the still air as the demon horde gathered.

"They've been waiting for us," said Rupert bitterly. "They must have spotted us the moment we entered the Darkwood. We never had a chance of reaching the far boundary. We came all this way for nothing."

"You've faced the demons before, and beaten them," said the Champion.

"I had a magic sword then," said Rupert. "I don't have it any more."

"Then we'll just have to do it the hard way." The Champion laughed quietly, and hefted his war axe. "Stand ready, guardsmen; this is where we earn our pay."

"If we win, I want a raise," said one of the guards, and the others chuckled briefly. Rupert wanted to laugh with them, but couldn't. They were his men, and he'd failed them. He'd promised them a chance to save the Forest Land, and instead he'd led them to their deaths. He looked around at his guards, waiting patiently for his orders, and felt a fierce surge of pride for them. They'd taken the worst the Darkwood could send against them and thrown it back, and now they stood ready to do it again, even though they were hopelessly outnumbered.

Rupert grinned suddenly, proud tears stinging his eyes. Whatever happened next wasn't important. The dark had tried to break him and his men, and the dark had failed, and in the end that was all that really mattered. Rupert looked out at the watching bloodred eyes, and laughed. For all their vast weight of numbers, the demons were still scared to come into the lamplight; they preferred to wait until the light ran out before attacking again. And then Rupert's laughter broke off short as an idea struck him, an idea so obvious he could have kicked himself for not thinking of it earlier.

"The lamps!" he yelled joyously, whirling on the startled Champion, "The bloody oil lamps! That's our way out! Guards; take the oil cannisters and spread a circle of oil around us. Use the reserves first, but if that's not enough start emptying lamps until it is. Well don't just stand there; move it! We do have a chance, after all!"

The guards jumped to obey. Beyond the lamplight the demons stirred restlessly, and Rupert grinned so hard his jaws hurt.

"Get the idea, sir Champion? All we have to do is wait for the demons to attack, and then set light to the oil. The Darkwood trees might not burn, but the demons will. It won't stop them for long, but it should hold them back while we cut our way out of here. We can't be that far from the boundary."

"It's not much of a chance," said the Champion carefully.

"I know," Rupert admitted cheerfully, "But at least it's a fighting chance."

And then the demons surged forward out of the dark. Rupert yelled to the guards, and a dozen torches dipped into the oil. Bright yellow flames roared up, throwing back the dark. The first demons to reach the blazing oil plunged straight into the flames and were consumed in a moment, and behind them came more demons, throwing themselves at the leaping flames like moths at a lantern. They began to smother the fire by the sheer number of their bodies, and more creatures of the dark used the charred bodies of the fallen as stepping-stones from which to hurl themselves at Prince Rupert and his company. *A nice try,* thought Rupert resignedly as he cut down the first demon to reach him, *but not good enough.* He realized he was going to die, and was vaguely surprised to find he felt more annoyed than anything. There were so many things he'd intended to do, and now never would. He'd never even told Julia that he loved her. He could feel her favor beneath his jerkin, pressing lightly against his heart. The demons came swarming out of the darkness, and Rupert raised his sword and stepped forward to meet them.

But even as the demons pressed eagerly forward, the flames leapt suddenly higher. The oil had reached the surrounding trees, which caught alight and blazed like torches. Rupert backed away from the searing heat, and his men moved back with him. The demons slowed to a halt, confused and uncertain. Rupert stepped back another pace, and a blinding light filled his eyes. For a moment he thought the flames had overtaken him, but all around him he could hear his men crying out in joy and relief. Rupert knuckled at his watering eyes and laughed breathlessly. They were safe. They'd reached the boundary of the Darkwood.

His sight quickly returned. It was late afternoon, shading into evening. Rupert looked blankly at the sinking sun. When he'd led his company into the Darkwood, it had been barely midday.

Time moves differently in the Darkwood.

Rupert swallowed dryly, and watched the last of his guards stumble out of the darkness and into the light. The demons didn't follow. Rupert couldn't see past the Darkwood boundary, but he knew the demons were there, watching. He turned his back on them and grinned at his men, and only then did he realize how small his company of guards had become. He counted them slowly. Twenty-five. Twenty-five men out of fifty. Rupert looked away. He felt sick.

"Don't take it so hard," said the Champion.

"Why not?" said Rupert bitterly. "Half my men are dead. Some leader I turned out to be."

"You've not done so badly. Given the odds we faced, it's a wonder any of us survived. If it hadn't been for your quick thinking, we'd all have been dead long before we could reach the boundary. All right, you lost half your men, but you saved the other half. No man could have done more. All in all, I'm quite pleased with you, Rupert. I'll make a Prince of you yet."

Rupert looked at the Champion warily. "I'm just a second son, remember?"

"I remember," said the Champion. He turned away to stare at the Darkwood boundary. "We can't hope to fight our way back through the darkness, but there isn't time to go round it. One way or another, we have to convince the High Warlock to return with us."

Rupert nodded tiredly. "Get the men ready to move out, sir Champion. One more mile, and then perhaps we can rest for a while."

"Rest?" said the Champion. "At the Dark Tower?"

"Right," said the unicorn, moving in beside them. "From what I've heard of this Warlock, we might have been safer in the Darkwood. Just how powerful is the High Warlock anyway?"

"Hopefully, powerful enough to stop the demons in their tracks and banish the darkness," said Rupert.

"But how far can we trust him?"

"About as far as you can spit into the wind."

"Great," said the unicorn. "Absolutely bloody wonderful. Why don't we just all kill ourselves now, and get it over with quickly?"

"Come on," said Rupert affectionately, taking the unicorn's reins in his hands. "You'll feel better once we're moving."

"Don't put money on it," growled the unicorn. "I have a bad feeling about this."

Rupert shrugged. "Legends don't impress me as much as they used to. The High Warlock left the Court when I was very young, but I can still remember the wonderful fireworks he made for my fifth birthday party. The rockets that flared against the night, and the catherine wheels that looked like they'd spin forever. He told me stories, and tried to teach me card tricks. You were at Court even then, sir Champion; you must have known him. What was he really like?"

The Champion hefted his war axe, his eyes cold and distant.

"He was a traitor, Sire. A traitor, a coward, and a drunk."

Rupert stumbled doggedly on through the freezing slush, head down to keep the sleet out of his eyes. The wind howled around him, tugging at his hood and cloak and buffeting him from every side. Rupert growled and cursed and hung on tightly to the unicorn's reins. Every third step he looked at his right hand to make sure the reins were still there. The cold had taken all the feeling from his fingers, despite his thick gloves, and he didn't want to get separated from the unicorn. Rupert slowly raised his head and peered slit-eyed into the rising storm. There was still no sign of the Dark Tower.

And last month it was still summer, he thought disgustedly. *What the hell's happened to the weather?*

He staggered and almost fell as the raging wind changed direction yet again, and the unicorn moved in close to try and shield him from the worst of the storm. Rupert patted the unicorn's neck gratefully, and glared into the swirling snow. He was worried about the unicorn. The animal was moving more and more slowly as the cold seeped into his bones, and even wrapping him in blankets hadn't helped much. Icy crystals glistened in his mane and tail, and his harsh breathing was becoming as unsteady as his footing. Rupert knew that if they didn't find shelter soon, cold and exhaustion would take their toll, and the unicorn would just lie down in the snow and die.

The storm had fallen on Rupert and his company only a few minutes after they'd left the Darkwood behind them. Dark clouds had gathered as they watched, and the chill evening air grew bitter cold. Rain fell in torrents, quickly turning to sleet as the company pressed on into the rising storm. The wind rose, howling and raging, and still Rupert led his men on. He hadn't come this far just to be beaten by the weather.

He stamped his feet down hard with every step, trying to drive a little warmth into them. The snow fell thickly, filling the air. It was cold, and getting colder. Every now and then Rupert caught a brief glimpse of the bloodred sun, hanging low on the sky, and tried to force himself to move faster. Once the sun had dipped below the horizon, the demons would be loose in the Land. He looked back over his shoulder. His guards were trudging steadily after him, huddling together to share their body warmth. The Champion walked by himself, as always. Hoarfrost had covered his armor in silver flurries, but of all the company the cold seemed to affect him the least. His back was straight, his head erect, and his massive legs carried him tirelessly on through the deepening snowdrifts. Rupert frowned. He ought to have found the sight inspiring, but somehow he didn't. There was something almost inhuman about the Champion's calm refusal to bend to the wind. Rupert looked away, and stared back the way they'd come. The wind dropped suddenly, and the snow parted, taunting him with a brief glimpse of the Darkwood, covering the horizon like a monstrous shadow. Rupert scowled, and turned his back on it.

And then the storm stopped. Rupert staggered on a few paces, before stumbling to a halt. He slowly raised his head and looked around him, the sudden silence ringing in his ears. The grass at his feet was summer green, untouched by sleet or snow. The sky was the deep blue of the summer evening, and the air was still and calm. He was standing at the edge of a wide clearing, bounded on all sides by a solid wall of flying snow. And one-by-one, as Rupert watched, his guardsmen stumbled out of the snow and into the summer, leaving the cold behind them. Rupert sank wearily down onto the soft grass, and stretched out his legs before him. Pins and needles savaged his hands and feet as the circulation slowly returned.

"Sanctuary," he said slowly. "We've found sanctuary, unicorn."

"I wouldn't be so sure of that," said the unicorn. "Look over there."

Rupert followed the unicorn's gaze. In the center of the clearing, atop a small hillock, stood a tower. Some forty feet tall, it was built entirely from a dark gray stone, battered and eroded by the passage of time. Ivy crawled across the stonework, and hung like curtains over the shuttered windows.

"The Dark Tower," said the Champion quietly. "I always imagined it would be taller."

Rupert looked up, startled, and then scrambled to his feet and glared at the Champion. "Will you stop sneaking up on me like that! My nerves are bad enough as it is."

"Sorry, Sire," said the Champion calmly.

One of these days . . . , thought Rupert, and then shook his head resignedly. "All right, sir Champion; get the men settled, and check we haven't lost anyone to the storm. I'll tell the High Warlock we're here."

The Champion bowed slightly, and moved away to take charge of the small knot of guardsmen, who were warily studying the Dark Tower with their swords in their hands. Rupert smiled grimly; he knew exactly how they felt. He pushed back his hood, and beat the snow from his cloak. He eased his sword in its scabbard, and sighed softly. He was just putting off the moment when he'd have to face the High Warlock, and he knew it. He also knew he daren't put it off any longer. The evening was still pleasantly warm in the clearing, but the light was fading fast. While there was obviously some kind of magic holding back the storm, there was no guarantee it was strong enough to keep the demons out once night fell. He had to get his men safely under cover, and there was only one way to do that. Rupert sighed again, pushed back his cloak so that it wouldn't get in the way of his sword hand, and started slowly up the slight incline that led to the Dark Tower.

"Watch your back," called the unicorn quietly, and then lowered his head to crop tiredly at the thick grass.

Rupert circled the tower twice, but although he counted no less than seventeen of the shuttered windows, there was no sign of any door. The windows themselves varied from less than a foot in width to over a yard, the lowest of them set into the brickwork a good five or six feet from the base of the tower. Rupert stopped in front of one of the lower-set windows, and frowned thoughtfully. The High Warlock had always been somewhat . . . eccentric.

Not to mention drunken and bad-tempered. During his many years at the Forest Castle, the High Warlock's excesses had been almost as legendary as his magic. His main interests had always been wine and women, not necessarily in that order, and an uncomfortably high regard for the truth, none of which had endeared him to Castle Society. When King John finally exiled the High Warlock, everyone for miles around breathed a heartfelt sigh of relief and stopped locking up their daughters and their wine cellars. Rupert bit his lip, scowling. For as long as he could remember, no one had ever talked openly about why the High Warlock had been exiled. He'd been a resident at Court since Eduard's time, and had been a tutor to King John; apart from Thomas Grey, the Warlock had always been the King's most honored adviser. And then Queen Eleanor died.

Within the hour, the High Warlock had gathered his few possessions and ridden off into the Forest. As soon as he heard, King John summoned his Court and read the Edict of Banishment upon the Warlock. Tears of anger and despair streamed down the King's face as he formally denied the High Warlock food or water, friendship or lodging, within the boundaries of the Forest Land. It wasn't long before travellers brought the news that the High Warlock had settled in an old border tower, on the far side of the Forest. Rupert could still remember the look on his father's face when the Champion had finally confirmed the news. At the time he'd been too young to understand the emotion he'd seen so clearly, but looking back, he now recognized it as helpless rage. The Warlock had defied the Edict, and there was nothing the King could do about it. He did try, for his pride's sake.

He summoned magicians to him from the Sorcerers' Academy, but all their spells and curses came to nothing against the High Warlock's power. He sent a troop of guards to tear down the Warlock's tower. They never came back. And so, finally, the King turned to other matters, and the Warlock was left to himself. Time passed, and dark tales grew about the Dark Tower, and the magics the High Warlock practiced there. But though there were many tales, there were few facts, and as the long years passed and the Warlock never left his tower, he gradually faded out of history and into legend, becoming just another boogeyman with which harried mothers could frighten their children into obedience.

He was a traitor. He was a traitor, a coward, and a drunk.

Soft footsteps sounded behind him, and he dropped his hand to his swordhilt as he looked quickly round. The Champion stared past Rupert at the Tower, and smiled coldly.

"Snakes have their holes, rats have their nests, and the Warlock is still in his Tower. He never did care much for the light of day. Have you found the door, Sire?"

"There doesn't seem to be one, sir Champion."

The Champion raised an eyebrow, and then leaned forward and knocked loudly on the shutters of the nearest window. For a long moment nothing happened, and then the shutters flew open to reveal a gray-haired old man dressed in sorcerer's black. He glared impartially at Rupert and the Champion, yelled "Go away!" and slammed the shutters in their faces. Rupert and the Champion exchanged glances.

"We're going to be polite," said Rupert determinedly. "We can't afford to be left stranded out here when night falls. Try again."

The Champion nodded, and knocked on the shutters. "Please come out, sir Warlock, we need to talk to you."

"No!" came the muffled reply.

"If you don't come out, we'll come in and get you," said the Champion calmly.

"You and what army?"

"Us and this army."

The shutters flew open again and the High Warlock looked past Rupert and the Champion at the twenty-five guards gathered together at the foot of the tower's hillock. Rupert glanced back at his men, trying to see them as the Warlock would. Their armor was battered and bloodied, but they hefted their swords with a grim competence. They looked tired, disreputable, and extremely menacing; more like bandits than guardsmen. The Warlock sniffed, and fixed the Champion with his gaze.

"This your army?"

"Yes."

"Get them off my lawns or they're all frogs."

The Warlock slammed the shutters again. Rupert turned to the Champion.

"Now what do we do?"

"Well," said the Champion, thoughtfully, "First, we get the army off his lawns."

Rupert glared at the Champion's departing back. There were times when he wondered just whose side the Champion was on. He sighed, turned reluctantly back to the closed shutters, and tapped on them politely.

"Sir Warlock? Are you still there?"

There was no answer, and the shutters remained firmly closed. *Oh great,* thought Rupert disgustedly, *we've upset him now.* He looked back at his men. Under the Champion's orders, they'd sheathed their swords and moved away from the tower. They were now standing at parade rest and trying hard to look harmless. They weren't being noticeably successful. Rupert glanced up at the darkening sky, and his frown deepened into a scowl. Night was almost upon them. Already the air was growing colder, and it seemed to Rupert that the swirling wall of snow was just a little closer to the Dark Tower than it had been. He hammered on the shutters with his fist, but still there was no reply. Rupert swore harshly. He was damned if he'd let his men face the dark again while there was shelter at hand. He studied the closed shutters thoughtfully. They didn't look all that strong. He grinned suddenly, and carefully inserted his sword between the two shutters. It was a tight fit at first, but Rupert leaned on the sword and it slid gradually in until the crosshilt stopped it. He waited a moment, listening, but there was no reaction from the Warlock. *Probably stomped off in a huff,* thought Rupert hopefully. *He always did have a rotten temper.* Rupert hesitated, remembering the transformed messenger who now guarded the Castle Moat, and then shook his head fiercely. His men needed shelter.

He grasped the swordhilt firmly with both hands, and

slowly leaned his weight against it. He knew he dare not put too much pressure on the blade in case it snapped, but try as he might, the shutter wouldn't give. Rupert glanced up at the evening sky. The last of the light was fading away. He glared disgustedly at the shutters, and threw his full weight against the swordhilt. The right-hand shutter flew suddenly open, and Rupert fell flat on his face. He lay still on the thick grass, his heart beating frantically, but long moments passed and there was no reaction from inside the tower. He scrambled to his feet, hanging grimly onto his sword, and looked cautiously through the open window.

The room was a mess. Crude wooden tables and benches lined the walls, all but buried under assorted alchemical equipment. Glass retorts and earthenware beakers covered every available surface, including the bare earth floor. Half the room was taken up by a battery of stacked animal cages, each filled to bursting with its own noisy occupants. There were birds and monkeys, rats and salamanders, and even a few piglets. The smell was appalling. A large wrought-iron brazier squatted commandingly in the middle of the room, its coals still glowing redly. And everywhere, scattered throughout the room, a forest of interconnected glass tubing that sprawled across the wooden tables, crawled along the walls, and spread its roots and tendrils wherever it could force a space.

There was no sign of the High Warlock. Rupert sheathed his sword and pulled himself up onto the narrow windowsill. He glared down at the crowded table-top below him, and carefully lowered himself into the largest gap he could find. He winced as glass cracked and shattered under his boots, and jumped hastily down onto the floor. The room seemed much bigger from the inside. It was easily thirty feet in diameter, and brightly lit by a single glowing sphere hanging unsupported on the air, just below the high-raftered ceiling. Rupert frowned. From the size of the room, it had to be the entire first floor of the tower, but there didn't seem to be any way of reaching the other floors. There was a trapdoor in the ceiling, but no obvious way of getting on it. He shrugged, and moved cautiously round the room, fascinated by the various magical paraphernalia. The caged animals studied him curiously as he passed, and one sad-eyed old monkey reached out to him past the bars of its cage, as though mutely beseeching Rupert's help. He smiled guiltily at the monkey, and moved on. A clear liquid pulsed continuously through the glass tubing, occasionally emptying out into carefully positioned beakers. Rupert leaned forward to sniff at one, and then stopped as his foot kicked against something on the floor. He stooped down and picked it up. It was a human skull, with the lower jaw missing. Rupert put it down on the nearest bench, and dropped his hand to his swordhilt.

"I don't recall inviting you in," said a mild voice above him, and Rupert's heart jumped as he looked up at the ceiling. A sturdy rope ladder hung down from the open trapdoor, and as Rupert watched open-mouthed, the High Warlock climbed agilely down to join him. Seen close up, the Warlock wasn't particularly impressive. He was a short man, his head barely coming up to Rupert's chest, and his black sorcerer's garb only accentuated his bony, slender frame. Deep lines etched his narrow face, and his eyes were vague. "What are you doing here?" he asked Rupert pleasantly. "And why are all those soldiers cluttering up my view?"

"We need your help," said Rupert cautiously. The Warlock seemed to have entirely forgotten his previous bad temper, and Rupert didn't want to upset him again. "The Darkwood . . ."

"Terrible place," said the Warlock. "It's so dark." A glass of white wine appeared in his hand from nowhere. "Care for a drop?"

"Not right now, thank you," said Rupert politely.

"It's good stuff," insisted the Warlock. "I brew it myself." He waved his free hand at the glass tubing, and then leaned forward confidentially. "I put a dead rat in every new barrel, to give it a little body."

Rupert decided not to think about that. "We can talk about the wine later, sir Warlock; right now, I need your help."

The Warlock smiled crookedly. "Do you know who I am, young man?"

"You're the High Warlock," said Rupert. "The last hope of the Forest Land."

The Warlock looked at Rupert sharply, all the vagueness gone from his eyes. "Don't you people ever learn? I don't give a damn about the Forest Land. Your whole stinking little Kingdom can rot in Hell for all I care! Now get out of here! Get out of my home and leave me in peace, damn you."

"That's no way to speak to your Prince," said a cold voice from behind Rupert. He looked quickly around, and was relieved to find the massive figure of the Champion filling the open window. The Warlock glared at the Champion, and then all the strength seemed to run out of him. He lifted his wine glass to his lips, but it was empty. His mouth worked, and he threw the glass away.

"Why can't you leave me alone?" he whispered. "Just go away and leave me alone."

"If it was up to me," said the Champion, climbing carefully down from the windowsill, "I'd leave you to hide in your hole until hell froze over. Unfortunately, the King needs you."

"I'm not going back," said the High Warlock flatly. "And there's not a damn thing you can say that will change my mind. There's nothing to call me back to the Forest. Nothing at all." He stopped suddenly, and for the first time looked closely at Rupert. "The Champion said you were a Prince. Are you really one of John's boys?"

"I'm Rupert. The youngest son."

"Of course; Rupert. I thought you looked familiar." The Warlock's face softened. "You look a lot like your mother."

"I have twenty-five men outside," said Rupert. "Will you give them shelter from the night?"

"They're safe enough out there," said the Warlock. "No demons can pass my wards. Your men can camp outside tonight, and leave in the morning. Of course, you're welcome to stay here, Rupert. It's been a long time since I last saw you."

"Twenty-one years," said the Champion. "Twenty-one years since you turned traitor."

"I'm not a traitor! I was never a traitor!" Bright crimson spots burned on the Warlock's cheeks as he stepped forward to glare up at the Champion, his hands clenched into fists. "I left because I chose to! For more than forty-five years I watched over the Forest Kings, keeping the Land from harm. I was John's protector when you were still learning which end of a sword to hold! Why I finally decided to leave

is my business, not yours. I gave forty-five years of my life
to the Forest Land; you've no right to ask any more of me."

"Take a good look, Sire," said the Champion calmly.
"There was a time, long ago, when this drunken old fool
was a hero. The most powerful magician the Forest Land
had ever known. His deeds are legendary. There are dozens
of songs about him; you probably know some of them.
There were even those who said he had the makings of a
Sorcerer Supreme. But somewhere along the line, he decided to throw it all away. He turned his back on his duty,
and frittered away his magic on fireworks, illusions, and
pretty baubles for the ladies. He could have inspired a
generation, but he preferred to spend his time getting drunk
and chasing the tavern whores. The High Warlock of legend; a coward and a renegade who betrayed his King when
his King most needed him."

"It wasn't like that!" screamed the Warlock. "You bastard, it wasn't like that at all!"

The Champion laughed. The Warlock howled wordlessly
with rage, and a pure white flame roared from his outstretched hand, smashing into the Champion's chest and
throwing him back onto the crowded table top under the
window. Glass tubing shattered as the Champion crashed
into it and lay still. Blood ran from his nose and mouth. The
nearby animals screamed shrilly, and ran to and fro in their
cages. The Champion stirred, and reached for his sword.
The Warlock gestured again, and crackling white flames
sprang from his fingertips to press the Champion back against
the tower wall. Rupert drew his sword and started forward.
The Warlock blasted him off his feet without even looking
around. Rupert tried to get up, and couldn't. All he could
do was watch helplessly as the Warlock's balefire slowly
lifted the Champion from the table and pinned him to the
wall a good twenty feet above the floor.

"I never liked you," said the Warlock. "You and your
precious duty. You don't know the meaning of the word!
What did duty ever mean to you, except as an excuse to kill
people? Well, there's no King to protect you now, sir Champion. I've waited a long time for this . . . ."

Rupert looked frantically around for his sword. Already
the Champion's chain mail was glowing cherry red under the
relentless heat of the balefire. Individual links sagged and

ran away in tiny rivers of molten steel. Rupert finally spotted his sword, lying just out of reach under a nearby table. He gritted his teeth and dragged himself forward inch by inch until he could reach the blade. His head still buzzed angrily from the knock it had taken during the fall, but he could feel his strength rushing back as he wrapped his hand round the familiar swordhilt. He grabbed the table edge and pulled himself to his feet. The High Warlock had his back to him, intent on his victim. The Champion's eyes were closed, and he didn't seem to be breathing. Rupert staggered forward and set the point of his sword against the Warlock's back.

"Let him down," he said harshly. "Let him down, now."

"Go to hell," said the Warlock. "No man calls me a traitor and lives."

"I'm your Prince," said Rupert. "In my father's name, I order you to release his Champion."

The balefire vanished, and the Champion floated slowly down to a gentle landing on the table top below. Rupert pushed the Warlock aside, and ran forward to examine the Champion. His chain mail had melted and fused together, and the leather jerkin beneath had been charred and consumed by the intense heat, but the bare flesh under the gaping hole was completely unharmed. The Champion's breathing was calm and even, and already he showed signs of returning consciousness. Rupert turned to stare at the High Warlock, who shrugged uncomfortably.

"A simple healing spell. He'll be all right in a while."

"Would you really have killed him if I hadn't stopped you?"

"Probably not," said the Warlock. "I always was too soft-hearted for my own good. Not to mention extremely loyal to your father. You fight dirty, Rupert."

"Of course; I'm a Prince."

They shared a crooked smile. Two glasses of white wine appeared in the Warlock's hands. He offered one to Rupert, who accepted gratefully. After all he'd been through, he felt he deserved a drink. He took a good sip, and raised an appreciative eyebrow.

"Not a bad vintage, sir Warlock."

The High Warlock smiled modestly. "One of my more useful spells. Now, Prince Rupert; what brings you to the Dark Tower after all these years?"

"The Darkwood," said Rupert. "It's spreading. We think the Demon Prince has returned."

The Warlock stared into his glass. "Damn," he said quietly. "Oh, damn. How fast is it spreading?"

"Half a mile a day, when we left. Of course, with the Blue Moon rising . . ."

"Wait a minute, wait a minute!" The High Warlock closed his eyes briefly, as though in pain. "Are you sure about the Blue Moon?"

Rupert stared at him. "Haven't you looked at the moon lately?"

"I haven't been outside this tower in twenty-one years," said the Warlock. "I've never felt the need."

He gestured with his free hand, and he and Rupert rose slowly into the air until they were on a level with the open window. Outside, night had fallen. Stars shone brightly against the dark, and the waiting guardsmen had built themselves a fire, but the main light came from the three-quarter full moon. It hung fat and swollen on the night, its lambent flesh mottled with thick blue veins. The Warlock stared, horrified, at the tainted moon. Clearly shaken and confused, it was some time before he could tear his gaze away and turn to look at Rupert.

"I didn't know," whispered the Warlock. "I should have known, but I didn't. What else have I missed?"

He frowned worriedly as he and Rupert sank gently back to the floor. "I'm sorry, Prince Rupert; I seem to have lost touch with what's been going on in the world. Has it really been twenty-one years? Where did all the time go? Ah well; that's what being a drunken hermit does for you. I suppose your father sent you to bring me back to Court? Yes, I thought so. Typical of the man. Wait until things have got completely out of hand, and then dump the whole damn mess in my lap and expect me to work miracles. So help me, if it wasn't my neck as well I'd just sit back and let him stew in his own juices. Unfortunately I can't do that, and he knows it. Despite all I may have said and done, the Forest is my home, and I can't turn my back on it. It'll be strange, going back to my old quarters in the Castle, after all these years. I hope they've been redecorated; I never did like the color scheme. I take it John has lifted the Edict of Banishment?"

"Of course," said Rupert, glad to get a word in at last. "He needs you, sir Warlock."

The High Warlock grinned suddenly. "And I'll bet that sticks in his craw something horrible! Aye, well, I suppose we'd better get a move on; it's a fair way back to the Forest Castle. The sooner we make a start, the better."

"You want to leave now?" said Rupert. "While it's still night? We wouldn't make it to the Darkwood! Sir Warlock, my men are in no condition to fight demons. They must have time to rest, and regain their strength."

"Not to worry," said the Warlock airily, "We won't have to go back through the Darkwood; I know a shortcut."

Rupert gave him a hard look, and then froze as a cold angry growl came from somewhere behind him. Rupert spun round sword in hand, and then dropped into his fighting stance, as with a clatter and a crash the Champion jumped down from the table the Warlock had left him on. His face was flushed with rage, but his eyes were cold and dark. He smiled grimly, hefted his sword once, and advanced slowly towards the High Warlock.

"You're a dead man, sorcerer," said the Champion. "You should have killed me while you had the chance."

"Oh, hell," said the Warlock tiredly. "I'd forgotten about him. Would you care to explain the situation to him, Rupert; or shall I turn him into something less aggressive? Like a dormouse."

"He'll listen to me," said Rupert quickly. The Warlock shrugged, and wandered off to talk to the animals in their cages. The Champion started after him, and Rupert moved hastily forward to block his way. "Sheath your sword, sir Champion. The High Warlock has agreed to help us against the Darkwood."

"Get out of my way, Rupert."

"We need his magic."

"He tried to kill me!"

"Yes," said Rupert slowly. "If I hadn't stopped him, I think he probably would have killed you. But even if he had, and you lay dead and cold at my feet, I'd still bargain with him. He's our only hope against the darkness, the only chance for survival the Forest has. And that makes him more important than you or I will ever be. So sheath your sword, sir Champion. That's an order."

The Champion growled something under his breath, sheathed his sword, and glared at the Warlock, who was rummaging through the clutter on one of the far tables and muttering to himself.

"The High Warlock was an old man when I first came to Court," said the Champion. "He'd have to be in his nineties by now. How do we know he's up to helping us against the Darkwood?"

"I'm not," said the Warlock, without looking around. "But I will be. Ah, that's the one." He picked up a wooden beaker, sipped cautiously at the frothing liquid it contained, and pulled a face. "One of these days I'm going to have to work on the taste."

He glowered at the beaker, and then drained it in several hasty gulps. He then slammed the beaker down on the table, screwed up his face and bent suddenly forward, clutching at his chest. Rupert ran over to the Warlock and grabbed his shoulders as he collapsed against the table, shivering and shaking. Rupert winced as he helped support the Warlock's weight; there was nothing left of the man but skin and bone. And then Rupert felt his hackles rise as the Warlock's flesh writhed under his hands. He snatched his hands away, watching disbelievingly as new bands of muscle swelled and crawled over the Warlock's bony frame. His shoulders widened and his back slowly straightened, the vertebrae cracking and popping like wet logs in the fire. Rivulets of black ran swiftly through the thickening gray hair. The Warlock sighed deeply and straightened up, and Rupert watched in awe as the Warlock tugged casually at his beard until it came away in his hands, revealing fresh baby-smooth skin glowing with health. A thick mane of jet black hair fell to his shoulders, and all that remained of his beard was a rakish black moustache. His back was straight, his frame was muscular, and all in all he looked no more than thirty years old at most. He grinned broadly at Rupert.

"Not much use being able to transform things if you can't do it to yourself as well, eh, lad?"

Rupert nodded speechlessly.

"Now then," said the Warlock briskly, "I suppose you're here about the Darkwood."

"We already told you that," said Rupert.

"Did you? My memory isn't what it was. I really should

do something about that, but I keep forgetting. Anyway, our main problem isn't the Darkwood; it's the Demon Prince."

"We figured that out for ourselves," said Rupert.

The Warlock fixed him with a steady glare. "Interrupt me again and you're an aardvark. Got it?"

Rupert nodded silently. He wasn't altogether sure what an aardvark was, but he had a definite feeling he wouldn't enjoy finding out first-hand.

"The Demon Prince," said the High Warlock thoughtfully. "Evil that walks in the shape of man; the never-born, the soulless. One of the Transient Beings, the stalkers on the edge of reality. His power increases as the Blue Moon rises, but if we can get to him before the Moon is full . . . before the Wild Magic is loosed in the Land . . ." The Warlock's voice trailed away, and his shoulders slumped. He suddenly looked very tired, despite his new youthfulness. "Listen to me; I'm talking as though we actually stood a chance against the Demon Prince. Even at my peak, I was never that good. And I'm a long way from my peak. My power stems from the High Magic, but the Darkwood is of the old, Wild Magic."

"What's the difference?" asked Rupert.

The High Warlock smiled grimly. "The High Magic can be controlled; the Wild Magic owes no allegiance to anything save itself." He stopped suddenly and shrugged, frowning. "Ah hell, I don't know; there's always the Infernal Devices in the Castle Armory. They might make a difference."

For the first time, Rupert realized that, when it came to the Darkwood, the mighty and awesome High Warlock was just as scared and uncertain as he was. "You show me a way to fight the darkness, and I'll follow you anywhere," he said impulsively. "Even if it means going back into the Darkwood."

The Warlock looked at him, and then grinned suddenly. "Practical, aren't you?"

Rupert grinned back. "I've had good teachers."

"All right," said the Warlock decisively, "Let's give it a try. Who knows; we might get lucky."

"Can we go now?" said the Champion. "We've little enough time as it is."

"Oh sure," said the Warlock amiably. He glanced at Rupert. "Race you to the window?"

"Wait a minute," said Rupert. "Just out of curiosity, sir Warlock; why aren't there any doors?"

"Windows are easier to defend," said the Warlock craftily. "And besides; I never needed a door, till now. I never went out." He paused to peer wistfully around the crowded room. "What a mess. I always meant to get organized one day, but I just never got around to it. I suppose I'd better put the animals into hibernation before I go. Kinder than . . . ah well. It's all for the best, I suppose."

He sniffed and shrugged, and walked toward the nearest window. "You know, Rupert; I should never have left the Sorcerers' Academy. I was quite happy there, changing gold into lead."

"Shouldn't that be lead into gold?" asked Rupert.

"Why do you think I had to leave?" said the High Warlock.

The wall of swirling snow pressed close around the Dark Tower, and the still night air was bitter cold. A fresh silver frost covered all the grass and sparkled on the ancient brickwork of the Tower. The Warlock was leaving, summer was over, and already the bleak midwinter laid claim to the land so long denied it. Every now and again, Rupert glimpsed strange dark shapes moving purposefully through the howling blizzard, watching and waiting for the High Warlock to step outside the protection of his remaining shields. Rupert scowled, and rested one hand on the pommel of his sword. His guards were tired, battered and bloodied from their trip through the Darkwood, and now he had to ask them to do it again. The Warlock had said something about a shortcut, a way to avoid the long night, but Rupert knew better. The maps were clear enough. There was only one route that would get his people back to Forest Castle before the Full Moon, and that was the way they'd come. Through the Darkwood.

"I'm hungry," said the unicorn.

"You're always hungry," said Rupert. "How can you think of food at a time like this?"

"Practice," said the unicorn. "What are we waiting for now? I hate hanging around like this."

"Well, not to worry. We'll be heading back into the Darkwood soon enough."

"On second thought, let's hang around here for a while."

Rupert laughed briefly, and patted the unicorn's neck. "It shouldn't be so bad this time; we'll have the High Warlock with us." He looked up and saw the sorcerer approaching. The Warlock was drinking wine and singing a bawdy song. The unicorn studied him carefully.

"This is the High Warlock? Our great hope against the Demon Prince?"

"Yes."

"Then we're in big trouble."

"Shut up," growled Rupert, and moved quickly forward to greet the Warlock.

"Ah, Rupert," said the Warlock vaguely, draining his goblet. "Are your men ready to leave?"

"Yes, sir Warlock. They're good men; you can rely on them to protect your back once we enter the Darkwood."

"I'm sure I could," said the Warlock. "But luckily that won't be necessary. We're not going back through the Darkwood. I'm going to transport us straight to the Forest Castle."

Rupert's heart sank. His mouth was suddenly very dry. "That's your shortcut? A teleport spell?"

"Got it in one, dear boy."

Rupert tried hard to hold on to his rising temper. "Possibly I'm mistaken, sir Warlock, but as I understand it, there are an awful lot of things that can go wrong with teleport spells."

"Oh, hundreds of things," said the Warlock. "That's why nobody uses them any more. Except in emergencies."

"Sir Warlock," said Rupert slowly, "I did not lead my men clean across the Forest Kingdom and through the long night itself, just to throw their lives away on a sorcerer's whim! Look at you; the state you're in, they'd be safer facing the demons."

The Warlock looked at him steadily. "Prince Rupert; if there was any other way to reach the Castle in time, I'd take it. But there isn't. A teleport's our only chance."

"A teleport could get us all killed! Look, if it was just me and my men, I'd risk it, but I can't allow you to put your life at risk. You're the last hope of the Forest Land, sir Warlock; with you gone, there'd be no one left to stand against the darkness."

"Don't rely on me," said the Warlock. "That's a good

way to get killed." His voice was soft and tired and very bitter. "I've lived too long with myself to harbor any illusions, Rupert. I'm nowhere near as powerful as I used to be, and I never was as powerful as the legends had it. I could have been, but I threw it all away on wine and women, just like the Champion said. I make no apologies; I had my reasons. Good ones. But don't be under any illusions about my magic. I can't just snap my fingers and make the Demon Prince disappear. What magic I have is at your disposal, along with whatever knowledge and low cunning my tired old mind still retains. If I can get us to the Castle in time, I think I can help. But I'm not indispensable to your fight, Rupert; I'm not that important anymore. I never was, really."

Rupert shook his head slowly. "I don't doubt your magic, sir Warlock; it's that goblet in your hand that worries me. Anybody can make a mistake when he's the worse for drink."

The Warlock smiled crookedly. "I'm not much of a sorcerer when I'm drunk, Rupert, but I'm worse when I'm sober. There are too many memories in my old head, too many unhappy memories. It's only the wine that keeps them quiet. The Champion was right, you know; I could have been a Sorcerer Supreme. I could have been a hero out of legend. Unfortunately, I just wasn't up to it. Not everybody is. When all is said and done, I'm not the stuff heroes are made of. I'm not particularly brave, or clever. I have a talent for magic, I've studied the Art all my life, but your family always expected so damn much from me! Every time some new magical menace appeared, they'd send me off to deal with it; never mind the risk to my life! Every ogre and demon and natural disaster . . . Eventually, I just got tired. Tired of the responsibility, the pressure, of being scared all the time. That's when I started drinking. It helped, at first. And still your family piled more and more responsibility on me, until finally I broke under the weight of it. Simple as that. And then I fell in love with a Lady who turned out not to care for me, and . . . well, it's a familiar enough story, I suppose.

"Look, Rupert; what I'm trying to say is . . . this is a kind of second chance for me. Don't ask me to stop drinking, because I can't. But if you'll trust me, I'll give you everything I've got. My word on it."

Rupert looked steadily at the High Warlock. All the sorcerer's new youthfulness couldn't disguise the tired, defeated set of his shoulders, but still he held his head high, his pride ready to stand or fall by whatever answer Rupert gave. The Prince smiled, and reached out to clap the Warlock lightly on the shoulder.

"Prepare the teleport spell," he said gruffly. "It'd be a long, hard struggle, fighting our way back through the Darkwood; I'd rather get my men home safely."

"Thank you, Sire," said the Warlock. "You won't regret this, I promise you."

Time passed, and the night wore on. The blue-tainted moon shone brightly down as the Warlock chivied the guardsmen into a small, compact crowd. At first, the guards hadn't been all that impressed by the Warlock, with his wine-stained robes and absentminded airs, but after seeing what the Warlock had done to the Champion's chain mail in a fit of pique, they suddenly developed a new respect for him. The Champion moved over to join Rupert and nodded at the High Warlock, who was sitting cross-legged in midair, staring at nothing.

"You mustn't go ahead with the teleport, Sire. We can't trust him."

"I've made my decision, sir Champion."

"He's a traitor and a drunkard. He . . ."

"Shut up!"

The Champion blinked in surprise, taken aback by Rupert's sudden anger.

"I don't want to hear another word from you," said Rupert quietly. "Go back to your men and stay there. That's an order."

The Champion looked at him steadily for a long moment, and then he bowed slightly and moved away to take his place among the guardsmen.

"Was that really necessary?" said the unicorn.

"Yes," said Rupert shortly.

"There are times," said the unicorn, "when you sound a lot like your brother."

The blizzard pressed closer, its solid wall of snow devouring the clearing inch by inch. The demons watched and waited in ever-increasing numbers, impervious to the unrelenting cold and the howling wind. Hoarfrost enveloped the

Dark Tower in an icy cocoon, and shimmered whitely on
the men's armor. Rupert's breath steamed on the freezing
air, and his bare face ached from the cold. A light snow
began to fall within the clearing. And then, finally, the high
Warlock dropped his feet to the earth and nodded briskly to
Rupert.

"Sorry about the delay, Sire; just checking the arrival
coordinates. Get the decimal point wrong, and we might all
appear several hundred feet above the ground. Or even
under it."

The guardsmen exchanged glances.

"Start the teleport," growled Rupert hurriedly, and the
Warlock nodded.

"Very well, Sire. If you and the unicorn would care to
stand just here, beside me . . . thank you. And now, we
begin."

He raised his arms in the stance of summoning, and his
gaze became fixed on something only he could see. For a
long moment, nothing happened. The Warlock's brow furrowed as he concentrated. Outside the clearing, the wind
raged and the storm intensified. And then the air within the
clearing seemed to dance and shimmer. A deep sonorous
tone shuddered through Rupert's bones, on a level almost
too deep for hearing. The ground shook beneath his feet.
Space itself ripped apart before the Warlock, revealing a
wide silvery tunnel that seemed to fall away forever. The
Warlock rose slowly into the air, and then, one by one,
Prince Rupert, the unicorn, the Champion and the guardsmen
left the ground behind them and followed the Warlock into
the tunnel.

The rip in space slammed together and was gone, with no
trace to show it had ever been there. The last of the Warlock's shields collapsed and fell apart, and the howling storm,
unfettered at last, swept forward to swirl helplessly around
the empty Dark Tower.

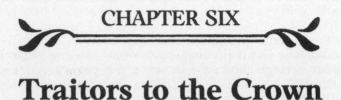

CHAPTER SIX

Traitors to the Crown

"But darling . . ."

"Get the hell away from me or I'll flatten you."

King John sighed tiredly. Harald and Julia were at it again. The King leaned back on his throne, and tried to pretend he couldn't hear the raised voices outside his Court. He had more than enough to worry about without having to deal with his potential daughter-in-law as well. A dozen petitioners from the outlying farms waited patiently before him, leaning tiredly on their great longbows, their home-spun clothes battered and begrimed with the dirt and dust of long days on the road. They'd arrived on foot little more than an hour ago, pounding determinedly on the closed Castle gates as night fell early across the Forest. On hearing the nature of the news they bore, King John had cursed softly to himself, and granted the farmers a private audience. And now they stood before him in the empty Court: tall, broad-shouldered men with sturdy muscular bodies formed by continuous backbreaking work from dawn to dusk. There was nothing soft or weak about the harsh planes of their faces, but in their haunted eyes the King saw a naked fear and desperation that chilled him to his bones.

"Julia, my sweet, if you'll only let me . . ."

There was the sound of fist meeting flesh, followed by a pained if somewhat muted howl from Harald. King John's mouth tightened angrily, and he gestured for one of his Royal Guard to approach the throne.

"Your majesty?"

"Take my compliments to my son Harald and the Princess

Julia, and tell them I will see them after this audience is
ended. You will further add that if I hear one more word
from either of them before that time, so help me I'll have
them chained together and cleaning out the Castle cess
pits!"

"Yes, your majesty," said the guard, and headed quickly
for the closed antechamber doors.

King John shook his head slowly, and turned back to the
waiting farmers. "Sorry about that; my eldest son's courting."

The farmers smiled and nodded, and seemed to relax a
little for the first time since entering the Court. King John
searched for something else to say that might help put the
farmers more at their ease. It was clear they needed to talk,
but none of them seemed to know where or how to start.
The King leaned forward, chosing his words with care, and
then the double doors slammed open as the Seneschal came
limping furiously into the Court, followed by a protesting
guardsman. The Seneschal glared him into silence, and then
advanced, still glowering, on the King.

"Dammit, your majesty, this time you've got to do
something!"

The King closed his eyes briefly, and wished wistfully that
he was somewhere else. Anywhere else.

"What is it this time, sir Seneschal?"

"It's those damned goblins again, what else?" The Seneschal lurched to a halt before the throne, nodded brusquely
to the mystified farmers, and then leaned heavily on his
walking stick and glared at the King. "You should never
have let those disgusting little creatures into the Castle,
Sire; they've been nothing but trouble since they got here. I
don't know what possessed Prince Rupert to send them to
us in the first place; I've known Barrow Down guttersnipes
that were more civilized! It took us three weeks to teach
them to use the toilets. And another three weeks to stop
them using the sinks. It's not as though they contributed
anything to the Castle's defenses; they can't fight worth a
damn, and they won't take orders from anyone except their
own leaders. They're passable scouts, when I can persuade
them to set foot outside the safety of the Castle walls, but
they will keep setting traps for the demons and then forgetting where they put them. You wouldn't believe how many

trackers we've lost that way. It's keeping the poachers on their toes, I'll admit, but that's not the point . . ."

"Sir Seneschal," said the King, cutting in firmly, "What exactly is your problem? What have the goblins done now?"

The Seneschal sniffed a couple of times in an embarrassed sort of way, and studied his shoes. "Well, Sire; for want of anything better to do with them, I put them in charge of manning the battlements. It seemed a good idea at the time, mainly on the grounds that anything which got them out of sight and out of mind had to be a good idea. I mean, what harm could they get up to on the damn battlements? I should have known better. You will be interested to learn, your majesty, that I have finally discovered why the kitchens are always short of cauldrons these days. It's because those damned goblins have been stealing them to mix their boiling oil in! We only just got to them in time to stop the little bastards from testing their latest batch by dropping it on the three Landsgraves as they rode in from their day's hunting!"

The King tried hard to look shocked, but a smile kept tugging at his mouth as he savored the thought of a cauldron of bubbling boiling oil being slowly tilted over the Landsgraves' unsuspecting heads . . . He finally hid his grin behind a raised hand, and had a quiet coughing fit.

"Were any of the noble Landsgraves injured?" he asked the Seneschal, when he felt he could trust his voice again.

"Well, not actually hurt, Sire, but if they hadn't been wearing cloaks and chain mail . . ."

Several of the farmers had a quiet coughing fit. It seemed the Landsgraves weren't that popular outside the Court, either. The King made a mental note to look into that; he could always use more allies against the Barons.

"I'm glad to hear no one was hurt," he said solemnly. "How did the Landsgraves take it?"

"You can ask them yourself, your majesty; they should be here any minute."

King John glared at his Seneschal. "Thanks for the advance warning. Round up the goblins, and send the lot of them out into the Forest. I need to know how fast the Darkwood is advancing, and the troop of guards I sent to find out hasn't come back. If nothing else, goblins do make excellent reconnaissance scouts. Mainly because they have a positive gift when it comes to hiding from anything even remotely threatening."

"Very good, Sire," said the Seneschal. "I'll send them on their way." He hesitated, and then glanced at the King. "They do mean well, your majesty, it's just . . ."

"Yes," said King John. "They are, aren't they."

The Seneschal grinned, bowed, and left. As he walked out, the three Landsgraves walked in. The two Royal Guardsmen glanced at each other, and then moved protectively closer to the throne, their hands ostentatiously near their swords. Ever since he'd been dragged senseless from the Court after his assassination attempt, Sir Bedivere had been careful to wear an empty scabbard at all times, but even so, there wasn't a guard in the Castle that trusted him an inch. Or the other two Landsgraves, for that matter.

Sir Bedivere, Sir Blays, and Sir Guillam marched silently forward, and the farmers gave way to them, stepping passively aside so that the Landsgraves could take their center position before the throne. They knew better than to protest to men who represented the Barons. Farmers might work the land, but the Barons owned it.

King John studied the three Landsgraves warily. There was a calm sureness about them that worried him. Still, when in doubt, attack. He leaned forward in his throne and glared coldly at Sir Blays.

"This is a private audience, sir Landsgrave. I have business with these men."

"The peasants can wait," said Sir Blays. "We have business with you."

"And what might that be?"

"Demons overrun the Barons' lands. What are you doing about it?"

King John scowled at the Landsgrave's bluntness, and struggled to keep his voice calm and even. "You know damn well what I'm doing; my guards are running themselves ragged fighting the demons, training peasant militias in those towns nearest the darkness, and helping to stockpile provisions in case of seige."

"While the Castle itself stands virtually unprotected," said Sir Blays sardonically.

King John smiled sardonically. "There's always the goblins, my dear Landsgrave. I'm told they're very good with boiling oil."

Sir Blays stiffened angrily, and Sir Guillam laid a restraining hand on his arm. The two Landsgraves stared at each other; Sir Guillam shook his head slightly, and Sir Blays subsided.

Now that is interesting, thought the King. *I always knew there was more to Guillam than met the eye.* He glanced quickly at Sir Bedivere, who was staring off into the distance as though nothing that had been said was of any interest to him. *Probably it isn't,* thought the King sourly. *He's just a killing machine, waiting for his next set of orders. But who gives those orders; Blays or Guillam?* He stared at the timid little man standing passively before him, and tugged pensively at his beard. Why had the Barons sent Sir Guillam? He wasn't a diplomat, like Sir Blays, and he certainly hadn't the makings of an assassin. He claimed to be an accountant, but so far he'd made no attempt to inspect the Castle's finances. Not that the King would have let him, of course . . .

King John frowned uncertainly. If the Landsgraves hadn't come to complain about the goblins, what the hell were they here for? And why were they so interested in his guards? The King sighed quietly. Now that the Astrologer was no longer on hand to advise him, it seemed he'd have to keep digging for answers the hard way.

"Well, Sir Guillam," he said heavily, "Perhaps you'd care to tell me why you've chosen to interrupt this private audience. Sir Blays doesn't seem too sure."

Sir Guillam smiled politely. "There are . . . questions . . . which need to be answered, Sire."

"Such as?"

"Such as what's happened to the High Warlock." Sir Guillam smiled diffidently. "He does seem to be rather overdue. Months overdue, in fact."

"He'll be here."

"When?"

"How the hell should I know?"

"You don't seem too unhappy about his tardiness," said Sir Blays. "Anyone would think you didn't want him to come."

"Sir Blays," said the King slowly, "I don't care to be

interrogated in this manner. You know very well how I feel about the High Warlock; you were here the night I read the Edict of Banishment upon him. Now, my noble Landsgraves; it's been a long day, and I still have much to do. What exactly do you want from me?"

"We want action!" snapped Sir Blays. "Fine words and promises won't stop the Darkwood. I know I speak for my fellow Landsgraves when I say the Barons will not stand idly by and watch the Forest Land fall into ruin while you dither and prevaricate and do nothing!"

"I'm doing all I can!"

"It isn't enough," said Sir Bedivere. He stepped forward a pace, and the two guardsmen drew their swords. The huge Landsgrave ignored them, his eyes fixed on the King. "If you won't do what's necessary, there are others who will."

"That sounded like a threat," said the King evenly. "Perhaps you've forgotten what happened the last time you dared threaten me?"

"Ah yes." Sir Guillam smiled. "Where is Thomas Grey these days? Still hunting for the . . . lost . . . Curtana?"

"It won't find itself!" snapped the King. "The Astrologer's worked day and night, trying to discover who stole the Curtana from my Armory."

"Assuming it was stolen." Sir Blays stared mockingly at the King. "You slipped up there, your majesty. It was just a little too convenient that the Sword of Compulsion should vanish into thin air the moment the Armory was rediscovered, thus putting the Curtana beyond the reach, and control, of the Court."

"You tread dangerous ground, my noble Landsgrave."

Sir Blays and Sir Guillam smiled, and Sir Bedivere chuckled openly.

"When you took the Sword of Compulsion for yourself," said Sir Blays, "you lost all claim to our loyalty."

"We cannot accept such a threat to the Barons," said Sir Guillam diffidently. "We therefore demand, in their name, that you hand the Curtana over to us, for . . . safekeeping."

"You demand?" King John rose to his feet, shaking with anger. "You demand nothing in my Court! Now get out, or I'll have you whipped from my sight! Get out!"

Sir Bedivere laughed softly, and King John shuddered at the barely restrained madness in that laughter.

"You really shouldn't have done that," said the huge, smiling Landsgrave. "I'll have your heart's blood for this insult."

"You dare . . ."

"There's no Astrologer to protect you now, King John. All that stands between you and me are those two guards. And that isn't going to be enough. Give me your sword, Blays."

Sir Blays glanced at Sir Guillam, who hesitated, and then nodded quickly.

"You'd better get out of here, Sire," murmured one of the guardsmen. "We'll hold him as long as we can."

King John stared numbly at Sir Blays as he slowly drew his sword. "Why are you doing this, Blays? We've known each other more than thirty years . . ."

"Will you please get the hell out of here!" hissed the guardsman. "You must raise the alarm!"

"That won't be necessary," said a quiet voice. "The King has nothing to fear as long as we are with him."

There was the faint whisper of flexing wood, and the King and the three Landsgraves turned to stare dumbly at the farmers as they deftly fitted arrows to their longbows and held them at the ready.

"How dare you?" whispered Sir Guillam. "How dare you defy the Barons! I'll have your farms burned for this!"

The twelve farmers stared steadily back, their arrows strung and ready.

Sir Bedivere studied them impassively, and then held out his hand to Sir Blays. "Give me your sword. They're just peasants."

Sir Blays glanced at the farmers, taking in the cold implacability of their faces, and shook his head slowly.

"Give me your sword!"

"No," said Sir Blays, and he sheathed his sword. "There's no need for this."

For a moment King John thought Sir Bedivere would attack the farmers empty-handed, but Sir Guillam and Sir Blays held his arms and talked quietly and urgently to him, until the killing glare had faded from his eyes. He finally threw off their arms, glared once at the King, and then turned and left the Court. Sir Blays and Sir Guillam followed him out. At the doors, Sir Blays hesitated and looked back.

"You brought this on yourself, John," he said quietly, and then he was gone.

King John sank back into his throne, his heart still racing. There was a general relaxing of breath from the guards and the farmers as they sheathed their swords and put away their arrows, and they glanced at each other respectfully. The King smiled on them all, and inclined his head slightly.

"Thank you for your support, my friends. I shall not forget this."

He settled back in his throne, and rubbed slowly at his aching forehead, not really hearing the farmers' muttered replies. King John shook his head slowly. By losing his temper with the Landsgraves, he'd played right into their hands. The only reason for their visit had been to insult and humiliate him before the farmers; to make it clear to them who wielded the real power in the Forest Land these days. The King frowned worriedly. The Landsgraves had moved beyond treason and into open rebellion, secure in the belief that he wouldn't dare have them arrested for fear of starting a civil war. They might just be right, at that. He couldn't fight the invading demons without the Barons' support, and they knew it. The King swore silently to himself. There must have been some way he could have avoided all this, but without the Astrologer at his side to advise him . . .

He shook his head wearily. These days, the Astrologer was his only link with his widespread forces. His guards and militia were scattered all over the Land, fighting to hold back the dark. By using his magic, the Astrologer could get messages to the various troops much faster than any horseman or carrier pigeon. Unfortunately, there was so much communications work for the Astrologer that he had little time for anything else. Including searching for the Curtana.

In the meantime, events in the Land went from bad to worse. Until he had to cope by himself, King John hadn't realized how much he'd come to depend on his old friend. There were taxes to be set, tithes to be gathered; all the endless paperwork of running a Kingdom, that never stopped even when the Land was under seige. It had been bad enough when he'd just had to sign the damn stuff . . .

He'd managed to unload some of the more routine matters onto his Seneschal, but with the Darkwood pressing ever farther into the Forest, each new day brought more news of refugees on the march, fleeing the approaching darkness with whatever possessions they could carry on their backs. Horses were in short supply, and the guards had commandeered all carts to carry what little of the harvest had been gathered in. The long strung-out trails of homeless people were sitting targets for looters, outlaws, and demons. Guardsmen protected the main roads as best they could, but there just weren't enough men to go around.

In the towns, prices soared as food grew scarce. Guards had to be diverted from the roads to put down riots. No matter where the King sent his men, it never seemed to help. They were always too few, and too late. Even with his Astrologer and his Champion to help, it would have been a logician's nightmare, but without them, the King could only stand and watch as his Kingdom slowly tore itself apart.

He sighed, and gently massaged his aching temples. Some days his crown seemed heavier than others. How had he come to rely on the Astrologer so much? There was a time he'd had dozens of advisers and favorites to stand as a buffer between him and his Court, the Barons, and all the other troubles of his reign. But over the years all the ones he'd liked and trusted had either died, or fallen away, or been proven base and false, until now only his Astrologer and his Champion remained, to stand at his side and help him bear the weight of kingship. And neither of them were here now he needed them.

The sheer querulousness of that thought sobered him suddenly, and a cold rush of shame ran through him. The Astrologer was working himself into the ground keeping the communications moving, and the Champion had rode unhesitatingly into the Darkwood in search of the High Warlock. If they could do so much in defense of the Realm, how could he, as King, be expected to do any less? King John frowned, and beat gently on the arm of his throne with his fist. Rupert and the Champion were months overdue, and with every day that passed, the chances of their ever returning grew steadily less. As far as the Court was concerned, everyone on that ill-fated expedition was dead, and had been for some time. The King sighed quietly, and finally admitted to himself what he couldn't admit in public; that Rupert and the Champion wouldn't be coming back. The admission hurt him strangely. Deep down, he'd still somehow clung to the belief that the High Warlock would return from exile, and drive back the demons and the darkness with his sorcery, and all would be well again. It came hard to the King to realize he'd wasted so much hope on an empty dream.

"Your majesty?" said one of the guards uncertainly, and King John snapped out of his reverie to find the farmers' deputation still standing patiently before him. The King stared at them blankly, shocked at how long he'd kept them waiting while his mind wandered.

"I'm sorry," he said quickly. "The Castle migration began last week, and I have much on my mind. What exactly is it that you want from me?"

The farmers looked at each other, and finally one middle-aged man stepped forward from their midst to be their spokesman. He was plainly ill at ease in the grandeur of the Forest Court, and he didn't seem to know what to do with his hands, which were large and awkward and tattoed with ground-in dirt from working the earth all his days. But when he finally began to speak, the King forgot all these things, and saw only the simple dignity of a man weighed down with pain, yet still unbroken and unbowed.

"I am Madoc Thorne, of Birchwater demesne," said the farmer slowly. "I farm twelve acres, as my father did before me, and his father before him. The land is yet kind to my family, though we must work it hard and long to make our living, and still pay our taxes and our tithes. For nigh on seven generations my family has raised the corn and gathered it in, harvest after harvest. It was my intention to some day hand this on to my eldest son, as it was handed on to me, but I no longer have any sons. The plague has taken them from me."

King John shuddered suddenly, as though a cold wind had blown over his grave. "The tales are true, then. Plague has come to Birchwater."

"And passed beyond, Sire; spreading faster than a bushfire fanned by the wind. Through all the Birchwater demesne, there's not a town nor a village nor a hamlet that hasn't felt its touch. Four hundred dead, to my certain knowledge, and ten times that number lie trembling in their beds, wracked with pain as their fever slowly consumes them. Nothing helps; not prayer, nor medicines, nor magic. Men, women, and children are struck down without warning, and waste away to nothing as their families watch, helpless. Livestock fall in their byres, never to rise again. Corn stands rotting in the fields, blighted by the early Winter, because there is no one left to harvest it.

"I had four sons, your majesty; four fine sons who worked the land beside me. Good boys, all of them. So far, I've had to bury two of them, and their mother. The other two cannot leave their beds. By the time I return home, it seems likely I'll have to dig another grave. That's why we've come to you, Sire; because we couldn't sit at home and do nothing while the plague takes our families, wasting the flesh from their bones and twisting their limbs till they cry out from the pain of it.

"We're not young men, you and I, your majesty. We've seen hard times before, and know the hardest time passes eventually. But this time, if you cannot help us, I fear no one will be left to see its passing."

There was a long silence, as King John searched for something to say. The farmer had told his tale with a simple honesty that was almost brutal, sparing himself nothing to be sure the King understood what was happening in Birchwater. The King understood only too well. The plague had appeared out of nowhere less than a month ago, starting at the Darkwood's boundaries and then spreading outwards with ferocious speed. At first it was thought that rats carried the disease, and then blame fell upon the refugees, but as more and more deaths were reported in all corners of the Land, it soon became clear that there was only one possible source for the contagion; the demons were carrying it out of the Darkwood.

And now the plague had come to Birchwater, less than a week's travel from the Castle.

"I will send you priests and surgeons," said the King finally. "As yet they have no cure to offer, but they can perhaps ease the pain of a victim's passing. I can't guarantee how many will reach you; I no longer have enough men to safeguard the highways. The demons . . ."

"The demons! It's always the demons!" Madoc Thorne stared desperately at the King, tears of rage and despair starting to his eyes. "Without a cure, what use are priests and surgeons to us? Send us men, Sire; men who can fight, and will teach us to fight. If we can't defend our homes from the plague, we can at least defend them from the demons that carry it. A bow can only do so much! I know the Barons have always forbidden us from training in the sword and the axe, but it's our only chance to stop the plague and turn it back!"

King John looked at his hands, so that he wouldn't have to look at the farmers. How could he tell them that all their long journey, all their sacrifices, had been for nothing? He sighed briefly, quietly, and lifted his great leonine head. He sought for some comforting words with which to cushion his answer, but as he met the farmers' hopeful eyes, he knew he couldn't lie to them.

"My friends; I cannot help you. I have no men to send you, either to guard your fields or train you in the arts of war. The Barons no longer heed me; what men they have, they will not relinquish. I've had to strip this Castle of guards just to keep the main highways open. I have no shortage of weapons; you are welcome to as many as you can carry, but I cannot spare one man to go with you."

The farmers stared at the King, and then at each other.

"Is that it?" said one of the youngest farmers, moving forward to stand beside Madoc Thorne. "We came all this way, fighting off outlaws and footpads and creatures of the dark, leaving our families and our farms unprotected, just to hear you say there's nothing you can do?"

"I'm sorry," said King John.

The young farmer started forward, his fists clenched, but Thorne grabbed him by the arm and held him back. "That's enough! Leave the King be; he's said his piece. He could have lied to us, told us everything'd be all right, but he didn't. He told us the truth. We may not like it, but at least now we know where we stand."

"Aye," said the young farmer. "We know that." And he turned away, so that no one could see he was crying.

Thorne let him go, and stared awkwardly at the King. "He meant no offense, Sire. He hasn't been himself since he lost his wife and both his babies to the demons."

"I'd help you if I could," said the King.

"We know that," said Madoc Thorne. "Sorry to have troubled you, your majesty; it's clear enough you've worries other than ours. If you could have your men sort out a few weapons for us, we'll head back to Birchwater come the morning."

"Of course," said the King. "I'll detail some guards to escort you the first few miles."

"No, thanks," said the farmer politely. "Reckon we can manage on our own."

He bowed his head briefly, and then he turned and left the Court. And one by one the farmers bowed to their King, and followed their spokesman out. King John sat on his throne and bowed to each farmer in turn, and the naked pity in their eyes as they looked on him hurt worse than anything they could have said. They had fought their way through the darkness to reach him, they had defended him against the Landsgraves, but when they turned to him for help, he had none to offer them. He had failed them, but they forgave him, because he was their King. And, troubled as they were, there was still room in their hearts for pity at what he had become; a tired old man who couldn't cope. One by one, the farmers left the Court, and the King watched them go, knowing that with the morning's first light they would be on their way back into the Forest, going home to die with their families. The last man closed the doors quietly behind him, but the sound echoed on the silent Court as though he'd slammed them.

"Your majesty," said one of the guards, and the King waved him to silence.

"Go after the farmers," he said brusquely. "Both of you. Find them quarters for the night, and have the Seneschal issue them whatever weapons they choose. Then find the Commander of the Royal Guard, and tell him I want to see him. Tell my son I'll see him and Julia when I'm ready, and not before. Now get after those farmers. Move!"

The guardsmen bowed quickly, and left the Court in silence.

King John leaned back in this throne, and stared out over his empty Court. Outside, night had fallen, and darkness pressed against the stained-glass windows. The many-candled chandeliers spread a golden glow across the Court, and a roaring fire blazed in the huge fireplace, but still the shadows gathered up among the rafters, and there was a chill to the night air that would take more than a simple fire to dispel. The King stared grimly about him, trying to see his

Court as it must have looked to the farmers. A quiet horror filled him as, for the first time in a long time, he saw the Court as it was, instead of how it used to be. The timbered floor hadn't been waxed in months, the portraits and tapestries were blackened and begrimed by smoke from the fire, and even the marble dais upon which his throne stood was cracked and chipped. And under all the superficial evidences of neglect, there was also a feeling of age, of something whose time had passed. The Forest Court had been ancient when King John first came to the throne, but never before had it seemed so faded and shabby to his eyes. As with so many other things, it had fallen apart gradually, over the years, and he just hadn't noticed.

How has it all come to this? thought the King, picking at the ragged ermine collar of his cloak. He'd always done his best for the Kingdom, done everything that was required of him. He'd made a good marriage, and they'd been happy together, until illness had taken her from him, twenty-one long years ago. King John sighed wearily, remembering. That had been his first real lesson in Kingship. It had seemed such a simple thing at first; a chill; after a summer swim. And then the chill became a fever, and the fever became something worse. At the end she lay in her bed, her face gaunt from all the weight she'd lost, her head rolling back and forth on the sweat-soaked pillow. Again and again she coughed bright red blood, in long painful spasms that wracked her frail body. All through the long days and longer nights, King John sat by her bed and held her hand, but she didn't even know he was there. The greatest surgeons and priests and magicians had come at his call, but none of them could save her, and at the last, for all his power, the King could only sit beside the bed and watch the one he loved slowly die.

King John sat on his throne, and looked out over his empty Court. He'd done his best. Fought the Kingdom's battles, defended the Land against its enemies, and all for what? To sit alone in a dusty, echoing Hall, and know his best hadn't been good enough.

Out in the antechamber, Harald and Julia glared at each other and argued in whispers while they waited for the King's summons.

"Look, Julia; you're going to marry me, and that's that. It's all been arranged."

"Then you can damn well unarrange it."

"The contract's been signed."

"Not by me."

"Your signature isn't necessary," said Harald calmly. "Neither is your consent."

He ducked at the last moment, and Julia's fist just brushed his hair in passing. Harald took the precaution of stepping back a pace while the Princess regained her balance. Being around Julia was doing more for his combat reflexes than all the Champion's years of training put together.

"Julia, we've been through all this before. This marriage is going to take place no matter how we feel about it. Why not just accept it, and make the best of things?"

Julia glared at him. "Look, Harald, I'm going to say this once and once only, so listen carefully. I don't love you. I don't like you. I have about as much feeling for you as I have for what they shovel out of the stables every morning. I wouldn't marry you if the alternative was leprosy. Got it?"

"You'll learn to love me, after we're married," said Harald complacently. Julia kicked him in the shin. Harald hobbled up and down for a while, swearing under his breath so as not to upset his father. He'd learned to anticipate the punches, but the kicks were still getting through.

Julia turned her back on him and indulged in a quiet fume. Given her somewhat precarious standing in the Court, the last thing she needed was an open feud with the heir to the throne, but she just couldn't help herself. Any woman in the Court was Harald's for the asking, and he had to pick on her. She'd known rabbits that were less determinedly amorous. He brought her presents and paid her compliments and couldn't seem to understand why he wasn't getting anywhere. Julia had to admit that Harald could be pleasant company on occasion, but the persistence of the man was matched only by his infuriating assurance, and sometimes just the sight of Harald approaching was enough to set Julia's palm itching for the hilt of her sword. Her hand dropped automatically to her side, and caressed the pommel briefly.

It felt good to have Rupert's sword on her hip again. After her journey into the South Wing, she'd lost no time in throwing away her formal gowns and replacing them with a simple tunic and leggings. Fighting in that damn dress had nearly got her killed. If demons could get into the South Wing, no part of the Castle was safe any more. Julia wore a sword at all times now, and at night her scabbard hung from her bedpost, close at hand.

Strange, she thought sardonically, *when I was living with the dragon in his cave, all I ever dreamed of was being rescued by a dashing Prince who'd take me to live in his Castle. And what happened? I got rescued by the most undashing Prince I've ever known, and now that I'm at the Castle I can't wait to get out of it.*

"Sweetness . . ." said a plaintive voice behind her.

"Lay a hand on me and I'll tie your fingers in knots."

"I hadn't even considered it," said Harald earnestly, and Julia's mouth twitched. "Why don't you like me, Julia? Everyone else does."

Julia turned back to face him. "Harald, I don't love you. Can't you understand that?"

"People like us don't marry for love."

"I do."

"But I'm going to be King one day," said Harald, with the air of a man laying down his fourth ace.

"I don't want to be Queen," said Julia, trumping him.

"Every woman wants to be Queen."

"I don't."

"Then what the hell do you want?"

Julia looked away. "I don't know."

There was a pause, and then Harald moved forward to stand beside her.

"It's Rupert, isn't it?"

"Maybe."

"He's only a second son. He'll never be King."

Julia whirled on him furiously. "That's all you can think about, isn't it? You and everybody else in this damn Castle. Well I'll tell you this, Harald; Rupert may not be the eldest son, and he may not be good enough to sit on your damned throne, but he was good enough to make the Rainbow Run, and good enough to stand beside me and the dragon when we fought off the demons!" Julia's voice broke suddenly, and tears started to her eyes. Somehow, she fought them back. She wouldn't give Harald the satisfaction of seeing her cry. When she looked at him again, her eyes were dry and her voice was steady. "Rupert is the finest and bravest man I have ever known; a warrior and a hero."

Harald raised an eyebrow. "Are we talking about the same person?"

"He had the guts to go back into the Darkwood again, to summon the High Warlock! I don't remember you volunteering to go!"

"That would have been foolish," said Harald. "It's quite straightforward, if you think it through. We couldn't both go; if by some misfortune we were both killed, it would leave the Forest Kingdom without a direct heir to the throne. At the very least, that would mean chaos; at worst, civil war. On the other hand, it was quite clear that one of us had to go; only a Prince of the line stood any chance of persuading the High Warlock to return. So, it had to be me, or him, and Rupert was the most expendable."

"He volunteered. You didn't."

Harald shrugged. "My place is here, defending the Castle from its enemies. Let Rupert run around playing the hero if he wants to; I have more important considerations."

"Such as what? Chasing me round the Castle like a billy goat in heat?"

"I won't dignify that comment with an answer."

"Rupert should have been back months ago! He's your brother! Don't you care about him at all?"

Harald stared at Julia steadily. "If Rupert dies, I'll avenge him."

"I'm sure that'll be a great comfort to him."

Harald smiled crookedly. "Don't expect anything more, Julia. Court life isn't conducive to brotherly love. You should know that; how many of your sisters stood up for you, when you were sentenced to death?"

"That was different. I was guilty."

"No more than any of us, Julia; you were just unlucky enough to get caught. When father dies, Rupert and I could end up fighting on opposite sides of a civil war, to decide who finally inherits the throne. We've known that since we were children. You can't afford to get too close to someone you're probably going to have to kill someday.

"But I promise you this, Julia; if Rupert is dead, I won't

rest till I find out who's responsible. And even if it turns out to be the High Warlock himself, I will avenge my brother."

Julia looked at Harald sharply. His voice had gradually become cold and hard, quite different from his usual casual tones, and for a fleeting moment, harsh lines showed in his bland, placid features. The moment passed, but Julia didn't look away, holding his eyes with hers.

"You think he is dead, don't you?" she said quietly.

Harald nodded slowly. "It's been five months now. Face it, Julia. He's not coming back."

And then they both fell silent, as a guardsman entered the antechamber and hurried past them into the Court, carefully closing the doubledoors behind him. There was a long pause. Harald and Julia looked at each other in silence. Eventually the doors swung open again, and the guardsman bowed to them both.

"Prince Harald, Princess Julia; the King will see you now."

"Remember the cess pits," murmured Harald, as he and Julia entered the Court side-by-side.

"How could I forget?"

"Then smile, dammit; it won't kill you."

"Want to bet?"

With heads held high, and wearing gritted-teeth smiles, they walked quickly forward to bow and curtsey respectively before the throne. The King regarded them both, and grinned sardonically.

"Drop the smiles, my children; you're not fooling anyone." He gestured for the guard to leave, and waited patiently for the doors to shut behind him. King John studied Harald and Julia a while in silence. Harald stared calmly back, while Julia shifted impatiently from foot to foot, her hand never far from the pommel of her sword. The King had made a decision about them; she could see it in his face.

"You two aren't getting on at all, are you?" said King John, finally.

"Early days yet, father," said Harald brightly. Julia sniffed audibly.

The King stared at her, and sighed audibly. "Princess Julia, how can anyone cause so much trouble in so short a time?"

"Practice," said Julia briskly. "What have I done wrong now?"

"According to the latest report, you've been organizing the Castle women, everyone from the scullery maids to the Ladies-in-Waiting, into a last-ditch militia. This has apparently included drilling them in swordsmanship, archery, and dirty tricks. Such as where best to kick a man when he's down, and how to smear your swordblade with fresh dung so that any wounds you make will fester."

"That's right," said Julia. "Some of my ladies are shaping up rather well."

"That is not the point!" snapped the King. "Women don't fight!"

"Why not?"

King John spluttered speechlessly for a moment. "Because they're not suited to it, that's why not!"

"That right?" drawled Julia. "Want to strap on a sword and go a few rounds with me? I'll give you a two-points start and still beat you three out of five."

"What are you grinning at?" growled the King to Harald. "I suppose you've been supporting her in all this!"

"No," said Harald. "I hadn't heard about this latest venture, but I really don't see the harm in it. If and when the demons decide to storm this Castle, we're going to need all the defenders we can muster. I don't care if there's a man or a woman guarding my back, as long as they know how to use a sword."

"Every now and again, you have moments of sanity," said Julia approvingly. "Not often, I'll admit, but it's an encouraging sign."

King John took a deep breath, held it, and let it go. It didn't calm him as much as he'd hoped. "I am also told, Princess Julia, that when my guards quite properly tried to break up your latest training session, you and your ladies drove them off at swordpoint. Is this true?"

"Pretty much," said Julia. "Served them right for interfering; it wasn't any of their business. And what's more, half your guards turned out to be really lousy swordsmen. They should have stayed and watched. They might have learned something."

The King shook his head disgustedly. "I don't know why I waste my time arguing with you. You have no sense of the fitness of things."

"None at all," said Julia cheerfully. "Is that all? Can I go now?"

"No you can't! You're here to discuss your forthcoming marriage to Harald."

"I'm not marrying him!"

"We've been through this before, Julia; you don't have a choice in the matter. Twenty-two years ago, your father and I signed a Peace Treaty to end the Border War between our two countries. Part of that Treaty was an arranged marriage between my eldest son and the Duke's youngest daughter, as and when said daughter should come of age. You are of age, Julia, and the marriage will take place as planned. I will not risk another war because of your stubbornness. The postponements are at an end, Julia. I have spoken to the Castle chaplain, and the wedding will finally take place two weeks from today."

"Two weeks?" Julia shot a furious glance at Harald, but he seemed just as surprised as her.

"Two weeks," said King John firmly.

"Last I heard, you'd put it off till next month," said Harald. "Why all the rush?"

"Yeah," said Julia suspiciously. "What's happened?"

The King gave her a grudging smile. "I have received a communication from your father, my dear. From what I can gather, he wasn't at all surprised to learn you'd survived your encounter with the dragon. Now that he knows you've arrived here safe and sound, he states quite clearly that it is his wish that your marriage to Harald should take place as soon as possible. In fact, he was most insistent. Vague threats of invasion and war hovered in between every line."

"Right," said Julia. "That sounds like Dad. Once he's made up his mind about something, he won't budge an inch, come hell or high water. Damn him."

"He wouldn't really go to war," said Harald. "Would he?"

"Oh yes," said Julia bitterly. "If he thought he was being insulted, he'd fight to the last drop of everybody else's blood." She stared grimly at the King, her hands curling into fists that trembled impotently at her sides. "It seems you were right after all, your majesty; I don't have any choice in the matter."

The King looked away, unable to meet her accusing eyes.

Harald reached out as though to comfort her, but drew back his hand when she turned her glare on him.

"I take it my father won't be attending the wedding himself?" said Julia harshly.

"No," said the King. "Apparently he's very busy just at the moment, and with travel as hazardous as it is . . . He did send you his love."

"No, he didn't," said Julia.

King John and Harald looked at each other, and for a long time nobody said anything.

"Come with me, both of you," said King John, rising suddenly from his throne. "There's something I want you to see."

He made his way carefully down the dais steps, waving aside Harald's offered help, and led the way to the rest of the Court. Next to the door leading to the King's private chambers hung a huge, faded tapestry. King John pulled at a concealed rope, and the tapestry slid jerkily to one side, revealing a hidden alcove in which stood a simple glass display case, some seven feet tall and six wide. Beyond the dusty fly-specked glass stood two wooden mannequins, each displaying an ancient and intricately stitched wedding outfit.

"Splendid, aren't they?" said King John. "These are your wedding robes, my children. Nine hundred years and more, it has been the tradition of this family that the first-born son and his bride shall wear these robes at their wedding. Your mother and I were married in them, Harald. There's no call to look at them like that, Julia; they're a great deal more comfortable than they appear."

Julia studied the two outfits skeptically. The groom's robe was a dark somber affair in black and gray, relieved only by a few silver buttons. The bride, on the other hand, was to appear in a light frothy concoction of laces and silks, all in purest white. Julia glanced at Harald, and then shook her head solemnly.

"I don't think much of yours, Harald. White just isn't your color."

"That's your gown!" snapped the King, keeping a firm hold on his temper.

"I can't wear that," said Julia. "There's nowhere to hang my sword. And anyway, why does it always have to be white?"

"It stands for the purity and wholesomeness of the bride," said King John coldly.

"Ah," said Julia, thoughtfully. She studied the wedding gown a moment. "Do you have it in any other colors?"

Harald got the giggles. The King turned to him slowly. Harald immediately had an extremely unconvincing coughing fit.

"Is something amusing you, Harald?" said the King icily. "No? I'm glad to hear it, because I want to make something clear to you and I want your full attention. From now on, there is to be no more quarrelling with the Princess Julia in any public place."

"But Father . . ."

"Be quiet! Now, Harald, I want you to do something for me. I want you to go down to the dungeons, find the dungeon master, and ask him to show you the cells directly under the moat. They are damp, dark, not a little cramped, and the smell is appalling. They are also apparently infested with a kind of fungus that eats insects and small rodents, and would no doubt love the chance for a crack at a human prisoner. When you've had a good look, go away and think about them. Because if you and Julia raise your voices again in front of the Court I swear by Blood and Stone I'll have you both locked up in one of those cells and not let you out again till your wedding day! Not one more word from you, Harald! Go! Now!"

Harald looked thoughtfully at his father, quickly decided that this was one time when discretion definitely was the better part of valor, and left the Court with as much dignity as he could muster. Which wasn't a lot.

King John waited until the doors had closed behind Harald, and then turned to stare steadily at Julia.

"You don't think much of Harald, do you?" he said finally.

Julia shrugged. "He has his good points, I suppose."

"He's a pain in the backside," said King John firmly. "Don't try to whitewash him to me, girl; I've known him a lot longer than you. Underneath the spoiled-brat image he so studiously cultivates for the courtiers, Harald is what I raised him to be; hard, ruthless, and self-sufficient. In other words, perfect material for a man who will one day be King. Rupert, on the other hand, takes after his mother too much;

thinks with his heart more than his head. I've always done my best as King, but I was never really cut out for the job. No more is Rupert. But Harald . . . he could be the best chance this country's got to get back on its feet again.

"Even after we've thrown back the long night, the Forest Land can never be what it was before. Too much has happened. The Barons have tasted power, and they'll not willingly give it up. Things will probably hang together for a while out of sheer inertia, but whoever succeeds me to the throne will have to be ruthless, determined, and much more of a diplomat than I ever was. Where I once commanded loyalty, Harald will have to fight and bargain for it. He should do well enough at that; he's always shown a natural talent for deceit and double-dealing. But he's never made friends easily, and he's going to need people he can trust at his side if he's to hang on to the throne. Especially if he has to fight a civil war to keep it.

"Harald has the makings of a great King, but he'll always need someone beside him to be his conscience, to temper his justice with mercy, to teach him compassion. Someone he cares for, and respects. You'll make a good Queen to his King, Julia."

"I don't want to be Queen!"

"Nonsense."

"I don't love Harald!"

"You don't have to. In a royal marriage, duty is more important than love. And don't frown like that, as though duty was an ugly word; it is, but we can't escape it. Just by being born into royalty, you and I took on responsibilities along with our privileges. We get the best of everything because we have the hardest work to do. We live in luxury because we give up everything else that matters. We weigh ourselves down with duty so that others can be free. And unlike àny other job, we can't walk away if the work gets too hard, or we don't want to do it.

"You're a strange lass, Julia, and sometimes I don't understand you at all, but in many ways you remind me of Rupert. You're honest and you're loyal, and you'll fight to the death for something you believe in. That's a rare combination these days. There are a great many pressing reasons for this marriage to take place, but as far as I'm concerned there's only one that really matters; the Forest Land needs you.

"So you see, my dear, I don't have a choice in the matter either. What you or I may want is no longer important; we must both do what we have to. The contract has been signed, and the marriage will take place two weeks from today, even if you have to be dragged to the altar by armed guards."

There was a long silence. Julia stared at the white frothy wedding dress, her eyes cold and hard.

"Can I go now, Sire?"

"Rupert isn't coming back," said the King quietly.

"Yes," said Julia. "I know. You sent him to his death."

"I had to," said King John. "That was my duty."

Julia turned her back on him, and left the Court.

Out in the antechamber, Harald glared coldly at Sir Blays.

"I know I'm late for your little gathering, Landsgrave; my father insisted on seeing me."

"Of course, Prince Harald," said Sir Blays calmly. "I quite understand. Unfortunately, the gathering of friends you insisted on has been underway for well over an hour, and if the promised guest of honor doesn't make his appearance soon, I fear the party may be over before it's even properly begun. These people need to see you just as much as you need to see them, Sire."

"I'll be along in a while," said Harald.

"It would be better if you were to accompany me now," said Blays, and Harald didn't miss the sudden coldness in the Landsgrave's voice.

"Better?" said Harald. "Better for whom?"

"Better for all of us, of course. We're all in this together, Prince Harald."

"I'll be there."

"You'd better be."

The two men stared at each other warily. Something was changing between them, and neither was sure exactly what it was.

"That sounded almost like a threat," said Harald softly.

"Think of it more as a friendly warning," said Blays.

"Like the warning Sir Bedivere so nearly gave my father

not an hour ago? If those farmers hadn't been there, that bloody berserker of yours would have killed him!"

Blays inclined his head slightly. "A regrettable incident."

Harald let his hand drop onto the pommel of his sword. "Is that all you've got to say about it?"

"I'll deal with Bedivere later."

"That's not good enough."

Sir Blays smiled politely. "I'd hate to see our alliance fall apart, Sire, especially after we've all invested so much time and effort in it. Right now, there are a great many people waiting to meet you, Prince Harald, all of them gathered together in one place at your request, at no little inconvenience and danger to themselves. I therefore strongly suggest that you don't keep them waiting any longer. This way, Sire."

Harald didn't move. "You seem to be forgetting which of us is in charge."

"No," said Sir Blays. "I haven't forgotten."

"Without me, everything we've discussed comes to nothing."

"Precisely. You need us, Harald, and you've come too far to back out now. My fellow Landsgraves and I can always leave this Castle and return to our masters. Sooner or later the King's forces will become so thinly spread they'll be unable to defend him and, when that happens, the Barons will just move in and take over. They won't need your help, and they certainly won't need you as King. Of course, if we have to wait that long, much of the Forest Land will have been destroyed by the demons. And you can be sure that when we finally storm the Castle, you and your father will not be given the option of exile. Do I make myself clear, Harald?"

"Yes. Very clear."

"Good. Work with us, and we'll make you King. Certainly the Barons would prefer it that way; they can see a great many uses for a constitutional monarch."

"You mean a figurehead."

"Yes, Harald. That's exactly what I mean. Now, I think we've wasted enough time on unnecessary discussion, don't you? It's time to go; your guests are waiting to greet you."

Harald's shoulders seemed to slump a little, and he looked away, unable to face the open disdain in Blays's eyes. "Very well, Landsgrave. It seems I have no choice in the matter."

And then they both jumped as behind them the double doors flew suddenly open, and Julia stalked out of the Great Hall and into the antechamber. She slammed the doors shut behind her, swore loudly, and then glared resentfully at the watching Prince and Landsgrave.

"Ah, Julia," said Harald quickly. "I'd like a word with you, if I may."

Julia shrugged angrily. "Suit yourself." She folded her arms, and leaned back against the bare panelled wall, frowning at nothing.

Harald turned back to Sir Blays. "I will join you at the party in a few minutes. I give you my word on it."

Blays glanced at Julia, and then smiled tightly at Harald. "Of course, Sire, I understand. Please accept my congratulations on your imminent wedding. I shall speak with you further at the party. In a few minutes."

He bowed to the Prince and to the Princess, and left the antechamber. Harald looked at Julia, and frowned worriedly. Her head was bowed, and her eyes stared blindly down in quiet desperation. There was a simple tired, defeated look to her that touched Harald strangely. In all the time he'd known Julia, he'd never once known her to give in to anybody or anything. But now all the strength seemed to have gone out of her, until she had nothing left with which to hold the hostile world at bay. He moved forward to stand beside her.

"Julia; what's the matter?"

"Nothing."

"Something's wrong. I can tell."

"Wrong? What could be wrong? In two weeks' time I'm marrying a man who's going to be King!"

Harald hesitated. He knew instinctively that if he said the right thing now, he could win her over to him in a moment, but say the wrong thing, and he'd lose her forever. He was surprised how much not losing her mattered to him.

"Julia, things will be different between us after we're married, you'll see. I know how much Rupert meant to you, but you'll get over him. Whatever happened, I'm sure he died bravely and honorably. As soon as this business with the Darkwood is over, we'll take a troop of guards and search the Forest until we find out what did happen to him.

And then, together, we'll take a vengeance the Forest will never forget."

"Thanks," said Julia quietly. "I'd like that."

"He is dead, Julia."

"Yes. He is." Julia stared listlessly at Harald. "I've known that for ages, but I could never quite bring myself to believe it. I didn't want to believe it. For a long time I kept hoping, but there's no hope left now. Not after all this time. No hope . . . I should have gone with him, Harald; I should have gone with him!"

Harald took her in his arms. She tensed, and then relaxed against him, her head resting on his shoulder.

"If you'd gone with him," said Harald, "the odds are you'd have been killed as well. He knew that; that's why he made you stay behind."

"I know that," said Julia. "It doesn't help. I wasn't there to stand at his side, and now he's dead. Rupert's dead. Every time I think that, it's like someone hit me in the gut. It hurts, Harald."

"I know, Julia. But you'll get over it, once we're married."

It was the wrong thing to say, and Harald knew that the moment he said it. Julia stiffened in his arms, and when she lifted her head to look at him, her face was cold and unyielding. Harald let her go, and stepped back a pace. He searched for something else to say, something that would bring back the closeness they'd felt, but the moment had passed. Harald shrugged mentally. There'd be other times.

"What did Sir Blays want?" asked Julia evenly.

"He was reminding me I'd agreed to attend a party of his. I really ought to be getting along; I'm late as it is."

"A party? Why didn't I get an invitation?"

Harald raised an eyebrow. "I thought you had a woman's army to train?"

Julia smiled sweetly. "I thought you had a dungeon to visit?"

Harald laughed. "Touché, my dear. The dungeons under the moat are something of a family joke. Father's been threatening me with them for as long as I can remember. The more upset he gets, the more he dwells on their gruesome details. I suppose there are still cells of some kind under the moat, but nobody's used them for centuries. Our dungeons are little more than holding cells; once the prisoners have been to trial, we send them out to work off their sentences on the farms. Why waste manpower?"

"What happens when they run away?"

"They can't. The Court magician puts a compulsion on them before they leave."

"Never mind all that," said Julia, suddenly realizing just how far Harald had led her from her original question, "About this party . . ."

"You don't really want to go, do you? You wouldn't enjoy it, you know."

"No, I don't know," said Julia, rather nettled at being openly excluded from the party. Not that she actually wanted to go, but . . . "Who's going to be at this party?"

"Oh, the Landsgraves, some High Society, a sprinkling of others. I'm not too sure myself. Trust me, Julia; you wouldn't enjoy it. And anyway, this is one party where admission is most definitely by invitation only. Now, if you'll excuse me, I must be going. I'll talk with you some more later, I promise."

And with that he hurried out of the antechamber, before she could ask him anything else. Julia glared at his retreating back. Just for that, she would go to his damn party, and heaven help anyone who tried to keep her out. She frowned thoughtfully. A party the size this one would have to be, couldn't be easily hidden away. Somewhere, there was a servant who knew, and who could be persuaded to talk. And then . . . Julia grinned. What with one thing and another, she was just in the mood for a little rowdy gate-crashing. She chuckled earthily, and strode off to look for a weak-willed servant.

Prince Harald strode casually down the dimly lit corridor, his hand resting lightly on the pommel of his sword. His footsteps echoed dully back from the oak-panelled walls; the slow, regular sound eerily loud on the silence. From time to time, as he drew closer to Lord Darius's quarters, a guardsman in full chain mail would emerge from some concealing shadow to challenge him, only to fall back on recognizing Harald's grim features. The Prince ignored them, but was quietly impressed by the thoroughness with which Darius protected himself. Obviously he didn't intend for his little party to be interrupted, and by setting his guards in ones and twos he avoided the attention that a large number of men would undoubtably have drawn. As it was, Harald estimated that a full troop of guards stood between Lord Darius's chambers and the rest of the Castle, acting as both an advance warning system and a strategically placed fighting force. Harald smiled slightly. The rebellion seemed well planned, if nothing else. He was quite looking forward to seeing who would be waiting for him at the party.

Two tall, brawny guardsmen stood before Lord Darius's door. They wore a featureless leather armor, with no colors to indicate allegiance. Their faces were impassive, but their eyes were cold and distrustful, and they held their swords at the ready as Harald approached them. They inclined their heads slightly as they recognized the Prince, but made no move to step aside. Instead, the taller of the two guardsmen indicated with his sword a small table to his left. Harald moved forward, and picked up a plain black domino mask from a pile on the table. He looked at the guardsmen, and raised an eyebrow.

"With the compliments of Lord Darius," said the guard. "A masked Ball, in your honor, Sire."

Harald chuckled softly. "Masks; how delightfully apt. But I don't think I'll bother, myself."

He tossed the mask back onto the pile. The guard sheathed his sword, picked up the mask, and held it out to Harald.

"The Lord Darius was most insistent, Sire," said the guard. "Nobody gets in unless they're wearing a mask."

"He'll make an exception in my case," said Harald. "Now stand aside."

The guard smiled, and shook his head slowly. "I take my orders from the Lord Darius," he said calmly. "Just as you do, Sire. Now put on your mask."

"And if I don't?"

"Then I'll put it on for you . . . Sire."

Harald hit him just below the breastbone with a straight finger jab, and all the color went out of the guard's face. He bent slowly forward, as though bowing to Harald, and then fell to lie still on the floor. The other guard lifted his sword and stepped forward, only to freeze in place as the point of Harald's sword pricked his throat. The guard lowered his blade, and tried hard not to swallow. He'd heard the Prince was good with a sword, but he'd never seen anyone move that fast . . .

"Who do you take your orders from?" asked Harald, his voice calm and quiet and very dangerous.

"You, Sire," said the guard. "Only you."

"Glad to hear it," said Harald. He stepped back a pace, and sheathed his sword. "Open the door for me, guardsman."

"Yes, Sire." The guard glanced quickly at his companion, who was still lying on the floor, curled helplessly around the bright agony in his chest, and then moved forward and knocked twice on the door. There was the sound of heavy bolts being drawn, and the door swung smoothly open. Harald stepped over the fallen guardsman and strode unhurriedly into Lord Darius's quarters.

All conversation stopped as Harald entered the Hall. The great babble of voices died quickly away to nothing, the musicians stopped playing, and the dancers froze in their places. Even the roaring flames in the huge open fireplace seemed muted by the sudden silence. Harald stopped just inside the doorway and looked about him. A vast sea of masks stared impassively back.

Darius's Hall wasn't all that large, as Castle Halls went, and the two or three hundred people present filled it comfortably from wall to wall. The number was about right for a Castle party, large enough to be impressive without being intimidating, but somehow the masks made a difference. Simple black domino masks predominated, but at least half of Darius's guests had chosen to wear their own individual masks; ornate and bizarre, gorgeous and grotesque, the masks watched Harald with a fixed intensity that came close to unnerving him. Their unmoving expressions, their exaggerated glees or sorrows or snarls, were so far from anything human as to be almost demonic. Directly before Harald, to his left, a white-faced Pierrot stood arm-in-arm with a horse-headed mummer. To Harald's right, a grinning Death leaned companionably on the shoulder of a shrieking Famine. A Fish stared goggle-eyed, and a Cat winked. And everywhere; simple black dominos and painted faces and lorgnettes of beaten gold and silver. Harald stared at the masks, and the masks stared back.

And then the sea of false faces suddenly parted, as two

figures came forward to meet him. A little of Harald's tension drained away as he recognized Lord Darius and the Lady Cecelia, and he moved his hand away from his swordhilt. Darius wore long heavy robes of dusty gray, whose cut and style fought in vain to make him appear slimmer. His mask was a black silk domino. Cecelia wore an ornate ball gown of blue and silver, studded with semiprecious stones, that covered her completely from neck to ankle without concealing any of her splendid figure. Silver bells hanging from her cuffs and hem chimed prettily with her every movement. Her mask was a dainty lorgnette of beaten gold on a slender ivory handle. Darius bowed to Harald, and Cecelia curtsied. Behind them, the sea of masks also bowed and curtsied. Harald nodded briefly in return, and Darius gestured urgently to the musicians at the far end of the Hall. A lively music sprang up, and the sea of masks was suddenly just a gathering of party guests as they broke apart to talk, or dance, or sample wines and sweetmeats and sugared fruits from the well-stocked buffet tables. Two servants moved forward and quietly closed the door behind Harald. He heard the heavy bolts slam home.

"Welcome, Sire," said Lord Darius. "We've been expecting you for some time."

"So Sir Blays informed me," said Harald, smiling politely.

"Did you have any trouble getting here, Sire?"

"None I couldn't handle."

"Would you like me to get you a mask, Harald?" asked Cecelia brightly. "I'm sure I can find just the thing to suit you."

"Indeed," said Darius. "My guards were under strict orders to provide you with a mask."

"They did try," said Harald. "I convinced them it was a bad idea. After all, I am here to be recognized, aren't I?"

"Of course, Sire, of course." Darius gestured quickly to a passing servant, who stopped and presented Harald with a tray of drinks. Harald took a glass of wine, drained it, put it back on the tray, and picked up another glass. Darius waved the servant away before the Prince could try for a third, and then studied Harald warily. Something was wrong; he could feel it.

"Why did you choose a masked Ball, my Lord Darius?"

asked Harald, sipping at his wine in a manner that suggested
only politeness kept him from pulling a face.

"To be honest, Sire, it was the only way I could persuade
most of them to come. No doubt the masks give them a
comforting sense of anonymity. There will be an unmasking
later, once we've all had the opportunity to . . . get to know
one another a little better."

Harald nodded solemnly. "Then if you'll excuse me, my
Lord and Lady, I'd better go and mingle with my fellow
guests, hadn't I?"

"That is the purpose of this party, Sire."

Harald smiled, and moved away into the crowd of bobbing masks. Darius and Cecelia watched him go.

"Something's wrong," said Darius slowly, his right hand
moving absently to the poison dagger concealed in his left
sleeve.

"Wrong? I don't see anything wrong, darling." Cecelia
took an elegant sip from her wine glass, and peered quickly
round the Hall. "The party's going splendidly; everyone's
here that should be."

Darius shook his head stubbornly. "It's Harald; the way
he's been acting. He should be more . . . well, *excited*,
dammit. The people in this room could put him on the
throne, if they choose to, but to look at Harald you'd think
he didn't give a damn what they thought of him."

Cecelia shrugged prettily. "Dear Harald's never given
much of a damn what anybody thinks. He doesn't have to;
he's a Prince."

"You could be right," said Darius. He drank deeply from
his wine glass, and on lowering it was surprised to find it
empty. He frowned, and put the glass down on a nearby
table. This was no time to be getting the worse for drink.
"Come, my dear; our guests are waiting, and if Harald
won't charm them, we'll have to do it for him, damn the
man."

Cecelia laughed. "You mean Gregory and I will have to
charm them; you'll be too busy making political and business deals."

"Of course," said Darius. "It's what I do best."

They shared a smile, and then moved away in different
directions.

Harald strolled slowly through the party, nodding politely

to those he recognized, and smiling coldly at those he didn't. He ignored all invitations to stop and talk, and wandered back and forth across the Hall until he was sure he'd seen everybody at least once. He finally ended up before the blazing open fire, and stood with his back to it, quietly enjoying the heat as it seeped slowly into his bones. Even the many thick stone walls of the Castle couldn't seem to keep out the unnatural cold that had fallen across the Forest. Bitter frosts blighted all the Land, and every morning the snow lay more thickly on the Castle battlements. Even the moat was beginning to ice over.

Harald shrugged, and sipped at his wine. Across the Hall, Darius was glaring at him. Harald looked away. He wasn't ready to talk to anybody yet. Instead, he amused himself by watching the masked guests as they moved gracefully through the intricate measures of a dance, or gathered in hungry little groups round the buffet tables and scandalmongers. It seemed to Harald that, for all the different kinds of masks, there was still a definite pecking order. High Society had their own individual and highly stylized masks, each with its own subtle clues as to who's features lay concealed beneath. The lesser nobles wore the wilder and more bizarre masks, as though making up in originality what they lacked in social standing. The traders and the military made do with the simple black domino masks that Lord Darius had provided.

Directly opposite Harald, three men wearing no masks stood together. Harald inclined his head slightly to them. The three Landsgraves nodded in acknowledgment, but made no move to approach him. Harald frowned, and met their eyes in turn. Sir Blays stared calmly back, Sir Guillam bobbed his head and simpered nervously, and Sir Bedivere . . . Despite himself, Harald shivered suddenly as he tried and failed to meet Sir Bedivere's cold, dark eyes. He knew now, beyond any shadow of a doubt, that if he had fought the Landsgrave that day in Court, Sir Bedivere would have killed him easily. Harald glowered into his empty glass. He hadn't forgotten or forgiven the Landsgrave's insult to his father, but he vowed to himself that if it ever came to a fighting insult again, he'd have more sense than to challenge the Landsgrave to a duel. He'd just stab the man in the back, or put ground glass in his wine.

"Welcome to the party," said a chill voice, and Harald

looked up to find himself face-to-face with a black-and-white Harlequin mask. Its rosebud mouth smiled politely, but no humor showed in the pale blue eyes behind the mask.

"I know that voice," murmured Harald. "Lord Vivian, isn't it? You're in charge of the Castle's guards, in the Champion's absence."

Lord Vivian reached up and slowly and deliberately removed his mask, revealing a gaunt, raw-boned face so pale as to be almost colorless, topped with a thick mane of silver-gray hair. There was a calm and studied stillness to the face that suggested strength and determination, but the eyes were hard and unyielding. Fanatic's eyes. His frame was lean and wiry, rather than muscular, but there was a deadly grace to his few, economical movements, and Harald noticed that Vivian's right hand never strayed far from his swordhilt.

"I command the Castle guards," said Lord Vivian slowly, "Now, and always, my King."

"I'm not King yet," said Harald.

"You will be," said Vivian. "The Champion isn't coming back. His body lies rotting in the Darkwood. I speak for the guards now, and every man-to-arms in this Castle follows my orders. With us at your side, no one will dare dispute your claim to the Forest throne."

"Indeed," said Harald. "But why should you support me, rather than my father? You swore an oath of allegiance to him, upon your life and your honor."

"That was before the coming of the Darkwood," said Vivian flatly. "My oath to protect the Land takes precedence over all other oaths. My loyalty is to the throne, not who sits on it. The Forest is endangered, and your father is no longer capable of doing what must be done."

Harald raised an eyebrow. "I take it you have something in mind for me to order as King?"

Vivian smiled coldly. "Take the fight to the enemy, Sire. Unite all the guards and men-at-arms into a single great army, and send them forth against the darkness. Under my command, they will butcher the demons and drive them back."

"And then?" asked Harald.

"And then, my troops will set a wall of fire between us

and the demons; a searing, bright-burning flame that will drive the foul creatures back into the darkness from which they came!"

"Even assuming such a tactic would work," said Harald thoughtfully, "hundreds of the outlying farms would be lost in the fire. Thousands of peasants would die."

Vivian shrugged. "Regrettable, but necessary. If the Darkwood isn't stopped, they'll die anyway. What does it matter if a few peasants must die, if by their deaths they ensure the survival of the Forest Kingdom? I'm a soldier; my men and I take that same risk every time we go out into battle. Afterwards . . . we can always build more farms, and the lower classes breed like rabbits, anyway."

"Quite," murmured Harald. "Still, I fear the Barons would not take kindly to such widespread destruction of their lands."

"My army would stand ready to support their King against any foe," said Vivian calmly. "No matter where such enemies might be found."

"A comforting thought," said Harald. "I will think on your words, my Lord Vivian, and your most generous offer of support."

"In return for my position as High Commander of the Guard, Sire."

"Of course, Lord Vivian. But of course."

Vivian bowed slightly, and replaced his Harlequin mask. Faded blue eyes glittered coldly behind the black and white silk, and then Lord Vivian turned away and disappeared into the milling crowd. Harald frowned, and shook his head as though to clear it. Vivian's presence at the party was hardly a surprise, but somehow Harald felt almost disappointed. He'd expected better of the man.

He glowered into his empty glass, tossed it over his shoulder into the fireplace, and casually acquired a fresh glass from a passing servant. The wine was lousy, but Harald was damned if he could face this party entirely sober. He looked up to see a masked Lord and Lady heading uncertainly in his direction. Harald sighed, and nodded politely to them. He'd better speak to somebody, or some of the guests might get nervous and leave. And that would never do. He bowed to the Lord and to the Lady, and they bowed and curtsied deeply in return.

The things I have to do, thought Harald sardonically. *The things I have to do . . .*

More masked figures came and went as the Ball wore on. Harald met three Lords he had suspected, two he hadn't, and a handful of local traders; it seemed the Darkwood was bad for business. The vast majority of those he met turned out to be courtiers, which was pretty much what he'd expected. On the one hand, courtiers tended to be conservative by nature for, as landowners or Sherrifs of the King's land, they had much to lose and little to gain from any political change. But, on the other hand, when all was said and done, most courtiers were lesser nobles who wanted very much to be greater nobles. And the only way to achieve that was to acquire more land, or move to positions of greater influence within the Court. Which was why they came to Harald, hiding behind their masks of silk and leather and thinly beaten metal. The masks changed, but the story was always the same; support in return for patronage. After a while, Harald stopped listening and just said yes to everyone. It saved time.

Cecelia and Gregory paraded arm-in-arm the length of the Hall and back again, smiling and chatting and making sure that everyone's wine glass was full to the brim. With her beauty and his firm masculine good looks, they made a handsome couple, bold and bright. Cecelia was at her sparkling best, her malicious little quips and barbed comments reducing even the most stern-faced to indulgent smiles and open laughter. Whilst not the most diplomatic of men, Gregory could be charming when he put his mind to it, and with Cecelia at his side to inspire him, the young guardsman strolled amiably among the uncertain, radiating confidence. Bluff and hearty, his sure manner and calm good humor steadied quavering nerves and spread a sense of purpose among the wavering. There were few glances at Cecelia's arm linked through his; everyone knew, or at least suspected. There were a few sidelong glances in Darius's direction, but nobody said anything. Since Darius knew and apparently didn't object, the subject was closed, at least in public. Among the courtiers, eyes met and shoulders shrugged. Politics made for strange bedfellows. Sometimes literally.

Darius missed none of this as he circulated among his

guests. Fools. He knew well enough that where reason couldn't sway a man, charm often would. Possessing but little charm himself, Darius needed someone else to front for him on occasion; someone with good looks, an easy manner, and not enough brains to double-cross his master. Gregory might have been tailor-made for the position. It helped that Cecelia liked him. But then, Cecelia wasn't exactly brilliant, either.

Darius sighed quietly, and looked around him. At least Harald had finally condescended to talk to his fellow guests, even if he did seem to be attracting mainly the lesser nobles of no real influence or importance. Darius sniffed cynically. About time Harald started pulling his weight and getting his noble hands dirty. Darius thought of the hard bargaining he'd just been through to get the two leading Forest grain merchants on his side, and smiled grimly. It wasn't just politics and force of arms that made a rebellion, as Harald and the Barons would find out to their cost. In return for certain future concessions, Darius now owned all the stocks of grain remaining in the Forest Land. Not so much as one cart-load would leave the carefully hidden silos without his permission. The Landsgraves might think they owned him, but the Barons would soon learn better when they had to come cap in hand to the Lord Darius for grain to feed their troops . . . He chuckled coldly, and then quickly composed his face into calm inscrutability as Sir Blays approached him. Darius looked surreptitiously about for Guillam and Bedivere, but as yet there was no sign of them.

"Sir Blays, my dear fellow," said Darius, bowing formally, "I trust you are enjoying my hospitality."

"Your wine's lousy and the company stinks," said Blays. "Still, when you're dealing with traitors, you learn to ignore things that would normally sicken you. I take it you've noticed Harald's growing popularity? Courtiers who'd normally run a mile to avoid him are fighting each other for the chance to shake his hand in public."

"Dear Harald does seem to be doing rather well," murmured Darius. "Possibly because he's been a little overgenerous in his offers of patronage. Still, let him promise what he likes; it keeps the courtiers happy, and we can always put things right, later."

"You mean the Barons will put things right, Darius."

"Of course, Sir Blays. But of course."

"Something's worrying your guests," said Blays suddenly. "Something that's got them so scared they don't even dare discuss it here. Have you any idea what's got into them?"

"Curtana," said Darius flatly. "They don't believe it's been stolen, any more than you or I do. No, my dear Blays; they're afraid that John and his pet Astrologer now have the Sword of Compulsion, and are planning to use it against them, setting geas after geas upon them until they're nothing more than slaves, with no will of their own."

"It's possible, I suppose," said Blays carefully. "How about you? Do you think John has the Curtana?"

Darius shrugged. "What does it matter? If he has, there's nothing we can do about it. If he hasn't, then he's defenseless against us. Besides, I've no doubt the sword's powers have been greatly exaggerated over the years. All magic fades, in time."

Sir Blays shook his head. "Legend has it that Curtana derives its power from the Demon Prince, himself. If that's so, then the Curtana is once again one of the deadliest weapons ever to be wielded in this Land. If by some chance the King really hasn't got it, we'd better find out who has, and quickly. John might hesitate to use the Curtana; there are a great many others who wouldn't."

"That's a problem for another day," said Darius. "In the meantime, the longer the Curtana stays missing, the better; its main value to us is as a weapon with which to isolate King John from his Court. The more scared they are of the King, the more likely they are to side with us."

Sir Blays smiled cynically. "It won't be that easy, Darius. It's not enough for these sheep to be scared; they have to be pushed into action. And to do that we have to be able to offer them some kind of protection against both the Curtana and the King's Royal Guard."

"You really think they'll be a problem?" Darius frowned thoughtfully. "With Lord Vivian as High Commander of the Guard . . ."

"The Royal Guard will still support King John," said Blays flatly. "They're loyal to the King, himself—almost fanatically so. The other guardsmen might or might not obey Lord Vivian rather than the King; more likely they'd hang back and wait to see which way the wind blows. No, my dear Darius; we need a weapon strong enough to ensure our safety against all attacks, no matter which quarter they might come from. Luckily, there are such weapons available to us, now that the Armory has been reopened.''

Darius looked sharply at Blays. "You're talking about stealing the Infernal Devices."

"Exactly."

Darius stared into his wine glass. "Curtana's bad enough, Blays. I don't think I'd trust any man who wielded one of the Damned blades. Those swords are evil."

"It's a little late to be getting particular, Darius. Look around you; out of all the Castle, barely three hundred people have turned out to openly support us. There should have been five times that number. Even with all that's happened, most of the Court are still loyal to the King. Or at least, they're more frightened of his wrath than they are of ours. We're going to need every weapon we can lay our hands on, and that includes the Infernal Devices. It's too late to get soft now, Darius."

Darius raised his glass and drank steadily until it was empty, still not looking at Blays. When he finally lowered the glass and spoke, his voice was calm and even. "Very well, Sir Blays. But I'll not wield one of those blades. Not for the throne itself and all the Forest Land."

"I never intended that you should," said Blays.

Darius stared at him a moment, and then bowed formally and walked away. Sir Guillam and Sir Bedivere came over to join Sir Blays.

"The noble Lord Darius doesn't seem too happy," said Guillam, smiling unpleasantly. "I do hope he isn't going to be a problem."

"He won't be," said Blays curtly. He didn't bother to keep the disdain from his voice; he might have to work with Guillam, but he didn't have to like him. Sir Guillam was such a *nasty* little man, when all was said and done. If he wasn't so necessary to the Barons' plans . . . Blays sighed regretfully, and then winced as Guillam's gaze wandered over the more comely of the Ladies present, blatantly undressing them with his eyes.

"Try to keep your gaze polite, dammit," growled Blays. "We're supposed to be persuading these people to our cause, not providing jealous husbands with grounds for a duel."

Guillam sniggered, and drank deeply from his glass. His round, bland features were flushed, and his smile was ugly. "Now, now, Blays; we all have our preferences. In return for my services, the Barons promised me I could have anything I wanted. Anything, or anyone. Since I've been here at the Castle, I've seen the most delightful creature; such a sweet young thing . . . I want her, and I'm going to have her. I'm sure she'll grow very fond of me, eventually."

Blays looked away. What little he'd heard of Guillam's private life had been enough to turn his stomach. It seemed the Landsgrave liked a little blood with his pleasures. And sometimes more than a little. Guillam stared hungrily at a tall and slender masked Lady as she and her husband stepped gracefully through the measures of a dance. She caught his eye, shuddered, and looked quickly away. Guillam licked his lips, and the husband glared at him.

"Damn you," snarled Blays, "I told you . . ."

"I don't take orders from you!" said Guillam fiercely. He turned suddenly to face Blays, a vicious little skinning knife in his hand. His mouth trembled petulantly, and his eyes were very bright. "I'm a Bladesmaster, and don't you forget it! Without me, you'll never control the Infernal Devices, and without them your precious rebellion hasn't a hope in hell of succeeding. You need me, Blays; I don't need you. My private life is none of your damn business! No one tells me what do do! Not you, or the Barons, or . . ."

A large hand closed over his, and squeezed. Guillam cried out with pain, and his face went white. Tears ran down his cheeks as Bedivere crushed his hand in an unyielding grip.

"You do anything to upset our plans," said Sir Bedivere quietly, "and I'll hurt you, little man. I'll hurt you so badly you'll never walk straight again."

He let go, and Guillam cradled his wounded hand to his chest, sniffing sullenly.

"Afterwards," said Sir Bedivere, "you can do whatever you like, you revolting little man. But not yet. Until Harald is securely on his throne, and safely under our control, you don't do one damn thing that might jeopardize our mission. Is that clear?"

Guillam nodded quickly, and Bedivere turned away to stare calmly out over the milling throng. The crimson glare had already faded from his eyes, but the madness remained, as it always did.

Blays shook his head slowly as Guillam awkwardly made his knife disappear. Not for the first time, Blays wondered how he'd come to this, plotting treason against his King with a berserker and a pervert. It was all John's fault, for being a weak King. If he'd been stronger, more capable, done what was so obviously needed, none of this would have been necessary. *You should never have gone after the Curtana, John. Anything else, and we might still have struck a deal, but once you'd opened the Armory there was nothing more I could do for you.* Harald would do better. He understood the realities of power. A strong King on the Forest throne, working with the Barons, not against them; that was what was needed. And then the Darkwood would be driven back, the demons destroyed, and everything would be the way it used to be. Everything.

Damn you, John! Damn you for making me a traitor!

Cecelia glided confidently through the loudly chattering crowd, making bright conversation with people she couldn't stand, and smiling till her jaws ached. The air was growing dull and stuffy despite the Hall's many air vents, and the constant roar of massed voices grated on Cecelia's nerves till she thought she'd scream. Finally she decided enough was enough, and taking Gregory firmly by the arm, she led him forcibly off to the punch bowl, in search of a little peace and a very large drink.

"How many more do we have to talk to?" she demanded, gulping thirstily at her punch.

"As many as it takes," said Gregory calmly. "We can't afford to let anyone leave who isn't a hundred percent convinced that it's in his best interests to side with us."

Cecelia emptied her glass and held it out to be refilled. "You know, Gregory; I can remember when I could dance and sing and drink all through the evening and on into the early hours of the morning, sleep for four hours, and still wake up bright-eyed and cheerful, ready to do it all again. Look at me now; I've only been here a few hours, and already I'm out on my feet. I'm getting too old for this."

"Nonsense," said Gregory gallantly.

"I am," Cecelia insisted mournfully. "I'm forty-one, I've got a double chin, and my tits are sagging."

"Rubbish," said Gregory firmly. "You're as young and lovely now as you've always been. I should know."

Cecelia smiled, and leaned tiredly against the young guardsman's chest. "Dear Gregory; you say the nicest things. I suppose that's why I keep you around."

"Not the only reason, surely."

Cecelia chuckled earthily, and pushed herself away from him. "Later, dear; later. We have work to do." And then she hesitated, and looked at him thoughtfully. "Gregory . . ."

"My Lady?"

"Why do you stay with me? You know I'll never divorce Darius."

"Yes," said Gregory. "I know."

"Do you love me?"

"Perhaps. What difference does it make, as long as we're having a good time together? Worry about tomorrow when it comes; for now, we have each other, and I've never been happier. Never."

Cecelia reached up, and taking his ears in her tiny hands, she pulled his head down to hers, and kissed him tenderly. "Thank you, my dear," she said quietly, and then let him go. "Now do me a favor and go and talk to those ghastly people for a while. I'm going to sit here and have a headache until I get my stamina back."

Gregory nodded amiably, and strode manfully off into the milling crowd. Cecelia stared dubiously at the punch in her glass, and then shrugged and sipped daintily at it. One more glass wouldn't hurt her. Darius came over to join her, mopping at his brow with a silk handkerchief that had seen better days.

"How are we doing?" he asked, looking longingly at the punch bowl.

"Not too bad," said Cecelia. She offered him a sip from her glass, but he shook his head. "Don't worry, Darius. Most of them are with us; the rest just need to be talked into doing what they want to do, anyway."

"Let me know at once if anyone makes a move to leave."

"Of course. I take it you have your poisoned dagger handy?"

"Of course. And the guards have their orders. No one gets out of here alive unless I vouch for them. We've come too far to risk being betrayed now. All our heads would roll."

Cecelia nodded soberly, and shivered suddenly. She reached out a hand to Darius, but he was looking round the Hall at his guests. Cecelia let her hand drop, and moved to stand beside him. The dancers had become a trifle unsteady on their feet, but seemed to be making up in enthusiasm what they lacked in skill and timing. Voices were growing loud and raucous, and the ever-present laughter was boisterous and shrill by turns.

"We'll be running out of wine soon," said Cecelia. "When do we start the unmasking?"

"Soon, my dear; soon. It's not something we can rush; it's the first real sign of trust, the first committment to our cause. When I think they're ready I'll give you the signal, and we'll both unmask. Once we've broken the ice, the rest will follow. I hope."

"What if they don't?" asked Cecelia quietly. "What if we haven't convinced them?"

"We must," said Darius, just as quietly. "If we don't, we'll be the ones who won't leave here alive."

Julia strode briskly down the brightly lit corridor, absently rubbing her bruised knuckles. No damn guardman was going to tell her which passageways she could and couldn't use. No doubt he would regret his insulting tone of voice, when he finally woke up. Julia grinned, and then stopped and peered cautiously about her. She could have sworn she heard something . . . She looked back the way she'd come, but nothing moved in the shadows between the torches. Julia shrugged, and continued on down the corridor. She rounded a corner, and then jumped back, startled, as an armed guardsman appeared suddenly from a concealed doorway. Julia's hand flew to the sword at her hip, and then she relaxed as she recognized the guard.

"Bodeen! What are you doing here?"

"Dying of thirst, mainly, Princess." The short, stocky guard lowered his sword, and sheathed it. "Three hours I've been on duty, and not so much as a cup of mulled ale to warm my bones."

"It's a hard life in the Guards," said Julia amusedly. "What exactly are you guarding?"

"Oh, just some party," said Bodeen. "Private get-together for some of the Lord Darius's friends. I didn't know you'd been invited, Princess; I wouldn't have thought you were the type."

"I wasn't, and I'm not." Julia grinned. "I'm just going to gate-crash the party to annoy Harald."

"Prince Harald?" said Bodeen. "I don't think he's in there. Certainly he hasn't passed by me."

"Oh." Julia frowned. She was sure she'd followed the servant's directions exactly . . . the damn Castle must be up to its old tricks again. Ah, well. "What are you doing here, though, Bodeen? With all those jewels you picked up in the counting house, you could have retired from the Guards and bought yourself a tavern."

"That's what I thought," said Bodeen grimly. "Unfortunately, the King made me hand over everything I'd found to the Seneschal."

"Not everything, surely?"

"Everything, Princess; right down to the last gold coin. Makes you weep, doesn't it. All those jewels . . . I mean, it wasn't as if the King would have missed a few, after all. If it hadn't been for you and me, he'd never have seen any of them again. Well, I've learnt my lesson. You can't trust the aristocracy; not even your own King."

"But . . . didn't you at least get a reward for helping rediscover the South Wing?"

"Just doing my job, Princess. That's what they pay me two silver ducats a week for."

"That's disgusting," said Julia flatly. "I think I'll have a word with the King about this."

Bodeen raised an eyebrow. "I wasn't aware you had any pull with him."

"When you get right down to it, I don't," said Julia wryly. "But it's worth a try."

"Yeah; sure. Thanks anyway, Princess."

"I'll tell you what I can do; I can break into Darius's party and bring you back a drink. How's that?"

"It's a nice thought, Princess, but if you haven't an invitation I can't let you pass."

"Oh, come on, Bodeen; you can let me sneak pass. I won't tell anyone."

"I'm in enough trouble as it is, Princess; I don't need any more. Thanks for the offer, but no."

"Bodeen . . ."

"Get away from him, Julia."

Julia spun round to find King John standing at the corridor intersection, staring grimly at Bodeen. Behind the King, filling the corridor from wall to wall, stood a full company of guardsmen, each man wearing the distinctive scarlet and gold markings of the Royal Guard.

"Stand aside, Julia," said the King. "You don't want to get blood on your dress."

Prince Harald wandered over to the punch bowl and refilled his glass. So far, the punch was the only thing that made this party bearable. He sat on the edge of the buffet table and stared sardonically about him, one leg idly swinging. Now that Darius and Cecelia had ostentatiously removed their masks, others were following suit. Mask after mask fell away as the revellers gained in confidence, but the faces revealed were flushed with anxiety and too much wine, and their laughter was forced and harsh. Harald smiled sourly and sipped his punch. Treason didn't come easy at the best of times. He stretched tiredly, and wondered how much longer the party would last. He'd had his fill of the courtiers and businessmen and Lords and Ladies, and all their many promises of what they'd do for him when he became King. And, of course, what they expected from him in return. Harald grinned suddenly.

He had a few surprises in store for them.

"Prince Harald; if we might speak with you a moment?"

Harald looked up at the three Landsgraves standing before him, and nodded curtly. "Of course, Sir Blays. After all, this is your party as much as mine. What can I do for you?"

"We need your decision," said Guillam, smiling unpleasantly. "And I'm afraid we must insist on knowing it now."

Harald surged to his feet in one smooth motion, and stood towering over the Landsgrave, his hand resting on the pommel of his sword. "You *insist* to me again, my noble Landsgrave," said Harald quietly, "And I'll cut your heart out."

Guillam flushed pinkly, and Blays stepped quickly forward to stand between him and the Prince.

"I'm sure Sir Guillam meant no offense, Sire; it's just that we don't have much time. The unmasking has finally begun, and soon the party will be drawing to its close. You must understand that we are all at risk the longer we stay here; if by some chance we were to be discovered together, it might prove a trifle awkward to explain."

Harald laughed. "You do have a talent for understatement, Sir Blays."

"Quite," said the Landsgrave, smiling mirthlessly. "We need an answer, Prince Harald, and we need it now. Are you with us, or not?"

"I need more time to think about it," said Harald.

"Your time just ran out," said Sir Bedivere. "What's there to think about? If you're not with us, you're against us. And if you're against us . . ."

"Then what?" said Harald. "Then what, sir Berserker?"

A crimson glare came and went in the giant Landsgrave's eyes, but when he spoke his voice was cold and emotionless. "If you're not with us, Prince Harald, we'll just find someone else and make him King."

"Like who?" Harald smiled crookedly and waved his glass around to indicate the crowded Hall. "Rupert's not coming back, and there's no one here with any claim to the throne. For better or worse, I'm the last of the Forest Kings; the line ends with me."

"Precisely," said Guillam. "So what's to stop us establishing a new line of Kings?"

Harald looked steadily at Blays. "You'd have to kill me first."

"That's right," said Guillam, and he laughed richly, as though he'd just made an excellant joke.

"There's no need for all this talk of killing," said Blays, glaring at Guillam. "The Barons would much rather have someone they can trust on the Forest throne; someone they know they can work with. They want you, Prince Harald. Everyone in this Hall wants you as their King. All you have to do is say yes."

"Supposing I did agree, just for the sake of argument," said Harald. "What do you get out of it? I mean, you three personally. What exactly have the Barons promised you; money, power, what?"

Blays thought furiously as he stared impassively at the Prince. Something was happening here, and he wasn't sure what. Harald seemed . . . different . . . somehow. When he'd gone to summon Harald to the party, Blays would have sworn the Prince's spirit was all but broken. And yet now Harald stood before him, his usual mask of flippancy thrown aside, his voice cold and unyielding. He was far too self-assured for Blays's liking, and his steady gaze seemed almost mocking, as though he knew something the Landsgraves didn't. Blays scowled. For the time being he'd play Harald's game, but later . . . later, there would be a reckoning.

"We serve the Barons," he said slowly. "That is our duty and our privilege. No doubt we'll all be well rewarded for our part in this, but our loyalty lies with Gold and Silver and Copper."

"Bull," said Harald. "No one's listening, my dear Landsgrave; no one can overhear us. For once in your life, forget diplomacy and tell me the truth. You know what I stand to get out of this deal, but if we're to work together I want to know where you're going to be, and what you're going to be doing, while I sit on the Forest throne. In other words, I want to know what's in it for you, my noble Landsgraves."

There was an uncomfortable silence, and then Blays bowed coldly to the Prince. "I speak for Gold, Prince Harald, as I have always done. In return for my part in this rebellion, and for my many past services, the Baron has most graciously named me as his successor. A marriage has been arranged between myself and the Baron's eldest daughter. A most charming young Lady; perhaps you remember her? She was most upset when you broke off your engagement to her, in order to marry the Princess Julia. Her father was even more upset. Still; at least now the Baron has a son-in-law he knows he can trust.

"When he dies, I will be Baron Oakeshoff. I have no wish to take over a demesne crippled by debt and overrun by darkness, just because the Forest has a weak King. With you on the throne, and the Barons to guide you, the Forest Land will grow strong again, and with it Oakeshoff demesne. That's what's in it for me, Prince Harald."

"Sir Bedivere," said Harald, turning slightly to face the tall Landsgrave.

For a moment it seemed he might not answer, but finally he stared at Harald and said simply, "I shall serve you as your Champion, Sire. It is all I want. It is all I have ever wanted. Your enemies shall fall before me, and I will bring you their heads to set upon your gates. I shall be your right hand, dealing out death and destruction, blood and terror, to any who dare oppose you. I will be your Champion, Sire; and all who live will fear your justice."

There was an unfocussed, faraway look to his eyes, and Harald shivered suddenly. He'd always known Bedivere was a killer, but now he stared into the man's eyes and saw a bloody madness staring back. There was something in the giant Landsgrave that called for murder and sudden death, and would never be satisfied. Harald swore silently to himself that, come what may, Sir Bedivere would have to die.

"Sir Guillam?" he said coldly.

Guillam looked up from his glass of wine, spilling some down his chin as he tried to empty his mouth too quickly. He swallowed hard, and then dabbed daintily at his mouth with a folded silk handkerchief. "The Barons promised me I could have anything I wanted," he said finally. "And I've seen what I want. She's tall and graceful and very beautiful, and she's going to be mine. She's too proud to have anything to do with me now, but she'll come to heel quickly enough once I've broken her spirit. They always do." He giggled suddenly, fingered the skinning knife in his sleeve, and drank more wine.

Harald turned away in disgust, pitying whatever poor woman the Landsgrave had set his mind on.

"Lovely girl," said Guillam softly, his eyes very bright. "Julia's such a lovely girl."

"What the hell's going on?" demanded Julia.

Bodeen drew his sword and stepped back a pace, blocking the narrow passageway. Behind the King, several of the Royal Guard raised their swords, and Julia could see fresh blood on the blades.

"Treason," said the King. "And this man is a part of it. Aren't you, Bodeen?"

"I'm afraid I can't let you pass, Sire," said Bodeen calmly. "I have my orders."

"Will you cut it out, Bodeen," hissed Julia. "These people are serious."

"So am I," said Bodeen. Candlelight shimmered on his sword as he hefted it, and the nearest of the Royal Guard stirred restlessly.

"I trusted you," said King John. His voice was flat, but his eyes were confused and angry. "You taught my son swordsmanship; you fought beside me in the Border campaign. And now you betray me. Put down your sword, Bodeen; at least that way you'll live to stand trial."

"That's not much of a choice," said Bodeen.

"You can't fight a whole company of guards," said Julia urgently. "Come on, Bodeen; do as he says. If you don't, they'll kill you."

"I think you may well be right," said Bodeen, and before anyone could react he grabbed Julia by the arm and pulled her to him, twisting her arm up behind her back. The King and his guardsman surged forward, and Bodeen set his sword against Julia's throat.

"One more step and she dies!"

"Stay where you are!" thundered the King, and the guardsman stopped. The King stepped forward.

"That's far enough," said Bodeen. His sword moved slightly, and Julia felt her skin part under the blade's keen edge. Blood trickled down her neck to stain the high collar of her tunic. The King stopped where he was. Julia tried to breathe as lightly as possible.

"Let her go," said the King.

"I don't think so," said Bodeen calmly. "She's my way out of here. I'm going to back down this corridor, and you're going to let me do it. Because if you don't, you're going to have to invite the Princess Julia's father to a funeral."

Julia tried to ease the strain on her twisted arm, but Bodeen immediately hauled it back into place. Her head jerked as she cried out in pain, and more blood ran down her throat.

"Keep still, Princess," said Bodeen. "I don't want to hurt you, but I will if I have to."

He means it, thought Julia wildly. *He really means it.*

King John gestured for his guardsmen to stand steady,

and glared at Bodeen. "All right, traitor; how do you want to play this?"

"First of all, everybody puts their swords on the ground," said Bodeen, unperturbed. "Then Julia and I are going for a little walk. I have some people to warn. And Sire; if I see anyone following me, I'll cut this young lady's throat from ear to ear."

Julia slammed the back of her head into Bodeen's face. There was a muffled crack as his nose broke, and his grip loosened as he groaned with pain. Julia elbowed him sharply in the ribs, ducked under the threatening sword, and broke free of Bodeen while he was still off-balance. He lashed out blindly with his sword and Julia threw herself to one side. The blade whistled past her face, and Julia's sword flashed from her scabbard as she dropped automatically into her fighting stance. Bodeen shook his head to clear it, and cut at her again. There was a ring of steel on steel as Julia parried the blow, and then she beat aside his blade, lunged forward, and stabbed him just under the heart. For a moment the tableau held; Julia in full lunge, Bodeen staring down at the sword piercing his chest. He tried to lift his sword, and then blood gushed from his mouth, and he crumpled limply to the floor. The King started forward with his guardsmen, but Julia waved them back. She eased the sword from Bodeen's chest, and knelt beside him. He grinned up at her with bloody teeth.

"I forgot what a fighter you are," he said indistinctly. "Damn. *Damn.*"

"Would you really have killed me?" asked Julia.

"I don't know," said Bodeen. "Probably."

"Why?" said Julia fiercely. "Why did you betray the King?"

Bodeen chuckled painfully. "The Barons paid me better." And then he died.

Julia looked up as King John laid a gentle hand on her shoulder. "Come away from him, Julia. It's over now. One of my guards will see you safely back to your chambers."

"It isn't over yet," said Julia. She got to her feet and stared steadily at King John. "I want to meet the men who bought my friend."

"You don't have to do this," said the King. "This isn't really your business."

Julia put her hand to her throat and showed King John the blood on her fingers. "Isn't it?"

The King looked at her a moment, and then looked away. "Very well, then. But don't get in our way. This isn't going to be pretty."

"Treachery never is," said Julia, wiping her bloodstained hand on her leggings.

The King signalled to his guards, and he and his party moved purposefully down the corridor, heading deeper into the East Wing. Again and again the King's men discovered others guarding the corridors, but none of them put up a fight. Faced with a full company of the Royal Guard, a few ran and were cut down; most surrendered. Finally the party rounded a corner and surprised two guardsmen standing before a closed door. The King watched broodingly as the two guards were disarmed and taken to one side, and then he gestured brusquely to his Guard's Commander, who bowed formally, walked forward, and hammered on the closed door with his mailed fist.

"Open, in the name of the King!"

Chaos filled the Hall as the revellers ran frantically back and forth, shouting and screaming, and drawing swords and daggers. Some clapped their masks to their faces again, as though the flimsy disguises could still somehow protect them. Tables were overturned as the crowd surged this way and that, and those who fell in the crush were trampled blindly underfoot. Lord Darius tried desperately to quell the panic, but his voice was lost in the shrieking din. Cecelia clutched at his arm, her face pinched and white with shock, but Darius didn't even know she was there. Gregory fought his way through the milling crowd to join her, but the sheer press of bodies slowed his progress to a crawl.

The three Landsgraves stared at each other.

"The bookcase in Darius's study," said Blays. "We'll use the secret passage to escape, and then . . ."

"And then *what?*" whimpered Guillam, the cold sweat of fear already running down his face. "We've been betrayed! The King will have us all executed!"

"He's got to catch us first," snarled Blays. "Pull yourself together; you're supposed to be a Bladesmaster, dammit. If need be, you should be able to fight your way out of here;

unless you've been exaggerating your abilities all this time. Now calm down, and think. That door is solid oak, and bolted top and bottom; it'll take the King's men a good hour and more to cut their way through, and by then we'll be long gone. All we have to do is get to the stables, and we can be on our way back to Oakeshoff demesne before the King even knows we've left the Castle. Once we're safely inside my master's Keep, no one can touch us."

"Where's Harald?" said Bedivere suddenly.

The three Landsgraves looked quickly about them, but Harald had disappeared. The huge door shuddered suddenly under another thunderous knocking, and once again the voice without demanded entry in the name of the King. Businessmen and courtiers drew together into their tight little cliques, swords at the ready. Lords and Ladies stood together, and strove for dignity. The cries of fear and rage died quickly away, replaced by sullen mutterings and grim bravado. And then everyone in the Hall was suddenly silent as a new sound cut across the quiet; the unmistakable sound of a heavy steel bolt being drawn from its socket. They looked to the main door just in time to see Prince Harald pull back the second bolt, and then casually throw open the door. King John nodded calmly to his son as he walked slowly into the Hall, his company of guards fanning out around him. Harald raised an eyebrow when he spotted Julia among the guards, but shook his head when she started to say something to him. Julia nodded understandingly; there'd be time for explanations later. The King moved slowly forward into the Hall and the silent conspirators fell back before him, until only Darius, Cecelia, and Gregory remained to face him. Darius stared blankly at Harald, who leaned against the doorjamb and shook his head sadly.

"Sorry, Darius," said Harald. "You can't trust anyone these days."

The conspirators stared at the Prince speechlessly. Darius stepped forward, his mouth working.

"Why?" he asked finally. "*Why?* We would have made you King!"

Harald shrugged casually, but his eyes were cold. "If you'd betray one King, no doubt you'd betray another if it suited you. Did you think I was blind, Darius? You threatened my father, you threatened me; your schemes would have endangered the whole Forest Land! I know my duty to the Land, Darius; it's more important than you or I will ever be. Did you really think I'd give it into your keeping? You've never cared for anyone but yourself in your whole damn life."

"Enough, Harald," said the King. "You've done well. Are there any other exits to this Hall?"

"Just the one, Father, the door in the far right-hand corner; it leads to Darius's private chambers. They can't escape that way; it's a dead end."

Darius spun round to face his fellow conspirators. "Don't just stand there, damn you! We outnumber the guards three to one. Kill the King, and the Land is ours. Kill the King, or we'll all face the Headsman!"

The conspirators stared at Darius, and then at the King.

"Put down your swords," said King John calmly. "Those who surrender to me will be granted exile. I give you my word on it."

The conspirators looked at each other.

"Fight, damn you!" howled Darius, his face mottled with rage. "We can still win!"

One by one, the businessmen and the courtiers and the Lords and Ladies dropped their swords and daggers onto the polished wooden floor. Darius stared at them unbelievingly, his eyes wild and desperate. Gregory moved in close beside Cecelia, his sword at the ready.

"It's over, Darius," said Lord Vivian, his slow chill voice echoing on the silence. "Better an honorable exile than a traitor's death."

Darius turned and ran for the far door. Cecelia and Gregory followed him.

"After them!" roared the King, and twenty Royal Guard set off in hot pursuit. Julia ran with them, sword in hand. Bodeen was dead because of Darius and his schemes, and Julia had promised herself a vengeance. Pursued and pursuers disappeared through the far door, and once again a tense stillness fell across the Hall. Together, side-by-side, King John and Prince Harald walked slowly forward to confront the three Landsgraves, the only men in the Hall still holding swords. Half the Royal Guard moved protectively after the King.

"Hello, John," said Blays. "All in all, it's been an interesting day, hasn't it?"

King John smiled sadly. "Did you really think my son would betray me, Blays?"

The Landsgrave shrugged. "It seemed a reasonable possibility."

"We've known each other more years than I care to remember, Blays. Time was when you were one of my staunchest allies; as close to me as my own family. And now this. Why, Blays? Why did you turn against me?"

"Curtana," said Blays simply. "When you decided to draw that cursed sword, you became a threat to my master. You must have known I couldn't stand by and do nothing."

"And so you took the Curtana, for fear I'd use it against the Barons." King John shook his head wearily. "That was never my intention, Blays. Now more than ever, I need the Curtana to throw back the darkness. Return the sword to me, and I promise you'll face nothing more than exile."

Blays's eyes narrowed, and his smile was openly contemptuous. "What kind of a deal is that, John; you know we don't have the sword. Or are you just looking for an excuse to order our execution?"

"I order you to hand over the Sword of Compulsion, Blays."

"I don't have it."

"You stole it from my Armory, traitor!"

"Liar!"

Blays threw himself at King John, the point of his blade seeking the King's throat. Harald parried the blow, and two guardsmen ran Blays through. The Landsgrave fell heavily to the floor, and lay still. Blood welled out from under his body in a widening pool. Sir Bedivere roared and charged forward. Blood flew on the air as his heavy sword sheared through one guardsman's chain mail, and then buried itself in another's chest. Harald cursed under his breath and stepped forward, putting himself between Bedivere and the King. Bedivere jerked his blade free from the dying guard, and cut savagely at the waiting Prince. Harald ducked under the swinging sword, and lunged forward. His sword punched clean through Bedivere's chain mail and slammed between the giant Landsgrave's ribs. Bedivere growled once, and then knocked the Prince flying with one blow of his arm.

Harald fell backwards, still hanging onto his sword, and
Bedivere cursed once as the sword was jerked out of his
side. Blood streamed from the jagged wound as Bedivere
cut down guard after guard, doggedly fighting his way forward to where King John stood grimly waiting, sword in
hand.

The King stared at the blood-spattered Landsgrave with
horrified fascination. The sword in his hand was a comforting weight, but he knew it wasn't going to be enough to stop
Bedivere. His Guard Commander had already suggested he
should withdraw rather than risk himself, but he couldn't do
that. It wasn't enough for a King to be brave; he had to be
seen to be brave. Besides, if he didn't face Bedivere now,
he'd always wonder if he could have beaten the man. And
then the guards nearest him fell suddenly away in a flurry of
blood as Bedivere burst through their ranks. For a moment
the two men stared at each other, no more than a few yards
between them. Bedivere's chain mail hung in bloody tatters,
but his sword was still steady in his hand and his eyes were
filled with a constant crimson glare. King John could see
more of his guards moving forward to attack the Landsgrave,
but he knew they'd never reach Bedivere in time. The man
was going to kill him. Bedivere drew back his sword, and
King John braced himself for the blow he'd never feel. And
then Harald stepped in and hamstrung Sir Bedivere from
behind. The giant Landsgrave screamed with rage as he fell
heavily to the floor, his severed leg muscles no longer capable of supporting him. The impact of his fall knocked the
sword from his hand, and King John watched grimly as a
dozen guardsman ran Bedivere through again and again
while he lay helpless on the floor. Sir Bedivere died frothing
at the mouth and trying to bite the hands that wielded
swords against him.

"Sorry, Father," said Harald. "But he would have killed you."

King John nodded curtly, and turned to Sir Guillam. The
sole surviving Landsgrave stared desperately about him, his
sword trembling in his hand. John wondered briefly why the
man hadn't made a run for it, and then realized that both
Blays and Bedivere had fought and been killed in less than a
minute. He glared tiredly at Guillam, and then turned away.
There'd been enough killing for one day. He nodded to the
two nearest guards, and they snapped to attention.

"Take Sir Guillam away," he said gruffly, and the two guardsmen moved confidently forward.

Guillam stabbed the first guard through the heart, and cut the throat of the second while his first victim was still crumpling to the floor. For a moment nobody moved. The Landsgrave had moved so quickly his attack had been little more than a blur. And then somebody screamed, and everything happened at once. More guards moved forward, and Sir Guillam met them with his blade. He moved among the guards with murderous ease, deflecting every blow aimed against him with movements almost too fast to be seen. Guardsmen died without ever knowing what killed them.

"Dear God," said King John faintly. "The man's a Bladesmaster. I wondered why the Barons made him a Landsgrave . . . What better assassin could there be than a man who's literally unbeatable with a sword in his hand? I should have guessed . . . but they're so rare these days. So very rare . . ."

"You'd better get out of here," said Harald quietly. "Those guards aren't going to hold Guillam long; he's more of a danger than Bedivere ever was."

"I think you may well be right," said the King. "But I'm not running until I have to. Sir Guillam may be unbeatable with a sword, but let's see how he fares against a couple of crossbows."

He gestured to the two waiting guardsmen, who stepped quickly forward, loaded crossbows already in their hands. At the King's nod they moved a few feet apart, to be sure of catching Guillam in a crossfire, and then each man nestled the heavy wooden stock of his bow comfortably into his shoulder, and took careful aim. Guillam shrieked when he saw them, and without any warning turned and ran for the far door at the end of the Hall. He lashed out viciously at those courtiers who didn't get out of his way fast enough, and unarmed men and women fell in bloody heaps to mark his passing. And then two bowstrings twanged as one, and Guillam was slammed violently against the right-hand wall. He whimpered once, quietly, and then his sword fell from his limp fingers, and he hung still and silent from the two heavy steel bolts that pinned him to the wall.

Julia burst into Darius's private chambers just in time to see the huge bookcase swing slowly open, revealing a concealed passage. Darius stood beside the bookcase, waiting impatiently for it to open wide enough for him to enter. Cecelia clung frantically to his arm, sobbing uncontrollably with shock and panic. Gregory turned to face Julia, sword in hand. She hesitated in the doorway, sweeping her sword back and forth before her. She'd easily outdistanced the guards, weighed down by their heavy armor, and Julia quickly realized that they weren't going to catch up in time to help her. She smiled grimly; at best the odds were only two to one against her. Gregory hefted his sword and glanced back at Darius.

"Get Cecelia out of here," he said quietly. "I'll hold them off."

Darius tried to force his bulk into the slowly widening gap between the wall and the bookcase. Cecelia pressed close beside him, sobbing and clinging tightly to his arm as though for comfort. Darius pushed her away, but she only tightened her grip, wedging them both into the narrow gap. There was a rising clatter of approaching feet, and then the first of the guards burst into the room, followed quickly by a dozen more. Gregory moved forward to block their way. His sword trembled in his hand, but in his eyes Julia could see a cold determination to sell his life dearly. He grinned mockingly at the guards and then glanced back at the bookcase, just in time to see Darius draw a dagger from his sleeve and stab Cecelia again and again until she let go of his arm and fell limply to the floor. Gregory screamed her name, threw his sword away, and ran over to crouch beside Cecelia's unmoving body. Darius disappeared into the concealed passageway, and the bookcase slowly closed itself behind him. By the time the guardsmen got to it, the gap was once again too narrow to let them pass. They couldn't even stop the bookcase closing.

Julia approached Gregory cautiously, her sword held out before her, but he just sat on the floor, cradling Cecelia's body in his arms. Her eyes stared wildly, and blood seeped steadily from her tattered bodice, staining Gregory's tunic where he held her to him. He looked up at Julia, and she realized sickly that the young guardsman was crying.

"There wasn't any need for this," said Gregory. "No need for this. Cecelia? Cecelia, love?"

Julia sheathed her sword. "Come on," she said gruffly, "Leave her. There's nothing you can do for her now."

"Cecelia?"

"She's dead, Gregory."

He didn't hear her. He just sat there, rocking Cecelia in his arms, and crooning to her as though she was a sleeping child. The tiny bells of her dress chimed, quietly, with every movement. Tears ran unheeded down Gregory's cheeks, and his eyes saw nothing, nothing at all.

The quietly crackling fire was warm and comforting, but Julia was too tired even to hold out her hands to the leaping flames. Exhaustion had crept up on her in the short time it had taken to walk from Darius's Hall to the King's private chambers, and now a harsh persistent pain beat dully in her back and legs, and it was all she could do to keep her eyes from closing against her will. Julia tried to sit up straighter in her battered, overstuffed chair, and knuckled her bleary eyes. It would be only too easy to just lie back and doze off in the gentle warmth of the fire, but she couldn't let herself rest. It had been a long, hard day, and it didn't seem to be finished with her yet.

She hid a yawn behind her hand, and Harald smiled tiredly at her from the chair opposite. Unlike Julia, he slumped bonelessly in his chair, his long legs stretched out onto a footstool, his toes quietly toasting before the fire. Fatigue had shaded heavy bags under his eyes, giving him a dissipated, brooding look. His crooked smile suggested that he'd like to be pleased with himself, but was too tired to make the effort. A cup of hot mulled cider stood on a small table beside his chair, and he sipped at it from time to time, in an absentminded way, as though seeking to rid his mouth of an unpleasant taste. Julia smiled at the thought. She'd tried some of that cider herself, and how anyone could drink the stuff voluntarily was beyond her.

King John sat between the two of them in an old, high-backed chair, pulling thoughtfully at his beard and frowning into the fire. He still wore his thick fur coat, wrapped around his shoulders like a grandmother's shawl, and every now and again he shivered suddenly, as though in response to a cold wind only he could feel. Julia watched him worriedly. Tired though he obviously was, he should have been elated, or at the very least pleased; when all was said and done he had broken the rebellion before it even got started, killed most of the ringleaders, and avoided a civil war that would have destroyed the Forest Kingdom. But instead his mouth was grim and his gaze was troubled, and in some subtle way he looked . . . older.

Julia looked away. The King's private chambers were much smaller than she'd expected. Her father had lived in rooms large enough to drill troops in. Fabulous tapestries had hung from every marble wall, gorgeous mosaics covered the floors, and huge glass windows filled every room with a blaze of light. Of course, the Duke's palace was drafty as hell and impossible to heat, but the Duke never gave a damn. He had a position to maintain and appearances to keep up, and on bad days the Duke seemed to believe that if he so much as entered a room less than fifty feet square, he was slumming. Julia smiled tightly. There were things about Hillsdown she missed, but her father's palace definitely wasn't one of them. Neither was her father, come to that.

King John's rooms were altogether different. Not one of them was more than fifteen feet square, and they all seemed to have been furnished with comfort rather than fashion in mind. Julia looked approvingly about her at the combined sitting room and bedchamber, and smiled indulgently. The room had that comfortable, cramped cosiness that only men living alone can achieve. Books lined the walls from floor to ceiling and overflowed onto the tables and chairs, where they fought for space with plates and cups and papers of state. Chipped statuettes and faded miniatures filled every nook and cranny, jostling each other for position. Much of the room's furniture was worn and battered, and had the look of objects retained long past the time when their usefulness was over, simply because they were old and familiar. Even the many rugs that covered the floor from wall to wall were threadbare in patches. And then a log cracked loudly as it shifted position in the fire, and John stirred uneasily in his chair.

"Can't get used to being in my winter quarters this early," he grumbled. "Feels all wrong. Here it is barely autumn, and already there's snow drifts a foot deep and ice covering the moat. The leaves have barely left the trees, and yet without a roaring fire close at hand day and night, my old bones ache from the cold. And the damn servants set up my furniture all wrong. They did it on purpose, just because I shouted at them a few times."

"We did make our migration a little early this year," said Harald. "You have to make allowances."

"No, I don't," snapped John, "I'm the King!"

Harald and Julia laughed, and after a moment John smiled sheepishly.

"You're right; I shouldn't have shouted at them. But when you get to my age, the little things in life become more important than they should. In my rooms there's a place for everything; everything in its place. Oh you can smile, Julia, but all you see is a clutter. Well, maybe it is a mess, at that; but it's a mess of my making, and I'm used to it. If I wake in the night and it's dark, I know I can just reach out my hand and find the candle in its usual place. Not that it ever is dark now; I have to be sure the damn fire is properly banked before I go to bed, or risk spending half the night shivering under the covers. Can't stand that fire. It sits there while I'm trying to sleep, making me jump with sudden noises, and all the time glaring at me like a great red eye."

He broke off as the door swung suddenly open, and Lord Vivian strode calmly into the room with a guardsman's blade at his back. He stopped where the guard told him, a fair distance away from the King, and stood quietly at ease, ignoring everyone. His scabbard was empty, but his hands were unbound. King John nodded curtly to the guard, who bowed formally, and left. Lord Vivian looked at the King.

"Do you trust me enough to leave me unguarded in your presence?" he asked slowly.

"Of course," said Harald easily. "You're unarmed."

Vivian smiled coldly.

"You're here because I want to talk to you," said the King, shooting a warning scowl at Harald. "The Landsgraves are dead, and Darius is still missing; that makes you the nearest thing to a leader the rebels have. They'll listen to you, where they might not believe me. So, what I'm about to say to you is intended for their ears as well. Is that clear?"

"Of course," said Lord Vivian, his pale blue eyes disturbingly direct and unblinking. "But then, I'm hardly in a position to disagree, am I? My life is in your hands."

"You're to be exiled, not executed."

"We're dead either way. Traditionally, exiles are allowed neither weapons nor shelter till they're beyond the Forest boundaries. Once outside the protection of the Castle walls, my fellow traitors and I will be sitting targets for the first demons to come along."

"You could always beg protection from the Barons," said Harald.

"Hardly," said Vivian. "The Barons don't have enough food to feed their own people, never mind three hundred more mouths. And without their providing an armed escort, it's extremely unlikely any of us would survive the journey through the Forest. I've led scouting parties from one end of this Kingdom to the other; the demons are everywhere. Put us outside these walls unarmed, and you're condemning us to death."

"There is an alternative to exile," said the King, slowly.

Lord Vivian smiled coldly. "I thought there might be."

"Earlier this evening," said the King, "I granted an audience to a deputation from the outlying farms. They're overrun with demons, and fighting a losing battle against the plague. They came to me for help, and I had to tell them there was nothing I could do. But now it seems to me that, just possibly, there is some help I can offer, after all.

"Go with them, Lord Vivian; you and all your fellow rebels. Escort the deputation back to their farms, defend them against the demons, and teach the farmers how to defend themselves. I'll supply you with weapons, horses, and whatever provisions we can spare. It's not much of a choice I'm offering you; if the demons don't get you, the plague probably will. But all those who serve me in this matter will receive a full Pardon, and when the dark has finally been defeated, those of you who survive may return to the Forest Castle with a clean slate."

"You're right," said Vivian. "It isn't much of a choice. I accept your offer, on behalf of myself and my fellow traitors."

The King nodded stiffly. "I won't deceive you, my Lord Vivian; the odds are that none of you will survive to claim that Pardon."

"It's a fighting chance, Sire. And that's all I've ever asked for."

Lord Vivian stood straight and tall before the King, his

head held high, and for the first time since he entered the
King's chambers, there was something about him that might
have been dignity and pride. Julia studied him warily, impressed in spite of herself. It occurred to her that just
because a man is a traitor, it doesn't automatically follow
that he's a villain or a coward. Harald sipped at his drink,
and made no comment. King John stared into the fire,
rather than at Vivian, but when he spoke his voice was calm
and even.

"My Seneschal will take you to the farmers. Their leader
is a man called Madoc Thorne; obey his orders as you would
mine. Give them all the support you can, Lord Vivian; they
were true to me, even after I failed them."

"We will defend their lives with our own, Sire. My word
on it."

King John looked up from the fire, and stared at him for
a long moment. "Why did you betray me, Vivian?"

Vivian smiled. "Ambition, Sire. I wished to be High
Commander of the Guard."

"No other reason?"

"No, Sire," said Lord Vivian quietly. "No other reason
worth the mentioning."

Harald shot Vivian a quick glance, but said nothing.

"Well, then," said King John slowly, "I'll see you again,
my Lord, when all this is over."

"Of course, Sire," said Lord Vivian. He bowed formally
to the King, and then turned and left, ignoring Harald and
Julia. For a while nobody said anything, lost in their own
thoughts.

"Do you really think he's going to stay with the farmers?"
asked Julia.

"Of course," said Harald. "He gave his word."

Julia just looked at him.

"He's a strange chap, is Vivian," said the King. "I've
known him half my life, and I still don't understand what
goes on behind those cold, empty eyes of his. He firmly
believes in looking out for his own best interests, and yet in
his own strange way he's intensely loyal to the Land. He
follows no cause save his own, but he's never been known to
break his word. He wants to be reinstated, and he wants to
do penance; I've just given him the chance to do both. He'll
hate taking orders from peasants, but he'll do it, and cut

down any of his fellows who refuse. A strange chap, Vivian; but always loyal to the Land and its needs."

"Don't worry, Julia," said Harald. "Vivian's a cold bastard, but he knows his duty. He won't betray us again."

"Well," said the King, pulling thoughtfully at his beard, "That's two problems solved, anyway. Unfortunately, we're still no nearer finding the Curtana."

Julia looked at him sharply. "I thought the Landsgraves had it?"

"Apparently not. I've got my guards searching the traitors' quarters, but I don't think they're going to find anything. Blays swore till the end that he hadn't taken it, and I'm beginning to believe him."

"Guillam or Bedivere could have taken it."

"Not without Blays knowing."

"I'm inclined to agree," said Harald, staring soberly into his empty cup. "And that means somewhere in this Castle there's a traitor we haven't found yet."

"Damn right," said Julia. "The same traitor who let demons into the South Wing."

"I'd forgotten about that," said Harald.

"I haven't," said Julia. "I've still got the scars to remind me."

"Time to worry about that tomorrow," said the King, yawning openly. "All in all, it's been a fairly successful day, I suppose. Considering how easily it might all have gone horribly wrong."

"True," said Harald. "If you hadn't brought those crossbowmen with you, there's no telling how many Sir Guillam would have killed."

"Quite," said John. "I was lucky there. The Landsgraves openly threatened me earlier this evening, when I was meeting with the farmers' deputation, only to back down and leave when the farmers supported me. That intrigued me; what on earth did the farmers have that could route the Landsgraves so easily? The answer was simple; my guards had swords, but the farmers had longbows. So, I played a hunch, and it worked out."

There was a long, thoughtful silence.

"Three hundred and forty-eight traitors," John said finally, all the satisfaction gone from his voice. "Three hundred and forty-eight. Not as many as I'd feared, but a damn sight more than there should have been."

"Don't blame yourself," said Harald sternly. "They're the ones who failed the Land, not you. Besides, I talked to most of them at the party; believe me, you're better off without them."

"How could you play along with such people?" asked Julia. "Living a double life; different lies for different people . . . how could you stand it? Why didn't you just turn Darius in when he first approached you?"

"He did," said John. "I persuaded him to carry on with the deception, but keep me informed. The party was Harald's idea, and thanks to him we caught all the rats in one fell swoop. Now I know who I can trust, and who is false. And, I know my son is loyal."

Harald raised an elegant eyebrow. "Was there ever any doubt?"

"No," said King John fondly. "But it was nice to be proved right."

"What's going to happen with the Barons now?" asked Julia. "More plots; more conspiracies?"

"They won't be any trouble," said John, smiling grimly. "They wanted to find out which of us was the stronger, and now they know. They'll just disown their Landsgraves, publicly condemn the rebels, and promise me anything as long as I don't withdraw my troops and leave them to face the demons on their own. No, Julia; they won't risk rocking the boat again."

"Then it's all over," said Julia. "The rebellion is dead."

"Not quite," said Harald. "There's still no sign of Lord Darius. We did finally force that damn bookcase open, but all we found was a tunnel leading into the air vents, and they go on for miles. I'd no idea so many of the interior walls were hollow."

"But that means he could be anywhere," said Julia. She stared quickly about her, and shivered.

Harald shrugged. "Just another rat in the walls. We'll get him, Julia; never fear. The guards are searching the tunnels for him even now. We'll have him by morning."

"How's Gregory?" asked Julia suddenly.

Harald and John looked blankly at each other.

"Who?" said Harald.

"Cecelia's lover."

"Oh, him." Harald frowned. "Hanged himself in his cell, poor bastard."

"I never liked him," said Julia. "But somehow I felt sorry for him. He wasn't a bad sort, at the end. He deserved better than Darius and Cecelia."

John shrugged. "I've no doubt he would have killed any one of us, if the Barons had ordered it. He was just in the wrong place, at the wrong time."

"And he loved the wrong woman," said Julia.

"Yes," said Harald. "I suppose he did."

"I'm tired," said Julia. "Unless you want me for anything else, I'm going back to my chambers and get some sleep."

"I'll walk part of the way with you," said Harald.

Julia looked at him. "All right," she said finally. "I think I'd like some company."

She levered herself up out of her chair, and Harald was there to steady her as she swayed tiredly on her feet.

The King nodded benignly. "Get yourself some rest, my children; you've earned it. It's been a long hard day for all of us."

They were almost at the door, when the King suddenly stirred in his chair.

"Julia . . . Bodeen was a friend of yours, wasn't he?"

"No," said Julia. "I didn't really know him at all."

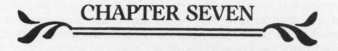

CHAPTER SEVEN

The Long Night

Darkness lay across the Forest Land from boundary to boundary, complete and unbroken save for an uncertain pool of light surrounding the Forest Castle. Demons moved silently through the smothering dark, sharpening their claws on the decaying bark of dying trees. No sun shone, and though a moon sailed endlessly on the night skies, its light was foul and unhealthy. Plants died for lack of sunlight, and wildlife either starved or fell prey to the demons' never-ending hunger. Snow and ice covered all the ground, and the freezing air drew the warmth from everything it touched. Men barricaded themselves and their families inside whatever shelter they could find, and prayed for a dawn that never came. Cold and dark and utterly merciless, the long night held dominion over all.

A new sound suddenly rang forth into the Darkwood: a deep sonorous tone like the peal of a huge iron bell. The sound grew steadily louder, building into a mighty roar that reverberated through the long night, shaking the ground and the trees, and challenging the silence. Demons snarled and shuddered and tried to flee, but the unrelenting sound came from everywhere and nowhere, and there was no escaping it. And then the great bass roar climaxed and fell silent as space itself ripped open, and a blinding silver light poured out in the Darkwood, Prince Rupert and his party had finally come home.

Rupert stared dazedly about him as he floated down from the shimmering silver tunnel, and staggered slightly as the ground rose suddenly up to slam against his feet. He was sure he'd spent no more than a few seconds in the tunnel, but in that brief moment the world had moved on, and everything was changed. A familiar stench of decay and corruption filled his nostrils, and the horrid numbing oppression fell upon him like an old familiar cloak. He gripped the unicorn's reins tightly as he stared wildly around, convinced the Warlock had bungled the spell and dropped them back in the Darkwood they'd just passed through, but then the last of the guards landed safely òn the uneven trail, and the silver tunnel suddenly snapped together and disappeared, taking its brilliant light with it. Abandoned in the unrelenting dark, Rupert's eyes went automatically to the only remaining light; the dim wavering glow surrounding Forest Castle.

For a moment Rupert hurt so bad he couldn't breathe, and he shook his head in wordless denial. He'd made it to the Dark Tower in time; there was no way in which the long night could have reached this far into the Forest. But there before him stood the Castle, shimmering whitely under a thick blanket of snow and ice and hoarfrost. Long jagged icicles hung from every window and turret, and the moat seemed no more than a single great slab of ice. Torches flickered at regular intervals along the battlements, but their dirty yellow glow did little to throw back the encroaching night. Rupert shuddered uncontrollably, but it had little to do with the bitter cold that was already seeping into his bones. It was one thing to fight his way through the Darkwood as part of the quest, or because it stood between him and the High Warlock, but it had no right to be here, threatening his home. The Darkwood had always been something that happened somewhere else; somewhere comfortably far away. Until now, he'd never actually believed that the Castle which had served the Forest Kings for thirteen generations could ever really fall to the darkness. It was impossible; it couldn't be happening . . . Rupert fought hard against his rising hysteria, and slowly brought himself back under control. His mind turned frantically this way and that, searching for an answer, any answer, as to what had gone wrong. How could the Darkwood have spread so fast? And then, finally, Rupert looked up.

Directly above him, floating on a starless night that went on forever, hung the Full Moon. Its color was that of tainted cheese or leprous flesh; the only color the eye can see at dead of night. The Blue Moon had risen.

Time moves differently in the Darkwood.

Rupert turned slowly to stare at the High Warlock. "What have you done?" demanded the Prince, his voice little more than a whisper. "Damn you, what have you done?"

The Warlock looked at him, and swallowed dryly. His face was blank with shock. "I don't know," he said finally. "Something must have interfered with my teleport spell. This is the right place, but the wrong time. I can't understand it . . ."

"We can discuss this later, Sire." The Champion's voice was calm and even, but his knuckles showed white where they gripped the long shaft of his double-headed war axe. "There are demons all around us. Our arrival seems to have startled them almost as much as it did us, but they won't stay startled much longer. We'd do well to get out of here while we still can."

Rupert glanced briefly at his guardsmen, already set up in a tight defensive circle of drawn sword and glowing lanterns, and nodded slowly. Their quiet competence steadied him, and he ruthlessly suppressed the last vestiges of fear and panic that still moved deep within him.

"You're right, sir Champion; let's get the men moving. You and I will take the lead, the High Warlock will guard the rear with his magic. You can do that much, can't you, sir Warlock?"

The High Warlock flinched, and then nodded stiffly. Rupert drew his sword, hefted the familiar comforting weight, and turned to his guards.

"Stay close together, watch your backs, and once we've started don't stop for anything. It can't be more than five hundred yards to the Castle, and after all we've been through, it's going to take more than a few damn demons to stop us going home! All right; let's go. Last man in pays for the beer."

It wasn't much of a pep talk, and Rupert knew it, but the guards raised a ragged cheer, anyway. Rupert grinned savagely back, fiercely proud of all of them, and then turned abruptly away so they wouldn't see the tears that stung his eyes. He took a firm hold of the unicorn's reins and started forward; not hurrying, but not dawdling either. If the demons thought the party was running from them, they'd attack. A show of confidence might just hold the creatures off while the party gained some precious yards. At this stage, every little bit helped. Rupert glanced surreptitiously about him. The Champion strode at his side, hefting his massive war axe as though it was weightless. The guards and the Warlock padded quietly along behind him in a tight bunch, alert and ready for any sudden sound or movement in the surrounding dark. The Warlock made more noise than all the guards put together. Rupert couldn't hear the demons that moved along with the party, but every now and then there was a sudden gleam of watching bloodred eyes, glaring in the dark like angry coals, or a fleeting glimpse of silent misshapen figures as they darted from shadow to shadow before and behind the party.

Rupert scowled, and tried to shrug his cloak more comfortably around him. The bitter cold grated painfully in his bones, and he couldn't seem to stop shivering. It had been a long time since he'd known anything but the snow and sleet and freezing air of the winter come early. He was beginning to forget what it was like to feel warm. A sudden movement caught the corner of his eye, and he glared helplessly into the darkness. The Castle was drawing steadily nearer, but its light didn't penetrate far into the Darkwood. Rupert smiled grimly. He didn't need to see the demons to know they were there, and it didn't matter a damn how many there were. If it came to a fight, the odds were that none of his party would survive to reach the Castle. Their only hope was to get as close to the Castle as possible, and then make a run for it. It wasn't much of a hope.

Rupert gripped his swordhilt until his fingers ached, but his hand still shook. The unremitting weight of the Darkwood beat down on him in all its old familiar horror, and it was no easier to bear now than it had been before. Every time his duty forced him back into the darkness, he hoped against hope it would be easier to deal with, but it never was. Every time, it was worse. Fear and panic and mind-numbing despair sank into him like icy water in his soul, until all he wanted was to lie down, curl into a ball, and scream for it to go away. But he couldn't do that. He wouldn't do that. He hadn't brought his men this far, just to give up on them when they were nearly home. Rupert stared at the Castle before him, drawing nearer with every step. Nearly there. Nearly home. So bloody near . . .

The unicorn lurched tiredly beside him, and Rupert reached up and patted the animal's neck comfortingly.

"Not much longer now," he muttered gruffly. "One last stretch of the legs, and then we can all take a rest."

"You keep telling me that," said the unicorn dourly. "A nice long rest in a warm, dry stable . . . I'll believe it when I see it, and not before. I just hope they've got some decent food. I've had nothing but grass for weeks. I think I'd kill for some barley."

"Once we're safely in the Castle, I'll bury you in barley."

"Given our present situation, I don't think that remark is in the best of taste."

Rupert and the unicorn shared a look, and then chuckled quietly together.

"It's been a strange journey, all told," said Rupert.

"I wouldn't argue with that," said the unicorn.

"You know we're probably not going to make it."

"The thought had crossed my mind."

"I just want to say . . . thanks. For being with me, when I needed you."

"Wouldn't have missed it for anything. You're not a bad sort, Rupert. For a human."

"Thanks; I think. Friends again?"

"Sure; why not."

"Great."

"I still want that barley you promised me."

Rupert laughed aloud, and the Champion looked at him strangely. Rupert hefted his sword, and was pleased to discover that his hand was now a little steadier. In a way, he almost wished the demons would attack, and get it over with. When he was fighting, there wasn't time to be scared. He breathed deeply to calm himself, and instantly regretted it as the Darkwood's constant stench of decay was suddenly strong in his nostrils again. Rupert shook his head grimly, and glanced back over his shoulder. The guards were still moving silently along behind him, swords at the ready, but Rupert's heart missed a beat when he realized the High Warlock was no longer with them. For a moment panic froze him in place, and then he relaxed with a great sigh of pent-in breath as he looked up and saw the Warlock had

taken to the air, floating silently and serenely a good ten
feet above the ground. The Warlock's eyes were closed, and
a deep scowl furrowed his brow, as though he was concentrating on some problem not immediately apparent. His
hands seemed to be glowing slightly, and for the first time
Rupert realized his party was moving in its own narrow pool
of light. Rupert looked away. At least the Warlock's magic
was good for something.

The Castle drew steadily nearer, shimmering palely like a
giant stone ghost in its own torchlight. There were no guards
on the battlements, but the drawbridge was up. Rupert
smiled dourly. If the demons ever decided to overrun the
Castle, they wouldn't bother using the drawbridge, they'd
just swarm right over the walls. He remembered the last
time he'd ridden into the Castle courtyard, only to find it
silent and deserted .... He shook his head angrily. He
couldn't have come this far, only to find he'd returned home
too late; he just couldn't.

Where the hell are the demons? What are they waiting for?

The Castle was three hundred yards away. Two hundred.
One hundred. And then the demons came for them.

Rupert barely had time to raise his sword before the
demons were all around him, and then there was only a
confused melée of steel and blood and reaching clawed
hands. He swung his sword in short, vicious arcs, cutting
through demon flesh with controlled, economical strokes,
and the fresh stink of demon blood was heavy on the air.
They came from every direction; twisted, malformed creatures with fangs and claws and eyes that knew nothing but
an endless, never-sated hunger. The earth trembled under
Rupert's feet and then cracked sluggishly open. Hundreds
of pale slimy tentacles whipped up out of the broken earth
and reached for the struggling guardsmen with a horrid
single-mindedness of purpose. Rupert glared down into one
of the wider cracks as he cut through a writhing tentacle; the
crack was filled with hundreds of needle-fanged mouths and
a single great staring eye, easily a dozen feet across. Rupert
shrank back, and the eye moved slightly to follow him.
Three tentacles wrapped themselves around a guard and
tore him to pieces, all in a matter of seconds. He barely had
time to scream. Something with wings and black-furred spider legs swooped down onto a beleagured guard, tore out

his throat, and disappeared back into the dark before the body hit the ground. Exhausted almost beyond the point of pain, Rupert put his back to one of the gnarled dying trees, and swung his sword mechanically back and forth before him. The demons were packed so closely about him, it was impossible to miss.

And still the demons came; some on two legs, some on four, and some came slithering on their bellies in the dirt. In the unsteady light it seemed to Rupert that many of the nightmare shapes shifted and ran like watery clay even as they pressed slightly forward to attack the beleaguered party. Strange unhealthy hybrids of plant and animal and insect rose and fell before him, loathsome creatures that could never have survived in the natural world. Rupert fought on. There were always more to replace those who died under his blade. A heavy weight fell on him from above, and something cold and scaly clung tightly to his shoulders while its slender clawed hands groped eagerly for his eyes and throat. Rupert howled in fear and rage, and reached desperately for the creature with his left hand. The demons ringed before him surged forward, and he cut frantically at them with his sword. Out of the corner of his eye, Rupert saw the grinning elongated head behind him swing suddenly forward, and then hundreds of jagged serrated teeth buried themselves in his left shoulder. He cried out sickly as the long jaws snapped shut, and dropped his sword as the creature on his back tightened its grip. The demons before him leapt for his throat, and then a blast of searing white light ripped through them, leaving behind nothing but a few charred, distorted bones.

Rupert lurched forward, still feebly clawing at the demon on his back, and another blast of balefire tore the creature from him. Only the head remained, clinging grimly to his shoulder even in death. Rupert fell to his knees, and retrieved his sword from where he'd dropped it. He tried to get up again, and couldn't. The Champion was suddenly at his side, prising open the demon head's jaws with his dagger. Rupert looked away, unable to watch. All around him, the demons were falling back into the surrounding shadows, unable to face the High Warlock's balefire. The blood-smeared tentacles withdrew into the earth and were gone, and within seconds the Darkwood was once again utterly still and silent. The Champion finally worked the demon head loose, and threw it to one side. He helped Rupert to his feet, and the unicorn moved quickly forward to stand beside the Prince. Rupert leaned thankfully against the animal's side as some of his strength slowly returned to him. The pain in his shoulder showed no sign of dying away, but at least now he could think through it. He could feel blood running down his left arm in a steady stream, but there was no feeling at all in his left hand.

I'll worry about that later, he thought determinedly. *I'll worry about a lot of things later.*

"Sir Champion!" he called thickly.

"Sire." The Champion stood beside him, his back straight and his head unbowed. His tattered chain mail was drenched with demon blood.

"We've got to get to the Castle, sir Champion. There's nothing left but running now; if we stand and fight, we're all dead. Get the men together, and tell them we're moving now. The High Warlock can run interference for us. Am I making sense? Yes. Good. You lead the way, sir Champion; we'll follow."

"Yes, Sire. We'd make better time if you were to ride the unicorn."

Rupert looked at the unicorn. Even in his dazed state, he could clearly see the blood that dappled the animal's heaving sides. The unicorn had looked like this once before; the time he'd nearly died in the Darkwood clearing . . . Rupert thrust the memory away.

"How about it, unicorn?" he asked quietly. "Can you carry me that far?"

"Sure; no problem. I'm barely scratched. Climb aboard, Rupert."

The Champion made a stirrup with his hands, and half lifted, half placed Rupert onto the unicorn's back. Rupert swayed a moment in the saddle, and fought hard not to pass out. He glanced down at his right hand, and smiled grimly. Somehow, he was still hanging onto his sword. A good omen; if you believed in omens.

Out in the darkness, something stirred.

"Run for the Castle! Now!" Rupert's voice was little more than a harsh rasp, but his guards were off and running almost before he'd finished speaking. He clung desperately to the unicorn's sides with his knees as the animal started forward, and stared grimly about him. The Champion ran before him, his war axe at the ready. The High Warlock flew overhead, balefire crackling and hissing around his hands. And fourteen guardsmen followed Rupert home.

Fourteen. Fourteen out of fifty. Rupert leant wearily forward against the unicorn's neck as the last of his strength flowed out of him. His hold on his sword slowly loosened, and only the awful pain that shuddered through him with every jolt of the uneven trail kept him awake. He didn't mind failing; he was used to that. But his men had followed him and trusted him, and all he'd done was lead them to their deaths. Just as he'd once led the unicorn to his death, lying broken and bloodied in a small clearing in the Darkwood. Only this time, there wasn't any Rainbow to drive back the dark.

His eyes kept dropping shut, even with the pain in his shoulder. Rupert knew he was probably going into shock, but didn't care. The shock seemed to be numbing both his pain and his memories, and he'd settle for that. The giant trees of the Forest loomed in and out of the darkness as the unicorn carried him steadily toward the Castle, and Rupert swallowed sickly when he saw the vast patches of open decay that mottled their bark. For all the darkness and the swarming demons, he hadn't been able to accept that the Forest was dead; the very idea was unthinkable. The Forest had existed for endless centuries before man, and deep down Rupert had always believed that it would still be there centuries after man had vanished and been forgotten. To see the great and ancient trees already dead and rotting hurt Rupert even more than his own likely imminent death; for if the Forest itself could fall to the darkness, what chance was there for anything or anybody. The last of Rupert's hope died in that moment, and slowly the world began to fade away around him, taking the pain and the heartbreak with it.

And then a grinning demon came flying out of the darkness at him, and his reflexes threw his sword up to meet it. The long spindly creature impaled itself on the blade, and fell away snarling soundlessly. Rupert stared blankly at his bloody sword, and then shook his head fiercely as a slow steady anger burned through him, shocking him awake again.

He might be too late to save the Forest, but perhaps he could still avenge it. More demons came pouring out of the darkness, and Rupert cut about him with his sword as the unicorn struggled to find one last burst of speed that would get him to the Castle before the demons could drag him down.

The Champion cut his way through the demons without even slowing, his eyes fixed on the raised drawbridge ahead. The guardsmen ranged themselves to either side of the unicorn, and fought furiously to hold off the solid heaving mass of demonkind that had erupted silently out of the surrounding dark. Rupert watched helplessly as three more of his men died horribly under the flailing claws and fangs of the demons, and concentrated on hanging onto the unicorn as best he could. He tried to at least grasp the reins with his left hand, but his fingers wouldn't obey him. The Castle was only fifty yards away, but it might as well have been fifty miles. The way ahead was completely blocked by the demons. A swiftly choked scream to his right told Rupert that he'd lost another guard, but he couldn't spare the time to look. The demons pressed close around him, and the unicorn's pace dropped a little more. Rupert felt a sudden almost overpowering urge to turn the unicorn around and ride back into the darkness, to kill and kill until he and his blade were drenched in demon blood. To die fighting, rather than running. The impulse passed as swiftly as it came, and Rupert grinned savagely as he cut through a reaching demon; he hadn't come this far just to throw his life away on a gesture. He'd fought his way through the Darkwood to summon the High Warlock from his Dark Tower, and now he was going home. And to hell with anyone or anything that got in his way.

The unicorn struggled on, step by step. Rupert's sword arm rose and fell in steady butchery. The Castle drew gradually closer . . . and still the demons came. Forty yards. Thirty. Twenty-five. *We might just make it after all*, thought Rupert. *We might just make it!* Eerie, distorted faces loomed out of the darkness around him, and he cut at them automatically with his sword. A slow, heavy thudding began somewhere far behind him; a deep muffled sound, like the beating of a giant heart. At first Rupert thought it was thunder, and it wasn't until the ground itself began to shake in time to the deep bass rhythm that he realized he was listening to the sound of something indescribably huge and heavy moving slowly through the Darkwood after him. Rupert risked a quick glance back over his shoulder, but the impenetrable darkness turned aside his gaze with contemptuous ease. And then the hair on the back of his neck rose as a vile, choking roar sounded on the long night; a deafening bellow of unthinking malevolent rage. The ground shook violently as the creature drew nearer, and Rupert realized that something different was coming out of the darkness; something huge and old and unspeakably powerful. He remembered the great white worm he'd fought in the Coppertown pit, and urged the unicorn on.

Light blazed suddenly in the long night, throwing back the dark, as the High Warlock finally unleashed his power. Trees were uprooted and thrown aside, and demons died howling silently as a vast invisible force slammed them to the ground and crushed the life from them. The earth rose and fell like a great slow wave as the Warlock's magic moved across it, and deep in the darkness something huge howled in pain and fear. Rupert shuddered as he felt the Warlock's power pulsing on the fetid air, coursing through the darkness, wild and unstoppable. There was something primal and savage in the magic the High Warlock had set loose in the world, something held at bay only by the Warlock's will. It seethed and crackled on the air, destroying everything outside of Rupert's party, and yet somehow, deep in his soul, Rupert knew that it was only the High Warlock that kept this awful power from flying free, to attack the Castle and the Forest and all that was, in one vast orgy of destruction. The demons fled back into the darkness, and the power followed them. Rupert slowly lowered his sword, and the unicorn broke into a ragged trot as he realized the way to the Castle was suddenly clear again. The Warlock flew after them, slowly twisting and turning in mid-air, as though in response to a wind only he could feel.

Rupert swayed in the saddle as the Castle Keep loomed suddenly up before him, and he knew the last of his strength was finally running out. He clenched his fingers around his swordhilt, desperate not to drop it, and something squat and hairy and many-legged came flying out of the darkness and dropped onto the unicorn's neck. The unicorn staggered, and almost fell. The demon clung tenaciously, its weight almost forcing the unicorn to a halt. Thin runnels of blood trickled down the unicorn's neck as the demon's barbed legs tightened their grip. The unicorn reared up and shook his head fiercely, neighing shrilly as the demon clawed for his eyes.

Rupert struggled to stay in the saddle, and cut viciously at the demon with his sword. The blade sliced clean through the clinging creature, but it didn't die. No blood ran from the wide cut, and even as Rupert watched, the edges of the wound knitted together and were gone. Rupert drew back his sword for another blow, and the demon's squat body writhed and flowed from one loathsome shape to another as it slithered along the unicorn's neck toward him. It left a trail of tiny bloody wounds on the unicorn's pale white skin, as though its belly concealed hundreds of little sucking mouths. Somehow the unicorn still staggered on, shrieking and neighing piteously, half out of his mind with shock and pain. Rupert cut at the demon again and again, aiming his blows carefully to avoid harming the unicorn, but still the creature wouldn't die. Mismatched arms and legs sprouted continuously from its hairy body, and were as quickly reabsorbed. Rupert ran the demon through from end to end, and it surged forward along the blade to seize his sword arm with half a dozen bony hands. Its touch burned like acid. Two sickly yellow eyes peered at him over a wide slavering mouth filled with hundreds of sliding, grating teeth. Rupert swore grimly, and struck at the creature with his numb left arm. The fingers of his left hand sank deep into the demon's flesh, just above its eyes, and then slowly started to close. The demon struggled to break free, but Rupert somehow ignored the mounting pain that seared through his arm and shoulder again, and concentrated on forcing his hand deeper and deeper into the demon's flesh. His fingers suddenly came alive, screaming agony with every movement, but past the pain he could feel something soft and yielding pulsing frantically in his hand; the demon's heart. The creature released his sword arm and launched itself at his throat, its slavering mouth stretched impossibly wide. Rupert laughed, and with the last of his strength, threw the demon to the ground. The unicorn trampled it under his hooves again and again, neighing hysterically. The demon finally stopped moving, and the unicorn rushed blindly for the Castle.

The ice-covered moat lay straight ahead, and within moments the unicorn's hooves were drumming loudly on the ancient sturdy wood of the drawbridge. Rupert shook his aching head to clear it. He hadn't seen the drawbridge being lowered. The Champion had already entered the Keep, and was standing before the closed inner doors, hammering on them with his mailed fist. The doors swung slowly open before him. Rupert entered the Keep, and then reined in his unicorn, and waited impatiently for the doors to open wide enough to admit him. He heard a movement behind him, and looked back over his shoulder. Ten guardsmen were slowly approaching the drawbridge, exhaustion showing in their every movement. What remained of their armor was soaked in blood, but every one of them still carried his sword. The High Warlock floated slowly after them, power surging from him in great shimmering waves that bowed the huge trees like a mighty gale. Demons lay writhing on the ground as his magic moved over them, their misshapen bodies melting and running away into the gore-spattered earth. The Champion yelled that the doors were finally open, and the unicorn lurched forward. Rupert brandished his sword defiantly at the darkness, and rode through the gatehouse into the safety of the Castle courtyard. The doors started to close behind him.

"No!" yelled Rupert, his voice almost inhumanly harsh from pain and fatigue. "Leave the doors! My men are still out there!"

"To hell with your men!" screamed back a furious man-at-arms. "There are demons out there! Close the doors!"

He broke off suddenly as Rupert reined the unicorn in beside him, and then leant forward and set the point of his sword at the man-at-arms' throat. Their eyes met, and the man-at-arms' objections died away to nothing. He stared up at the torn and bloodied figure leaning over him and knew, beyond any doubt, that this man was more dangerous than any creature from the Darkwood.

"Those doors are staying open till all my men are in," said Rupert. "Now give the order, or I swear I'll cut you down where you stand."

"Hold the doors!" yelled the man-at-arms, "And stand by to repel demons; we've got men coming in!"

Rupert lowered his sword and turned away to stare out into the darkness, the man-at-arms already forgotten. His men were finally coming home, and tired and battered and bloodied as he was, a grim pride welled up in him as his ten remaining guardsmen helped each other across the draw-bridge and into the courtyard, waving away all offers of help from the Castle men-at-arms. Even after all they'd been through, after all the Darkwood had thrown at them, they were still determined to finish their journey on their own two feet. The High Warlock's light suddenly flickered and went out, and he flew down to stand in the middle of the drawbridge, glaring out into the darkness. The High Magic he'd unleashed no longer beat upon the air, but some trace of its ancient power still remained, lending his short frame a dark and brooding dignity. Demons gathered on the edge of the Castle's pool of light, but made no move to approach the Warlock. He turned his back on them, and stalked through the Keep and into the courtyard. The demons surged forward.

Men-at-arms howled orders to the gatehouse, and the two huge double doors swung slowly together. Rupert just had time to glimpse the drawbridge rising into the air, already overrun with clinging demons, and then the great oaken doors slammed shut, and men rushed forward to slide the heavy steel bolts into position. Rupert finally sheathed his sword, and slumped exhausted in the saddle. Thousands of demons pounded frustratedly on the outer walls of the Castle, the deafening sound rising and falling like a never-ending roll of thunder. And far away, deep in the rotten heart of the darkness, something awful and inhuman howled its cheated rage.

Rupert swung unsteadily down from his saddle, managed a few uncertain steps, and then sat down suddenly with his back to the inner wall. Even through twenty feet of solid stone, he could still feel a faint vibration from the demons hammering on the outer wall. He cradled his left arm in his lap, and for the first time in too many months, allowed himself to relax. His head was swimming madly, he was starting to shake with delayed shock and reaction, and only the jagged pain in his left shoulder kept him from passing out on the spot, but he didn't give a damn. He was back in the Forest Castle, and that was all that mattered. For good or bad, whatever the consequences, he'd come home.

Bit by bit the demons stopped their assault on the Castle wall, and the great roar of sound slowly died away to an unbroken silence that was somehow even more ominous. Rupert closed his eyes and just let himself drift for a moment. He'd done everything he'd been asked to do, and now he was entitled to a rest. Just for a while. A quiet, tired whickering close to hand jerked his eyes open again, and he looked up to see the unicorn standing beside him, his great bony head hanging wearily down, his hooded crimson eyes staring at nothing. Rupert smiled fondly at the animal.

"Good run, unicorn," he said hoarsely.

The unicorn snorted, and fixed him with a sardonic eye. "You'll never see better, that's for sure. I've never run that fast in my life. It's amazing what you can do when you have to. How are you feeling?"

"Awful, bordering on lousy. I think I'd kill for a drink of water. Assuming I could find the energy."

"Never mind the malingering; where's that barley you promised me?"

Rupert managed a kind of laugh, and for the first time found the strength to raise his head and look about him. The courtyard was packed with people from wall to wall; farm folk, villagers, and townspeople, who must have fled to the Castle for protection when the demons overran their homes. Rufugees from the long night, they huddled together in small family groups, their few remaining possessions scattered around them in pathetic little heaps. Open fires burned fitfully throughout the courtyard, fighting off the dark winter with a little heat and light. But still the courtyard remained bitter cold, and dark shadows gathered between the fires. There were a few ragged tents and lean-tos, providing an illusion of privacy, but little actual shelter. Animals wandered freely from fire to fire, grubbing quietly for what scraps of food they could find. With so many people and animals packed together, the smell was appalling, but nobody seemed to notice. They were too used to it.

The worst part was the silence; people huddled together for warmth and comfort, but said nothing. They just stared lethargically into their fires, with eyes that had seen too much horror and too little hope, and waited for the darkness to come and take them. Rupert smiled sourly. Even the Castle walls, and the magic they contained, weren't enough to keep out all of the Darkwood's influence. Fear and uncertainty and despair hung upon the air like a thick choking fog, reflected clearly in the helpless terror that showed in every refugee's face. Darkness had entered their souls, and laid its mark upon them. Rupert looked away. After all his travels, and despite everything he'd faced and accomplished, he'd still failed in his mission. He'd got back too late. The Blue Moon had risen, and the Forest had fallen to the endless night. And out of the fifty men who'd followed him on his quest to the Dark Tower, only ten had returned.

I tried, thought Rupert dejectedly. *At least I tried.*

He fought off a wave of self-pity that would have drowned him if he'd let it. He'd feel sorry for himself later, when he had the time. He hadn't reported to the King yet, and he ought to take a look at his men and make sure they were all right. They'd had a rough time of it, at the end. Rupert looked around for the Champion, but he was nowhere in sight. No doubt he'd gone straight to the King, to inform him of the High Warlock's return. Rupert frowned. As leader of the party, it was his place to report on the mission, not the Champion's. At the very least, the Champion should have checked with him first. Rupert smiled grimly as the answer came to him. The Champion had only sworn to obey his orders until the mission was over. Now they were back at the Castle, Rupert was once again nothing more than a second son, and what little control he'd had over the Champion was at an end. In fact, he'd do well to start watching his back again. Boots scuffed on the cobblestones close at hand, and Rupert looked up to find the man-at-arms from the gates glaring down at him. Tall, broad-shouldered and muscular, he would have been an impressive sight even without the anger that darkened his scarred face. He was carrying a rusty-headed pike in two huge hands, and behind him stood several more men-at-arms, all of them cold-eyed and menacing. Rupert stared at them calmly.

"You want something?"

"My name's Chane," said the man-at-arms from the gates. "Remember me? Thought you might. You could have got us all killed, you stupid bastard, just for a few damn guards! I don't know what the hell you were doing out there, or how you got the gates open, but by the time we're finished with you, you're going to wish the demons had got to you first."

Great, thought Rupert. *I fight my way through half the demons in the Darkwood, just to get beaten up by my own men-at-arms. Typical.*

He rose unsteadily to his feet, his left arm hanging limp and useless at his side. The unicorn moved in beside him to protect him. Chane hefted his pike, grinning unpleasantly. And then ten dirty, blood-stained guards burst out of the surrounding refugees to stand between Rupert and the unicorn and their attackers. Chane and his friends took one look at the grim figures confronting them, and started to back away. There was a sudden echoing rasp of steel on leather as the guards drew their swords, and the men-at-arms backed away even faster.

"That's our leader you're threatening," said one of the guards quietly. Rupert recognized him as Rob Hawke, the Bladesmaster. "He brought us back from the dark. If he hadn't stopped you, you'd have slammed those gates in our faces and left us to die out there. So, you can either lower those pikes, or you can eat them. Got it?"

"Who the hell are you people?" blustered Chane, his eyes darting nervously from one grim-faced guard to another.

"How long have you been a man-at-arms in this Castle?" asked a cold, familiar voice, and Rupert looked around to find the Champion at his side, his war axe in his hands.

Chane's jaw dropped, and all the color drained from his face in a second. "Sir Champion . . ." he whispered faintly. "They told us you were dead! But . . . if you're alive, then he must be . . ."

He stared wide-eyed at Rupert, who smiled sardonically back. And then, to Rupert's utter amazement, Chane lowered his pike, knelt before him, and bowed his head. The other men-at-arms did the same.

"Forgive me, Sire," said Chane, his voice breaking with emotion. "Forgive me for not recognizing you, but it's been so long . . . we'd given up all hope . . . everyone said you were dead! Everyone!"

"Well I'm not," said Rupert shortly. "Or if I am, I'm a bloody thirsty ghost."

Rob Hawke immediately offered Rupert his canteen. Rupert nodded gratefully to the guard, and sheathed his sword. He took the canteen, pulled out the stopper with his teeth, and sucked greedily at the lukewarm water. He'd never known water to taste so good. His thirst finally died away, and he reluctantly handed the canteen back. Chane and the other men-at-arms were still kneeling before him, and he gestured uncomfortably for them to get up. Their continued devotion was becoming embarrassing.

"Welcome back, Sire," said Chane, rising quickly to his feet, his eyes shining with something that might almost have been religious awe. "Welcome home, Prince Rupert."

His words echoed loudly on the stillness, and then a murmur ran quickly through the crowded refugees. Heads turned to stare in Rupert's direction, and here and there people stood up to get a better look. The murmur ran swiftly back and forth, growing louder all the time, building to a roar. Within seconds everyone in the courtyard was on their feet and advancing on Rupert, laughing and cheering and chanting his name over and over again. Rupert's guards moved forward instinctively to protect him, and Chane and his men-at-arms were quick to join them, forming a human barrier between Rupert and the heaving, cheering throng. Rupert shrank back against the Castle wall, staring about him in bewilderment as the crowd pressed forward against his line of guards. Everywhere he looked there were shouting, cheering faces, many streaked with tears. Some of the refugees were actually jumping up and down with joy. Rupert looked to the Champion.

"What the hell is going on here?"

The Champion smiled. "Apparently we were all given up for dead long ago, and with your mission to the Dark Tower a failure, what hope was there for the Forest Kingdom? But now here you are, back from the long night at the last possible moment, bringing with you the legendary High Warlock, who will of course put everything to rights again with one wave of his hand. You're the answer to all their prayers, Sire."

Rupert snorted. "Are you going to tell them the bad news, sir Champion, or shall I?"

The Champion smiled dourly. The refugees were pressing forward again, paying no attention to the guards' warnings, or their drawn swords. The crowd's voice was slowly changing, becoming desperate and angry. Rupert wasn't just a returned hero, he was also their Prince; they wanted to know where he'd been, what had happened to him, why the journey had taken so long, why he hadn't returned in time to save them from the darkness. They didn't see the blood and tiredness on him, they saw only the hero and savior they wanted to see; the miracle-worker who would throw back the demons, defeat the long night, and make everything the way it used to be. Their voices became querulous and demanding, and they pushed and shoved at one another, jostling the guards and reaching out to try and touch Rupert himself, to compel his attention. The crowd's voice changed yet again, becoming harsh and ugly as the refugees slowly realized Rupert wasn't making them the promises they wanted to hear. Different factions tried to outshout each other; some pleading for more food or water for their families or their livestock, others demanding living quarters inside the Castle, away from the dark. Their voices rose and rose as they demanded hope and comfort and answers Rupert didn't have. He tried to talk to them, to explain, but they were too busy shouting to listen. Rupert couldn't really blame them; he was so tired and confused his explanations didn't make much sense even to him. The refugees surged angrily back and forth, their cheering excitement of only a few moment before gone, as though it had never been. The guards looked at Rupert for orders as the crowd pressed forward yet again.

"Get the hell away from me!" roared the Prince, and drew his sword. The guardsmen immediately fell into their fighting stance, and waited for the order to attack. The men-at-arms levelled their pikes, and the Champion hefted his war axe thoughtfully. The blood-smeared blades and heavy pike-heads gleamed dully in the torchlight as the refugees fell suddenly silent. The uncertain hush lengthened as Rupert glared round at the sullen faces ranked before him.

"I'm tired," he growled, finally. "I'm going up to my chambers now, to get some rest, and anyone who disturbs me will regret it. I don't care what your problems are, they can all damn well wait until I've got some sleep. Now get out of my way, or I'll have my guards open up a path for me."

There was a long, strained silence.

"Ever the diplomat, eh Rupert?" said an amused voice, and Rupert looked over the heads of the crowd to see Harald walking unhurriedly down the steps from the main entrance hall. He strode casually among the refugees, positively oozing reassurance and competence, and weary as he was, Rupert had to admire the performance. Harald's calm voice promised everything but committed him to nothing, and yet it seemed to satisfy the refugees, who slowly drifted back to their fires and their animals, muttering to each other and shaking their heads dolefully. None of them so much as spared a glance for Rupert. Their returning hero had let them down by being only human. Rupert watched Harald moving confidently through the dispersing crowd, and shook his head slowly. Harald had always had the gift of words, when he chose to use it. That empty-headed routine of his might fool the Court, but Rupert knew better. Ever since they were children, Harald had always been able to manipulate people and situations so that he came out on top; usually at Rupert's expense.

For all his faults, and there was no denying Harald had many, he was an excellent organizer. Before the evening was over, he'd have drafted a list of all the refugee's complaints, and have set up a system for dealing with those that really mattered. Rupert sighed disgustedly, sheathed his sword, and leaned back against the Castle wall. There was a time when he'd thought Harald only did such things in order to look good, while still leaving the bulk of the work to other people, but now he saw it was just another reason why Harald would someday be King, while he never would. Harald was a diplomat. Rupert shrugged. Stuff diplomacy. Try using tact and reason with a demon, and it'd rip your head off.

He turned away and nodded gratefully to Chane and his men-at-arms. "Thanks for standing by me. It could very easily have turned nasty."

The men-at-arms hefted their pikes bashfully, and bowed quickly in return.

"Sorry about the refugees, Sire," said Chane. "You can't really blame them; they lost everything they had when the dark came. I doubt there's a family here that hasn't lost a child or a parent to the demons. They've been frightened and helpless for so long, they needed someone they could strike back at. It just happened to be you."

"Yeah, well," said Rupert tiredly. "Thanks, anyway."

"Sure," said Chane. "If you ever need us again, you know where to find us. We'd better get back on duty, I suppose; the demons could come anytime."

He bowed again, and led his men-at-arms back to the gatehouse. Rupert watched them go, and frowned thoughtfully. Either Chane was the most forgiving man he'd ever met, or there was something going on here he didn't know about. Or maybe . . . Rupert smiled suddenly. Or maybe he was just getting paranoid again; coming home to the Castle could do that to you. He sighed, and turned back to his waiting guardsmen. At least he didn't have to worry about them; they'd been loyal to him since the very beginning. Even though they had no real reason to be . . . After all, the Champion only obeyed him because the King ordered him to . . . Rupert shook his head angrily, but the thought wouldn't go away. He knew he had to ask the question, if only because he was so afraid of what the answer might be. Either way, he had to know. He ignored the patiently waiting Champion, and moved on to confront Rob Hawke.

"Why have you remained loyal to me?" he asked bluntly. "When I started out, I had a full troop of fifty guards; I've only brought ten of you back. Don't you blame me for your friends' deaths?"

Hawke shook his head slowly. "We don't blame you for anything, Sire. We didn't expect to survive the Darkwood, never mind the Dark Tower. We figured to stick with you till we were safely out of sight of the Castle, and then we'd all desert. No offense, Sire, but what little we'd been told of you wasn't exactly encouraging. According to the Castle gossip, you'd never led guards before, you told impossible lies about having been through the Darkwood twice, and you were a coward. We'd no intention of following a man like that into battle.

"And then we saw you take on your brother and the Champion, right here in the courtyard. You drew the Champion's blood; twice! No one's done that since he became Champion. After seeing that, it seemed likely the gossip was wrong. Taking on the Champion wasn't a particularly bright thing to do, but it proved you were a fighter. So, we figured we'd stick with you just long enough to talk you out of going to the Dark Tower, and then you could desert with us. The Champion would just have woken up one morning, and found us all gone. Simple as that.

"And then we came to Coppertown. We saw what lived in the pit, and we saw you fight it, and win. After that . . . well, we started to believe in you, and your mission. And maybe we started to believe in ourselves, as well. It hasn't worked out too badly, all told. No one's ever faced the odds we have, and survived. We don't blame you for anything, Sire. We're proud to have served with you."

Rupert nodded stiffly, too overcome with emotion to speak. "Thank you," he said finally. "I couldn't be more proud of you. I'll talk to my father; assuming we survive the darkness, there'll be a grant of land for each of you. My word on it."

"Just doing what we're paid for," said Hawke. "Mind you, the combat bonuses on this little jaunt should add up very nicely. Assuming you'd be willing to do one small favor for us, Sire."

"Anything," said Rupert.

"Well," said Hawke carefully, "If the Champion were to report anything about our planning to desert, we wouldn't get a penny."

"He won't report you," said Rupert. "Will you, sir Champion?"

The Champion looked at him thoughtfully, and then bowed his head slightly. "As you wish, Sire."

The guards grinned broadly at one another, and then Hawke suddenly held up his sword in the warrior's traditional oath of fealty. The other guards were quick to join him, and within seconds there were ten swords raised in the ancient salute. For a moment the tableau held, and then the blades crashed back into their scabbards, and the guardsmen turned and left, heading for their barracks and some much needed rest. Rupert watched them leave, and wished he could go with them, back to the security and camaraderie of their fellows. But he couldn't. He was a Prince, which meant he was going back to an empty room, and the politics and intrigues of his family and his Court. He looked away, to discover the Champion regarding him speculatively.

"Something wrong, sir Champion?"

"I don't know, Sire. I'll have to think about it."

"I'm still only a second son."

"Yes," said the Champion. "I know." And then he turned, and walked away.

Rupert thought about going after him, and then decided it could wait till tomorrow. Come to that, everything could wait until tomorrow. Or the day after. Hurrying footsteps close by caught his attention, and he looked round to see a tall, portly young man in flashing silks bearing down on him. His shoulder-length blond hair was carefully styled in the latest fashion, and in a courtyard full of hungry people, he looked almost indecently well-fed. He drew himself up before Rupert, struck a dignified pose, and then bowed elegantly. Rupert nodded warily in return, and the man straightened up again.

"Your pardon for intruding, Sire, but on hearing of your miraculous return, I dropped everything and rushed here immediately."

"You did?" said Rupert.

"But of course, Sire! You have come back to us out of the very darkness itself; come back to save us all! What a song I shall make of this!"

Rupert looked at him. "A song?" he said, slowly.

"Well yes, Sire. I'm the new official Court minstrel. But not to worry, Sire, the song I shall make of your daring exploits will be a tale of great heroics and selfless deeds, of honor and adventure and miraculous escapes . . ."

His voice trailed away as he caught sight of Rupert's face. He started backing away and when Rupert drew his sword, and then turned and ran as Rupert advanced on him with murder in his eyes. Rupert gave up after a few steps, but the minstrel had the good sense to keep on running.

"Was that really necessary?" asked the unicorn.

"Definitely," growled Rupert, sheathing his sword and leaning back against the Castle wall. "It was minstrels and their damn stupid songs on the joys of adventuring that got me into this mess in the first place."

"You don't look too good," said the unicorn.

"You might very well be right about that."

"Why don't you go and get some rest, Rupert. Before you fall down."

Rupert closed his eyes, and for the first time allowed himself to think luxurious thoughts about a hot bath and a soft bed. He sighed contentedly, and then opened his eyes and looked at the unicorn. Bloody streaks covered the animal from head to haunches where the demons had clawed him. His head was hanging down, and his legs were trembling with strain and fatigue.

"You don't look so good yourself," said Rupert. "You're a mess, unicorn. Those demons really got to you."

"Flattery will get you nowhere," said the unicorn. "I'll be fine in the morning; it's just a few scratches. You're in worse shape than I am. I've seen people being buried who looked healthier than you do right now. For once in your life, listen to reason and go to your bed, damn you. I'm looking forward to my first good night's sleep in weeks, and I've enough to keep me awake as it is, without having to worry about you as well."

"I'll walk you to the stables."

"No you won't; the condition you're in, I'd end up having to carry you, and my back's killing me. Go to bed, Rupert. I'll be fine once I get to the stables. With luck, I'll find a groom I can terrorize into giving me some barley. Assuming I can stay awake long enough to eat it."

"All right, I give in," said Rupert, smiling in spite of himself.

"About bloody time," growled the unicorn, moving slowly away. "And get that shoulder seen to!"

"Yeah, sure," muttered Rupert. He leaned his head back against the wall as a sudden chill rushed through him, shaking his hands and chattering his teeth. The chill passed as quickly as it came, leaving him weak and dizzy. He pushed himself away from the wall, but only managed a few steps before he had to stop. The ground seemed to drop away under his feet, and he had to fight to keep from falling. The world grew blurred and indistinct, and then snapped back into focus as he concentrated. Rupert breathed deeply, blinking away the sweat that dripped steadily into his eyes. Having fought his way through the Darkwood and an entire horde of demons to get home, he was damned if he'd cap it all by fainting away in the middle of the courtyard. He'd walk out of here on his own two feet all the way back to his own chambers. Then he'd faint.

He moved slowly and cautiously through the tightly packed refugees, taking it one step at a time. Whenever anyone tried to talk to him, he just glared at them and dropped his right hand onto the pommel of his sword, and that took care of that. His left arm was completely numb again, but he could see the fresh blood coursing down his sleeve and dripping from his hand. He carefully tucked the numb arm inside his jerkin and laced it tight, forming a makeshift sling. The pain in his shoulder flared up with every step, but he was so tired now he could almost ignore it. Many of the refugees shrank away as he passed, and Rupert began to wonder what kind of picture he presented to them. No doubt their precious hero looked rather different when seen close up; tired and irritable and covered in blood and gore, most of it his own. He tried keeping his hand away from his swordhilt, but it didn't make any difference. The steps to the main entrance hall loomed suddenly up before him, and Rupert started toward them. He'd just put his foot on the first step when Harald stepped out of the crowd of refugees to block his way.

"Welcome home, dear boy. We were getting a little worried about you."

Rupert looked at his brother tiredly. "Were you, Harald? Were you really?"

Harald shrugged. "You've been gone a long time. We'd pretty much got used to the idea that you wouldn't be coming back. I was beginning to fear I'd have to go out and avenge you."

Rupert looked at him closely. "Why should you risk your life to avenge my death?"

"You're family," said Harald. "I know my duty. You'd do the same for me."

"Yes," said Rupert slowly. "I suppose I would."

He nodded gruffly to Harald, genuinely touched. Harald smiled briefly in return, his face as impassive as ever.

"Well," said Rupert, "What's been happening while I've been away?"

"Not a lot," said Harald. "The Darkwood's been here almost a week. It could just as easily be more than a week, I suppose; it's hard to keep track of time when there's no sun in the sky. We've been using marked candles and water clocks, but they're not exactly reliable. Still, now you've brought the High Warlock back to us, no doubt things will take a turn for the better. You did bring the Warlock back, didn't you?"

"Oh yes," said Rupert. "He's back."

"I don't remember much about him, to be honest," said Harald. "Is he really as bad as he's painted?"

Rupert thought for a moment. "Yes and no," he said finally. "Does it matter? He's got the power, and that's all anyone here will care about."

"Power enough to throw back the long night?"

"I don't know. Maybe." Rupert turned away, and looked out over the crowded courtyard. "How many refugees are we sheltering here in the Castle?"

"About twelve thousand. God knows how many more are trapped out there in the dark, unprotected. We took in as many as we could when the darkness fell, but then the demons came, and we had no choice but to bar the gates and raise the drawbridge. It all happened so suddenly, Rupert; we had no warning at all. The demons haven't mounted any kind of attack yet. They just sit outside our walls, watching and waiting. From time to time they call to us in human voices, begging to be let in. We don't open the gates to anyone anymore."

Rupert looked at him, and raised an eyebrow. "What led you to make an exception in our case?"

"We didn't," said Harald. "The drawbridge lowered itself, and the gates swung open of their own accord. That's why I assumed the High Warlock must be with you."

"Where's the dragon?" asked Rupert suddenly. "Why didn't he come out to help us against the demons?"

"Apparently he still hasn't got over his last encounter with the demons. According to Julia, he was hurt much more seriously than any of us realized. He's been hibernating for months, trying to heal himself. It's beginning to look as if he may never wake up again."

Rupert looked sharply at Harald. "Julia. How is she?"

"Oh, she's in excellent health, I'm happy to say. Actually, you got back just in time. Julia and I were to have been married weeks ago, but what with one thing and another, there just hasn't been the time. Still, Father assures me the ceremony will finally take place tomorrow. It'll do no end of good for Castle morale. I'm so glad you're back, Rupert; it wouldn't have been the same without you there beside me, as my best man."

Rupert stared at him silently, and Harald stepped back a pace. The tiredness and pain had vanished from Rupert's face, and had been replaced by a cold, calculating rage. Harald's eyes narrowed, and he dropped his hand to his swordhilt.

"Do you think," said Rupert thickly, "that I fought my way through all the demons in the long night, and braved the High Warlock in his Tower, just so that you could take Julia away from me? I'll see you dead first."

Harald fought down an urgent need to step back another pace. He couldn't afford to appear weak. He swallowed dryly, remembering the last time he'd fought his brother in the courtyard. He still carried some of the scars. This time, Rupert was obviously weakened by his wounds and loss of blood, but still Harald hesitated. There was something in Rupert's eyes; something cold and dark and very deadly.

"Things are different now," said Harald finally. "You've been gone a long time, almost seven months, and Julia's had time to think. Time to see things differently. Julia and I . . . we've come to know each other very well, in your absence. Very well, indeed. She's marrying me of her own free will, Rupert, because she prefers me to you."

"Liar!"

Harald smiled coldly. "Talk to Julia, if you wish. She'll tell you the same. You've lost her, Rupert. Just as you'll always lose to me."

He turned to go. Rupert snatched his sword from his scabbard, and lunged after him. Harald spun round, sword in hand. Their blades met in a flurry of sparks, and then Rupert collapsed on the steps as his legs betrayed him. He tried to get up again, and couldn't. He'd used the last of his strength in the darkness, and now there was nothing left. He lay sprawled and helpless across the marble steps, panting harshly, still somehow hanging onto his sword. He slowly raised his head and there was Harald, standing above him, sword in hand. Harald smiled down at him.

"Get some rest, dear fellow," he said calmly. "You've

been through a lot, and I'd hate for you to have to miss my wedding."

He sheathed his sword, and turned and walked away, leaving Rupert lying in his own blood. Rupert tried to get his legs under him, but there was no strength left in them. His wounded shoulder was filled with a sickening ache, and the foul stench of the demon gore soaked into his clothes was suddenly overpowering. Rupert lowered his head onto his sword arm, and closed his eyes.

I'm tired, he thought fretfully. *I've done all I can; let somebody else carry the bloody burden for a while. I'm just so damn tired . . .*

He heard someone coming down the steps toward him, but he didn't even have the strength to raise his head and see who it was. The footsteps stopped beside him, and a firm hand took him by his uninjured shoulder and turned him over. Rupert moaned despite himself, and looked up to see the High Warlock scowling down at him.

"Why the hell didn't you tell me you'd been hurt?"

"Just a few scratches," muttered Rupert blearily.

"Idiot," snapped the Warlock. He knelt down beside Rupert, and at a gesture from his stubby fingers, Rupert's leather jerkin slowly peeled itself away from the jagged wound in his shoulder. Blood ran freely as the barely formed scabs broke open again, and the Warlock whistled softly.

"Will you look at that . . . bit clean through to the bone, and then broke it in half a dozen places. It's a wonder you lasted this long. Now hold still."

The Warlock's fingers writhed through a series of intricate movements too fast for Rupert to follow, and then the pain in his shoulder was suddenly gone. Rupert twisted his head around, and watched in amazement as the splintered bone in the open wound slowly knit itself together again. The wound closed over it, and within seconds nothing remained but a long white scar. Rupert stared at it breathlessly for a moment, and then cautiously flexed his arm. It worked fine. A slow grin spread across Rupert's face as he worked his arm again and again. It felt great. The Warlock chuckled quietly, and a full wine glass appeared in his hand from nowhere.

"Drink this. It'll do you good."

Rupert sniffed the cloudy white wine suspiciously, and

then gulped the stuff down. It tasted even worse than it smelled, and it smelled pretty bad. He shook his head quickly, and handed the glass back.

"A very poor vintage, sir Warlock."

The High Warlock grinned, and the glass disappeared from his hand in a puff of brimstone smoke. "You should taste what it's like before I dissolve it in wine. It'll help replace the blood you've lost, and clear some of the toxins from your system, but right now what you need more than anything is a good night's sleep. Go and get some. Now, if you'll excuse me, it's time I had a word with your father. We've a lot to discuss."

He hesitated, as though considering whether to say something further, and then he turned and walked back into the entrance hall. Rupert lay back on the marble steps, luxuriating in the wonderful peace that follows a release from pain. He tried his left arm again. His shoulder seemed a bit stiff, and the new scar tissue tugged uncomfortably with every movement, but all in all Rupert decided he felt better than he had in months. A pleasant lethargy flowed through him, and he was sorely tempted to just lie back and go to sleep right there on the steps, but he knew he couldn't do that. Sleeping on cold marble would leave him good for nothing when he finally woke up. He sighed regretfully, and tempted himself with thoughts of a steaming hot bath, to be followed by a soft bed in a warm room. Heaven. Sheer heaven. He rose slowly to his feet, sheathed his sword, stretched and yawned, and finally started up the steps to the main entrance. After all the many months, he was actually going to sleep in civilized surroundings again. And anyone who got in his way would live just long enough to regret it.

The constant fear and oppression of the Darkwood gradually diminished as Rupert made his way deeper into the Castle, putting layer after layer of thick stone walls between him and the long night. It was a long trek back to his chambers in the NorthWest Tower, but somehow the anticipation made it all worthwhile. After so long a time away, it felt good to be back among familiar sights and sounds, and yet Rupert found himself frowning more and more as new, ominous changes caught his eye. The refugees were everywhere, spilling out of their quarters into the corridors and passageways. Most of them just watched blankly from where they sat as Rupert passed, their eyes listless and empty. It was the children who got to Rupert the most; they sat where their parents put them, and watched the shadows around them with wide, frightened eyes. Rupert recognized the signs; they'd been in the Darkwood too long, and the long night had set its mark upon them. He tried to talk to some of the children, but they turned away from him, and would not be comforted.

Roaring fires blazed in every fireplace, filling the air with more sooty smoke than the over-worked air vents could hope to handle, and yet still the Castle corridors remained cold and bleak, and light whorls of hoarfrost pearled the ancient stone walls. Wherever Rupert went, the passageways and common rooms were only dimly lit. Forest Castle had always depended on the foxfire moss for its light, and now there was none; the bitter frosts of the winter come early had seen to that. There were still torches and oil lamps, but their uncertain light filled the narrow stone corridors with too many unquiet shadows.

A few minor courtiers came and walked with Rupert a while, filling him in on the latest news and gossip, and sketching out some of the things that had happened while he was away. Rupert listened unbelievingly as they told him of the abortive rebellion and its consequences, but he wasn't in the mood for conversation. Finally, they started telling him things he didn't want to know, and he drove them from him by dropping his hand onto his sword and glaring steadily at them until they got the message. Rupert walked on, alone. Some of what the courtiers had said had been interesting, but he was too tired to care or concentrate.

The solid oak door of Rupert's private chambers had never looked more welcoming. He leaned tiredly against the closed door, putting off the moment when he could finally rest, just so that he could savor it that much longer.

"Rupert! Damn you; where the hell have you been?"

Rupert straightened up and turned around, and Julia threw her arms round him and crushed him to her, not waiting for any answer. Rupert hugged her fiercely in return, and buried his face in her long, blonde hair. For the first time in a long time, he felt happy and at peace. Finally, Julia pushed Rupert away, and they held each other at arm's length, staring hungrily into each other's eyes. Both of them were grinning so hard their mouths hurt. And then Julia's smile vanished as she took in the harsh lines of pain and fatigue etched deeply into Rupert's blood-smeared face.

"Rupert; you've been hurt! What happened?"

"Several hundred demons were foolish enough to try and stop me coming back to you. I'm fine now, honest. How are you, lass; you're looking great."

"Well, I was," said Julia dryly, "until some great oaf of a Prince got blood all over my new gowns."

Rupert stepped back and took his first good look at her. Julia's robes were a curious mixture of fashion and practicality, and though her face was painted and rouged in the latest Court style, her long hair fell unfettered to her waist, held out of her face only by a simple leather headband. She wore a sword openly on her hip.

"It's your sword," said Julia. "You gave it to me in the Darkwood, remember?"

"Yes," said Rupert. "I remember."

His voice was suddenly flat and cold. Julia looked at him curiously.

"What is it, Rupert?"

"Harald just invited me to your wedding tomorrow," said Rupert.

Julia looked away, unable to meet his gaze. "We all thought you were dead. I thought you were dead. You don't know what it's been like here, on my own. It's not as if I was given any choice as to whether or not I wanted to get married. And Harald . . . Harald's been very good to me while you were away."

"Yeah," said Rupert. "I'll bet he has."

Julia spun on her heel and stormed off down the corridor. Rupert shook his head disgustedly. Why the hell hadn't he kept his mouth shut? Now he'd have to go after her, and apologize, and . . . His shoulders slumped. What was the point? She'd admitted she was going to marry Harald. Rupert looked down the corridor after her, but it was empty. He turned his back on it.

He opened his door, stepped into his room, and shut the door behind him. He then locked and bolted it. He leaned back against the solid oak door, let out a long heartfelt sigh, and stared round his room. Fifteen foot by fifteen, most of it taken up with his bed, wardrobe and wash basin. Threadbare carpets covered the floor, but the bare stone walls were cold and featureless. The only other door led to his private jakes. Rupert had never been the sort to accumulate possessions, and the simple bedchamber would have seemed stark and utilitarian to anyone but him. As a Prince of the line, he was entitled to a full suite of rooms and half a dozen personal servants, but he'd never wanted them. Servants just got in the way when he wanted to be alone, and besides; how many rooms can you live in at one time?

Rupert started toward the bed, and then he turned back and checked the door was securely locked. He checked the solid steel bolt, too, running his thumb over the cold metal again and again to be sure the bolt was all the way home. Ever since he first returned home from the Darkwood, Rupert had been grateful his room had no windows. It meant he only had to guard his door against demons. With his sword in his hand he could face any number of demons, but ever since that first trip through the endless night, he was afraid of what might creep up on him in the dark while he was asleep and helpless. He needed to rest. He needed to sleep. But he knew he wouldn't be able to rest or sleep until he was sure he was safe. He moved over to the wardrobe, shook his head disgustedly, and gave in to his fear, one more time. He set his shoulder against the side of the massive wardrobe, and slowly pushed it forward to barricade the door. And only then did he stumble over to his bed and sit on it.

An oil lamp burned steadily on the simple wooden stand that held his wash basin. Metal brackets on the bed's headboard held two unlit candles. Rupert used the lamp to light both the candles, and then put the lamp back on the stand, taking care not to disturb its flame. He couldn't bear the thought of waking up to find his room in darkness. He slowly unstrapped his sword belt, and placed it on the floor beside his bed, safely at hand, should he need it. And finally, he just sat there on his bed, staring at the bleak stone wall before him.

The Blue Moon was full. Darkness had taken the Forest for its own, because he hadn't got back in time. And Julia . . .

I could have loved you, Julia.

Rupert lay back on his bed, bloody clothes and all, and fled into sleep. His dreams were dark and restless.

*   *   *

Lord Darius scuttled endlessly through the pitch dark tunnels, muttering to himself as he went. The thin, querulous sound of his voice echoed hollowly back from the thick, stone walls to either side of him, and seemed to reverberate on the dank, still air long after he was gone. From time to time there was a faint patter of many running feet as the air vent rats retreated into their holes to let him pass. Darius ignored them. They were too small and too timid to hurt him, as long as he kept moving. A faint gleam of light showed in the darkness ahead, like a single star on a moonless night. Darius stopped running and crouched motionless in the dark, peering warily at the unsteady glow before him. Apart from his own labored breathing, all was still and silent. After a while, Darius drew his dagger from his sleeve and started cautiously forward.

Thick streams of dirty golden light fell from a side vent set high on the tunnel wall. A rusty metal grille split the light into a dozen gleaming shafts, choked with swirling dust and soot from the tunnel air. Darius crouched just outside the falling light, and bit his lip nervously. This much light meant he was close to an inhabited area of the Castle, and that meant food and drink and a chance to strike back at his enemies. But he had to be careful. Ever since he'd first fled into the network of hidden tunnels and air vents within the thick Castle walls (how long ago? he didn't know anymore) he'd been afraid to go back into the Castle itself. Even when hunger and thirst finally drove him to leave his tunnels for a time, he lived in constant terror of being found and trapped by the King's men. He had no doubt the guards would kill him on sight. He'd have given such orders. It was only sensible. And so he left the darkness only when he had to, slipping out of hidden panels and concealed air vents at times when he was sure there was no one around to see. He stole bread and meat and wine, never enough to be missed, and never enough to satisfy the gnawing hunger that burned in his belly all his waking hours.

Darius stared into the golden light before him, and fought down an impulse to leave his tunnels and take his chances in the Castle, just to be able to move and live in the light again. The constant darkness of the interconnecting tunnels weighed remorselessly down on him like water dripping on a rock, gradually wearing it away with an endless patience. Darius snarled silently, and shook his head stubbornly. He couldn't leave the dark yet. It wasn't time. He'd sworn to stay in the tunnels until his dark master called him forth, and in return he'd been given power over his enemies. Real power. Sorcerous power. He could feel it, burning within him, growing stronger all the time. The dark one had taken Darius's long-neglected talent and stirred it into awful life. Darius smiled. Soon his power would blaze like a beacon, and then he would leave the dark and gain his revenge. Until then, he waited, for as much as he wanted to walk in the light again, he wanted revenge more. Much more.

Darius moved forward into the golden light, and stood on tiptoe to stare into the side vent. The light hurt his eyes, and tears ran down his dirty stubbled cheeks, but he couldn't look away. After a while, his ankles began to hurt. He ignored the pain as long as he could, but finally he was forced to move away from the side vent, and the golden light that comforted him. He stood thinking for a moment, weighing the pros and cons, and then he reached into his sleeve and took out his last precious stub of candle. He used his dagger hilt to strike sparks against the side vent's metal grille, and the candle wick finally lit. All at once the tunnel seemed to spring into being around him, as though it had been waiting eagerly for that little extra light to make it real and solid again. Darius cringed away from the roof of the tunnel as it pressed down bare inches above his head. The walls crowded in around him as the sudden light once again made clear how horribly narrow and enclosed the tunnel was. Darius staggered around and around in a tight little circle, and everywhere he looked a wall of ancient brickwork stared mockingly back, only inches away. A cold sweat ran down his face, and he moaned and whimpered and flapped his hands aimlessly as the panic rose in him. Darius spun around and around and around, unable to stop. He was buried alive deep in the stone guts of the Castle, miles away from light and air and freedom. He screamed suddenly, and attacked the wall before him with his fists, and then he tripped and fell and lay sobbing in the filth that coated the tunnel floor. He lay there for some time in the darkness, blind to anything but his own panic, and then his sobs slowly died away as his fear receded, leaving behind nothing but a simple, overwhelming tiredness. He sat up, and wiped at his face with the back of his hand. He felt something move in his closed hand, and opened it to find he'd crushed his candle stub into a shapeless mass of crumbling wax. Darius sniffed once, and then threw the wax away.

He scrambled awkwardly to his feet, retrieved his dagger from where he'd dropped it, and moved back into the golden light falling from the side vent. He brushed at the foulness that soaked his clothes, and wished fleetingly for a mirror. He often wondered how he looked now. He could tell he'd lost weight from the way his robes hung loosely about him, but he felt there'd been other changes too, though he couldn't quite name them. He was cold and tired all the time, but he'd got used to that. Darius shrugged, and stopped thinking about it. It didn't matter. Nothing really mattered any more, except the face that floated always before him, even in the deepest and darkest of the tunnels; Harald's face, smiling calmly as the Prince betrayed him to his enemies.

You can't trust anyone these days, Darius.

Darius crouched down on his haunches in the golden light. To either side of him, he could just make out the dirt and smoke-smeared walls, running with slime and sooty water. A thin, slippery mud squelched under his feet. The centuries old brickwork surrounding him was pitted and uneven, and the drainage channels that should have carried away the condensation and other deposits were all hopelessly blocked. The Castle was getting old, falling apart. Much like him. Darius scowled, and muttered to himself, remembering all the things he'd planned, all the things he'd meant to do. He'd had so many plans . . . all worthless now. His rebellion was over. Finished. Beaten before it had even begun. Darius chuckled softly, and the unpleasant sound took a long time to die away into whispering echoes. There was still his revenge. All the people who'd tricked and lied and driven him into the darkness were going to pay in blood for what they'd done to him. The dark master had promised him this.

Darius hefted the dagger in his hand, admiring the way the golden light shimmered on the narrow steel blade. Dirty brown specks of dried blood still crusted the blade near the crosspiece. Darius frowned. It was a pity about Cecelia.

There was no doubt he was better off without her; she was always getting in his way, slowing him down. Always *pawing* at him. And yet still he missed having her there, at his side. He'd always been able to talk to Cecelia, even though she hadn't understood half of what he had to say. A pity about Cecelia. But she shouldn't have got in his way.

Darius tensed suddenly as he heard voices rising and falling, not far off. The voices became steadily louder as they drew near, but there was a sinister blurred quality to the sound that made the words indecipherable. Darius shrank back against the wall as the voices boomed like thunder in the narrow tunnel, and then suddenly they stopped, cut off in mid-word, and all was still and silent again. Darius smiled uncomfortably, and relaxed again. Sound travelled strangely in the air vents, echoing and re-echoing until it faded into whispers, but every now and again some freak of acoustics would bring Darius voices and conversations from the inner Castle, as clearly as though he was there in the room with those who spoke. Darius knew what had happened to his fellow rebels. More than once he'd been tempted to leave his tunnels and beg for exile too, but his pride wouldn't let him. He had to have his revenge, or all his time in the dark had been for nothing.

He turned away from the side vent and set off down the tunnel, leaving the golden glow behind him. Darkness soon returned, as though it had never been away. Darius muttered constantly to himself as he scurried down the long narrow tunnel, happily contemplating all the bloody revenges he planned for his many enemies.

Soon, he promised himself. *Soon*.

The High Warlock was bored. The Champion was in conference with the King and not to be disturbed, Rupert had disappeared, and everybody else was too busy or too tired to talk to him. The Warlock wandered back and forth through the endless Castle corridors, to see what there was to see, but he soon grew tired of that. He needed some fresh air and some open space. The Castle held too many memories. He found an empty corner, sat down and sank quickly into a trance. His astral spirit floated up out of his body, and flew back down the corridors, through the entrance hall and out into the courtyard; an invisible presence, like a passing breeze.

The square was packed solid with refugees, and even in the open courtyard the high stone walls were unbearably oppressive. The Warlock flew quickly over the bent heads of the apathetic refugees, up over the Castle wall, and out into the long night.

The ice-bound Castle shimmered eerily in its own silver light, like a single huge snowflake. The light didn't travel far into the Darkwood. Once the Forest had been full of life, but now nothing moved save the demons, stalking silently through the endless night. And though the trees themselves were rotten and decaying, they were still, somehow, horribly alive. The Warlock could hear them screaming.

All around him, the darkness beat on the air like a continuous roll of thunder and, high above, the Blue Moon howled ceaselessly. The Warlock's senses revealed much more of the world than most humans ever saw, and what would have seemed a static, motionless scene to any other observer was full of sound and fury to the High Warlock. To his left and to his right, the ghosts of yesterday retraced their movements again and again; moments caught in time like insects imprisoned in amber. Every now and then, a ghost would vanish from his sight like a bursting soap bubble, as the presence of today finally overcame that dim remainder of the past. Paths of power, old and potent, burned all around the Castle, their blinding light undiminished by the Darkwood. The Warlock frowned suddenly as he sensed something moving, deep in the earth. Ancient and inhuman, it stirred fitfully, and then returned to its long sleep. The Warlock relaxed a little. The Forest was far older than most people realized, and some traces still remained of creatures that rose and fell long before the coming of man. Too few realized how lightly such creatures slept.

The Warlock looked up sharply as a demon stalked forward out of the Darkwood. It walked uneasily on two legs, and though its shape was vaguely human, an oily green fire dripped steadily from its jaws to spark and sputter on the ground. Its wide slash of a mouth was filled with huge slablike teeth, and its eyes burned yellow in the dark. The Warlock's eyes narrowed, and the demon stopped its advance. The High Warlock raised one hand, and the demon snarled soundlessly and turned and loped back into the Darkwood. The Warlock smiled tightly.

As the demon disappeared back into the endless night, something deep in the darkness roared its hunger, and the Warlock frowned thoughtfully. Toward the end of the last demon attack, he'd sensed something huge and awful making its way toward the Castle. At the last moment it had held back rather than test his power, but already the Warlock could feel changes taking place in the Darkwood. The demons were massing for another attack, and with them . . . The High Warlock shivered suddenly, although he no longer had a real body. Under the Blue Moon's light, creatures that should have slept till the end of time now walked the world of men once more. Nightmares and horrors made flesh and bone stirred restlessly in the endless night, and waited impatiently for the order to move against the Castle.

The Warlock shrugged, and took to the air again. Things happened as they would, when they would; and it made no sense to worry about them. He brushed the grim thoughts from his mind and flew slowly over the moat, staring speculatively down at the massive sheet of ice covering the water. A great dark shadow moved slowly under the ice, following his path. The High Warlock hovered in place above the ice, and the shadow stayed still beneath him. The Warlock frowned curiously. It seemed there was something still alive in the moat, but he couldn't quite make out what. Even more interesting, it could apparently see his astral spirit. Whatever it was, it was trapped under the ice. The Warlock sank down over a crack in the ice, and peered intently at the dark shape in the water. It stirred uncertainly, and then the Warlock jumped back instinctively as the shape surged suddenly up against the underside of the ice. The crack widened and broke apart, and a single eyeball on a long pink stalk emerged through the gap. The Warlock drifted down onto the ice, a cautious distance away.

"Hello," he said politely. "Who are you?"

A thick bubbly voice came softly to him, though whether through the crack in the ice or directly to his mind, he wasn't sure.

I live here, said the voice. *In the water. In the moat.*

Home. My name . . . that was a long time ago. Long time ago. Who are you?

"I'm the High Warlock. I'm a sorcerer."

The eyeball swivelled back and forth on its stalk to get a better look at him. *I remember you, I think. From the Dark Tower.*

"Ah yes," said the Warlock. "That was some years ago, wasn't it? You disturbed me at my work, and I changed you into something and sent you back here."

Long time ago, said the thick, inhuman voice. *Long time. I live here now. In the moat. Home.*

"I hadn't realized it had been so long," said the Warlock. "I'm sorry. I'll change you back . . ."

"No! Please; no. I'm happy here, guarding the moat. It's all I want; all I ever wanted. In the summer there are fish and birds and insects, and I hear their voices, hear their songs. The wind and the rain and the Forest are a part of me now, and I am a part of them. I can feel the seasons change, and the world turn, and the slow steady pulse of the living. I can't give that up. I can't go back to being human. To being only human.

"Yes," said the High Warlock. "I know. I couldn't give it up, either. But isn't there anything I can do for you?"

The eyeball nodded thoughtfully. *Come and talk to me,* said the bubbling voice. *Talk to me, sometimes. I do get lonely here, for someone to talk to in the speech of men.*

"I'll come when I can," said the Warlock.

Promise?

"Promise."

Good. Good. The eyeball turned to stare past him, taking in the darkness. *The long night has fallen, sorcerer. You'd be safer inside the Castle.*

"So would you."

Bubbling laughter. *The demons don't bother me. They know better. Go back into the Castle, High Warlock. Go back into the light, and the safety of company. Come to me again, when the night is over. Please?*

"Of course," said the Warlock. "Farewell, my friend."

He turned and soared back into the air. The eyeball watched him go until he dipped behind the Castle wall, and was lost to sight. The eyeball turned briefly to stare at the encroaching darkness, and then disappeared back under the ice with a faint slurping sound. The crack in the ice froze over, and the dim dark shape below swam slowly away through the freezing waters of the moat.

Rupert woke slowly to an insistent hammering on his door. He rolled onto his back and stared blankly at the ceiling for a moment, as his dreams fell reluctantly away, and then he sat up suddenly and reached frantically for his sword on the floor by his bed. He felt safer with the sword in his hand. He glanced at his oil lamp, and smiled sourly as he saw the oil had run out, while his candles were still burning. He glared at the shadows that filled the corners of his room, and tried to remember what had woken him. The knocking came again, and the back of Rupert's mind screamed *demons demons demons!* He shook his head stubbornly and breathed deeply, and the wild unreasoning fear that had set his heart racing slowly subsided, dying away to its familiar background murmur. He swung cautiously out of bed, wincing at the tired ache that still filled his muscles, and after a moment's hesitation, he sheathed his sword and laid it on the bed. *Whoever it is, they'd better have a damn good reason for disturbing me,* he thought grimly. He knuckled his gummy eyes and moved reluctantly over to the wardrobe blocking his doorway. Outside, his visitor knocked again, putting some muscle into it.

"Who is it?" growled Rupert, indulging himself in a long, slow stretch that set his joints creaking.

"The Champion, Sire. You're needed."

Since when? thought Rupert sardonically. "All right. Wait a minute."

He put his shoulder to the wardrobe, and the massive piece of furniture slid jerkily back to its original position. Thick welts in the rugs before his door showed where the wardrobe had stood while he slept. Rupert stooped down and carefully turned the rugs over, to hide the markings. If word got out he had to barricade his door before he could sleep, he'd never hear the end of it. Rupert unbolted and unlocked the door, taking his time about it. Whatever the Champion wanted to tell him, the odds were it wasn't going to be anything he wanted to hear. He finally pulled the door open, and glared unsympathetically at the waiting Champion.

"This had better be important, sir Champion."

"I see you're feeling better, Sire."

Rupert just looked at him. The Champion shook his head sadly.

"You can't still be tired, surely? You've had almost four hours sleep."

"Four hours?" Rupert looked around for something heavy with which to brain the Champion, and then gave up on the idea as being too much of an effort. He leaned wearily against the doorjamb and stared disgustedly at the Champion, who looked, as always, calm and rested and ready for anything. "All right, sir Champion; tell me the bad news. What's happened while I've been resting?"

"Not a lot, Sire. The demons are still waiting outside our walls, and the King and the High Warlock have done nothing but scream abuse at each other since they met."

"Great," said Rupert. "Just great."

"So," said the Champion casually, "I thought it might be a good idea for you to go down to the Court and talk some sense into them."

"And what makes you think they'll listen to me?"

"You have immense personal knowledge of the Darkwood, Sire. No man has ever passed through the darkness as many times as you, and returned to tell of it."

"And?"

"And," said the Champion, "You're quite possibly the only remaining member of the Court who doesn't have his own axe to grind."

"It's worth a try, I suppose," grunted Rupert, dourly. He moved back to the bed and buckled on his swordbelt. He'd worn it for so long he felt undressed without the familiar weight on his hip. All in all, he did feel a little better for his four hours' sleep. The stiffness was gone from his left shoulder, and he could barely feel the new scar tissue pulling when he moved his arm. He was still tired, but he could handle that. He'd had a lot of practice, recently. He ran his fingers through his tousled hair, pulled his jerkin straight, and then looked down at his blood-soaked clothes. Four hours of restless sleep had not improved their appearance. Rupert thought about changing into clothes more suitable for the Court, and then thought, *Forget it*. If the Court didn't like it, tough. He settled his swordbelt comfortably, and strode over to the patiently waiting Champion.

"All right; let's go."

The Champion glanced at Rupert's gory attire, and his mouth twitched. "Well, that should get their attention, Sire, if nothing else."

"Good," said Rupert, and strode out the door.

Prince Rupert and the Champion paused in the Court antechamber, and shared a sardonic smile. Even with the great double doors securely closed, the roar of raised voices within the Court came clearly to them. Rupert shook his head, stepped forward, and threw the doors open. A solid wave of sound came rushing over him as he stood in the doorway, staring about him—a vast animal roar of naked fear and fury. The courtiers had finally seen the darkness of the long night, and that sight had sent them to the edge of madness. The Lords and Ladies of the Court milled back and forth with shrill voices and wild eyes, moving from one faction to another in the same muddled, apparently aimless way that bees move from flower to flower. Other courtiers huddled together in sullen, frightened knots, and would listen only to their own comforting lies. Every man in the Court wore a sword at his hip, even those who had obviously never drawn a sword in anger in their lives. And everywhere there were raised voices and shaking fists, and faces made ugly by rage and fear and open hysteria. The Darkwood had come to Forest Castle.

At the far end of the Court, King John sat stiff-backed on his throne, with two guardsmen to either side of him. *How long has he needed the protection of armed guards in his own Court?* wondered Rupert, frowning. The King leaned forward on his throne and glared coldly at the High Warlock standing proudly before him, and Rupert didn't need to know what they were saying to know they were arguing. His frown deepened as he studied their faces. Anger was written plainly there for all to see, and so was fear, but beyond the obvious and the expected lay something else; something that might have been betrayal, on both sides.

He was a traitor. A traitor, a coward, and a drunk.

Rupert looked away. Standing at the King's right hand was Harald, swathed in gleaming chain mail, every inch the Prince. His muscles rippled impressively as he casually changed from one heroic pose to another. Rupert smiled

grimly; Harald had always looked the part much more than
he did. And then he saw Julia, hanging on Harald's arm,
and his smile was suddenly gone, leaving only the grimness
behind. Rupert watched silently as Julia smiled gaily and
patted Harald's arm with an easy familiarity. Harald smiled
at her, and said something that made her laugh. And then
some hidden instinct called to both of them, and they looked
out into the Court and saw Rupert watching them. Julia
flinched away from his steady gaze, and then stared coldly
back, daring him to say anything. Harald smiled and bowed
politely. Rupert looked away. Suddenly he felt tired. So
very tired. For a moment, he wanted nothing more than to
just turn and walk out of the Court and back to his room,
there to sleep and sleep and sleep, until everything went
away and stopped making demands on him. The moment
passed, but the weariness remained. Rupert sighed, quietly.
No rest for the wicked.

"Look at them," said the Champion disgustedly, nodding
at the courtiers. "The long night has finally fallen, and all
the Court can do is squabble and catcall like children in a
playground. They'll be pulling each other's hair next."

Rupert smiled in spite of himself. "You know, sir Champion; there was a time I actually believed the High Warlock
might *solve* some of our problems . . . I should have known
better."

The Champion glared coldly about him. "I did warn you,
Sire. I trust the High Warlock about as far as I could throw
a wet camel."

"Then why did you risk your life riding with me, on a
journey whose whole purpose was to try and persuade the
Warlock to come back with us?"

"Because my King ordered me to," said the Champion.
"No other reason."

"Ah, hell," said Rupert. "I suppose I'd better go and
break this shouting match up, or we'll never get anything
done. At this rate, somebody is bound to upset the Warlock
once too often, and we'll end up with a Court full of bemused-
looking toads."

"He wouldn't dare use his magic here," said the Champion.

"Don't bet on it," said Rupert. "The High Warlock has
all the practicality and self-preservation instincts of a depressed lemming."

He strode forward into the Court, and the milling crowd closed around him. The noise was appalling, and the people were packed so tightly together that Rupert quickly found himself hard put to make any headway. He saw a gap in the crowd and made for it, but a courtier got there first. Rupert tried to get past him, but the courtier just shot him a spiteful glance and deliberately moved to block his way. Rupert took the courtier by the shoulder, turned him around, punched him out, and walked over him. The nearest Lords and Ladies turned angrily on the Prince, and then took one look at his face and backed hastily away. Rupert strode on toward the throne, and the constant babble of voices died gradually away, as one by one the courtiers became aware of the grim, bloodstained figure in their midst. They fell away to either side of him and watched silently as he passed.

Rupert finally came to a halt before the throne. The King and the Warlock went on arguing, too wrapped up in each other to notice either Rupert's presence or the sudden hush that had fallen across the Court. Rupert stared past the King, and caught Harald's eye. His brother stirred uneasily, and a slight frown marred his placid features. Rupert's time in the Darkwood had changed him, and for the first time Harald felt a faint prickling of fear run down his spine. The blood-spattered, cold-eyed stranger before him had nothing in common with the quiet, indecisive brother he'd dominated for so many years. Harald looked away, unable to meet Rupert's gaze any longer. Without really knowing why, Harald was suddenly frightened. Death seemed to hang about Rupert like a shroud, as though he had brought something of the endless night with him into the brightly lit Court. Or perhaps it was simply that his eyes held more pain and horror than any man should ever have had to face. Harald started to shiver, and found he couldn't stop. He tried to concentrate on what the King and the Warlock were arguing about, and ignored the cold sweat beading on his forehead.

"We can't hide behind these walls forever!" shouted the King. "If we don't take the battle to the demons, it won't be long before they come looking for us!"

"You're either mad, or blind," growled the High Warlock. "You're talking as though the Forest was still under siege from the Darkwood. Get used to the idea, John; the

Forest is gone. There's nothing left but the night. Outside these walls there's no light, no life; nothing but the dark, and the demons that live in it. And there are an awful lot of demons in the dark. The creatures of the night outnumber any force you could hope to put together by more than a thousand to one. Anyone who leaves this Castle isn't coming back. Ever."

"So what are we supposed to do?" demanded the King tightly. "Hide in our little bolt hole while the dark grows even stronger? Wait until the Demon Prince himself comes to fetch us? I don't have enough men to guard the Castle walls as it is. It's only a matter of time before the demons come swarming over the walls and slaughter us all!"

"I need time," said the Warlock. "There are spells I can use, spells that should drive the demons back, but they take time to put together. Surely you can hold off the dark just a little longer?"

"What with?" howled the King, his face mottled with angry patches of red. "My men are dying. I'm running out of food, water, firewood . . . if the demons were to storm us right now, I couldn't be sure we'd throw them back. You've got to do something, damn you! You're the High Warlock! Do something, or we're all dead!"

"It's always me, isn't it? It always comes down to me, and my magic. You ever stop to think that just possibly I get bloody tired of having to clean up your messes for you? Just once, why don't you try taking responsibility for your own foul-ups? You know, you haven't changed a bit, John; you sit on your damn throne and mumble and dither until things get really out of hand, and then I'm supposed to step in and put everything right again, just like that! Never mind I've got my own life to lead. Never mind how much I have to risk my life in the process. Well, this time we're going to do things my way. I'm not putting my neck on the chopping block just because you're too impatient to wait!"

"I'm your King! I order you—"

"You can take your order and . . ."

"SHUT UP!" Rupert's sudden roar cut across their voices, bringing them both up short. Silence fell across the Court. A courtier standing beside Rupert opened his mouth to say something, and found himself staring with horrified fascination at the sword point pressing lightly against his belly.

"One more word from anybody," said Rupert quietly, "And I'll gut them."

Everybody looked at his determined face, and the blood-smeared sword in his hand, and quickly decided he might just mean it. Rupert stared about him at the silent, watchful Court, and grinned tightly.

"Now that I've got your attention, perhaps we can discuss the situation calmly, instead of screaming and shouting and running around like a chicken that's just had its head chopped off."

He sheathed his sword, and a quiet sigh of relief travelled around the Court, not least from the courtier Rupert had used to make his point.

"You're learning, Sire," said the Champion approvingly.

Rupert looked around and wasn't particularly surprised to find the Champion standing just behind him. Rupert nodded politely to him, and turned away. He wasn't altogether sure how much support he could depend on from the Champion, now that their mission was over, but for the moment at least it seemed he had an ally in his father's Court. If only because they both disliked the courtiers so much . . . Rupert stepped forward a pace, and bowed curtly to his father. The King stared at him for a long moment, his face and cold steady gaze giving nothing away.

"I thought you were dead," he said finally. "After so many months, and no word of you from anyone, I was sure I'd never see you again."

"So I gathered," said Rupert dryly. "In the courtyard, half of them acted like they'd seen a ghost. Hey, wait a minute; didn't the goblins tell you I was still alive? They did get here all right, didn't they?"

"Yes," said the King. "Unfortunately. But that was months ago. You were supposed to be back long before this."

There was a pause as they just looked at each other, their faces carefully impassive; each waiting for the other to say something.

"You could at least say you're glad to see me again," said Rupert, finally. "Or wasn't I supposed to come back from this quest, either?"

"You haven't changed," said the King. "You haven't changed at all, Rupert."

"Don't bet on it," said Rupert, and there was a sudden,

unyielding harshness in his voice that startled the King, and drew another thoughtful frown from Harald. Rupert ignored them both, and turned to the High Warlock. "Now you've had time to think about it, sir Warlock, perhaps you'd care to tell me what the hell went wrong with your teleport spell. We should have arrived here long before the Blue Moon was full. You promised me your spell would get us here in time. I trusted you, High Warlock."

"It wasn't my fault," said the Warlock, almost defiantly. "Somebody in this Castle interfered with my spell, so that we arrived at the right place, but the wrong time."

"Somebody here?" said Rupert. "Are you sure?"

"Of course I'm sure! I'm the High Warlock! Whoever it was, he isn't very powerful; he couldn't break or distort the spell, just deflect it. As far as I can make out, we were supposed to arrive even further in the future, after the Castle had fallen, but his magic wasn't strong enough."

Rupert shook his head slowly, trying to follow the explanation. "How could anyone here have interfered with your spell? Nobody here knew we'd be coming back by teleport."

"The Demon Prince knew," said the High Warlock.

A quiet murmur rustled through the Court, and several courtiers looked nervously about them, as though just the mention of his name might somehow be enough to summon the Dark Prince in person. The King leant forward on his throne, scowling and tugging angrily at his beard.

Rupert looked closely at the Warlock. "Are you saying the Demon Prince himself had something to do with your spell going wrong?"

"Indirectly, yes. He has no power outside the Darkwood, but he can work through human agents. Somewhere in this Castle, there is a traitor who serves the dark."

"That much we already know, sir Warlock," growled the King. "But can you name him?"

"Not easily; he's covered his tracks too well. Given time, perhaps . . ."

"We don't have the time," snapped Rupert. "We can worry about unearthing traitors after we've done something about the demons outside our walls. Father; how many armed men can we put in the field at one time?"

"Not many, Rupert; the plague hasn't left us much in the way of manpower."

"Plague?" Rupert's skin crawled suddenly, and a cold breeze seemed to caress the back of his neck. "What plague?"

The King smiled sourly. "A great deal has happened since you left, Rupert. The plague has been with us for months; a sickness and a fever that weakens and finally kills. We've tried everything, but nothing works against it. It swept across the Forest like a flash fire, and entered the Castle a good week and more before the darkness finally fell."

"How many people have we lost?" asked Rupert quietly.

"Hundreds," said the King. "Possibly thousands. There's no way of telling anymore."

"Damn!" The High Warlock screwed up his face, as though he'd just bitten into something sour, his eyes burning with sudden insight. "I knew it! As soon as Rupert told me about the unicorn losing his horn to the demons, I knew there had to be a reason!"

"I don't follow you," said Rupert. "What has the unicorn's horn got to do with the plague?"

"Everything," said the Warlock. "Two facts, Rupert. First; it is the Demon Prince's nature to corrupt. Second; a unicorn's horn has one special property, to detect and cure poisons. Put these two facts together, and the source of the plague becomes obvious; a debased unicorn's horn that spreads poison instead of curing it. In the Demon Prince's hands, that horn has produced a sorcerous plague, spread by his demons, incurable by any natural or unnatural means."

"If there is no cure," said the King slowly, "Then we've no way of stopping it. Eventually, everybody in the Land will be dead, no matter what we do. I can't accept that, sir Warlock; there must be something we can do!"

"There is," said the High Warlock. "Destroy the Demon Prince, and his plague will perish with him."

"This is all very interesting," said Harald dryly, "But we do seem to be drifting away from the point. The Demon Prince and the plague are problems for the future, assuming we have one. In the meantime, in case everybody has forgotten, we are still under siege from the demons outside our walls. As I recall, Rupert, you claimed to have some kind of answer to that problem. That was, after all, why you halted our discussion of the matter so . . . abruptly."

"Discussion?" said Rupert derisively. "Far as I could tell from the babble, your *discussion* had done nothing but

divide you into two trains of thought: Brute Force And
Ignorance, and Close Our Eyes And Maybe It'll All Go
Away. Keep thinking like that, people, and we're all going
to end up dead."

"I take it you've got a better idea?" said Julia.

Rupert looked at the Princess, who was clinging ostentatiously to Harald's arm. "Yes," he said finally. "I have.
Father; where's the Astrologer?"

"In seclusion," said the King. "He's using his magic to try
and discover who stole the Curtana, and where it's hidden."

"The Curtana?" Rupert blinked confusedly. "How could
anybody steal that? It's still in the lost South Wing!"

"Not anymore," said Julia. "I helped discover a way into
the South Wing. Unfortunately, when we finally got to the
Old Armory, the Curtana was missing."

Rupert's head whirled as he struggled to take all this in. *A
great deal has happened since you left, Rupert.* He sighed,
and firmly suppressed an urge to begin a series of questions
he could tell would probably last for hours, with no guarantee he'd be any better off at the end.

"You have been busy, haven't you, Julia?" he said finally. "Still, we can talk about that later. In the meantime,
Father, you'd better send for the Astrologer. If my plan's to
work, we're going to need all the magic we can muster."

"What do you want the Astrologer for?" growled the
Champion. "What's he going to do; read the demons' horo-
scopes and tell them it's a bad time of the month for attacking Castles?"

"He's a sorcerer," said Rupert. "And magic is the key to
this whole mess."

"Sorcery is the Demon Prince's way," said the Champion,
glaring at the silent High Warlock. "Fight fire with fire, and
we'll all get burned. This is a time for cold steel, Sire; for
human strength and valor."

"We tried that in the Darkwood, remember?" snapped
Rupert. "Cold steel isn't enough anymore! Demons don't
care how many of their number they lose, as long as they
bring us down. There are thousands of the damned creatures outside our walls, and God knows how many more
waiting to replace them when they fall. No, sir Champion;
the Darkwood is a thing of magic, and must be met with
magic."

The King opened his mouth to say something, and then looked around, startled, as the Court's double doors flew suddenly open, and the Astrologer entered the Court.

"Sorry I'm late, Sire; while searching for the Curtana, I had something of a breakthrough. As far as I can tell, the Sword of Compulsion no longer exists. Whoever took it from the Armory must have destroyed it. I have to admit, I'm not sure whether that's a bad thing or not."

A quiet muttering among the courtiers suggested they weren't sure, either.

King John pulled thoughtfully at his beard, frowning. "That sword still might have saved us from the darkness, Thomas. I take it there's no way of telling who stole it?"

"Without the Curtana? No, your majesty." The Astrologer turned to the High Warlock, and bowed deeply. "It's good to see you again, after all these years, sir Warlock. What small magics I possess are yours to command."

"Thank you, sir Astrologer," said the High Warlock politely. "I'm sure you'll be a most valuable ally."

"Look, we can all shake hands later," said Rupert testily. "Right now, we've still got a few hundred thousand demons to deal with."

"Ah," said Harald, "We're back to your famous plan again, are we?"

"Harald," said Rupert slowly, "You're getting on my nerves. One more interruption from you, and I'm going to knee your balls up around your ears. Got it?"

There was an uncomfortable silence, as everyone pretended not to have heard that.

"Your plan, Rupert," said the King finally.

"It's fairly straightforward," said Rupert. "Unlike most of you here, I've fought the Darkwood before. Swords aren't the answer, and neither is magic, but put them both together and we've got a chance. So, first we put together the biggest army we can; anyone who can still stand and wield a sword. Second, we back them up with spells from the High Warlock and the Astrologer, plus any other sorcerers and magicians we can find. Then, we attack the demons outside our walls and hit them with everything we've got. If we can drive the darkness back just this once, we can turn the tide. The demons aren't unbeatable; kill enough of them and they'll retreat. And without the demons to lead the way, the long night can't advance. If we make a stand, here and now, there's a chance we can throw back the night. It's not much of a chance . . . but . . . well, what have we got to lose?"

There was a pause.

"That's not really much of a plan," said the King, tactfully.

"It's a bloody awful plan," said Rupert, "But it's the best chance we've got. The demons aren't going to get any weaker. But hit them hard enough and often enough, and you'll find they die just as easily as any other creature."

The King nodded reluctantly. "Unless anyone has anything constructive to add . . . *constructive*, Harald . . . very well. In just over three hours from now, the clocks say it will be dawn. Half an hour before that time, I want to see all able-bodied men assembled in the courtyard. With luck we'll have found somewhere to put the refugee families by then. Don't anyone be late; if you're not there, we'll start without you. The gates will open at dawn. And then we'll show the demons a fight they'll never forget. That's all. Court is dismissed. Rupert, Harald, join me in my private chambers, please. Now."

The King rose from his throne, nodded curtly to the bowing courtiers, and strode briskly off to his private quarters, followed at a respectful distance by his guardsmen. The Court buzzed for a while in a subdued fashion, and then broke up into its various factions, and left. The High Warlock and the Astrologer went off together, calmly discussing magical tactics. The courtiers filed out in their little cliques, heading back to their quarters to ready their swords and their armor and their courage, knowing that in a few short hours they would have to go out and face the demons and, most probably, die. For all his contempt of the courtiers in general, Rupert was quietly impressed by the way they took it. For once in their life, they didn't whine and they didn't argue. They were clearly scared spitless, but Rupert had no doubt that, when the time came, most of them would be waiting in the courtyard, sword in hand. And those few too scared to turn up probably wouldn't have been much use in a battle, anyway.

He looked over to where Julia stood talking with Harald. They both seemed very interested in each other, and not at all in him. Rupert wanted to look away, and couldn't. At first, he'd thought Julia was just playing up to Harald to make him jealous, and that deep down she still cared for him. But now he knew better. For the first time, he realized how natural Julia looked in her formal gown and cloak. She looked somehow right beside Harald, as though she belonged there. Rupert glanced down at his own torn and bloodstained clothes, and the thought of that tall, stately Princess on his arm was totally ridiculous.

I'm a second son, he thought bitterly, *And that's all I'll ever be. It didn't take Julia long to discover where the real power is in this family.* He took one last look at the gorgeous blonde Princess laughing with Prince Harald, and turned away. *That's not the woman I knew,* he thought tiredly. *That's not the woman I fought beside in the Darkwood . . . the woman I came to love. That Julia was just an illusion; a dream born of need and shared danger . . . and loneliness. I should have known better.*

He strode stiffly past the empty throne toward the King's private chambers, and his duty lay heavy on his shoulder. He didn't care. It was all he had left.

Julia watched him go, and bit her lip. She wanted to call after him, but her pride wouldn't let her. It was his place to come to her; she was damned if she'd give him the satisfaction of seeing her crawl. After all she'd been through, after all the months of believing him dead and gone, when word had reached her that Rupert had finally turned up safe and sound, she'd been so filled with joy and disbelief she hadn't known whether to laugh or cry or jump up and down on the spot in sheer exuberance. She'd bullied the Seneschal into telling her where Rupert's rooms were, and had run all the way there to welcome him back, only to find him cold and insulting. She would have explained about Harald and the marriage, if he'd just given her time, but no; he was too busy being hurt and angry. He had no right to be that way. He didn't know what it had been like in the Castle, on her own, with the darkness closing in. With him gone, and the dragon sleeping, maybe even dying, it wasn't surprising she'd turned to Harald. She'd needed somebody, and there wasn't anyone else . . . Julia watched Rupert leave the Great Hall, and her hands closed into fists so tight they ached.

She glanced at Harald, who was staring thoughtfully at

the slowly closing door through which Rupert had just passed.
There was no doubt that Harald had become a major part of
her life in the past few months, but Julia still wasn't sure
how she felt about him. He was kind, attentive, even charming, and yet sometimes she'd look up from his smile and
find herself staring into eyes so cold they made her shiver.

There was no denying Harald had his faults, but Julia had
been very impressed by the quiet, competent way he'd taken
charge of things, as the darkness grew steadily nearer and
day by day the situation deteriorated. King John had done
his best, but with more and more refugees streaming in from
the ravaged countryside, events had quickly proved too
complicated for any one man to handle, and the King had
reluctantly been forced to admit he could no longer cope
without help. Harald and the Seneschal had taken most of
the load off his shoulders, but King John had grown increasingly bitter and depressed over what he saw as his failure to
retain control of his own Kingdom. He spent less and less
time at Court, with the result that Harald had gradually
taken most of the responsibility upon himself, until now he
was most often in command. He seemed to be doing a good
job, or at least as good a job as anyone could have managed
under the circumstances.

And yet, despite all his problems, Harald still found the
time to come and talk with her, and keep her company.
He'd come a long way from the brash, insensitive bastard
who'd pursued her so relentlessly in the early days. Julia
grinned suddenly. If nothing else, it seemed she'd had a
civilizing effect on the man. She stared at Harald almost
fondly, and then her smile faded away as his expression
suddenly changed. Harald was still staring at the closed door
that led to the King's private chambers, but as Julia watched,
Harald's normally calm and pleasant features disappeared,
to be replaced by hard unyielding lines that completely
changed his face. Julia stared at him, fascinated; it was like
discovering a whole new person underlying the one she was
used to. She frowned thoughtfully; she wasn't at all sure she
liked this new Harald. She could see strength in his face,
and determination, and obviously an iron will, but there was
also fear, and in a sudden flash of insight Julia realized that
Harald was afraid of Rupert. And then the moment passed,
and Harald's usual calm mask reappeared. He turned to

smile at her, and surely it was only her imagination that made Julia see a cold, killing fury in his eyes.

"Well now, Julia," said Harald pleasantly, "I'm afraid I've got to go and see Father now, but I expect there'll still be a little time afterwards, before I have to lead our troops out to battle. Why don't you join me in my rooms in an hour or so, and we can spend some time together before the dawn."

"Yes," said Julia. "Of course. Harald, I . . ."

"It's Rupert, isn't it?" said Harald. "Don't worry about him, my dear; you'll forget him soon enough, once we're married. You won't even have to talk to him again, if you don't want to. In fact, that might be best. Rupert's been something of a bad influence on you, Julia, though to be honest, I never did understand what you saw in him. Still, as soon as our meeting with Father is over, I've no doubt he'll find somewhere to hide until he has to come out and fight with us at dawn. For all his fine talk, Rupert's never really been much of a one for fighting."

"He beat you in your last duel, didn't he?" said Julia, and then wondered why she'd said that.

Harald looked at her sharply. "That was a fluke. He'd learned a few new tricks, that's all. Next time . . ."

"Wait a minute." Julia's eyes narrowed suddenly. "Did I miss something, or did you really just say that Rupert would be going out to fight again at dawn?"

"Well, of course he'll be there," said Harald. "It's his duty."

"You can't be serious! You saw him in Court; he's exhausted!"

Harald shrugged coldly. "He doesn't have any choice in the matter. Rupert, Father, and I will be leading the charge against the demons; it's expected of us. After all, you can't expect the rabble to follow if royalty won't lead, can you? Not that it actually matters whether Rupert turns up or not, as long as I'm there. I'm the eldest son, and I'm the one they'll follow."

"He'll be there, and you know it," said Julia. A slow, cold anger wrapped itself around her like an old, familiar cloak. "Rupert knows his duty. He's always known his bloody duty. And he's not a coward."

Harald laughed unpleasantly. "Rupert's always been a

coward. He still needs a nightlight in his room before he can sleep!"

Julia turned her back on him, and started down the dais steps. Harald hurried after her.

"Julia! Where are you going?"

"I have to see Rupert. I have to talk to him."

Harald grabbed her by the arm, and stopped her at the foot of the dais steps. She jerked her arm free, and clapped her hand to her swordhilt.

"Get away from me, Harald."

"No, Julia," he said firmly. "It's too late for that now. You made your choice, and you can't go back on it."

"Don't be too sure about that, Harald."

"Oh, I think I can be, my dear. Or do you really believe Rupert would take you back, once he's found out just how *close* you and I have become during his absence?"

"I thought he was dead!"

"I doubt that'll make any difference to Rupert. He's always been rather . . . old-fashioned . . . in such matters. Face facts, my dear; you've made my bed, and now you must sleep in it. Forget Rupert. You're going to be my wife, Julia, and as such you must learn to obey me."

Julia brought her knee up sharply, and Harald doubled over, gasping for breath. Julia left him there before the throne, and hurried, almost running, to the door through which Rupert had already passed. It was horribly clear to her that if she didn't talk to him first, Rupert would go out to face the waiting demons believing that she didn't care for him. And she couldn't let him go to his death believing a lie.

She hurried out of the Great Hall and down the corridor that led to the King's private chambers. She soon came to the King's door, and stood there a moment, composing herself, before knocking politely. Nobody answered, and when she tried the handle it wouldn't turn. She beat on the thick wooden panels with her fist, and then fell back suddenly as a single glowing eye opened in the' wood of the door, and looked at her. Julia shuddered uncontrollably as she faced the shining, metallic eye. All her instincts were telling her to turn and run, but still she stood her ground and glared defiantly back.

This door is sealed, said a cold voice in her mind.

"You must let me in," said Julia shakily. "I have to see the King."

Prince Harald, Prince Rupert, and the High Warlock may enter, said the cold voice. *To all others, this room is sealed. Leave now.*

"I have to see the King! It's important!"

Leave now.

"Damn you, let me in!"

Julia reached for her sword, and a bright flash of balefire sent her sprawling to the floor. She shook her head to clear it, and then clambered unsteadily to her feet, carefully keeping her hand away from her sword. The eye in the door stared calmly back at her, bright and metallic and utterly inhuman.

Leave, said the cold voice. *Leave now.*

Julia glared helplessly at the unblinking eye, and then turned and walked back down the corridor. The eye watched her go, and then closed, disappearing back into the wood of the door. Julia slowly made her way back to the Great Hall. Whatever King John wanted with his sons and the High Warlock, it must be pretty damned important to justify such a strong warding spell. She'd just have to talk to Rupert later, that was all.

She had to talk to him, while there was still time.

Deep in the endless gloom of the South Wing, a concealed door swung slowly open, and Lord Darius stepped out into the corridor. He looked cautiously around him, but nothing and no one moved in the wide, empty gallery that stretched away to either side of him, cold and dark and silent. Darius smiled slowly, and pulled the door shut behind him. It closed with only the faintest of clicks, and no trace remained in the panelled wall to show where it had been. The only light came from a single foxfire lamp set high up on the wall, but Darius's eyes had grown so used to the dark that even this dim glow was enough to light the corridor clearly. He glanced uneasily about him, uncomfortable in such an open space after so long in the cramped and narrow tunnels, and then crouched down on his haunches next to the wall. His once fashionable clothes were fouled and dirty, and hung loosely on his thinning frame. His unhealthy flesh was blotched and waxy pale, hanging in ugly folds and flapping jowls, from having lost too much weight in too short a time. No fine Lord or Lady from the Court would have recognized Lord Darius now, in the half-mad, scarecrow figure that crouched like an animal in the shadows because it preferred the darkness to the light.

His puffy eyes glistened brightly as he peered quickly about him, ready to turn and run at the first sign of danger. Again and again, his hand moved nervously to the dagger concealed in his sleeve, but no shadow stirred, and no sound broke the silence, save for his own unsteady breathing. The South Wing waited, as it had waited undisturbed for so many years, but still there was a tension on the unmoving air, as though the very Stones themselves were aware that something evil walked the empty corridors.

There was a cold, brooding look in Darius's face, as though he held some awful secret within him, of things done or planned in the dark because they could not stand the light of day. Rupert would have recognized the look. He had passed through the endless night, and something of that darkness was in him too, and always would be. The Darkwood had placed its mark on both their souls, but whereas Rupert strove to throw the darkness off, Darius had surrendered to it willingly, in return for what it had promised him.

Darius held up his left hand, and flames licked around his fingers without consuming them. He had power now, power from his dark master, and with that power all debts would be repaid, all insults revenged. Darius laughed softly, and the flames disappeared. He crouched alone in the gloom, saying nothing, thinking little; waiting for those he feared and hated to come to him, there in the quiet and the cold and the darkness of the deserted South Wing.

King John sighed, and watched dourly as his breath steamed on the chill air. He pulled his cloak tightly about him, and moved his chair a little closer to the banked, glowing fire. Even in his private rooms, deep in the heart of the Castle, it seemed there was no escaping the bitter cold of the Darkwood. He stared thoughtfully at the High Warlock, sitting opposite him on the other side of the fireplace. The Warlock sprawled inelegantly in his chair, chewing on a chicken leg, his short tubby legs propped up on a footstool. The cold didn't seem to bother him at all.

Lamps and candles filled every spare niche in the overcrowded room, but still the overall impression was one of gloom. Always, in the past, the King had been able to draw strength and comfort from the many layers of ancient Stone that surrounded him, from the magics and the mysteries of Forest Castle, his legacy and birthright. For twelve generations before him, the Forest Kings had defended the Land from all that threatened it, and something of that strength and determination had come to reside in Forest Castle itself, or so John had always believed. But now the long night had come, and all the ancient magics in the Castle walls had not been enough to keep out the Darkwood. The King scowled testily; times were hard indeed when a man couldn't even find a little peace and comfort in the security of his own rooms. John smiled briefly, recognizing the pettiness of his thoughts, and pushed them firmly to one side. He glanced again at the High Warlock, and memories ran swiftly through his mind, not all of them bad. He and the Warlock had never been especially close, but they'd worked well together, for many years. There was even a time he'd thought of the High Warlock as his strong right arm, but that was a long time ago. A very long time ago.

The Warlock stripped the last of the meat from the chicken leg and then, as John watched, casually broke the bone in two and sucked at the marrow like a child with a stick of candy. When he'd finished, he threw the bone into the fire and wiped his greasy fingers on the front of his robe. King John looked away. The High Warlock he remembered would rather have died than behave in so uncivilized a manner. The Warlock he remembered had been gracious and courtly, and even something of a dandy. Always the height of fashion, and never a lock of hair out of place. Right to the very end, his poise had never faltered; the tavern-keepers said he was the most dignified drunk they'd ever known. John smiled slightly in spite of himself, and then the smile vanished as he remembered other things. He closed his eyes, and after a while the awful memories subsided, though some of the pain remained to haunt him, as always. He looked again at the High Warlock, who was staring absently into the fire. The

Warlock's face was calm and impassive, and John had no
idea what the man was thinking.

"I wondered how I'd feel when I saw you again," said
King John slowly. "Whether I'd hate you, or fear you. It's
been a long time, hasn't it?"

"Yes," said the High Warlock. "It has."

"You look pretty much as I remember you. You haven't
aged at all."

"Transformational magic; I can be whatever age I wish.
Of course, the younger I choose to be, the faster I burn up
what remains of my life. I'm an old man now, John; older
than you and your father put together. You know, I miss
Eduard, sometimes. I could talk to him. You and I, we
never really had much in common."

"No," said the King. "But your advice was always good."

"Then you should have listened to it more."

"Perhaps."

They both fell silent, and for a long while neither of them
said anything. The fire stirred uneasily in the fireplace, and
the sound of the crackling flames was eerily distinct on the
quiet.

"There was no need to banish me, John," said the Warlock finally. "I'd already banished myself."

The King shrugged. "I had to do something. Eleanor was
dead, and I needed to do something."

"I did everything I could for her, John."

The King stared into the fire, and said nothing.

"What do you think of young Rupert's plan?" asked the
Warlock.

"It might work. We've tried everything else. Who knows?"

"I like Rupert. He seems an intelligent lad. Brave, too."

"Yes," said John slowly. "I suppose he is."

They looked at each other awkwardly. Too many years of
pain and rage and hoarded bitterness lay between them, and
they both knew it. They had nothing to say to each other; it
had all been said before. The High Warlock got to his feet.

"I suppose I'd better have a word with Thomas Grey. His
powers appear to have grown somewhat in my absence;
perhaps he can be a help to me, after all. Good night, John.
I'll see you again, before we go out to battle."

"Good night, sir Warlock."

The King stared into the fire, and didn't relax until he'd

heard the door open and close. Even after all the years, the memories wouldn't let him be. He closed his eyes, and once again he and the Warlock were standing together beside Eleanor's bed. The bedclothes had been drawn up over her face.

She's dead, John. I'm so sorry.

Bring her back.

I can't do that, John.

You're the High Warlock! Save her, damn you!

I can't.

You haven't even tried.

John . . .

You let her die because she didn't love you!

The King buried his face in his hands, but no tears came. He'd shed them all long ago, and there was no room in him for tears anymore. The door opened behind him, and he quickly sat up straight again, composing his features into their usual harsh mask. Rupert and Harald moved forward to bow respectfully before him. They stood shoulder-to-shoulder, but still there was a coldness between them. King John smiled tiredly. The day there was anything but coldness between those two, he'd eat his boots, buckles and all. Rupert and Harald waited patiently, staring calmly at a point somewhere over the King's head. John braced himself. Neither Rupert nor Harald was going to like what he had to say to them, but he had to have their support.

"Sit down," he growled finally. "You make the place look untidy."

Harald sank quickly into the chair the Warlock had just vacated, leaving Rupert to go in search of another chair. John tried not to wince, as the sound of bumped furniture and falling objects told him exactly where Rupert was at any given time. Rupert finally returned, dragging a chair behind him. Harald had a coughing fit behind a raised hand, until the King glared at him. John didn't turn around to see how much damage had been done to his room; he didn't think his patience would stand it.

"Sorry," said Rupert, as he carefully placed his chair midway between Harald and the King.

"Not at all," said John politely. "It is a little cluttered in here."

He waited patiently while Rupert settled himself in his

chair, and then tugged thoughtfully at his beard as he wondered how best to start. The silence lengthened, and still he hesitated. He knew what he planned to do was both right and necessary, but that didn't make it any easier.

"You wished to see us, Father," said Harald, eventually. "Is it about the wedding?"

"No," said the King, not missing the way Rupert's hand rested casually on his swordhilt. "Though the wedding will have to be postponed again, I'm afraid."

"Oh dear," said Rupert. "What a pity."

"Yes," said Harald. "Isn't it."

"So why are we here?" demanded Rupert. "Is it something to do with my plan to fight the demons?"

"I'd hardly call it a plan," said Harald. "Mass suicide would be closer to the mark."

"If you've got a better idea, I'd love to hear it!" snapped Rupert. "What would you rather do; hide behind these walls until the demons come looking for us? Believe me, Harald, it's better to die fighting."

"It's better not to die at all," said Harald. "There has to be another way. Perhaps the High Warlock . . ."

"No," said the King flatly. "Even at his peak, he was never that powerful. But you're right, Harald; there has to be a better way. And I think I might just have found it. If nothing else, it should improve our chances against the demons."

"I don't understand," said Rupert, frowning. "If there is another way, why didn't you mention it at Court?"

The King met his gaze squarely. "Because the Court wouldn't have approved."

"It's something to do with the Curtana, isn't it?" said Harald suddenly.

"In a way," said the King. "I had planned to use the Curtana against the demons, but that sword is lost to us now. There are, however, other swords just as powerful, if not more so."

Rupert and Harald looked at each other, and John found a small amusement in their equally shocked faces, as they realized what he was talking about. If nothing else, it seemed he'd finally found something they could agree on.

"You're talking about the Infernal Devices," said Rupert, incredulously. "You can't be serious, Father!"

"Why not?" said the King.

"The Infernal Devices are forbidden to us," said Harald, but King John didn't miss the cold calculation that had entered Harald's eyes.

"We can't use them," said Rupert. "The Curtana was bad enough, but those blades . . . I'm not sure which scares me most; the demons, or those cursed swords."

"Understandable," said Harald, "But then, you're scared of lots of things, aren't you?"

Rupert looked at him, and Harald stirred uncomfortably in his chair. "Keep talking, Harald," said Rupert calmly. "It's all you're good for."

"That's enough!" snapped the King. "Save your feuding until we've found a way out of the darkness. That's an order!" He glared at his sons until they both reluctantly inclined their heads to him. John leant back in his chair, and when he spoke again, his voice was calm and measured. "The Infernal Devices are swords of power; power great enough to save the Land from the long night that threatens it. Nothing else matters."

"But we don't even know what the swords do," protested Rupert. "It's been so long since anyone dared draw the blades that even the legends have grown vague. Rockbreaker. Flarebright. Wolfsbane. Those names could mean anything! For all we know, we could be waking an evil greater than the one we already face."

"Even an evil sword can be put to good use," said Harald. "Providing it's kept under careful control."

Rupert shook his head stubbornly. "I don't trust magic swords."

"What choice do we have?" said John quietly. "You said it yourself, Rupert; the Darkwood's strength is based in magic, and it must be fought with magic. According to the legends, the Infernal Devices were the most powerful weapons ever created by Man."

"And the last time they were drawn," said Rupert, "they laid waste to half the world before they could be sheathed again. According to the legends."

"This time, they could save the world!"

"Or damn it, for all time."

"What difference does it make?" said Harald. "Outside these walls, there's nothing left but darkness now. The Land has fallen. The Infernal Devices may be our last chance, our last hope . . . or they might destroy us all. It doesn't really matter. We're damned if we do, and damned if we don't. Personally, I think I'll settle for a chance to take our enemies down with us."

Rupert scowled, and slowly shook his head. "There has to be another way."

"No," said John simply. "We've run out of choices, Rupert. The Infernal Devices are all that's left."

"Then God have mercy on all our souls," said Rupert.

John, Harald, and Rupert sat in silence a while, staring into the fire rather than face each other. They knew that shortly they would have to make their way to the South Wing, there to draw the forbidden swords from their ancient scabbards, but not yet. Not quite yet. They stared at the sinking flames of the guttering fire with quiet desperation, each lost in his own thoughts. Rupert found himself remembering the Coppertown pit, and the worm he found there, but most of all he remembered the magic sword that had failed him.

Rockbreaker. Flarebright. Wolfsbane.

Rupert started to shiver, and found he couldn't stop.

In the silent, deserted hall that marked the boundary of the South Wing, the Castle grew a little darker. There were blazing torches, and oil and foxfire lamps, but none of them made much impression on the gloom that filled the air like a dirty fog. Rupert stood in the hall's North doorway, staring dubiously at the closed double doors on the opposite side of the vast, echoing chamber. Somewhere beyond those doors lay the Armory and the Infernal Devices; perhaps the only hope left for the Forest Land. Rupert frowned, and shifted uncomfortably from foot to foot. The hall was the beginning of the South Wing, and he didn't like it at all; it reminded him too much of the Darkwood.

Rupert had made a point of arriving before the others; partly because he needed some time to himself, but mainly because he'd wanted a damn good look at the newly discovered Wing before he ventured into it. A great many rumors had accumulated about the South Wing in the thirty-two years it had been missing, and all of them were bad. Over a hundred parties had sought to plumb the secrets of the lost

Wing at one time or another, but the only ones that came back had been those who'd failed to find a way in. And now Julia and the Seneschal had found a way in, and returned to tell of it. Rupert looked about him, and shook his head slowly. From what he'd seen of it so far, the South Wing should have stayed lost.

One of the lamps suddenly guttered and went out, and the shadows grew that much darker. Rupert stirred uneasily. Rather than give in to his nerves, he strode determinedly into the hall and took the lamp from its niche. A quick shake revealed that the lamp had run out of oil. Rupert smiled dourly, and relaxed a little. The hall didn't seem quite as large and forbidding now that he was actually inside it, but there was still something disquieting in the silence, and the utter stillness of the air. Rupert was suddenly aware of soft dragging footsteps behind him, and he spun round sword in hand to discover the Seneschal glaring acidly at him from the North door. Rupert smiled apologetically, and sheathed his sword again.

"Sorry, sir Seneschal."

"Oh, don't mind me," said the Seneschal, leaning heavily on his stout walking stick as he limped into the hall. "I'm just a servant, after all. No one else pays me any mind, so why should you be any different? I mean; I'm only the man who singlehandedly discovered and destroyed the barrier that kept people out of the South Wing. But does anybody listen to me? Stay out of the South Wing, I tell them. It's not safe in there, I tell them. But does anybody listen? Do they hell as like. I'd have a nervous collapse, if I could only find the time."

"Has somebody upset you, sir Seneschal?" asked Rupert diffidently.

"Ha!" said the Seneschal, bitterly. "Upset! What is there to be upset about? I've only been dragged from my bed and escorted to the Great Hall by half the Royal Guard! When I finally got there, a neanderthal with dragging knuckles and the lowest forehead I've ever seen curtly informed me that I had been granted the signal honor of leading the Royal family back into the South Wing, starting Now. No *Please*, or *Would you mind?*" The Seneschal slumped his shoulders, and looked tired and defeated and put upon. He was very good at that; he'd had a lot of practice recently. "Never mind I haven't had a free moment to myself since the refugees arrived. Never mind I've been run ragged chasing up and down the corridors looking for somewhere to put them all, because the King keeps changing his mind. Now he wants me to lead him to the Armory, at an hour in the morning when any man with half a brain in his head is fast asleep! The old man's getting senile, if you ask me. He'll be needing help to find his own privy next."

Rupert grinned happily as he listened to the Seneschal rant and rave. It was nice to know some things didn't change.

"Now then, sir Seneschal," said Rupert finally, when the Seneschal had slowed down enough for him to be able to get a word in edgeways, "Aren't you going to tell me what happened to your leg?"

"My leg?" The Seneschal stared at him blankly, and then glanced down at the thick oaken staff he was leaning on. "Oh, that. Julia and I found some demons hiding in the South Wing. Not to worry, though; they're all gone now."

He didn't volunteer any details, and after a moment Rupert decided not to ask. He didn't think he really wanted to know.

"I haven't even had time to say hello to my own grandfather," grumbled the Seneschal. "Not that we've ever had much to say to each other, but still . . ."

"Your grandfather?" said Rupert.

"The High Warlock," said the Seneschal. "Must be twenty years since I last saw him."

Rupert heard footsteps behind him, and turned around just in time to see Harald and the King entering the hall. The Seneschal sniffed angrily, and pointedly turned his back on them all. Rupert and the King shared a knowing look.

"Has somebody upset you, sir Seneschal?" asked the King, politely.

"Ha!" said the Seneschal.

"Rupert," said the King, "Why is the Seneschal sulking?"

"I am not sulking!"

"Then what's keeping us?" said Harald. "The South Wing is waiting."

"Just a minute," said Rupert. "Is this all of us? No guards, no escort? According to what the Seneschal's been telling me, the South Wing is still pretty dangerous."

"You can always stay behind," said Harald, "If you're worried . . ."

"I was thinking of the King's safety," said Rupert.

"Of course you were," said Harald.

"That's enough!" said the King sharply. "We aren't taking any guards, Rupert, because if the Court were to even suspect what we plan to do in the Armory, they'd probably try and stop us. And we haven't got time to put down another rebellion."

"What happens when we come back with the swords?" said Rupert. "The Court isn't going to take kindly to being kept in the dark on this."

"You can say that again," muttered the Seneschal.

"We've been through this already, sir Seneschal," said the King firmly. "You have agreed to help."

"Besides," said Harald, "Once we've got the swords, what the Court thinks won't matter any more."

"There'll be time for discussion later," said the King. "The dawn is drawing steadily closer, and we haven't even got to the Armory yet. Sir Seneschal, if you please . . ."

"Oh, very well," said the Seneschal grudgingly. "We might as well make a start, I suppose, since I'm here. It's my own fault; I'm just too easygoing, that's my trouble. I let people take advantage of my good nature."

The Seneschal continued to mutter and grumble under his breath as he led the way out of the hall, and into the South Wing. Harald and the King followed close behind him, and Rupert brought up the rear, his hand resting lightly on the pommel of his sword. He stared covertly about him as the small party moved briskly through the dim, foxfire-lit corridors and passageways, and at first he was almost disappointed that everything seemed so . . . ordinary. After all the songs and legends he'd heard on the missing Wing, he'd been expecting something more intimidating. Rupert smiled sourly; he of all people should have known that songs and legends were wrong more often than they were right. And yet there was something about the South Wing . . . something *disturbing*. Rupert had felt it first in the hall at the boundary, but as he made his way deeper into the heart of the rediscovered Wing, it seemed to him more and more that there was an unfinished air to the empty, echoing corridors; as though something was about to happen, or was already happening; something that had no end . . . A cold breeze stirred the hackles on the back of Rupert's neck, and he shook his head quickly. This was no time to be letting his paranoia get the better of him. And then a new thought came to him, and he increased his step so that he could walk alongside the Seneschal.

"Sir Seneschal; why is this Wing still empty, when the rest of the Castle is packed with refugees? Can't we billet some of them here?"

"Nobody will live here," said the Seneschal quietly. "Thirty-two years ago, something happened in this Wing; something so terrible that the echoes still remain. It's in the floor and in the walls, and even in the air itself; a sense of something evil, that happened here long ago and is still happening, even after all these years. The Stones remember. You feel it too, don't you, Rupert? Everybody does, after a while. The first people we settled here came running out after only a few hours. The others we tried didn't even last that long. Eventually, we gave up, and left the South Wing to itself. Whatever's in here, hiding in the dark, it doesn't want company."

Rupert swallowed with a suddenly dry throat. "So this Wing's completely empty?"

"Apart from your disgusting friends," said Harald.

"Ah yes," said the Seneschal. "I'd forgotten about them. The goblins live here, Sire. They seem quite happy and unaffected. Either they're simply not superstitious, or they're all completely insensitive."

Rupert smiled. "That sounds like them."

"Got it in one," growled a deep bass voice from the shadows. "Welcome back, Prince Rupert."

Rupert's party came to a sudden halt as the goblin leader stepped forward into the dim light, followed by half a hundred other goblins from the surrounding shadows. They all wore some kind of armor, and knives and short swords and axes gleamed in every hand. For a long moment nobody moved, and then, as one, the goblins knelt and bowed to Rupert. Even the goblin leader tucked his head quickly in and back, in what might just have been a bow. Rupert looked around him, a delighted grin spreading slowly across his face. Regular food and better living conditions had put meat on the goblins' bones, and removed some of the gaunt-ness from their faces. More important, most of them now handled their weapons with the quiet competence of the seasoned fighter. Altogether, the goblins looked a great deal more impressive than when Rupert had first met them, back in the Tanglewood. He almost felt that he should be kneeling to them.

"On your feet," he said finally, not even trying to hide the warmth in his voice. "You're warriors, now."

"Well; they try," growled the goblin leader, glaring disgustedly around him as the goblins scrambled awkwardly to their feet. "It's good to see you again, Sire. They told us you were dead, but we didn't believe them. Not one of us."

"Thank you," said Rupert. "It's good to be back among friends."

Harald chuckled mockingly. "Trust you to make friends out of goblins, Rupert. But then, anyone else wouldn't need to associate with such creatures, would they?"

The goblin leader made a casual gesture, and the nearest half-dozen goblins took a firm hold of Harald and unceremoniously turned him upside down. Harald sputtered with outrage and reached for his sword, only to stop short as the smallest goblin stepped forward and pressed a jagged-edged knife against his throat.

"Just say the word," said the smallest goblin cheerfully, "And we'll skin him for you, Prince Rupert. Or just nod, if you like; we're not fussy. Dead informal, that's us. Or maybe you'd like him fricasseed? We can do some very nasty things with a banked fire."

"I wouldn't doubt it for a moment," said Rupert. "Unfortunately, we need Harald alive, for the time being. You can let him loose now; I'm sure he'll mind his manners in the future."

"Can't we at least bounce him off the walls a little first?" pleaded the smallest goblin.

"Maybe later," said Rupert.

The goblins dropped Harald in a heap on the floor and moved reluctantly away, muttering disappointedly. Harald sat up and glared about him. He made a tentative move toward drawing his sword, but stopped as he realized half a hundred well-armed goblins were glaring back at him. Harald decided to ignore them. He scrambled to his feet, and set about rebuilding his injured dignity.

King John studied Rupert as the Prince spoke quietly with the goblin leader. At first, the King had been rather amused by the goblins' awe of his son, but he was slowly coming to see that, underneath the ridiculous adoration, there was a very real respect and reverence. In all the time they'd been at Court, the goblins had never once bowed to their King. If anyone had ever suggested it, the revolting little creatures would probably have split their sides laughing. But they bowed their heads to Rupert. So did the guards who'd come back with him out of the long night. To hear the stories they'd been telling in their barracks, you'd think Rupert was one of the great heroes of legend. Even the Champion's report had been full of praise for Rupert's valor and skill in battle. Even the Champion . . . King John scowled, and tugged at his beard. He was going to have to think about this. Rupert was finally showing signs of becoming a warrior and a hero, and that . . . was dangerous.

"I've got to go now," said Rupert to the goblin leader. "We're rather pushed for time. You do know we're going out against the demons in a few hours from now?"

"Of course," said the goblin leader gruffly. "Some of us will be there with you. We still remember what the demons did to our homes, our families. They came at night, and there was no moon in the sky. They killed our children first, and then our women, and only those of us who turned and ran survived to tell the story. We knew nothing then, of fighting or hate or revenge. We have learned much in a short time. They say humans know how to forget, Prince Rupert. Perhaps one day, you will teach us this. There are so many things we need to forget, but we don't know how. For us, the blood and death lies forever before our eyes, and our ears still hear the screams.

"All we've learned so far is how to kill demons. For the moment, that's enough. If we can't have peace of mind, we'll settle for revenge. Perhaps we can learn to be brave too, now we've no choice."

Rupert put out his hand, and the goblin leader clasped it firmly with his own gnarly hand.

"We'll make you proud of us yet, Prince Rupert."

"I already am," said Rupert. "I already am."

The goblin leader nodded quickly, and then turned and stalked back into the shadows, and was gone. Within seconds, the rest of the goblins had also disappeared from the corridor, sliding back into the darkness as silently as they had arrived. Rupert found his eyes were a little too moist, and blinked rapidly until the feeling went away, and only then did he turn back to face the rest of his party. The King looked at him strangely, but said nothing. Harald was doing his best to pretend that nothing had happened, while still trying to get the wrinkles out of his clothes. The Seneschal was leaning against the far wall, staring at the ceiling, and tapping his foot impatiently.

"Can we get on now?" he asked coldly, apparently of the ceiling. "All this conversation may be very interesting, but it's not getting us any closer to the Armory."

"A moment, sir Seneschal," said the King. "You have found us a route that avoids the missing Tower?"

"Amateurs," said the Seneschal. "I'm dealing with amateurs. Of course I've found us a way around it! That's my job, remember? That's why I was dragged out of a nice warm bed to lead you through this damn warren. Now follow me, if you please, and stay close; I've got more than enough to worry about, without having to waste valuable time searching for strays."

"Of course, sir Seneschal," said the King soothingly.

The Seneschal growled something under his breath and hobbled off down the corridor, and after a moment the others followed him. Rupert once again brought up the rear, scowling thoughtfully as he considered the Seneschal's words. What the hell was this missing Tower, and why was it so important they avoid it? Come to that, how had the demons the Seneschal mentioned got into the South Wing in the first place? Rupert shook his head grimly. There were a lot of things he wasn't being told; as usual. Obviously a great deal had happened during Julia's rediscovery of the South Wing, but then, knowing Julia, it was only to be expected that anything she was involved in would be far from easy or straightforward. Rupert smiled slightly at the thought, and then deliberately thought of something else. Thinking about Julia still hurt too much.

Lights grew few and far between as the party moved deeper into the South Wing. Corridors gave way to galleries, which gave way to halls, rotundas, and apparently endless stairways, until finally they came to the Armory. The

Seneschal unlocked the great double doors and then stepped back for the King to lead the way in, but for a long moment nobody moved. Rupert stared at the Armory doors, and felt his flesh creep with something that was neither fear nor awe, but some strange mixing of the two. For almost fourteen generations, the Armory had been the weapon house of the Forest Kings. Somewhere beyond those doors lay all the mighty blades of history and legend; of heroes and villains and defeated enemies of the Realm. And somewhere, in the darkness beyond the doors, lay the Infernal Devices: Rockbreaker, Flarebright, and Wolfsbane.

Rupert glanced at the King, who had still made no move to enter the Armory. His face was tight and drawn, and beads of sweat showed clearly on his forehead beneath the crown. Rupert looked quickly at Harald, but his brother's placid mask was firmly in place, showing nothing but a polite, patient interest. And perhaps it was only Rupert's imagination that made him see an extra, hungry gleam in Harald's eyes. Rupert looked back at the unlocked, inviting doors, and then stepped forward and pushed open the left-hand door. It swung smoothly back under his hand, the ancient counterweights barely whispering despite their long years of neglect. The Seneschal was quickly at his shoulder with a flaring torch as Prince Rupert entered the Armory of the Forest Kings.

The great hall stretched away before him, its boundaries lost in the gloom beyond the torch's light. To his left and to his right and straight ahead stood blades he'd heard of all his life, but never expected to see. Rupert moved slowly forward down the narrow central aisle. Swords and axes and maces filled the weapon racks and hung proudly on the walls, their richly worked metal and leather scabbards still perfectly preserved by the Armory's spells. Hanging beneath a simple brass plaque bearing its name was the great broadsword Lawgiver, wielded by seven Forest Kings in succession, until the blade finally became too battered and nicked to take an edge. Not far away stood the slender silver blade named Traitor, wielded by the infamous Starlight Duke during his short-lived usurpation of the throne. And more, and more . . . A sudden, overwhelming sense of history and ages past rushed over Rupert like an endless tide as he slowly made his way to the rear of the hall. The

Forest Kingdom was a great deal older than most people realized, or cared to remember.

Many of the weapon stands lay empty and abandoned, their blades gone to arm those who presently defended the Castle against the demons. Other swords had been left behind, having seen too much wear and tear to be useful as anything more than objects of ceremony and history. But still there were thousands upon thousands of weapons, waiting patiently in their ranks for the day they would once again be drawn in defence of the Forest Land. Some blades Rupert recognized by name or reputation, while others had passed out of history completely. More than once Rupert found himself staring at some nameless sword, and wondering what tale of triumph or tragedy lay locked within the enigmatic blade. But even though he'd never seen them before, he still knew the Infernal Devices when he came to them.

They stood together in their own little alcove; three huge longswords in chased silver scabbards. Their foot-long hilts were bound with dark, stained leather, and from the size of the scabbards the blades had to be at least seven feet long, and six inches wide at the crosspiece. Rupert stood before them and knew why his skin had begun to crawl outside the Armory. The swords stank of blood. As quickly as he recognized the smell, it was gone, leaving Rupert to wonder if perhaps he'd only imagined it. The blades stood before him, cold and majestic, and apparently no more dangerous than any other sword. But still Rupert felt a deep-rooted sense of forboding, as though close at hand some ancient and awful creature was stirring uneasily in its sleep. He shook his head angrily to clear it, and reached for the nearest blade. The Seneschal quickly grabbed him by the arm and pulled him back.

"I wouldn't, Sire; the swords are Protected. Try and touch one before the spell is removed, and we'll be carrying what's left of you out of here in a bucket."

"Of course, sir Seneschal," said Rupert. "I didn't think." He could feel his face burning, and silently damned himself for a fool. It should have been obvious, even to him, that blades as powerful as the Infernal Devices wouldn't have been left unguarded. "I take it there is a counterspell?"

"There is," said the King. "I learned it from my father, as he learned it from his. I never thought I'd have to use it."

Rupert and the Seneschal moved aside to let King John approach the Infernal Devices. Harald held back a way, watching closely from behind his mask of indifference. The King stood a while before the three great swords, and then, finally, he said three words in a harsh, guttural language unlike anything Rupert had ever heard before. The King's words seemed to hang on the air, echoing and re-echoing. And then the swords answered him.

Rupert's hackles rose as the soft, eerie voices came to him from everywhere and nowhere, rising and falling and blending into strange and unnatural harmonies that seemed to hint at meaning without ever achieving it. The result was complex, liquid, and altogether inhuman. The King spoke occasionally in reply, his voice harsh and strained in comparison to the gentle, almost seductive speech of the swords. And then the blades fell suddenly silent. The King's voice took on a strange, unpleasant rhythm, and then fell to an almost inaudible whisper. The hall grew steadily colder, and Rupert watched his breath steam on the air before him. The old runes etched into the silver scabbards seemed to writhe and curl like living things, and Rupert felt a sudden sense of pressure nearby, as though something was fighting to break out . . . or in. The air stank of freshly spilled blood. Something moved in the shadows beyond the torch's uncertain light. And then the King forced out three last words, and the Infernal Devices laughed softly; a greedy, eager sound. Rupert shuddered sickly, as though just hearing the sound had somehow dirtied him. The last of the echoes died quickly away, and all was still and quiet again. The torchlight flared and flickered, but the shadows were only shadows. The air grew warmer, and the overwhelming stench of blood was nothing more than an unquiet memory. King John stared impassively at the Infernal Devices, and when he finally spoke, his voice was once again calm and even.

"Three swords," he said quietly. "One for each of the Royal line, to wield against the endless night. I choose . . . Rockbreaker."

"And may God deliver us from evil," whispered the Seneschal.

King John reached out and took the left-hand sword from

the stand. The giant blade appeared almost weightless in his hand, but he made no move to draw it from its scabbard. He simply stared at it for a moment, and then slung it over his left shoulder and strapped it firmly in place. The blade hung down his back, the tip a bare inch above the floor, its long hilt standing up behind the King's head. He hitched his shoulder once, to settle the weight more comfortably, and then stepped back and gestured for Harald to make his choice.

Harald approached the two remaining swords cautiously. His eyes flickered from one blade to the other, undecided, but finally his gaze came to rest on the right-hand sword. His mask of unconcern suddenly fell away, revealing a harshly lined face with dark, determined eyes, and a grim smile that had nothing at all of humor in it. "Flarebright," said Harald softly, reading the ancient runes graven into the sword's crosspiece. "I choose Flarebright." He took the sword from the stand and slung it quickly over his left shoulder, fumbling at the buckles in his eagerness until the Seneschal had to help him.

King John gestured for Rupert to approach the weapon stand. Rupert looked at the one remaining sword, but stayed where he was. *Go ahead,* whispered a voice deep inside him. *It's only a sword.* The silver scabbard gleamed enticingly in the torch's unsteady glow. Wolfsbane. A sword of power.

And Rupert stood again in the Coppertown pit, holding up his sword, calling and calling for a help that never came.

"No," he said finally, and turned away. "I don't trust magic swords anymore. Let someone else have it."

"Take the sword," said King John. "You are of the Royal line; the sword is yours by right and duty. The people need symbols to follow into battle."

"No," said Rupert. "There are some things I won't do, father; not even for duty."

"Take the sword!" snapped the King. "That's an order!"

"Go to hell," said Rupert, and walked away. His footsteps echoed dully on the silence as he made his way back down the central aisle. All around him, the swords of countless heroes watched reproachfully as he turned his back on them. Rupert walked on, his head held high. He'd done enough, more than enough; no one had a right to ask anything more of him. He'd face the demons again because

he had to, but he'd do it with honest steel in his hand, not
the foul and terrible evil he'd sensed in the Infernal Devices. A wave of bone-deep weariness surged slowly through
him, and Rupert wondered if he had time for just one more
hour's sleep before dawn. He was so damn tired . . . He
shook his head and smiled wryly. There'd be plenty of time
for rest after the battle, one way or another. All the time in
the world. He walked out of the Armory and into the
corridor, and Lord Darius was waiting for him.

Rupert glimpsed a brief flash of light from Darius's dagger
as it sliced through the air toward him, and he threw
himself desperately to one side. Darius's blade cut through
Rupert's chain mail as he fell, but somehow just missed his
ribs. Rupert hit the floor rolling and was quickly on his feet
again sword in hand as Darius came toward him, snarling
and muttering to himself.

The tiny discolored knife swept back and forth in quick,
vicious arcs as Darius pressed forward, and Rupert backed
away. He knew poison on a blade when he saw it, and he
wasn't about to take any chances. The extra reach of his
sword should be enough to keep Darius at bay until the
others answered his call.

Harald and King John appeared at the Armory doors,
and Darius snarled at them. Black dripping balefire flew
from his pointing hand. Harald drew Flarebright from its
scabbard and was on guard in one swift motion, and the
balefire soaked into the great gleaming length of steel and
was gone. Darius turned on the King, but he'd already
drawn Rockbreaker. Darius stepped back from Rupert, and
raised his hands in the stance of summoning. A long jagged
crack appeared in the stone floor before him. A dirty blood-
red mist boiled up out of the widening crack, followed by a
rush of clawed and taloned devils with murder in their
glowing eyes. The air was full of the stench of brimstone.
Both Harald and the King froze for a moment as deep-
buried atavistic terrors ran through them, and then the
moment passed, and they leapt forward, roaring their war
cries. Flarebright and Rockbreaker gleamed ruddy in the
crimson hell light. The devils screamed and mewled as the
Infernal Devices cut them down, but ever and always they
rose to the attack again, their wounds healed and gone in

the blinking of an eye. Harald and the King stood back to back, and fought on.

Darius turned on Rupert again, and backed him up against a wall, shifting eagerly from foot to foot as he searched for an opening in Rupert's defense. He wanted to kill Rupert with his dagger, if he could. Feel the blade turning in the Prince's flesh. It would be so much more satisfying. Rupert swayed back and forth to match Darius's movements, and searched frantically for some way out of the mess he'd got himself into. There was nowhere left to retreat to, and from the look of things, Harald and the King needed his help desperately. The poisoned dagger cut at him again and again, and Rupert could feel the sweat running down his sides as he struggled to parry every blow. Darius was leaving himself wide open, but Rupert didn't dare relax his guard long enough to make an attack. Even a scratch from that blade might be enough to kill him. On the other hand, he didn't need the growing ache in his arms to tell him he couldn't keep this up for long. Despite the High Warlock's spells, he was a long way from being fully recovered from his wounds, while Darius's strength and fury seemed never-ending. Rupert scowled. He had to do something, while he still had the energy to bring it off.

Rupert parried yet another blow, and then swung his sword in a flat, vicious arc at Darius's eyes. Darius fell back instinctively, and Rupert threw himself at Darius's waist, groping for Darius's knife hand. They fell to the ground in a tangled heap, and the devils and the crack in the floor vanished in the blinking of an eye, with no trace remaining to show that they had ever been there.

Rupert and Darius scrambled to their feet. Darius laughed breathlessly, and threw himself at Rupert's throat. Harald cut him out of midair with one sweep of Flarebright's massive blade. Blood flew in a wide arc as the impact of the blow threw Darius crashing back against the corridor wall. The huge sword had almost cut him in two, and yet still somehow Darius tried to turn and run. Harald stepped forward, and ran him through from behind. Darius snarled once, and then slid slowly down the wall, leaving a wide smear of blood on the ancient panelwork.

Harald tried to pull the blade out of Darius's back, but the sword wouldn't move. A slow red flush crept up the long steel blade as Flarebright nuzzled deeper into the wound it had made. Harald tugged at the sword with both hands and finally, reluctantly, it jerked free. The whole length of the blade had acquired a grim, crimson sheen.

"Well," said the Seneschal quietly from the Armory door. "If nothing else, the Infernal Devices do seem to be living up to their reputations. Barely drawn a few minutes, and already christened in blood."

"Yes," said Harald. "They like blood. And they love to kill." He stared thoughtfully at Flarebright's red-tinged steel, and then slipped the sword back into its scabbard. His face quickly regained its usual calm, but his eyes remained vague and uncertain, as though he was only just beginning to realize what he'd let himself in for. He suddenly noticed that his hands were spotted with blood, and wiped them clean on his jerkin with quick, compulsive movements.

"Anyway," he said quietly, "The important thing is that finally we've caught our traitor. Darius must have let the demons into the South Wing through the air vent tunnels he knew so well, and he must have used his newfound magic to interfere with the High Warlock's teleport spell." He looked down at Darius, lying broken on the ground. "Luckily, he's no great loss. No one's going to miss him."

CHAPTER EIGHT

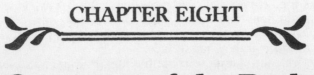

Creatures of the Dark

Even before he left the main entrance hall, Rupert could feel the cold waiting for him out in the courtyard. The temperature in the hall dropped steadily as he approached the main doors, and suddenly his breath was steaming on the air before him. Rupert pulled his cloak about him, and nodded brusquely to the guard at the doors. The guard opened the doors a crack, and Rupert slipped quickly out onto the main stairway. The doors slammed shut behind him, to keep in what little warmth remained, and Rupert winced as the bitter cold of the courtyard cut at him like a knife. Coal braziers and banked fires glowed bravely here and there across the crowded courtyard, spreading all too little heat or light. Thick snow and ice covered the battlements and stable roofs, and shining hoarfrost pearled the inner walls. Torches blazed at regular intervals along the walls, but the main light was the bright blue glare of the Full Moon, riding high above on the endless dark of the starless night. And in that courtyard, under that unhealthy light, the last army of the Forest Land slowly gathered itself together.

Rupert stamped his feet and beat his gloved hands together as he stared down at the milling crowd that packed the courtyard from wall to wall. The refugees and their camps were gone, moved into the Castle for the time being at least, their place taken by grim-faced men and women preparing themselves for battle. There was little talk or chatter. Outside, the Darkwood pressed close about Forest Castle, nuzzling at its walls like some huge, determined hound searching for the prey temporarily denied it. Rupert shuddered suddenly as the old familiar sense of oppression and forboding settled upon him once again. He fought the fear down, refusing to give in to it, knowing that if he ever did, even for a moment, he'd never be free of it for the rest of his life. He studied the gathering army below him, and wondered how they'd react when they finally went out into the Darkwood, and discovered that the demons were only part of the evil they had to face.

He watched dourly as some five hundred men and half a hundred women strapped their armor about them, and tested the balance of whichever weapon they felt most comfortable with. All too many had obviously never drawn a weapon in anger in their lives. The guards and men-at-arms ran through their exercises with quiet competence, while the courtiers and traders, farmers and townspeople copied the fighting men as best they could, sweeping their blades awkwardly back and forth before them. Priests moved calmly from group to group, talking quietly and reassuringly, giving comfort where they could. The grooms led the few remaining horses out of the stables, keeping a firm grip on the reins and murmuring soothingly to the nervous, suspicious animals. Rupert frowned thoughtfully. The last time he'd tried to take horses into the Darkwood, they'd had to be blindfolded and led in by hand. Hopefully the Castle war chargers were made of sterner stuff.

He looked away, and then smiled slightly as he spotted a small group of goblins sitting quietly by the stables. They were happily engaged in filing jagged barbs into the edges of their swords, and then smearing the barbs with fresh horse dung, so that any wounds they made would be sure to fester. Up on the battlements, the rest of the goblins were preparing cauldrons of pitch and boiling oil. Rupert shook his head mournfully. For all their good points, there was no getting away from the fact that the goblins had absolutely no sense of honor or fair play. They should do very well in the coming battle.

The High Warlock was sitting at the bottom of the main entrance steps, drinking wine straight from the bottle. Rupert started down the steps toward him, only to stop short when he realized the Warlock's eyes were unfocussed and far away. There were fresh wine stains on his robes, and he swayed slightly from side to side in time to some old song he was singing quietly to himself. Rupert watched the Warlock a while, and felt a little of his hope go out of him. With so much at stake, he'd been depending on the Warlock to stay sober and keep his wits about him, but apparently that had been too much to ask. Rupert's hands closed into fists, and then opened again. It wasn't the Warlock's fault he wasn't the man the legends had made him out to be. *It's not as if he was the only one to let me down,* thought Rupert tiredly. He remembered Julia, hanging on Harald's arm at Court. *You'd think I'd have learned by now; I can't depend on anyone but myself.* Rupert continued on his way. He walked right past the Warlock, but the Warlock didn't even notice.

Rupert threaded his way through the packed crowd, nodding and smiling absently to those who spoke or called to him. He knew he ought to be doing his bit as a Prince, by rallying the army with pep talks and rousing speeches, but somehow he just couldn't bring himself to do it. The words would have turned to ashes in his mouth. Harald would have handled it easily enough; he'd have clapped the guardsmen on the back and told them comforting lies, and promised the farmers and the traders honor and glory in battle, with undying fame for those who fell. Rupert moved on through the crowd, his face set in tired, brooding lines. He'd fought the demons too many times already to harbor any illusions about the forthcoming battle. There was nothing but the dark, and the creatures that lived in it, and the things you had to do to defeat them; with little honor, and damn all glory for the quick or the dead.

The crowd finally thinned away as Rupert approached one of the old stables. The huge, rambling structure seemed unnaturally quiet and deserted, as though recently abandoned. All the windows had been boarded over, and the single great door was locked. Icicles hung in clumps from the guttering, and inches of snow lay undisturbed on the windowsills and doorframe. Rupert took out the key the Seneschal had given him, and unlocked the door. It swung slowly open at his touch, the warped frame protesting quietly with a series of brief creaks and groans. Rupert put away the key and stood in the doorway, looking into the gloom. Everything was dark and still and silent. He stepped back a pace, took a torch from its bracket by the door, and then slowly entered the stable.

"Dragon?" he called softly. "It's me; Rupert."

There was no answer from the darkness. Rupert held the torch high, and at the rear of the stable dark green scales shimmered dully in the unsteady torchlight. Rupert slowly approached the sleeping dragon, shadows stirring uneasily around the pool of light he moved in. The air was dry and dusty, with a strong musky smell hanging over everything. The dragon lay curled in a circle in a nest of dirty straw, his head resting on his tail, his wings wrapped around him like a huge emerald blanket. The massive wings moved slightly, continuously, in time to the dragon's slow breathing. Rupert put the flaring torch in a nearby wall bracket, and then crouched down by the dragon's head. The great golden eyes were closed, and the wide grinning mouth hung slightly open. Rupert reached out a hand, hesitated, and then tapped gently on the creature's bony forehead.

"Dragon? It's Rupert; I need to talk to you. I need your help."

The dragon slept on, undisturbed. Rupert crouched among the filthy straw and stared forlornly at the sleeping creature. A sudden wave of despair swept over him. Deep down, he'd always believed the dragon at least would be there beside him when the time finally came for him to go out and face the Darkwood again. *I should have known better* . . . First Julia, then the High Warlock, and now the dragon. He had no claim on any of them, and wouldn't have used it if he had. But it would have been nice if just one of them could have been there at his side. So that he wouldn't have to face the dark alone. Rupert sighed quietly, and the memory came to him of the dragon standing tall and proud in the Darkwood clearing, spilling a liquid fire onto the demons, destroying them by the dozen with his fiery breath. And then he remembered the dragon lying sprawled and broken in that same clearing, one wing half torn away, golden blood streaming down his side. The dragon, dying in the dark, because Rupert had led him into the Darkwood, and the dragon had trusted him.

"Sleep on, my friend," said Rupert quietly. "I've no right to ask any more of you."

He got to his feet, took the torch from the wall bracket, and walked back to the stable door. He hesitated in the doorway, and looked back at the sleeping dragon. He wanted to say goodbye, but didn't. He turned and left the stable, locking the door securely behind him. Darkness filled the stable again, the only sound the slow steady burr of the dragon's breathing.

The High Warlock leaned back on the entrance steps, glowered about him, and took another drink from his bottle. The wine was a lousy vintage, but he couldn't be bothered to change it. He was doing his best to get drunk, but somehow it just wasn't working. He could feel the wine lying sullenly in his belly, while his mind remained stubbornly alert. His eyesight was a little blurred, and his legs a little unsteady, but all the old tormenting memories were with him still. More or less. The Warlock frowned, and shook his head irritably, trying to remember the words of the song he'd been singing, and somehow they eluded him. He hated it when he couldn't remember things like that. Hated it. More and more there were gaps in his memory where there never used to be; little things, for the most part, but gaps nonetheless. *Getting old,* he thought sourly. *Too many years gone by. Or too much booze. Or both. Yes, probably both.* He took another drink from the bottle, spilling wine down his chin. He wished he could remember the words of the song. Eleanor had always loved that song.

They stood together on the balcony, watching the fireworks splash color across the night skies. Behind them, in the Great Hall, the Victory Ball was well under way. A light summer breeze swirled the Warlock's robes, and toyed lazily with Eleanor's hair. Her hair was the color of corn, and she wore a dress of blue and gold, but he couldn't remember her eyes. Minstrels were playing the song in the background, almost drowned out by the constant chatter of the courtiers. The Warlock watched the fireworks closely. He'd planned the display down to the last detail, but there was always time for something to go wrong. Tempermental things, fireworks. A rocket burst against the night, its fires spilling out to form the shape of a lion's head. The Warlock smiled, and relaxed a little. Eleanor put her arm through his, and snuggled up to him. He couldn't remember her eyes.

The fireworks are very beautiful.

Thank you, your majesty.

Must you be so formal, sir Warlock? On a night like this,

there should be no formalities between friends. Call me Eleanor.

As you wish; Eleanor.

That's better. Now, won't you tell me your name?

To know a sorcerer's name, is to have power over him.

I'm sorry. I didn't know that.

No reason why you should.

Oh, look at that rocket! It's a waterfall; how clever of you. Isn't it a wonderful night, sir Warlock?

Indeed it is, Eleanor.

I don't think I've ever been happier. John is coming home victorious from the Border War, the harvest is safely gathered in and stored, and . . . and my best friend in all the world has given me such marvelous fireworks for my birthday! It almost feels wrong to be so happy. And the minstrels are playing my favorite song! Dance with me, sir Warlock. Please.

I'm . . . not sure that would be proper, Eleanor. The Court . . .

Then dance with me here, on the balcony. Just the two of us, alone.

Her perfume filled his head as they danced together, hand-in-hand, face-to-face, their bodies moving slowly, gracefully to the dimly heard music. Fireworks blazed silver and gold upon the night. When he kissed her, her lips trembled but her arms were strong.

He couldn't remember her eyes.

The High Warlock stared at the half empty bottle in his hand, and cursed himself bitterly for ever having left the Dark Tower. He should never have come back to Forest Castle. He'd been safe in his Tower, with his booze and his work, hidden away from the world. Safe from his past, his memories, and all the things people expected of him. He should never have come back.

He looked out across the courtyard, and nodded to Rupert as the Prince came over to join him. Rupert glanced at the bottle in the Warlock's hand, and his mouth set in a cold line.

"I know," said the Warlock. "You don't approve. But sorcerer or no, I need a little something to lean on." He took a long drink from his bottle, and wiped his mouth on his sleeve. "I keep telling you I'm not the all-powerful sorcerer everyone thinks I am. There are no real magicians

left any more. Not like there used to be. Magic is going out
of the world, Rupert; and all because of us."

"Us?" said Rupert.

"Man," said the Warlock. "All because of man. His logical, rational mind will be the death of magic yet. Magic
works by its own rules, and they don't pay much attention
to cause and effect. That's why all the truly great sorcerers
have always been eccentrics; they mastered magic because
they were as whimsical and contradictory as the sorcery they
studied. Magic has its own structure and logic, but it's not a
human logic. There are rules that magic obeys, but even
those tend to be contracts of agreement rather than natural
laws. I'm confusing you, aren't I? Magic's a confusing business. Every year there are less and less people who can
bend their minds enough to control magic. Fewer and fewer
mad enough to understand sorcery, while still sane enough
not to be destroyed by it.

"All too soon, magic will be gone from this world, Rupert; driven out by Man, with his need for logic and reason
and simple, understandable answers. Science will replace
magic, and we'll all be a damn sight better off. Science
always works. All we'll have lost will be a little poetry, a
little beauty . . . and perhaps a little of the wonder of the
world. No more dragons. No more unicorns, or goblins, or
wee folk."

"No more demons," said Rupert.

"Win some, lose some," said the Warlock. He started to
lift his bottle to his mouth, but stopped when Rupert looked
at him. He shrugged, and put it down again. "It's ironic,
really. The one thing that could ensure the survival of magic
is the Blue Moon itself. But that's Wild Magic, and a world
ruled by the Wild Magic would have no room in it for Man.
There's nothing rational or logical about the Wild Magic, no
subtlety, no control; just sheer naked power. Power to
reshape reality itself. It we lose this battle to the Demon
Prince, Rupert, it'll be the end of everything. The Darkwood
will be all there is, and nothing will move in it save the
demons.

"Nothing human, anyway. Some life will survive. It always does. There's something unusual living in the moat,
under the ice. A fascinating creature."

"The moat monster!" said Rupert.

"If you say so," said the Warlock. "He used to be human, you know. I put a change on him, a long time ago."

"That's right," said Rupert. "If nothing else, that's one thing I can see put right. Change him back."

"I beg your pardon?" said the Warlock.

"Change him back," said Rupert flatly. "He was born a man, and it's only right he should have the chance to die as a man, not . . . some creature."

"He doesn't want to be changed back," said the Warlock firmly. "He's quite happy as he is. In fact, he was most insistent about it when I talked with him."

Rupert looked at him incredulously. "You're kidding."

"I never kid," said the Warlock frostily. "It was only a temporary spell, after all. He could have changed back any time after it wore off. If he hasn't, it's because he likes his new form better."

Rupert looked at the Warlock, but his face remained serious.

"I think I'll go and have a word with my unicorn," said the Prince finally. "If you'll excuse me . . ."

The Warlock chuckled quietly as Rupert disappeared back into the milling crowd, shaking his head slowly in a confused kind of way. The Warlock took a long drink from his bottle. When he lowered it again, King John was standing before him, his face twisted with open disgust. Torchlight gleamed ruddy on the shining chain mail that wrapped the King from head to foot, and the Warlock didn't miss the ancient leather-bound swordhilt standing up behind the King's left shoulder.

"Hello, John," he said politely. "You're looking very . . . impressive. I'd offer you a drink, but I've only the one bottle."

"Can't you leave that stuff alone even for a moment?" said the King harshly.

The Warlock shrugged. "I need a drink."

"You always did," said the King.

The Warlock looked sharply at the King. "I see you're carrying Rockbreaker. Who's idea was that?"

"Mine," said the King flatly. "The Infernal Devices are our last hope against the dark."

The Warlock smiled sardonically. "I thought that was me."

"No," said the King, looking at the bottle in the High Warlock's hand. "Not anymore."

"Don't use the sword, John," said the Warlock quietly. "You can't trust the Infernal Devices; between them they have the power to destroy the world. If you awaken that power, you don't have a hope in hell of controlling it."

"We'll use the swords," said the King. "We have no choice any more."

The Warlock sighed quietly, and looked away. "You're quite right, you know," he said finally. "I shouldn't drink as much as I do. It's affecting my mind, distorting my spells, and I suspect it's slowly killing me."

"Then stop," growled the King.

"I can't," said the Warlock simply. "Do you think I haven't tried? I don't drink because I want to, John; I drink because I need to, because I can't get through the day without it."

"Same old excuse," said the King, and the Warlock looked at him pityingly.

"You never did understand, John. But then, you never wanted to. You never needed a drink in your life. You've never *needed* anything. To hell with it. We can't all be perfect."

"You're nothing but a drunkard!"

"I'm what you made me, John. You and your damned family. Pulling your precious hides out of one damn scrape after another. I wasn't always a drunkard."

"Only when it mattered."

"I got the job done, drunk or sober!"

"All except once," said the King. "The one time it really mattered."

"Don't," whispered the Warlock. "Please."

"My Eleanor was dying, and you were nowhere to be found. I had to send men out to search the ale-houses and taverns and drag you back. And all the time I waited by her bed, my wife . . . my Eleanor . . . You could have saved her!"

"I didn't get back in time."

"You were drunk!"

"Yes," said the High Warlock. "I was drunk."

He looked at the bottle in his hand, and after a moment he started to cry.

*   *   *

Prince Harald stood impatiently before the closed main gates, hiding his growing irritation behind his usual calm mask while a servant fussed around him, adjusting the buckles on his armor. The many layers of interlapping chain mail were hot, heavy, and very restricting, but Harald was a great believer in armor. No matter how good you were with sword and buckler, sooner or later you were bound to face someone better or luckier than you, and that's when a good suit of chain mail came into its own. Harald frowned slightly as he remembered his last fight with Rupert, here in the courtyard. His armor hadn't saved him then. Harald's face slowly cleared as he dismissed the thought. Things were different, now. Now, he had Flarebright. The Infernal Device hung down his back, the long hilt standing up behind his left shoulder. He kept catching glimpses of the hilt out of the corner of his eye every time he turned his head. Flarebright was eerily light for so large a blade, but Harald could still feel its presence with every move he made. There was a dull, unpleasant warmth the length of his back, as though the sword burned constantly like a hot coal in its scabbard. And sometimes, for no reason at all, Harald thought of how good it would feel to draw the Infernal Device, and cut down enemies without number . . .

The servant finally finished his work, and Harald waved him away. He drew his usual sword from its scabbard at his side, and began a series of warming-up exercises. The solid weight of steel in his hand was a comfort to him, and he could feel some of the tension going out of his muscles as he moved gracefully through the familiar routine. He'd been taking his training a lot more seriously since Rupert beat him, and he could feel the difference. He'd always been good, but now he was even better. Rupert's grinning face hung before Harald's eyes as he stamped and lunged and circled, his sword sweeping from cut to parry to slash and back, over and over again. Flarebright's scabbard slapped against his back with every movement, as though reminding him it was still there. Harald whirled and spun, his sword flashing brightly in the torchlight, but still he knew that once he was out in the long night, his own sword wouldn't be enough, for all his skill and training. His only chance against the demons was to use the Infernal Device. Somehow, he wasn't as eager to use it as he'd thought he'd be.

He saw the King making his way toward him, but deliberately continued his exercises. He waited until the King had almost reached him, and only then looked up and came to a stop. He lowered and sheathed his sword in one fluid movement, and leaned casually back against the closed gates. He mopped at his sweating face with a handkerchief, and bowed slightly to the King, who nodded brusquely in return.

"Ready for the battle, Harald?"

"Of course, Father."

King John stood silently a moment, as though waiting for Harald to say something more. Harald let him wait.

"You wanted to speak to me, Harald?"

"That's right, Father." Harald wiped the last of the sweat from his brow, and slipped the handkerchief back into his sleeve. "I want you to marry Julia to me before the battle. There is still time."

King John looked at him incredulously. "You want what?"

"I want Julia as my wife, and I want the ceremony performed now. It will do wonders for the morale of our people, and settle once and for all the somewhat nagging question as to whether I or Rupert is the favored son. I need to be sure the people will follow me."

"Your marriage has been postponed," said the King evenly. "Apart from the fact that this is neither the time nor the place for a wedding, I don't want Rupert upset. It won't be long before he'll be riding out into battle alongside us, and there are those who will follow him where they won't follow you."

"Precisely my point," said Harald. "I am the eldest son, the firstborn. I am the one whose orders they should follow. Besides; there are other reasons for the marriage. It's entirely possible that you and I and Rupert could all die in this battle, leaving the Forest Land without a ruler. If Julia and I were married, the Royal line could still continue through her. And if, by some calamity, you were to die while Rupert and I both survived, my being married to Julia could well ensure my succession to the throne. Either way, holding the marriage now would make your wishes in the matter quite clear. Otherwise, we could win this battle against the darkness, and still lose the Land to civil war."

"No," said the King. "I've given you my answer, Harald, and I don't like to repeat myself. The wedding is postponed; indefinitely."

"I see," said Harald. "So that's the way the wind blows."

For a long moment the two men faced each other silently, their eyes locked. From all around them came the clamor and hubbub of the last army of the Forest Land, as it slowly readied itself for battle, but Harald and the King were deaf and blind to everything but the moment of conflict between them. King John studied his eldest son coldly. Harald and Rupert had always been at odds; it was only to be expected, given their situation. But this sudden vehemence on Harald's part had caught the King by surprise. In the past, Harald had always been ready and able to deal with Rupert on his own. He never lost his temper, and he knew how far he could go. But now . . . this was the first time Harald had ever turned to his father for help. King John frowned thoughtfully. Either Harald was genuinely fond of the Princess Julia, or he was seriously worried about Rupert's rising influence in the Court. The latter was by far the most likely reason, but you could never tell with Harald. You could never tell anything with Harald.

King John sighed, and looked away. He was sorely tempted to just turn and walk away, but he knew he couldn't do that. It wouldn't do to have Harald thinking the King was afraid to face him. It wouldn't be . . . safe.

"You are my eldest son," said the King slowly, carefully meeting Harald's gaze again. "When the gates finally open, you will ride out beside me, at my right hand. But Rupert is also my son, and he will ride at my left hand. It is vital for the morale of our troops that the three of us present a united front against the dark. Our army is going to have enough to worry about without having to decide whose orders they will and won't obey. We don't have time for politics any more. So; there is to be no more open dissension between you and Rupert. Is that clear, Harald?"

"Perfectly clear," said Harald.

"Good," said the King. "Then there's nothing more we need to discuss, is there?"

"I saw you speaking with the Warlock," said Harald. "Is he still drinking?"

"Of course. But he'll do what's needed, when he has to."

"Tell me," said Harald easily, "I've always wondered; were the stories true?"

"Stories?" said the King. "What stories?"

"The stories about him and mother, of course. They say he loved her. They also say . . ."

King John lifted his hand to strike Harald across the face, and then slowly lowered it again. Harald didn't flinch, but his eyes were wary and watchful. The King sighed quietly.

"Harald . . ."

"Yes, Father."

"You've the makings of a good King, Harald. You know politics and intrigue and law. You even understand the paperwork, which is more than I ever did. But you'll need more than that, if the people are to support you. Oh, you've charm enough, when you choose to use it, but . . . I don't know where your heart really lies, and I doubt if anyone else does, either. Sometimes I worry about you, lad. You're my son. My blood and kin. Yet I swear you're as much a stranger to me now as the day you were born."

"I'm what you made me," said Harald, and then wondered why his father flinched at the words.

The main stables stood dark and abandoned on the far side of the courtyard. Its doors gaped open, unattended, and the horses and the grooms were gone. Inside the stables, a single lantern shed a golden glow over the end stall as Rupert saddled his unicorn. All around them small sounds magnified strangely on the quiet, and echoes seemed to whisper on forever. The still air was thick with the smells of dirt and hay and horse dung. Rupert knew he should find the abandoned stable disturbing, but somehow he didn't. If anything, he rather liked the quiet. It felt good to get away from everything and everybody, even if only for a while. Outside the stable doors, the constant babble of voices rose and fell like the dim, far-away pounding of surf on a beach; something too far away to have anything to do with him.

Rupert settled the unicorn's saddle comfortably into place, and then set about the many dangling straps. The unicorn looked a lot better than the last time Rupert had seen him. His wounds had been cleaned and roughly stitched, his mane and tail had been cleaned and combed, and there was even a little barley left in his feeding trough.

"So how are you feeling?" asked Rupert.

"Bloody awful," said the unicorn. "If I felt any worse you'd be making glue out of my hooves. I can't believe we're actually going to fight the demons again. Who's bright idea was that?"

"Mine, actually," said Rupert.

"I might have known," muttered the unicorn.

"There's no need to be like that. Just once more into battle, and then it'll be all over."

"That's what I'm afraid of. Isn't there something else we could try?"

"Like what?"

"Running away leaps to mind."

Rupert laughed tiredly as he tightened the cinch strap. "Where could we go? The darkness is everywhere now. No, unicorn; we either stand and fight, or wait to die. There's nothing else left to us."

For a long while, neither of them said anything. Shadows pressed close about the lantern's golden glow, and the air grew steadily colder. Rupert finished readying the unicorn, and then sank wearily down onto a pile of dirty straw. An hour at most, and then he'd have to go out and face the Darkwood again. Face the demons and the darkness and the horror of the endless night. Rupert yawned, and leaned back against the side of the stall. He was too tired to be really scared. The unicorn snorted suddenly, as though in response to some inner argument, and turned his head to stare at Rupert with calm, bloodred eyes.

"Rupert . . ."

"Yes?"

"You once asked me my name. I told you then I'd sworn never to use my name until I was free again, but now . . . well, it seems to me that if I don't tell you now, there might not be another chance."

Rupert shifted uncomfortably under the unicorn's steady gaze. "You don't have to tell me, if you don't want to."

"You're my friend," said the unicorn. "My name is Breeze."

Rupert got to his feet, and hugged the unicorn's neck tightly. "Breeze," he said, and then had to stop. When he felt he could trust his voice again, he let go of the unicorn and stepped back a pace so that he could meet the unicorn's eyes. "Breeze, if by some miracle we actually survive this mess, you're free. I swear it, by Blood and Stone. I'll check the records to find which valley you were taken from originally; some of your old herd might still be there. Perhaps we could . . . go and look for them. Together."

"Yeah," said Breeze. "I'd like that, Rupert."

"You don't believe we're going to survive this one, do you?"

"No, I don't."

"All right, then. By the authority vested in me, by blood and kin, by Blood and Stone, I hereby free the unicorn named Breeze from any and all obligations to me, and to my family. Okay, Breeze; that's it. You are now a one hundred percent independent individual. Or as near as any of us ever get to it."

"Is that all there is to it?"

"What did you expect; a fanfare of trumpets? Or isn't my word good enough for you?"

"Your word has always been good with me, Rupert. But is it legal?"

"Of course. I am a Prince, after all."

"I had noticed," said the unicorn dryly. "Free. *Free.* I always thought I'd feel different."

"How do you feel?"

"Strange. Naked. I don't know yet."

"Well, if nothing else, you don't have to go back into the Darkwood again. I freed you from all obligations, remember?"

"You wouldn't last five minutes without me."

"That's not the point, Breeze."

"Yes, it is," said the unicorn firmly. "I could have left you any time in the past. You gave me enough chances. When all is said and done, I stayed with you because you were my friend, and you needed me. No other reason. So let's have no more nonsense about you going back into the Darkwood without me. We're a team, and don't you forget it."

"Still," said Rupert. "You are officially free now. I've said the words."

"Don't we need a witness?"

"You have one," said the Champion.

Rupert and the unicorn looked quickly round, to find the Champion standing in the stable doorway. He inclined his head slightly to Rupert, who bowed warily in return. The Champion was wearing full plate armor. The burnished steel gleamed coldly under the lanternlight, its entire surface etched and engraved with heraldic signs and ancient magical wards. He carried a featureless steel helm under his arm, and his huge hands were sheathed in massive steel gauntlets. He looked impressive, menacing, and totally unstoppable.

"Sir Champion," said Rupert steadily. "Is it time to go?"

"Soon, Sire. The King tells me you refused to bear one of the Infernal Devices when it was offered to you."

"That's right."

"It was your duty to take the sword."

"My duty is to the Land, sir Champion. And those cursed swords are so much a threat to the Forest as the Darkwood itself."

The Champion nodded slowly. "You may well be right, Sire. But then, I've never had much use for magic, myself."

Rupert looked sharply at the Champion. He seemed almost on the point of telling Rupert something; something important.

"Have you seen the Warlock?" asked the Champion suddenly.

"Yes," said Rupert. "We talked awhile."

"He's drunk again."

"I've never known him when he wasn't."

"I have," said the Champion. "But that was a long time ago." He leaned back against the stable wall, his cold dark eyes staring past Rupert and into memory. "He was impressive, then. Could have been a Sorcerer Supreme. Could have been the legend everybody said he was. He could have been the greatest hero this Land has ever known."

Rupert listened carefully. There was hatred and bitterness in the Champion's voice, but underlying all of that . . . something else. Something that might have been betrayal.

"Sir Champion; why did the High Warlock leave the Castle after my mother died?"

"He could have saved her. If he'd been sober. If he'd been there." Rage twisted the Champion's face, and Rupert wanted to look away. It seemed almost indecent to see such naked emotions in the face of a man who normally showed such control. "The Warlock was why I came to Forest Castle, Rupert. He was famous, and I wanted to be part of that fame, that legend. And so I came to serve your father, as his Champion.

"That's when I learned the truth about the legendary High Warlock. Your mother was a great beauty, Rupert. Everybody said so. When she fell ill that Summer, all the Land prayed for her recovery. The Warlock was supposed to be with her, that afternoon. Instead, he left her by herself, and went off somewhere, drinking. By the time we found him and dragged him back, it was too late.

"And then, he ran away. He ran away! I all but worshipped that man, Rupert; I believed in him. And he turned out to be nothing but a drunk and a coward. I could have forgiven him many things, but not that. Never that. He let your mother die, and then he ran away rather than face what he'd done.

"And now he's back, and once again all our fates rest in his trembling hands. After all these years, despite everything I've achieved as Champion, the Land's destiny will be decided not by heroes and warriors and cold clean steel, but by one drunken coward and his magic!"

The Champion turned suddenly and stalked out of the stables, his hands curled into massive impotent fists at his sides. Rupert watched him disappear back into the waiting crowd. A memory came to Rupert, of the two of them standing together on a hill, looking down over the Coppertown pit. Of the Champion telling him how he'd run away from the mines as a small child, and how he would never run from anything, ever again.

Julia elbowed her way through the growing crowd, ignoring the glares and muttered curses of those she left in her wake. It had started out as a thoroughly rotten day, and it showed no signs of improving in its last few hours. She stopped and looked about her, hoping against hope to catch a glimpse of Rupert somewhere in the courtyard, but he was nowhere to be seen. Julia sighed, and once again headed for the far corner where her troop of fighting women were waiting for her. She'd promised to lead them through one last weapons drill before the battle, not that it would make much difference. They'd come on well, much better than she'd expected; and certainly a great deal better than the Castle guards had ever expected. A few more months training, and they would have been good enough to . . . Julia smiled sourly. They didn't have a few more months, or even a few hours. The gates would open at dawn, and shortly after that, her women would either be warriors, or dead.

Julia's hand tightened round the pommel of her sword till her knuckles ached. So much to do, and never enough time. Rupert had to be here somewhere, but nobody had seen him for ages. It was as though he'd fallen off the face of the earth. She had to find him before the battle began, she had to; but her women were waiting for her. Julia's mind worked frantically as she plunged on through the crowd, searching desperately for a way out of her dilemma, and then a sudden calm fell across her as she realized there was no way out. Her women needed her, and she'd given them her word that she'd be there. Rupert would have understood. He knew a lot about duty.

The crowd suddenly broke apart before her, and Julia stumbled to a halt as King John stepped out of the crowd to block her path. Harald stood at the King's side, carrying a huge sheathed longsword in his arms as though it was both infinitely precious and utterly repellent. Julia eyed Harald and the King warily as they bowed to her. They were being polite and formal, which could only mean that they were up to something. She watched their faces change as they realized she was no longer wearing formal Court robes, and smiled politely at them, daring them to say anything. She'd had to search half the Castle laundry to find the sensible, hard-wearing clothes she'd worn in the Forest during her time with Rupert, but it had been worth it. For the first time in months, she actually felt comfortable.

Besides; she couldn't use a sword properly while wearing formal robes.

"Princess Julia," said the King slowly, "Your garments are hardly suitable for a Lady of the Court."

"Probably not," said Julia. "But they're quite suitable for a battle. If you think I'm going out to fight demons wearing high heels and a long flowing gown, you're crazy. Now, did you have something in particular you wanted to say to me, or were you just indulging in a little fashion criticism?"

"We have something for you," said Harald.

"Oh yes?" said Julia suspiciously. "And what might that be?"

"A sword," said Harald. "It's called Wolfsbane."

He held out to her the long silver scabbard he was carrying, and Julia looked at it for a long moment before finally taking it from him. Despite its seven feet and more in length, the sword seemed practically weightless in her hands. The scabbard was covered in ancient, deeply etched runes that teased her eyes with hints of meaning. *I don't like this sword,* thought Julia suddenly. *It feels . . . unhealthy.* She started to hand the sword back to Harald, and then stopped as she realized both he and King John were wearing similar swords strapped to their backs. The long leather-bound hilts peered over their shoulders like watchful eyes. And that was when Julia remembered the name Wolfsbane.

"This is one of the Infernal Devices," she said slowly. "One of the most powerful and evil swords ever created. And you expect me to use this?"

"They're our only hope now," said the King. "We need their power."

"Wait a minute," said Julia suspiciously, "Why are you offering me this sword, and not Rupert?"

"He didn't want it," said Harald.

"Why not?"

Harald smiled slightly. "Perhaps he was afraid of its power."

"Perhaps," said Julia, "he had reason to be."

The King shifted uncomfortably as Julia turned her searching gaze on him. "We did offer him the blade, Julia, but he refused to take it. He said . . . he said he didn't trust magic swords anymore. Do you understand what he meant by that?"

Julia frowned, and worried her lower lip between her teeth. "No," she said finally. "I don't." She hefted Wolfsbane in her hand, and made as though to draw it. Harald and the King both sucked in a sudden breath, and stepped back a pace.

"I wouldn't," said King John quickly. "You might unleash the sword's attribute."

Julia studied the sheathed sword, and frowned thoughtfully. "Three Infernal Devices, each with a different attribute. I remember the stories my father told me, when I was very young. Of three magic swords, and the evil and destruction they caused before they could be brought under control. Rockbreaker. Flarebright. Wolfsbane. I never thought

I'd hold a legend in my hand. What is Wolfsbane's attribute? What does it do?"

"We're not actually sure," said the King. "It's been so long since anyone dared draw any of the blades . . ."

"Great," said Julia. "Just great. All right; what do you know about the Infernal Devices?"

"They like blood," said Harald quietly. "And they love to kill."

Julia looked at him sharply. There had been something in Harald's voice . . . something that might have been fear, or loathing . . .

"But why me?" she said suddenly. "All right, Rupert wouldn't take the sword, but why does it have to be me? Why not the Champion, or the Astrologer, or . . ."

"You're of Royal blood," said the King.

Julia smiled wryly. "Of course. A sword like this could make any man a King; and there's no one else you can trust with that kind of power."

"That's right," said the King. "No one, but you."

"And I'll bet that sticks in your craw something fierce," said Julia. "A woman with a sword, what is the world coming to? All right; I'll use Wolfsbane. But only if I have to. I don't trust magic swords, either."

She slung the scabbarded sword over her left shoulder, and buckled it securely into place. Harald moved forward as though to help, but stopped short when Julia fixed him with a sardonic eye.

"Have either of you seen Rupert around?" she asked, her voice carefully casual.

"I've no doubt he's here somewhere," said the King. "But I haven't seen him since Darius died."

"Yeah, right," said Julia. "I heard about that. Good to know Darius finally got what was coming to him."

"Quite," said Harald. "I haven't seen Rupert at all, but then, he hasn't had much to say to me since I told him he was still going to be best man at your wedding to me."

Julia looked at him, and then at the King. "You can't leave him alone, can you? Even now, you can't leave him any peace, or hope of peace. You're beneath contempt, both of you. Get out of my sight."

"Julia . . ." said the King.

"Get away from me, damn your eyes!"

King John bowed stiffly to her, and turned and walked away. Harald opened his mouth to say something. Julia rested her hand on the pommel of her sword. Harald smiled politely, and followed his father into the crowd. Julia watched him go, and was surprised to find herself shaking with the strength of her emotions. She breathed deeply, filling her lungs with the freezing courtyard air, and slowly some of her calm came back to her. *Rupert, my dear . . . what are we going to do?* She shook her head slowly, and then started as a long, leather-wrapped swordhilt suddenly appeared at the corner of her eye. Julia scowled, and looked away. Wolfsbane was a solid, uncomfortable presence at her back, for all its lightness, and she wasn't at all sure she'd done the right thing in accepting it. She felt happier with the blade she knew, hanging in its usual place at her left hip; the sword Rupert had given her, long ago, in a Darkwood clearing when all had seemed lost . . .

Julia looked around the packed, milling courtyard. *Wherever you are, Rupert; watch your back.* She sighed tiredly, once, and then strode off into the crowd, heading for where her troop of women were waiting for her. And the Infernal Device on her back seemed to grow a little heavier with every step.

Rupert stood in the shadows of the stable doors, watching Julia drill her troop of women. Swords and spears and hand-axes gleamed in the torchlight as the women stamped and lunged, their movements still somehow graceful despite the cumbersome chain mail they all wore. Julia strode back and forth before them, stopping briefly to smile and encourage, or demonstrate a difficult cut or parry. As she moved through the flickering, uncertain light, sword in hand, her tall, lithe form seemed like that of some ancient warrior goddess, teaching the arts of war to her worshippers.

She was dressed as she had been when Rupert first knew her, and he wasn't sure why that hurt him as much as it did. With her old clothes, and her long, blonde hair tied back in two simple, functional braids, she was like a bitter accusing memory of the time they'd had together, before he'd brought her back to Forest Castle. He'd been so happy, then.

"I wish you'd go and talk to her," said the unicorn.

"You're getting on my nerves, standing there all frowning and broody."

"There's nothing left to say," said Rupert quietly. "She's marrying Harald, of her own free will."

"Yeah," said the unicorn. "And demons are vegetarians. You're too hard on the girl, Rupert. If she's marrying Harald, it's only because the Court pressured her into it. It's not as if she had any choice in the matter, now is it?"

"I don't know," said Rupert tiredly. "I don't know anything any more."

"Buck up," said the unicorn gruffly. "We'll be going out into the dark soon. Think of all the fun you can have, taking out your troubles on the demons. They won't know what's hit them."

"Yeah. Sure." Out in the courtyard, Julia turned suddenly to face the stables, and Rupert backed quickly away from the doors before she could see him. He didn't know why he was so angry. If was her life, and she had a right to live it as she chose. He hadn't even known her long. They'd spent a few months together, and then he'd had to leave her at the Castle while he went off in search of the Dark Tower. After so many months apart, with every reason to suppose him dead, it was only to be expected that Julia would turn to somebody else. And Harald always was a charming bastard. Their marriage had been all but inevitable.

That's as may be, thought Rupert grimly. *But I'm still not going to be the bloody best man!*

He turned his back on the open stable doors and tugged irritably at his new chain mail. The vest had obviously been fashioned for someone a few inches taller and a great deal broader than him, and in the few places where it did fit, it chaffed him unmercifully. The arms were too long, the leggings were baggy, and the waistline was a joke. And to top it all, his hood kept falling forward over his eyes. Rupert stomped back and forth between the stalls, trying to get the feel of the armor, but soon gave up in disgust. It could take weeks to get a new suit of chain mail fitting just right, and he didn't have weeks. It would just have to do as it was.

"Typical," he said finally.

"What is?" asked the unicorn.

"Well, here I am, all dressed up in bright new armor,

about to go back into the dark and fight evil, and all I can think of is how much I need to visit the privy!"

The unicorn sniggered unfeelingly. "It's just nerves, lad. Think about something else."

"It's all right for you. You can take a piss any time you feel like it. I have to unbuckle half my damn armor first."

"Don't worry," said the unicorn. "Once we get outside the gates, one good look at the demon horde will undoubtedly scare the piss right out of you."

"You're a great help."

"You're welcome."

"Ah, to hell with it," said Rupert suddenly, and before the unicorn's startled gaze, he began unbuckling his chain mail.

"Rupert; what the hell do you think you're doing?"

"First, I'm going to get rid of this damn armor, and then I'm going to empty my bladder. Any more questions?"

"Just the one; how long do you think you're going to survive out there without any armor? They'll rip you to pieces!"

"I'll burn that bridge when I come to it."

"As I recall," said the unicorn, watching interestedly as piece after piece of chain mail fell to the stable floor, "The last time you threw away your armor, we were immediately ambushed by a bunch of goblins, and you terrorized the lot of them. Who knows; maybe you'll get lucky again."

"I fight better without armor, anyway," growled Rupert, gazing vacantly into space as he emptied his bladder against a convenient wall post. "Chain mail's not as bad as plate armor, but this stuff fits like a sack, and just gets in the way. I'll keep the vest; I'm not entirely daft. Did you say something, unicorn?"

"I wouldn't dare."

Rupert sniffed, and walked back to the unicorn, readjusting his sword belt.

"Feeling better now?" asked the unicorn.

"Much," said Rupert.

"Then perhaps you'd like to tell me just what you think our chances are of coming out of this mess alive."

Rupert looked away from the unicorn, and shrugged tiredly. "I don't know, Breeze. We've got the High Warlock on our side, if he sobers up in time. And the Infernal Devices should make quite a difference, if we can keep them under control. Our own chances . . . aren't particularly good, but we've beaten long odds before, haven't we?"

"In other words," said the unicorn quietly, "we're going to die out there."

"It looks like it," said Rupert finally. "We've pushed our luck as far as it will go, my friend. Only a miracle will get us out of this one. Still, at least this way we have a chance to take some of the demons with us."

"Then that will have to do," said the unicorn.

"Rupert . . ." Julia's voice was quiet, hesitant. "I need to talk to you."

Rupert looked around quickly. Julia was standing half-silhouetted in the stable doorway. She moved slowly forward into the lanternlight, and Rupert didn't know whether to smile or bow or turn and run. In her old familiar clothes, she looked just the way she used to be, and he didn't want to be reminded of that.

"I'm busy right now, Julia. Can't this wait?"

"No," said Julia. "It can't."

She studied Rupert in silence, taking in the dark bruises of fatigue beneath his eyes, and his watchful, wary stance. There was a grim, defeated look to him that she'd never seen before, and for a moment it was like looking at a stranger. The moment passed, and Julia smiled suddenly. When in doubt, go to the heart of the matter.

"I love you, Rupert."

He flinched as though she'd hit him. "Of course you love me. That's why you're marrying Harald."

"No, Rupert. They can threaten and plead, and they can drag me kicking and screaming to the altar, but they can't make me marry him."

"Sure." Rupert couldn't seem to raise enough strength to be angry; he was too tired to be anything but bitter. Julia reached out and put a hand on his arm, and it seemed heavy even in its gentleness.

"Rupert; I don't want you to go off into battle believing a lie. I don't give a damn for Harald, or being a Princess, or anything but being with you."

"I saw you in the Court," said Rupert thickly. "I saw you with Harald . . ."

"I was angry," said Julia. "I wanted to hurt you, to make you jealous, because . . . oh, Rupert . . ."

She moved forward and took him in her arms. He clung to her desperately, like a drowning man, his face buried in her neck. She hugged him fiercely back, not flinching even when his strength hurt her.

"Don't leave me," Rupert said hoarsely into her neck. "You're all I've got left."

"I'll never leave you," Julia promised him quietly. "Never again, my love."

"Me neither," said the unicorn, butting them gently with the side of his head. Without looking round, Rupert reached blindly out with one arm and hugged the unicorn's neck.

After a while, Rupert regained control of himself and straightened up. Julia immediately let go of him, and brushed at his clothes and pulled his chain vest straight, so that she wouldn't have to see his face while he composed himself again. Rupert was funny about things like that.

"How long before they open the gates?" she asked, her voice carefully calm and steady.

"Not long now," said Rupert. He smiled at Julia as she fussed over him, and then frowned suddenly as he caught sight of the leather-bound swordhilt standing up behind her left shoulder. "Julia, where did you get that sword?"

Julia heard the tension in his voice, and stepped back a pace so that she could face him squarely.

"The King wanted me to have it. He said you'd turned it down."

"That's right, I did. I wish you had, too."

"It's only a sword, Rupert."

"No, it isn't! That thing on your back is an Infernal Device; an evil so great my ancestors kept it locked away in the Armory for over five hundred years rather than risk using it."

"How can any sword be that evil?"

Rupert looked at her steadily. "According to legend, the swords are alive; and they corrupt the souls of those who bear them."

Julia shook her head impatiently. "A sword is a sword. All right, it feels . . . wrong, somehow. But as long as it kills demons, I'll have a use for it. Anyway, you carry a magic sword yourself." Julia stopped suddenly, and looked at Rupert thoughtfully. "The rainbow sword; I'd forgotten all about it. Why can't we use that against the darkness? It worked before, remember?"

Rupert shook his head. "I've already tried, Julia. It doesn't work anymore."

Julia's face fell, and for a moment they stood together in silence. Julia glanced out the stable door. "Rupert; I can't stay much longer. My women are waiting for me."

"Yes; I watched you drilling them. They looked . . . promising." Rupert smiled suddenly. "I don't know, lass; it hardly seems fair to send you out into the dark, carrying an Infernal Device and leading a company of fighting women. I mean, we just want to kill the demons, not terrorize them."

Julia laughed. "I'll make you pay for that, after the battle's over."

"Promise?"

"Promise."

They looked at each other steadily. Rupert reached out and took Julia's hands in his.

"Julia, whatever happens . . . I love you, lass. Never doubt it."

"I love you, Rupert. You watch your back, when we finally get out there."

"Right. And after we've won . . ."

"Yes," said Julia. "There'll be time for lots of things, after we've won."

They kissed once, lingeringly, and then Julia turned and walked out of the stables, back to her waiting women. Rupert watched her go and, for the first time in a long time, he felt at peace with himself. He reached inside his chain mail vest, and from under his jerkin he brought out a crumpled, battered handkerchief spotted with faded bloodstains. "My Lady's favor," he said softly. He touched the cloth to his lips, and then tucked it carefully back into place, over his heart.

"Lancers, mount up! Gate keepers, stand ready!"

The Champion's voice came roaring across the courtyard, and for a moment the voice of the crowd fell silent, before rising again in a bedlam of shouted orders and whinnying horses. Rupert breathed deeply, straightened his shoulders, and led the unicorn out of the stables and into the courtyard.

The Champion sat astride a massive, evil-eyed charger,

the torchlight gleaming ruddy on his freshly polished armor. Impressive and invincible, and towering above the milling crowd, a hero out of legend. He gestured impatiently with his war-axe, and a hundred lancers urged their horses forward to take up their position behind him. The couched lances stabbed proudly up at the starless night sky, their gleaming shafts bedecked with brightly colored ribbons and lady's favors, like so many brilliant banners. The guards and men-at-arms moved in behind the lancers, laughing and joking and passing around flasks of wine. They stamped their feet against the cold, and glanced at the closed gates with eager anticipation, glad that the waiting was almost over. And behind them, bringing up the rear, came the courtiers and farmers and traders, uncomfortable in their ill-fitting armor, but quietly determined not to be found wanting when the time came. Men and women stood side-by-side, carrying swords and pikes and hand-axes, and no one thought it strange. Women were fighting for the same reason as men; because they were needed, and because there was no one else.

Rupert mounted his unicorn, and slowly made his way through the crowd to take his place at the head of the army. A handful of guardsmen appeared out of nowhere and formed themselves into an honor guard around him. Rupert bowed his head to them, and the ten guards he'd brought back from the Darkwood saluted him with their swords.

"What the hell do you think you're doing here?" demanded Rupert. "You should be taking it easy in your barracks; you're walking wounded."

"If we can walk, we're not wounded," said Rob Hawke. "That's the orders. Besides, why should you have all the fun? We were just getting the hang of killing demons when you dragged us back into the Castle."

"You know the odds are stacked against us," Rupert began, and then had to break off as the guards laughed derisively.

"When haven't the odds been stacked against us?" grinned Hawke. "We're getting used to that."

"Doomed!" moaned another guard. "We're all doomed!"

Several of the guards started wailing a funeral dirge, but quickly grew bored and changed it to an upbeat tempo. People around them stared at the guards, and then looked hastily away. Rupert couldn't speak for laughing. By the time the small party reached the Castle gates, he was leading his men in a bawdy marching song in which the word *doomed* appeared at regular intervals.

King John was kneeling beside his horse in the shadows of the inner North wall, struggling with a stubborn girth strap. His tousled gray hair was held in place by a simple leather headband, and his chain mail bore the scars and repairs from a hundred old campaigns. Rockbreaker clung to his back as though it was a part of him, but he still wore his old, familiar sword on his left hip. The Astrologer stood beside him, watching patiently. Finally he reached down and deftly pulled the girth strap into place.

"Thanks," said the King gruffly, getting to his feet. "Never was much good with horses."

"You're welcome, John."

"I'm glad you're here, Thomas. It seems there's nobody else in this Castle who gives a damn whether I live or die."

"There's always your family."

"Family," said King John. "I haven't had a family since my Eleanor died. My sons and I . . . aren't what you'd call close. No reason why we should be. Harald is a brave enough fighter, and a better statesman, but his heart is as empty as a pauper's purse. I don't think he'd know an honest emotion if it bit him."

"And Rupert?"

For a moment Thomas Grey thought John was going to tell him to mind his own business, and then John's shoulders suddenly slumped, and the King looked somehow older.

"Rupert. Not once in his life has that boy done what I expected of him. He shouldn't even be here now, by rights. When I sent him off on his quest, I never expected to see him again. Certainly, he was never supposed to actually track down and fight a dragon; he was supposed to do the sensible thing, and just keep on going into exile, as I intended. But no, he had to be different. He had to do his duty. Ah well, he's not a bad lad, in his way."

"Then why isn't he here, with you?"

"No reason why he should be. Since the day he was born, he's known nothing but loneliness and despair, and all because of me. I didn't need or want a second son, and the

Court is very quick to pick up on things like that. They made his life a misery, and I let them do it. I could have protected him, advised him . . . loved him. But I never did, because I always knew that one day I might have to order his death, to secure the throne for Harald. I had to be that way. The Land couldn't survive a civil war, not so soon after the Border War with Hillsdown. And now, after all these years . . . I can't help thinking the Land would be safer in Rupert's hands than Harald's. At least Rupert has a heart."

John turned back to his horse, gave the stirrup a quick tug to make sure it was secure, and then pulled himself up into the saddle. The horse tossed its head impatiently, eager to be off. John settled himself comfortably, refusing to be hurried, and then smiled at Thomas Grey.

"We'll be off soon. Wish me luck."

"Good luck, John. And watch your back."

King John urged his horse forward, and slowly made his way through the packed ranks of the waiting army to join his sons before the Castle gates.

Rupert's hands closed tightly on the unicorn's reins as he watched his father moving slowly and purposefully toward him. His back muscles tensed painfully as he struggled to appear calm and unconcerned. *What do you want now?* he thought bitterly. *There's nothing more you can do to me, nothing left you can take from me.* The guards surrounding him grew silent and watchful as the King carefully maneuvered his horse into position, midway between Rupert and Harald. The two Princes bowed briefly to their King.

"You got here just in time, father," said Harald smoothly. "We were becoming concerned about you."

"Thank you, Harald," said the King. "Now, if you'll excuse me for a moment, I want to speak to Rupert in private."

Harald stiffened slightly, and shot a quick searching glance at Rupert before bowing coldly, and moving his horse several yards away. He sat rigidly in the saddle, studying the huge oaken doors before him, and his face revealed nothing, nothing at all. King John ignored him, and looked meaningfully at Rupert's honor guard. The guardsmen stared calmly back. Several of them ostentatiously rested their hands on their swordbelts. The King smiled grimly.

"Call off your dogs, Rupert. Before I decide to have them muzzled."

The guards looked at Rupert, who nodded reluctantly. The guardsmen bowed to him, stared coldly at the King, and then withdrew into the crowd, though not very far. Rupert studied the King thoughtfully.

"Whatever you want, Father, the answer's no."

"You always were a cautious one, Rupert."

"I've been given enough cause."

The King looked away, unable to meet Rupert's steady gaze. His horse fidgeted uneasily as the King's hands played aimlessly with the reins.

"Rupert . . ."

"Father."

"How long now, before we go out?"

"A few minutes, at most."

"Do you hate me, son?"

The sudden question caught Rupert off-guard, and he stumbled over his reply. "Sometimes, I suppose. You've given me damn little reason to love you, but . . . you're the King, and the Land must come first. I've always known that."

"Politics," sighed the King. "It all seems so petty now, set against the long night waiting outside our walls. I've always done my best for the Land, done what I believed was right, even when it cost me the things I treasured most, but none of the things I fought for seem to matter much anymore. Rupert, you're my son, my blood and kin, and I want you to know that I'm proud of you. Despite . . . many things, you have always been true to the Land, and your duty."

"Why wait till now to tell me?" said Rupert. "Why not tell me when it mattered; just once, in front of the Court!"

"And make you even more of a target for the Court intrigues?" said the King softly. "I kept you isolated from the throne and the Barons so that Harald's supporters wouldn't see you as a threat. Was I really so wrong, to want you alive rather than hanged as a pretender to the throne?"

"That isn't why you did it," said Rupert flatly. "You did it for Harald's sake, not mine."

King John nodded quietly. "I did my best for you," he said finally. "What happened to your chain mail? Why aren't you wearing it?"

"It got in the way. I do better without armor."

The King looked unconvinced, but let the matter drop rather than risk breaking the tentative bond between them. "Watch yourself out there, son. I want you coming back in one piece."

"I'll do my best to oblige you," said Rupert solemnly, and they both chuckled briefly.

There was a pause, as they looked for something else to say, and found they'd said it all. They never did have much in common, and Rupert knew that he and his father were already beginning to drift apart again.

"I don't know what everyone's so worried about," he said finally. "How can we lose, with the Champion leading us?" He gestured at the Champion, sitting impassively astride his armored war charger like an ancient heroic statue come to life.

King John glanced briefly at his Champion, and frowned. "The Champion isn't necessarily a touchstone for success, Rupert. He's not been defeated in battle since he became my Champion, over twenty years ago; and that makes him dangerous. To us, and to himself."

"Dangerous? How?"

"He's overconfident. By the time he realizes he's not invulnerable after all, it might be too late to do him or whoever he's fighting beside any good."

Rupert nodded soberly. "I'll keep an eye on him."

"It might be wise." King John took up his reins and turned his horse away from Rupert. "And now, I'd better have a word with your brother, while there's still time."

"Father," said Rupert suddenly, "If you'd thought it necessary, you would have ordered my death, wouldn't you?"

The King glanced back over his shoulder. "Damn right I would have," he said calmly, and then urged his horse on into the packed crowd, heading for where Harald was waiting on his charger. Rupert shook his head slowly, and looked away.

"So, here we go again, Breeze. Out to face the darkness one more time."

"Good," said the unicorn. "I'm fed up with all this waiting. Anything would be better than this. Well, almost anything."

"Yeah. I'm scared, Breeze."

"So am I, Rupert."

"My guts are churning like you wouldn't believe."

"Take it easy. The gates will be opening any minute, and once the fighting starts you won't have time to be scared."

"Yeah. Sure. Oh hell, I need to take a leak again."

"No, you don't."

"Look, whose bladder is it?"

"Stand ready, the gatehouse!" called the Champion, and a sudden hush fell across the army for a moment as everyone realized that the gates were finally about to open. Half a dozen men-at-arms moved into position before the doors, ready to draw back the great steel bolts at the King's command. Rupert slipped his left arm through the straps of his buckler, and tightened them securely. The heavy weight of the shield on his arm was deeply reassuring. He took a firm hold of both reins with his left hand, and then drew his sword. The familiar feel of the swordhilt was a comfort to him.

His guardsmen jostled their way back through the crowd, and took up their positions around him again. They shifted restlessly from foot to foot, hefting their swords impatiently, their eyes fixed on the great oak doors. Rupert felt a strange calm seeping through him, now that the moment had finally come. One way or another, this could well be the last time he'd have to face the darkness. Julia called out to him, and he looked back to see her slowly maneuvering her horse through the crowd toward him. Her troops of fighting women formed a guard of honor around her. They looked hard and competent, and ready for battle. Rupert wondered wistfully if he appeared anything like as intimidating to them. He bowed politely to the women, and exchanged a grin with Julia as she steered her horse in beside him.

"Looks like we're finally off," said Julia.

"Looks like it," said Rupert.

"Ready for the fray?"

"Ready as I'll ever be. How's the Warlock?"

"Doing his best to appear confident, but it's an uphill struggle. The Astrologer's rounded up half a hundred minor sorcerers and witches, but none of them are worth much. The Warlock's got them working together to support his spells, but there's no telling how successful that'll be."

"Julia, do you think my plan's going to work?"

She laughed. "Not a chance. But we've got to do something, haven't we?"

Rupert sighed. "It would be nice if *somebody* believed in my plan."

"Would you rather we lied to you?"

"Frankly, yes."

"Stand ready, the army!" roared the Champion, and a sudden quiet fell across the courtyard, broken only by the stamping and snorting of the impatient horses. Rupert eased his buckler into a more comfortable position, and gripped his sword firmly. All around him, the combined breathing of more than five hundred men and women seemed strangely loud and distinct on the hush, rising and falling like an endless tide. Swords and maces and lances gleamed blood-red in the flickering torchlight. The fear and the tension that had filled the courtyard was gone, replaced by a fierce determination that ran through all the army, binding them together like a single giant heartbeat. A simple determination; to make the demons pay dearly for what they'd done to the Forest Land. King John held up his sword.

"Open the gates!"

The heavy steel bolts slammed back into their sockets, the huge oak doors swung open, and the last army of the Forest Land surged forward to meet its destiny.

The horses' pounding hooves echoed thunderously back from the Keep's walls, and then they were out and charging across the lowered drawbridge. The torchlight fell away behind them, and the army plunged forward into the endless night. The leprous moon floated overhead, blue and full and malevolent. Demons rose in their thousands from the concealing shadows of the Darkwood, twisted and malformed and horribly eager. Not one monstrous shape was much like any other, but the same hunger filled their glowing eyes, and they moved in obedience to a single dark purpose. The mark of foulness was upon them all, the mark of the Demon Prince. Sickly blue moonlight gleamed dully on the fangs and claws of the creatures of the night as they walked and crawled and slithered up out of gaping cracks in the earth. And then the army slammed into the waiting demons, and the slaughter began.

Swords rose and fell against the seething darkness, and

demon blood flew on the stinking air, but the first force of the charge was quickly soaked up by the sheer numbers of the demon horde. The lancers pressed stubbornly onward, followed by some of the guards, but the vast bulk of the army soon found itself trapped only a few hundred yards from the ice-covered moat. Horses reared and screamed as the demons swarmed around them, and often it was only the press of bodies that saved the animals from hamstringing or worse. The army milled confusedly at the edge of the Darkwood, already broken apart into a dozen embattled groups, fighting desperately to hold their ground against the never-ending tide of demons that came pouring out of the darkness. The air was full of shouts and screams and war cries, and the harsh tearing sound of steel biting into flesh, but the demons attacked in silence, never making a sound, even when they died. In the unreal light of the Blue Moon, the demons seemed like monstrous ghosts, or nightmares come alive and solid. And bravely though the army fought, more than half of them were pulled down and butchered in the first few minutes, their screams mercifully short. There were just too many demons.

Light blazed suddenly against the night, a crackling white flame that burned unsupported on the air high above the battle. Jagged bolts of lightning stabbed down into the Darkwood, scattering the demons. Dozens of the creatures staggered blindly through the battle, howling silently as they burned like torches. Other clutched at their throats and fell choking to the ground as the air suddenly vanished from their lungs. Balefire blazed silver on the night, and the High Magic was everywhere. Demon turned on demon and tore each other to pieces, the few survivors running amok through the demon horde until they too were brought down. Slowly the demons began to give ground, and the army pressed forward, cheering the High Warlock's name as they eagerly pursued the retreating demons. And then the balefire was suddenly gone, and the High Magic no longer beat upon the air. Darkness returned to the Forest, and the only light was that of the Blue Moon.

Rupert leaned out of his saddle and cut through a leaping demon, and then had to duck sharply as a barbed tentacle lashed at him from an overhanging branch. He started to aim a blow at the tentacle, but the unicorn had already carried him out of reach. The battle had degenerated into an unholy mess. There was no pattern or structure to the demons' attack; they came from every side at once, and for every creature that fell there were a hundred more to take its place. The army and the demons surged back and forth in a bloody confusion of swords and axes and fangs and claws, and the ground grew thick with unmoving bodies. Rupert glared about him, searching for some kind of cover. His guardsmen were gone, separated from him when the army fell apart. He swore harshly, and cut viciously at the demons that milled around the unicorn. With the High Warlock's magic gone, the army had lost what little advantage it had seized, and already some of the smaller groups were falling back as the demons tore into them with renewed ferocity.

Rupert hewed at a demon that clung tenaciously to his boot even as he hacked it in two, and looked quickly about him. Less than half of the Forest army were still on their feet and fighting, and all but a few were being forced steadily back by the demons. There were no wounded, on either side; the demons were hungry. Rupert swallowed sickly as he realized how many of his army were already dead, with the battle barely begun.

They never had a chance, he thought slowly. *I promised them a chance to save the Forest Land, and all I did was lead them to their deaths. Damn it all to hell! There's got to be something that'll stop the demons! There's got to be.*

He slashed about him with his sword, trying to open up a space around him, but no matter where he turned there were always more demons, closing in on the unicorn from every side. Slowly, foot by foot, the demons pushed the army back, the battle now nothing more than a slow, dogged retreat to Forest Castle. Blood streamed across the torn ground, dark and viscous. Some of the demons turned aside to drink it, thrusting their muzzles deep into the dripping mud. The army fell back and the demons went after them; leaping from the shadows, falling down from out of the night, reaching up from cracks in the earth. The night grew steadily darker, and the shadows were pus-filled with distorted life.

Harald gutted a demon with one well-calculated blow, and then clung tightly to his horse's reins as it trampled the

writhing creature under its hooves. His gleaming chain mail
was scarred and broken and soaked in blood, some of it his
own. His sword rose and fell steadily, and still the demons
came at him. He met them coldly, calmly, as hard and
unyielding as the sword in his hand, but still the demons
came. He glanced quickly behind him every chance he got,
checking and rechecking how much farther it was to the
edge of the moat. The King hadn't given the order to retreat
yet, but the battle was lost, and everyone knew it. Harald
felt no guilt, or even regret; no one could have won against
such overwhelming odds. The Forest army had been beaten
even before it crossed the drawbridge. The moat wasn't far
away now, and Harald tried to turn his horse around, but
the sheer press of bodies made it impossible. All he could
do was back his horse away from the demons, step by step,
following the rest of the army back to the moat. He felt
suddenly trapped and helpless, and panic flared up within
him. He fought it down, using all his old habits of self-
control. Lose his head now, even for a moment, and he'd
live just long enough to regret it. He glanced to his right,
and saw Rupert slowly retreating on his unicorn. Rupert's
sword was a silver gleam against the darkness, cutting through
the demons like a scythe through wheat. Harald looked
away. He already knew his brother was good with a sword.
He still had some of the scars to remind him.

You could be the better swordsman, whispered a quiet
voice in his mind. *All you have to do is draw Flarebright.*

Harald shuddered, and hacked savagely at the nearest
demon. He'd draw Flarebright when he had to, and not
before.

King John fought to stay in the saddle as his mount
plunged this way and that, half out of its mind with fear and
pain. He lashed about him with his sword, missing as often
as not, but somehow still managing to keep the demons at
bay. The sword grew heavier and more awkward with every
blow. His breath was getting short, and his heart hammered
painfully against his breastbone. Sweat ran down into his
eyes, and he had neither the time nor the energy to wipe it
away. *Too old,* thought John bitterly. *Too damn old.*

Rockbreaker slapped at his back with every movement, as
though reminding him it was still there. King John ignored

it. He wasn't ready to draw the Infernal Device yet. Not quite yet.

Princess Julia looped her reins around her arm and swung her sword with both hands, holding back the demons by sheer ferocity. Her fighting women were scattered among the army, but Julia had already seen most of them fall to the demons. They'd fought well and died bravely, but they never had a chance against so many demons. *If only I'd had more time,* thought Julia. *What an army I could have made of you.* Her horse suddenly lurched beneath her, and screamed shrilly. Julia kicked free of her stirrups and threw herself clear as the horse collapsed. It kicked briefly as the demons tore its throat out, and then lay still. Some demons were already feeding at the great rip they'd torn in the horse's belly. Julia was quickly on her feet and fighting, but the fall had shaken her. Everything was happening so *fast.* She backed quickly away as the demons moved to surround her, cutting her off from the main bulk of the army. Julia set her back against the trunk of a decaying tree, and glared desperately about her. The army was being forced farther away with every movement, and there was no way she could rejoin them. The demons moved slowly forward, taking their time, enjoying her fear. Julia swept her sword back and forth, her breathing coming short and hurried. Alone and on foot, all her strength and skill with a sword wasn't going to be enough to save her, and she knew it. She swore harshly, sheathed her sword, and drew Wolfsbane.

The sword seemed almost to leap into her hand, clearing the long silver scabbard with ease. The wide steel blade gleamed dully before her, and then pulsed with a sudden sickly yellow light. The demons froze in their tracks, staring at the glowing sword as though mesmerised. The hilt was unpleasantly warm in Julia's hands, and there was a new feeling in the night as something stirred, something that had slept for centuries and was now awake, and aware . . .

A demon leapt for Julia's throat, and she cut it in two with one easy sweep of the blade. The huge sword weighed almost nothing in her hands, and its edge didn't even grate on the demon's bones. Julia grinned harshly as the demon fell, and then her grin disappeared as the two halves of the demon's body rotted and decayed and fell apart, all in a few seconds. More demons threw themselves forward, only to collapse into putrid decay when the sword bit into them. The Infernal Device glowed with an unhealthy yellow light, like a corpse fire on a cairn. The demons fell back uneasily, but something made Julia pursue them, cutting viciously at anything that moved. The demons died screaming silently as corruption took them.

Wolfsbane, thought Julia. *Bane; that which causes death, ruin, destruction, or decay.*

She swung the blade in wide, eager arcs, killing all within her reach. The demons did not die cleanly, and yet Julia found nothing of mercy in her. The creatures of the night fell beneath her sword in ever-growing numbers, and a bleak savage grin slowly fixed itself to her face. There was no humor in that smile, and only a distant coldness in her eyes. It felt good, killing demons; hurting them as they'd hurt others, destroying them as they'd destroyed the Forest Land. Her sword rose and fell, and the demons died horribly. She laughed aloud, though no one would have recognized her voice in that awful sound.

Harald clearly heard the snap of breaking bone over the battle's roar, and then his horse collapsed under him. He swung easily out of the saddle and down onto the blood-soaked ground, and moving quickly forward, he killed the grinning demon that had broken his horse's leg. The horse moaned and rolled its eyes piteously as the demons closed in around Harald and the fallen animal. Harald sheathed his sword and drew Flarebright. The demons hesitated, and Harald thrust the Infernal Device deep into his horse's chest, killing it instantly. He waited a second, and then withdrew the sword. The long steel blade dripped a vivid crimson flame. The demons fell back a little. Harald bowed briefly, regretfully, to his dead mount. He'd always been rather fond of the animal, but he couldn't leave it to suffer. And besides, he'd needed the horse's blood to activate Flarebright. The demons pressed suddenly forward, and Harald went to meet them, sword in hand. And wherever Flarebright bit into demon flesh, the creature immediately burst into searing crimson flames that left behind nothing but ashes. The sword drank the demons' blood, and their blood fueled the sword's flames. It seemed to Harald that he had always known this, and he couldn't understand why he was suddenly so reluctant to use the sword.

He moved confidently among the demons, leaving death and destruction in his wake, but he found no joy in it. For perhaps the first time in his life, he could feel events slipping out of his control. He shook his head constantly, as though to clear it, and it slowly came to him that he was no longer sure whether he was using the sword, or the sword was using him. Flarebright's flames grew more and more intense as the Infernal Device sated itself on demon blood, until Harald could barely stand the heat blazing from the sword. He held the blade at arm's length, and still the bloodred flames rose higher, higher. Flarebright burned against the dark, but it was not a healthy flame, or a natural light. And Harald knew, deep down, that as yet the sword was barely awakened, and was using only a fraction of its power. Demons burned around him like so many misshapen candles, and the sweat that ran down his face was only partly due to the heat from the sword's flames.

King John's sword shattered on a demon's scales, and he threw the broken stub in the creature's face. The demon fell back a step, and before it could come at him again, the King drew Rockbreaker and cut the creature in two. The longsword was unnaturally light in his hands, and the great steel blade had a curious golden sheen. King John hacked viciously at the demons that clustered round his horse, trying to drag him down, and the blade sliced cleanly through their flesh without even pausing in its arc. The King frowned, impressed, but knew there had to be more to the Infernal Device than a keen edge. He could feel the ancient power stirring impatiently in the long blade, waiting for him to use it. He scowled uneasily, and then, without quite knowing why, King John swung down out of his saddle and stood beside his horse. The animal reared suddenly, pulling the reins out of his grasp, and in a moment it was off and running, back to the safety of the Castle. The demons dragged it down before it made twenty feet. King John turned away from the horse's dying screams, and holding Rockbreaker high above his head, he brought the blade swinging down to sink deep into the Forest floor.

The ground split apart with a grating roar, long jagged cracks opening up for hundreds of yards in every direction. The earth groaned loudly as it rose and fell like a great ponderous wave. Demons disappeared into gaping holes, and were crushed to death as the sides of the chasms slammed together again. Deep in the earth, something huge and alien stirred uneasily in its sleep, and then screamed horribly as the earth moved around it, grinding it unmercifully beneath the overwhelming weight of the Forest. The King stared grimly about him, satisfied at the destruction he'd wrought, and then his slight smile vanished as he saw men and women from his own army struggling to climb out of the huge crevasses before the sides slammed shut again. King John quickly pulled Rockbreaker out of the ground, and the broken earth grew still.

There is power in this sword, thought the King slowly. *Power to break and reshape the earth itself. Power that could level mountains, or raise up new ones. Rockbreaker.*

And it wasn't until later that he remembered how many of his own people had died under that power.

The demons died in their hundreds under the three Infernal Devices, and still they came swarming out of the darkness. The army came to the bank of the moat, and there made its stand, as best it could. The Castle drawbridge was raised, and would not be lowered until the King called the retreat. Of the five hundred and fifty men and women who had followed King John out of the Castle, less than a hundred now remained. The lancers were gone, pulled down and slaughtered in the first few minutes. Most of the farmers and traders and townspeople were dead, along with half the guards and men-at-arms. The survivors now huddled together in a single defiant knot at the edge of the frozen moat, and swung their crimson blades with savage desperation. The demons were everywhere, filling the night, and there were always more to replace those who died.

Rupert swayed tiredly in his saddle, and almost fell. He caught himself just in time, and took a firmer hold on the reins. His muscles ached fiercely, and his head was swimming with fatigue, but still he continued to fight. At first he thought of his duty, and then of survival, but finally he carried on fighting simply because he was damned if he'd give in to the darkness. He'd been beaten many times before, but he'd never once given in, and he wasn't about to start now. He could see the Champion to his left, standing at the head of the army and swinging his massive war axe like a toy. There was no sign of his war charger, and his armor was rent and bloodied, but the swarming demons broke about him like the pounding surf on a rocky shore, unable to wear him down. Rupert supposed he ought to find the sight inspiring, but somehow he was just too damn tired to care.

The ice covering the moat suddenly exploded, as the moat monster roared up out of the freezing waters. Forty feet long from jaws to tail, it snatched up the nearest demon threatening Rupert, and tore it to pieces. The moat monster's vicious jaws gaped wide as it threw back its gargoyle head and howled a challenge to the darkness. Its long scaly body bulged with thick cables of muscle, and the earth of the moat's bank seemed to sink a little under the monster's immense weight. It glanced quickly at Rupert to make sure he was all right, and then threw itself at the demons. Its foot-long claws and rending fangs ripped through the demons in a flurry of blood and gore.

So that's what the moat monster looks like, thought Rupert. *I often wondered. He's certainly . . . impressive.*

A demon sprang out of the darkness, and Rupert gutted it in midair. It grabbed at his buckler as it fell, and Rupert had to cut the shield free from his arm before the demon's weight could drag him out of his saddle. Something with steaming bloodred eyes came flying out of the shadows and slammed into his chest, almost throwing him from the saddle. The creature clung to his chain mail vest with a dozen legs, and snapped at his unprotected throat. Rupert brought up his left arm to guard his throat, and the demon sank its jaws into his flesh, biting clean through to the bone. Rupert groaned, and tried to reach the creature with his sword, but it clung too closely to his chest, its jaws locked on his arm. Other demons were quick to spot his vulnerability, and came racing toward him out of the night. Rupert tried again to lift his sword, but all he could think of was the awful, tearing pain in his left arm.

And then the Champion's axe came out of nowhere and sliced clean through the demon's guts. Its jaws relaxed as it died, and Rupert was finally able to tear his arm free. He turned to thank the Champion, but the press of the fighting had already carried him away.

For a moment Rupert found himself in a quiet part of the battle, and he took advantage of the lull to check his injured arm. White shards of splintered bone showed clearly in the wound, but he could still move his fingers. Rupert gritted his teeth against the pain, and slipped his left arm under his swordbelt, pulling the belt tight to hold the arm securely. Not much of a sling, but it would have to do. *I'm not having much luck with this arm,* he thought shakily. *That's another healing job for the High Warlock.* The thought reminded him of the way the supporting magic had suddenly stopped, and he twisted around in the saddle to look back at Forest Castle. The battlements were brightly lit with dozens of flaring torches, but there was no sign of any of the magicians. Rupert swore harshly, and then turned quickly back as the demons pressed forward again.

Step by step, he was forced back with the rest of the army, and yet, although there were as many demons as ever, the press of battle was slowly easing, as the piled-up bodies of the dead and the dying now formed a high barricade between the army and its attackers. Rupert looked vaguely around him, searching for familiar faces among the survivors, and frowned as he realized he couldn't see Julia anymore. He sat up straight in the saddle, and then froze as he spotted Julia standing alone with her back to a tree, surrounded by demons, a good dozen yards outside the barricade.

Rupert took a firm grip on his sword and urged the unicorn forward, but the animal only managed a few steps before he stumbled and almost fell. Rupert looked down and swallowed sickly as he saw the blood running thickly down the unicorn's heaving sides. He quickly dismounted, and checked the unicorn for other wounds. A demon came scrambling over the barricade. Rupert killed it before it hit the ground, and turned back to the unicorn.

"What the hell do you think you're doing?" snapped the unicorn breathlessly. "Get back in the saddle before the demons get you."

"Why didn't you tell me you were hurt?"

"We're all hurt, Rupert."

"You're in no condition to carry me any farther. Move back to the edge of the moat, and get yourself across the drawbridge the moment it's lowered. That shouldn't be long now."

"Forget it. You wouldn't last five minutes without me."

"Breeze . . ."

"No. I'm not leaving you."

"I'm giving you an order!"

"Stuff your order. You freed me, remember?"

"Breeze, for once in your life will you please do as I ask? I've got to go and help Julia; she needs me. We'll both join you the moment my father calls the retreat, I promise. Now move yourself, while you've still got the strength."

"I hate it when you're right," growled the unicorn. He started toward the rear of the embattled army, his head hanging limply down. Rupert watched him just long enough to be sure he'd get there all right, and then turned and headed for the barricade. He had to get to Julia . . .

Harald and King John fought back-to-back, the two Infernal Devices keeping the demons at bay. Blood dripped steadily from their torn armor, not all of it demon blood. Rupert waited a moment to be sure their attention was fully on the demons, and then pulled himself up onto the barricade. He didn't think his father would try and stop him, but he couldn't take the risk. The piled-up bodies shifted and stirred under his weight, and Rupert froze where he was, crouched in shadows. Most of the demons seemed to be concentrating on breaking through the barrier, rather than looking for people coming out over it. Soon there was another lull in the fighting in his area and, choosing his moment carefully, Rupert scrambled down the other side of the barricade, wincing and cursing under his breath as every jolt or sudden movement shot pain through his injured arm. And then he was on the ground and running toward Julia, sword in hand.

Julia kept her back pressed against the rotting tree, and swung Wolfsbane back and forth before her in wide, killing arcs. Decaying bodies lay piled around her, but still the demons came, leaping and clawing. Julia hacked viciously at the foul-grinning creatures before her, knowing it was only a matter of time before she grew too tired or too slow, and then they would drag her down. She hoped it would be a quick death, but feared it wouldn't. Her blade faltered as her concentration slipped, and a demon ducked under the sword and lunged for her throat. A backhand slash cut the creature in two, but left Julia's defenses wide open. The demons surged forward.

Rupert slammed into them from behind, and the demons scattered as he fought his way through them to stand at Julia's side. For a long time there was nothing but flashing steel and flying blood, and then the demons suddenly retreated back into the shadows, leaving Rupert and Julia standing alone before the rotting tree. They slowly lowered their swords and stared warily about them. The darkness still seethed with misshapen life, but the demons seemed to be falling back into the Darkwood. The army watched suspiciously from behind its barricade, and made no more to pursue them.

"It's not like the demons to give in that easily," panted Rupert, leaning heavily on his sword as he fought to get more air into his heaving lungs. "They're up to something. Have to be."

"Seems likely," said Julia. She sat down suddenly as her legs gave out, and after a moment Rupert joined her. He glanced dubiously at Wolfsbane.

"That thing any good, as a sword?"

"I've known worse."

Rupert stared glumly at the dead bodies lying heaped around them, purulent with decay. He looked sideways at Julia, and raised a sardonic eyebrow. "You know, lass; there has to be an easier way to make a living."

They grinned at each other, too tired to laugh. Rupert looked closely at Julia's wound, and frowned.

"You're hurt," he said harshly.

"So are you," said Julia. "But you still managed to save my life."

"You'd have done the same for me."

"How bad is that arm?"

"Bad enough, lass. How are you feeling?"

"I've felt better."

Rupert put his good arm around her shoulders, and she leaned against his chest. They sat in silence a while, easing their hurts by sharing them. Rupert knew he should be getting Julia back to the rest of the army while the demons were still quiet, but he hadn't the strength.

"If nothing else," said Julia, "I'll have a few more interesting scars to add to my collection."

"Same here," said Rupert.

Julia stirred restively against his chest. "Rupert, this battle isn't going very well, is it."

"It's been a bloody fiasco, lass. Most of us are dead, or dying. Without the High Warlock's magic to back us up, we were nothing more than sitting targets. It's a wonder any of us have survived."

"Rupert . . . can you hear something?"

"What?"

"There's something out there, Rupert; something big. And it's coming this way."

Rupert looked out into the night, and then scrambled to his feet, sword in hand. Julia slowly got herself up and stood beside him, leaning heavily on Wolfsbane for support. Deep in the night, a soft blue glow was forming; the same vile shade as the Full Moon overhead. The blue glow came slowly forward out of the Darkwood, rising and falling and shifting constantly from one vague shape to another. Demons stirred uneasily in the shadows, and shrank back into the darkness. *What the hell's out there?* thought Rupert. *What could be so bad that even the demons are afraid of it?* He remembered the worm in the Coppertown pit, and moved forward a little to put himself between Julia and whatever was coming out of the darkness. The army watched unmoving from behind its grisly barricade.

A deep bass roar sounded on the night, a long deafening bellow of unreasoning malevolent rage. The sound echoed on through Rupert's bones, even after the roar had died away to a low menacing growl, and then to silence. Rupert shot a quick glance at the army's barricade, but quickly decided against making a run for it. Whatever was coming wasn't going to be stopped by a simple barricade. A slow muffled thudding began, like the beating of a giant heart, and Rupert felt his hackles rise. He'd heard that sound before, when he first brought the High Warlock back to the Castle. The ground shook beneath his feet, and once again Rupert felt a coldness in his soul as he recognized the sound for what it was; the steady ponderous footsteps of something huge walking in the night, coming closer, closer. The ever-present stench of decay and corruption grew worse as the shapeless blue glow drifted nearer, and the giant footsteps jarred the earth like hammer blows. The hovering blue light finally came to a halt some twenty yards short of the army, and the footsteps stopped with it. The light pulsed once, outlining the rotting trees with its shark brilliance, and then faded away, revealing the horror it had hidden.

It had obviously been dead for some time, but it moved and was aware. Its dull white flesh was dry and mummified, eaten away in places to reveal the discolored bones beneath. It stood nearly fifty feet tall, its squat, wedge-shaped head half hidden in shadows. Its wide slash of a mouth was filled with huge, serrated teeth, and balefire burned where its eyes should have been. It had two arms and two legs and it stood erect, but there was nothing in the least human about it. A long barbed tail swept back and forth behind it, smashing apart the decaying trees as the creature moved among them. It was dead, and it was aware. It had lain in the ground for years beyond counting, but something had called it up and sent it out to kill again. The ground trembled under its feet, and its hatred thundered on the stinking air.

"The swords!" cried King John. "The Infernal Devices! They're our only hope!"

He scrambled up and over the barricade, with Harald close behind him. The army made as though to follow, but the King waved them back. King John stalked forward to meet the creature, and Harald and Rupert and Julia moved in behind him. The creature's head turned to follow them, the flames in its eyesockets flaring and jumping from the sudden movement. The King came to a sudden halt, glared up at the creature, and then thrust Rockbreaker deep into the ground before him. The earth heaved and tore itself apart, groaning like a wounded animal, but still the creature stood, braced securely on its huge legs and tail. The King withdrew Rockbreaker, and Harald stepped forward and lifted Flarebright above his head. Scarlet flames caressed the length of the blade, and then a bloody balefire leapt out from the sword and splashed against the creature's chest. It screamed its rage, but the flames barely marked its dead flesh. Julia circled round to the creature's left, Wolfsbane at the ready. The creature moved its head to follow her, and Rupert circled round to its right. He wasn't sure what good he could do against something that was already dead, especially when all the Infernal Devices had done was anger it, but he had to do something. Flarebright's flame cut off suddenly as Harald lowered the sword, and the creature lurched forward. It reached for Julia with a clawed hand, and Wolfbane gleamed brightly as it sliced clean through the mummified flesh. The creature snatched back its hand. Even in the dim light, Rupert could see that Wolfsbane had laid the hand open to the bone. There was no blood, but the wound was already corrupt and gangrenous. The creature growled once, and reached for Julia again.

Harald lifted Flarebright, and vivid crimson balefire forced the creature to a halt. King John thrust Rockbreaker into the ground, and left it there. The sword stood upright, glowing fiercely against the dark, and jagged cracks opened up in the earth, racing away from the sword and toward the creature. Gaping crevasses appeared all around the towering creature, but still it wouldn't fall. Julia ran forward and cut at the creature's legs. It howled with murderous rage, and Julia had to throw herself flat as a huge clawed hand swept viciously through the air where her head had been. It reached for her again, and Rupert moved in behind the creature and hacked clean through its left ankle. The exposed tendon snapped like an over-stretched cable, and the creature roared deafeningly as its leg collapsed under it. It lurched backwards, and then fell full length into a gaping crevasse. The loose earth gave way beneath Rupert's feet like shifting sands, and he suddenly found himself sliding into the chasm after the creature. He tossed away his sword, threw himself at the edge, and just made it, hanging on grimly with his one good hand while his legs dangled over the long drop. The crumbling earth started to come apart under his fingers, and then Julia grabbed him by the wrist, and held onto him until he could scramble up onto firmer ground.

King John pulled Rockbreaker out of the ground, and the earth grew still again. Rupert retrieved his sword, and he and Julia helped one another to their feet, leaning on each other as much for comfort as support. And then a long angry roar echoed up out of the earth, and a huge dead-white hand appeared out of the crevasse and sank its claws deep into the earth. The great wedge-shaped head appeared over the edge of the chasm, its balefire eyes glowing brightly as the creature sought to pull itself out of the pit. Harald lunged forward and thrust Flarebright deep into the creature's neck. Bloodred flames consumed the creature's flesh, and it howled horribly. It jerked back its head in agony, pulling the sword out of Harald's grasp. Crimson flames roared up about the creature's head, but it wouldn't release its hold on the side of the crevasse. Julia moved forward and plunged Wolfsbane into the creature's throat, all the way to the hilt. The dead-white flesh decayed and rotted before her eyes, and Flarebright's flames surged even higher. The creature released its hold and fell back into the pit, taking Flarebright and Wolfsbane with it. It disappeared from sight, and then the sides of the crevasse slammed together, and the night was still and quiet again.

Rupert stood beside Julia, who was staring quietly at where the chasm had been. "You let go of the sword," he said softly. "Why?"

"I didn't like what it was doing to me," said Julia, and turned her back on the broken earth.

King John looked back at what remained of his army, huddled together at the edge of the moat behind their barricade of piled-up bodies. Out in the darkness, he could hear the first faint stirrings of the returning demon hoard. He stared out into the endless night, and a soft blue glow appeared, deep in the heart of the darkness, followed by another, and another, and another. King John hefted Rockbreaker in his hand, and a sudden temptation ran through him, to unleash all the sword's power in one final gesture that would destroy the Forest and everything in it. The moment passed, and he shook his head wearily. Perhaps it would come to that, and nothing would remain to him but to avenge the Land's destruction, but not yet. He would wait, until there was no more hope, and the Castle had fallen, and then . . . he would make his decision. The demons were getting closer. The King turned back to his waiting army.

"Retreat!" he called harshly. "There's nothing more we can do here. Stand ready, the gatehouse! Lower the drawbridge!"

There was a distant clanking of chains and counterweights from the Keep, and the drawbridge slowly lowered itself over the moat. Tired, broken and defeated, the survivors of the last army of the Forest Land streamed across the drawbridge as fast as their wounds and exhaustion would allow. Their banners lay torn and bloodied beneath the bodies of the dead, and there was no hope left in them. Harald and King John stood together by the drawbridge, giving what comfort and encouragement they could to the warriors who shambled past them. They had led the army out to battle, and they would be the last to retreat; it was expected of them. Rupert and Julia stood to one side, their arms around each other, their eyes dull with a bone-deep weariness. The Champion stood alone a few yards from the drawbridge, staring out into the dark. His face was calm and cold, and though his armor was caked with blood, his back was still straight and his head unbowed.

There was a sudden roaring in the darkness close at hand, and the moat monster crashed out of the shadows, surrounded by leaping, clawing demons. The monster fought savagely, despite his many wounds, but there were just too many demons, even for him. He dragged himself across the broken earth and threw himself into the moat. The ice cracked open under his weight, and then froze over behind him as he disappeared back into the dark waters. He took a dozen demons with him, and none of them returned to the surface.

More demons came pouring out of the darkness, and the few men and women still on the drawbridge panicked, and fled into the Castle. Harald and the King went after them, carefully not running, followed by Rupert and Julia. The Champion stood alone at the edge of the drawbridge, his war axe in his hands. The demon horde came streaming out of the long night, the vile blue moonlight shimmering on their fangs and claws. The Champion smiled slightly and waited for them to come to him.

The demons threw themselves at him, and he stood them off easily, sweeping his axe in wide killing arcs that tore through flesh and bone alike. The demons tried to go around him, only to fall and scramble helplessly on the moat's ice. The drawbridge was the only way into the Castle, and they had to get past the Champion first. The demons came boiling up out of the shadows in a never-ending stream, but still the Champion stood his ground, and would not retreat.

Rupert stopped at the inner gates, and looked back. The banks of the moat were thick with demons, and a small knot of dark, twisted figures were swarming around the beleaguered Champion. He was fighting well and strongly, but it was clearly only a matter of time before the demons would drag him down. Rupert started forward, and Harald was suddenly at his side.

"What's happening out there?"

Rupert pointed wordlessly, and Harald turned quickly away to shout orders to the gatehouse. Rupert moved out into the Keep.

"Sir Champion!" he yelled desperately. "We're all in! Get back here, dammit; they're raising the drawbridge!"

The Champion didn't hear him. The demons fell again and again under his axe, and there were always more. It felt good to be fighting, to be proving himself as Champion, to be killing those who threatened the Realm. The demons came at him without end, and he met them with cold steel and a colder smile. He knew he was going to die, and he didn't care at all. The Castle needed him, and that was enough. The huge axe was weightless in his hands, and the demons fell before it like over-ripe wheat. Demon blood flew on the air, and the drawbridge became slippery with gore and offal. The Champion fought on, one man against an army, and the army slowed and was stopped.

But in the end he was only one man, and no man can stand against an army for long. The demons tore at him again and again, ripping through his armor. He never felt the wounds, or the blood that streamed down his sides and legs. The Castle was under his protection, and he wouldn't turn and run.

He wouldn't run away.

The demons surged forward, and pulled him down. He never felt the claws that tore out his throat, and he died still trying to swing his axe. The demons poured over his body, and raced across the drawbridge toward the Keep.

There's no time to lower the portcullis, thought Rupert suddenly, *and the demons will be here before they can close and bar the gates . . . unless somebody stops them . . .*

He ran through the Keep to meet the demons, sword in hand. All he had to do was hold them back for a few minutes, and then the gates would be securely shut. He reached the base of the drawbridge, and the first few demons jumped him. He cut them down with swift, savage strokes. *Why me?* he thought bitterly. *Why does it always have to be me?* And then he was facing the main body of the demons, and they came to a sudden halt as he blocked their way, hacking about him with his sword.

"Shut the gates!" he screamed hoarsely. "Shut the bloody gates!"

The demons ripped and tore at him, and he sobbed aloud at the pain, but still he held the demons back. A few more minutes; just hold them off for a few more minutes. *Julia, my love; if only we'd had more time together* . . . And then the demons dragged him down, and he fell beneath them, still clinging to his sword.

In the courtyard, Harald and a handful of men-at-arms stood ready to slam home the heavy steel bolts, once the main windlass had closed the gates. Julia leaned against the inner South wall, and stared blearily about her.

"Rupert? Where are you, Rupert?"

She straightened up when she realized he wasn't with her anymore, and glanced quickly around the packed courtyard. She couldn't see him anywhere, and a sudden cold panic seized her heart. Julia pushed herself away from the wall, and started toward Harald. He'd know where Rupert was. And then she stopped dead as she glanced between the slowly closing gates, and saw Rupert brought down by the demons. Julia ran over to Harald, and grabbed at his arm.

"Stop the gates! Rupert's still out there!"

"He's already dead," said Harald harshly. "He died buying us the time we needed to close these gates. Now either help us with these bolts or get out of the way."

"You wanted him to die out there!" screamed Julia, and snatching her old sword from its scabbard, she ran unsteadily between the closing doors, and out into the Keep. She heard running feet behind her, and glanced back to see King John close on her heels, Rockbreaker in his hands. They just had time to share a brief smile, and then they were among the demons. The first few fell easily to Julia's rage, and those she missed or never saw were no match for Rockbreaker. Julia swung her sword with both hands, and a demon folded forward in midair, trying in vain to stuff its guts back into the wide slash in its belly. It fell squirming to the ground, and Julia kicked it out of her way as she fought her way down the narrow stone tunnel to the place where Rupert had fallen. The King was at her side, Rockbreaker cutting a wide swathe through the demonkind, but Julia could tell he was at the last of his strength. They forced the demons back to the drawbridge, step by step, and then Julia and the King slammed into a small knot of struggling demons. The creatures fell away as Julia and the King pressed forward, and a tall blood-soaked figure surged to his feet, scattering the demons in all directions. He swayed unsteadily and one arm hung limply at his side, but he was still swinging his sword. He wiped away some of the blood that masked his face, and grinned crookedly at Julia.

"What kept you?" asked Rupert, cutting down a demon that tried to get between them.

Julia laughed, and moved in beside him, swinging her sword with fierce abandon. The demons came at them in never-ending numbers as Rupert and Julia and the King retreated back through the Keep, a step at a time. Blood splashed against the stone walls, and streamed along the ground. Julia didn't look back at the Castle gates. She didn't think they'd actually slam the gates on their own King, but if they had, she didn't want to know about it. As long as there was still hope, she could go on fighting. *There are worse ways to die than fighting to save the one you love,* she thought suddenly, and realized she was grinning crazily even as tears ran down her cheeks. *Rupert, my Rupert; we've gone through too much together for me to lose you now.*

The demons surged forward, and Rupert and Julia and King John met them with their swords.

Balefire blazed suddenly against the darkness, scattering the demons as it exploded among them. Lightning jumped and crackled the length of the Keep, striking down those demons in its path. Rupert looked back at the gates, and saw a brightly glowing figure standing alone in the narrow gap between the two motionless doors. The glare was so blinding Rupert had to look away, but he knew who it was. He could feel the High Magic all around him, beating strongly on the night. Julia took him by his good arm, and began hurrying him back toward the gates.

"The Champion," he said thickly.

"He's dead, lad," said the King, moving in close on Rupert's other side. "The demons didn't leave enough of him to bury."

Together, Julia and the King half-led and half-carried Rupert back to the open gates, while the glowing figure's balefire threw back the demon horde again and again. A grimy smoke rose from the growing pile of demon dead that lay blocking the entrance to the Keep. Julia and the King hustled Rupert through the gates and into the courtyard. The glowing figure stepped back to join them, and the huge oaken doors finally slammed together. Harald and the men-at-arms pushed home the steel bolts, and began pulling barricades into position.

Rupert collapsed by the inner East wall, and Julia hadn't the strength to hold onto him. He stretched out full length on his back on the cobbles, and blood welled steadily out from beneath him. Julia sank down at his side, cradled his head in her lap, and gave herself up to what few tears she had left. King John sat with his back to the inner wall, his head hanging wearily down. Rockbreaker lay unnoticed by his side. The glowing figure at the gates moved slowly toward them, his light dying quickly away to reveal the High Warlock. His face was drawn with fatigue, and his hair was entirely gray.

Outside, the demons hammered on the closed gates till they sounded like some huge, unearthly drum.

CHAPTER NINE

In the Darkwood

Rupert lay on his back in the courtyard and wondered who was crying. The tear-choked voice seemed somehow familiar as it called his name, but he couldn't quite place it. He wanted to comfort whoever it was, but he didn't know how, and after a while the tears died away. Rupert knew he was in the courtyard, he could feel rough stone cobbles pressing into his back, but everything else seemed vague and far away. He didn't seem to hurt much anymore, and for a moment that worried him; but only for a moment. There was blood on his face and in his eyes, and when he tried to wipe it away, his hands wouldn't obey him. Someone was tugging at his chain mail, and the voice was calling his name again, but he didn't respond. It didn't seem important, and he was tired, so very tired.

Julia tried to remove Rupert's mail vest so that she could get at his wounds, but the buckles were slippery with blood, and she was so tired she couldn't even see straight any more. She struggled stubbornly with the buckles, cursing her clumsy fingers. Rupert hadn't moved since he collapsed, and the more Julia examined him, the more frightened she became. There was so much blood she couldn't tell one wound from another, and she couldn't seem to wake him. She started to wipe the blood from his face with a piece of rag, only to stop suddenly when she discovered he didn't have a right eye anymore. The empty socket stared blindly up at her, and she would have broken down and cried again, if there'd been any tears left in her. She started to call for help, but the words died unspoken on her lips as she stared around her.

The courtyard was a slaughterhouse, with the dead and the dying and the wounded lying side by side. Some of the army survivors just lay where they had fallen, too tired or too shocked by what they'd been through to move, even for food or water or help for their injuries. A few servants moved among the wounded, helping where they could, and women and children guarded the Castle battlements with improvised weapons.

High above the courtyard, the Blue Moon stared pitilessly down from the starless night, and outside the gates the demons beat unceasingly against the shuddering oaken doors.

King John got slowly to his feet, picked up Rockbreaker, and sheathed the sword without even looking at it. For all their legendary power, the Infernal Devices had been no match for the Darkwood. Now two of the blades were lost, and he had nothing left to set against the endless night. *It's all over,* he thought slowly. *We've lost. I tried everything I could think of, and we still lost.* For a moment he wanted to run away and hide, to barricade himself in his quarters and wait till the demons came for him, but he knew he couldn't do that. He was the King, and he had to set an example. Even if there was no point to it anymore. He nodded brusquely to Harald as his son approached, and then the two of them turned to look at Rupert and Julia.

"How is he?" asked the King, and then had to fight not to look away as he realized the extent of Rupert's injuries.

"He looks bad," said Harald, and Julia rounded on him fiercely.

"You left him out there to die, you bastard!"

Harald met her furious gaze calmly. "If the demons had got past him, we'd never have been able to close the doors in time. By holding the demons back, even if only for a few minutes, Rupert helped to save the lives of everyone in this Castle. He knew he didn't stand a chance when he went out into the Keep, but he also knew his duty. My duty was to get the gates closed, so that his sacrifice wouldn't have been in vain. I did what was right, Julia. I did what was necessary."

"You always do, Harald," said the King. He knelt painfully beside Julia, and put an arm round her shoulders.

"There must be something we can do," pleaded Julia. "We've got to do something. He's dying!"

"Yes," said King John softly. "I think he is. It was a

brave stand, while it lasted. The bravest thing I've ever seen."

"You can't die!" shouted Julia suddenly, and taking Rupert by the shoulders, she shook him desperately. "Wake up, damn you; I won't let you die!"

Harald and the King tried gently to pull her away, and she fought them.

"Let me through," said a tired voice, and Julia stopped struggling and looked quickly round as she recognized the High Warlock's voice.

"Help him! You're a sorcerer; help him!"

"If I can, lass." The Warlock moved slowly forward, walking carefully and deliberately, like an old man whose bones pained him. And then Julia realized with something of a shock that the Warlock was an old man. The hair that had been jet black was now a dirty gray streaked with white, and his face had sunk back to the bone, the flesh heavily lined and wrinkled. His hands were gnarled and twisted, and they trembled constantly as he held them over Rupert's bloodied chest. A brilliant light flared briefly at the Warlock's fingertips, and Rupert's wounds knit gradually together. The bleeding slowed and stopped, and Rupert's face relaxed a little, but he didn't waken. The High Warlock nodded grimly, and turned to Julia. She felt a warm glow move swiftly through her body, and then it vanished, taking her pains with it. Only her tiredness remained; that, and the bone-deep despair that tore at her heart every time she remembered how close she'd come to losing Rupert.

"Is that it?" she asked the Warlock anxiously. "Will he be all right?"

"I don't know, Julia. There's not much magic left in me now, but I've done all I can for him."

"What happened to your magic during the battle?" growled the King.

"We were betrayed," said the Warlock simply. "Just before the gates opened, a servant appeared with several jugs of wine, and presented them to us with your compliments. We were all very touched at the gesture, so we joked and laughed and drank you a toast. Several toasts, in fact. There was enough poison in that wine to kill an army. My magic was strong enough to throw off the effects, eventually, but the others never stood a chance. They started to fall just after the gates opened, choking and clawing at their throats. I held on as long as I could, and then the poison took me. When I finally recovered consciousness, I was surrounded by bodies, and the battle was over. I did my best for you, John, for as long as I could. I only wish it could have been more."

"Thomas Grey!" said the King suddenly. "He was with you!"

"He was lucky," said the Warlock. "He didn't care for the vintage, so he only drank a little. He and I were the only survivors; just the two of us, out of more than fifty."

"Who did this?" said Harald. "Who stabbed us in the back? I thought all the traitors were dead."

The Warlock shrugged. "The servant who brought us the wine is dead. Somebody used him, and then killed him so that he couldn't tell us who it was."

He broke off as Rupert suddenly stirred, and tried to sit up.

"Julia?"

"I'm here, Rupert." She put an arm around his shoulders to support him, and he shook his head slowly to clear it.

"How do you feel, son?" asked the King.

"Terrible," said Rupert. "But I'll survive."

"Of course," said Harald. "You always do."

"My eye hurts," said Rupert, and then froze as his fingers found only sealed eyelids where his right eye used to be. "My eye; what's happened to my eye?"

"Easy, lad," said the King, and Julia quickly grabbed Rupert's hand to stop him clawing at his face.

"I'm sorry, Rupert," said the High Warlock, quietly. "There's nothing more I can do."

Rupert swallowed hard, fighting back his panic. He felt maimed, crippled, even more than if he'd lost an arm or a leg. The world looked strange and different, seen through his one eye; it looked flat and somehow unreal, and he couldn't seem to judge distances properly. He remembered an old guard with one eye, who'd once told him something about depth perception, and how it had stopped him being a swordsman, and the panic surged up in him again.

"How the hell am I going to use a sword, with only one eye to guide me?"

"I wouldn't worry about it too much," drawled Harald.

"There are so many demons, all you have to do is keep swinging and you're bound to hit one, sooner or later."

For a moment Julia thought she would kill him for being so callous, and then she took her hand away from her sword as she realized Rupert was laughing.

"You bastard, Harald." Rupert grinned. "Trust you to put things in perspective."

"One of my more useful talents," said Harald. "Now, if you'll excuse me, I want to make sure the battlements are secure."

He bowed politely, and moved off into the courtyard. Julia watched him go, and shook her head.

"There are times," she said slowly, "when I don't understand that man at all."

"You're not alone," said the King dryly. He rubbed tiredly at his eyes. Julia looked at him closely.

"You look exhausted, John. How did your part of the battle go? Are you hurt?"

"Just cuts and bruises, my dear. And there's not much to tell about the battle. I led my men out, and I brought some of them back. For a time, I almost felt like a King again." He looked unflinchingly at the bodies lying heaped together on the bloodstained cobbles, and shook his head. "It wasn't worth the price."

"You went back with me to help save your son. I've never seen anything braver."

"Bravery isn't enough anymore," said the King. "Look around you, Julia. My army is broken, the Castle's under siege, and I haven't even got enough men left to guard the battlements. Twelve generations of my family built the Forest Kingdom and kept it strong. It only took one generation to see it all destroyed; one incompetent King."

"It wasn't your fault . . ."

"Wasn't it? The King is the Land, and the Land is the King. I failed as King, and now the Land is paying the price."

"Bull," said Julia. "You're a man like any other, and you did the best you could with an impossible situation. You mustn't blame yourself, John. The Darkwood doesn't care how brave or strong you are; it's a part of Nature, like an earthquake or a storm. You can't hope to beat it with swords and axes and armies."

"So what should I do? Give in?"

"No," said Julia sharply. "We go on fighting, but in a different way. We've tried armies and we've tried magic, and they've both failed us. Now there's only one way left. Think, John; what's the real heart of the Darkwood, what gives it life and purpose? The Demon Prince! Destroy him, and you destroy the Darkwood!"

"I don't believe I'm hearing this," said Rupert. "It's all we can do to hold the Castle against the demons, and you expect us to go traipsing off into the Darkwood in search of the Demon Prince himself? We wouldn't last five minutes out there!'"

"We've got to try!" said Julia. "It's our only hope now."

"Wait a minute," said Rupert. "I hate to suggest it, but how about another teleport spell? If he got it right, the Warlock could take us straight to the Demon Prince."

"No," said the Warlock quietly. "I don't have enough magic left to power that kind of spell."

"The dragon!" said Rupert. "He could fly us over the Darkwood!"

The High Warlock looked at him. "You've got a dragon? Here?"

"Sure," said Julia. "He's sleeping in the stables."

The Warlock shook his head slowly. "Nobody tells me anything."

"The last time I tried, I couldn't wake him," said Rupert. "Maybe you can, sir Warlock."

"It's worth a try. But I'll need to rest first."

"Very well," said King John. "I suggest we all get whatever rest we can. We'll meet again in an hour's time. Unless, of course, the demons get here first."

"You always were a gloomy bastard, John," said the High Warlock.

The Warlock sat alone at the bottom of the main entrance steps, brooding over the empty wine bottle in his hand. Only a few hours ago, he could have called up another bottle just by thinking about it, but now . . . He sighed glumly, and put the bottle down, carefully out of his line of sight. He remembered the drugged wine the servant had brought him, and smiled wryly. Maybe it was time he gave up drinking wine. Right now, he'd settle for a good brandy.

He wistfully considered raiding the King's wine cellars, but decided against it. The demons could come swarming over the walls at any time, and he had to be ready for them. He sighed again, and then glanced up as King John appeared before him.

"You look terrible."

"Thanks a lot, John."

"Your hair's gone gray."

"That's what being sober does for you."

King John smiled in spite of himself. "You're losing your magic, aren't you?"

"Looks like it. It's hardly surprising; I've cast more spells in the last twenty-four hours than I'd normally cast in a year. And fighting off the poison took a hell of a lot out of me. Now, every spell ages me a little more. I can feel the winter in my bones, and I'm starting to forget things. I hate it when I can't remember things."

"I know," said the King. "I feel the same way, sometimes. But in a way, it's a kind of blessing. After all, we both have things we'd rather not remember."

Julia unstrapped the long, silver scabbard from her back, and studied it thoughtfully. It looked different, now that it no longer contained the Infernal Device. The silver itself seemed dull and lusterless, and the ancient runes set deep into the metal held no meaning at all. Julia hefted the scabbard in her hands, and then threw it away. It fell among a pile of discarded weapons left by the returning army and, from a distance, it was just one more scabbard among many.

Julia leaned back against the inner East wall, and closed her eyes. If felt almost sinful to be resting, when everyone else was racing around the courtyard like a chicken about to have its head chopped off, but until the Warlock decided he was ready, there was nothing for her to do. So she sat down, leaned back against the wall, stretched out her legs, and had a little rest. She let one hand drop to the sword at her side, and smiled slightly. Rupert had given her that sword a long time ago, or so it seemed, and it had done good service by her. Which was more than she could say for Wolfsbane. She'd never been happy with that sword in her hand. She could have hung onto it, rather than letting it vanish into the earth along with the creature it was killing, but she'd chosen to let it go, and still felt she'd done the right thing. Wolfsbane was more than just a sword; much more. It was alive, and it was aware, and it had wanted her mind and her soul. And Julia knew that if she had used the sword long enough, it would have had them both. In the end, she'd given up the sword because she'd wanted so much to keep it.

She heard footsteps approaching. She opened her eyes just long enough to recognize Harald, and then closed them again.

"I see you've got rid of the scabbard," said Harald. "Probably a wise move. According to some legends, the Infernal Devices can never be destroyed, and if they're ever lost or thrown away, they will eventually find their way back to their scabbards."

"You believe that rubbish?" asked Julia, not bothering to open her eyes.

"I've seen a great many things recently that once I would never have believed possible," said Harald calmly. "That's why I threw away my scabbard."

Julia opened her eyes and looked at him. The scabbard was gone from Harald's back, and it seemed to Julia that he stood a little taller without it. Their eyes met for a moment, sharing a knowledge they would never reveal to anyone else, of how close they had come to being seduced and overpowered by the swords they'd carried. After a while, they looked away, perhaps because they didn't want to be reminded. They just wanted to forget.

"Do you think the Warlock will be able to wake the dragon?" asked Harald.

"I don't know. The dragon's been hibernating for months. Rupert thinks he may be dying."

"Well, Rupert has been known to be wrong, on occasion."

Julia looked at Harald steadily. "You would have shut those gates on him, wouldn't you?"

"How many more times, Julia? It was necessary. Somebody had to defend the Keep, so that the gates could be shut."

"Then why didn't you do it?"

Harald smiled. "I never was the heroic type."

"So I've noticed," said Julia, and getting to her feet, she walked away in search of Rupert.

*   *   *

Rupert leaned back against the locked stable door, and waited impatiently for the others to join him. It was still bitter cold in the courtyard, and he was beginning to wish he'd gone into the Castle proper and found himself a good thick cloak. He beat his hands together and blew on them, and then crossed his arms tightly across his chest. Cold. Always cold, these days. He looked hopefully round the bustling courtyard, but there was still no sign of any of the others. *I don't know why I bother being on time,* thought Rupert bitterly. *Nobody else ever is.* He drew his sword and put himself through a series of simple exercises, but the numbing cold made him awkward, and his lack of depth perception kept throwing him off. He finally gave up in disgust, and slammed his sword back into its scabbard. Like it or not, his days as a swordsman were definitely over. Maybe he should take up the axe instead; it was a lot harder to miss with an axe.

He gently ran his fingers over his sealed eyelids, and swore softly. His eye was gone, but it still hurt. He flexed his left arm and shoulder, and sniffed dourly. He supposed he should be grateful that at least something was working right again.

He frowned, remembering the way the unicorn had looked, lying sleeping in the stable. The groom had dosed the animal with a sleeping draught. He assured Rupert the unicorn would recover from his wounds eventually, but there had been more hope than conviction in the man's voice. Rupert sighed tiredly. Long before the unicorn could wake from his drugged sleep, the final battle would be over—one way or another.

He looked out across the crowded courtyard, and smiled suddenly as he spotted a familiar goblin hurrying past, carrying a bucket of steaming pitch almost as big as he was. Rupert called after him, and the goblin looked back, startled. He grinned broadly on seeing Rupert, and came back to join him. He dumped the bucket on the ground beside them, swearing horribly at the pitch when it looked for a moment as though it might slop over the sides. He started to offer Rupert his hand, but saw the condition of it just in time, and decided on a snappy salute instead.

"Hello, Princie," said the smallest goblin cheerfully. "How you doing?"

"No so bad, considering," said Rupert. "I just wondered if you knew how your friends got on in the battle. I got separated from the main bulk of the army early on, and I rather lost track of things."

"They all died," said the goblin matter-of-factly, "Every single one of them. They did their best, but goblins weren't made for fighting, or being brave."

"I'm sorry," said Rupert. "I didn't know."

"Our leader died with them," said the smallest goblin. "He insisted on leading his men into battle. He was never really happy as leader, but he was all we had. He tried hard. Poor bastard; he never really got over the death of his family in the first demon raid."

"So who's leader now?" asked Rupert.

The smallest goblin grinned broadly. "Me, of course; who else? I may not know much about fighting and heroics, but I'm an expert when it comes to dirty tricks and booby traps. Now then, if you'll excuse me, I'd better get this bucket up to the battlements before the pitch cools off. Wait till those demons try climbing up the outer walls; they won't know what's hit them!"

He chuckled nastily, grabbed up his bucket, and scurried back into the crowd. Rupert watched him go, while in his mind's eye he saw again the biggest goblin he'd ever known, hunched inside ill-fitting bronze armor, and growling sarcastically behind an evil-looking cigar. A goblin who'd once asked Rupert if he could teach the goblins how to forget, because they'd never learned how, and there was so much they wanted to forget . . .

Someone called Rupert's name, and he quickly turned to see Julia and the High Warlock come walking out of the crowd toward him.

"I've got something for you," said Julia cheerfully, and handed Rupert a length of black silk. He looked at it dubiously.

"It's very nice, Julia. What is it?"

"It's an eye patch, silly. Try it on."

Rupert opened it out, and after a few false starts, pulled the strap over his head and eased the patch into position. He glanced self-consciously at Julia. "Well? How does it look?"

"You look very rakish," said Julia, cocking her head on

one side to better admire the effect. "Just like the pirates in my story books when I was a girl."

"Thanks a bunch," growled Rupert. He glared at the Warlock, daring him to say anything, and the Warlock turned quickly away to study the stables. He gazed skeptically at the rambling, broken-down building, and looked distinctly unimpressed.

"Are you sure you've got a dragon in there?"

"He chose the stable," said Julia. "And I for one wasn't going to argue the point."

"Quite," said the Warlock. "How did you persuade him to come here in the first place?"

"I rescued him from a Princess," said Rupert, and Julia nodded solemnly. The High Warlock looked at them both, and decided not to ask any more questions. He didn't think he really wanted to know.

Rupert unlocked the door, and pushed it open. Darkness filled the old timbered building, though bare slivers of light showed through the boarded-up windows. Rupert took a torch from its bracket by the door, and lit it with his flint and steel. The sudden flame pushed back the darkness, and the stable leapt into being before them. The empty stalls were full of shadows, and the low, thatched ceiling showed dimly through the gloom. Rupert moved slowly forward into the stable, followed by Julia and the High Warlock.

Their footsteps echoed dully on the still air, and the torchlight constantly jumped and flickered, though none of them could feel any draught. They found the dragon at the rear of the stables, curled up in a nest of dirty straw. His great folded wings rose and fell in time to the slow steady burr of his breathing. Rupert stared silently at the sleeping dragon, and felt a hot flush of shame run through him. The dragon had been hurt in the Darkwood, because of him. Hurt so badly that the creature was still sleeping off his wounds months later. Hurt, and maybe dying. And now here he was again, hoping to wake the dragon so that he could ask him to risk his life in the Darkwood one more time. Rupert felt tired, and guilty, and not a little ashamed, but he was still going to do it. The dragon was the only chance the Forest Land had left.

The High Warlock whistled quietly as he took in the size

of the dragon, and nodded thoughtfully. "How long has he been sleeping like this?"

"Two, three months," said Julia. "He never really got over the beating he took on our first journey through the Darkwood. Once we got here, he took to sleeping most of the time, until finally we couldn't wake him at all."

The Warlock frowned. "Odd; dragons don't usually take long to heal. Either a wound kills them, or it doesn't."

He moved in close beside the dragon, and passed his hand slowly over the creature's head. A pale, scintillating glow formed briefly around the sleeping dragon, and then vanished. The dragon slept on, undisturbed. The High Warlock stepped back, nodding grimly to himself.

"As I thought; he's been under this spell for months."

"A spell? You mean this sleep isn't natural?" burst out Rupert. "Somebody's been deliberately keeping him like this?"

"I'm afraid so," said the High Warlock. "And whoever cast this spell must still be around somewhere, or it would have collapsed by now."

"I can't believe it," said Julia. "I just can't believe it. *Another* damned traitor? There can't be! The only ones with a grudge against King John were Darius and his conspirators, and they're all either dead or in exile. Who else is there that could be a traitor?"

"No use looking at me," said the Warlock. "I'm rather out of touch with Forest politics."

"Whoever it is would have to be after the crown for himself," said Rupert slowly. "Nothing else would be worth taking these kind of risks for. So we're looking for someone who wants to be King . . . or who can't wait to be King."

"No," said Julia. "It can't be."

"Why not?"

"Because . . . he just wouldn't, that's why not. He turned against the conspirators who would have made him a King!"

"From what I can gather, if he had gone along with them he'd have ended up as nothing more than a figurehead for the Barons."

"Perhaps I'm being a little slow," said the Warlock testily, "but who the hell are you talking about?"

"Harald," said Rupert grimly. "My brother, the Prince Harald. He always was . . . ambitious."

"Harold," said the Warlock thoughtfully. "I remember him as a boy. Big, healthy lad; very fond of hunting. I was his tutor for a while, but I don't recall him ever showing much aptitude for magic."

"There you are," said Julia quickly. "Our traitor has to be a pretty powerful magician."

"Not necessarily," said Rupert. "They never did find the Curtana."

"The Sword of Compulsion!" said Julia. "Of course; that was what the King intended to use against the demons in the first place."

"Exactly," said Rupert. "Only it got lost during the conspiracy. The Landsgraves swore they never had it, and I'm inclined to believe them. I've seen the wards that protected the Infernal Devices, and they were specifically keyed to the Royal line. Anyone else trying to take the swords would have been killed instantly. It seems only logical that the Curtana would have been protected in the same way."

"So whoever took the sword had to be a member of the Royal family," said the High Warlock slowly.

"Yeah," said Rupert. "My father, Harald, or me. Now I was away when the sword disappeared, and it doesn't make sense for the King to have taken it, so that only leaves . . . Harald."

"That doesn't make sense, either," said Julia stubbornly. "If he had the Curtana, he would have used it by now. He certainly wouldn't have gone out to face the demons without it."

Rupert shrugged. "Maybe there's some reason why he can't use the sword yet. Look, it has to be Harald; there's nobody else it can be."

"No," said Julia. "I don't believe it."

"You mean you don't want to believe it," said Rupert. "From what I've heard, you and Harald got pretty close while I was away."

"And just what is that supposed to mean?"

"You know damn well what I mean."

"Don't you shout at me!"

"I am not shouting!"

"SHUT UP!" roared the High Warlock, and glared impatiently at both of them until they fell silent. "Worse than children, the pair of you. Now is it too much to ask, or could we please concentrate on the matter at hand? Namely, the sleeping bloody dragon!"

"Sorry," muttered Julia, and Rupert mumbled something conciliatory. The two of them traded apologetic glances and smiles as the Warlock turned away to study the sleeping dragon. He stood glowering a moment, and then stretched out his arms before him. A faint, shimmering glow fell from his hands, only to fade away before it reached the dragon's scales. The Warlock scowled, and tried again. This time, the glow was much brighter, but it still couldn't reach the dragon. The High Warlock muttered something extremely vulgar under his breath, and raised his arms above his head in the stance of summoning. A brief crimson glow flared around his hands and was gone, and a vivid crackling flame was suddenly dancing unsupported on the air before him. It sank slowly toward the sleeping dragon, and then flared and sputtered, bobbing back and forth on the air as though pressing against some invisible barrier. The Warlock spoke a few words in a strange, fluid language that echoed disturbingly on the still air. His face beaded with sweat, and his hands shook, but still the flame hovered in midair, unable to move any closer to the sleeping dragon. The High Warlock braced himself, and spoke aloud a single Word of Power. His mouth gaped wide in agony as, for a moment, a brilliant light roared up around him, and then it was suddenly gone, and the crimson flame sank slowly down and into the dragon's gleaming scales. The air in the stable felt suddenly different, as though a barely felt tension had just snapped, and disappeared. The dragon stirred fretfully, and then his great golden eyes crept open, and he lifted his massive head up out of the dirty straw. Julia threw her arms around his neck, and hugged him fiercely.

"Oh dragon . . . dragon!"

"Julia? What's wrong, Julia?"

"Nothing. Nothing's wrong, now that you're back."

The dragon looked at Rupert, and his eyes widened slightly.

"Rupert," he said slowly. "You're back. How long have I slept?"

"Two or three months," said Rupert, smiling. "Welcome back, dragon. It's good to see you again."

"It's good to see you again, Rupert. Julia and I were getting rather worried about you. Did you say *months?*"

"That's right," said Julia, releasing him. "The Darkwood has fallen over the Castle, the demon horde is battering at our gates, and any moment now they could all come swarming over our walls and slaughter the lot of us."

"Nothing changes," said the dragon, yawning widely. The High Warlock studied the hundreds of gleaming teeth, and was visibly impressed. "I don't suppose you brought me anything to eat, did you?" said the dragon.

"Dragon . . ." said Julia.

"I know," said the dragon mildly. "We're all in imminent danger of being killed. But I've been asleep for months, and used as I am to hibernating for long periods, right now I'm hungry. Very hungry. Several roast chickens for starters, I think, and then maybe a cow or two. Or three."

"Dragon," said Rupert. "We need you to fly us over the Darkwood, in search of the Demon Prince. Will you do it?"

"Of course," said the dragon. "Right after dinner."

The Warlock looked at Rupert and Julia. "I always knew there was a reason why dragons never caught on as pets."

Ice formed on the inner Castle walls, and the cobblestones became treacherous underfoot. A dozen wrought-iron braziers burned fiercely in the courtyard, but did little to dispell the bitter cold that hung about the Castle like a numbing shroud. The wounded had all been taken inside the Castle, where some warmth was still to be found, and the dragon sat alone in the middle of the courtyard, eating his way steadily through a large pile of assorted meats. A few guards and men-at-arms were busy strengthening the barricades at the main gates, looking like slow clumsy bears in their huge fur cloaks and gloves. Outside the Castle walls, the endless night was still and silent.

Rupert and Julia stood at the bottom of the main entrance steps, wrapped in thick fur cloaks, talking quietly together. They stopped talking, and moved closer together, as King John appeared suddenly from the main entrance and made his way down the steps to join them. Rupert and Julia bowed formally, and the King nodded briefly in return.

"I like the eyepatch," said King John. "Very piratical."

"Now don't you start," said Rupert. "So help me, if one more guard asks me to sing him a sea shanty, I'll flatten him."

"Never mind, dear," said Julia soothingly. "When all this is over, I'll buy you a glass eye."

"I can hardly wait," said Rupert coldly.

King John decided it might be a good time to change the subject. "How long before the dragon will be ready to fly?" he asked quickly.

"Shouldn't be long now," said Rupert. "We've just about run out of meat."

"The Demon Prince," said Julia thoughtfully. "What does he look like?"

"Nobody knows," said the King. "No one's ever met him, and lived to tell of it."

"Great," said Julia. "Just great. How are we supposed to find him, if we don't even know what he looks like?"

"Thomas Grey will lead you to him," said the King. "Now, if you'll excuse me for a moment . . ." He bowed quickly and walked away, heading for a nearby brazier where the Astrologer and the High Warlock were warming their hands and quietly exchanging trade secrets. The Astrologer looked up when he heard the King approaching, and then murmured something to the High Warlock, who immediately bowed politely and moved unhurriedly away to talk to the dragon. The King nodded brusquely to the Astrologer, and moved in beside him to warm his hands at the glowing coals.

"Thomas, we have to talk."

"Of course, John."

"The dragon's about ready. It won't be long now."

"Good. Every hour I think it can't get any colder, and every hour it does."

"Thomas . . ." The King gazed steadily into the brazier, as though looking for inspiration in the crackling flames. "I never imagined it would come to this. The Land in ruins, the Castle under siege, so many dead; and all because of us."

"Don't blame yourself, John. How could we ever have imagined anything like this?"

"We should have."

"We did what we thought was best."

"And my brave Champion is dead. If he hadn't made that stand on the drawbridge, the Castle would have been overrun by now. He saved us all. And he died out there, alone in the darkness, not even knowing whether he'd succeeded or failed. I miss him, Thomas. It feels strange, not having him at my side. He had his faults, but he was brave, and loyal, and even honorable, in his way. In all the Kingdom, he was perhaps the only man I ever really trusted."

The Astrologer raised an eyebrow. "The only one, John?"

The King laughed suddenly, and clapped the Astrologer on the back. "And you, of course, Thomas. I'd trust you with my life."

"I saw you talking to Rupert," said the Astrologer. "Have you told him we're going with him into the Darkwood?"

"Not yet," said the King. "He's going to take a lot of persuading. That's what I wanted to talk to you about. I think we should tell him the truth. All of it."

The Astrologer stiffened, and looked at him sharply. "Do you think that's wise, John?"

"I don't know, Thomas. But I do think it's necessary."

Rupert watched curiously as King John left the Astrologer and started back toward him. He saw the Astrologer reach out as though to stop the King, and then his arm slowly dropped as he changed his mind. And in that brief moment Rupert saw that the Astrologer was wearing a sword on his hip, carefully hidden out of sight under his cloak. Rupert grinned harshly. It would appear the Astrologer wasn't as confident in his sorcery as he liked to pretend, if he needed a sword on his hip to back him up. He quickly wiped the smile from his face as the King drew near. He felt Julia slip her arm through his, and he squeezed it gently against his side. Right now, he could use a little moral support. The King stopped before him, and then hesitated, as though unsure how best to proceed.

"You don't have to go back into the Darkwood, Rupert. You've gone through it so many times now . . ."

"That's why I have to do it again. No one else has the experience I have."

"And I'm going with him," said Julia firmly. "He needs someone to guard his back. Someone he can trust."

The King frowned. "How many people can the dragon carry, altogether?"

"Four, at most," said Rupert. "So far there's us, and the High Warlock . . ."

"No," said the Warlock, coming over from where he'd

been talking with the dragon. Rupert noted absently that the Warlock's hair was almost entirely white.

"What do you mean, no?" said Julia. "We need you!"

"I'm sorry, Julia," said the Warlock quietly, "But waking the dragon took practically everything I had. With so much Wild Magic loose in the world, it's all I can do to control what little magic I have left. Take the Astrologer instead; he still has some magic. I'll stay here, and give the Castle what protection I can. My power will return in time. If the demons would just hold off for twenty-four hours, I could still give them a run for their money."

"The *Astrologer?*" said Julia incredulously. "You've got to be joking! We need a real sorcerer. Look, the Castle can't stand against the demons no matter what you do, but you're the only one of us who stands any chance against the Demon Prince!"

"No, Julia," said the Warlock. "There's nothing more I can do for you."

"Thomas Grey is a fine sorcerer," said the King. "And he has a way to lead us directly to the Demon Prince."

Rupert looked at him quickly. "Us? What do you mean, *us?*"

The King met his gaze squarely. "I mean, I'm going with you."

"You can't," said Rupert flatly. "You're needed here."

"As Julia has just pointed out, the Castle will fall anyway if the Demon Prince isn't stopped," said the King evenly. "I have to go with you, Rupert; because, without me, you don't have a hope in hell of destroying the Demon Prince."

"Why? Because you're carrying Rockbreaker?" said Rupert, eyeing the long swordhilt standing up behind the King's shoulder.

"Partly," said the King. "But there is another reason."

"Let me tell them, John," said the Astrologer, moving quickly forward to stand beside the King. His face was pinched and drawn, and his hands clenched and unclenched at his sides. He looked quickly about him, almost angrily, and when he spoke his voice was flat and harsh. "John and I have to go with you. We were there at the beginning of this evil; we have no choice but to be there at its ending."

"I don't understand," said Rupert, looking from the Astrologer to King John and seeing something in their faces he couldn't quite put a name to.

"It's all our fault," said the King quietly. "All the deaths, all the destruction. All our fault."

"How?" said the High Warlock. "How is it your fault?"

"We were the ones who first summoned the Demon Prince back to the world of men," said King John.

For a long time, nobody said anything. The Astrologer looked almost pathetically defiant, his eyes darting from face to face like a cornered animal's. The King looked tired and defeated, but still his dignity hung about him in scraps and tatters, and he didn't flinch from Rupert's horrified gaze.

"Why?" said Rupert finally.

"The Barons were out of control," said the Astrologer. "They were ruining the Kingdom with their endless intrigues and jealousies. They had to be brought back into line. It seemed to us that a single, big enough threat might be sufficient to unite the Barons in a common cause, and bring them back under the central authority of the Crown."

"That was the plan," said the King. "We thought that if it didn't work out, all we had to do was reverse the spell, and we could send the Demon Prince back to the darkness he came from."

"You fools," said the High Warlock. "You bloody fools."

"Yes," said the King. "Old, frightened fools. But we were younger then, and we thought we knew what we were doing. It all went wrong, right from the start. We drew the pentacle, and Thomas set the wards. I lit the candles at the stars' points, and he set the holy water at the vales. I can remember it all so clearly, even after so many years. We said the words, and summoned him by name, and then the darkness fell on us like a ravening animal. I couldn't see, couldn't breathe, but I could feel something moving close at hand; something awful. And then I heard Thomas screaming, and I tried to get to him, but I couldn't find him in the darkness. Finally I passed out, and when I awoke the darkness was gone, and poor Thomas lay unconscious at my side.

"The years passed, and there was no sign of the Demon Prince. We thought we'd got away with it, and that he had simply returned to the darkness from which we'd summoned him. And then, just recently, demons appeared in the Tanglewood, and the Darkwood's boundaries began to spread."

"Wait a minute," said Rupert. "When exactly did you summon the Demon Prince?"

"Thirty-two years ago."

"But, that was when . . ."

"Yes, Rupert," said the King. "That was when we lost the South Wing."

"I was away from Court, that summer," said the High Warlock. "I always wondered why you were so evasive about what you'd been up to in that South Tower. Why didn't you talk to me first? I could have warned you . . ."

"You would have talked me out of it," said the King. "And I didn't want to be talked out of it."

"Figures," said the Warlock. "All right, where did you and the Astrologer get the kind of power you'd need for that kind of summoning?"

"We used the Curtana," said the Astrologer. "I teleported John and myself into the Armory, John took the sword, and I teleported us out again. Nobody ever knew we were there."

"I didn't know you could teleport," said Rupert.

The Astrologer smiled coldly. "There are lots of things you don't know about me."

"So you took the Curtana," said Julia. "No wonder the Seneschal couldn't find it. You sent us on a wild-goose chase!"

"No," said King John. "That was the problem. Thomas and I returned the sword to the Armory before we left the South Wing, thirty-two years ago. It should still have been there."

Rupert and Julia looked quickly at each other. "Then who's got the sword now?" said Rupert slowly.

The King shrugged. "Once I'd broken the protective wards, anyone could have taken the sword. Darius must have been in and out of the South Wing all the time, using those damned tunnels of his. He probably took the Curtana as insurance, in case his schemes came unstuck, and then forget where he hid it in his madness. And now that Darius is dead, the odds are we'll never find the Curtana. It could be anywhere in those tunnels; anywhere at all."

"Perhaps it's just as well," said Rupert. "The Curtana never brought anyone anything but grief."

"We seem to have strayed from the subject," said the Astrologer. "The point is that John and I have to go with you; since we summoned the Dark Prince in the first place, he can't be banished or destroyed without our cooperation."

Rupert glanced at the High Warlock. "Is that right, sir Warlock?"

"I'm afraid so, Rupert. That's what the legends say."

"Legends," muttered Rupert disgustedly. "It always comes back to bloody legends."

"I have a right to face the Demon Prince again," said King John. "Despite all I may have done, I am still King of the Forest Land, and I will have a reckoning for what has been done to the Land."

"John," said the High Warlock. "If you go back into the Darkwood, the chances are you won't be coming back again."

"I know that," said the King. "But we all aspire to moments of nobility. It's the best any of us can hope for."

"Let's go," said Rupert. "The longer we stand here talking, the likelier it is the demons will come scrambling over our walls. Dragon! Are you nearly ready?"

"Of course, Rupert," said the dragon calmly. "Climb aboard, and we can be on our way."

Rupert and Julia headed for the dragon, followed by the Astrologer. The King stopped short as Harald appeared from the main entrance. He waited patiently for his eldest son to come down and join him, and they stood together a moment, neither quite sure what to say.

"If we don't come back," said King John abruptly, "You will be King, Harald. Keep the Land alive, any way you have to. The night can't last forever. If the demons come over the walls or through the gates, fall back into the inner Castle and block off the entrance corridors. Keep pulling back; make them fight for every room, every gallery. This Castle was built to withstand any siege. There are enough secret passageways in this place to keep the demons running in circles for years. Keep your wits about you, and you might just make it. Don't fail the Land, Harald. Don't fail the Land."

"I won't, Father," said Harald. "You'd better go now; the others are waiting. Good luck."

Rupert and Julia watched from the dragon's back as Harald and the King embraced each other. Julia shot a glance at the

Astrologer, waiting patiently beside the dragon, and then put her arms around Rupert's waist, and leaned forward so that her mouth was by his ear.

"Do you think we should say something?" she asked quietly. "If Harald is the traitor . . ."

"What could we say?" murmured Rupert. "We've no proof against him. You heard the King; with the wards broken, anyone could have taken the Curtana."

"But leaving him in charge of the Castle . . ."

"There's nothing we can do, Julia. For now."

They fell silent as the King hurried over to the dragon and climbed awkwardly up onto his back, followed by the Astrologer. Everyone settled themselves more or less comfortably, and the dragon stretched out his wings and flexed them experimentally.

"Stiff," he muttered. "Very stiff."

"Are you sure you're up to this, dragon?" asked Rupert. "There are four of us, and it could be a long flight . . ."

"Do I tell you how to use a sword?" said the dragon. "Of course I'm up to it. You just hang on tight, and I'll get you there. I just hope someone knows where we're going. Oh, and Rupert . . ."

"Yes?"

"Next time, try and wake me before things get this desperate."

Rupert was still searching for a suitably venemous reply when the dragon surged suddenly to his feet. Rupert grabbed quickly for the dragon's neck as the huge membranous wings beat strongly to either side of him, and then, with a stomach-wrenching jolt, the dragon threw himself into the air. The courtyard fell slowly away beneath him, just as the demons finally came swarming over the Castle walls. Rupert watched in horror as they quickly fought their way past the defender on the battlements, and spilled down into the courtyard. The High Warlock stood alone, balefire blazing from his hands, as the demons came at him from every side. The main gates burst open, the thick oaken doors splintering like kindling, and the courtyard was suddenly full of leaping, clawing demons.

And then the Castle fell away behind the dragon, and was lost in the darkness. Below him lay nothing but the Darkwood, gleaming eerily under the light of the full Blue Moon.

*   *   *

"It's all over," said Rupert dully. "The demons have won."

"We've got to turn back!" said Julia. "Dragon . . ."

"No," said the King. "We go on. There's nothing else we can do."

The dragon flew on into the darkness, and for a long time nobody said anything. Bitterly cold air rushed past them, cutting fiercely at their bare hands and faces. Rupert felt Julia huddle in close behind him, and he tried to shield her body from the wind with his own. The night sky was empty of stars, but the Blue Moon filled the darkness with an ancient power. The Wild Magic roared upon the night like a giant heartbeat, strange and whimsical and utterly inhuman. Far below him, Rupert could sense things waking and moving that had no place in the time of Man. The world itself seemed to be changing subtly as the dragon carried his passengers deeper into the night. More and more, Rupert had the feeling that it was they who were out of place; that the world had moved on, and he and his kind no longer belonged.

The power of the full Blue Moon; to reshape reality itself.

Rupert shook his head quickly to clear it. So far, nothing had been done to the Land itself that could not be undone by the Demon Prince's death. At least, that was what he'd been told. Rupert frowned. He was no longer sure he believed much of what he was told.

"How are you managing, dragon?" Rupert asked, as much for the comfort of hearing his own voice as anything else.

"I feel fine," said the dragon, his wings moving easily in a strong steady rhythm. "I feel . . . young again. My bones no longer ache, my wind is sound, and I can see forever. I'd forgotten how good it felt to be young. It's the Wild Magic, Rupert; I can feel it, singing in my blood. The Wild Magic, loose in the world again, just as it was in my younger days. The days before the coming of Man."

"Was that a better time for you?" asked Rupert slowly.

"Better?" The dragon fell silent for a while, and his great brow furrowed as he flew steadily on into the night. "It was . . . different."

The Darkwood stretched away beneath them, an endless tangled mass of interlocking branches. Gnarled and twisted boughs curled together in an intricate embrace of rotting wood. Savage thorns thrust up through the Darkwood roof, some dappled with recent bloodstains. Shimmering blue moonlight glistened on the decaying branches, and the sweet stench of corruption was everywhere.

"This may well be a stupid question," said Julia, "But how are we supposed to find the Demon Prince through all that? It'll take us hours to cut our way through, with no guarantee we're even in the right place."

"I'll find the Demon Prince," said the Astrologer grimly. "My magic will lead us right to him."

"And what are we going to do when we find him?" asked Julia.

"Destroy him," said the King. "The Land cries out for vengeance."

"Sure," said Julia. "Destroy him. Just like that. You haven't the faintest idea of how to go about it, have you?"

"We'll do what we can," said Rupert. "We'll try cold steel first. If that doesn't work, we'll try magic. If that doesn't work, the dragon can breathe fire on him."

"And if that doesn't work?"

"Then we're in big trouble."

"Great," said Julia. "Just great."

The endless canopy of interwoven branches flowed steadily away beneath them like a solid unmoving ocean. The oppressive horror of the long night was a little easier to bear above the Darkwood itself, but still the darkness pressed in around the dragon. It weighed heavily on his wings, and grew stronger the farther he flew into the night, almost as though it was trying to force him back. Rupert could feel a pressure mounting against them as they flew on, and the dragon had to labor harder and harder to maintain his pace. The beating of his wings took on a more urgent rhythm, and his breathing became harsh and strained. There were voices in the darkness, muttering and laughing and screaming, and more than once Rupert felt a soft, unsettling touch on his hands or face. He didn't know whether the others could feel anything, and didn't ask. He didn't want to know. He kept wanting to let go of the dragon's neck and strike out at the darkness around him, to make whatever it was keep their distance, but he didn't. He couldn't afford to lose control now, not even for a moment. *Easy, lad, easy,* he thought determinedly. *They're just trying to spook you, that's all. Don't let them know how well they're succeeding.*

"Down there," said the Astrologer suddenly, pointing out and to his left. "There's a kind of clearing, covered over. That's where we'll find the Demon Prince."

"Are you sure?" asked the King.

"Oh yes, John," said the Astrologer. "I'm sure."

The dragon looked quickly back to see where the Astrologer was pointing, and then turned and glided down toward the roof of the Darkwood. The huge thorns rose up to meet him. At the last moment the dragon spread his jaws wide, and bright, roaring flames spilled out onto the thorns and branches, eating through them like acid. The flames couldn't seem to take a lasting hold on the dead wood, but they quickly opened up a hole in the canopy large enough for the dragon to fall through, his wings pressed tight against his sides. The moonlight was suddenly gone, and the dragon plummeted into darkness. He stretched his wings wide to slow his fall, and then he slammed into the ground, almost spilling his passengers from his back. For a long moment, nobody moved. All around them there was nothing but the night, still and silent and deadly.

"Did anyone think to bring a lantern?" whispered Julia.

The dragon coughed politely, and a brief gush of fire fell from his mouth. It caught hold on one small patch of lichens and oily mosses that covered the floor, and the clearing was suddenly filled with a leaping, wavering light. Rupert swung down from the dragon's back, carefully avoiding the fire. It seemed to be burning well and steadily, but showed no signs of spreading. Rupert nodded slowly, satisfied for the moment, and drawing his sword he moved quietly away from the dragon while the others were dismounting.

The clearing wasn't very large, no more than forty feet in diameter, with half a dozen pathways leading off. In the exact center of the clearing stood a single rotting tree stump, roughly fashioned into the shape of a throne. Fresh blood-stains spotted the decaying wood. Rupert glanced up at the break in the canopy overhead, but there was no trace of the Blue Moon or its light, only a darkness that went on forever. Julia came over to stand beside Rupert, her sword in her hand. They shared a quick smile, and then Julia went back to searching the surrounding darkness for signs of movement. The King and the Astrologer stood together beside the rotting throne.

"Is that fire wise?" asked the King quietly. "Surely the light will tell the demons we're here?"

The Astrologer smiled coldly. "They'll know we're here soon enough, John."

"This place is disgusting," said Julia, stepping gingerly over a pile of blood-spattered bones, some still with shreds of meat clinging to them. The mossy floor squelched blood as she trod on it.

"All right, sir Astrologer," said Rupert finally. "You led us here. Where's the Demon Prince?"

"You want him?" said the Astrologer. "Then I'll call him. Master! They're here! I've brought them to you!"

Rupert and Julia stared at him in horror, and then leapt forward, sword in hand, but before they could reach the Astrologer, a massive weight slammed them to the ground and pinned them there. Rupert struggled fiercely against the unseen force holding him, but it was all he could do to lift his face out of the blood-soaked moss on the floor. His sword was gone from his hand, and he couldn't even turn his head to see where it had fallen. He could just make out the King lying helpless on the ground nearby, while beyond him the dragon lay heaving and writhing at the edge of the clearing, unable to rise. The Astrologer laughed quietly. Inch by inch, Rupert raised his head to look at him. Thomas Grey was lounging at his ease on the rotting throne, and in his hands was a glowing sword with a dull black jewel set in its crosspiece.

"What's happening?" groaned Julia. "Why can't I move?"

"It's his sword," said the King painfully. "It's the Curtana. He must have had it all along."

"Of course," said the Astrologer. "I had to be sure you were in a fit state to greet my master."

"Welcome," said a soft, sibilant voice from out of the shadows. "Welcome, my dear friends. I've been waiting for you."

Rupert fought to keep his head up as he watched a tall spindly figure slowly form itself out of the darkness at the edge of the clearing. It gradually took on depth and weight and reality, like a nightmare creating itself in flesh and bone. The Demon Prince stood fully eight feet tall, his body emaciated to the point of starvation. His lambent dead-white skin was wrapped in black rags and tatters, and two crimson eyes burned unblinkingly from under the wide brim of his large, battered hat. What little could be seen of the Demon Prince's face gave the impression of being blurred and unfinished. He smiled slowly at his enemies lying helpless on the clearing floor, his wide slash of a mouth full of pointed teeth, and then he moved forward with the sudden darting grace of a spider, and snatched Rockbreaker from its scabbard on the King's back. The sword seemed almost to shudder in the long, skeletal hand.

"And interesting toy," said the Demon Prince. "There was a time when it might even have been of some use against me."

He broke the sword across his knee in one swift movement, and threw the pieces aside. Far away, Rupert thought he heard something scream in agony, and then fell silent. The Demon Prince turned to the Astrologer, and reached out an imperious hand. Thomas Grey leapt immediately to his feet and hurried over to present his master with the Curtana. The Dark Prince hefted the sword in his hand, and the glowing steel blade burst into searing flames. Within the space of a few seconds, nothing remained of the Sword of Compulsion but a pool of molten metal steaming on the ground, with a few dull jewels floating in it. Rupert quickly tested the compulsion that held him. It seemed a little weaker, but its hold still lingered on under the influence of the Wild Magic.

"You have done well, my slave," said the Demon Prince to the bowing Astrologer. "All my enemies are now gathered in one place, and the only remaining swords that might have harmed me are now destroyed."

He broke off suddenly, and darted over to where Julia was reaching out her hand to retrieve the sword she'd dropped. She'd just wrapped her fingers round the swordhilt when the Demon Prince brought his heel down hard. The sound of her bones breaking was eerily loud on the silence. The Demon Prince ground Julia's crushed fingers under his heel, but she wouldn't cry out. He chuckled quietly, enjoying the agony in her face, and then he lifted his foot away and turned back to the Astrologer. Even in the dim light, Rupert could see that Julia's hand was now nothing more than a mess of blood and splintered bones. She tried to lift her sword anyway, and it fell from her crippled hand. The Demon Prince didn't even look round. He seated himself elegantly on his throne of decaying wood, with the Astrologer at his right hand, and looked coldly upon his fallen enemies.

"Well?" said the Demon Prince, his quiet voice subtly grating on the ear. "Have you nothing to say to me? After all, you've waited so long to meet me . . . what about you, dragon? We're two of a kind, you and I. We can still remember when the world was young, and we were powers on the earth. Things have changed since then, since Man came into the world. You've grown old, dragon; old and weak. Magic was going out of the world, and you were going with it. But now the Blue Moon is full, and the Wild Magic has returned. Forget the humans, serve me; and watched the dragonkind grow strong again."

The dragon slowly lifted his great head, fighting grimly against the geas that held him prisoner.

"Answer me," said the Demon Prince.

"Rot in hell," said the dragon. "Julia and Rupert are my friends, and I'll not betray them to a Prince of decaying trees."

Fire roared from his mouth, only to fall harmlessly to the ground, unable to reach the Demon Prince. The flames sputtered on the oily moss, and went out.

"Foolish animal," said the Demon Prince. "Go to sleep."

The dragon's eyes closed, and his head fell heavily to the ground. The Demon Prince moved over to stand before him, and kicked him in the face. Golden blood trickled down the dragon's muzzle. The Demon Prince kicked him again.

Rupert slowly pulled one leg up under him, fighting the geas every inch of the way. He could see his sword, lying on the ground between him and the King, but it was well out of reach. One good jump would be enough to get him to it, but as yet the compulsion was still too strong. Rupert slowly brought his other leg into position, and waited with a cold and patient fury for the geas to die away.

"You planned this all along, Thomas," said King John dully. The light had gone out of his eyes, and his face was an empty mask, wiped clean by pain and shock. "You poisoned your fellow sorcerers."

The Astrologer chuckled happily.

"Why?" groaned the King. "Why turn against the Forest? Against me?"

"Answer him, slave," said the Demon Prince. "His despair amuses me."

"You, John," said Thomas Grey, smiling crookedly. "You and your damned throne. Thirty years and more I spent propping you up, making your decisions for you, but what did I ever get out of it? All those years living in your shadow, doing your dirty work, while you had all the wealth and the power. I could have been somebody, John! I could have been somebody in my own right, maybe even a Sorcerer Supreme! But I gave that up to go with you, because you needed me. I would have made a far better King than you. Lots of people said so, but no, I stayed loyal. You were my friend. And then, years later, I finally realized I had no more power or station or wealth of my own than the day I first followed you to Court to be your Astrologer!"

John stared at him, tears rolling unheeded down his sunken cheeks. "Thomas . . . we've been friends since we were children together . . ."

"Children grow up, John."

"Do you really hate me so much?"

"More than you can imagine, John. I've looked forward to this moment for years. A great many years."

"You . . ." said John slowly. "You were the one who first suggested we call the Demon Prince!"

"Of course," said the Astrologer calmly. "With his power, I could have made myself King."

He broke off as the Demon Prince laid a hand on his shoulder, and squeezed gently. Blood ran down the Astrologer's arm as the long claws sank deep into his flesh, but he didn't flinch or cry out.

"Such a foolish mortal, to think of controlling me," murmured the Demon Prince. "You were mine, body and soul, from the moment you decided to summon me out of the darkness. From that moment on, you became an agent, my slave, my . . ."

"Traitor," whispered the King.

"I have always been well served by traitors," said the Demon Prince.

John bowed his head and looked away. In the space of a

single day he had lost his Kingdom, his Castle, and his oldest friend. It didn't seem possible that a man could hurt so much and still go on living.

Rupert cautiously raised himself up on his elbows. The geas was almost gone, but the sword was too far away. The Demon Prince would stop him before he could get anywhere near it. The King, on the other hand, was almost on top of the sword . . . Rupert frowned. In order to stand any chance at all, the King was going to need a diversion, to distract the Demon Prince and the Astrologer . . . Rupert smiled sourly as the answer came to him. He might not be able to reach the sword, but he could certainly reach the Demon Prince. *Damn,* thought Rupert, *this is going to hurt.* He quickly caught his father's eye, and jerked his head slightly at the sword lying between them. Now, if the Demon Prince would just move a few steps closer . . . The Astrologer laughed suddenly, and the King slowly turned his head to look at him.

"Well, John"—the Astrologer grinned—"nothing more to say to me? No last minute appeals to my better nature, or the friendship we once shared?"

John just looked at him.

"I'm going to be King," said Thomas Grey simply, a world of satisfaction in his voice. "At long last, I'm going to be King. My master promised me your throne, for my part in this. Don't worry, John; I'll put the Kingdom back together, and run it as it should be run. And with the demons to back me up, there's not a Baron in the Land will dare stand against me."

"You're crazy," said Julia harshly. "King? King of *what?* There's nothing but the Darkwood now."

"Things won't always be like this," said the Astrologer calmly. "I shall rule the Forest Land. This was promised to me."

"Such a petty ambition," said the Demon Prince. "I offered you all the Kingdoms of the world."

"The Forest Land is all I want," said Thomas Grey. "It's all I've ever wanted. And now I shall be King, at last."

"I think not," said the Dark Prince.

The Astrologer turned suddenly to stare at the inhuman creature lounging carelessly on its decaying throne.

"I have no use for Kings," said the Demon Prince. "Only slaves. Come here, slave."

Thomas Grey shook his head slowly. "I'm to be King. King of the Forest Land. You promised me!"

The Demon Prince smiled, showing his teeth. "I lied."

He rose to his feet in one sudden movement, and started toward the Astrologer. Thomas Grey backed away, and then turned and ran. He barely made half a dozen steps before the night closed in around him like a living cloak. Grey fell struggling to the ground, wrapped in darkness, and screamed horribly as within his body he felt his bones and muscles moving, changing, twisting . . .

The screams finally died away, and King John watched horrified as the thing that had once been his friend rose slowly to its feet as a demon. A low-browed head squatted on broad, muscular shoulders, and its overlong arms fell down past its knees. Thick oily hair showed clearly through great rents in the sorcerer's torn robes. A simple, crafty intelligence showed in the glowing bloodred eyes, but there was no trace of recognition in them when the demon glanced briefly at the King before scuttling away to crouch fawningly at the Demon Prince's side.

"Well?" said the Demon Prince to the King. "How do you like your friend now?"

Rupert lunged forward and slammed into the Demon Prince. The creature staggered backwards and almost fell, but recovered his balance at the last moment. Rupert caught the Demon Prince in a bear hug, and hung on grimly, his head pressed against the creature's bony chest.

"Father!" he yelled desperately. "Get the sword! Get the damn sword!"

The Demon Prince's head snapped forward, the long spindly neck stretching impossibly. Rupert had only a brief glimpse of vicious teeth reaching for his throat before he released his hold and threw himself backwards. The jaws snapped together just short of his face, and then a hard bony knee shot up to slam into his side. Rupert groaned as he felt newly healed ribs break, and then the ground rose up to hit him. He rolled slowly onto his face and pushed himself up onto one elbow, just in time to see Julia try again to reach her sword. The demon Astrologer drove a fist into her gut, and she collapsed again, fighting for breath. The demon giggled. The Demon Prince moved slowly forward, chuckling softly. Rupert braced himself, and glanced quickly at his father. The King hadn't moved at all, and the sword still lay where Rupert had dropped it.

"Father!"

The Demon Prince stopped before the King, and smiled down at him. "I don't think he hears you, boy. He's broken now, just another of my slaves. Aren't you, John?" He reached down, and taking the King by the throat, lifted him easily off the ground. The Demon Prince held him out at arm's length and shook him playfully, grinning broadly as he watched the King's feet kicking a yard and more above the ground.

"Aren't you, John?"

The King tore feebly at the Demon Prince's hand, air rattling in his throat.

"You shall be the lowliest of all my slaves, little coward," said the Demon Prince softly. He drew the King's face close to his own, and laughed mockingly. King John spat in his face. The Demon Prince howled with rage, and his hand closed tight about the King's throat. His other hand ripped through the King's chain mail and sank its claws deep into the King's chest, searching for his heart.

Rupert staggered to his feet and started toward them, and the demon Astrologer came to meet him. Julia lunged forward, snatched up Rupert's sword from the clearing floor, and threw it to him. Rupert caught the sword in mid air, and turned quickly back to face the demon. It snarled once, and backed slowly away from him. The Demon Prince threw the King aside, and stalked toward Rupert, grinning broadly. Rupert stood his ground, hefting his sword in his hand. He could see Julia and his father, both struggling to get to their feet, their blood dripping onto the filthy moss. Even the dragon was stirring uneasily in his sleep. Rupert swallowed dryly. He knew cold steel wasn't going to be enough to stop the Dark Prince, but he had to try. His friends needed him. He lifted his sword above his head for one last desperate attack, and then all his rage and hope and need surged up into the sword and out, out into the long night and beyond, and the Demon Prince screamed despairingly as with the roaring of a mighty falls, the Rainbow slammed down into the Darkwood clearing.

Brilliant colors threw back the darkness, thundering endlessly against the long night. Rupert turned his face up into the cascading light, and laughed aloud as strength flooded back into him. Vivid shades and colors burned through the night, driving back the Darkwood. Rupert looked around him for the Demon Prince. He could just make out a tall spindly shadow struggling weakly among the colors, like an insect trapped in hardening amber. And then, even as he watched, the shadow melted away into nothing. The Rainbow blazed bright and glorious against the night, and then was gone.

Rupert slowly lowered his sword, and looked up into the night sky. For a moment he thought nothing had changed, and then, one by one, the stars came out, and the full moon overhead shone silver bright. The brooding oppression of the Darkwood was gone, as though it had never been, and already the first faint red gleam of dawn was spilling out onto the darkness. The long night was finally over.

Rupert sheathed the rainbow sword, and looked about him. The mosses and fungi that had covered the clearing floor were gone, replaced by a thick carpet of grass that glowed softly with its own inner light. The Demon Prince was gone, and with him the creature that had once been the Astrologer. The dragon was sitting up on his haunches, shaking the last drowsiness out of his head. His emerald scales shimmered brightly where the Rainbow had touched them. Julia was standing beside the dragon, happily flexing her newly healed hand, and staring about her in open wonder. Rupert went over to her and took her in his arms, and the rising sun was like a benediction.

King John sat beside the decaying throne with his head in his hands, and wept for the loss of his friend.

CHAPTER TEN

Endings and Beginnings

Out in the Forest, birds were singing. Leaves had begun to appear on some of the trees around the clearing, and the air was full of clean, familiar Forest smells. Sunlight poured down through the slowly widening break in the canopy overhead, and the early morning sky was so brilliant a blue it almost hurt Rupert's eyes to look at it. High above the Forest, the dragon soared effortlessly on the gentle morning winds, his scales shimmering brightly in the golden sunlight. Rupert could feel the winter cold finally leaving his bones, and the sun was warm on his face. All around him he could hear the quiet, furtive sounds of animals emerging from their hiding places to investigate the returning Forest. And yet, for every tree that stood wreathed in green or bronze, another stood stark and dead, its wood eaten away from within. For some, for all too many, the Rainbow had come too late.

"Half the Forest's still dead," said Julia. "I thought that, once the Demon Prince was gone, everything would just return to normal."

Rupert shook his head slowly. "Not even the Rainbow can bring back the dead, and some of these trees have stood in darkness for a very long time. The Darkwood may be gone, but it'll take the Forest centuries to recover from the damage done to it. No, lass; we're rid of the Demon Prince, but we still have to deal with the legacy he left us."

Julia suddenly stumbled over something lying hidden in the long grass, and bent down to pick it up.

"What have you got there?" asked Rupert.

"I'm not sure," said Julia. "Looks like a piece of bone, or horn, or something."

"A horn? Let me see that." Rupert reached out a hand for the object. Julia went to pass it to him, and then almost dropped it as her newly healed fingers refused to cooperate. Rupert caught the horn just in time, and smiled sympathetically at Julia. "How's your hand now, lass? Still stiff?"

"Yeah," said Julia wryly, kneading her injured hand with her good one. "The Rainbow healed the damage all right, just like before, but it's going to take a hell of a lot of exercise before this hand is supple enough to use a sword again."

"I know what you mean," said Rupert, wincing slightly as a too sudden movement brought him a warning twinge from his newly healed ribs.

"I wish the Rainbow could have done something for your eye," said Julia

Rupert shrugged carefully. "So do I, lass; but then again, I'm happy just to be alive." He studied the piece of horn in his hand. It was almost two feet long and thickly curlicued, the creamy white ivory cracked and discolored. Rupert nodded grimly. "I thought so."

"What is it?"

"It's the unicorn's horn. He lost it to a demon in the Darkwood, remember? The Demon Prince used it to spread his plague."

Julia looked at the horn warily. "Is it still dangerous? Maybe we ought to destroy it."

"The High Warlock will know what to do with it," said Rupert, slipping the horn into the top of his boot. "I'll give it to him when we get back to the Castle. Maybe he can find some way to fix it back onto the unicorn."

"Rupert," said Julia gently. "We can't be sure that either of them survived that last attack from the demons."

"Damn," said Rupert. "Oh damn. I'm sorry, Julia, I didn't think . . . It just doesn't seem possible that so many people could have died in so short a time."

Julia put an arm round Rupert's shoulders, and he hugged her to him. They stood together awhile, staring about them, enjoying the sunshine and breathing in great lungfuls of the fresh, untainted air. Losing themselves in the morning, so they could forget the horrors of the night.

"It's hard to believe it's finally over," said Rupert.

"It isn't over," said a quiet voice, and Rupert and Julia looked quickly at King John, sitting alone at the edge of the clearing and staring at the ground with empty eyes. "The Demon Prince isn't dead. All the Rainbow did was drive him back to whatever dark hell he came from. Since the Astrologer and I were responsible for summoning him out of the darkness, only we can truly banish him. One day, the Demon Prince will return. Even if it takes him hundreds of years, he'll be back."

Rupert and Julia waited patiently, but the King had nothing more to say. In all the time he was speaking, he never once raised his voice or looked up from the ground.

"Well," said Rupert finally, "Even if you're right, Father, if it's going to take him hundreds of years to return, I don't see how it's any problem of ours. As long as we take care not to lose the rainbow sword . . ."

"Right," said Julia. "We've saved the Forest, and that's what matters." She stopped suddenly, and looked at Rupert sideways. "Rupert . . ."

"Yes?"

"Can I ask you something?"

"Of course."

"Why did you tell me earlier that the rainbow sword didn't work anymore?"

Rupert smiled shamefacedly. "Just before I began the Rainbow Run," he said carefully, "the dragon told me that if I reached Rainbow's End, I'd find my heart's desire, but that might not be what I thought it was. When I made the Rainbow Run, all I wanted was something that would help me save you and my friends from the darkness. And that's what I was given. When I tried to use the sword again, down in the Coppertown pit, I was just trying to save myself. So it didn't work. This time, I didn't care about myself any more; I just wanted to save you and the others from the Demon Prince. So the sword worked again. Simple, really, when you think about it."

"If it's that simple, why didn't you think of it sooner?"

"I've had a lot on my mind recently."

They shared a smile, and then looked round suddenly as a long, loud roar sounded on the morning air, silencing the singing birds. The air shimmered and broke apart, and out of an endless silver tunnel floated the High Warlock. He dropped gracefully to the ground, and the rent in space slammed shut behind him. Rupert and Julia moved forward, grinning broadly, and took it in turns to clap the High Warlock on the back. Rupert finally stood back and took his first good look at the High Warlock, and felt his smile slip a little. The Warlock's hair and moustache were pure white, and if anything he looked older and frailer than he had when Rupert first met him.

"Well, sir Warlock," said Rupert uncertainly. "You're looking . . . uh . . ."

"Yes," said the Warlock dryly. "I know. That's what being sober and respectable does for you."

Rupert laughed in spite of himself. "All right; what happened to the Castle after we left? Last we saw, the courtyard was swarming with demons."

The Warlock shrugged nonchalantly. "They didn't stay long enough to do any real damage. We all retreated inside the main Castle and manned the barricades, and then the next thing we knew the demons were attacking each other. Without the Demon Prince to hold the horde together, it didn't take long for the demons to revert to type, as mindless animals. Most of them died at each others' hands, and the guards drove out the rest without too much trouble. I doubt the survivors will last long in the Forest, now there's no darkness to hide in." He stopped suddenly and looked searchingly to Rupert. "Tell me; how did you kill the Demon Prince?"

"With this," said Rupert simply, showing the Warlock his sword. "I found it at Rainbow's End; it calls down the Rainbow."

The Warlock gave him a hard look. "Why didn't you tell me you had the rainbow sword?"

"We're not actually sure the Demon Prince is dead," said Julia quickly. "King John says all we did was banish him."

The High Warlock frowned thoughtfully. "With a creature like the Dark Prince, it's hard to be sure of anything. Since it was never born, it can't really die. I'd better look into the matter some more."

They stood in silence for a while, looking about them. The Forest was ablaze with color once again, and from everywhere came the simple sounds of birds and animals and insects.

"I'm glad to see your powers have returned to you, sir Warlock," said Rupert eventually.

"Yes," said the Warlock wryly, "It was rather a good teleport, wasn't it? Now that the Wild Magic is gone, the remains of my magic are back under control again."

"What was happening at the Castle when you left?" asked Julia. "Did you take many losses?"

"Some," said the High Warlock. "Mainly on the battlements. But most of us came through it pretty much unscathed. They'd just started clearing up the mess when I left."

"That's going to take some time," said Rupert.

"Oh, I don't know," said Julia. "Harald'll keep everybody busy."

Rupert had to smile, knowing as he did his brother's fondness for organizing things and giving orders. The High Warlock took in the way Rupert and Julia were standing together, and smiled suddenly.

"I take it Harald's wedding is off, Rupert?"

"Definitely," said Rupert. "Julia and I are . . ."

"So I see," said the Warlock. "I hope you'll be very happy together."

"Wait a minute," said Julia, "Don't I get a say in this?"

"No," said Rupert, and kissed her quickly before she could say anything else. They finally broke apart, and Julia smiled at him sweetly.

"I'll get you for that," she said calmly, and then kissed him again. The High Warlock waited a moment, until it became clear that Rupert and Julia were no longer interested in anyone but themselves, and then he moved away to stand with King John and stare out into the Forest.

"John . . ."

"I know. You're leaving again, aren't you?"

"Yes," said the High Warlock. "I'll teleport you back to the Castle, and then I'm off. Magic is going out of the world, and my years are catching up with me."

"Feeling sorry for yourself?" said John.

The Warlock smiled tiredly. "Just a bit. I shouldn't complain, really; at least this way I can say I ended my life with one last great adventure."

"One last adventure," said the King. "Yes. That's a good way to end a life. I'm not going back to the Castle, either. You know Thomas Grey is dead?"

"Yes," said the Warlock. "I know."

"He turned against me and betrayed the Land, and at the end, he said it was all because of me. More and more, I think perhaps he was right. Trusting Thomas too much was just one of the many mistakes I made. I'm not going back to the Castle.

"I never wanted to be King anyway. All the work, the problems, the endless responsibility . . . I did my best, but somehow that was never enough. And now, more than ever, the Forest Land is going to need a strong King. There's a lot to be done; overseeing relief work for the towns and villages, saving what we can from the ruined harvests, reestablishing Royal control over the Barons . . . generally pulling the Land back together again. And I'm just not up to it. Let somebody else try; Rupert or Harald. Either of them would do a good job.

"All I want now is to be alone. Maybe here in the Forest I can find some peace, some absolution; some way to live with my memories of what I've done, and didn't do."

"John . . ."

"Goodbye, Warlock. I won't say goodbye to Rupert and Julia. If I did, I might not be able to go. You'll have to find a way to do it for me. I won't be seeing them again."

He smiled briefly, and then walked away into the Forest. The Warlock watched quietly as he disappeared into the dark green shadows between the trees. Rupert and Julia suddenly noticed that the King was gone, and hurried over to the Warlock.

"Where's my father?" said Rupert.

The High Warlock turned and bowed formally to him. "Your father is dead, Rupert. The King is dead. Long live King Rupert of the Forest Kingdom."

It was three in the morning, and the Castle was fast asleep. Stars shone brightly in the night sky, and the full moon lit the courtyard bright as day. A few weary guardsmen patrolled the battlements and manned the gatehouse, but only shadows moved in the empty courtyard. Rupert crept stealthily down the main entrance steps, and then ran silently through the moonlight to hide in the shadows of the inner West wall. He pressed close against the stonework, and waited patiently while his breathing slowed and his eyes adjusted to the sudden change in light. The guards moved slowly from post to post, occasionally staring out at the Forest. None of them so much as glanced at the courtyard. Rupert let out his breath in a quiet sigh of relief, and shrugged the heavy pack on his back into a more comfortable position. He moved quickly along the inner wall, keeping to the shadows, until he finally reached the old stable. He knocked once on the door, waited a moment, and then knocked again. The door swung open just wide enough to admit him, and then closed after him.

Julia unhooded her lantern, and a smoky yellow light filled the stable. Two saddled horses waited patiently in their stalls, while the unicorn glared nervously about him in the aisle. Rupert glanced quickly at the shutters to make sure they were secure, and then leaned back against the closed stable door and relaxed a little.

"You're late!" hissed Julia. "Where've you been?"

"I had a few things to attend to."

"Such as?"

"I left the rainbow sword in the Armory. Just in case father was right, and the Demon Prince does come back some day."

Julia's face softened a little. "Yes, well, the sword's probably more use to them than it would be to us. You did get yourself another sword?"

"Of course."

"And you did check the guards on the gate?"

"Yes, Julia. They're all loyal to me. And yes; the dragon is waiting for us in the Forest. Now calm down, will you; nothing's going to go wrong. Are you nearly ready?"

"Just about. Have you decided where we're going yet?"

"Not really. The important thing is to get out of this madhouse. The King hasn't been dead twenty-four hours, and already the vultures are gathering. There are more factions in the Court now than you can shake a stick at. The sooner I get out of here, the better."

"There's always a chance they'll come after us."

"I doubt it," said Rupert easily. "With me out of the way,

Harald will have a clear field. If I didn't leave, he'd probably have me exiled. Or killed."

"If we don't get a move on," said the unicorn sharply, "somebody's going to find us here, and Harald'll probably have you both hung as horse thieves."

"Harald won't grudge us two horses," said Rupert. "Well, he will, but he won't do anything about it."

"What do you want *two* horses for, anyway?" said the unicorn in a hurt voice. "The Warlock fixed me up fine before he left; there's no reason why I can't carry you."

"Ah," said Rupert. "Actually, there is a reason . . ."

"Oh yes? And what might that be?"

"I *can't* ride a unicorn," said Rupert, blushing slightly. "Not any more. I'm not longer . . . qualified. You see, Julia and I . . ."

"I get it," said the unicorn. "Spent the night celebrating, did you?"

"We still want you to come with us," said Rupert quickly. "I promised to help you track down your old herd, remember?"

"Yes," said the unicorn gruffly. "I remember. But after we've done that, where were you thinking of going?"

"I don't know," said Rupert. "Why?'

The unicorn snorted and tossed his head. "If you think I'm going to let you just go wandering off on·your own, you're crazy. You wouldn't last ten minutes without me, either of you, and you know it. Somebody's got to keep you out of trouble."

Rupert and Julia laughed, and took it in turns to hug the unicorn's neck. The lamplight shone golden on his horn.

"Hey, Rupert," said Julia suddenly. "What's in the backpack?"

Rupert grinned. "Another reason why I was a bit late." He shrugged off the pack, propped it on a nearby stool, and opened it. Julia gasped, and then swore reverently. The battered leather pack contained hundreds of glowing jewels. Julia reached hesitantly into the backpack, took a handful of gems, and let them dribble through her fingers in a stream of multicolored fire.

"Where the hell did you get these, Rupert? They must be worth a fortune."

Rupert laughed. "It's part of the treasure trove you and the Seneschal found in the Old Treasury. What with all the excitement, they never got around to locking it away securely. They just dumped it in a storage room, padlocked the door, and put up a simple warding spell, linked to the Royal family. And since we are rather short of guards at the moment, they left it at that. So, I just chose my moment carefully, broke open the padlock, and helped myself. By the time Harald figures out what's happened, we shall be long gone."

He buckled the pack together again and lifted it onto his back, grunting a little at the weight of it. "Now that my father is . . . gone, I think I'm entitled to an inheritance. And this is it."

Julia placed a gentle hand on his arm. "We don't know for sure that he's dead, Rupert. They haven't found his body yet, and the Warlock's disappeared."

"I can't really believe he's gone," said Rupert. "As long as I can remember, my father's always been there; a part of my life, like food or sleep or duty. We were never . . . close, but then we never wanted to be, before. And now, just when I was getting to know him, just when I was starting to like him . . ." Rupert stopped short, and looked away, swallowing hard. "He's dead, Julia. There's no doubt in my mind at all. He wouldn't just walk out on the Land. He couldn't."

"But you can," said Julia. "There's nothing to hold you here now."

"Yes," said Rupert, turning briskly back to face her. "And it's time we were on our way. Let's make a start."

"Hold on a minute," said Julia. "Assuming Harald doesn't send half an army after us to get his jewels back, have you thought about what we're going to do with ourselves, once we get out of here?"

"Not really, no," said Rupert. "I've never had to think about earning my living before. The jewels should help."

"Yeah," said Julia. "We could buy ourselves a tavern."

Rupert shook his head. "The hours are too long."

"How about a farm?"

"Too much like hard work."

"Well, what do you want to do?"

Rupert shrugged. "I don't know, lass. But preferably something that doesn't require me to use a sword. I've had enough of that."

"Right," said Julia. "I'll go along with that. At least until my sword hand's back to normal."

"Let's go," said Rupert. "I'm not going to feel safe until I've put several miles between us and the Castle."

"Rupert," said Julia slowly, "We don't have to go. You could stay, and make yourself King. After all you've done for the Land, you'd have no trouble finding support."

"I don't want to be King," said Rupert simply. "I'm not suited to it. And besides; it's going to be hard enough work rebuilding the Kingdom without having the Land torn apart by a civil war. I didn't put my life on the line to save the Land, just to see it destroyed again. No, Julia; the best thing I can do for the Forest is to leave. My last duty. And then, finally, I'll be free."

"And you're happy to leave Harald sitting on the throne?"

"Yes. For all his faults, and he's got enough of them, he'll make a good King. Certainly a better King than I'd ever be."

"I couldn't agree more," said Harald.

Rupert and Julia spun round to discover Harald leaning confidently against the closed stable door. "You really should have locked the door behind you," said Harald calmly. "You're getting careless, Rupert."

"Don't try and stop us, Harald," said Rupert.

"Wouldn't dream of it, dear boy," said Harald. "As you said, the Forest Land will be far better off without you. The Princess Julia, however, is a different matter."

"Oh yes?" said Julia.

"You're not going anywhere, Julia," said Harald. "You're staying here, with me, as my Queen."

"Like hell I am," said Julia. "Ours was an arranged marriage, set and signed without my consent. As far as I'm concerned, the marriage is now very much unarranged. Look, there's no need to worry about my father. Hillsdown must have taken nearly as much damage from the Darkwood as we did; he'll have far too many trouble of his own to worry about, without trying to invade the Forest. And if it's just an alliance you're after, I have several other sisters . . ."

"I don't want them," said Harald. "I want what's mine. I want you."

"Harald," said Julia firmly, "The marriage is off. I wouldn't marry you if the alternative was a nunnery. Got it?"

"Now how can you say such things, after all we've meant to each other?" said Harald calmly. "I mean, you have told Rupert all about us, haven't you?"

"She didn't have to," said Rupert. "I'd barely been back in the Castle an hour before your people had taken great pains to let me know that she'd been sharing your bed in my absence. And you know something, Harald; I don't give a damn. She thought I was dead, and you always were a charming bastard. No, Harald; what matters is that in the end she chose me over you, because she loves me, as I love her."

"Right," said Julia, moving in close beside Rupert. "I wouldn't take you on a bet, Harald."

"We've leaving now," said Rupert. "Get out of our way."

"I'll see you hanged first," said Harald.

He went for his sword, and Rupert punched him in the mouth. Harald reeled backwards against the stable door, caught off-balance, and Rupert slammed a fist into his gut. Harald bent sharply forward at the waist, and Julia rabbit-punched him. Harald fell to the ground, and lay still. Rupert knelt beside him and checked his pulse, and then rose grinning to his feet.

"He's going to feel that in the morning," he said happily. "You know; I've waited a hell of a long time to do that."

"So have I," said Julia. "So have I."

They shook hands solemnly.

"I hate to spoil the moment," said the unicorn dryly, "but it strikes me as rather unlikely that Harald would have come here alone. Hadn't you better check to see if he brought any guards?"

Rupert and Julia looked at each other, and then Rupert darted over to listen at the closed stable door, while Julia hooded her lantern, plunging the stable into darkness. For a moment, all was still and silent, except for the restless movements of the horses in their stalls, and the quiet rasp of steel on leather as Rupert and Julia drew their swords.

"Anything?" whispered Julia.

"Not a sound," murmured Rupert.

"I'm not being stopped now, Rupert."

"No more am I. Ready?"

"Ready."

Rupert hauled the stable door open, and leapt out into

the moonlit courtyard, Julia at his side. Outside the stable, a dozen goblins were busily looting half a dozen unconscious guards. The smallest goblin looked up, startled, and then grinned broadly at Rupert.

"Hello, Princie; how's it going?"

"A lot better for seeing you," said Rupert, sheathing his sword. "But hadn't we better get these guards into the shadows? They're a bit conspicuous out here."

"First things first," said the smallest goblin, tugging hard at a guard's stubborn signet ring. "The only ones who might spot us are the guards up on the battlements, and I've got a few of the lads keeping them occupied, just in case."

"And just what were you doing out here at this time of night?" asked Julia, still hanging onto her sword. She stared suspiciously about her, and glared meaningfully at a goblin who got too close to her. The goblin retreated in a hurry.

The smallest goblin grinned triumphantly at the signet ring now adorning his thumb, and then looked a little sheepishly at Rupert. "Well, to be honest, you're not the only ones planning on doing a moonlit escape. It didn't take much foresight on our part to realize that once the fighting was over we goblins were going to be about as welcome here as an attack of rabies. So, we decided to gather up our families, grab what goodies we could, and make a run for it. It's not as if we had any reason to stay; you're the only one at Court who ever had any time for us. And with your brother on the throne . . . Anyway, we saw you were in a bit of trouble, so we thought we'd help out. Just for old time's sake."

"Thanks," said Rupert. "Where are you headed?"

"Back into the Forest. We've never had much time for cities, or even towns. Too many walls make us nervous. Besides, I've come up with some great new schemes for waylaying defenseless travellers. Stick to what you're best at, I always say."

"Good luck," said Rupert dryly, holding out his hand. The smallest goblin reached up and shook it firmly.

"Good luck yourself, Princie. You're not a bad sort. For a human."

He whistled sharply to the other goblins, who quickly dragged the unconscious guardsmen away from the stable and into the shadows of the inner wall. In the space of a few

moments, nothing remained to show that they had ever
been there. The smallest goblin threw Rupert a snappy
salute, blew Julia a kiss, and disappeared into the shadows.

"Let's get out of here," said Julia. "This courtyard is
getting to be as busy as a market day."

Rupert nodded wryly, and they hurried back into the
stable. Julia led the horses out into the courtyard while
Rupert bound and gagged Harald, taking great care to do a
thorough job. He finally dumped Harald into an inconspicuous corner that just happened to be particularly filthy, and
then he and the unicorn hurried out of the stable to join
Julia and the horses. Sacking tied around the horses' hooves
kept the noise down to a bare minimum, but even so Rupert
felt horribly exposed and vulnerable in the bright moonlight. He glared quickly about him, grabbed his horse's
reins, and started slowly across the courtyard toward the
Keep. Julia followed close behind her horse, and the unicorn brought up the rear. The slightest sound seemed unnaturally loud in the silence, and Rupert hoped like hell that
the guards on the battlements were still occupied with their
goblins. Julia moved quickly up beside him as they drew
near the Keep. Four guardsmen were standing before the
closed gates with raised pikes.

"Are those your guards, Rupert?" asked Julia quietly.

"That's them."

"Are you sure we can trust them?"

"Of course I'm sure. They came back from the Darkwood
with me. We could trust them with our lives."

"We are," said the unicorn shortly.

The guards nodded respectfully to Rupert, and lowered
their pikes.

"We were beginning to wonder if you were still coming,
Sire," said Rob Hawke.

"I had a little business to attend to," said Rupert. "Any
problems at your end?"

"Not so far. Have you got everything you need?"

"Just about."

"Then let's get you on your way, before the master-at-
arms starts making his rounds."

The four guards pulled back the heavy steel bolts, and
then swung open the great oaken doors. The ancient wood
was scarred and rent, with whole strips torn away like kin-

dling, but the doors still stood. The guards came back, and Rupert shook them all by the hand.

"Best of luck, Sire," said Hawke.

"Thanks," said Rupert. "My brother's having a little rest in the old stable at the moment; you might want to go and discover him in a while."

"Oh sure," said Hawke. "Still, no hurry, is there?' '

"Won't you get into trouble for letting us pass?" asked Julia.

"I doubt it," said Hawke, grinning. "Everything's in such a mess that no one's sure where they're supposed to be; and that goes double for the guards."

"Look," said Rupert suddenly, "you're welcome to come with us, if you want."

"Thanks all the same," said Hawke politely, "But no thanks. The new King's going to need all the guards he can lay his hands on to put this Land back together again; and that's bound to mean extra money and promotions for old hands like us. Besides, we've got lands of our own to look after, remember? You granted them to us, and the old King ratified it himself, just before the last battle. Who knows, our descendants might even end up as Lords or Barons some day."

"That should shake things up," said Rupert, and all the guards laughed.

Rupert and Julia swung up into their saddles and rode forward into the Keep, the unicorn close behind. The gates closed slowly after them as they passed quickly under the raised portcullis and out onto the lowered drawbridge. The ice had all but vanished from the moat, but Rupert couldn't see any sign of the moat monster. He urged his horse on, and soon Rupert and Julia and the unicorn were safely among the first few trees at the edge of the clearing. Behind them, the drawbridge swung silently shut. *Good thing I ordered those gears greased,* thought Rupert. *Normally they're loud enough to wake the whole damn Castle.* It occurred to him that that order was probably the last he'd ever give. He frowned uncertainly. He wasn't quite sure how he felt about that, but if anything, he felt rather relieved. He led the way into the Forest until he was sure they were out of sight from the Castle, and then reined his horse to a halt. Julia and the unicorn pulled up beside him.

"Dragon?" called Rupert quietly. "Where are you?"

"Here," said the dragon, emerging suddenly from the trees to Rupert's left. The horses took one look at the dragon, and tried to bolt. Rupert and Julia fought them to a halt, and muttered soothing words in their horse's ears while glaring at the dragon.

"Sorry," said the dragon, moving cautiously forward to join them again.

"Whatever you do, don't smile at them," growled Rupert as his horse finally calmed down. "I don't think they're ready for that yet. Are you ready to go?"

"Of course, Rupert. By the way, do you think we could stop off at Dragonslair mountain so that I can retrieve my butterfly collection? I've seen some fascinating specimens here in the Forest that I'd love to add to it."

"Sure," said Julia. "Why not?"

"Good," said the dragon. "You know, I think I'm going to enjoy this trip, wherever we're going. You two are the most interesting humans I've come across in centuries. Always in the middle of things. Wherever we end up, I doubt it'll be dull."

Rupert looked up at the night skies with an expert eye. "The sun will be coming up soon; we'd better get a move on. Out there, somewhere beyond the Forest, there are countries that have never even heard of the Forest Kingdom. Let's go and visit them."

"Right," said Julia.

They set off down the dusty trail that led into the Forest, and so passed out of history and into legend. And wherever they went, and whatever they found, Rupert, Julia, the dragon, and the unicorn faced it together. Heroes, all.